2/22

Anybody
Here Seen
Frenchie?

LESLIE CONNOR

Anybody Here Seen Frenchie?

KATHERINE TEGEN BOOKS
An Imprint of HarperCollins Publishers

Katherine Tegen Books is an imprint of HarperCollins Publishers.

Anybody Here Seen Frenchie?
Copyright © 2022 by Leslie Connor
Map art © 2022 by Ramona Kaulitzki
Photographs courtesy of Leslie Connor
All rights reserved. Printed in the United States of America.
No part of this book may be used or reproduced in any manner whatsoever without
written permission except in the case of brief quotations embodied in critical
articles and reviews. For information address HarperCollins Children's Books,
a division of HarperCollins Publishers, 195 Broadway, New York, NY 10007.
www.harpercollinschildrens.com

Library of Congress Control Number: 2021946100
ISBN 978-0-06-299936-8

Typography by Laura Mock
22 23 24 25 26   PC/LSCH   10 9 8 7 6 5 4 3 2 1
❖
First Edition

To Carey,
Thanks for always looking out for the rest of us.
With my love,
LRPC

Aurora

The Letters

When our letters from the school come, we sit together on the deck at the A-frame to read them. Actually, I'll be doing all the reading.

Frenchie sits, spine straight, his freckled face tilted up. He works his fingers along the strap of the needlepoint purse he carries. In his other hand he holds his envelope. He squints and blinks at the breaks of the sun coming through the pines.

"Any birds up there?" I ask.

He doesn't answer. He never does. Not with words. But he arches his back a little.

"I saw your pine warbler early this morning," I tell him. The mention of birds is my best shot at getting his attention. But it doesn't always work. It's possible I will never figure out why. But that's okay by me.

I tear into the envelope addressed to me: Aurora Pauline Petrequin.

I shake the folds out of my letter as fast as I can. "Come on, Frenchie. Open yours too!" I say. He might not get how important these letters are. But I know, our entire sixth-grade destinies are typed inside.

"Okay . . . we're about to find out who our next teacher is," I tell him. I drum the soles of my sneakers on the deck boards.

"Can you feel that? That's suspense," I say. "Here we go!" I take a huge breath and hold it while I scan the page. It takes forever to zero in, but then . . .

"Ms. Beccia!" I shout. "Yes! We're in Ms. Beccia's class! Whew!" I fan myself with my letter, then go limp where I sit. Here's what I know: Ms. Beccia is brand-new. This is a small town and the only other sixth-grade teacher is Mrs. Hillsbeck. She's been around forever, and she's *spoken to me* on the playground during recess a good number of times. Her reasons for that have all been *unreasonable*: dangerous climbing on the climber, running too close to others, handling dirt, clogging the drinking fountain with a pebble and turning it into a sprinkler, which everyone loved. Except Mrs. Hillsbeck. She got soaked trying to make it stop. She got angry too. That's some pretty bad history. There was a better place for me to spend sixth grade.

"Ms. Beccia. Yes!" I sit upright again and turn toward Frenchie. "Can I open yours now?" He is holding his envelope so lightly it's easy to take it from him.

I pick the paper triangle open. No need to drum my feet. The suspense is over. His letter will look like mine, right down to the Ms. Beccia part. "It's so great getting the new teacher," I say. "I love a fresh start."

I unfold the page which is addressed to Nathan French Livernois. Makes me snort because nobody ever calls him Nathan. I clear my throat.

"Okay." I work my way down the page. What I see makes me quiet. (I am not a quiet girl.) I reread it. I look at Frenchie. He's still staring up into the branches.

"What the heck?" I whisper. I let the letter fall into my lap. Then I yell, "What the heck! How's that going to work?" I jump to my feet and run in through the open door of the A-frame calling, "Mom! Pop! Gracia! There's a mess-up of all mess-ups here! Frenchie and I got put in different classes!"

Aurora

The First Time We Met Jewell Laramie and I Tried to Play Softball

Mom and Pop are as surprised as I am about Frenchie being in one sixth-grade classroom and me being in the other. Pop even called the school to make sure the assignments are right. (They are.) They all tell me it will work out fine. Frenchie and I will still take the bus together. We'll see each other at lunch and on the playground.

Mom says things like: "Remember, Aurora, there was a time before Frenchie lived here and you survived just fine."

I say things like: "Yeah! That was three years ago! I'm not used to that anymore! And what about Frenchie? Can we agree that there is a little bit more to this than just two friends getting separated? Can we?"

I remember the summer before Frenchie and Gracia came. That was the year I tried playing softball, which I only did because the coach came to our house to recruit me. And it was a chance to play *something* with other kids. I already knew I had a darn-good throwing arm. That comes from me being a rock hound.

I don't have much of a collection. Yet. I am particular. I'm searching for tourmaline. Parts of Maine offer great gem hunting. I'd give up sour pickles for a month to go digging for minerals over in Oxford or Androscoggin. That's where the old mica mines are, and the really cool pegmatites. Those are veins of igneous rock, and that's where you find the good stuff like beryl, topaz, *and* tourmaline.

Around home, I pick up rocks all the time. They're mostly granite, and I have collected enough of that. I throw them far as I can so I don't refind them. Why let a rock disappoint you twicc? Pop says the lack of tourmaline in our part of Maine (fact) could be my ticket to the majors (joke). He says my arm gets stronger every time I *don't* find a piece of the good stuff, which is, so far, all the time. I like choosing targets. Mostly boulders so I don't hurt the trees—or anything else. Underhand, overhand, I've got good aim, and I can put enough speed on a rock to make it zing.

Our town has a girls' softball league, and Coach Jewell

Laramie wants every girl in town to play. That's why she came to see me. She thought we were new here because the A-frame was newly finished. The door was open because of the stinky new paint smell, and because Mom and Pop were bringing in the kitchen cupboards that day. Jewell called hello. Then she walked right in and thunked a hunk of something frozen all wrapped in plastic on our kitchen table.

"Hey, neighbors! I'm Jewell Laramie." She tipped her cap, which looked to be trapping a pouf of pale golden hair.

"I'm Aurora. Aurora Pauline Petrequin," I told her.

"Ah! Just the girl I'm looking for," said Jewell.

That was an even bigger surprise than seeing her sweep into our new house. I waited while Mom and Pop introduced themselves—Rene and Ed—and pronounced our last name twice over.

"Brought you folks some dinner!" Jewell nodded toward the hunk in the bag. "Venison tenderloin," she added.

"Oh, we don't eat that," I said. "That's deer meat. Deer are mammals. We don't eat mammals."

Jewell looked at Mom and Pop. "Oh. Tells it like it is, does she?" She cocked her head in my direction.

"She does," said Mom, and Pop nodded.

"If it makes you feel any different, there was no suf-fering. I took this deer during bow season. Had a clean, double-lung shot. The only shot I'll take."

Clean, double-lung shot.

How can that *not* cause suffering? I looked at the package on our table and thought about pointing out that it was dead.

"We appreciate the gesture," Pop said.

"Doesn't offend me," Jewell said, "and I hope I haven't offended you."

"You haven't, and we don't mean to be ungracious," Pop explained.

"But we still don't eat that," I repeated. "Oh. That sounds ungracious, doesn't it?"

"A little bit," Mom said.

I looked at Jewell. "I blurt things. I do that a lot," I told her.

"Nothing wrong with honesty. I like it," Jewell said. "Tell me, what do you eat?"

"We say feather, fin, and flora," Pop told her. "Local dairy and a little seafood."

"Yut, yut . . ." (Some Mainers will say *yut* instead of *yes*.) Jewell Laramie nodded like she was really paying attention. So when she started to tell us all about her girls' softball league, I listened to her. She practically begged me to come play.

"All levels are welcome, and U-eight is all about learning the game and having a good time," she said. "Think about it, Aurora. I bet there's an athlete in you." She

7

picked up her frozen deer meat, held it under her arm, and gave it a pat. "You folks should know . . . hunters are a fact of life in Maine."

"Acknowledged," said Pop. "We aren't new to Maine."

"Yeah, I've been here all my life," I said.

"And I've been here half of mine," Pop added.

"And about a third for me," Mom said. "We're not even new to town. Just new to this spot."

"Yeah, we moved out of our house on the bay, and now we rent it out to folks from away," I said. (If you are from away, it means you don't live in Maine; you are a visitor.) "And maybe you saw that little house right next door here?" I pointed. "We're going to rent that one out too."

"Gotcha," said Jewell, and she put up her thumb, which had one of those purple nails on it. Like she'd whacked it with a hammer or pinched it in a wood splitter, probably months before. There's something about a purple thumb like that—always makes me like the person who's got it. Enough to go try playing ball.

But, sheeshy-sheesh! That game is full of rules, and you stand around that diamond for hours and nothing happens. Ugh. Then if someone finally does hit a ball and you decide to run across the diamond to stop it, your own teammate by the name of Darleen Dombroski could decide to *cry* because you got in her way on the play. And stepped on her ankle. And gave it an accidental grinding. Never mind you made a perfect throw to first base and got the hitter out—*which I did.* That night Darleen got her mother to call my mother. (Darleen's mother has been calling my mother since we were in kindergarten.) This time, Mrs. Dombroski told Mom that there are *positions* in softball, and that maybe she could help her daughter (me) understand that so no one else would get hurt.

Well, Coach Jewell tried playing me everywhere. Not like a punishment. She tries everyone everywhere. She rotated me to the outfield, where there was *less than nothing* to do—except handstands. I pulled my glove off and kicked my feet into the air. I tried cartwheels next, and I figured out the cool trick of pulling up grass on the way over. Then throwing it like confetti.

Coach Jewell leaned out of the dugout, calling, "Aurora! Aurora P.! No gymnastics out there! Be ready! A hit could come your way."

"Yeah, I won't hold my breath about that," I called back. "I could take a nap out here." I faked a yawn, but it turned into a real one—noisy too. Some of my teammates giggled. They snorted and covered their faces with their gloves. "I could grow a year older waiting out here . . . am I nine yet? Am I ten?"

But before the game was over, my teammates, who were also my classmates at school, started to whisper that I was "not funny" and "so annoying." They were tired of me, and I was tired of softball.

Jewell Laramie came to the house the next day.

9

She brought us a brook trout. She set it down and said, "Feather, fin, and flora, correct? Well, here's some *fin*!" Then she showed me how the game of softball works by putting all our mugs and the salt and pepper shakers on the table in a diamond. She said *teamwork* at least five times. I propped my chin on the table and tried not to interrupt.

Finally, I said, "Coach, I know all that." Because I did. "But it takes way too long for something to happen. I can't stand it. I need more to do!"

Jewell looked me over a second. She nodded and said something nice about me and my raw talent. Mom gave Jewell a bag of apricot muffins. Muffins for brook trout. Like, all good. We're friends. But my days on the softball diamond were done.

I didn't miss it. Plenty of rocks to inspect and throw, and that's what I did pretty much all summer long. On my own. I didn't have my little brother, Cedar, yet, and I was the only kid living on our road. But that was about to change.

Aurora

Mainstreaming Frenchie

The first time I met Frenchie Livernois we were waiting for the bus at the end of the long driveway we share. That was three years ago. Third grade.

I ran, jumped, and hopped all the way there, rip-ready for the first day of school. Another whole summer gone, and now the bus was coming to get me again. I *loved* going places. Still do.

In fact, we'd just come back to Maine after a vacation with Gram and Gramp in Connecticut. That's why we weren't around to see our new neighbors move into the little house beside the A-frame. But Pop had said there was going to be a mom and a kid living there. A change like that is pretty big news where we live.

I remember feeling my heart leap when I spotted them at the end of the drive. I ran and skidded to a stop right next to the woman and sprayed little stones over her clogs and against her bare ankles. Mom pulled me back.

"Careful, Aurora," she said.

"Oops! Sorry! Sorry!" I said.

Our new neighbor was nice. She laughed and her brown curls bounced. I waited for the boy to laugh too. But he stood a few yards away from us, back turned, almost like he hadn't heard us come up at all. Weird, I thought.

I wanted to get to him, but his mom was talking to my mom, and I was working on being a good listener. Sort of my life project. She explained that her name was Gracia, and that her boy's name was Nathan French Livernois. But she had called him Frenchie from the day he was born.

There we go, I thought, because if she had not explained, I was going to have to ask about that name.

"I'm Aurora Pauline Petrequin," I said. I bopped from side to side and gave myself a knock on the head. "That's *Pet-ruh-quin*, just so you know. It's easy. But nobody gets it right. They say *Ped-a-guin*. And *Peterkin*. Pfft! Every year, I have to tell my new teacher, sound it out!"

"You would think they could do that," said Gracia. Total twinkle in her eye.

Mom stood behind me, her hands cupped loosely on my shoulders.

"Anyway, you can call me plain *Aurora*," I said, and I

12

roared my name to be friendly, and because Aurora is a name that likes to be roared, *and* I thought if I was loud enough that boy Frenchie might turn around.

Gracia leaned down and smiled. "I'm going to guess that there's nothing plain about you." She had a voice like butter.

"You might be right," I said. Then I skittered away from the moms and went over to Frenchie. Who in this world doesn't turn around to say hello? I shuffled up beside him. I took a good look at all his edges—his profile—and the way his dark hair was trimmed around his ear. His skin was light like seashells and sprinkled with summer freckles.

"Hey. I'm Aurora," I roared, but not too loudly. "Good to meet ya," I said.

Frenchie stared straight ahead.

"Hellooo?" I tried again. He didn't answer. I knew plenty of kids in town who were not too interested in me. But, sheeshy-sheesh, this was a brand-new one. Wasn't he even going to give me a try? I leaned in. "We're neighbors now, ya know."

That boy did not move.

I walked all the way around him. Took a good look at those tan pants of his. He had them pulled way up, belted so tight his plaid button-down shirt puffed out almost like a costume. That's all he has ever worn, for as long as I've known him.

Frenchie Livernois: plaid mushroom. I stood beside him. Tried to stare at whatever he was staring at. Was it our mailboxes on that post across the road? Something in the field? Maybe he'd seen something crawling around in the ditch.

"You know," I said, "there's a wood rat that travels along there. You like animals?"

Frenchie's elbows straightened by his sides. His hands twitched. Then stopped. He didn't quit staring, except to blink his long dark eyelashes—like slow motion.

"Wood rat." I said it again just to see if he'd move. Nope.

I spun on one foot, grinding the gravel. I leaped and landed in a lunge, arms wide, right into the middle of Mom and Gracia's conversation.

"Hey! What's with him?" I blurted. I pointed my finger behind me.

Mom said, "Aurora, try not to—"

"Interrupt," I said. "Yeah, sorry about that. But what the heck?" I jabbed my finger back toward the boy again.

Gracia smiled. She used her butter voice again. "Oh, Aurora, I was telling your mom, Frenchie doesn't talk. Not in words. But he does hear you."

I pulled my chin back. "Oh. Hears me, huh?" I wasn't so sure. Not that I thought she was lying. But I wondered if she was one of those moms who would say the thing she wanted to think was true even when it wasn't. Like Darleen Dombrowski's mom who kept saying all through second grade that Darleen was "a kind and patient soul."

I had news for her. Even way back then.

Darleen is a difficult acquaintance of mine. I'm not alone there. Other kids don't play with her, and since they don't play with me either, the school has been trying to pair us up for years. Exhausting is what that is. Unsuccessful too.

But I was heading into third grade that very morning. Fresh start coming up. I had my *strategies*. For one, I was aiming to do less blurting. (I aim for that every year.) It's tricky for me. Pop says I should be me, and that people learn by living and doing. Trouble is, I end up having to *undo* a lot of stuff that I mess up.

Anyway, I went up to Frenchie that first morning and stood close to his ear. "Sh-should be here s-s-soon," I told him. I put those *s*'s right into his ear. "The bus-s-s, that iz-z-z . . ." He twitched and pulled his shoulder up. Kept staring. I stepped back. His mom was right. He could hear. He was also ear ticklish.

"I bet you don't get in trouble, do ya?" I said, watching those eyelashes again.

I took two giant Mother-May-I steps toward the road and looked. Still no bus, which meant I had time to scratch open a few of my Connecticut-vacation mosquito

15

bites. Or maybe they were from when we'd made a pit stop in Massachusetts. I started counting off the states we'd driven through on our way home the day before. So I was thinking about states when I heard Frenchie's mom tell my mom, "So, I decided to bring him here, where I could *Maine stream* him."

I quit digging my skin. I popped straight up. I looked at that woman hard. Was she saying she'd moved here to Maine and was going to put Frenchie in a stream?

"Well, hey," I called. "Can he swim?"

Mom and Gracia both laughed.

Mom said, "Mainstream means Frenchie's going to attend public school and go to class like you, Aurora."

Gracia Livernois said, "But you ask a good question. Frenchie doesn't swim."

"Uh, well, knowing how to swim is a smart idea for anyone living around here," I said. "We've got a place where we can teach him."

Gracia knotted her hands together. She brought them up under her chin. "I want him to learn," she said. Then she added, "So many things."

She seemed hunched up and nervous, like she was worried about all the streams in Maine, and the ponds and the ocean too. But I get it now. It was more than that. She had a no-talk boy, heading off for a new start at a new school in a new town.

16

Frenchie

She Was Aurora

Frenchie Livernois stared at the field beyond the mailboxes. Birds were there. Low, in tall grass.

The girl came up from behind. Running, spinning, jumping. She landed beside him. She spoke at him.

"*Wood rat.*"

Quiet is good for seeing birds. So Frenchie kept watch, while the girl hissed right into the hole of his ear.

She told him, "*S-s-soon,*" and "*Bus-s-s.*"

The girl's voice was one. Single. Clear. It gave Frenchie the feeling of birds without seeing birds. Lightness in his fingers. It moved inside him on the path up his arms. Down his ribs. It made his shoulder inch up. A tug from somewhere inside him.

Pretty soon he knew she was Aurora.

She looked where he looked. At the field. When the birds flew up, Aurora called. "Whew-a whew-wheee! Did ya know those were there, all this time, Frenchie?" She flapped her arms.

Arms are like wings. They are not wings.

Hands are like wings. They are not wings.

Frenchie watched the birds put dark flicker shapes on the pale sky. They drew loops, then grew small as dots.

When the birds were gone, Frenchie flapped his hands. He meant to make birdsong. He thought he had. But there was a rumble—down-road from where he stood. It juddered the bottoms of his feet. He felt it at his middle.

Aurora called. Her one clear voice.

"Frenchie! It's coming! *Bus-s-s-s!*"

She was Aurora. And Frenchie was going with her.

Aurora

The Special Person

I remember Mom sticking a bunch of dot Band-Aids on my bites right before the bus came. (She still carries them in all her pockets.) She gave me a quick hug (because I don't like long ones), and I followed Frenchie onto the bus. He proved again that he could hear. How else would he have known what our driver, Helene (same one I had since kindergarten), meant when she told him to take that nice seat right behind her?

"And where do you want me?" I asked.

"Aurora, *baby*, sit anywhere you'd like." (Helene calls everyone *baby*. She draws it out real long, like, *baaaay-bee*.)

The bus was full of the kids who were always splitting off to make tight circles of themselves at school. And at the playground. And at the town beach every summer.

I picked the seat across the aisle from Frenchie. I waved to Mom with both arms, and she waved back with one because she had the other around Gracia's shoulders. Those two were going back to our house for coffee before work, and to become best friends.

I liked being back on the bus. I liked the smell of the rubber floor mats, and I loved the jiggly ride. I liked kicking my Band-Aid-dotted legs out in front of me and wiggling my butt to make the seat squeak. I liked humming a hum that was not a real song, and shouting up to Helene to ask how her summer was, and did she see that cat at the side of the road just now? How about that tractor tire full of black-eyed Susans in that yard right there? Was she surprised I didn't live at the beach anymore?

I liked feeling as if the year was new. No mistakes yet. When I looked over at Frenchie, he seemed pretty much the same as when he'd been staring off across the end of our road at the mailboxes, but now he was staring out the window. Made me wonder, does this kid know what new is? Does he feel that? Does he care? If I watch him real close will I be able to tell?

When we got to school, there was a classroom aide there to meet him, right off the bus. That was Mrs. Kingsley.

"He doesn't talk," I said. "Hope somebody told you that."

"Yes, Aurora. Thank you," she said. "Here we go. This way!" She was very cheery. She marched Frenchie Livernois down the hall with one hand on his back. I didn't think he liked that. He kept hurrying forward and scooting over. I ran up to try to tell Mrs. Kingsley that she should maybe stop doing that, and I accidentally stepped on her heel.

"Ouch!" she said, and she hopped twice.

"Sorry!"

Frenchie was hauling ahead of us. Mrs. Kingsley hustled after him.

Turned out we were all going to Mr. Ritter's room. Frenchie was going to be in my class.

The best thing about the first minutes of the first day of school is nothing has gone wrong yet. I bolted into that room to see if I could find kids to match up with. Like, get a spot at their table. That's always kind of hard for me. *Trying* to fit in does not work. It means folding yourself up into some shape that doesn't feel like you.

School is tough, and I don't mean the learning part. I do okay with that. But I've always had too much to say. I have trouble keeping still—big-time. Even way back in kindergarten, kids didn't like me doing frog-legged cartwheels across the little red rug and crashing through their board games. All my ideas were the loud kind. Hard to keep inside.

Every year, my teachers worked on good *strategies* for me, like:

Look at your friends when they're speaking.

Let them finish their sentences.

Listen to what they say.

I tried. I really did. At home, Mom and Pop tried to help too. They always said, "First things first, Aurora: you get to be who you are. Everyone does. The trick is to see if part of you can take a little time. Watch other people, and see if you can tell how they feel. Be aware."

I actually like that idea. But I'm not sure how well I did it. Until I met Frenchie. I did watch him. The great part was, he didn't care if I talked my head off while I was at it. You can do that; you can talk and watch at the same time. But I've noticed that it works better if I am quiet every once in a while.

The kids in our third-grade class watched Frenchie the first day. Stared at him, is what I mean. Probably wondering what was up with him, same way I did when I met him at the bus stop. I guess nobody was used to a kid who didn't talk and who seemed to like birds more than humans. He looked into the trees a lot. He flapped his hands like little wings, and it turned out he had a mess of bird pictures stuffed into his backpack. But kids stared at Frenchie, then looked away before they had to say anything. Then they stopped noticing him at all. That's what I saw. They leaned left or right to talk around him. They rushed past him to get to one another. Like he wasn't there. Frenchie Livernois. Invisible boy.

But for me, something started to happen those first weeks of third grade. Every time I turned around, there was Frenchie, right behind me. Staring. Not at me. Just at whatever. But he stayed near. Our families were spending time together at home, and like I say, our moms are best friends.

One day, Mrs. Kingsley said, "You do very well with Frenchie, Aurora."

"So do you," I said. It was true. She had stopped rushing him down the hallway. She'd quit putting her hand on his shoulder.

"Well, thank you. But what I mean is, you're very good at reading his behavior."

"What's that mean?" I asked. "You mean seeing how he feels?"

"Exactly," she said. "I think he's chosen you. You are Frenchie's special person."

I smiled. "Yeah. I am."

Aurora

Pebble Nest

Pebble Nest belongs to us. That's our big old house on Flanders Bay. Not fancy. Just awesome. The place can sleep ten people as long as they like each other. If you do two cartwheels down the lawn, then jump the scruffy hedge, you will wind up on a half-circle beach that is covered with a bazillion smooth pebbles, all colors and all kinds of rock. Pop always says there's no better spot for a salty swim and a nap in the sun.

We used to live there. Now we have the A-frame in the woods and we rent Pebble Nest out by the week from May to October. Mom and Pop say the money helps butter our bread. I say Pebble Nest is a reason to love Saturdays.

That's when it's ours again. Saturdays from 10:30 a.m. to 2:30 p.m.

There is a price to pay. We have to clean. The whole place. From top to bottom. Some people wouldn't like the work of it. But it's different when you love a place. Besides, we go at it like machines. We're almost always done by noon. (Best thing we ever did was buy doubles of all the linens so we can take the washing home and bring it back clean the next week.) Then, as long as the weather is even close to good, we can hit the beach to swim, hunt for rocks, or dig for clams. We have lunch up on the lawn. Feels like we live there again. We pack up at two thirty because there has to be no trace of us by three, when the next renters arrive. Sometimes it's families. Sometimes it's a bunch of yoga people or watercolor artists. It's always people from away.

Frenchie comes to Pebble Nest with us every week now, without his mom. But it didn't start out like that. The whole first year, Gracia came too, and she barely let Frenchie out of her sight. Gracia helped us learn to watch him, to *see* all the different ways Frenchie can be. He can get upset. Not often, and he's not a tantrum kid. But if he gets overwhelmed, he shuts down. He tucks up on the ground and wraps his arms over his head. Gets me right in the heart. But Gracia says it's Frenchie's way of claiming the space he needs to get through the upset. The best strategy is to catch it before it happens. But if it does, we let Frenchie know that we are there for him. I think he gets that.

Frenchie's comfortable with us. For two summers now he's been showing up at the door to the A-frame every Saturday morning, ready to go to Pebble Nest.

"It's nice for us and nice for Gracia," Mom says. "It isn't easy being a single parent."

I get that. Pretty sure all parents like breaks. Gracia beams when she sees Frenchie hop out of our van at the end of a Saturday. She gets him back again, and it's like her boy is all her eyes can see. Makes me smile even when I'm not thinking about smiling.

I love it that Frenchie comes to Pebble Nest. He helps! He knows to take the bin full of recycling out to our van. He slides the empty bin under the kitchen sink, right where it belongs. There are some things Frenchie gets. Can't tell you why.

In the upstairs bedrooms, I play tornado. I whip the sheets off the beds and spin the pillows right out of the cases. Frenchie piles the linens into the basket. I always take a few bounces on the naked mattresses. The twin beds are great for a back-and-forth. Of course, I'm not supposed to do that. Frenchie sees me. But he'd never rat me out. When the beds are done, we dust. He's not the best at it, but he follows behind me with his own cloth. Good enough.

The beach at Pebble Nest is where we taught Frenchie how to swim. We got right on that, like Gracia wanted. Mom knew what to do. She said Frenchie should learn two things first: to hold his breath underwater and to float on his back and breathe. The beach was perfect because he could wade into the chilly water nice and easy. I was super excited. I wanted to splash like a sea lion. But I kept calm for Frenchie, and Gracia too. We walked him out just far enough that all we had to do was bend our knees and lower ourselves underwater. I did all the demonstrating.

"Breathing place!" I said, stretching my arms high. Then I pointed down and said, "No breathing below." I took a breath and lowered myself under. It felt like baby steps. But then one Saturday, Frenchie did like I did. He went under! He never choked, not once. I laughed at the way he kept his eyes open, even in the salty water. He was mostly a stare-at-nothing boy, but it seemed like Frenchie looked right at me whenever he was coming up for air. When he did the same with Gracia, she didn't just laugh, she cried.

Teaching him to float was harder. I'm not sure the idea of lying down on top of the water made sense to him, even though I showed him a hundred times. "Sit back, then lie back." Even with Mom and Gracia on each side of him and their good old mom hands underneath him, he would not lie back. He kept *sitting*.

"Sheeshy-sheesh! Way to give yourself a good dunking!" I said.

Our skin was starting to wrinkle. Frenchie's lips were blue. He shivered. I watched him sit back and sink one more time. Enough, I thought. Time to warm up in the sun.

The sun!

"Oh! Wait! I got it," I said. "Frenchie, watch me." I motioned Mom and Gracia out of the way.

"Aurora, he's been watching you," Mom said.

"He's been staring," I said. "Frenchie. Look, look." I tilted my face up. "Are ya watching? Do you know what I feel right now? The sun. On my face. It's up there. You know it is. Now I'm going to sit a little, then I'm going to *lie* back. And I'm going to keep the sun on my face. I'm going to rest my whole self on the water." I slowly lay back. With my ears underwater and my eyes half-closed, I told him, "Here I am just lying on the water. Relaxing. Breathing. And there's the sun up there. Betcha I'll see a bird fly by. That's right, a bird! You've gotta try this, Frenchie."

Well, he did it. Face tilted up to the sun, he lay back and made his body straight.

"That's it, Frenchie! Relax and breathe."

He floated and floated, while Mom and Gracia and I clapped our hands and celebrated.

If there is one thing Frenchie loves as much as birds, it is the sun.

Aurora

Two Years Ago: When Cedar Came Home

With Frenchie and Gracia right next door, it was like our family got bigger. That first winter, I asked Pop if we could build a covered bridge to connect the little house to the A-frame. He said Frenchie and I should build it out of snow, and we tried. There was a melt before we finished. But when more snow came—and we can get dumped on here—Pop cleared a path with the snowblower, from our door to Frenchie's door. We must have gone back and forth ten times a day. We had two places to get a cup of cocoa.

When my little brother, Cedar, came along the next fall, Gracia and Frenchie helped like family would help.

Cedar was adopted, and that can take way longer than it takes to grow a baby. I mean, years. Mom and Pop couldn't have any more kids after me, so there was nothing to do but sign papers and wait. Forever. But, funny how one day when we weren't expecting it, the call came, and boy, did we hop to it. Mom and Pop got in the car, and I went to stay the night with Gracia and Frenchie. In the morning, we came back to the A-frame. We cleaned and washed up my old baby clothes and some of Frenchie's too. We hung the crib sheets in the sun. I was glad the three of us were together because I was worried. We had gotten ready for our new baby a few times before. And then . . . no baby. All of us cried. We felt like someone was missing.

But this time, Mom and Pop came home with our Cedar.

Here's what I remember about that afternoon:

First, our baby was crying his head off. He was pulling at his ears and leaving little bloody kitten scratches on his cheeks. "Poor little man," Mom said. "He's got double ear infections."

Second, he had shiny black curls all over his head that lay down like little *o*'s.

Third, even though he was not as weensie as the newborns I had seen, he was still the smallest, twisty-squirmy little person I'd ever held in my arms.

The fourth thing I remember was how I felt way deep

inside the middle of me. I decided it had to be my heart melting. That made me laugh and then cry, and look at my parents, then back at Cedar, and laugh again. I knew I was going to love that screaming baby for the rest of my life.

Cedar had fevers and misery for the whole first winter and on into mud season. He stayed up way past everyone's bedtime. He needed a lot of rocking, humming, and dancing with Mom and Pop, and even me. Frenchie and his mom came every day. Gracia would dance Cedar all around the open floor plan of the A-frame while Frenchie and I listened to bird calls at the computer and Mom and Pop took naps.

Cedar saw our pediatrician a lot. He sucked down syringes full of gloppy pink medicine. Then he threw it up and magically made it look like twice as much.

Mom and Pop took him to an ear doctor, and a man called the naturopath, and a woman called an acupuncturist. Finally, finally, summertime came and the ear troubles faded, at least for a while. It was like Cedar could start being Cedar. Mom and Pop think the warm, dry weather did it. Probably right. He had troubles again last winter. The infections come and go now. Not as bad. Still, we know there are times when Cedar doesn't hear us. The doctor said that might be why he doesn't talk much yet, and why he's hard to understand. The words probably sound right to him. They just aren't always clear to us. But he tries, so we try too. We listen. This year, Cedar finally calls me by my name. He says, *Awoh-wah*. And I love it.

Aurora

Darleen Dombroski

At Mountain View School, we celebrate new siblings. (I think it's nice that they say *new siblings*, because sometimes older kids are new too.)

Ever since kindergarten I have been meeting everybody else's new siblings, mostly tiny babies. I had to get to fourth grade before it was finally my turn. I was rip-ready to introduce my baby brother. Turned out to be the best day of school ever.

Mrs. Santiago had our class measure Cedar in inches. Then we converted him to metric. We had a talk about adoption. We sang "You Are My Sunshine" and "What a Wonderful World." We ate cupcakes in Cedar's honor, and I got to take one home for our freezer. Cedar could have it when Mom and Pop decided he was old enough. At the end, we set up for a photograph of all of us together. I sat in the center holding Cedar, and my classmates crowded all around us. I looked left, then right.

"Wait, wait! Where's Frenchie?" I wanted to know. He'd gotten inched out—all the way to one end, almost out of the shot. "Make way! Frenchie to the front!" I called.

Mrs. Santiago brought him up beside me. "This is our picture," I told him. "You, me, and this new baby bird." I rocked Cedar in my arms. We got the shot.

The next morning, Mrs. Santiago gave me two prints of the photo. "The large one in the frame is for your family," she said. "I laminated the smaller one for you, Aurora. Pocket-size, so you can carry it with you."

I thanked her, then I spun around the room, showing the picture to anyone who wanted to see it. During class, I put my picture into my desk, where I could sneak peeks at it. But Mrs. Santiago had to ask if maybe the photo was too great a distraction for me.

"Last time," I promised her. I pushed it into the back of my desk. Before lunch and recess, I put that photo in the pocket of my shorts.

Every day, Frenchie and I run, from the edge of the blacktop, across the playing field to the backstop. It's a fifty-yard dash according to our gym teacher. Of course we run back again, so it's really a hundred.

But this day, our art teacher, Mrs. Chandra, had put

out a big new bucket of sidewalk chalk. That always brings a swarm of artists. I couldn't resist. I grabbed a thick new stick of chalk and claimed a patch of blacktop.

Frenchie paced beside me. He went twenty feet away, then came back, again and again. I knew he wanted to run. He counts on things to happen the same way every day.

"One quick chalk picture," I told him. "Okay?" Then I heard a voice I knew.

"He doesn't know what you're saying."

I scraped the tip of my chalk down hard. *Darleen Dombroski.* If I had noticed that she was making chalk pictures too, I would have skipped it. (One of my strategies at school is to stay clear of Darleen. I came up with that one on my own.)

"He does know," I said. "Look at his hands." I waited for her to put eyes on Frenchie. Emma Bowman and Milo Robinette looked up from their chalk art too, and I figured, good. They will notice him. "See him making those little fist squeezes?" I asked.

"So what?" Darleen shrugged.

"That's what he does when something isn't quite right. Like now. He's impatient. And disappointed. He wants me to run with him."

Darleen huffed and shook her head. She swung her shoulders. *No, no, no.*

"He might be a little upset that we are talking *about* him instead of *to* him. Or he might not like the way you're talking to me," I added. "Just saying."

"You don't know that. You're not his mind reader, Aurora."

That made me think back to third grade, when Mrs. Kingsley said I was good at reading Frenchie's behavior. I watched the different ways he stood, and moved his hands, and fluttered his eyelids. Those things told me what his mind was up to and how he was feeling. So . . . maybe I *was* Frenchie's mind reader. To me, it was funny! I tried to hold back a snicker, but it flew out anyway— snort! That made Milo laugh. Then Emma laughed too. Darleen narrowed her eyes at me.

Frenchie swept by again, still squeezing his hands open and closed.

"Hey, I'm trying to draw a cardinal for you," I said. "But this red chalk is more like pink. . . ."

Then I remembered the photo in my pocket. Frenchie would love to hold it for me. I jumped up. "Hey, want to look?" I held the photo out. He put his hand up to take it, then paced away again, all one motion. "It's from our Sibling Day!" I called.

"He won't remember *Sibling Day*." Darleen bobbled her head as she spoke. "He definitely doesn't get that the baby is your brother. Your baby *bird*," she added, *not nicely*. That's when I should have walked away from Darleen. But in the next second Frenchie came striding up with the

36

photo in his hand. He was looking at it closely, the same way he studies his bird pictures. So I had to go and say it:

"Hey, Darleen. Check it out," I waved my chalk stick in Frenchie's direction. "See how he's looking at that photo? He knows every person in it, including Cedar."

"You can't be sure. . . ."

"Well . . . when Frenchie is at our house, which is almost every day, he's the first one to hear Cedar fussing when he wakes up. He goes and stands beside the crib until someone comes to get Cedar."

"Proves nothing," Darleen said.

"It proves everything!"

Then Emma Bowman piped up. "Well, it sounds like he knows there is a baby. And he pays attention to him." Then Milo Robinette agreed.

Then it got quiet. And then . . . there it was, Darleen's crumpled face. The cry. This is the tough thing about her. The inside of her head tells her that everything is somehow *mean to Darleen*. There had been plenty of times her crying didn't go so well for *me*. So I jumped in.

"Don't cry!" I said. "If you don't believe me, fine. Forget it."

She sniffled and whimpered. (I can't stand when she does that.) Both Emma and Milo got up and patted her back. "It's okay, Darleen. You're fine."

Mrs. Woodsum, who had recess duty that day, came

over. Darleen's voice shook while she told Mrs. Woodsum that I told a made-up story—*lied*—to make her feel bad. *And* laughed at her!

"Nope. Not a lie." I pushed my hands deep into my pockets. "It was a true story. An example, actually. And the laugh was just—a noise that came out of me."

Frenchie stood behind me, clenching the Sibling Day photo in one hand and making fist squeezes with his other.

Emma and Milo and some other kids—ones who don't play with me, or Frenchie, *or* Darleen—actually stood up for me. First time ever for that.

Mrs. Woodsum walked Darleen over to the corner of the blacktop, and I don't know what got said there. She told me to wait. I was next. I folded my arms on my chest. Frenchie stood beside me, in his full *no* pose now, chin jutting.

"Hey, Frenchie. It's okay," I said. "Just taking a bite out of recess, is all." I sighed. "Forget the chalk. We should be running our hundred-yard dash."

When Mrs. Woodsum took me to the corner, I told her exactly what had happened. "So you can see," I said, "Darleen was *terribly confused and wrong.*" Mrs. Woodsum walked me back to Darleen. She held us both by a hand— firm but gentle, which is infuriating—and she said, "Now, girls, Frenchie doesn't speak, but he is a human being just like each of you are. So let's always choose kindness, okay?"

What? Was she really saying that to me?

"Girls? Do you both understand?"

Darleen nodded, but I shrugged.

"Aurora?" Mrs. Woodsum pressed me.

"I am kind to Frenchie," I said. I twisted my hand out of Mrs. Woodsum's hand. "I should *not* be in trouble right now—"

"Aurora. You're not in trouble." Mrs. Woodsum sure sounded stern. "Remember that there's always something to learn from every disagreement."

I disagree, I thought. But I didn't say it.

"Can I go now? Please?"

Mrs. Woodsum said yes. I tossed my chalk back in the bucket.

"Frenchie! Time to run! Ready, set, go!"

Aurora

Back-to-School Shopping

Mom and Gracia are sticking to all our back-to-school traditions. They know it's bugging me that Frenchie and I won't be together.

Mom's a freelance writer. Most of her articles are for the *Great-State Travel Guide of Maine*. (There is a *Great-State Travel Guide of New Hampshire* too. And Vermont. Et cetera.) She makes space in her days by writing at night. She promises that we'll go to our usual lunch at the Picklonious Deli this year, with the stop at Taunton Bay Sweets afterward, and, of course, the back-to-school clothes-shopping trip at Renys. We always get that in before the crowds. And before all the plaid shirts are gone.

We're good at shopping. By that I mean we move

along so Frenchie doesn't get overwhelmed. A store like Renys can do that to him. Big space, bright lights. A lot of sounds, and people. What's new this year is that Cedar is fast on his feet. The second we wrestle our cart through the door he breaks away.

"Runner!" I cry.

Gracia is closest. She lunges and misses. Frenchie is gazing up at the ceiling lights. He's got his needlepoint purse tucked against his side like always. He's not much for running after Cedar anyway.

I am on it. Cedar's little sneakers slap along the tiled floor. I chase him through the shoe department, into the ladies' department. I run up behind him and almost knock him down. He points at a peg wall full of tote bags and pocketbooks.

"En-chee," he said. (That's what he calls Frenchie.)

"Yep, yep," I said. "Those purses are kind of like Frenchie's. But we don't need those today, Cedar Tree." I scoop him up. Lucky thing, he doesn't scream or twist—or worst of all, go limp. He can slide away like a hot stick of butter if he wants to.

I run him back to meet our cart in the boys' department. Gracia is holding a pair of khaki pants up to the backside of Frenchie, checking the fit. She gets him the same kind every year, except longer. Easy-peasy. Two pairs in the cart.

Mom hoists Cedar into the seat in the shopping cart.

"Let's hustle along," she sings, and Gracia laughs. All of us know, Cedar won't stay put for long.

"Next stop. Plaid shirts!" I say. (They *have* to be plaid.) I lead the way. Gracia makes a quick decision about size, then holds up three shirts in different plaids.

"Frenchie? Do you like these?" she asks. He doesn't answer, but he doesn't take the *no* pose either. In fact, he puts his arms around all three shirts and carries them to the cart. Sometimes, when he does stuff like that it makes Gracia cry.

As for me, I find things in the boys' and girls' departments. Today, it's three pairs of boys' sports shorts. Double mesh. Hems that hit below my knees, elastic waist with plenty of room, and my favorite thing, big deep pockets in front. I wear shorts all year, and leggings underneath when it's below freezing. But I'm not a kid who feels the cold much.

In the girls' department, I go round and round the racks, tapping every shirt on the shoulder with the palm of my hand. "Naw, naw, naw. Nope. Yuck."

"Take another look," Mom says.

"Eh. I got my old stuff. Still fits." (This argument is part of our back-to-school shopping tradition.)

"Understood," Mom says. "But your clothes have been worn hard, Aurora. It might be nice to have something without stains for picture day."

I groan. Then I spot a rack with tank tops on it. (They

can be impossible to find once fall comes.) "Yes!" I cheer. "Plain ones! No words or pictures!"

I grab up two, and Mom adds two more.

"Oh, and maybe . . . this!" I yank a zip-up hoodie off a circular rack. The hanger flips off the rack and flies over my shoulder. "Whoa!"

"Aurora. Go gently," Mom says, while Gracia hides a laugh.

"Can't help it!" I say. "They've got hoppin' hangers in here!" I bounce up and down and swing the hoodie in the air. Cedar is watching me. He starts to giggle.

Then I hear more giggling. I see two girls and two moms. One mom and daughter have dark tumbles of hair, almost exactly the same. They are wearing bright tunic tops with embroidery and mirror beads over their blue jeans. You could never find tops like that here in Renys. They look like something from India, I think. Then the mom speaks.

"How to put fun into a shopping trip!" Yep. I hear the Indian accent. Her dark eyes dance at Cedar. "That chuckle is so cute, don't you think so, Leena?" The girl grins and nods.

The other mom is redheaded, and the girl is very blond, with a pink sunburn on her nose, cheeks, and shoulders. Everyone is smiling, and I even see them notice Frenchie, who is being quiet beside our cart and staring up at the lights again. (Sometimes when there's a lot going

43

on, Frenchie picks one thing to focus on.) The blond girl looks up like she's trying to see what he is looking at.

"It's the lights," I say. "Unless a bird got inside. Or a clothes hanger!" We laugh. I hold the hoodie up and make a goofy face. "Guess I'll try this on." I hope they'll stick around. I want to make them laugh some more. But they wave and disappear around the next aisle. Oh well.

Gracia, who Mom says is the best shopping partner ever, finds me two pairs of leggings.

"Love 'em!" I say. "Even better than the ones you picked for me last year."

"Oh good!" Gracia laughs. "It makes me cold to see your bare legs in winter."

"New can be nice. Besides, I did go through the knees of the old ones during mud season."

Mom stands by, nodding. I peel out of the hoodie, and Gracia hands me a long-sleeve tee. I slip it over my tank.

"It's *you*," Gracia says. I love that she knows what I like.

"It's me . . . as long as we can get this scratchy tag out of the neck. . . ." I reach back and tug at the neck of the shirt. I let out a growl.

"Of course," Gracia says. "We'll have our annual detagging ritual."

"Oh . . . meanwhile . . . you need underpants," Mom says, in her loud-mom voice.

"Oh, underpants, you say? Not sure the people over in the birdseed aisle heard you, Mom!" I point across the store, and Mom laughs. She takes Cedar, who wants out of the cart now anyway, to go find underpants.

Gracia and I look around some more, and Frenchie makes sure my clothes and his clothes have a nice space between them in the cart. He likes some things to be done a certain way. But something else seems to be bothering him. He's making little fists by his sides. I get an idea in my head.

"Hey, you want to push?" I say, and he steps right up.

He wraps his hands around the bar and starts the cart rolling.

"There ya go. Come on. We'll find my mom and Cedar. See if they've found me some *underpants!*"

"Aurora, you are a thoughtful friend," Gracia tells me as we stroll.

"Well, he asked for what he wanted," I say. "So, it's a little bit him asking and a little bit me guessing."

"Guessing correctly." Gracia uses her butter voice. "You are truly special."

I smile and give a little shrug, and think, I am Frenchie's special person. Then I remember the placement letters from the school. I swallow hard. Because the thing is, Frenchie is my special person too.

I think:

It's coming, Aurora. You're going to be in Ms. Beccia's class, but Frenchie will be in Mrs. Hillsbeck's. Apart.

I cannot picture it! My heart begins to sink.

Cedar comes running. His dark curls bounce on his head; his chubby cheeks bounce on his face. He's holding a pack of underpants by one corner, swinging it hard. He runs right at us and wriggles by.

I go after him, calling, "Cedar! Come back here with that!"

He stops and flings the package up in the air. It spins right up over the top of the display. I cover my mouth and catch Gracia's eye. We hear the package land in the next aisle over. Then a lot of laughing.

I race around the end aisle and see the two girls and two moms. Again! The sunburned girl is bent over laughing. The girl in the bright tunic smiles. She holds the pack of underpants out to me.

"I think these are for you?" I love how she says it and asks it all at the same time.

"Yup." I jab a thumb toward Cedar. "He tossed them. Up and over!" I say as Mom and Gracia and Frenchie meet us in the aisle.

Soon we are talking to Joanie Waller and her mom, from Collingswood, New Jersey, and Leena Virani and her mom, from Atlanta, Georgia. Ha! I think. The girl from away, and the girl from farther away.

The moms talk to each other, and the girls talk to me. Cedar climbs the side of the shopping cart, and Frenchie waits, but he faces away. Maybe he understands, or maybe

46

he doesn't, but we are learning that both Joanie and Leena have moved to town. Both are new this year. And both will be in *my* sixth-grade class with Ms. Beccia.

"Beccia! Yes!" I whoop. I cover my mouth with both hands and bounce on the balls of my feet. I'm making Leena and Joanie laugh, and I love it.

The moms are agreeing that we should get together before the start of school—*and* that we should do that this Saturday at Pebble Nest. Leena and Joanie want to come! And me, I am thinking the strangest thing of all: it is possible that this is going well.

But then it starts. Frenchie sways and moans. There is too much going on inside of Renys now. Too much for Frenchie. These are new people. Everyone's excited, and we're talking too loudly, and all at once. He rocks and holds tight to the shopping cart. His moaning turns to a hollow woo-oo-woo-oo. All I can think is, we're going to have to leave, and I *so* don't want to.

I tell myself, Don't be *dirt*, Aurora.

I know Frenchie can't help this. He's in a super struggle. He's suffering. Gracia once said being upset gives him more pain than the times he's actually injured. We have to make it better for him. Right now.

Gracia is on it. She tells him, "I'm here. Frenchie." (The butter voice.) She takes a few steps with him. She turns to everyone and smiles her gentle smile. "We need to move on toward the checkout. So, Rene, follow whenever you're ready."

"We'll be right behind you," Mom says, and I know she means it.

"Right behind you," I echo. I feel pulled to go with them and pulled to stay where I am.

"Bye, Frenchie. Bye," Leena and Joanie and both their moms call after him softly. They seem to understand. Mom stays to get phone numbers.

"See you Saturday!" I tell the girls. I hustle to catch up to Gracia and Frenchie. She is cooing with him, letting him know she's there for him. She'll pull him out of this.

And she does. By the time we leave, Frenchie is more himself. He carries his new clothes in the Renys bag right against his chest. I'm more myself too. The Saturday plan with the new friends is a go! I am keeping a cork in my excitement. But I cannot fool Mom. She gives me a wink. She knows how I feel. I am over the moon!

In the evening, Frenchie and Gracia come to our house. Pop starts us a pancake supper. We like them fluffy, so he separates the eggs and whips the whites. Frenchie kneels on the kitchen stool and stares into the batter bowl. (He loves to watch the mixer.)

I hear Pop telling him, "See how it gets foamy first? Keep watching. Stiff peaks will form. . . ."

Gracia and Mom sit on the couch picking the stitches

out of the tags on some of the new clothes—mine and Frenchie's. We both go bonkers about tags. Sort of funny how the kid who likes his belt pulled tight can't stand tags. Me, I can't stand either.

I have built up some energy inside me tonight, and it wants out. I get on my back on the floor and do bicycle legs and fist pumps. I happened to look at Gracia as she leans down to bite a thread out of one of my new tops.

"Umm . . . pitooey!" she says. She picks the thread off her lip.

"Go, Gracia! Get 'em any way you can," Mom says with a laugh.

"Nice of you, doing all that thread picking," I say from my spot on the floor. I roll back and push up into a shoulder stand and continue to bike. "I don't have enough patience for that. Of course, if you know me, you know that."

"We're up to the challenge," Mom says. "I'm glad the back-to-school shopping is done." (She says that every year.) Mom mouths a thank-you to Gracia. She thinks I don't see her do it, but I do.

"Such a nice coincidence, meeting the new girls and new moms today," Gracia says. "I'm looking forward to Saturday."

"Umm," I say. But I hope she won't say much more about it. I let my shoulder stand go off-balance. Faking it.

"Whoa-whoa!" I grunt and pretend to concentrate.

I liked those girls, Leena and Joanie, and I felt like they already liked me back. Two new girls. In my class! Imagining what that would be like was getting all tangled up with knowing I wouldn't be with Frenchie.

How was he going do without me?

How would I do without him?

Aurora

The First Day of Sixth Grade

The last days of summer vacation are way different than any before. Joanie and Leena and their moms come to Pebble Nest. The Viranis surprise us all when they drive up in their shiny new food truck, with Leena's big sister, Zenia, on board. She is our server. We have Virani Family Indian Cuisine for lunch. I fall in love with potato-and-pea samosas with tamarind sauce.

I keep Frenchie in my sights—or I mean to. But I get busy sketching Leena and Joanie a map of the school. Everything will be new for them. When I look up, Frenchie is wading at the edge of the water and Gracia is sitting on the beach with Joanie's mom. Frenchie is on a break. A people break.

We keep all our end-of-summer dates with Frenchie and Gracia. He likes those days best, when he knows what to expect. But he and Gracia come for a lunch date at Joanie's house one day, and we all hike the Hidden Ponds Loop another. Frenchie is most comfortable staying off to the side, a bit ahead or behind. I am completely comfortable everywhere. I am having a ton of fun.

On the last weekend before school begins, we host a sixth graders' super-supper cookout at the A-frame. Gracia has us all making personal pizzas on the grill. Pop lights candle lanterns, and Mom builds us a campfire for toasting marshmallows and pineapple kebabs. We tell not-very-scary ghost stories.

And now I don't want summer to end.

It's a good thing school always starts just before Labor Day. Three days to get used to it. Three days off. Then a short week. It's like a break at the beginning.

The air still feels like summertime on our first day of sixth grade. I wait with Frenchie at our bus stop. I scuff up the gravel, pacing left, then right. I get the same old feelings. Fresh start coming. Helene will drive our bus again. The floor mats will smell clean and rubbery until someone spills milk or yogurt and sours them up.

For days I've been reminding Frenchie, "Mrs. Kingsley will meet us. Like always. And I'll walk with you to *your* classroom. But then I'll have to go down the hall to *mine*." He doesn't answer. Not in a way that anyone else would understand. But I see the little fist squeezes.

I lean toward him and whisper, "I know. I'm not so sure about this either."

He raises his shoulder up. "Oops. Sorry. Gave you an ear-tickler, didn't I?"

Then it turns out I am wrong. Mrs. Kingsley is not there—or at least she isn't there to meet us. I can see through the glass panel that the office is full of kids and parents with first-day-of-school problems to sort out. But I know where Frenchie's classroom is. (Our school is small.) We can get there on our own.

A guy meets us at the door. At first I think he's another kid. But then he speaks and his voice is deep. He's a man. He's young.

"Oh! Hello, you must be Frenchie," he says. Frenchie stares past him. Then the guy looks at me. "And you must be Aurora."

"Am," I say. "You already heard about me, huh?"

"I heard Frenchie would be coming in with you," he says. "I'm Mr. Menkis. I'm a very recent hire. I just got off the phone with Frenchie's mom. Mrs. Whilmer and I called to let her know I'm Frenchie's new aide."

I raise my eyebrows. "*You are?* Wonder what happened to Mrs. Kingsley," I say.

Mr. Menkis shrugs. "A last-minute change."

"Are you old enough to teach here?" I ask. "Because, um . . . you are small. I mean short."

"I am short. But yes, I can teach here. Today's my first day," he says.

"So you mean we're about to find out." I rock my head from side to side.

He sputters a little, and I think he's trying not to laugh.

I decide that Mr. Menkis is cheery but not in a drive-you-nuts way like some people are when they meet Frenchie. *Overly effusive* is what Mom and Gracia call that. It's when people are too loud and too happy, and talk fast. It makes me feel like they're afraid to leave any space between their words because if they do, something could go wrong in there. Frenchie and I both get some *overly effusive* greetings from adults when they first meet us. I shrug it off. But nothing makes Frenchie cross a room faster.

"We thought you'd be waiting out front," I tell Mr. Menkis. "That's how this usually works."

"Well, I was there. But your bus was delayed this morn—"

"Well, that happens a lot on the first day," I say. "Oh. Sorry for interrupting."

"Sure. The office was going to call me—"

"Oh. The office." I roll my eyes. "It's a circus in there. More first-day stuff."

"Right. Well, I came back down to steal a few minutes and set up Frenchie's desk. So thanks for escorting him,

54

Aurora. I've got it from here. You can go on to your class-room," he says. "The day is about to begin."

"Hmm. Well, I promised Frenchie I'd walk him *into* his room. He'll take that to heart," I say.

I point a finger and repeat, "*Into.*"

"That works for me," Mr. Menkis says, "at least for today." He steps aside.

Frenchie's classmates are sitting down, which means mine are too. Down the hall. His classroom teacher, old Mrs. Hillsbeck, is up in front getting ready to take attendance. I think she's been around since our school was built, and that was a long time ago. That's how it is in our town. Teachers either stay a really long time or a really short time.

I see Frenchie's name tag taped to the top of his new desk. There are three bird identification cards all in a row.

"Oh, hey. Great idea!" I say. I give Mr. Menkis a nod. "Frenchie is all about birds."

"This is what I hear."

"See his needlepoint purse? Get him to show you what's in there."

"I sure will," he says.

"Great . . ." I want to stay longer. Maybe until lunch-time. Maybe until the last bell.

"Okay, Aurora . . ." Mr. Menkis looks at his watch. I take the hint.

"Going," I say.

But first I tell Frenchie I'll see him at lunch and recess. I want him to be okay. My own armpits feel a little cold and sweaty as I go out that door.

Ms. Beccia is probably going to pronounce my last name wrong. My whole class is going to crack up.

"Can't wait." I sigh and roll my eyes on my way down the hall.

Then I remember that I'll have two new friends in my classroom. Joanie and Leena. The girl from away, and the girl from farther away.

"Yes!" I pull up on the straps of my backpack and go speed-walking down the hall.

Aurora

Preposterous Pursuits

The first morning of sixth grade flies by. Ms. Beccia is a funny, laugh-out-loud teacher! She gets my last name right! She lets Leena and Joanie and me push our desks together in a triangle. I don't have to worry about Darleen Dombroski because she is not in my class. She's down the hall with Mrs. Hillsbeck. And Frenchie. When I think about Frenchie, I want to run and peek inside that room. But Ms. Beccia's classroom is a busy place. We're doing math already. (Placeholders and rounding.) Since Frenchie and I were never in this room together, I'm not looking for him here the way I thought I'd be.

At lunchtime, I take hops ahead of Leena and Joanie. At the door to the multipurpose room, I point them to the small round table tucked up beside the stage. "Frenchie and I sit there, a little bit apart, because lunchtime gets noisy," I say. "But see? There's room for four."

They go in while I wait for Frenchie. He comes down the hall, taking long Frenchie strides, with Mr. Menkis beside him. I wave my arm overhead. "Hey, Frenchie! How was it? Did you have a good morning?"

Mr. Menkis answers for him with a nod.

"I'll meet you at the door after recess, Frenchie," he says. "Enjoy your lunch. You as well, Aurora."

"Thanks, Mr. Menkis! You too!" I turn to Frenchie. "Come on," I say. "Leena and Joanie are already at our table."

I make sure he gets the chair he is used to, the one that faces the stage. He twists it a hitch, so he is turned slightly away from us. He does that around the new friends, I have noticed. But he opens his lunch and begins to eat.

Leena opens a container of Indian food. In seconds, the air around our table smells unbearably fantastic. She digs into her backpack and brings out a notebook.

"Look," she says. Big smile. She flashes the cover. I see hand lettering.

Joanie reads. "'Preposterous Pursuits.'" She raises her eyebrows. "What's this?"

"Okay." Leena takes a breath like she's been dying to tell us. "I have been thinking about this since new students' orientation day. Preposterous Pursuits is a list

58

of activities to do during recess. The expected, *and* the unexpected. Think *challenges*," she says. "Think, *scavenger hunt*. The idea is, we put that playground to the test."

"You mean, explore its possibilities?" I ask.

"Exactly! And we work as a team. No winners or losers. Just things to do. All of us. Together."

"Wait. I need an example," Joanie says.

"Okay, sure." Leena opens the notebook. "So one of my ideas is the Acorn Carry. For this one, you pile as many acorns as you can onto *one* hand. Keep your other hand behind your back and walk from the oak tree back to the blacktop. The blacktop is our home base. The idea is to *collectively* bring as many acorns home as we can."

"Oh . . . I think I get it." Joanie nods.

I stay quiet because I'm thinking.

Leena reads more examples. "Dog and Bone. One person is the *dog* with a blindfold on, and they have to guess who snuck up and stole their bone. Human Sundial is the coolest. We'll need chalk for that one. High-Water Mark. We jump up and scratch a mark with a stone in the brick wall, as high as we can reach. And we can brainstorm more!" Leena holds her pencil ready.

I glance at Frenchie beside me. Still turned away and nibbling on his sandwich. I wonder how he'll do with Preposterous Pursuits. . . .

"Bird Search!" I blurt. "Oops. Sorry so loud."

"It's perfect!" Leena adds my idea to the list.

"Hundred-Yard Dash!" I lean toward Frenchie. "Every day, right? And we'll try the other pursuits too. Okay?"

He pulls his elbows in. Leena catches my eye.

"If anyone wants to opt out of a pursuit, that's totally fine," she says. "We can revisit any one of them any time."

"Ya know what?" Joanie tilts her head. "We should keep count. In the notebook. Add a tally mark for every hundred yards we run. For challenges like the Acorn Carry, we can try to best ourselves. We can keep a bar graph!"

Leena squeezes Joanie's arm. "Yes!"

"Record the results!" I clap my hands. "Genius! This whole thing is genius! And, Leena, you better give each challenge its own page."

"Oh. My. Gosh! Yes." She flips to a blank page and makes the first header: 100-YARD DASH.

Before we leave the lunch table for our first recess of the year, we have added half a dozen pursuits to Leena's list. When we get outside, we dive right in.

It goes okay. For Frenchie, I mean. He follows a few steps behind me for a round of Garbage Grab. That's Joanie's idea. We go around the edge of the playground picking up paper litter. (Nothing gooey.) We fill up the brown bag from her lunch in no time, and dump it in the receptacle.

"We need more bags!" I say. "Lot of litter!" We make Garbage Grab a Priority Pursuit. Leena stars the page.

Joanie writes the date and draws a picture graph: one bag.

I *love, love, love* the way this is coming together.

But Frenchie doesn't. He twists his fingers into the strap of the needlepoint purse and goes to pace at the edge of the blacktop.

I turn to Joanie and Leena. "It's time. Gotta dash," I say. "Hundred yards, that is." It splits me up from them. (They are not dashers.) I don't mind so much because Frenchie and I will earn two tally marks for the book.

I call to him. "Ready, set, go!"

By Friday, the third day of school, I am sure of three things: Preposterous Pursuits will be never ending. And never boring. *And* I have *friends*!

I run the second hundred-yard dash of the day with Frenchie. We've worn a pair of paths, from the edge of the blacktop to the backstop, and not because of Preposterous Pursuits. We started this way back. I do the math: 180 days of school each year (minus a few for bad weather), multiplied times three. Whoa! 540 days of running! We have wrecked the grass. We have left our mark.

We reach the backstop, tag it, and turn. Running back, I've got my eye on Leena and Joanie. They're on the blacktop together, notebook open. On the ground beside them is the yardstick Ms. Beccia let us borrow. We need it for measuring Hop, Skip, and Jump and High-Water Mark. We're trying to do both today because tomorrow is the start of a three-day weekend, and Leena likes setting goals.

Frenchie and I finish our run, and Joanie cheers, "The Hundred-Yard Dash page is filling fast!"

"Whew!" I lean over my knees and breathe. Frenchie switches to pacing. "Hear that, Frenchie? The tally is climbing. All because of you!"

Yesterday, we played Bird Search, with Frenchie in the lead, but I'm not sure he knew he was leading. We walked under the trees with him and counted all his flaps and tweets. Mrs. Woodsum came over to see what we were doing.

"Girls," she said, her eyebrows low, "this seems a bit unkind."

"What? Why?" I asked. Joanie and Leena stood beside me looking petrified.

"I see you writing in a notebook every time Frenchie flaps his hands." Mrs. Woodsum shakes her head. "And I hear a lot of giggling." She gives us a look. Stern and disappointed. "Girls, Frenchie's not able to control—"

"Wait. No," I said. "Sorry for interrupting. But it's *not* unkind. I get why you could think that, Mrs. Woodsum. But this is a game about spotting birds. Perfect for a kid who loves them."

"W-we're including him," Joanie whispered in a mouse voice.

Well, big surprise. Mrs. Woodsum accepted my explanation and left us to our bird search. Leena and Joanie thought I was brave for standing up to her.

"Well, I've had experience," I said. "If you mess up, admit it. But if you didn't, you should say so."

"Defend the truth!" Joanie said, her fist in the air. That made us laugh.

"Mrs. Woodsum should know better," I mumbled. "I've been Frenchie's friend for a long time."

"I bet she saw it differently because Joanie and I are here too," Leena said.

Things have been different, and nobody feels it more than Frenchie. I can see. He paces when I poke my nose into the Preposterous Pursuits notebook. He does hand squeezes if a pursuit takes too long. Then I have to stop and do another dash with him. A couple of times now, I've thought I should drop out of Preposterous Pursuits. But I like it too much to leave it.

Today, with two runs done, Leena and Joanie and I go on to Hop, Skip, and Jump. (I cannot get Frenchie to try, even when I remind him that birds hop too.) We take running starts and hop, skip, and jump. We use Ms. Beccia's yard stick to measure our distance. From the corner of my eye, I see Frenchie pacing.

"Hey," I say, "we already did two runs. Give me a few minutes, okay?"

It's not okay. I know it's not. But I feel a little burn. Frustration is what that is.

When Leena and Joanie gather up the notebook and the yard stick and head to the brick wall for High-Water Mark, I go. I'm in a jumping mood. I jump all the way to the wall, all of us laughing. Except Frenchie. I call for him to come. I wind my arm round and round. Joanie tries to get him. But he walks wide to avoid her.

Then I hear it. "Woo-woo . . ." and I stop in my tracks.

"Woo-woo . . ." At the edge of the blacktop, Frenchie sinks to the ground.

"Oh no . . ."

He tucks up like an egg.

"Frenchie! It's okay!" I go to him, but I'm too late.

He folds his arms over his head and shuts down.

I sit beside him while Joanie and Leena speak to the playground monitor. She sends them to get Mr. Menkis.

Aurora

Waiting on Frenchie

Mr. Menkis does exactly the right thing. He doesn't rush up. He arrives, and brings the calm with him. He sits down with Frenchie and me. He asks everyone to give us some space. Perfect word. This is Frenchie's space. Like Gracia told us years ago, it's the space he makes for himself when he needs it. Our job is to sit near and talk softly. That's what Mr. Menkis and I do.

The recess bell rings. I give Leena and Joanie the tiniest finger wave as they join the line to go inside because, of course, I'm staying with Frenchie.

"Any idea what happened?" Mr. Menkis asks.

"Yeah." I puff out a breath. "I've been doing stuff he isn't used to, and it messes with him." I explain about

Preposterous Pursuits and hundred-yard dashes. "The problem is, I need to be in two places at once," I say. "It's impossible."

"Ahh . . ." Mr. Menkis nods.

"I feel bad about it . . . but . . ." I shake my head and don't finish.

"You're having a new kind of year." Mr. Menkis says it for me. "Treat yourself sweetly, Aurora. Change happens. It's the world's number one constant." He pushes his feet out in front of him, and his hands behind him. He tilts his head back so his face is in the sun.

I do the same. I whisper, "S-s-sun sure feels good right now. Feel it, Frenchie?"

"Do I hear sparrows?" Mr. Menkis asks softly. He gives a low whistle, follows with a cheepity-cheep-cheep.

We are waiting for Frenchie to feel like himself again.

"Aurora," Mr. Menkis says, "keep in mind, having new friends doesn't mean you're leaving someone else behind."

"Thanks, Mr. Menkis. Nice of you to say it."

Beside me, Frenchie begins to relax. He lowers his arms. He stretches one leg forward.

"You're like a bird leaving the egg," I tell him. "You're hatching."

Ed Petrequin

In the Drop-Off Circle

Ed Petrequin arrived at Mountain View School's morning drop-off circle a little on the early side the first Friday in September. Cedar had a morning appointment with the ear doctor over in Ellsworth. Given the late-summer traffic, the sooner Ed got on the road, the better. Aurora and Frenchie both hopped out onto the sidewalk. In the back seat, Cedar cried out.

"Bye-baw! Bye-baw!"

His little boy had something to say. Ed was sure of it, and he was trying his darnedest to understand. But he had his eye on Aurora and Frenchie too. The boy was staring off, which he did quite often. Ed waited to make sure Aurora circled back to collect him. And she did. She turned him toward the front doors of the school. Ed felt proud. Aurora was a good human. Of course, he'd always known that. But this year, he'd seen her mature—and she'd done it in her own good time, by being exactly who she was.

"Love you, my girl. Love you," he whispered. Ed knew she was too far away to hear him. But he leaned and stretched his arm toward the passenger's side window, hoping Aurora would see him wave goodbye one last time. She and Frenchie merged with all the other kids—heads and backpacks—through the open door.

Cedar was upset now, arching his back and kicking his legs.

Doesn't like that car seat, Ed was thinking. Too confining for Cedar, who had skipped walking and gone right to running. Ed was an old father. He sighed a little when he thought about the hours ahead. Rene had a story to write, and she'd taken Gracia with her to Camden the previous afternoon at Ed's suggestion. A night away from home was a rare treat for both of them. Ed was in charge of the three kids. Aurora and Frenchie were easy. But Ed felt like he'd chased Cedar all evening long, and finally, into bed. Phew. Ed had collapsed on the couch, fallen asleep with his boots on.

Aurora had helped. She always did. Now she and Frenchie were in school. Ed was on his own. He'd be running after Cedar all day. The women wouldn't be back until after three o'clock.

"That's okay," Ed said, and he smiled. "They're getting a nice pampering." He was happy for both Rene and Gracia.

Ed was yawning, so he missed the moment when his little boy pointed his plump finger toward the side yard of the school.

"Bye-baw! Bye-baw!" Cedar cried, and he kicked.

"What is that about?" said Ed. He glanced into the back and saw Cedar put his finger into his ear.

Not another infection, Ed thought. Well, good time for a checkup.

"I'm so sorry, my boy. I don't understand . . ."

The toddler sat back in the car seat, gave a whimper of defeat. One last time, he whispered, "Bye-baw . . ."

Ed let the car idle forward. A few feet from the back bumper of the car in front of them, he gently pressed the brake again. Then again. "Well, little buddy. There's no use being anything but patient. The school circle is a traffic jam. That's why we like the school bus. How about we sing?" Ed said. "Want to sing?" He cleared his throat and found his old college choir baritone. "'I've been workin' on the railroad, all the live-long day. . . .'"

Cedar sang the next line along with his pop. "Yidee yidee yidee-YAY-yo . . . ahh-dah yah-yah-yah-yah YAY. . . ."

Frenchie

During Arrivals

Frenchie stood in the narrow side yard outside the school, looking back at the glass door. He could see himself in it. Tan pants and plaid shirt. Belt tight. On right. He watched himself pat the needlepoint purse at his side.

Frenchie waited to disappear. That would happen when Aurora swung the door to come out and go with him. The Frenchie in the glass would fold away, then come back again when the door closed. That was how the door with glass worked.

He waited.

Aurora didn't come.

He heard birds chattering in the skinny trees. Frenchie loved the way birds opened themselves. The wings. Turning colors off and on, flick quick, like his own blinking eye. He hugged the needlepoint purse. But he did not look up. He remembered something Aurora had once said:

You don't bother with birds at a time like this!

Aurora

Before Attendance

I'm leaning across the top of my school desk, belly and elbows. I'm holding half a split geode cupped in my hands. I'm keeping it out of sight for now. I've got a good story that goes with this old rock, and I'm dying to tell it to Joanie and Leena before attendance time.

"What do you have, Aurora? What's in your hands?" Leena's dark eyes shine.

"Yeah! Tell, tell!" says Joanie. She scoots her chair in to be closer.

"Well," I say, "have a look!" Slowly, I lift one hand away. All they see is a crusty brown rock in my palm.

"Oh . . . ," says Leena.

"What is it?" Joanie asks.

Very slowly, I turn the rock over and let them see the open side.

"Ooo! Crystals!" says Leena.

"Right!" I say.

"Like diamonds!" says Joanie. "Where did you get it, Aurora?"

"I'll tell you the story," I say. But that's as far as I get. Someone calls my name.

"Aurora?"

I slide back off the top of the desk and settle into my chair. I look around and wonder if it is someone who thinks they need to *speak* to me about climbing the furniture.

"Aurora." I hear it again. Then I see Mr. Menkis in our doorway.

"Oh, hey, Mr. Menkis." He takes a few steps into the room. I'm surprised to see him here.

"Aurora, did you see Frenchie this morning?" he asks.

"Yeah," I say.

"Did you come in together?"

"Yep."

"Okay," Mr. Menkis says. "Thank you."

He hurries out of the door.

"Huh. That was weird." I shrug at Leena and Joanie. "Bet Frenchie's looking out a window. Watching birds," I tell them.

"Probably," says Leena. She's seen how it is. How much he loves birds.

"Maybe he's in the bathroom," Joanie whispers.

"Yeah," I say. "Something like that."

Then our teacher, Mrs. Beccia, wants our attention. "Class, let's settle in and review today's schedule," she says. She turns to the whiteboard.

"Darn!" I say. There isn't time to tell the story of the geode.

Topher Menkis

Before Attendance

Topher Menkis knew when to expect Frenchie—*and* Aurora. The bus schedule had pretty well ironed itself out by the end of the second week of school. In respect for their friendship, and at the girl's suggestion, he'd been meeting the pair in the hallway, between the classroom door and the lobby. The distance was short. Administration had approved.

But this morning, Topher reached the ever-changing-tree mural in the school's front lobby without seeing either Frenchie or Aurora. He watched the stream of kids whose heads were, on average, about level with his own nose. He rose onto his toes, stretching upward for a better view of the bus circle.

Could he have already missed them?

Ah, there, he thought. He recognized the cluster of kids who were coming through the front door to the school. A back-of-the-bus bunch. This group was on his radar for two reasons. One, they rode Frenchie's bus. Two, he'd overheard one of them calling him Mini Menkis behind his back. Easy for Topher to shrug it off. No denying, he was probably the shortest school staff member these kids had ever met. He'd also been an elite college gymnast and knew the benefits of a low center of gravity.

So these were kids from the same bus . . . but something wasn't right. Frenchie and Aurora always sat up front. They should've entered the building well before this back-seat bunch—illustrious citizens of Mountain View School. Topher stepped into their path, stood tall and put up a hand.

"One second, please," he said, in his best Mr. Menkis voice. "Was Frenchie on the bus this morning? Or Aurora?"

The bunch shrugged in unison. Avoided eye contact.

But one voice answered. "We sit in the back. Never really see them. Probably gone down the hall already."

"Right," Topher said. "Onward, then. Thank you. Have a good day, people."

He thought to dash out and ask the bus driver, but it was too late. She had already pulled on through the loop.

Before he went in search, he leaned around the glass

partition to speak to the school secretary. "We don't have a sick call on Frenchie Livernois this morning, do we?"

"On Frenchie?" The secretary scrunched her brow. She checked all the Post-it squares on her desk, then her computer screen. She shook her head. "No...nothing..."

"Okay. Didn't really think so. I'm supposed to receive a message if he's going to be absent, and I don't have one. I must have missed him," he said, keeping his voice even. But in truth, Topher Menkis was mystified, and a little worried as he hustled on down the hall. Frenchie had had a terrific second week—and only the one upset on the playground last week. But Topher's concern grew when he didn't find Frenchie in his classroom.

There had to be an explanation....

Aurora.

He hurried down the hall and peeked into her classroom. There she was! At her desk—*on it*, actually—belly surfing, and talking to the two new girls. She had her feet hooked into the back of her chair, and it bobbed as if she were towing it behind her.

But no Frenchie.

He stayed only long enough for her to tell him that yes, Frenchie was at school today. He double-timed it into the boys' bathroom to see if Frenchie had made a stop, then back to his classroom for one last look. Empty desk.

Topher took no chances. He dialed the school office from the hall, as he turned in full circles, looking up and down the corridor still hoping to spot the boy. The secretary answered. Topher informed her that they may have a problem. He did not have eyes on Frenchie Livernois. "Please inform Principal Whilmer—*right away!*"

Less than three seconds later, Topher heard the weirdly pleasant-sounding *bong-bong* of the outer door alarms. In the now-quiet hall, he listened to the automatic dead-bolt locks slide and click into place on all the doors at Mountain View School.

Lockdown.

Aurora

As Class Begins

Ms. Beccia is still going over our schedule for the day when we hear a sound—a sort of *bong-bong*. It is coming from the hall. Every head turns toward the door. We ask, "What is that?" Did somebody lean on a button they shouldn't have? Ms. Beccia takes a call on the classroom intercom.

Next thing I know, our school principal, Mrs. Whilmer, and her assistant, Mrs. Delano, come into our classroom. They stoop beside my chair. We are eye to eye.

Am I in trouble?

In a whispery voice, Mrs. Whilmer says, "Excuse me. Aurora, we're looking for Frenchie. Did you see him this morning?"

"Oh yeah, I already told Mr. Menkis. He's here. Frenchie's here."

Mrs. Whilmer does not look convinced. "Wait," I say, "are you telling me Mr. Menkis didn't find him? Sheeshy-sheesh!" I rock my head from side to side.

"Sometimes he wanders a little. You know," I say, because Mrs. Whilmer has known Frenchie for three years, same as I have. "He never goes far." I push up out of my chair. "I'll help you look."

"Thank you, Aurora." Mrs. Whilmer stands and puts a soft hand on my shoulder, but it *is* a stop-you hand. "We will want your help in a few minutes. We have a procedure to follow, so it's important for all students to stay in their classrooms for now. But I will come get you as soon as the situation allows." Mrs. Whilmer and Mrs. Delano head for the door.

Situation?

"Well, okay," I call after them, "but I could be helping yoooouu . . ." I hold the note.

I sit back down. Joanie and Leena look at me with big round eyes. I flap a hand.

"He'll turn up," I say. "But why can't I go look for him? Why don't we all look for him?"

Aurora

Frenchie's Way of Whistling

I know my friend. If he's not in this school building, then he's outside looking up into the trees, searching for birds. I see him do it all the time. We go hiking and he will stop still, all of a sudden. I freeze in place too, and I whisper in the lowest whisper I can, "Bird?"

Frenchie answers by keeping his body still. He stares, more than he watches. I am never sure at what. I face the same way he faces. I scan all around us. Most of the time, I'll find the bird. We both stay still until it leaves. Then he flaps his hands and lets out a whistle. He doesn't smile. But I know that's Frenchie being happy.

Pop says Frenchie's whistle is musical. I'd say that's right. Little bit tweety, little bit twittery. He uses his lips to make a little hole to blow through. He does something with his tongue inside his mouth that breaks the sounds into short bursts. Pop said that's called staccato. Gracia told us Frenchie did that on his own; she never taught him. I believe her, because even though we got Frenchie to float, and even swim, it can be hard to teach him things.

Gracia said Frenchie never played with toys. But by the time he was three, he was all about birds. "There's no telling why." She said it with a soft smile. "He'd watch them at our feeder, and everywhere we went. He started to flap his hands like little wings, and raise his chin and purse his lips, like making a beak." Gracia laughed. "One day, he whistled!"

That pretty whistle is one of the only sounds that Frenchie Livernois makes, and it is like birdsong. But it isn't exactly like any of the bird calls I know. I thought about it once: birds have beaks, not lips, and I think they make sounds in their throats. Quite a bit different from Frenchie's tweet. He doesn't pipe like the Carolina wren, doesn't coo like a mourning dove. He doesn't make the cheepy-chatty sound of a finch, and he doesn't buzz like a chickadee. And thank heavens he doesn't scream like a blue jay.

If I had to pick, I'd say his song is closest to the oriole. Come to think of it, that's probably why the oriole call is my favorite.

Aurora

Anybody Here Seen Frenchie?

Mrs. Whilmer and Mrs. Delano are back again. Our security guard, Mr. Gessup, is with them.

"Quiet, please. May we have your attention?" Mrs. Delano speaks.

Then Mrs. Whilmer raises her hand and asks, "Has anybody here seen Frenchie Livernois this morning?"

Leena, Joanie, and I raise our hands. But every set of eyes is on me. People know that he's always with me. Has been for the last three years.

"You still haven't found him?" I say, waving my hand over my head.

"We have not," Mrs. Whilmer says. She asks each of us where we saw him.

"Coming in this morning," says Joanie. "At the front doors."

"Same," I say.

"And it was just for a quick second," Leena adds.

"Okay. Thank you, girls. Mr. Gessup has some thoughts for all of us," she says. "This is very important. Please be good listeners."

Mr. Gessup holds up Frenchie's school portrait. He smiles. "I think all of you already know what Frenchie looks like."

"But that's from last year," I say. "He has longer hair right now." I put a finger in the air and add, "Sorry for interrupting."

Mr. Gessup says, "That's okay. Details are important. For instance, Frenchie wears tan pants and plaid shirts, and he carries a big shoulder-type bag—"

"It is a needlepoint purse! He keeps bird pictures in it. Another detail," I say.

"Thank you, Aurora. So, we'd like everyone to think very hard about what you saw this morning. Retrace your path in your mind's eye. If you walked to school, did you see anything unusual? If you rode your bus, did you see Frenchie? Was he in the drop-off circle? Or somewhere else around the building?"

I shake my head. Frenchie doesn't do that.

"If you think of something—anything—even if it

doesn't seem important to you, we'd like to hear about it. Just ask your classroom teacher for permission. Feel free to talk to us." He sweeps his arm in a friendly way. Mr. Gessup is being chirpy this morning. It's a little weird.

"Nobody is in trouble," he says. "Nobody is *going* to get in trouble. We expect Frenchie will be found safe and sound, probably before lunchtime." He rubs his belly, like he's already hungry.

There are some laughs. Tiny ones.

"That's right," Mrs. Whilmer says. "We are a community, and we all want to find Frenchie. So do that little bit of work with us and use your memories. Think about this morning," she says, "and, please, if you have ideas, if you know things Frenchie likes to do, something you have seen him take an interest in, let us know. Our police and the security guards from our other schools are arriving to help us look."

The police?

"You'll see them outside the windows and in our hallways. They may pop into your room. Thank you all very much." She adds a soft smile. She and Mr. Gessup stand together near the door. They talk in low voices.

"Aurora," Leena whispers. "Are you all right?"

"Well, I think I am. But that part about the police? Sheesh."

"I know. . . ." Joanie scrunches her brow. Other kids

are looking at me. I think everyone expects me to be bonkers right now. Should I be?

I lean across the desks to get closer to Joanie and Leena. "Frenchie doesn't get lost," I say. "The more you get to know him, the more you'll see it. We hike all over the woods, bird-watching, and rock hunting, and Frenchie makes it home *before me* most of the time. He gets me unlost. Like a human compass."

Joanie nods. "He was the first one back to the trailhead the day we hiked Hidden Ponds Loop," she says.

"He always knows the way," I say.

I think how this past weekend Frenchie and I were out for hours in one of our favorite places, Sundrop Meadow. Right behind our houses. On the way home, I kept picking up rocks and stopping to throw them. Soon, Frenchie was out of sight. I don't worry when that happens. But I hustle a little to catch up. We crossed the blueberry fields, then I saw his plaid shirt and the reddish square of the needlepoint purse disappearing into the pines up ahead. I stopped at his house to make sure he was there. I wasn't even up the steps when Gracia called from the kitchen window, "He's here! Thanks, Aurora."

"Aurora?" Mrs. Whilmer is speaking to me. "Will you come now?" she says. "We could really use your help."

I'm on my feet. I follow the adults into the hall. Weird look to the place. Every classroom door is closed. Mrs. Whilmer says she's going to check in with staff members who are looking for Frenchie inside the building, then meet the police officers. So I'm with Mr. Gessup.

"Come on, my friend," he says. "Let's go outside and see if we can find the boy with the needlepoint purse."

Aurora

The Day Frenchie Got the Needlepoint Purse

I walk the playground ahead of Mr. Gessup. I look through the tree trunks, beyond the fence, and make chirping, cheeping sounds. A few police officers are picking through the woods. Seeing them puts a pit in my middle.

Across the schoolyard our custodian opens the utility shed. (They're searching everywhere.) Mr. Menkis is there too. He vaults onto the lid of the dumpster, then up to the shed roof, graceful as a cat. Wow! He stands at the roof ridge and scans the grounds.

I try to spot a patch of plaid in the woods, or a dash of red. The needlepoint purse.

I was with Frenchie the day he got that purse. Hot, horsefly kind of day in late July. It was the summer before we started fourth grade. I'm sure, because I know we didn't have Cedar. Not quite yet.

Gracia took us to our favorite Route 1 flea market at Baker's Field. She said for fun, but I knew it was because Mom and Pop wanted me out of their hair while they were painting our kitchen floor. (I can be quick and forgetful, and I step in things like wet paint.) Frenchie will always go to a flea market. There's no better place to find bird pictures on the cheap.

I watched his face as we bumped along looking for a parking spot in the shade. It was the chin-up face. That's a ready face. He loves scouting for bird pictures, and when he gets to the kind of place he can do that, he knows it. You won't see Frenchie jumping up and down about that—or anything else, really. But if you watch—if you really *see* him—his face will say it all: *I've got business here.*

There was a big summer crowd that day. We'd been there all of fifteen minutes when Frenchie stalled out at Mrs. Thrift's camper van. She's a regular. Her spot always looks like she opened her camper door and shook all the stuff out of it. Then she spends the day sorting everything onto blankets. From what I've seen, she finishes just about in time to pack it all up again. Her husband always helps her. She tells him what to do.

I'm thinking Mrs. Thrift is not her real name. But that's what it says on the pin she wears on her front. The pin is as big as a tea saucer with a lace ruffle around the edges. Cumbersome is how that looks. But the black letters on the yellow background do catch your eye. She always hangs a matching sign off the sideview mirror of her camper van. Good advertising.

Anyway, Frenchie picked up the wide, flat needlepoint purse. The stitches made a pattern of fall leaves, nuts, and pine cones in red colors mostly, with some dark green and brownish gold. It had a long shoulder strap on it with a brass buckle, and a zipper across the top to keep it closed. He worked his hands all along the edges of the bag.

"So, ya like it?" I asked. I leaned in and gave the bag a sniff. Kind of musty. I rubbed my nose. Slapped a green-headed fly off my arm. Boy, were we sweating.

"I like it too," I told him. "Useful-looking, I'd say. Take it hiking, carry a water bottle, school papers . . ."

Mrs. Thrift kept her eye on us while she dusted a blue glass water pitcher. (I wondered how that got to the flea market in one piece.)

"He does like it," I told her. "I can tell."

Frenchie went to stand in front of Gracia. He rocked on his feet with the purse all scrunched up tight against his chest, and the price tag dangling out below his elbow.

"What do we have here?" Gracia caught the tag in her hand and took a look. She sighed. She looked at Frenchie. Then at Mrs. Thrift. "We'll take it."

"He wants the purse, does he?" Mrs. Thrift set the vase on a blanket and stuck her chin toward us.

Gracia held out a ten-dollar bill. "Yes, please."

"You're sure? I don't do returns," Mrs. Thrift warned. "What do you think he wants with a needlepoint purse?"

"I don't know." Gracia grinned. "But he doesn't ask for much. So . . ." She waggled the bill.

Mrs. Thrift narrowed her eyes and nodded. She trapped her giant Mrs. Thrift pin under her chin as she dug into her belt pack. She pulled out a five-dollar bill. "Half price. Today only," she said. She took Gracia's ten and gave her back the five.

"Oh, hey! That's a deal! You're a good old one, Mrs. Thrift!" I said. I punched my fist in the air. I spun on one foot.

"Very kind of you to do this for my son," said Gracia. (She always says *my son*.) "Thank you."

Frenchie was already heading back to the car with his new old purse. He knew what he wanted it for. A place to keep his bird pictures.

Aurora

Last Year When Frenchie Found the Nuthatch

I've got a joke I tell to Frenchie: "If I am a rock hound, does that make you a . . . bird hound?" I don't think he gets it. But I swear he would agree with me that the point is not to find everything at once. You love the hunt, and if possible, you don't take all the treasure when you do find it. Also, no getting disappointed if it takes a while to find the thing you want. Like me with the tourmaline; *that* is taking forever. So I love helping Frenchie find his birds. I end up being as much a bird hound as a rock hound. Last October, we went to Blue Hill to catch the last farmers' market of the season. We walked around eating empanadas, then went into town for ice cream, and I spotted the shop.

"Hold everything," I said, arms wide. "We have got to go inside."

"Clean hands first," Mom said. She handed Frenchie and me wet wipes.

The place was called Troviosity. The sign hung on a chain by the door. Mom said it sounded like someone had put the words *trove* and *curiosity* together. I knew what *curiosity* meant, because I've always been full of that. But Mom had to tell me that a trove was a collection of things, valuable or delightful.

"Well, matter of opinion, then," I said.

Our moms had a few more bites of their ice cream cones to go, and Cedar was still working on his kiddie serving. They stayed outside, on a bench in the sun, while Frenchie and I rushed up the steps together.

I gave the Troviosity sign a poke to make it swing. (Had to.) I was pretty sure Frenchie and I were thinking the same thing as I let us in the door: this was the kind of shop that might have bird prints.

Inside, there was a lot of flea market stuff—colored bottles and old silver coffeepots—mismatched forks and spoons. But everything was shined up and set out on fancy little tables and shelves. The shop smelled like cinnamon instead of dust and hot grass.

"Yeah," I said to Frenchie, "there could be birds for you here. Could be."

We started our search. The shop woman watched us through her skinny-rim glasses. She looked young, like a college student, and had warm brown skin and super-close-cut hair. She was smiling one of those worry smiles.

"Hi," I said. "I'm Aurora. This is Frenchie. He doesn't talk. We are both eleven. We don't break stuff."

"Oh, I'm sure you are fine." She threaded one finger through her dangly earring. "Looking for anything in particular?" she asked.

"Birds," I said. "John Audubon prints. Not framed. And since you said 'in particular'—a nuthatch. At least that's what I'm guessing."

I didn't explain because that could be too much talking. But the reason I was thinking nuthatch was because Frenchie had been watching one the morning before. Funny little thing that went traveling round and round the trunk of an oak tree. I say funny because a lot of the time, it was upside down.

"Well, all our unframed prints are here," the shop woman said. She showed me a wooden V-shaped rack. "You're welcome to look through. There was a set of Audubons, if I am not mistaken. Take a look."

"Okay, thanks. And hey, if you want to know, we did just have ice cream cones but we both cleaned up with wet wipes." I flexed my fingers for her. "Our moms will be in a minute with my little brother. He'll be cleaned up too."

"Perfection!" She smiled the better kind of smile. Her

phone buzzed over on the glass countertop above a jewelry case. "Excuse me, just a second," she said. "Feel free to interrupt me if you need to."

I called to Frenchie. "Hey. Over here. Could be the jackpot," I said.

I started to flip through the prints. All of them were wrapped in plastic. Maybe sticky ice cream fingers would not have mattered. "Let's see . . . boat, fish, boat, another boat, lighthouse, another lighthouse . . . third lighthouse . . . sheeshy-sheesh . . . lobster traps, fisherman, rocks, farmhouse . . . ah, *bird*." (I think it was a pelican.)

I paused, but Frenchie stared at that bird print like it was nothing but another lighthouse.

"Okay, okay. Not what you're after. Guess I knew that." I went on flipping prints. I got to a pack of pictures tied to together with a velvet ribbon. I pulled the bundle out of the rack. A sticker on the plastic sleeve said *Audubon/set* in pale pencil. I could see that the one on top was cardinals.

"You already have this same exact one," I said. I gave it a tap.

Frenchie did the slow blink.

"Yo, excuse me. Ms. Troviosity? Mind if I untie these?"

"Sorry?" She looked up from her phone. I pointed at the ribbon, then whirled my hand around. "Oh, sure. Go right ahead. And by the way, I'm Sheree." She pointed to herself and gave me a wink.

I gave her a thumbs-up.

"Let's see what's in here, Frenchie." I opened the pack and started to fan out the pictures.

There were six in all, and before I even got a good look, Frenchie had one in his hands.

"Oh! The nuthatch!" I blurted. "I knew it!"

Sheree came right over. (She probably wasn't used to loudness in the shop.) Frenchie clasped the print to his chest.

"You have just what he wants!" I said. "Unbelievable!"

"Oh, you found the Audubon set! So it's for him, is it? He likes birds?"

"He is all about them. How much? How much for that one? It's the nuthatch in case you wondered."

"The one? Oh, it's a set." She put her finger on her upper lip and frowned.

"Oh . . . ," I said. "Poo." I looked at Frenchie holding the print. I wanted him to have it. "Well, how much for the set, then?" I scrunched up my nose.

"Let me see, I thought there was a tag attached to the ribbon. Oh, here. Must have fallen." She bent to pick it off the floor.

"Sorry," I told her. "That's probably me who dropped it."

"That's okay. . . . Let me see. . . . Oh, Sixty-two fifty."

"Sixty-two *dollars* and fifty cents? That's expensive!" I said. I wiped my mouth with the back of my hand. "Sorry.

Little bit of spit there."

Sheree shrugged, as if she didn't mind the spit.

"Eh," I said, "his mom probably isn't going to go for that. I get that it's a great set of birds. And you wrapped them nice with the ribbon, and all. But there's a bird budget," I said. "Slim chance of a sale here."

"Oh, I see," she said. She looked sorry. She whispered to me, "I—I hope he's . . . not going to get upset if his mother says no."

"Naw. He'll just leave. Right out your door. Don't get me wrong, he'll still *want* the print. But he won't throw a tantrum, and he won't tear up your shop."

"I'm so glad. I don't want to hurt his feelings." She tilted her head and looked Frenchie over, probably no more than a second, but it seemed longer.

When Mom and Gracia came into the shop, there was a short discussion about the nuthatch being part of a set. Gracia gently took the print from Frenchie. She told him, in her usual quiet way, that the set was too expensive. "We'll find you the nuthatch. Some other time."

On our way out, I called over my shoulder, "See that? He's okay!"

The young woman nodded and smiled as she wrapped the velvet ribbon back around the set of prints.

We tried to stop at a bookstore right after that. I say tried because we had to leave pretty quick. Cedar was going to town, wiping out the picture-book shelves with a few quick swipes. So before you knew it, we were on the sidewalk again, heading for the parking lot.

"Oh, there you are! Wait!" We heard someone calling, but we all ignored it until we heard the same voice call louder and say, "Frenchie? It's Frenchie, right?"

That was weird because in all the time I've spent with Frenchie Livernois, I have never seen anyone running toward him calling his name. But Sheree from Troviosity was doing that exact thing. Her flat shoes smacked along the sidewalk. She waved a skinny paper bag in the air. When she reached us, she stopped to catch her breath. "Whew! The set . . . It doesn't matter. Who cares if it's five instead of six? Five is still a set, isn't it?"

"Oh my goodness," Gracia said. She put her hand on her chest, which is a very Gracia thing to do. "Thank you, but I think it is still probably too expensive for us."

"No, no. I want him to have it. Please. Here, Frenchie. Here's your nuthatch."

Frenchie stared straight ahead, never looked at her. It's not his way. But he put his hand right up, and she slipped that package into it. He blinked. She smiled, then watched as he slid the bag into his needlepoint purse. Then he started walking again.

We said thank-you for him. "That's not going to go to waste," I told her. "It'll be with him all the time. Every day." Mom and Gracia agreed with me.

"Nice of you, Sheree! You are the Nuthatch Lady!" I turned and called back to her. I even pointed both my pointer fingers at her and said it again. "Nice! Of! You!"

Then I added, "Thanks for *seeing* him!"

Maxine Grindel

Mrs. Thrift's Engine Trouble

If Maxine Grindel hadn't had her head under the engine hood of the old Mrs. Thrift camper van, she might have heard the gentle clacking of four cloven hoofs stepping across the road. She might have seen that most unusual-looking deer just before it became part of the weave of the blond-and-brown field at the side of the house. She might have noticed the way the late summer grasses closed, curtain-like, behind the deer's flicking tail.

Maxine was experiencing the great gift of determination that morning. The squealing of the camper van's aging fan belt had become unbearable on last week's trip to the Baker's Field flea market. If there was one thing Maxine knew about keeping an old engine healthy, it was that she better keep the one part that drives everything else shipshape. It wasn't an easy repair, but she'd done it before. Years ago. Maxine was good with her hands. With her two strong thumbs and few good grunts, she worked the new belt onto the pulleys and finally into place with a pop. There it is! Maxine thought. Mrs. Thrift will ride again!

The only help she had that morning was her husband, Dudley. All she needed him for was to start the engine on her command so she could see the new belt spin. Tricky business this was, because with the hood up Maxine and Dudley couldn't see each other.

"How about now?" Dudley barked out the driver's side window—for about the fifth time. He took a sip of his coffee, spilled some down his front, and flipped a page of the morning paper, which he had opened across the steering wheel.

Maxine straightened up and banged the top of her head on the hood latch. "Ow! Who put that there?" She rubbed her head with her palm and cussed a little. She barked back at her assistant, "Not yet!"

"All set? Did ya say?"

"Not now!" Maxine squawked. Dudley never listened! "I haven't even gotten the pulley adjusted . . . ," Maxine mumbled to herself.

While Maxine mumbled, Dudley said, "Gotcha, darlin'."

And while she tapped two fingers on the belt to check the tension, Dudley stretched his foot out and pressed the clutch to the floor. He turned the key in the ignition.

The engine turned over beautifully. The belt spun swiftly—and when it did, it sliced the tip of Maxine's right ring finger clean off.

Maxine might have screamed. For sure, she staggered back from the open hood. She held her finger tightly in her opposite hand and stared at it. She felt sealed in— as if a bubble had enclosed her, and for a few seconds, there was nothing except that whitish-pink place on her finger. Maxine made her eyes large and round. That was *not* the bone, she was pretty sure. Then Maxine had the dizzying thought that somewhere around her in the pine needles—or perhaps stuck to the hood or the engine of the camper van—was a piece of fingertip. . . .

About one-third the size of a cannellini bean, she thought.

And it was *her* fingertip. . . .

That she was not likely to find . . .

Ever.

Maxine felt cold. Her knees weakened. Blood came up in the end of her finger and poured down the sides like a candle spilling wax. Maxine stumbled. She saw Dudley coming around the camper for a look. She blinked. The world was disappearing now, and Dudley was going with it. Maxine was falling backward toward the ancient lawn chair beneath the broad pine.

If Maxine hadn't been blacking out, and if Dudley hadn't been running toward her, spilling coffee down his arm the whole way, one of them might have seen the boy in the plaid shirt come striding across Bert Gray Road and into the meadow at the side of the yard. And if Maxine hadn't been sinking through the weather-beaten webbing of the old lawn chair, she might have seen that strange, beautiful, unspeaking boy. She might have recognized him *and* the needlepoint purse he was clutching. Maxine Grindel—Mrs. Thrift—never forgot a sale.

Aurora

Thinking Back to Morning

We circle the school. No Frenchie. Mr. Gessup and I come to the tiny side yard. It's a narrow little nowhere spot at one end of the building. The kind of place nobody ever has a reason to be. There's a little ridge with a row of saplings. Mr. Gessup and I go up, calling Frenchie's name. I wait and listen, hoping I'll hear a rustle. Or, better, Frenchie's tweeting. But there is nothing.

I do what Mrs. Whilmer and Mr. Gessup wanted us to do. I hit the replay button in my brain. I think back over the morning from the time we got to school.

When we pulled into the drop-off, Cedar was bouncing up and down in his car seat and trying like the dickens to tell us something.

"Bye-baw! Bye-baw!" He kicked his feet out in front of him.

I told him, "Sorry, Cedar Tree. I don't understand."

Neither did Pop, and if Frenchie did, well, he wouldn't be able to tell us. Besides, he was staring out the car window and—

My own thought stops me.

I get that feeling—like I've been dunked in ice water. I turn to face Mr. Gessup.

"I was wrong!"

Mr. Gessup's eyes are round. "About what? What's the matter, Aurora?"

"I forgot!" I tell him. I turn and run down to the side yard door. I see my reflection in the glass. I look wild. I tug hard on the door. Then push it even harder. It doesn't budge. Then I remember: *lockdown*.

"Mr. Gessup!" I call. "Hurry! You have to get me in!" He comes running with his keys. "I forgot! We didn't even take the bus this morning!" I tell him. "Everything was different. I've *got* to tell Mrs. Whilmer! Right away!"

Aurora

Why Pop Drove Us to School in the First Place

I get to Mrs. Whilmer's office and it's like she knew I was coming. She catches me by my shoulders.

"We didn't take the bus! I completely forgot!"

"I know. It's okay, it's okay," she says.

"What do you mean okay? Did you find him?"

"Well, no, not yet. But I talked to your bus driver, Helene, and she told us you and Frenchie weren't on the bus this morning."

"Oh yes, Helene," I say. My heart is pounding.

"I called Frenchie's mom, and when we couldn't reach her, we called your dad, and he told us—"

"They are together!" I can't help interrupting. I'm bursting to explain the whole thing, and Mrs. Whilmer lets me. "My mom and Gracia are together. See, my mom had a story to write, about a new spa that opened at the Seacliffe Inn over in Camden. They have this thing called a Himalayan salt therapy room. Ugh. Not important," I say. "The place gave Mom a one-night stay for two."

"Got it," says Mrs. Whilmer. She's been nodding and listening. Being super nice.

I'm remembering how Mom had hesitated to go. She wanted to do the story but she didn't really care about spending the night or having the total spa experience. But the minute Pop heard about it, he'd said that Mom should go and take Gracia.

"Have a nice dinner in town," he said. "Sleep late. Get massages. Eat kiwis and chocolates." He said Frenchie could stay with us. And I said I'd help with Cedar. We wanted them to go.

So they did. They left yesterday afternoon, with little overnight bags, and they giggled like Leena and Joanie and Cedar and I would if we were going out for ice cream. I liked thinking of Mom and Gracia having that much fun.

I look at Mrs. Whilmer. "So Frenchie's mom went with my mom, and he stayed at our house last night. That usually doesn't happen. When you and Mr. Menkis asked me if Frenchie was on the bus, my brain was thinking about *usually*. Today was different. I'm really sorry, Mrs. Whilmer. Frenchie came to school with me. *In our car.*"

"I understand how you forgot," she says.

"Pop brought us early because Cedar had a doctor's appointment in Ellsworth. He dropped us off. Right out front." I think for a second. "We met Leena and Joanie. We all came in together."

"Your dad says he saw Frenchie enter the building, just like you said." Mrs. Whilmer nods.

"I am one hundred percent sure," I say.

I have a little memory movie of that in my head. I see Leena . . . and Joanie. Trouble is, I can't see Frenchie.

I tell Mrs. Whilmer, "Frenchie was behind me. Indoors. But, I'm not sure if"—I take a swallow—"I don't remember stopping at his classroom door. Not today."

Aurora

The Ever-Changing Tree

I sit in the school office waiting for my parents and Gracia to pick me up. It's going to be a while. Pop will get home first but he'll have to wait for Mom and Gracia. They have a longer drive back to town. I keep leaning out to check the front doors. Mrs. Whilmer keeps promising me they are on their way.

This orange plastic chair is putting static electricity into my shirt. I can't sit still and I keep getting snapped. My hair is doing that thing where it flattens onto my face. Clinging. Like scared hair.

I see our art teacher, Ms. Chandra, through the glass. She's leading a small group of students. They're carrying neon-colored Post-its on their thumbs. They filter past

Ms. Chandra, then stop in front of the ever-changing-tree mural in the school lobby. It's a big bulletin board with a bare tree painted on it. Spreading branches. Like a yard maple. But that's not the point. Ever-changing. That's the point.

The winter I was in second grade, before I knew Frenchie, my class decorated the tree with snowflakes. Then we put up snow poems. I still remember mine:

Here comes the milk-white snow
I don't know the reason why.
Let's scoop it in our hands
And throw it back into the sky.

Then, last April, the third graders made pictures of bird's nests with eggs inside and put identification cards up to go with them. Frenchie and I stopped every morning to look at them. When school let out in June, there were illustrated folktales. For the start of school this year, there's a sign that reads: "Welcome, New Birds." Our seven new students, including Leena and Joanie, each have a colorful bird with their name and grade on it tacked to a high branch.

But the every-changing-tree is also a community board for all of us. We post news—everything from new kittens to losing a tooth. Birthday wishes and funny riddles. Even ice hockey scores. Darleen Dombroski once posted a note asking for help finding the heart-shaped locket she lost. (She got it back. She stopped crying.)

I watch the kids at the mural. They're sticking the bright Post-its onto the tree trunk. Ms. Chandra is close to me. I lean out of the doorway. "Hey, Ms. Chandra? What's going on there?"

"Oh, Aurora." Her dark eyes shine. "Some of my morning students felt distracted when they got to the art room. Everyone's thinking about Frenchie. They asked if they could write messages to him and post them on the tree."

"Messages, huh?"

"Yes. Good thoughts. Frenchie will see them when he returns." She dips her chin and smiles. "Meanwhile, we're sending positive energy to him." She hands me a Post-it and a marker.

"Positive energy. Like reaching him through the air?" I ask. Mrs. Chandra gives me a nod. But I am not sure that's possible. What's the energy source? Who or what steers the messages in the right direction—and if something out there knows which way to go to find Frenchie, why doesn't it give us a clue? Or better still, tell us where he is? Then I think this: If Frenchie is here, like hiding here in the school, I'm going to be mad. Because this is really starting to hurt. I curl back into the plastic chair in the office to wait.

Aurora

The Poem Barn

I have sat in this school office plenty of times. Usually because I'm in some sort of trouble and I am waiting to hear what Mrs. Whilmer has to say about it. Today, that stuff feels like nothing. I drop my head, and close my eyes. I try to get to better thoughts. Something I love to do. Or a place I love to go. No surprise, everything connects to Frenchie. He's in all my scenes. That thought takes me close to home.

Our friend Anzie Maylord owns the blueberry farm at the top of the place we call Sundrop Meadow. You could say, our big old backyard meets her big old backyard. But it's a good hike between our houses.

Pop jokes about this little piece of bad luck—that the

wild blueberries haven't managed to creep onto our part of the barrens. ("Still hoping Mother Nature will do us the favor." He says it every season.) The good luck is, we have an open invite from Anzie. July through the beginning of September, we head up with our buckets, a couple of times a week. We go in the early evening, after all the machine picking stops. We check the perimeter where berries get left behind. But handpicking in the low bush is tough. We work our way up to the enclosure where Anzie keeps her cultivated high-bush berries. That's the place to fill a bucket.

Anzie is neighborly. And we are neighborly back. We bring her bread or pesto or flavored vinegar. She gives us a rosy grin every time we see her, then tosses her thick curly braid over her shoulder. But her boyfriend, Carney Huggins, who lives with her now— eh—not so neighborly. Not so welcomey.

We see him more than I want to. Sometimes more than we see Anzie because her pie-baking business keeps her in the kitchen. Carney does the pie deliveries. But he finishes early. Come afternoon, he's doing this or that around the fields. He's tall, skinny, and scruffy. Suntanned to a crisp. His hair is even messier than mine, cap on or cap off.

Carney has never chased us out. But he scowls, and looks at our buckets like we're thieves. Don't know how he got Huggins for a last name. Hard to picture him doing much hugging, though I suppose he hugs Anzie. He's mighty more friendly when the parents come with us—even if that means Cedar too, running around the fields like a miniature tornado—which he does. When I'm up there with Frenchie, I can't help hoping we won't see Carney. Helps to stay low and stick to picking.

Picking is one of the things that Frenchie gets. From the first time he watched me do it, he understood how the string on the bucket went around your neck and left you two hands to pick with. He knows ripe from not ripe, and he cleans the bushes like he's a machine. The only thing that slows him down is stopping to watch the barn swallows skimming over the field, catching bugs. Or if he sees the cedar waxwings come in for a meal. They love the blueberries. So do the deer. Natural pruners, Anzie Maylord calls them. She always shrugs and says, "I've got no grudges with the wildlife."

Might have been three weeks ago Frenchie and I were up there filling buckets with berries to bring home for freezing. I was thumbing clusters of fat blues into my bucket, slapping mosquitoes and daydreaming. Suddenly, Frenchie was on the move. I knew why. He wanted to get to Anzie's barn.

"Wait up! I'm coming!" I started trotting. I held my bucket to keep it from bumping against my belly. My backpack wobbled. I opened my mouth wide and let out a—I don't know—a sound. Like a huge yawn.

"Fuh-fuh-Frenchie! Wait for me!" I was giggling as we came alongside the big barn near Anzie's house. The barn is covered in rows and rows of old shingles. There are words painted on the side of the barn in big white block letters. It's a poem that Anzie wrote:

SUN RAIN WIND SWEPT
BUD BLOSSOM BERRY
SWEET EARTH ROOTS KEPT
MAKE A SOUL MERRY

Every time we reach the barn, Frenchie stops. He waits for me to read. I used to go right up to his ear and say "S-s-sun," because I liked the way Frenchie brought his shoulder up when my breath tickled him. I'm a pest. I confess. But there was more to it. When I said "S-s-sun r-r-rain w-w-wind sw-wept" into Frenchie's ear, I was trying to put the words into him.

But I know his ear is not some sort of tunnel into the depths of him. One day I realized something so big I had to say it out loud—so I would hear it. "Why do you want to do that anyway, Aurora Pauline Petrequin? Why change him? He's perfect. Perfectly Frenchie."

I caught up to him—I always do—and stood beside him. We faced the side of the barn, I took a huge breath and recited the poem—loudly.

"'Sun rain wind swept. Bud blossom berry. Sweet

earth roots kept. Make a soul merry!'" I threw my arms wide. I shook out my shoulders. I took another breath. I was ready to go again when I heard—

"Aurora!" There stood Carney Huggins, backward cap and one eye closed like he might have a headache.

I popped my eyes open. Carney knew my name? Could not believe that!

"Be quiet." He pushed the words at me. Stuck a hard *t* sound on the end. He sighed. Then for a second or two it seemed like Carney Huggins looked past me, to where Frenchie stood still, staring at the poem on the barn. First time I ever saw Carney really look *at* Frenchie, and for once, Carney's face didn't look so cranky. I should have let that moment last longer.

"Sorry for being too loud," I said. "Frenchie likes the poem—"

"Yeah, that's fine." Carney looked back at me, scowling again. "But do you have to shout it?"

"Uh . . . well . . . no. But maybe it'll scare the fruit flies off the berries if I do," I offered.

His shoulders sagged.

"Or not," I said.

"Are you done picking?" He stuck his chin toward my bucket. "Late season, you know. Not much left. And Mr. Plaid?" Carney actually smiled for a second. "Looks like he did all right. How about you head out, now." He gave his head a little swing toward the back of the property.

"Oh! Not so fast," I said. I turned to show him my backpack. "Mom and Pop sent two loaves of sourdough for Anzie. And you too. I guess."

"That's really nice," he said, but he sounded like he had a stomach cramp. "Drop them off at the kitchen. Quietly, if you can. Huh?"

"Sure," I said, "anything to make your soul merry." I jumped and pointed at the barn. Almost spilled my berry bucket. I gave him a grin.

"Shh!" Carney shook his head once more.

"Oops, sorry. Too loud."

He turned away and set off for Anzie's vegetable patch. I turned to Frenchie and whispered, "Come on. Sheeshy-sheeshy. Nothing new there."

Frenchie followed me to Anzie's kitchen door. I pulled the two loaves of sourdough out of my pack. I decided not to knock, because maybe I'd done enough bothering. I left the bread in a delivery crate on her bench.

On the way home I told Frenchie, "Ya know, it's possible that Carney Huggins and I won't ever be a good mix. But ya know what, Frenchie? I think he kind of likes you. Maybe you're his kind of kid."

Aurora

Spotting the Spotted Deer

When I want to get outside, which is always, but Frenchie is feeling lazy or hard to reach, I make him a promise. "This will be a bird hike," I'll say. If that doesn't get him, I push harder. "Hey! This is the blue jay talking to you, Frenchie." I flap my arms. Let's get outside and fly!" That gets him up, and it's all good because we both get what we want.

About a year ago we started out on one of those bird hikes up Sundrop Meadow, not far from Anzie's. Good day for sightings. Frenchie was flapping, whistling, and tweeting every few minutes. I kept slowing to a stroll to make sure he caught up to me. I checked the ground for rocks. Nothing exciting there. I was starting to feel bored until—

On the path ahead I heard a swish. Then a clacking sound like rock against rock. A flash of white and brown streaked across the trail. I halted. So did Frenchie.

"Whu-hut . . . ," I whispered. I thought someone's goat was running loose. The animal stopped in the high grass under the twiggy trees. It turned back and looked right at us.

I caught my breath.

Not a goat.

A deer?

Yeah. Because, flyswatter ears.

But this deer was not like any I had ever seen. It was spotted from head to hoofs, with a lot of white on its coat. The tip of its nose looked extra round, like a black rubber ball. Its snout was white and broader than I'd ever seen on a whitetail, with a dark marking along the center. A pair of brown diamond-shaped patches gave the deer a perfect mask—pretty as a stuffed toy—with dark eyes shining out, and white eyebrows arching upward.

"Wow . . . ," I whispered so low. "Now, Frenchie"—I hoped he would get what I was about to say—"you don't bother with birds at a time like this!"

Then I tried not to breathe. Frenchie stood still right beside me. I was with the best, silent deer-watching person in the world. We'd seen plenty of white-tailed deer together. Enough to know they don't hang around for long. (Sometimes I wonder if they know there are a lot of hunters in Maine.)

Stay, stay. I sent that spotted deer a good hard-thinking message, and maybe that got through. Big long seconds went by while we looked each other over. The deer was small. Not the same way a fawn is small—even though I guessed it was young. This deer's body was thicker than a fawn's. Its legs were short but strong—or so I told myself. It watched us. It blinked, and it seemed unafraid.

I daydreamed: This deer had come on the path because of us—Frenchie and me. Like an end-of-summer gift. It must want to know us and take apples or sunflower seeds from our hands. (Except we didn't have any, and it wasn't quite that close. But almost.) I imagined it would let us touch its warm neck and lead us into the woods. Maybe take us to a deposit of stones, maybe to a vein full of chunks of dark green or blue tourmaline . . .

"Hello," I whispered. The deer twitched its ears. Slowly, I raised one hand, palm up. I stepped forward. A stick snapped. The deer sprang away. That spotty white coat flickered through the woods and was gone.

"Ah, dang," I said. "Sorry, Frenchie. I broke the spell." He was already heading back along the path for home. I caught up to him, passed him, and jumped in front of him. "Wait!"

Frenchie stopped.

"You saw it, right?"

Frenchie stared. Slow blink.

Come on, I thought. Tell me you saw that crazy strange deer, Frenchie.

All he did was hoist his needlepoint purse up into his armpit.

I stepped out of his way. He started walking again. I stayed behind him and mumbled, "Do you think I scared it off when I put my hand out? That was dumb of me, huh?" I followed his plaid shirt. "Weirdest creature ever. I didn't even know what it was at first. Never seen a deer like that. Never heard of a deer like that. I'll look it up though. See what I can find out."

I thought about some key words to use. "*Spotted deer. In the woods*. Oh. *State of Maine*. I guess that should be in there too, huh? I'll tell you everything I learn," I promised. "But what do you say we keep it a secret. For now?"

Easy ask.

Frenchie couldn't tell anyone about the deer. Of course, that also meant, if I went home and said I'd seen a most fantastically enchanting, rare spotted deer, and nobody believed me, Frenchie couldn't back me up either.

"Hope we see it again," I said. "Wait! I'm going to leave a marker before we get too far." I dug my heel into the ground and scratched out a big X. "Eh. Nah. A good rain will wash that right out." I picked up a thick stick, tall as me, and tried to twist it into the ground. It wouldn't go, so

I jumped on it and twirled it with all my weight, and don't you know, that stick broke and I fell. I put a big new scrape in my arm.

"Dang! Hey, Frenchie! Wait up!"

He didn't. I rubbed my bloody arm, and that stung like heck. But I couldn't care much. Not after seeing what we'd seen.

"Whoo-hoo!" I shouted. I wound my arms around like a double windmill and ran to catch up to Frenchie.

Aurora

About Piebald Deer

A few days after we saw the spotted deer, Frenchie had all his bird prints arranged on the floor like quilt squares. Corners matched up, just right. I settled beside him and inched the tips of my fingers right up close to the edge of the first row of bird prints. If I moved one, he would straighten it. (Gracia says he has a strong sense of order.)

"So," I said, "I learned all about our spotty deer. First, it's rare. Get what I'm saying? Not so many walking this earth."

I wasn't sure how much to tell him. I'm always guessing about that. But this time, it was more that I needed to talk.

"There's a sad part, Frenchie. Piebalds don't do so well. It's kind of like, if you see spots and patches on the outside, it means there's other stuff wrong on the inside. Like messed-up bones and weak organs. Piebalds don't live as long as most deer. Gets me right in my heart."

Frenchie stared at his bird pictures. He squeezed his hands into little fists.

He's listening, I thought, and he is sorry, like I am.

I flopped on my back, stared at the ceiling. "I hope we get to see the piebald again. I want to check up on it. Make sure it's okay," I said. "And if we see it, let's follow it. For as long as it'll let us. That means we can't scare it. So I won't reach at it, and you can't flap and tweet, okay? We just follow. Can you do that for me?"

Frenchie popped up off the floor and made a beeline for our kitchen. I hadn't even noticed but Pop was running the mixer. Making bread dough. Frenchie never misses that.

I rolled up on one elbow and looked at his bird pictures, laid out so perfectly. I reached for the nuthatch print, the one Frenchie got from the woman at that cinnamon-smelling shop Troviosity. There were two birds in the painting. One heading up the tree, one heading down. I turned it upside down, wondering if Frenchie would notice. When the mixer stopped, and he came back, he knew. In a millisecond. He turned the nuthatch picture right-side up.

"Okay," I whispered near his ear. "So if you get that, I'm going to count on you to get what I said about the pie-bald deer."

Frenchie pulled up his shoulder. I laughed. "You are so ear ticklish," I said.

Carney Huggins

Special Delivery

Carney Huggins was half done with the pie deliveries. He was coasting at a good clip along Punkinville Road when a strange *something* bounded out in front of him— and stopped.

It. Will. Move.

That's the last thought Carney had before he jammed on his brakes. He threw his arm in front of the stack of pie boxes on the passenger's seat beside him. A matter of reflex, that was. But in a sudden stop, everything that's not bolted down will keep going forward.

Carney did. His clipboard did. Five out of seven pies did. Even the pair of five-gallon buckets that had been riding in the bed of the pickup did. They rolled right up over the top of the cab and bounced off the hood of the truck. Now they were rolling in the road.

In the next few seconds Carney did several things. He slumped in his seat and swore. He pushed his cap back to the top of his head. He shut down his engine, *and* he smelled blueberry pie like he'd never smelled it before, which was saying a lot.

Carney blinked. He scanned the side of the road for the animal. What was that anyway? He'd seen something similar—a deer, but not a normal one—during a blinding sunset in the barrens a few days back. He'd gotten an only slightly better look today. But that *was* a deer. Had to be the same one. Peculiar as could be. Spotted, and prettier than a prizewinning pony. Or something that'd walked out of a fairy tale. Who the heck was he going to tell that to?

Carney looked around the cab of the truck. He'd managed to save only two of the pies—or so he thought. The three pie boxes that happened to be below his hand had probably hit the glove compartment. The two that happened to be above his hand must have hit the dashboard. Hardly mattered, because all five of those pie boxes had come to rest on the floor of the passenger's side of the truck. Some had their lids flung open, revealing a serious misarrangement of runny purple berries and broken golden crusts. As for the two pies Carney thought he had saved, well, a peek under each lid disclosed that they, too, had gone forward inside their boxes.

"Pie pileups," Carney muttered. Boy, did they smell good.

He popped his door and slid out of the truck. Best to get his buckets out of the road. They were still rolling side to side, seeking a level, Carney figured, and he laughed because there was nothing level about Punkinville Road. Both buckets were fatally busted. Not surprising. He set them into the bed of the pickup.

Now. What to do about the pies?

He opened the passenger's side, and the fresh-baked aroma struck him again. Ahh. Anzie did make the best blueberry pies. Carney lifted the boxes and their loose contents up onto the seat of the truck. He propped on one buttock inside the open door. The pies were unsalable . . . but not inedible.

Hand pies.

That's what Carney thought as he slid his fingers under a nice half-sandwich-size pocket of crust. Deftly, he dumped the oozing berry filling into his mouth and folded the pastry in after it. As he savored that cheekful, he glanced out through the truck's back window. He thought he saw something—a flash of plaid, was it? Plaid on Punkinville Road could only mean someone was around, and here he was in an embarrassing mess of pies and broken buckets. He was in no mood to chat. He stayed low, pushed another scrap of pie into his mouth. He snuck a few more peeks out the truck windows. Where did that plaid go? Had his eyes played a trick?

Some minutes later Carney was either sick of pie or about to be sick because of pie. He sucked purple syrup off his thumb. Time to go back and find out what Anzie wanted to do about the failed delivery. On the way he'd think how to describe the weird deer that had caused all the trouble this morning.

Carney shut the passenger's side door. He used his elbow and his shirtsleeve to polish the dust off the painted side of the truck. The letters spelled out Anzie's poem. That's what she called it—a poem. Carney wasn't so sure, though it hardly mattered. He did so love Anzie. But alone on Punkinville Road he had a few thoughts, such as, Wasn't it more a list of words? Could a list be a poem? Anzie sure thought so. She'd put it on everything that had anything to do with the farm, including the long barn, including this truck.

SUN RAIN WIND SWEPT.

He wondered, not for the first time, shouldn't that be WINDSWEPT?

BUD BLOSSOM BERRY. Okay. Yes. It was a blueberry farm, and alliteration was a happy thing.

SWEET EARTH ROOTS KEPT. Hmm. That seemed a bit out of order.

MAKE A SOUL MERRY.

"Bah," said Carney. That last line seemed especially discordant because the only way he could hear it now was the way that neighbor girl had recited it—no, screamed it—on an otherwise-serene evening.

Aurora. That was her name. She was Ed Petrequin's kid. Carney knew Ed from around town, and as a neighbor since Ed owned all that land adjacent to Anzie's and had built the A-frame down the hill. Nice enough folks, and Anzie was very fond of them. But, oh, that Aurora. And her busy little brother, whose name Carney could never remember. Birch? No. Oakley? No. But it had something to with some tree or other.

"Pine cone," he said out loud. Then he snorted a laugh, which burned of blueberry. Anyway, those Petrequin kids were out of control. Carney wasn't much of a kid person, and he knew it, which is why he was surprised by the brand-new soft spot he felt for Aurora's friend—the boy who didn't talk. Wasn't that all kinds of ironic? The quietest kid he'd ever run across paired with the loudest one on earth? Carney remembered looking at the boy as he'd stared at Anzie's poem on the side of the barn. Unremarkable pose, and Carney wasn't sure he could read. If he'd thought anything, it was that the kid had always seemed absent or empty. Wrong. That boy was taking in something from having Anzie's verse shouted at him. Carney could still see the boy's dark eyelashes closing down—that slow blink. Why did some scenes stick in the memory? Then he remembered something else about the boy: the plaid shirt.

Frenchie

The Truck

Something inside Frenchie told him it would not be good for the deer to leap just then. But it did. Into the road. It stopped and looked back at Frenchie.

The truck halted. It threw buckets at the deer.

Bump-bah-dah—bang! Bang!

The deer sprang into the woods on the other side of the road.

Frenchie could see the opening between the trees. He knew where to go. But first he watched Carney Huggins pick up the buckets and get back inside the truck.

Quiet. Quiet is what Carney likes.

Frenchie saw the words on the truck. Same as on the barn:

SUN RAIN WIND SWEPT.

He remembered.

SUN SUN SUN.

That's what Frenchie always thought should come next. But it didn't. Aurora always said something else. But she wasn't there to say it now. So Frenchie tilted his face up and thought:

SUN SUN SUN.

His nose holes filled with the scent of blueberries. Warm and heavy. The way they are when Anzie pulls them from her oven. When Ed puts them in pancakes.

SUN SUN SUN.

Frenchie crossed the road, he slipped behind the truck, in a hurry to catch up with the deer. He saw Carney Huggins sitting in the truck. Down low. Eating the warm berries.

Quiet.

Frenchie stepped into the cool slice of shade between the trees. The deer place. A thin trail. Pretty soon, he saw the spots. Pretty soon, he began to watch his feet again. Hike, hike, hike.

And still, he thought Aurora would be behind him.

SUN SUN SUN.

Aurora

Messages for Frenchie

Ms. Chandra and her students have gone back to the art room. A few more kids have stopped by to leave Post-its on the ever-changing-tree mural. I look at the handwriting—some curly, some printed, some block letters. I read the messages:

> So sorry you are missing.
> Come home soon, Frenchie L!
> God is watching over you.
> Wherever you are, I hope you are seeing some great birds.
> Chirp-chirp!
> Come home safe.

(I'd like to take my marker to that one. It should say *safely*.)

> I think you are in my math class and we miss you there.
> Dear Frenchie, we are on the lookout for you!
> Hope you are warm enough.

(That one is odd. It's not even cold out.)

The messages are nice, I guess. But this is a change to the ever-changing-tree mural that I wish had never had come. I'm trying not to be sour about it, but a lot of the notes are from kids who have never bothered with Frenchie before today, kids who walk right by him in the hall—because most kids do.

There is one bright green Post-it note that says this:

> I owe you an apology. Please come get it.

No one was watching when that one went up. I know for sure, because it's from me.

Aurora

A Worst Possible

This is the feeling of a Worst Possible. I mess up a lot. I say I am sorry about ten times day. Mom and Pop tell me that's okay, and to move on from those things. But a Worst Possible is bigger than that. It sticks harder. I think the only cure is a time machine. That's what I want now. I want to go back to this morning, walk through the doors of the school and *not* have Frenchie behind me. I would put him beside me, I'd get him to his classroom, and I'd see him go in.

I close down hard on my eyes. The Worst Possible wells up in me.

"Frenchie," I whisper into the air. "Where did you go?"

It happened this past July. A Worst Possible a lot like this one. I made the same mistake. I forgot what was behind me. Mom and Pop and Gracia said that Frenchie and I could take a short hike while they were making dinner. Nothing unusual about that *until* I asked if we could take Cedar, and Mom and Pop said yes!

"Really? We can? Hear that, Cedar Tree? Want to go walking with Frenchie and me?" Well, my little brother headed for the door. He was going to get out before someone changed their mind. "Frenchie, come on!" I said, jumping up and down. Frenchie and I were the big kids. Apparently, we could be trusted. Especially me.

I've always tried to help with Cedar. I've done everything I can for him, including sometimes loving him up too hard and making him cranky. But I also have it in my head that I am my best self around him. Better than I am with other kids—except Frenchie; I feel pretty *best* with him too.

"Keep your eye on the little sprinter," Mom warned.

"Frenchie," Gracia said. She looked up from a platter of portobello mushrooms she was oiling for the grill. "You'll help Aurora with Cedar, yes?"

"He will," I said. "We'll be back in thirty minutes. Sound good? Okay, great." I loved answering my own questions.

"Fifteen," said Pop. "Grill's already lit."

"Okay, twenty," I said, "and we'll stay where we can *smell* dinner cooking. How's that?"

"Fairly reasonable," Pop said. "Twenty minutes, then." He pulled his phone out of his pocket. He set the timer, then held it out to me.

"When it rings, start back home," he said. "And, Aurora, I don't need to say it, do I?"

"Yeah, yeah. Take good care of the phone."

"No!" He scoffed. "Take good care of Cedar!"

"Oh! Right!"

What a feeling that was, walking out with Frenchie *and* Cedar, with Pop's phone swinging in the deep pocket of my shorts. Cedar didn't even look back. He wrapped all his little fingers around three of mine and off we went, with Frenchie a little way behind us. I knew we could make it to the crest and catch those couple of minutes when the sun goes low and the tree trunks are all lit up and glowing on their west-facing sides.

Sure enough we did.

"Look at that. Looks like the trees are on fire, doesn't it?" I said.

Neither Frenchie or Cedar could give me much of an answer. But Cedar was in a big-boy mood without our parents. He nodded his head like he understood. Frenchie stared and blinked a little.

"When I see the light do that, that's when I start to get

what artists do," I said. "Light and dark make shapes, but also, I think shape is the reason you see light and dark. Something like that. . . ."

"Yah," said Cedar, nodding again. "Yah, Awoh-wah."

I loved him so much for trying to use his words. But most of the talking was up to me, of course. As we walked, I said, "Feel that? How it's warmer down around your legs? The grass is holding on to all the heat from the sun today. But up here"—I swung Cedar's arm up—"the air is cooler." Cedar turned his chin up at me and giggled. I let his arm down again. "It's like the grass was baking all day. Like bread. You can even smell it." I gave the air a big sniff.

Cedar tried to do the same, but he did what he always does; he blew out instead. I folded over, laughing. Then Cedar laughed too. Frenchie stared ahead, and that was one of those times I wished he could get what laughing is—the unstoppable way it happens.

I used the hem of my tank top to wipe Cedar's nose. He stood for it way better than usual. "Good job, Cedar. I think we got it all. What do you think, Frenchie?" I looked and he was doing the stare. Like he was actually seeing something. I looked where Frenchie was looking and—zow! Right there in front of us, no more than the space between first base and second base, stood the piebald deer. Again!

"Ooo!" I whispered. "Down! Down! Get low." I tugged

on Cedar. Not hard. Frenchie dropped too. There we were on our bellies and elbows.

"Look, Cedar. See that deer? See the spots? And all those colors? That is called a *piebald* deer."

Cedar blinked as he peeked through the grasses. The deer picked up its head. "Shh . . ." I put my finger on my lips, and Cedar folded his lips in. The deer went back to grazing. Every so often its ears flicked at a halo of bugs.

"Oh, he's a boy," I whispered. "Nubs up top. He's got baby antlers."

The three of us lay still, watching, even Cedar.

"Cedar Tree," I whispered. "Don't ever forget this, okay? Don't forget that you got to see a piebald deer." Would he remember? Could he? What did I remember from being two and half years old? Not so much. "Try, Cedar. Try not to forget."

"'Kay, Awoh-wah," he whispered.

The deer raised his head again. Then he began to walk.

"We've got to follow," I said. "Stay low." Frenchie wasn't much for crouching, but Cedar did what I did. We walked into the ferns, leaving about twenty feet between us and the deer. The low light caught his coat as he headed into the woods. He had at least as many colors on him as Anzie Maylord's calico barn cat.

I looked behind me and motioned for Cedar to keep coming. He was holding back a grin, as if smiling might make too much noise. The deer hopped over a fallen pine branch. I wove a path between the skinny trees, hugged my way around the boulders. I looked back and saw Frenchie standing tall, stepping along. I kept following that piebald, stopping whenever he stopped, my heart beating hard. We'd never been able to follow the deer for so long. I scratched a bug bite while I drank in the sight of him. He was weird and beautiful, and he was *letting* us be this close, and—

Brr-ba-ding! Brr-ba-ding!

I jumped right out of my mosquito-bitten skin. The deer raised his head, then leaped.

Brr-ba-ding! Brr-ba-ding!

Pop's phone buzzed and rang and buzzed and rang. I jammed my hand into my pocket and yanked the phone out. I shut down the alarm. I growled. Then I roared. The piebald was gone.

"Can you believe that?" I said. I turned around to face Frenchie and Cedar. "Darn it!" I stamped a foot down and cracked a dry stick. Frenchie stood, tall and plaid, and stared at one of those non-places off behind me, and Cedar—where was Cedar?

"Cedar!" I stood on my toes, looking over into the ferns and grasses. "Cedar Tree?" I could *not* see him. And right then is when my heart felt like it was puking inside of me—the Worst Possible filling my insides. "Oh my— Cedar!" I called. "Frenchie! Wh-where is he? Where?"

Of course, Frenchie just stood there, opening and

closing his hands. This was up to me. I suddenly had no idea how far I had tracked the piebald.

It was only minutes. Not far. Right?

I couldn't think when I had last turned to check on Cedar. *My tiny little brother!*

I scrambled to the top of a high rock. I scanned the woods and called for Cedar. Why wasn't he answering? "Cedar? I have a game for you! Say my name!" I had never heard so much silence. "Cedar, if you can hear me! Say my name right now!"

And he did. And when he did, Frenchie started walking toward him. And I started breathing again. I jumped down and crashed over dead branches to get to him, scraped my legs in the puckabrush and didn't care one bit.

Cedar was fine. He wasn't far away, crouching low in the ferns. A little nest. I hugged the heck out of him. He looked at me with big round eyes.

"'Kay, Awoh-wah?" he said. It sounded like a question, so I answered.

"Yeah, yeah. I'm okay." But I had to hold back tears. That never happens to me. I sniffed hard. "Hey, come on, you guys. We better hustle home."

I put Cedar on my back. Hitched his little legs under my arms. I brushed a tiny trickle of blood from a scratch on his shin. "You're okay, you're okay," I told him.

Frenchie walked us out of the woods. I called up to

thank him. He always knows where he's going. He made it home first, like always.

The thing about a Worst Possible is, even when it's over, if you let yourself think back on it—even for a second—it gets you all over again.

And it always will.

Aurora

Waiting with Mrs. Whilmer

Mom and Pop, where are you? Come on, come on!

I stare at the ceiling tiles in the school office, and I wonder if I can stand another minute. I tell myself, Stay positive!

I think of all the things that Frenchie knows that can keep him safe.

He can swim. . . .

He knows how to cross the road. . . .

He's a strong, fast walker. . . .

Uh-oh. If Frenchie is out there fast-walking, he could be pretty far away by now. But what would ever make him do that? This morning is not a typical Frenchie morning.

Mrs. Whilmer swishes in.

"How are you doing, Aurora?" she asks. "Need anything? Can I get you a snack?"

"No, thanks," I say. "I just wish my parents would get here. And Gracia too."

Then I cover my face and think, Oh, Gracia! What will she say to me? My heart sinks—in a backward way, like it's going to hit my spine from the inside.

"They will be here soon," Mrs. Whilmer says. She glances at her watch.

"Yeah . . . I know." I dig my fingers into the sides of my face and work my cheeks like putty. "This is what an eternity is," I say. I pull up my feet and wrap my arms around my knees. Then I wiggle and reach into my pocket and pull out my geode. I squeeze it in my hands until the crystals pinch me.

Mrs. Whilmer covers my hand with hers, but then she leaves it too long. I'm uncomfortable. I do the only thing I can think of: I take back my hand, open my palm, and show her.

"Oh, a geode! And it's a beauty," she says.

"Frenchie and I split it," I tell her. I stare into its shiny center and wonder, Where's the other half now?

Aurora

Reedie's Rock Shop

The geode is new. We drove to Reedie's Rock Shop in Verona Island on Labor Day Saturday. The trip was for me, the rock hound with an allowance to spend. I planned to zero in on the tourmaline. But when I saw the geodes in a crate by the cash register, I bought one on the spot.

The whole idea with a geode is to open it, and Reedie's is all set up for that. The girl in the shop brought me the safety glasses, the chisel, and the ball-peen hammer. Frenchie knew I was going to crack that geode. He did not approve.

Everything about his body told me so. He blinked with his eyes looking up hard to his left. His chin jutted forward—the *no* pose. In case that message wasn't clear enough, he went right out the open door and stood beside the car, looking up into the trees.

"Frenchie. Come back in. Please! It'll be all right!" I called to him from the steps. He didn't budge. I leaned on the jamb, cupping the geode in both hands. It was about the size of a medium russet potato, and it looked like one too. I rubbed the dry brown surface with my thumb and wiped the dust on my shorts. I turned the geode over a few times.

Reedie's couldn't tell me where it'd come from.

"A rock shop worth its salt ought to know," I'd told the girl at the counter before I'd paid.

She'd said, "Maybe Missouri, because the riverbeds are full of them and they come up after storms."

"But you aren't sure, are you?" I'd said. And she said no, she was not.

But I'd made my choice, and I wanted to split it and find out what kind of crystals had formed inside of it. All Frenchie wanted was to get back in the car.

I looked over my shoulder into the shop. Mom and Gracia and Cedar were stopping beside barrels of tumbled stones.

"Ahhh! Yocks!" said Cedar. He pushed both his little hands deep into a barrel of polished pink quartz.

"Yes. R-r-rocks," I heard Mom pronouncing it for him. "Scoop. But don't throw, Cedar boy," she added.

Gracia leaned into Mom with something in her hand. "Rene, look at this blue one with the black and white veins running through it. What is this?" Together they searched for a label.

"Sodalite," I called from the door.

"Oh, good guess, Aurora!" Mom called. "You're right."

I shrugged. Had I wasted several weeks' allowance on a rock-hard potato? Yeah, I was a geode owner for the first time in my life. That was pretty cool, even though it was store-bought. But I'd had a special reason for buying it, and if Frenchie wasn't into this, it was going to bum me right out. I don't spend for rocks easily. Buying seems like cheating. If I add a rock, I want to be the person who found it.

Pop had once said, "Aurora, your rules for rock hunting could make for a small accumulation."

I had told Pop, "I am planning to grow at least as old as you. I have years of searching ahead of me. Someday, I'll ride my bike all the way to Androscoggin County for a real mineral hunt. Someday, I'll borrow the car from you and Mom and drive all the way to the state of Oregon to look for thunder eggs."

Pop had thrown his arms over his chest and pretended to faint onto our couch. All six foot six of him, laid out, with big work boots hanging over the armrest.

The memory made me snort as I stood in the doorway watching Frenchie.

"Hey," I called. "It's not really breaking it; it's more like opening it. Something amazing could be on the inside. Shiny stuff." It probably wasn't worth telling him all the fun facts about geodes, like how it takes decades for one to form, and how you never know what sorts of crystals might be lining the hollow—anything from quartz to purple amethyst. Even agates and jaspers. I wasn't about to lie and say a bird would come flying out, but I thought about it.

"I got it so we could share it." I told him. "I figure we'll each have a half to take to our new sixth-grade classrooms since we're not together this year. It'll be two things that fit right together even though they are apart. Ya know?"

Frenchie turned from the car to face me, though as usual, he didn't really look at me.

"I'll take the smaller half," I promised. Then I rolled my eyes. "Well, there you go. That's a sentence that makes no sense. If they were actually halves, they'd be the same size. That's not too likely to happen. Geodes break where they want to break. But I'll try for equals, Frenchie, and if I blow it, you can have the bigger one. Promise."

And that's when he came back inside Reedie's Rock Shop.

I was not going to let him change his mind. I stuck the safety glasses on my face and set right to tapping a line into that potato-looking geode. Mom took a video of the whole thing. That's how I know what my breath sounded like when the geode fell into two pieces. You can hear me say, "Aww! It's a beauty! Nice crystal cavity. And look! Look! We got ourselves a snowball burr on one side! See that nice round part in there?" Mom followed me with her phone as I leaned toward Frenchie. "Oh! And another! One in each piece. I don't think that happens a lot." I said it right to the camera. "This second one's pretty tiny. See? But I'd say that's still a *snowball*."

Then you can hear Cedar say, "No-baw! No-baw!" He leans forward, and before any of us can stop him, he sticks the tip of his tongue into the bigger geode half and gives it a lick!

The picture goes tilty and blurry, and you can hear Mom laughing. Gracia too. And me, being so happy that Frenchie went along with cracking the geode.

We ran our pinkies all along the cavities, and felt the edges of the crystals. We looked at both pieces with magnifying glasses. Then I slid the larger piece of the geode across the top of the hammered-up table at Reedie's until it sat right in front of Frenchie with all its crystals shining up at him.

"Yours," I said. Then he reached for both pieces of the geode. Slowly, he fitted them back together like he was fixing a broken egg. Frenchie gets stuff, but I didn't expect that. Neither did Gracia. She got teary. Then he held the smaller piece close to his chest and pushed the larger one in front of me.

"Me?" I said. "You want me to have the bigger piece?"

Frenchie didn't speak. But he did answer. In a very Frenchie way. He opened the flap on his needlepoint purse and dropped the small half of our geode inside. Then he walked back out of Reedie's Rock Shop and stood beside the car again, ready to go home.

Aurora

The Glue

Mom, Pop, Gracia, and Cedar *finally* walk through the front door at Mountain View School. I slither off my orange chair to the floor, then bounce to my feet. I peel around the glass partition and fall against them all. We hug—oh my gosh, we hug! It's not that perfectly happy sort of hugging. It's more like, time to glue ourselves together. We are all going to find Frenchie.

I see how much Gracia needs him back. She presses her palms together and takes shivery breaths. There is a little crying but no apologizing—no time for that. The town is taking over the search for Frenchie. They are setting up headquarters down at the Fire and Rec Center. We need to be there.

I run for the van shouting, "I'll take the way-back seat!"

I keep watch out the windows all the way down Bert Gray Road. I am looking for Frenchie, hoping to spot him, waiting in a yard or a field. The words sit ready on the tip of my tongue. I want to say them *so* much: *There! He's there!*

But I don't get to.

We drop Gracia at her house. I watch her on the step. She's hunched, like she is folding up with worry. But she straightens and flings the door open and slips inside quickly. She's going ahead of us to the Fire and Rec Center. No point in her waiting while four Petrequins get organized. Mom has to change her clothes. We'll need our boots and water bottles. We are about to start the most important hike of our lives.

"Let's hurry," I say. I rock in the seat, even though home is only yards away now. Cedar rocks too.

Mom and Pop are talking.

"We'll need the carrier for Cedar, or we'll be no help at all," Mom says.

"The carrier, diapers, and the *vests*," Pop says sharply.

"That's tomorrow," Mom says. "Archery season opens tomorrow. Designated areas only."

Oh right, I think. Orange Days. Hunting season. Every year, Mom blocks the days onto our family calendar with a neon-orange marker. Early September to mid-December. Those are the days we wear bright orange safety vests for hiking *anywhere*, or even filling our own bird feeder, or raking leaves in our yard.

"Take no chances," Pop says.

Before Pop speaks again, Mom says, "Vests. Yes. Of course."

"I wonder how they're going to organize this search." It's the last thing Pop says before we hop out of the car at home.

This search.

The words sound awful to me. My guts are yuck. I want to find Frenchie so much. "I guess they'll start near the school. Since he was there this morning." I say it mostly to myself. I feel a pull inside me to go back there and look. But the place I picture him in my mind is up at the blueberry barrens. Sundrop Meadow. Our big back-yard. Maybe it's just because we go there so much. But what if it's a hunch?

I am in my boots and ready, but Mom and Pop are still putting Cedar on the potty, and finding bug repel-lent, and filling water bottles. "Hey, please can I go up to Sundrop Meadow and cross over to Anzie's?"

"Right now?" Mom breathes out. She's exasperated.

"I want to look there first."

"We can drive up. It would be good to let Anzie know—spread the word that Frenchie is—"

"No, I mean I want to hike up. I want to look for

Frenchie. He could be up there bird-watching in the woods beside the meadow. Or maybe even picking . . ." Although, I know the crop is pretty spent for the year.

"He knows the way," I say. Those words puff me up. Frenchie in the present tense. Frenchie *now*. Because he *is* now. I'm sure he is.

"Aurora, he knows the way when he starts from home," Mom says. She has her doubtful face on. "But he didn't start from home today. . . ."

"Mom, I know. I still want to look there. Please!" I say.

Pop hears me. He follows Cedar out of the bathroom. He has fresh diapers for the day tucked under his elbow.

"So you drive it; I'll hike it. Meet me in her driveway. I can't wait anymore. I can't!"

My parents look at each other.

"No harm," says Pop. "We'll meet up at Anzie's." He puts a finger up. "No meandering, Aurora."

That's all I need to hear. I am out the door. Forget hiking. I am running. A dozen sprint steps and suddenly I hear Pop hollering my name.

"Aurora! You forgot!" I turn and see him jogging toward me. He's flapping an orange vest at me.

"Sorry, Pop! Sorry!" He wraps me into the vest and hugs me, hard. I hug him back.

"See you up the hill, my girl. Love you."

"Love you, Pop!"

Aurora

My Quick Stop in the Barrens

I hike faster than normal today on my way up to Sundrop Meadow. I talk the same way I always do—even though I am alone. Usually, I have Frenchie walking beside me, never answering, of course. But his pants always swish together, and I know all the different ways he breathes. And what his burps sound like. There's that whisper of breath he takes in before he tweets like he does. Today, there is a whole lot of silence coming back at me. It's different than not hearing answers from my friend. My person. The person who chose me to be his person. It's bigger.

I hold the bottom hem of the orange vest as I go. If only Frenchie was wearing one, he'd be easier to spot.

At the top of the meadow I turn in a slow circle,

looking and looking hard as I can. I think about the math of it, and I tell myself, he'll be along this radius, or this next one. But as I come around, I haven't spotted him, so I go round again.

I look west toward Anzie's farm, south toward home. Then I head into the East Woods. But I am not going to be a dope about this. I won't go deep. I have not forgotten that I was a little bit lost here a few weeks ago, following that piebald deer. I've still got scars from crashing through the puckabrush to get to Cedar that day. That would be a bad thing to repeat, and besides, if I get lost, well, I'm one less person to go searching for Frenchie.

That makes me stop still.

"Frenchie!" I call out. "Frenchie, can you hear me? Give me a tweet! Or come on out." I wait. Nothing. "If you're hiding, stop it! If you're crouching, quit it! Stand up! Now!" First, I'm mad. Then I'm brilliant. "Hey, want to go to Anzie's and read the poem off the barn? You know the one." At the top of my lungs I holler. "'SUN RAIN WIND SWEPT BUD BLOSSOM BERRY SWEET EARTH ROOTS KEPT . . .'" I stop to take a breath. It doesn't seem right to go on and holler out the next part: MAKE A SOUL MERRY. There's nothing merry about this. I tilt my head back, push my shoulders forward. I call, "Fren-CHEE! I'll read you the rest, but you have to come with me!" I wait. I breathe again and again.

He doesn't come.

I can't stay any longer. Mom and Pop will worry. They could be at Anzie's by now. I jam my hand into the pocket of my shorts and wrap my fingers around my geode for a second. "Come on, Frenchie," I whisper.

I scan the woods one more time. Then I turn and sprint toward Anzie's farm.

Aurora

Encountering Carney

I'm going in through the gate, breathing hard, when I see Carney Huggins. He's got some rocks by his feet (nothing special, I'm pretty sure) and a shovel in his hands. He's plugging up a gopher hole. He stops digging and squints at me.

"Hey," I say as I get near, but I try not to slow down. "Weird seeing me here this time of day, isn't it?"

He pulls his chin under. Looks like he is thinking that over. "Yeah, I guess. It is."

"Well, it's due to something bad," I tell him. "He's gone missing. In case you haven't heard." I'm still on the move, trying to sweep on by. I do *not* have time to chat with Carney.

"Wait, wait. Say again?" he says.

Now I do have to stop. "Frenchie Livernois," I say. "You know him. Comes up here with me all the time."

Carney raises one arm, reaches to scratch under the back of his hat. He's got a long purple stain running from his wrist to his bony elbow. Now that I am standing still, and kind of close to him, I am pretty sure he smells like blueberry pie. Maybe that's what he and Anzie eat for breakfast. Pie. Or maybe his clothes fill up with the smell of them when he's driving deliveries.

"Seems like he left the schoolyard early this morning," I say. "First thing."

Now Carney tilts his head. Looks like he has a question but he's not getting around to asking it.

"There's going to be a search. We'll use all the help we get," I say.

"Oh. I might . . . uh—"

"Yeah, yeah," I interrupt. "If you can't search, then spread the word. Tell three people and ask them to tell three more. Get the math? I think you kind of like him. Not me. But him. And that's okay. A lot of people think I'm too much."

"So, wait. There's a search, you say?"

"Yep." I point toward the farmhouse. "My parents are letting Anzie know. I'm here to meet them. We're going down to the Fire and Rec Center to get our assignment.

NOW." I finish up loud hoping he'll get the point. I have to go!

"Aurora!"

"What?" I turn, but I keep trotting backward. Carney Huggins has his hands cupped around his mouth like he's going to yell something at me. Sheesh, Carney! And you think I drive you nuts? Think it's easy running backward? Think I'm not worried about my friend?

"What school?" he calls. "Where did he leave from?"

"The elementary!"

"Where's that?"

"Up Bert Gray Road!" I scream back. Under my breath I say, "How can you live here and not know that?"

Maxine Grindel

Maxine and Dudley at the Hospital

Maxine Grindel sat in a chair in the exam room at the walk-in clinic. Best not to wait up on that high table, lest she get woozy again and tip over. Dudley might not be quick enough to catch her.

A nurse had firmly instructed Maxine to hold her hand high, above her heart, and to apply pressure on the end of that ring finger, which had bled through a wad of paper towels—and was *throbbing*.

It'd been over an hour since Dudley had packed Maxine—half-passed-out—into the passenger's side of the Mrs. Thrift camper van. It made sense to drive the van to the clinic; it had a new fan belt and was running like a dream.

"Where is that doctor?" Maxine's patience was eroding.

Finally, a woman who was much too young to be anybody's doctor arrived and snapped a pair of rubber gloves on. She took a good look under Maxine's clump of bloodied paper towels.

There was good news: Maxine's topless ring finger would heal, as long she followed instructions to the letter. The doctor predicted, that when all was said and done, the healed finger would look only the littlest bit misshapen, and only to someone who was really giving it a look.

"Don't care what it looks like!" Maxine exclaimed. "I need to be able to use the dang thing! I have work to do! And by the way, it *hurts!*"

The doctor gave Maxine two pills for the pain, then slipped out of the room. Again, Maxine and Dudley waited.

"It's a pity," Dudley said. He rested his hand gently on his wife's knee. "I'll miss that little bit of your finger, Maxie."

"Well, when we get home, you can look for it. Find it, and it's yours," Maxine said.

Dudley chuckled his best chuckle.

The doctor swished back in. "Starting to feel better?" she asked, her sweet young head tilted in sympathy.

Seconds later, she poured a *stinging fire* of antiseptic on Maxine's wound. Maxine moaned and thunked her forehead on Dudley's shoulder. The doctor set to wrapping Maxine's finger in cloth, followed by several layers of snowy-white gauze. Maxine watched as the doctor worked, going around and around the finger until, to Maxine's sleepy eyes, her finger had become triple-thick. Maxine started to laugh.

"Look, Dudley! I've got a little finger puppet." She wiggled it. (It didn't hurt anymore.) Maxine laughed harder.

"Don't be swinging it around, now," Dudley warned. Maxine ignored him.

"I think I'll call her Miss Mummy." She made the finger bob and bow. "Hello, hello! Do you like this show? No!" She tilted her head back and cackled.

A short time later, Maxine was half-asleep on the bench outside the clinic with Miss Mummy resting in her lap. The September sun warmed her face. Dudley had gone to get the camper van from the parking lot. Maxine heard the engine rev up in the distance.

The Mrs. Thrift-mobile, she thought, and she smiled because that new fan belt sounded so right.

Maxine waited. She observed a few cars out on Dixon Way. Watched the garbage truck backing up over at the Dental Associates building. *Beep-beep-beep.* It was a terrible noise. But everything seemed pleasant to Maxine.

Soon, she heard voices nearby. Folks standing in the circle right beside her. Maxine narrowed her eyes. Were those uniforms? Looked like it.

"There's a missing boy . . . ," someone said.

"We're heading out to join now . . . the search . . . underway . . ."

Maxine tried very hard to tune in.

"Sixth grader," she heard. "So, how old is that? Ten or eleven?"

Maxine knew the answer. She tried to speak. She might have said, "Eleben." Then "Whu-bere?" and "Whu is dis do say?" Then she might have asked, "Whu-appened?"

The uniforms were not answering. Maxine listened harder.

"Poor kid. . . . There's something about him. . . . They say he doesn't talk."

Wait . . .

A thought bubbled up in her head. Didn't she know a boy who didn't talk? Maxine's eyebrows arched. Oh, but her lids felt heavy. And Lord, she was tired.

The camper van rolled to a stop right in front of her. And there was Dudley, sweet old Dudley, helping her up and in.

On the way home Maxine wondered many things. Why didn't her finger hurt anymore? Why was her mind floating through with thoughts of that boy . . . *Frenchie?*

Frenchie, who's momma had bought him the needlepoint purse. Maxine slowly remembered the day. Baker's Field. Right off Route 1. Hotter than a Tater Tot. Horrid with buzzing flies. Hmm. Last July? Or the one before?

Jewell Laramie

Stuck in Traffic

Jewell Laramie had everything she needed for her softball league's end-of-season picnic. She liked to wrap up with a decent celebration, and she always chose the first Friday in September. Fact was, Jewell found endings rather bittersweet. Best way to get through? Have a party! Tonight was the night.

She was nearly back to town, having spent the morning packing her Jeep with paper plates, napkins, and red-checked tablecloths. She'd been to the Picklonious Deli—league sponsor—where she'd fetched gallon-size jugs of sweet relish, mustard, ketchup, *and* three huge jars of famous Picklonious sour pickles.

"Lot of vinegar in the Jeepy today." Jewell had joked

with Sid and Berkley from the deli as they'd shouldered the jars and jugs to her car.

Jewell had thought it all through—how to pack the back of her Jeep in a particular order. The boxes of softball mini trophies—which she'd purchased on her own dime—were already snugged up against her bow and quiver, which were mounted on the rack behind the Jeep's rear seat (another end-of-summer ritual). The paper goods and condiments were nestled in next. The two coolers full of hot dogs, slaw, and potato salad—currently filling up Jewell's fridge—would fit in the center, and the three large bags of charcoal would go in last because she'd need them first.

Yep. Jewell Laramie knew how to be efficient.

It would've been nice if she could have trusted someone else to fire the grills. But Jewell believed that if she wanted this celebration done right, she had best do it herself.

As she reached the center of town, traffic moved in that slow, parade-like way that was typical of Maine in summertime. "Even post–Labor Day weekend," she muttered. "Well, this is *Vacationland.*" Maine license plates had been embossed with the slogan. "Since 1936! Fun fact." Jewell chuckled and waggled a finger in the air.

She hovered her foot over her brake pedal, pressing down as needed. The traffic crept along, in barely broken, bumper-to-bumper stretches in both directions. When

Jewell reached the Fire and Rec Center, the two cars in front of her took righthand turns into the lot. She gave the place a glance as she let her Jeep snail forward. Lot of activity—

HONK-*honk-honk!*

Jewell hit the brakes. Her blood rushed. An insistent old Chevy in the oncoming lane turned in front of her. A second car tailed the first, as if hitched together. That driver waved to Jewell as if to say, *Yut, cutting you off! Thanks!*

Jewell set her foot on the gas. She powered forward a few yards before another car could attempt to cut across.

"Perfectly lawful on my part," she said. She shot a last look into the Fire and Rec parking lot. Maybe she could make a little stern eye contact with that pair of blockheads. Instead, she noted a whole lot of folks standing around outside the building.

Huh.

Jewell focused on the road home again, but she had a feeling now, and it nagged her. Something out of the ordinary was going on in her little part of *Vacationland*.

Oh, there! She recognized the Petrequin minivan, coming toward her. Jewell lowered her window to flag them, thinking there'd be time for a neighborly ask: Where the heck is everyone going? As they got close Jewell noticed that Rene was driving, and that her eyes were fixed on the road ahead. Ed, too, was leaning forward in a purposeful way in the passenger's seat, as if they needed to be somewhere. The van rolled on by.

Jewell wondered if they had the kiddos with them. Neat family, they were. Jewell often thought about the day they'd met. The Petrequins had turned down her offering: a beautiful venison tenderloin. They'd made it clear; they didn't eat mammals, *and* they didn't fancy hunting. Jewell chose not to be offended.

However, she thought about Aurora—all the dang time. Oh, how she had wanted that kiddo for her team—still did! "Great throwing arm. Not going to give up on that one," she said out loud. Jewell was sure that girl would mature into an excellent player. *More raw talent in her pinkie finger than I ever had in my whole body....* She mused.

Jewell grinned, remembering what the girl had told her back in March when Jewell had, for the third straight year, come recruiting at the Petrequins' place.

"Trust me, Coach. You're better off without me." Aurora had flapped a hand. "I'll be scratching bug bites in your outfield and crawling out of your dugout, heading for the monkey bars between ups." Then she'd said, "Softball. Ugh! Too much standing around!" Aurora had faked a loud yawn to drive her point. Hard for Jewell to keep a straight face. Aurora had lasted almost four games the one season she did play. Jewell still cracked up every time she remembered the last one. Aurora had managed to stuff several softballs into the deep pockets of her shorts. She'd waddled onto the field for the start of the third inning, shorts sliding severely to the south.

Jewell slapped a hand down on her steering wheel in the Jeep, and sighed. "Ohh . . . what a kiddo!"

Once again, traffic slowed in front of her. She stepped on her brake pedal, stretched up and glanced in her rearview. She spotted the back of the Petrequin van, turn signal flashing cherry bright.

"By golly . . . they're heading to the Fire and Rec Center too," Jewell said.

There happened to be a slim opening in the stream of oncoming vehicles. Jewell Laramie, pulled a tight U-ey and joined the caravan.

Aurora

How to Organize a Search

At the Fire and Rec Center there is a lot of standing around. Never seen such a swarm of orange safety vests in one place. Hunting season coming. People are playing it safe. This is a different kind of hunt, I think. This is the hunt for Frenchie.

I catch sight of Coach Jewell as she pulls into the lot in her Jeep. "Huh. And here we are, standing around. Like at a softball game," I mutter. But I am glad to see her. She knows the woods, and since the woods are all around us, and Frenchie hasn't been seen anywhere else, there's a good chance he is in them. But where?

I'm standing alone because Mom and Pop (with Cedar on his back) and Gracia are at one of the check-in tables that have been set up. They are calling it headquarters. Everyone is to pick up a map, instructions, and a water bottle if they need one. I get the feeling the rescue organizers have some ideas about where to look for Frenchie. As if there are only a few places all lost kids end up.

My heart keeps taking down dives. I keep hauling it back up.

Chief Nash has a megaphone in one hand, and notes in the other. He looks like he's about to make an announcement. I do a slow 360 where I am standing. It's too much for me that so many people have turned out. It makes this real. This is a Worst Possible. I swallow hard.

Chief Nash's voice booms, "Folks! Folks! Your attention, please! May I?"

Everyone quiets down. They look up from their maps to listen.

"Thanks, people. We are grateful you are here. We have a few things to cover. Then we'll turn our parties out to various locations of interest."

"Time's a-wasting!" someone shouts.

"Giddyap!" shouts another.

Chief Nash puts up a hand, keeps his cool. "Now, we ask that you take note of some information." He turns to a pair of whiteboards set up on risers where everyone can see them. Written across the top of the first board are the words WHAT WE KNOW. Chief Nash reads them out loud, then shakes his head.

"We wish we knew more." He draws a line under the words. "Now, we are looking for our eleven-year-old boy." He begins to make a list.

BOY. 11 YEARS OLD.

"His name is Frenchie Livernois." Up goes Frenchie's name. "He is nonvocal, folks. Does. Not. Speak." He writes that down, then taps the board with the tip of his marker. "He can hear. So we want to use his name when we are out there."

I try to picture "out there." I can't see it but it feels huge—beyond huge. I wonder what searching will be like.

"He was last seen at the Mountain View School on Bert Gray Road at approximately seven forty-three this morning." He adds to the list, then says, "We know that he entered the building. For some reason, he did not enter his classroom."

For some reason named *me*, I think. I wait for Chief Nash to say it: *Aurora Pauline Petrequin*. She messed up. Forgot her best friend.

"The school has been thoroughly searched. We have determined that he is not in the building." He mentions Frenchie's clothes and backpack and the needlepoint purse. And birds. He asks if anyone has seen anything this morning—anything at all. A boy on his own. An abandoned backpack. "Please come talk to us," he says. "Even if it didn't seem important at the time. I can't stress that enough."

I am looking at my feet now. I scuff them around in the grit. When I look up, Darleen Dombroski's face is in my face. Right away, I think it: Here's something I don't need. Somehow, I keep from blurting it.

"Hi, Aurora," she says. She's got her hands behind her back. She swings her body from side to side.

"Hi." One-word answers are about all I have. I glance up at the sky, trying to avoid eye contact with Darleen. There is one of those perfect September suns straight overhead. I look down again. Darleen is still here.

"I bet you feel terrible," she says, still swinging.

"I want to find Frenchie," I say.

"We're going to help," she says. "My mom came and took me out of school early, just for this."

I nod at her.

"Nice," I say, because it is nice. Then I want to say, *What the heck, Darleen? Not like you ever did anything but screw your face up at Frenchie Livernois before today.* But I don't because we need searchers.

"We'll find him," I say. I would like to weasel away from her now, but there are people everywhere. I feel stuck. Darleen gives a little shrug.

"My mom said it'll be a good lesson."

"Lesson?" I stare at her.

"Yeah. Seeing how a search works. I've never seen what they do. I mean, of course we want to find him—"

"A lesson?" I say it again. "Are you kidding me? Frenchie

is a person. You don't get to make a lesson out of him! A lesson is a hip-hop class!" I sputter. "Or learning to knit a *s-s-something!*"

Two seconds, and there it is. The Darleen crumple face. She is going to cry. I don't get to see that through because she goes shoulder-shoving through the crowd, bouncing off people on her way. I figure she will be back. With her mother. That's another thing I don't need today.

I get a little mercy when Mom and Pop and Cedar and Gracia come to get me. "We are starting up at the school," Mom says. She waves a paper map.

As we hurry to our car, Gracia asks, "Did the app load?"

"We're loading an app?" I say. "Now? What for?"

"It's a search-party tool," Pop says as he leans into the car and settles Cedar into his seat.

"Oh. Really?"

"Yes, it's genius!" Moms says. "They asked all the volunteers to purchase it. For a few bucks, it creates a digital map and tracks us. So there will be a record of where everyone has walked, and what time each area was searched."

"Oh . . . ," I say, I think I hear my own voice brighten a little. "That's pretty cool, huh?"

"If the data show that we are retracing the steps of others, they can drop us a digital pin," says Gracia. "We'll move to an area that hasn't been covered. It should be very helpful." Her voice seems a little stronger now too.

Still, she rubs the knobs of her knuckles into her palms.

Pop gets Cedar buckled up and hands me the phone. "Watch for the download, Aurora."

I look closely at the screen.

"It's got about a quarter of the way to go," I say.

Mom and Pop hurry to the front seats while I jump into the van on one side of Cedar and Gracia goes around and slips in on the other.

I buckle in and hold the phone tighter, as if I have the power in me to speed up the download. Come on, phone, come on! Gracia needs this. We all need this. I lean around Cedar and give her a smile.

"It's happening," I say. "The dot is filling."

Before it is even done loading, and before we know if it will even work, the app seems like the greatest invention ever; it's something to believe in. Right now.

"You ready, Cedar Tree?" I say. "We're going to take a *big* hike. Going to look for Frenchie."

"En-chee," he says. His word for Frenchie.

"That's right," I say. "Frenchie." It must seem strange to Cedar that Frenchie isn't with us in the minivan right now. We are always together. Always!

"Bye-baw!" says Cedar.

He's kicks his feet and bounces. Pop turns in the passenger's seat and tells him, "Take it easy, Cedar. Easy."

Mom pulls our van out of the fire station lot, while more volunteers roll in.

"Wow. See that?" Pop says. "No doubt, we will be joined by others up at the school."

"No doubt," says Mom. She presses the gas pedal. We head off toward Bert Gray Road.

Topher Menkis

Good Intentions

Topher Menkis sat in Frenchie's chair, devastated but desperately trying to buck up. Last thing he needed was for administration to be worried about him. There was a kid to find! His plan was to hydrate and eat something, but the almond butter with apples and honey on flax bread didn't look as good as it had when he'd assembled it early that morning.

Topher had unique skills to offer for the search, *and* he had called for backup: two friends on their way. But he had to pull himself together mentally, or he'd be useless.

He looked at the collage of bird pictures taped to the top of the boy's desk in front of him. They'd made that together. Topher had brought Frenchie a new paper cutout of a feathered friend each day since the first day of school. For his part, Frenchie loved to pull out long pieces of Scotch tape, snap them off the roll, and use them to stick the birds down. They'd already gone through a whole roll of tape.

"Bird of the Day!" Topher would announce, and there were signs that Frenchie was beginning to anticipate this. That was progress. Maybe it was true that birds were the way into this silent, seemingly closed-off boy. Topher was determined to reach Frenchie. New job. Good intentions.

Now Topher tucked two fingers into his shirt pocket and tweezed out the would-be Bird of the Day, a green-eyed vireo, clipped from an old *National Geographic* magazine. He turned it over in his fingers, then let it fall onto the desk.

How had day seven become so nightmarish?

How had he lost the kid? A vulnerable kid!

Topher felt 100 percent responsible. His job was to focus on *one* boy, to encourage him and protect him.

All day.

Every day.

Topher slammed his hand flat on Frenchie's desktop. *Fail!*

Aurora

The Search Begins

Mom pulls our van into the school parking lot. This feels weird. I have anything *but* school on my mind. I see people we know. Whole families have come. But a lot of kids are still in class, and a lot of parents are still at work.

But this is good. Helpers are here. We will find Frenchie.

Then don't you know it, the folks in charge ask everyone to gather up.

"Ugh! All we do is gather up," I say. "Gather, gather, gather. Can we please start searching?" I scruff around in a circle on the school driveway.

"I know it seems that way," Pop says. "But come on, let's

listen." He hauls me in against his side, where I squirm.

"An organized effort is paramount," Mom says. She stands close to Gracia, but keeps her eye on Cedar. He is on the ground for now and wants to run. They are letting him be loose as long as they can. He'll be riding in the backpack, and it could be a while. He's not going to like that.

I let myself think it: Maybe we will find Frenchie right away.

Gracia draws in a big breath and sighs. "This waiting is very hard," she whispers. Her jaw is tight. She presses praying hands to her forehead. Not the first time I've seen her do it.

The organizers wanted her to wait for news at headquarters. But Gracia told them no, she had to join the search for her boy, and she needed to be with her friends (us). They could reach her on her cell with news or questions. They promised to stay in touch.

"A reminder," the organizer calls, "we are working from *point last seen*. That's where we start a search for a missing person."

"Here," I whisper, pointing my finger at the ground. The guy goes on.

"We know Frenchie was dropped off at the school this morning. We believe he either left the building shortly after entering, or never entered at all. So right here, is the last place anyone saw him."

I glance at Pop. We are pretty sure he's the last one who saw Frenchie. Well, except for Cedar. Maybe. He could have been watching from our van when Frenchie walked into the school. Pop shakes his head and sighs. I think he feels the same kind of awful I feel. I bet we want the same thing: a do-over, starting from about 7:43 this morning. But he's not the one who lost Frenchie. That was me.

"We are focusing our search on the two-mile radius all around the school." The guy draws a wide loop with his finger. "Check your phone apps for the map. Images should be coming up any second now, thanks to Dottie Sylvania—our librarian and tech specialist at headquarters. She is on it! You'll see the circular area of the search cut up into pie slices." He shows us with his hands. "Each group walks a widening triangle outward from this center point—a pie slice."

"So let's go-o-o . . . ," I growl.

"Your work is to crisscross within your pie slice. Cover it all. Refer to the app to stay on track. Headquarters will keep us in the loop. In the event of changes you'll get new instructions."

"Changes? Like what?" I ask.

Pop shushes me and gestures at the speaker. "Keep listening," he says.

"What we mean is the development of a last known position. It's different from a last point seen. A last known position means Frenchie Livernois has been seen, *or* a clue has been discovered that lets us know he was most likely in that location. Could be anything from a footprint to a lunch bag, to a piece of clothing. Watch as you travel. If you find anything, message headquarters immediately. *A last known position, or LKP, can change the focus of our search.*"

I can't listen anymore. I'm ready to walk—a pie slice, a doughnut hole. Whatever. I turn in a circle looking out and think, Where would I go?

No. That's wrong thinking. The question is: Where would Frenchie go?

I think of how the sun strikes the front doors of the school on clear mornings. Frenchie lets it shine on his face before he goes inside. Did he do that this morning? If he left the school grounds, would he walk toward that sun and across Bert Gray Road? What would matter most to him?

"Okay, here it is." Mom waves the phone, then holds it low for all of us to see. "There's our triangle in the yellow highlight." She looks up. "So . . . back of the school and to the northwest. That's our slice of the pie." She smiles at Gracia. Gives her a nod.

It's good to know that we are about to actually do something.

I keep looking up because . . .

Birds.

Birds would matter to Frenchie. Birds in trees. There

are gosh-darn trees all around us.

"Okay. Stay safe out there and stay in touch. The search begins!"

"The search *resumes*," I say. "Some people have already been looking all morning."

As soon as I say it, I see one of them. Mr. Menkis. With Frenchie missing there is no one for him to watch over today. Instead, he is sitting on the curb, orange vest and backpack on, lacing his hiking boots. He sees me too. He lifts his chin at me. I wave back, but then I duck my head. What if he's wondering why I wasn't careful this morning—why I didn't bring Frenchie to him?

I watch my own feet as I follow Mom and Pop and Gracia to the back of the school, to our slice of pie—the worst kind ever—with Cedar running along beside me.

Carney Huggins

Seeing Clearly

Carney Huggins stopped at the kitchen door, two pairs of hiking boots under one arm and a couple of well-worn day packs slung on the other. He dropped all that gear and leaned on the jamb, watching his sweet Anzie at work. She was carefully sliding the remains of the smashed pies from his Punkinville Road mishap out of their tins and into her deep-dish baking pan. Carney thought she was doing an artful job of fitting the sections together, like a miniature landscape of dark purple rivers, with islands of amber-colored crusts. Odd-looking pie, but it had the look of something you'd scoop with a big spoon and feed to a crowd. Fitting.

Carney and Anzie would be heading down to the Fire

and Rec Center soon to join that search for the silent boy. When Ed and Rene Petrequin delivered the news, Anzie's double oven was hot and stacked full of half-baked pies. Excruciating choice, but they'd decided to let the pies finish while they gathered their gear. Then they'd dash out—about a half hour behind their neighbors.

"Nice repair," Carney said as Anzie used a spatula to pat a flat top on her reconstructed pastry.

"It'll do. We'll take it to headquarters with us," she said. "If the search goes long, they'll want to feed people. Or, if not, the firefighters will appreciate it. I hope we get there and learn that Frenchie's been found, safe and sound. Poor kid." She released a worried sigh. "He must be terrified," she muttered.

Carney held his bottom lip between his teeth. He managed to nod, but he was thinking that Anzie might not be right in this case. The boy called Frenchie didn't strike him as one who knew terror; the kid *was whatever he was*, wasn't he? Carney let out a nearly silent sound like *Hunh*. Who else could he say that about? And what would one call that anyway?

"Hey, Carne, clean T-shirt for you, maybe?" Anzie pointed at the evidence of spilled pies and garden mud, staining the front of Carney. "Seventeen minutes to go," she said, checking her kitchen timer.

"Yes, my beloved," he said. He peeled off his shirt at the sink and ran suds up his arms. He found the trail of blueberry stain running from his pinkie to his elbow. He scrubbed, then cupped water in his hands to wash the garden grit out of his eyes. He blinked. Twice. What Carney wanted was to see clearly. To see what had really happened earlier in the day. Then he would know. He'd be sure.

Was it a patch of plaid? Or a sparrow flying by? Could it have been the boy everyone was looking for? He shook his head. He should know the difference between a boy and a sparrow. But sometimes things flitted by so fast, and if you didn't know that you were going care about it later, you didn't take note. Should he say that he might have seen a boy following a deer—a deer that looked like it'd stepped out of a storybook? Carney used the hand towel to dry his eye sockets. He pressed hard enough that he made himself see spots.

"You know, Anz . . . I keep thinking about something," he said. "This morning was so weird."

"Why is that?" she asked, bringing their water bottles to the sink.

"Like I told you, I stopped for a deer . . ."

"Yes. You've seen deer before, haven't you?" Anzie teased.

"This one was weird. But thing is, I took a minute there. I sat in the truck," Carney continued. "You know, collecting myself and . . . stuffing my chops with your good pie. . . ."

Anzie felt flattered. She snickered.

"But, Anz, I'm not sure . . ."

"Of what, Carney?" Anzie squinted at him. "Don't be a weirdo. Tell me!"

"I might have seen something . . . and it might have been . . . *plaid*."

"Plaid?" Anzie looked nonplussed—but only for an instant. "Oh. *Plaid?* Are you saying what I think you are saying?"

"I—I think I might be."

"What? Carney! You saw him? Why didn't you say?"

"I don't know," he said thoughtfully. "I'm not sure, and I don't want to steer them wrong. But I'm starting to think I did see Frenchie this morning out on Punkinville Road."

Carney could hear Anzie's next breath catch in her windpipe.

"Pity's sake!" she hissed. She flicked off her apron and snapped it at Carney's knees. He jumped aside. "You've been sitting on vital information!" She gave him an exasperated cussing out as she shut down the fire on her double oven.

"Anz? Your pies!"

"Pies be darned, Carney! Get your shirt on. Grab that pan. We have to go!"

Aurora

Crisscrossing

In the beginning, I run ahead of Mom and Pop and Gracia, tweeting and whistling. This feels like a race to me, the most important race I will ever be in. I'm quick, crisscrossing the skinny part of our pie slice. Sticks snap and pop, and ferns brush my knees, and sometimes I have to duck under a bough, or unstick my hair from an old grabber branch.

Here in the narrow point of our pie shape, I reach the boundaries quickly. Pop is not far behind me. He looks at the map on his phone and he says, "Turn, Aurora. Turn again. That's right. Criss and cross."

At first, we can see other groups on both sides of us. Orange vests moving in and out of the trees. Then the pie slices widened, and we all spread out. The groups are going at different paces. Every so often someone calls Frenchie's name. Sometimes it's Gracia. Sometimes me. Sometimes we hear it off in the distance.

Frenchie!

Frenchie?

Cedar, riding in the pack on Pop's back echoes, *"En-chee. En-chee."*

I realize something: I should have grabbed that mega-phone back at the school and made a few announcements. I know things. I know Frenchie likes to stop and run his hands through a patch of cinnamon ferns and pat a head of Queen Anne's lace. But he doesn't like the scratchy feel of lichen-covered boulders. I know he doesn't climb trees. But if there are birds in a tree, he will stand below, looking up. Then he'll flap and tweet when they fly away. I stop still.

That's important!

It's one of the only sounds he makes. None of these searchers know that. I cup my hands around my mouth and yell.

"Hey! Everybody! Frenchie can whistle!"

There is silence. Then voices calling back, asking questions. But they are muffled by the land and the trees. If I can't hear them clearly, they didn't hear me right either.

"No!" Pop booms. "Not found! Neg-a-tive!" He makes a call on his cell right away, and I know I've done wrong.

"Aurora!" Mom comes running forward to speak to me. "You must not shout out like that. You'll confuse the searchers."

"Sorry," I say, and you can bet I'm whispering now.

"It's okay, Rene," says Gracia. "Don't scold." She tells me I am right to want the searchers to know everything that I know. "Details can help. They said so at headquarters." She's being sweet. But I want to shrink down to mini-mushroom size.

Pop pockets his phone again. "We're all set," he says. "Headquarters will message everyone, and they'll share the fact that Frenchie can whistle. The search continues," he says, and he swings his arm into the air. Cedar likes that. He copies him.

I would like to apologize one more time, and make it as loud as my blurt. But I'd be repeating a mistake. I go back to hiking, and back to what I was thinking about.

Birds. Frenchie's all about birds. A lot of birds live in trees. It's worth looking up every so often, I decide.

The sun is high and it shines down on the woods. I think I have never noticed the light and dark and light and dark of the woods—not quite this way. This is how the deer hide. How the birds blend in. I think of the day I couldn't find Cedar. The Worst Possible. I watch for khaki pants now, and a plaid shirt, and the dark berry-red of a needlepoint purse. I take a deep breath. The way it comes into my chest reminds me of reading the poem on Anzie's barn. I don't yell. I whisper.

"'SUN RAIN WIND SWEPT...'"

I know the rest the way Anzie wrote it. It's a poem to her farm, for everything that's true there. But what about here? What's true about now? I look around me, then change the next line.

"LEAF SHADOW SHINE..."

I step along to the new words. I add more.

"SWEET FERN SECRET KEPT..."

What else? I keep hiking.

"BOULDER BLOSSOM VINE."

I whisper the lines.

"SUN RAIN WIND SWEPT
LEAF SHADOW SHINE
SWEET FERNS SECRET KEPT
BOULDER BLOSSOM VINE."

It's a poem now. A poem I can walk to.

Jewell Laramie

Zooming In

Jewell Laramie changed all her plans for the day. She had a thing or two to take care of before she could join the search. But join she would. First, she went home and sent out a message postponing the softball league picnic. She added a note about the missing boy and requested that all "fit and able" folks lend themselves to the search. Then she packed her Jeep—almost the way she had planned for earlier in the day, but now her purpose had changed.

She was back at the Fire and Rec Center filling the big fridge with the hot dogs and salads she'd purchased for the softball league picnic. Those would be supper for the searchers now. The garden club had offered to cook and serve. She backed her head out of the fridge as Carney Huggins and Anzie Mayfield arrived with a pan of deep-dish pie. Blueberry, from the purple looks of it. To be helpful, Jewell went to take the pan from Anzie. That put her close enough to hear Carney telling Chief Nash about a deer having jumped in front of his truck on Punkinville Road earlier that morning.

Jewell turned with the pan, and on her way to the fridge and thought, Well, didn't that happen all the time? Deer in the road? This was Maine. And why had Carney Huggins chosen this moment to tell a deer story, anyway? What did it have to do with the search? She stowed the pie quickly and came back to eavesdrop.

She heard Carney say something about buckets rolling in the road. Then she saw Anzie give her fella a good knuckle to the arm. "Tell them the rest, Carne!"

Then Carney told about a possible—but not definite—flash of plaid. Jewell's ears perked up at that. She'd seen it written on the whiteboard: Frenchie Livernois, was last seen wearing a plaid shirt.

Those in charge checked the large map on a big screen that librarian Dottie Sylvania had set up special for the search. They discussed terrain, saying moderate to easy in terms of hiking. They estimated the distance and looked at the time.

"Seems unlikely," Chief Nash said. "The boy started the morning here." He moved the cursor along the map and stopped at Mountain View School near the top of Bert Gray Road. "How would he make it to Punkinville Road? And what? Fly up over a fifty-foot rock face here at the preserve?"

"North," Jewell heard Carney say, though he was talking behind one hand, in a sort of thinking pose. "It happened closer to here," he said, and he tapped the screen with his finger.

"That's still a lot of open land to cross and it—"

"Flattens out," Jewell interjected. "Much more level overall if you're crossing farther north." With all eyes on her now, she added, "Ask any deer. Ask any hunter." She worked her eyebrows up and down. She turned to Carney. "You say you saw a boy and a deer. It could be they're using the same trail."

"Wait. Are you saying this boy and a deer are traveling together?" Chief Nash squinted at Jewell.

"No!" Jewell said. "I am saying my fellow sporting folks and I have tracked deer for miles, using their paths. I'm saying walking a trail, even an animal trail, is easier than bushwhacking." She elbowed her way up to the large screen, Dottie shifting quickly to let her in. "Carney, come take a look at this with me."

Jewell traced her finger along the screen.

"There's a known deer trail about here. Weaves down from upper Bert Gray Road like so. Not far from the school," Jewell noted. "Heading west to east, the trail crosses Punkinville Road right about here." She looked at Carney. "Yes?"

"That's the place. Roughly," said Carney.

"The hiking would be easy enough for a healthy, woodsy kiddo," Jewell said. "There are several deer 'bedrooms,' along the trail and one ends here." She drew a circle with her finger. "Just southeast of where you were."

"Hmm," said Carney Huggins. He cupped his chin in his hand and closed one eye at the map on the screen.

"What?" Anzie said. "Carney, say what's on your mind."

"Hmm . . . direction," he said. "Both the deer and the boy—if it was a boy at all—they came from the other side of the road. Both were traveling east to west."

Jewell closed herself off from the ensuing chatter. She did not like the idea of getting steered off a solid lead. There was a vulnerable boy out there, and he needed to be found. She helped herself to the cursor and manipulated the map to reveal a plot of land deeper to the east, closer to the river, and not so far from the seashore. She switched the aerial view and zoomed in on the broccoli-like tops of trees, and the pale trapezoid of a farm field. Closer, closer. Ah! She found what she was looking for.

"Yo," said Jewell. "I say, yo!" Everyone huddled behind her. She traced a faint line that cut across the corner of the field. "This is trampled earth, as seen from above," she said. "It's the deer path, and see, it disappears into the woods here." She pointed out what looked like a small dark, depression in the landscape.

"See that?" she said. "Slight clearing. The path ends here. Because, if they kept going, the deer would reach the seashore before too long, and I don't need to tell you, deer prefer the woods, meadows, and barrens. So what they do here is they rest." Her eyes were on the screen now, and Jewell was trancelike in her belief that this was an area of interest. "This is a deer 'bedroom.' They'll stay here, usually all day, but not always. Then, like most creatures when they reach the end of a trail, they turn around and head back." She took a breath. "That, my friends, could explain why the boy was heading east to west."

Aurora

Last Known Position

"Hold up!" Pop calls.

We have been out for over an hour when the message comes in.

"There's news?" Gracia asks, and her voice pipes with hope.

I hold my breath and do not blurt, but I am wishing, wishing, wishing.

Have they found him? Is Frenchie all right?

But the news isn't quite that good.

"They're bringing us in," Pop says.

"What?"

"Yep." He wipes his forehead with his bandanna.

"There's an LKP—last known position. Apparently, somebody saw Frenchie late this morning." Pop smiles like it's good news, and Gracia takes a big breath in and grabs Mom's arm.

"Really? Where?" she asks.

"Punkinville Road," says Pop, and Mom and Gracia fall together in a hug.

"Punkinville? Huh. So now what?" I say.

"I imagine we start over again inside a new two-mile radius," says Mom. She grunts a little as they transfer Cedar from Pop's shoulders to hers.

"So we go back to the school now?"

"That's right," says Pop. "Then to headquarters at the Fire and Rec Center for our new assignment."

I am wilting inside, but I try not to show it. This feels wrong. I feel pulled, like I want to keep walking the way we were going. I don't want to leave our slice of lost-person pie unsearched. It's hard not to feel as if we have walked this far for nothing, and now it's going to take us almost as long to get back, except we won't bother to crisscross. We will walk a straight line. Then I remember something from math class: the shortest path from point A to point B is always a straight line.

Mom and Pop and Gracia are already on the march, heading back to the school, and I know I have to go with them.

I look over my shoulder, and call out one more time,

"Frenchie! Frenchie?" Then I whisper, "Coming to get you, wherever you are."

A straight line *is* a lot shorter. I am surprised when we step back onto the playing field and see the school. Everything looks a little weird. This is not the way we come to school. I wonder if the day is going on like normal, except for me, out here searching, and Darleen Dombroski, who is out here somewhere having her lesson.

We hustle in to use the bathrooms. Cedar gets a fresh diaper, and Mom gives him a belly buzz and a good-egg award. He's ridden a long way in the pack today. Mom sets him on his feet and lets him run up and down the halls of school. He's laughing his curly head off. I crack a big grin, and take a run with him. He rounds the corner, and I hurry to grab him before he reaches the classrooms and I hear my name.

"Aurora!" I turn.

"Leena! Joanie!" I am so happy to see them. They come running up to hug me.

"We have been so worried about you," Joanie says.

"About me?"

"Yes. Because Frenchie is your friend, and this is scary," Leena says. I feel my next swallow go down hard.

"I'm fine but so worried about Frenchie," I say.

"We are too. Everyone is. The ever-changing tree mural is full of notes for him." Leena smiles. I know she wants me to feel better. "If the notes were leaves, you could rake them into a pile and jump in!"

"Saw that." I nod. "Even before I left school this morning there were lots of them."

I tell them about the search—quickly. I think to myself:

SUN RAIN WIND SWEPT
LEAF SHADOW SHINE
SWEET FERNS SECRET KEPT
BOULDER BLOSSOM VINE.

"They want us to move to a new area," I tell my friends. "Somebody thinks they saw him."

"Oh, that's good! So good!" Joanie gives my arm a pump. Then Cedar comes running and bashes into all three of us and wraps our knees in his arms.

"Ugh!" We almost fall over. Joanie and Leena laugh and cuddle Cedar.

"Are you helping?" Leena asked him, and he nods. "You're searching for Frenchie?"

"Yeah. En-chee," says Cedar. "Bye-baw, bye-baw."

"What's that?" Leena asks.

"No idea," I say with a shrug.

"Hey, I better go catch up to my family. Frenchie's mom is with us," I add.

"I wish I could come with you, Aurora." Joanie frowns. Her shoulders drop.

"We hope our parents will let us help after school," says Leena. "But my mom's working on the food truck straight into suppertime."

Suppertime. Wow. I think about all the walking we have done and wonder if they'll still assign search areas (pie slices) so late in the day. For the first time I think about how the sun will go down. I try to remember what time that happens now that the days have grown shorter. I think of the chilly evenings.

We have got to find Frenchie.

I take Cedar's hand to leave, and Joanie says, "Hey, Aurora. we still want to know what you were going to tell us. Your story."

"What story?"

"About your geode. You were about to tell us this morning. But Mr. Menkis came in, and then Ms. Beccia started class. And then ... well ..."

"Oh. Right," I say. I reach into my pocket and curl my fingers around my half of the geode. "It can wait," I tell them.

Outside in the parking lot volunteers are handing out apples, bananas, and energy bars to the searchers as they come out of the woods and back across Bert Gray Road.

I see Darleen Dombrowski. She has one shoe off and she's leaning against the water truck. Her mother is dabbing Darleen's ankle with damp paper towels. Looks like she got scraped up out on the trail. She wipes her eyes, and her lip quivers. I know that an ankle-skinning can sting like heck. I feel bad for snapping at her when she said searching for Frenchie would be a good lesson—not that it doesn't still grind my insides. But now she is sniffling and miserable. I actually think it: Poor Darleen.

"Ah! Fuel!" Pop says, eyeing the snacks.

"Take one of everything," a lady tells him. "There's plenty, and you're all working so hard out there. You'll need calories to find that boy. Then go see Charlie and Edna to get your water bottles filled. Tank is right there on their pickup."

Pop thanks her and calls me over.

"Aurora. Come grab a bite."

"Or two or three!" the lady says. She holds up apples in both hands.

I shrug. Pop motions to me—being pushy this time. I shrug again. But when I see that probably every searcher is choosing a snack too, including Mom and Gracia, I take an energy bar and an apple.

"How about you, Cedar Tree? Hungry?"

He's not shy. He grabs two bars.

We get into the car and roll out of the lot.

"Oh, food!" Mom says.

"I'm not sure I can eat," says Gracia. "Maybe a nibble."

I am not sure I can eat anything either. I've felt a hollow in me all day. Every so often it fills up with worry. I make myself bite into the apple. It is crisp and sweet. Suddenly, I can hardly cram it in fast enough. It's like the lady said: calories. Calories for finding Frenchie. Cedar polishes off both of his energy bars and grabs at my apple core. Mom gives him a banana. Gracia's eating one too. She takes small bites and deep breaths.

"I feel like we are going to find him now," she says.

I look out the window. It's so weird. I've got no proof. I've got no reason at all, but I still feel like we're headed in the wrong direction.

Frenchie

Eat Sleep

Frenchie marched in under the trees right behind the piebald deer. Half a dozen more deer popped their heads up out of the ferns.

Plain deer. No spots.

They looked at Frenchie with their dark eyes. He heard a snort, then saw all the white tails flip up as they ran away.

The piebald deer looked as if it might go with them. But it stayed. It ate green leaves. Frenchie ate the sandwich from his backpack.

Soon the piebald deer settled in one of the lie-down places the other deer had left behind. Frenchie chose one too. He rested and listened.

He heard birds.

Insects.

People.

Someone said his name.

Frenchie stayed low and quiet. The piebald deer had closed its triangle-patch eyes. It was sleeping.

Quiet is for sleeping.

Aurora

Seeing Home

I have Pop's phone in the back seat of the van. I'm look-ing at where we have been. There's the search circle with the school as the center point, and all the slices of the pie, including ours. I can see the path we took and where we stopped when we got word to come back in.

"See anything yet, Aurora?" Pop asks.

"Nope," I say. I'm watching for a new circle to come up on the screen.

"Oh, I hope it's not a glitch. We don't need that." Gra-cia sighs.

"Well, Mrs. Sylvania is a technology supergenius," I say. "She's probably working on it right now." I look at the screen, and a new circle appears on the map right before my eyes.

"Ha! Hey, you guys," I say, "here it is! The new circle overlaps the first one. Looks like a Venn diagram. You know, with stuff in common in the middle?" If Frenchie were not missing, I might love all of this.

"Ahh . . . ," says Gracia. "That's why they wanted the searchers on the east side of Bert Gray Road to stay on the job and finish hiking their pie slices. That area falls inside Aurora's Venn diagram."

I don't know how Gracia can do it on this awful day, but she gives me a smile.

"That makes sense," says Pop.

I still have the phone. I study the new circle. Then I shout.

"HOME!"

They all gasp. Pop taps the break and the van lurches.

"Good grief, Aurora!" he says. "I thought I was about to hit something!"

Outbursts are worse inside a car.

"Sorry, so sorry," I say. "But you have to see this! The new search includes *home*. Look, look. Bottom of the circle." I pass the phone up to Gracia. Mom turns in the front seat and they share. Pop keeps his eyes on the road.

"Aurora is right," Gracia says.

"Sure is," says Mom. "So . . . the new center point is

partway up Punkinville. That must be where someone saw Frenchie."

Thinks they saw him. I keep it to myself. I am wondering lots of things, but one of the biggest ones is this: If Frenchie was that close to home, why didn't he go home? He always knows the way.

Gracia keeps looking at the new search circle. "All of Flanders Pond is included, then the edge of the circle taps the southern part of Lake Road and sweeps just south enough to include our houses, and Baker Hill and Tucker Mountain."

"He's been to all those places before," I say, but I am quiet about it. "We all have. We've hiked them together."

By the time we reach the meetup on Punkinville Road, a message has come in. Mom has the phone now. She reads, then tells us, "No pie slices this time. They are focusing on areas. This is good," she says. "The Pond Association is activating a search all around their shores and beyond. A hiking club is covering Tucker Mountain. We're to focus on a network of deer trails."

"Near home?" I ask.

"Not really." She shakes her head. "North of home, heading west to Bert Gray. Back to the school."

"So, wait a minute. Frenchie started at the school, cut all the way over to Punkinville Road, and now they think he's going back to the school? Sheesh! Why didn't we stay there? We weren't done searching our pie slice!" I

bounce my head against the seat back—several times—
and think:

SUN RAIN WIND SWEPT
DARN IT DARN IT DARN IT

There is nothing to do but follow directions. That's
how you can be the most helpful. Mom and Pop and Gracia have said it again and again. We go where they send
us, and begin to walk a narrow path on the west side of
Punkinville Road.

Sometimes it seems like the trail has ended or tapers
down so thin, or opens up so broad, we aren't sure we are
on it anymore. It's a little nutty to say, but we are following the path we see on the phone, even when it doesn't
seem like the ground is doing the right thing.

Sometimes we meet up with other groups. Crossing a
stretch of meadow, Jewell Laramie spots me.

"Aurora P.!" she calls. "Oh! And all the Ps!" She plows
through the grass, smashing down the goldenrod on her
way. When she realizes that Gracia is with us too, she hugs
her extra tight. "I'm so sorry. I know this must be excruciating."

"Thank you," Gracia says. "I am grateful to everyone
for helping us search for my son. Please tell others I said
so, will you?"

"Of course. And listen, we will not stop," Jewell says.

211

The grown-ups talk and sip water.

I march in place. I'm an object in motion, and I'm going to stay in motion.

When Jewell asks me how I am doing, I tell her. "I won't be all right until Frenchie is found."

"I'm with ya, kiddo." She offers me a knuckle bump. When we touch, she wraps her other hand tight around both our fists. I have to smile. Otherwise I don't think she'll give me back my hand. She says, "If Carney Huggins is right abou—"

"Carney Huggins?" I blurt.

"Yut. Carney's the one who spotted Frenchie on Punkinville."

"You don't say?" says Pop. "News to us."

"All we heard was *somebody*," Mom says. "We know Carney, and of course we know Anzie, very well."

"Yut," says Jewell. "If you ask me, he had some useful information—and all because of a near miss! Whew!" She leans back on her heels.

"A near miss?" Gracia tilts her head at Jewell.

"He stopped for a deer in the road. That's when he saw a flash of plaid. You know, just happened that they were all in the same place at the same time. But it sure got me thinking that it makes all sorts of sense that Frenchie is walking these deer trails," says Jewell.

"I don't get it. Why do you say so?" I want to know.

Jewell stoops down low, eye level with the tops of the

grasses. "Easy passages," she says. "Look at that. That's a kiddo-shaped space if I ever did see one. A path is a sweet discovery. It's already there for us, so we take it. Don't you think?"

I shrug. "I kind of like climbing over stuff," I say.

Jewell laughs out loud. She says, "I guess you do, Aurora P. Always honest!"

Jewell leaves us—to do some retracing and recalculating, she says. It's late afternoon, the sun shines like a little fire on my forehead. I look left and right. I swish the grasses with my hands on both sides of the trail and look in, as if I might see Frenchie curled up in a ground nest. Waiting for us.

Mom and Pop let Cedar get down again. He runs up the trail. I pass everyone to stay close behind him.

"If he ducks into the grass, we could lose him!" I shout.

But then I see that Cedar takes the path. Only the path. Because it's already there for him, like Jewell said.

Maxine Grindel

Upon Waking

Maxine Grindel opened her eyes. She was sitting in a chair at her front window. Same spot she'd been since late morning when she and Dudley had returned from the emergency clinic. Same old view of Bert Gray Road between the trunks of the tall pines. Her orange cat was resting on her lap, and in turn, Maxine rested her wrapped finger on the cat's ample back. Dudley had kept her apprised, between her many unintentional naps that day, about the search for the missing boy.

"Any more news?" she asked groggily. "Are they still up at the . . . ooo-ahhh . . . sssch . . . coool?" She lost that sentence in an enormous yawn, but Dudley understood her.

"Believe so," he said.

"Oh, me . . . wish we could be out there helping," Maxine sighed. "Did I tell you, I've met that boy? Charmed me into a Mrs. Thrift deep discount on a pretty-pretty needlepoint purse without speaking a word. Hmm . . . Did I tell you that, Dudley?"

"You did. A dozen times, darlin'."

"Oh no, I did not!" Maxine protested.

"You did. It's fine."

"Well, it's breaking my heart," she said. "I want to join that search."

"Me too," said Dudley. "But we need to tend to you today."

Maxine knew that her immediate future was all about sleeping off that wild medication and taking care of her finger. She was going to miss the flea market in Searsport the next morning anyway. "Mrs. Thrift takes a sales hit," she mumbled. "Doctor's orders." She glanced at her bandaged finger, a.k.a. Miss Mummy. "Piddling," Maxine said, because nothing was more important than finding that boy—oh, his poor mother, and his poor little loud friend. She must ache for him. Mrs. Thrift knew a special bond when she saw one.

Soon, the purring of her cat and the sunshine beaming in the window between the tall pines combined forces and sent Maxine back to napping. But not for as long this time.

When she woke, Dudley was bringing tea and crackers for her, and a late lunch with an early beer for himself. Maxine thanked her fella. She took a slow steamy sip, and oh, that tea tasted good. A few sips later, she felt like she might finally be coming back to life. She looked out at her busted lawn chair. She vaguely recalled having taken a hard landing on it. Oh, in fact and she'd gone *through* it. Right. She was fainting at the time. The webbing had not held.

Heavens! Was she ever going to regain her handle on this day? The crumpled chair frame and torn webbing still lay on the carpet of pine needles that spread right out to the edge of the road—and the road, Maxine noticed, seemed busy now.

"Lot of traffic. Looks like it could be coming down from the school," she said.

"Maybe they're on the move," Dudley said. He took a look at his phone.

"Think it means he's been found?"

"Naw . . . I think Charlie and Edna would have sent a message in that case. They're up there. Took a tank of drinking water in the back on of their truck. But you're right, Maxie. That is a lot of cars."

"Curious," Maxine said. She suddenly felt bored and thought she might like to get up. She shifted under the weight of the cat and got back an offended look. She purred at him, and he settled again. He was a sweet cat—when he wasn't sneaking outside to taunt the back-yard birds.

Oh, the birds.

"Dudley," Maxine asked, "did you remember to fill the feeder?"

"Oh. I remember now," he said.

"Well, you know what? I want to do it," she told him.

"Oh, Maxie, are you sure?" Dudley did not put down his sandwich.

"Yes," she said, and she eased herself out from under the cat. She waggled Miss Mummy at Dudley.

"I think *we* can handle the task," she joked, and Dudley laughed with his mouth full. "We'll holler if we need you."

"I'll listen for you," he said. "Steady now, darling."

Maxine did feel steady. She stepped into her slippers (no laces to tie), and made her way to the kitchen pantry. She protected her injured finger and scooped a pitcher full of sunflower seeds, one-handed. She popped the latch on the back door with her elbow and swung it open. She stopped on the step and took in a deep breath of the warm September afternoon. Ahh! This was just what she needed.

She glanced into the yard. There was a *spotted* animal standing at her birdfeeder. She opened her eyes wider than she had all day. Maxine blinked. Twice.

What a strange jewel of a creature—oh, a deer! *Was it*

a deer? Since when did deer wear patches of all those colors—chestnut and chocolate, snowy white, and roan red.
It looks *quilted*! Maxine thought.

She stood stock-still. She watched the deer give the
feeder a good nudge with its black bulbous nose. With its
pretty-pretty lips, it swept the last of the sunflower seed
out of the lowest feeder hole.

"Dudley . . . ," Maxine whispered, though not loud
enough to be heard. What to do? He *must* come see this.
Maxine was in a pickle; if she went to get Dudley the deer
might well be gone by the time they came back. If she
called for him too loudly the animal would scare.

Maxine stayed stuck for several long minutes. If only
she had been able to take her eyes off that magnificent
deer, she might have seen the boy in the plaid shirt and
khaki pants. He was standing with one cheek pressed
against the smooth gray trunk of a beech tree, no more
than thirty feet away from Maxine and her back door.

Frenchie

The Cool Tree

The tree trunk felt cool on Frenchie's cheek. It smelled good too. Outdoor things often did smell good. The deer was eating seeds like birds eat seeds. Frenchie could hear the cars going by on the road. Not far.

Cars are not a good time to cross.

But Frenchie thought the deer would cross like it had in the morning because it was going back now. He remembered:

Let's follow. For as long as it'll let us.

He was still thinking that Aurora would come. The school was close again, and Frenchie knew the way.

He heard a latch click and a person came out the door. Slippers on the feet. Not shoes. She was Mrs. Thrift.

Frenchie squeezed the needlepoint purse against his side. Mrs. Thrift had lots of things. She might have more seeds for the deer. But she didn't come off the step.

She stood as still as a cool tree.

Aurora

Just Over a Year Ago;
Ezelda Trink's Quarry

This search for Frenchie is taking us over all sorts of Maine terrain. We scuff through the gray dust and peastone beside a gravel pit, and it makes me think of the day we visited the quarry.

Mom had a story to write about an artist who owned a quarry. Or part of one. Inactive, is what Mom told me. Except, hey, a quarry means a whole lot of rock. And trees and water mean a whole lot of birds. *And* the place was open to the public. I knew it probably wasn't the place to find a nice tourmaline specimen, but it sounded cool, and it wasn't far from home.

"Close as the crow flies," Pop said. He says that about

a lot of places, because our roads do wind the long way around.

We took a picnic on a hot day last summer. Frenchie and Gracia came with us. We packed a cooler because mom was scared our sandwiches would turn putrid before we got to eating them.

We followed the signs up a loopy road that turned to dirt and parked our van in a scrubby, sloped lot. Pop and I had to drag the cooler up a path. At the top were giant pieces of granite sunk into the ground all in a row—all of them taller than Pop. We wedged our way between them.

"Sheesh!" I said. "Good thing we're not hauling a double-wide, Pop. Good thing we don't mind banging up our cooler and scraping off our hip bones."

"I'll say! Phew!" Pop sat down hard on the cooler and fanned himself with his hat. Mom let Cedar slide off her hip. She took a few photos and scribbled some notes while Gracia took a brochure out of a box on a post. Frenchie and I walked a few more feet. We stood shoulder to shoulder looking over the place.

"Whoa!" I said. "It's like a rock fun park! Cut right into the earth. Mom! You should put that in the story!" There were pools of black and green water, and clusters of lily pads with pink star-shaped blooms sitting on top, and purple pickerel weed. Plants grew up out of cracks in the gray rocks. There were granite sculptures everywhere, carved with suns, swirls, whales, and fish. There was a bank of heaped-up, jagged rocks—all sizes—from the quarry's old working days. I knew because I'd seen photos of the mines in Androscoggin.

Way out across a big pool of dark water, I could see a tall gray wall of granite, the highest side of the quarry. It was at least as high as the peak of our A-frame.

"Mom! Pop! Did you know it would be like this?" I called to them. "How come we've never been here before?"

"Welcome!" There came a woman with a crinkly smile, her gray hair in a floppy bun. She had on a heavy apron and spatters of clay had dried on her arms. "I take it you are the writer?" she said to Mom. "I see you found the brochure. Map is on the flipside. Do you have any questions?"

"I do!" I said. "How'd those monster stones get there? I mean, right in the way and all?" I jabbed my thumb over my shoulder at the tall standing rocks.

"Those are my megaliths," she said. "Took me a whole summer working with Gorgeous, sun up to sun down to plant them. Had some help from my friends to set them upright into the holes and backfill."

"Wait, wait. Working with Gorgeous? Who's he?"

"She! Gorgeous is my backhoe. She's rusty, trusty, and good."

"And what about you?"

"I'm rusty, trusty, and not as good."

"No! I mean what's your name?"

"Ezelda Trink. Welcome to my quarry."

"Ee-zelda Trink," I repeated. "And this is your own quarry. Wow. So do you want to be called Ms. or Mrs. Trink?" I asked.

"Call me Ezelda."

"Okay. So Ee-zelda, about those *megaliths*, did you ever think people might want to drive their cars right up to the top here?" I asked.

"That's exactly what I thought," she said. "But I wanted to keep cars down there, and artistry and natural beauty up here." She stretched her arms wide.

I gave my sweaty head a scratch. I looked at Mom and Pop and Gracia. They were going to let me handle this. "Well, what about wheelchair access? Ever think of that?"

"Did. That's when I call up to the house for Gary. He's an artist in residence. Came for two months and stayed for two years." She chuckled. "We go down together and help anyone who needs us—if they need us, that is. It's an incline, after all, not a ski slope. Wheelchairs and baby strollers fit between the megaliths. Gorgeous and I made sure of that."

She shut one eye at me. "You're a thoughtful girl," she said.

"Oh. Thanks. A lot of people say I'm annoying."

Ezelda the artist snorted. "Unimaginable," she said.

She smiled a gentle kind of smile at Frenchie. "Quiet soul," she said. She looked at the three parents. Maybe wondering who he belonged to.

"He's a *silent soul*," I said. "Well, maybe not." I looked right at Gracia. She smiled and nodded. "What I mean is, he doesn't talk with words. So you have to *look* for his answers."

"Makes things interesting for you, then, doesn't it?" Ezelda said.

"Yeah." I shrugged. "But I get him. Like right now, he looks like he's having a big old stare at nothing. But he's really looking for birds. They're his favorite. He's birds. I'm rocks. Hey, mind if I do some rock hunting here? On your property?"

"That's fine. As long as rocks is all you're hunting. After anything in particular?"

"Tourmaline," I said. "I'm always after tourmaline. It's here. I mean, probably not right here. But it is in Maine. In case you didn't know. One of these days I'm going to visit a mine and find a vein." I sighed. I looked all around her place. "But thanks for letting me look. Oh, and if I do find it, can I keep it?"

"You're welcome to take all the stone you can carry."

Well, that was all I needed to forget all about lunch. I was off. Except Mom grabbed the tail of my T-shirt before I got away. I kept marching. I made windmill arms.

"Ah, Aurora, let's please take a look at Ezelda's map first."

"And a few safety rules," Gracia added.

225

The quarry had parts. Right close was the picnic area and a wading pool. A short walk across some flat rock and there was a shallow swimming pond.

"The most important note," Ezelda said, "is that there's no admittance beyond the fence. You see?" She pointed to a split rail that circled a huge, watery hole surrounded by the high wall of granite. "That's a deep-water quarry. Cold as can be, and not safe."

"Got it," I said.

"Best way to view it is through these." She flipped open the lid on a wooden box attached to a post and pulled out an old set of binoculars. "You'll find more binocular boxes on the property. Maybe your birder will enjoy them."

I put them right up to my eyes and scanned all around the quarry.

"What's that hill full of crunchy-looking stone?"

"Grout," she said. "It's scrap from the mining days. Jagged cast-offs. I banked it up with help from Gorgeous. Another deterrent for those who ignore fences and think they want to go dip in the deep water. I can't have that."

"Oh . . . I see," I said.

I was still looking through the binoculars, imagining the old quarrying days, and looking at the stripes in the granite, and the way plants had taken root in the stone. I already knew that granite was superhard igneous rock with mica, quartz, and feldspar in it. Some of the crystals were catching the sun. I traced my way up the farthest and highest part of the quarry wall, all the way to the top.

"Hey!" I said. "P-people up there! Right now! You said no hiking allowed up on that ledge."

"I don't allow them," Ezelda grumbled. "They ride their ATVs and motorbikes in from the town parcel, and completely ignore the property markers. They've tamped a path up there, wide as a logging road. But there is little I can do." She sighed.

"Back to work with me," she said. "I'll be off this way, in the clay studio." She waved her muddy arm. "Drop in and visit. Enjoy the place!"

Well, I didn't find a piece of tourmaline that day. But Mom got her story, and I sure did like the shallow ponds of Ezelda Trink's quarry. Frenchie and I floated there, and Cedar sat splashing in the puddles with Pop. I thought about what it must have been like years ago when they cut and dragged giant slabs of granite out.

"Huh. That's kind of destructive, taking rock out of the earth like that, isn't it? Look how it's all scarred up. . . ."

Frenchie couldn't hear me that day; his ears were underwater.

Now here we are searching for him, passing by this gravel pit—and talk about scarred up. It's a funny thing, both this pit and the quarry are for harvesting stone. But the quarry is beautiful, and I'd call this gravel pit ugly. Ghost gray. Dry and weedy. But as we walk out, I remember something Ezelda Trink said. Something that I liked, because I could see it with my own eyes.

Nature has been taking back the quarry—growing it over and healing it up.

That's what I want—to get healed up. We are not finding Frenchie, and now every step leaves me with a fresh hollow in my gut.

Aurora

Trespass Trail

The land turns woodsy again. The air is cooler under the trees. The brush and boulders are taller than we are, and wider than a six-person hug. Ferns and reindeer lichens cling to them like wild heads of hair. I would love to climb them—if everything about today were different, that is. Frenchie would stay below. He doesn't like lichens. Too rough—like a tag in the neck of a shirt, I guess.

I ask for a turn carrying Cedar in the backpack. He's heavy as rocks and thinks this is a game. He pulls my hair and puts his fingers over my eyes; he bounces and hollers, "Goh! Awoh-wah! Goh!"

We walk a sponge of reddish-brown pine needles now. We step over roots. We kick up pine cones, hard little green ones and big open brown ones. My legs feel like rubber. I teeter one time too many for Mom. She takes my brother off my back.

When we reach a yard, or a clearing, it can seem like the trail has ended. And maybe it has. But headquarters drops new pins on the GPS that have us winding toward Bert Gray Road—back to the school—so we keep going.

All day long we have not really known whose land we were on. When we do see people, we explain why we are trespassing.

Gracia tells them, "My son is lost. Have you seen a young boy come through? Eleven years old."

We hand them the photocopy of his school picture. (I tell them his hair is longer now.)

Some say, "Oh! Heard about that. Went missing, huh? So sorry. Terrible thing." People promise to keep an eye out for him. They invite us to fill our water bottles. Everyone is kind.

But nobody—nobody—has seen Frenchie.

Frenchie

The High Place

The trail stopped in a high place. Frenchie stood on the edge looking out.

All rock.

He knew this place. From over there. Across. In the low.

Aurora liked all this rock. She liked the deer too, so he followed it all day long. But she had not caught up, and now Frenchie couldn't see the deer, but that might be it, making swishing sounds off in the green leaves.

A loud, dark bird made him look up. He had some loud birds in the needlepoint purse. But not this one. There was light and dark and shine, and light and dark and shine up there.

Then the bird flew out. "Caw-caw!" Black wings tilted into the blue.

Frenchie stared.

Nothing holds birds up.

Nothing keeps them up.

Now the bird was gone, so Frenchie flapped and tweeted. The needlepoint purse swung at his side. The ground under his heels made sounds. Then it broke into crumbs. Slow. Fast. Smash! His teeth clanked together. He was on his butt.

Sliding.

The high place let go of Frenchie. The branch caught him. Let him go. The rocks caught him. Let him go. He grabbed. But everything let him go.

Frenchie could not stay up on nothing.

Ezelda Trink

Things Fall

Most days, by three in the afternoon, Ezelda Trink was done working in her pottery studio. That's when she could be found—or, not found, as she preferred—leaning on the split rail fence, gazing over the deep-water quarry, and coddling a mug of good Earl Grey tea.

But this Friday afternoon harbored a rotten surprise for the artist.

She trimmed her last pot of the day from the wheel and nestled it under the long sheet of plastic at her front table with the rest of the day's successful turnings. She scrubbed her hands and toweled them dry. She turned from the sink, and when she did, she caught the loop of her apron tie on . . . something.

That something was the corner of the tall drying shelf, where a dozen pots sat ready for the kiln. Darned if Ezelda and her apron tie didn't pull the whole setup off its supports. The shelves and the clay pots came down with a crash.

Ezelda spent the next hour softly cussing to herself, and picking up shards of leather-hard pottery and tossing them into a vat of water. It was a lot of lost work at the potter's wheel. But the pieces were unfired, so they'd absorb the water and become soft clay again.

So it went. . . .

And so it was that Ezelda was *not* peacefully sipping tea in full view of the deep-water quarry at three o'clock that afternoon when Frenchie Livernois took his dreadful fall. She did *not* see him tumbling down the granite ledges, losing his belongings as he went. She neither saw nor heard the splash he made as he hit the dark cold water.

Frenchie

Right After the Fall

Frenchie's butt was killing him. Lots of stones on that slide down. And plants. Everything he'd grabbed had let him go.

The way down had taken his shoes. A branch had taken his purse with his birds inside. Now he was under the dark water. In a place of no breathing. Cold was filling his clothes, and the spaces between his toes. It seeped into the tunnels of his ears and ached there.

Above, he saw the September sun. A shiny blur.

SUN SUN SUN.

He would like to go up. But his pants were caught by one cuff on something below.

Frenchie reached down and tugged. Tried again.

Raked his finger across some hurting thing. A bubble went up. He wanted to follow it. With cold fingers he worked his belt back through the buckle. He popped the snap. Pushed the zipper down. His pants let him go. Up. Toward that sun. He burst into the breathing place.

He lay his body on the top of the water.

That's it, Frenchie! Relax and breathe.

SUN SUN SUN.

Frenchie

The Small Flat Place

Frenchie floated, and while he floated, he looked through his half-open eyes. The sun was still shining. A few birds flew by in the space between Frenchie and the sun. He was on the wrong side for seeing feather shine. The birds went like dark flickers. Like shadows, but not shadows.

The cold was taking the ache out of his backside, but it was putting an ache at his temples. He flipped over in the water. He paddled and kicked to where the rock had a spot for him. Right below where he had come down. He pulled himself onto the sun-warmed ledge.

It was a flat place.

Like a front step.

But no house and no door. There wasn't much room. Only enough for Frenchie, one tiny tree, and a patch of pale green lichen, which he wished was not there. Too scratchy. Too peely.

Aurora

Bringing Folks In

The sky has that look that reminds me of all the times I have been late for supper. Of course, it's September and the days are shorter. I already get it: headquarters will want to pull us off the search before dark. Secret decision: I won't go. Not until we find Frenchie.

At six thirty Pop gets the message.

"They are bringing folks in," he says, and the news falls hard on all of us.

Gracia gives a nod—like, trying to be brave. She and Mom hug each other. They cry a little. They whisper on each other's shoulders, then wipe their faces. Cedar leans around from the pack on Mom's back, asking, "'Kay, Mam? 'Kay?"

No. Not okay, Cedar Tree. Not.

We use this time to rest, all of us lined up on a log. Pop stares at his boots. Mom is hunched; Gracia looks like she is studying her palms. Even Cedar is silent.

I hear Gracia breath in, then out. "Well, I'm going to stay strong for my son." She stands up and looks at Pop. "Okay, Ed. What's the plan? What do they say?"

"We finish out this way," he says. He stands and points us in the direction that we've been traveling. "We're close to Bert Gray Road. Should come out not far from the school. They'll have a bus waiting to take us all back to Fire and Rec for some supper. Then to our cars from there. We'll start again in the morning."

"Not me," I say. "I'm not stopping. We don't have Frenchie."

"Aurora . . ." Mom cups her hand on the back of my head. "Another hour and it'll be too dark to see—"

"Uh-uh. Our eyes will adjust," I say. "The dark is only dark if you've been looking at light. You just have to stay out in it. Keep your pupils dilated."

"Well, I'm not sure about your theory, but . . ."

"I'm not getting on that bus. I'm going back to that land behind the school. It's a feeling I have. A feeling about Frenchie."

There, I said it. I ball up my fists and add, "I can't stop searching."

"Oh, we won't stop. But we need to make sure we are

at our best," Gracia says softly. She comes to me and cups her hand around one of my fists. "We need food and rest for our bodies. And sleep for our brains." She strokes my hand until my fist uncurls. Then she holds my open palm like it's the middle of a sandwich and her hands are the bread. Her eyes pool. "We need to dream our best dreams about Frenchie. And tomorrow morning, we'll begin to search again. Okay, Aurora?"

Cedar echoes. "'Kay, Awoh-wah? 'Kay?"

"Please?" Gracia says. Her tears spill.

I cannot say no to her.

Pop thinks we have a half hour to go. We walk on. Cedar starts crying, like he's doing it for all of us. I look around for something to give him—maybe a pine cone, which he'd probably love to throw at me. Instead, I find a stick with a foot-long piece of old-man's beard hanging from it. I hand it up to Cedar—on Pop's back now. It makes him so happy, he hums! He reaches out of the pack, swishing the stick like a wand. The wispy lichen floats beside him. Cedar dusts the tall boulders, the tree trunks, and me.

Frenchie

Pink Sun

The sun that had warmed Frenchie and dried his shirt, underpants, and hair was huge now. And pink. Suppertime sun. Frenchie looked around him. He did not want to eat lichens, little green pine needles, or tree bark. So he inched right to the edge of the flat spot that held him, made a cup with one hand, and slurped cold water from the quarry. He spilled. But there was lots more if he wanted it.

He scooted himself back, away from the edge, careful to set his hurting parts down gently. He tucked up and wrapped his arms over his head. He peeked out through the space between his elbows. The pink sun made a rosy glow on the dark water of the quarry.

And the rocks. Big.

And the stones. Small.

Down, down, down, the pink sun dropped. Frenchie watched it all the way.

Slice.

Sliver.

Dash.

Done.

Aurora

Twilight

The trees aren't so thick, and the boulders aren't as huge. Looks like another meadow up ahead.

"Close, close," Pop tells us. He looks at the map on the phone. "One last property to cross. We should see the road soon."

Soon is usually a good word. But when Pop says it now, I tug on the ends of my hair and don't let go. All seems lost. I feel lost. *Soon* means we'll stop. How can we do that when we haven't found Frenchie?

Then I see something. "Wait. What is that?" My heart pumps, like it's starting me up. "There's something in the trees!" I bound forward.

I keep it in my sights. It's round enough to be a person's head!

Right size!

Right height!

And is it moving? I swear I see it moving.

I keep clawing forward.

Frenchie? Frenchie? Please be you!

But it isn't Frenchie. It's a ball-shaped burl on a tree trunk. I drag my fingers across it—rough, old brain-shaped thing. How could I mistake a bump of bark for my best friend?

Mom and Pop and Gracia catch up to me.

Mom puts her hands on my shoulders, give them a squeeze. "Did you meet with a trickster, my girl?"

"Yeah," I mumble. "Sorry. Sorry, Gracia."

"Don't be," she says. "It's hope that makes us see things. And I won't lose hope."

We reach the roadside, and we can see other searchers heading to the school. Not far. Gracia pauses. She looks at the horizon line. The sun is gone. A narrow streak of pink is left behind.

"Gracia?" Mom asks. "What is it?"

"The twilight," she says, looking up and all around. "Seems so *inky*."

And I bet she is thinking what I am thinking: her no-talk boy, her son, is somewhere out there in the almost dark.

Aurora

Dinner Stop

When we get to the Fire and Rec Center there is food. A lot of food. And long tables all set up. This could be a party. Except it's not. The volunteers tell us, "Take a plate. Please eat!" Groups of searchers start to fill the tables, stepping over the benches with their full plates in their hands. I don't think I've ever seen the center so busy.

Some of the food is not what we eat, like there must be a hundred boiled hot dogs and big squirty jugs of ketchup and relish. There are two giant jars of the Picklonious Deli's famous sour pickles. Any other time, I'd go elbow-deep for one of those. Tonight, I don't want anything.

Mom tries. She steers me toward a tray of mac and

cheese. She spoons some out for Cedar, even though she usually keeps him from eating too much dairy—like it will gum up his ears or something. "Aurora? Some for you too?"

I shake my head.

"Baked beans? How about a scoop? This is dinner. You should try to eat some—"

I flap my hand at her. "I'll get us a table," I say.

I find a nice clean one. Some older kids are clearing and wiping. I sit down on the long bench. I fold my arms on the tabletop and set my forehead on them. I stare down at my lap and my feet. My legs are tired. The weird way. Where they can't stop moving. I let them swing, and I breathe. The space around my face fills with my own warm air. It's noisy on every side of me. I hear, but don't listen. Don't have to. No one is talking to me.

My mind talks to itself—and to Frenchie.

What the heck? Where did you go?

And why?

Was it a bird? When?

Couldn't you have waited?

I ask myself, what have I not thought of? Or just forgotten? Frenchie gets ideas—kind of the same way I sometimes blurt—and suddenly, he slips away. Whenever we've had to look for him—like fetch him for supper—we find him nearby, under the overhang at the A-frame, or staring up a tree beside the house. Or sitting with eyes closed, loving the feel of the sun on his face down at Pebble Nest.

What could've been different about today?

I feel somebody slip onto the bench beside me—two somebodies, one on each side. I feel a hug, arms close around my ribs. I see the sleeve of a bright pink silk tunic top wrapping across my middle. Leena. She squeezes me. On my other side, Joanie puts an arm on my shoulders. Her fingers pat my neck.

"Hi," I say. I feel kind of bad for not picking up my head, and I know my neck must be the sweatiest, dirtiest thing on the planet.

Then I see something even dirtier under the table across from me: a pair of caked-up work boots and muddy cuffs.

A deep voice asks, "Is she okay?" I keep my face in my warm space but think the voice is asking about me—am I okay.

"She misses her friend," says Leena.

"Frenchie Livernois is her bestie. And she's his," Joanie adds.

Now I wonder who wants to know.

I feel a hand on my forearm. Rough fingers. I pick up my head. Carney Huggins. Lucky for him, I have no words, and for sure, no loud ones.

"Hey, Aurora," he says, "want pie?" He slides a paper

248

bowl full of crackled-up blueberry pie right against my arm and sticks a spoon into it for me. I could cry. But I'm not a crier.

"Thanks," I say. I'm raspy as a frog. "I heard you're the one who saw him."

"Wild coincidence," he says, and he shakes his head.

"And he was fine? Or at least he looked okay?" I ask.

"I only got a quick look. But I think so." Carney nods. "So, listen, keep your chin up, okay?" He doesn't stick around but turns back to wave as he goes.

Mom and Pop and Gracia and Cedar come join Leena and Joanie and me. I don't feel good, exactly, but I do feel surrounded by good people.

Everyone is eating, and I try a bite of the mac and cheese that Mom pushes at me. I pick at it, and I see Gracia picking too. She makes a little *yum-yuck* face at me, as if to say it's good but who can eat? She feels the way I feel.

Leena's big sister, Zenia, comes over with a plate of potato-and-pea samosas. "Hey, guys. An offering from the food truck," she says. She stays because Cedar is making everyone laugh. He pinches at a slippery baked bean with his fingers and chases it around his plate.

Leena says, "Aurora, I'm wrapping a samosa for you, to go."

Joanie runs off and comes back with two spoons. She hands one to Leena. "Come on, Aurora, grab your spoon. We're going to help you eat that pie."

Later, Anzie Maylord comes over to say goodbye. "Gracia, if you hear anything in the night, no matter what time, please call," she says. "We are close by. Otherwise, we will see you all in the morning. First light."

Pop asks if Anzie could give him a ride to our minivan, which is still parked at the side of Punkinville Road.

"Sure! We've got the truck, but we'll squeeze you in," says Anzie. "I'll take the middle."

I watch Pop go. The back of his shirt is pressed with the shape of Cedar's carrier straps. Carney holds the door open for Pop and Anzie, then he looks over his shoulder at me and gives me a nod.

Mom says we should clean up our table and be ready for when Pop gets back. I'm glad to have something to do. I gather up our mess and make my way to the dish tubs and trash cans. While I am there, I hear my name.

"Aurora!" It's Mr. Menkis, Frenchie's classroom aide. He motions to me. He's sitting at a table with a man and a woman. They are young, like Mr. Menkis, but taller. I go to them and right away, I see that they have a whole lot of gear with them. Serious outdoorsy stuff, like packs with neon reflectors, and loops of rope and straps hitched up to carabiners.

Mr. Menkis introduces us. "Aurora, meet my friends, Mr. Reesick and Ms. Schneizik."

"Really?" I say. "Sheesh. Your friends rhyme." All three of them let out snorts.

"I know!" Mr. Menkis says. "What were the chances? Hey, guys, Aurora is Frenchie's best friend. I am talking *superlative*." It sounds like something good, so I smile.

Mr. Reesick tells me, "Hey, Aurora, I know you have to call him Mr. Menkis because he's a teacher. But you can call me Dave."

Ms. Schneizik points to herself and hurries a swallow. "And I'm Jordanna," she says. "We know this has been a hard day. So sorry."

Dave says, "But listen, we are going out right after we fuel up here."

"Out? To look for Frenchie?"

"Yep."

"In the dark?" I ask.

"Yep." Jordanna taps her headlamp and it flashes. She pats her pack and a row of lights blinks across the strap.

"Dave and Jordanna are my climbing buddies," Mr. Menkis tells me. "We took search-and-rescue training together this summer."

"For real?" I can hardly believe my ears.

"Yep. I called them to come help us find Frenchie."

"All for one and one for all!" Jordanna pumps her fist.

"Can you train me?" I ask. "Can I go out there with you?"

"I wish," Mr. Menkis says. "But I'm afraid there is more to it than we could teach you in one night. A lot of parts, and equipment, and you have to be eighteen."

"Yeah. I figured," I say. "How long are you going to search?"

"Through the night," says Dave.

"Until when?"

"Until we find him," Mr. Menkis says. He holds up his elbow, and I knock it with mine.

Aurora

Before Bed

"How to get through these next hours until day break," Gracia says. Her voice is shaky. She holds her hands in two small fists against her chest. Her face is a map of worry lines.

"Stay here with us," Mom tells her.

"We'll make up the sofa for you," Pop tells her.

"Or my bed," I say. "You can have my bed tonight." I mean it.

"Thank you. But I need to be home in case Frenchie turns up—"

"And he could!" I sit straight when I say it. I want it to be true. "Sorry for interrupting, but he knows the way home. He always does."

Silently, I think, then why isn't he back? And then I hear it in my mind, the bad thing I have not been able to say.

What if it's because he can't get back?

Gracia comes to me, her arms open. She's forcing a tiny smile, I can tell.

"Quick hug, Aurora?" she asks, which is like promising not to overdo it, because she knows I'm a short hugger, same as she knows Frenchie rarely takes a hug at all.

"For good luck," she adds. We squeeze each other, and I make sure I don't let go first.

Then Mom walks Gracia next door. Their shoulders touch the entire way; I see them in the light from the porch lamp. Reminds me of the day we all met at the bus stop, the day all of us started to be best friends.

It's impossible, I think. Impossible for us to go to our beds knowing that Frenchie is not in his.

Frenchie

The Dream

Frenchie Livernois fell asleep in the dark right where he was, all hunkered up close to the wall of the narrow ledge. Soon he was dreaming. In the dream, he was very small. Small enough to be sitting way down inside of a bowl a lot like the one Ed Petrequin used when he made pancakes in the kitchen at Aurora's house. The needlepoint purse was high and away. Frenchie wanted his birds. So he called to them. He made sounds in his dream.

One by one papers came blowing out of the purse. One by one birds lifted off the papers into the air. They flew. One by one they came down into the bottom of the bowl and perched where Frenchie could see them *so well*. He saw their knees tucked up under their wings. He saw every feather stripe. And the holes where the feathers grew out of the bird skin. He heard the birds breathing through their hollow bones. He saw their purple beating hearts. And he saw their long naked bird toes right next to his.

Aurora

Bedtime

Mom puts Cedar down for the night. She checks with me to see if I want anything to eat. I don't. She sends me to the shower. I soap up my arms and legs and scrub about a hundred fresh bug bites and scratches clean. Then I let the water run on my face and my sweaty neck. I get it all done fast—too fast. Because the only thing left to do then is go to bed. Before they send me upstairs, Mom and Pop want us to make up a list of positives.

"Good luck," I say. Mom starts.

"This night is unseasonably warm, and clear," she says. "Frenchie might feel a little chilly, but he's safe from bad weather."

"He's a strong boy and a good hiker," says Pop.

"Mr. Menkis and his two friends will search through the night," I say. "So at least somebody is out there. It makes me feel like Frenchie is less alone."

"Agree," says Mom, and Pop nods. "And Frenchie likes being outdoors—and he even loves the night sky," Mom adds.

"Yeah. And like Gracia said, he's not as worried about himself as we are about him. I think it's true." I twist the hem of my sleep shirt and remember back on some of the places we searched today. There are pictures in my mind, like Frenchie tucked into a circle of ferns. Or grass. His own nest.

"Maybe if we think of that we can relax enough to get some sleep," Mom says. "Then we'll be better in the morning. Better for Frenchie."

I get into my own bed, gather my quilt close, and I think I will sleep. But my legs hiked all day, and they are still hiking now. They kick out all their own, like I brought somebody else's legs to bed with me. I press my elbows to my ribs, try to make myself still. My mind sees Frenchie in all the places we've been, and it makes me wonder if we'll be in those places together again. Ever. Why did this happen? Why can't we be having a campout together right now? Why can't he be with his mom next door where he belongs? How long can I lie here not sleeping?

My bedsheet looks like a fat twist of rope. My quilt is in a bunch. I sit up and wonder where the comfortable spot in my bed has gone—where's the place that usually holds on to me?

I go downstairs and find Pop snoozing in the recliner. Mom is on the couch, sipping a mug of tea.

"Aurora," she whispers. She pats the spot beside her with her hand. I settle next to her and pull my feet up. I inch my toes close to Mom's thigh, and she lets me tuck them under where it's warm, and where she can weigh them down for me so they'll stop twitching. She sets down her tea and wraps me with one arm. We don't speak, not at first. I sit by her warm side and think about everything, everything, everything. This day . . .

"I'm scared, Mom. And I really miss him."

"Aurora . . ." She pulls me close, and I let her. "I know. I'm so, so sorry."

"Mom, you know how Frenchie likes birds? And the sun? And even the night sky, like you said."

"Yes," Mom says, and I can hear her smiling.

"I think he likes tree leaves and clouds and even rain too. Everything that is up, off the earth." I turn to look up at her. "It's like that's where his big world is."

"Hmm . . . ," says Mom. "I've always thought how positive he looks when he tilts his face up." She raises her chin the way Frenchie does.

"I hate this, Mom. I lie in my bed just waiting for morning. . . ."

"These are the hardest hours of anyone's life." Mom's

lips are on my head. She's twirling a loose piece of my hair. I can almost never sit still for someone fussing with me that way. But tonight, I do.

"Mom, promise me we will go back to searching. Like Anzie said, first light."

"We will." It's Pop who answers.

"Did we wake you, Pop?"

"Naw, not really. I've been in and out," he says. "Been thinking . . ."

"About what?"

"Well, Frenchie, of course, and Gracia. Poor Gracia. But also, about tomorrow because it's going to be tricky. At some point we have to go deal with Pebble Nest."

"Right." Mom sighs.

"Pebble Nest?" I sit up. "What about it?" Then I remember. "Oh. Tomorrow is Saturday. Well, forget it!" I say. "We can't do the cleaning. Call the renters. Tell them the deal's off."

"Can't do that. The house has to be made ready," Pop says, but he is shaking his head like he wishes that wasn't so. "We can't neglect our business."

"But what about Frenchie!" I say it loudly. Mom puts her hand on my knee.

"Hang on, now," she says. "We will all go back to the search first thing in the morning. That is a given," Mom says, and Pop agrees with her. But then they talk about Pebble Nest, and how maybe Mom should leave the search around noon with Cedar and give Pop's back a rest from the carrier pack. Or should Pop go? Would starting at noon give anyone enough time to do all the cleaning and make all the beds on their own? Would Cedar be wild and cranky? Maybe Pop and I should keep Cedar and . . .

They keep discussing.

I rub my face with my hands. I think about tomorrow. All the impossible parts. Suddenly, I know that Mom *cannot* go to Pebble Nest.

I interrupt them.

"It has to be Pop," I say. "I'll go with him, and we'll take Cedar too." My parents are both looking at me and listening. "Gracia has to stay with the search because Frenchie is her boy. And Mom has to stay with Gracia." I look right at Mom. "She needs you the most."

"That's good reasoning," says Pop.

"So thoughtful," says Mom.

"Pop, promise me we'll work really fast when we get there." A big jaw-stretcher of a yawn catches me. I lean on Mom.

"Never faster," Pop says, and I know he means it.

Frenchie

Waking and Remembering

Frenchie opened his eyes as darkness was going away.

His sleep was going away too.

He sat on the flat ledge. He remembered how he came down. And lost his shoes. And the needlepoint purse with all his birds. He didn't have pants now. He had cool white legs. He had one arm wrapped around them. His other hand held tight to a tiny pine tree that had its root stuck into the rock.

Frenchie wanted some sun on him. But the high, high rock at his back kept him wrapped in shade. If he could get home, the sun would be there, he was sure. He knew the way. But there was no path here where he was. No place to take a step. No way to go up. He held on to the pine and leaned forward—only a little because it hurt to unbend his body. He looked all around as far he could see.

He remembered one more thing that he had lost. That piebald deer.

Aurora

First Light

We are up at first light, and back at the Fire and Rec Center before 6:00 a.m. People are pouring in, a swarm of orange vests. Way more people than yesterday. I remember that it is Saturday. More people are available. The check-in is organized.

Chief Nash speaks through the bullhorn. "Please see a volunteer for instructions at the tables marked with an A. Move on to tables marked B if you'd like one of our student volunteers from the high school to help you download the tracking app. . . . Please refer to the large screen to understand the scope of our search thus far."

I cover my ears and move away. That bullhorn is not morning-friendly. Pop is handing coffees to Mom and

Gracia. Cedar is sprinting through the crowd from one wall of the Fire and Rec Center to the other. I could stop him. But people smile every time he weaves by. Besides, Mom and Pop are keeping an eye on him.

There is food. Again. Breakfast.

I do a double take when I spot Darleen Dombroski. It looks like she is in charge of a bagel basket. I'm so tired my gaze turns into a stare.

I'm thinking about Frenchie. Best days. Like, when Cedar came home. And family dinners and pancake Sundays. Bird hounding and rock hounding, and me cheering Frenchie on the day he learned to float. Him going along with me, the times we trailed the piebald deer. And him knowing the way home. Having a true friend—the thing I am aching for this morning.

I blink. There's Darleen. And her bagel basket. She sees me seeing her. I bite my bottom lip. Darleen doesn't have a person like Frenchie Livernois.

Poor Darleen. I mean it, for real. *Poor Darleen.*

She doesn't know how good that can be. She can't even ache like I'm aching right now. But she still came here today.

I go on over to her.

"Hey," I say. "I'm sorry you got all scratched up yesterday. That puckabrush will get you if you don't watch out. And sometimes it just gets you anyway, huh?"

She dips her head a little and nods.

"I got a bee sting too!" she squeaks, as if that sting is still happening right now.

"Oh yeah? Super sorry," I say. "It's hard out there," I tell her. "It means a bunch that you came to help. Thanks."

"I'm helping indoors today," she says. She even smiles a little. "I'm going to serve lunch. It's a better assignment for me."

"Right. People will be huge-hungry!" I offer her a high five. She looks a little worried, but she takes it. Her eyelids flutter when our palms smack. I probably did that too hard. I decide to scoot back to my family.

"What do you think, Aurora?" Pop nods toward the table full of fruit, breakfast bars, and Darleen's bagels. "Want to grab some grub along with our assignment? You could stand to eat something, my girl."

I shrug. Then I'm saved by the bullhorn.

Chief Nash says something about a progress board up in the front of the room. I tell Pop, "I'm going to go see."

The word *progress* has me curious, but when I get to the Progress Board, I see that it's mostly the same stuff as yesterday. The list: missing boy, eleven years old, plaid shirt and tan pants, nonverbal, dark hair. They have added the LAST KNOWN POSITION at Punkinville Road, and another note that says they are dropping digital pins in areas that have been searched BUT (in big letters) they believe the SUBJECT (why not say Frenchie?) has been on the move.

I have to agree with the last part. Frenchie can walk for hours once you get him going—or once *something* gets him going. But when he decides he wants to go home, he does. So if he's on the move, why hasn't he *moved* home yet? It bothers me about like a bur caught in the arch of my shoe.

Here's another bother: if you ask me, "progress" would be having a lot more than the same list from yesterday with a few guesses added on. I stand in front of that board, shifting my weight from foot to foot.

"Pfft!" I say. "How do we even know it's *progress* until we actually find him?" I say this to no one, except there is a woman standing beside me, and I'm pretty sure she hears me. I watch her tie a bandanna around her close black hair. Then she adjusts her glasses on her nose and looks back at me. We both open our mouths and say, "Oh!"

Loud as a girl with a bullhorn, I say, "Hey! You're the Nuthatch Lady!"

"Yes, I guess I am," she says.

"Yeah! You're, umm . . . Shcree! Right? You gave Frenchie Livernois the Audubon print. You broke up that set of six for him and left yourself with five. And now you're here to help find him?" I ask. "Did you know that's who we're looking for?"

"Yes. I saw his picture on the news last night. I recognized him right away. The boy who loves birds. I've never forgotten him. I guess I feel connected."

"You are," I say. "I see you're not wearing your flat little-shop shoes today."

"Oh no. Hikers all the way," she says.

"Good thing," I say. I am about to tell her more when Mr. Menkis stops on his way out.

"Ready, Aurora?" he asks. "It's a brand-new day." He bounces in place to settle his pack on his shoulders. His carabiners jingle, and his ropes swing.

"I'm ready," I say. "Mr. Menkis, did you really search all night?"

"We did. Sorry I can't tell you that we found him," he says.

"I know you tried. Did you sleep?"

"Hmm . . . no. But my energy is up," he says. "I'm optimistic. We have a lot more help today. Did you hear? There's a group of mountain bikers, and the cross-country team from the high school is here. Some folks from an ATV club got special permission to ride some of the trails north of the school. Dave and Jordanna are still with me, right outside. And you're here," he says. He smiles at the Nuthatch Lady and me, then waves as he pushes on the door.

"And you're here too." I cup my hands and send him an echo. Then I think, Yep, we're both here. Mr. Menkis and Aurora Petrequin. The ones who lost Frenchie Livernois. And now we're going to be a part of finding of him. With lots of help.

I turn to the Nuthatch Lady. Sheree.

"Thanks for coming. I mean, a lot, a lot, a lot. And thanks for that nuthatch print. Frenchie loves it. Did you get a bagel? Do you like coffee? Right over there. It's free." I point her in the right direction, and when I do, I feel a little burst in my chest. It's like a firework lighting up.

I feel optimistic. Like Mr. Menkis said.

Maxine Grindel

Orientation at the Fire and Rec

Maxine Grindel felt bolstered when she saw the crowd at the Fire and Rec Center so early in the morning. She was relieved to finally join the search party. Her head was free of the previous day's cobwebs—not drowsy in the least. She was keenly worried about that boy, and could not stop picturing him, so slight and silent. So vulnerable. And already he'd spent an entire night outside on his own.

He'll be found today, she told herself with resolve. Safe and sound.

In the next second a speeding toddler with a headful of dark curls brushed by Maxine. She instinctively clutched her bandaged finger to her chest. (It would hurt like the dickens if it got bumped.) She heard the little one laughing, a mingle of mischief and glee. An older child was right behind him, giving chase, and insisting that it was time for them to go.

"Mom and Pop want you!" the older girl called.

If Maxine had gotten a better look, she might have recognized the chaser as the talkative girl who came by Mrs. Thrift's booth at Baker's Field two Julys ago. Maxine might have remembered that she was the girl who had been with the now-missing boy the day his soft-spoken momma had bought him the needlepoint purse.

Instead, Maxine and Dudley continued on their way to Table A for the brief orientation. Maxine recognized Jewell Laramie right away. She knew they'd lucked into a competent instruction-giver. Jewell had a reputation: she was a hunter; she knew the woods. This morning, she was on the job as Maxine and Dudley approached.

Jewell spoke between gulps of coffee. She explained about the tracking system, and about the significance of the last known position.

"I shared a hunch yesterday," Jewell confided as she referred Maxine and Dudley to the map on the screen. "The boy was seen crossing there at Punkinville Road, and I happen to know there is an identifiable deer path right there. Just waiting for a kiddo to come along, if you know what I'm saying." (Maxine wasn't entirely sure, but she nodded nonetheless.) "You can see where the search has been focused, going on up through town roughly east to west, on a bit of a diagonal." Jewell resketched the highlighted line with her finger. "We've been thorough. The catch is, the timing. It's late summer, and in the world of white-tailed deer, that means the does have been out on their own, fattening up for mating season. They've cut a lot of little trails to get to their favorite edibles and liedowns."

"Umm-hmm. So we have a lot of those little trails to search," Dudley said with a nod.

Maxine squinted at the large screen. "Look at that, Dudley. That main trail goes right beside our yard! See the shape of the lot? That's us. I never knew . . ."

"Ah. You're on a main thoroughfare," Jewell said.

"And we do see deer," Maxine said. "Six to eight at a time." She paused a moment. "Speaking of deer," she began to address Jewell, who would surely be interested, even though she seemed to be looking past Maxine now, "I saw one at our bird feeder yesterday, and it had the most amazing spotted co—"

"Yut, yut. So sorry to cut you off, Maxine," Jewell interrupted. "I'm seeing quite a bottleneck at the door, folks coming my way. I'm afraid I've got to move you on over to Table B. The kiddos will help you put the search app onto your phone." She pointed, took a sip of coffee, and waved to the students, seemingly all in one motion.

"Little help here for these folks. Yut, yut. Again, apologies, Maxine."

"Not at all, Jewell! We are on a mission here," Maxine said. She cupped her injured finger close again, and she and Dudley shuffled along to Table B.

Aurora

Forward, Then Back

I'm eating the bagel that Pop brought for me. I chew in time with my footsteps and wash each bite down with a gulp from my water bottle.

You felt optimistic! Now stay optimistic! I tell myself this again and again.

Trouble is, the day feels cut short every way I look at it. Pop and I cannot go far today. We will need to head back to the car and go to Pebble Nest. What if we don't find Frenchie before then? Then after we finish cleaning, we'll be starting all over again—and who knows where that'll be?

"Wherever they drop us a pin," I mumble to myself. "But then how long before the sun is gone again?"

Frenchie cannot stay out another night. We have to do better.

I think about all the times I have messed up and had to fix something. What did I do? My only answer: I tried harder. So here I am wondering, how can I search harder? Do I stomp my feet down firmer? Open my eyes wider? (I know it's ridiculous, but I try it anyway.) How do I do more than I'm doing?

"Hey, can I go off the trail?" I ask. "I'll stay with you. I'll just be about ten feet away."

"What's your purpose?" Mom asks.

"To walk wider," I tell her. I spread my arms open. "To see more."

"Sure. Give it a try," Moms says. "But do keep up, Aurora."

I lunge into the puckabrush, even if the hiking isn't as easy—and it's not. Even if it means more scrapes and scratches—and it does. I call for Frenchie. I try to tweet the way he does—almost like an oriole. I see birds, and I watch where they go until I can't see them anymore. I flap my arms, wishing I could be an eye in the sky.

There are other searchers nearby, covering side trails, nooks, and crannies. I see their heads and shoulders. I cover my mouth with my hand and hold back a bagel burp. Nobody needs to hear what's been building in my stomach.

The sun is moving up in the sky. I want Pop to forget

about Pebble Nest. But I know he's watching the time. I am dreading that hike back to the car.

I have a good thought: there are so many people who want to bring Frenchie home. He gets ignored a lot, it's true. He's the kid nobody is sure what do with. But this morning, whole families from school arrived at the center as we were leaving. And people like Sheree, the Nuthatch Lady. She remembered him! How *wow* is that? I didn't actually see Mrs. Thrift with my own eyes, but I saw her camper van in the lot. And Anzie's truck was there. Leena and the whole Virani family said they'd join the search today, and Joanie and her mom too. Even Darleen had found her own best way to help.

The time comes. No trace of Frenchie, but Pop and Cedar and I have to turn back. We check the charge on Gracia's phone and make sure the app is working. We hug each other, then we split up.

I follow behind Pop, looking right and left and up, while Cedar bobbles in the pack. I can tell Pop is worried that he hasn't left enough time to spruce up Pebble Nest before 3:00 p.m., when the new guests will arrive.

"Pop, we'll get it all done!" I call up to him. "I'm already stripping beds. In my mind."

"What's that? The 'think' system?" He laughs. He is taking long strides. I try to match him but I have to double step.

"Ya know, retracing doesn't mean we stop searching,"

I say. "Jewell was retracing on purpose yesterday. Remember?"

"Right, my girl," he says.

That's all I need to hear. I believe it: there is a chance we will find Frenchie. Wouldn't that be something? I can picture it: suddenly he comes out onto the path with his plaid shirt all tucked in.

The geode swings inside the pocket of my shorts. I keep it going, and I keep up with Pop. I call my friend's name. I look left and right—

Boof! I walk my face smack into the back of Pop, and the carrier. I plant my eye into the heel of Cedar's sneaker.

"Ow!" I spin and grab my face.

Pop stumbles forward, on account of me bashing into him, then turns around. "Oh, girl! Are you all right?" I squirm while he does a close-up check.

"It's fine," I say, though my eye is aching and does *not* want to be pried open.

"'Kay, Awoh-woh?"

"Yeah, Cedar Tree," I grumble. I reach up and give him a pat. "I'm okay."

But I am not.

I am miserable, and it isn't about the bump in the eye. It's about this feeling I have that the three of us are heading in the wrong direction now. Like Frenchie's somewhere behind us. The only thing good about that is Mom and Gracia are behind us now too.

Aurora

Putting a Fast Shine on Pebble Nest

We rush in the door with our baskets of fresh sheets and towels and the empty recycling bins. Pop and I hold our breath and do a quick scan. I let out a cheer, because the Poets of Guilford have left Pebble Nest in tip-top shape.

"Phew! And glory!" says Pop.

I run to up the stairs to check the bedrooms. I call down. "The poets stripped their own beds!"

"Oh, love those poets! Love them!" He sings it out loudly. He has to. Cedar is banging on the piano down in the living room. "Start with the sinks and tubs, will you?" Pop hollers. "I'll be up in a minute, and we'll make the beds together."

I scrub a shine onto every inch of porcelain. I dust the night stands and dressers and empty all the wastepaper cans into one. When Cedar comes up the stairs with the duster, I send him around all the edges. "Do a good job. Like Frenchie," I say.

He looks at me funny. Like he's concentrating. He says, "En-chee."

"Yep, Frrr-enchie," I say. Mom wants us to try to get Cedar to hear the difference.

"En-chee en bye-baw."

"Bye-baw? That again?" I snort a laugh. Cedar looks back at me, his eyes narrow. He whispers it one more time.

"Bye-baw."

I shake my head. "Come on, Cedar Tree. We have work to do."

"En beech-en-yoks?" he asks. This one I know: And beach and rocks?

"Yep, yep. We'll go down to the water as soon as we finish here. But only for a few minutes. Understand?"

He nods, a big nod.

"'Kay, Awoh-woh."

Ezelda Trink

Something Autumnal

On Saturday afternoon, Ezelda Trink rested her mug of tea on the split rail fence and looked out over the deep quarry pond. Tea at three, as it should be. What a relief to have things back to normal after yesterday's no-good shelf collapse in the studio. All those leather-hard pots in pieces on the floor. She'd planned to fire them today, dang it all. Instead, she'd pushed the ruins all back into the vat to soak. A few days, and they'd all be soft clay again.

"Could've been worse," she muttered. She cupped her mug in her hands, admired the sea-green glaze for a moment. She looked out across the still dark water of the pit quarry, and to the broad, high wall of granite beyond.

Something caught her eye. Way up, there was a square of color. It was reddish, not bright but autumnal perhaps, set off by the backdrop of gray granite.

Ezelda reached into the wooden box on the post and lifted out the binoculars.

"These old eyes . . ." She mumbled as she hunted through the lenses for that claret-colored square. There! There it was! A leafy-patterned piece of fabric. Some sort of handbag, was it? Embroidery? Needlepoint? Ezelda could see that it was dangling by its strap on a skinny, bent sapling. There was something familiar about it.

Ezelda scoffed. People were always roaring through that parcel of town land on motorbikes or snowmobiles and stopping up there to catch the view over her quarry. Often, they'd stay and watch the sunset. She didn't mind that. Beauty belonged to everyone. But she *did* mind the campfires, often left burning up on the rocks; she *did* mind when people tossed trash and other unwanteds over the edge. Her quarry was *not* a dump. Most of all, she feared someone would make a mistake and either drive or dive off that ledge. The pit quarry was legendarily deep and perilous, with its projections of granite, and who-knew-what-else rusting away down below.

Whoever had tossed that bag had failed to give it a good enough fling. "Got it hung up on that twiggy tree, now did ya?" Ezelda mused. She kept her eyes pressed against the cool circles of her binoculars, and traced the path the handbag would have taken had it fallen all the way down. There was the bit of ledge there at the water's edge—

"My stars!" Ezelda Trink said right out loud. "What is that?"

Aurora

Last Sweep

"**R**emember, Cedar, we can't stay long. So soak it in now." He grabs two fists full of pebbles and throws them into the water. He kneels and scrapes more into a pile. I kneel beside him. I close my eyes. Let the breeze blow two days' worth of uncombed hair out of my face.

Pebble Nest, you are the best.

But for the first time in my life I feel restless on this beach. I need to go. Pop is inside doing the last sweep before we go rejoin the search.

Cedar's mound of pebbles shines in the sun. Most Saturdays, I am here with Frenchie hunting for tourmaline in the surf. I never find any. I like the hunting. I like that Frenchie is beside me. I pull my half of the geode out of my pocket, nestle it into the tiny pebbles. I cup water in my hands and let it spill into the miniature crater.

I turn my face up to the sun. September bright. And then everything hurts. My middle cramps up, like my own heart has tied itself into a knot. And now it's pulling extra hard.

I want him back!

Ezelda Trink

Through the Lens

E zelda peered at the small-looking someone, all tucked up on the low, narrow ledge of granite far across the water. It was his legs, pale as fish bellies, that had caught her eye, even before the bands of bright red that ran through his plaid shirt. Hadn't that boy visited the quarry before? With a girl about the same age? Hard to tell from this distance—and through a cloudy old set of binocular lenses.

Slowly, it all came back to her. About a year ago, a writer had brought her family and friends. She wrote a quarry story. The girl had been a ripe talker. The boy couldn't or wouldn't. He'd had that needlepoint pocketbook with him—stuffed full of bird pictures.

Yes! He was all about birds. That's what the girl had said.

Through the binoculars Ezelda could see the boy clinging to a white pine sapling that had taken root on the granite shelf. How had he gotten there? She raised her hand to signal him. "Are you hurt?" she called. Her voice bounced back to her. Then she remembered, he wouldn't answer.

Ezelda bit her knuckle. It was going to be near impossible to reach that boy. No one should climb that bank of grout—too jagged, too shifty—let alone portage a rescue float over it. And then back again? Ezelda thought not.

"Oh! Say! Young one! Could you wave to let me know that you're all right?" she called.

The boy sat still.

"I'm getting help! Don't move!"

Ezelda pulled her phone from her canvas apron. She hurried to the clearing by the studio. As soon as she saw that she had a signal—blessed signal—she poked in the numbers: 911.

Aurora

What Cedar Said

"I want him back!" I whisper. My jaw aches. "I want Frenchie back." I bring my hands, still dripping with water, up to my face. I feel it spilling down my front. I lean down to scoop more. I stare into my hands, like I've got a whole ocean cupped right here. I think of Frenchie. I see him hiking, swimming, flapping his hands, and tweeting like a bird. I make a list in my mind of all the tiny things he understands—things most people wouldn't guess he knew, like when the picture of the nuthatch is upside down, how to fill a berry bucket faster than anyone, and how to find his way home. . . .

Cedar pats me on my hip bone with his little hand. I look down and see him standing on his toes, like he wants to be right in my face. "En-chee," he says.

"Yeah, En-chee." I ruffle his hair. I don't care about correcting his speech. Not right now. I hold his hand and look into his serious brown eyes.

"En-chee en bye-baw," he says.

I shrug and I shake my head. I don't know what he's saying.

Frenchie and . . . something? Frenchie has my ball?

"En-chee en bye-baw!" Cedar says. He pushes those word at me so hard. Then he says, "Bye-baw *dee-yah*." Suddenly, I hear it.

"Piebald deer!" I say it out loud.

Cedar's eyes open wide.

"Are you saying piebald deer?"

His face breaks into an enormous grin.

"Aurora!" I hear Pop holler.

I squint toward the house. He barrels out the door, waving his phone in the air.

"It's Frenchie!" he calls.

I push my tongue between my lips. Taste the salt. What does Pop mean?

"They've spotted him!" Pop calls. He circles his arm. "They've found him!"

Found?

I gather Cedar in my arms and sweep down to grab my geode out of the pebbles. My little brother holds tight, and I run for the car while he giggles. Pop comes from the house. I hear the keys in his hand. We yank the car doors open.

I hitch Cedar into his car seat. My fingers are wet and shaking. I double-check his buckles, then click my own. "We're in, Pop! Both in!"

He spins the steering wheel with the heel of his hand and reverses.

I push my back against the seat and breath out. "Go! Go!" I say.

"Goh-goh!" cries Cedar.

Pop hits the gas. The gravel sprays back against the storage shed. We are off.

Aurora

Following Jewell Laramie

"Do you know where to go, Pop?"

"Roughly. He's out west of the school. At the back edge of quarry."

"The quarry! Where we went that time? But isn't that kind of far?"

"Not as the crow flies!" Pop says. "And we are to go in a different way, which is the part I'm not sure of. But north of the school, there's a town-owned parcel," he says. "Mom said something about snowmobile trails."

I'm craning to see out the front of the car. We reach the bottom of Bert Gray Road; I see a white Jeep tucked close to the pond, emergency lights flashing.

"Pop! That's Jewell! She's waving. I think she wants you to stop."

"Good gosh!" says Pop. He takes the turn and pulls off the road in front of the Jeep. He leans out the window and twists back to speak to Jewell. I can't catch a word she says. But I can hear Pop.

"Great! I'll be right behind you!" he says. He pulls his head back inside and waits while Jewell steers onto the road ahead of us.

"That Jewell is a gem!" Pop says. "She came down to lead us in. Phew!"

I take the phone and check the search app. There are no more highlights on the satellite view. No pie cuts, no assignments. There's just one pin now. It is off to the west behind Mountain View School.

This! This is the way I wanted to go!

Beside the pin is something that looks like a dark pool of water—the quarry! When I zoom in, I can see a dirt road that narrows into a windy, come-and-go line. It's the back way in. It's the path to Frenchie! And this feels like the longest trip up Bert Gray Road ever.

We take a turn just past the school, staying right behind Jewell's Jeep. We roll along a bumpy, gravelly road until it becomes too narrow for cars. Other vehicles have arrived before us, including emergency trucks from three different towns. The sight of them gives my heart a jump.

Jewell pulls over into the ferns behind them. Pop does the same. The second we park, I'm out of the car. I can see where to go—the trail is clear.

My feet hit the ground, and I run.

"Aurora! Wait! You wait!" Pop hollers. "Wait. For. Me."

I turn and see him tugging Cedar out of the car with one arm and jostling the carrier in his other.

"I can't!" I scream. I start fast-walking instead, arms swinging so hard they ache in the sockets. I hear the car door slam. I hear Pop yelling and Cedar calling to me. Then I hear Jewell Laramie.

She says, "Give me the baby, Ed. You need to run."

Aurora

Knots

Pop has me by the back of my shirt—like making a suit-case handle out of the armholes of my tank top. I haul him for at least a quarter mile. Three times he has told me, "There's a dangerous drop at the end of this trail. So help me, Aurora, you are *not* going off it."

"I won't! Pop, are you serious?" I say. "Think I don't want to be *alive* when I see Frenchie again?"

We see people up ahead, and I pull Pop harder. I see the light of the sky behind them. It's not the same as a clearing. It's like Pop has been saying, we are coming to the place where the land drops away and the forest ends. I catch sight of Mom. She's been watching for us and now, *now*, Pop finally lets me go.

I run at Mom, and she runs at me. She catches me in a full-stop bear hug. She holds me tight. She walks me back a few steps. "He's all right; he's all right!" she says, her breath in my ear. I want to believe her, but she keeps me walking me backward. I'm scared—scared there is something she doesn't want me to see.

"Mom! Let me go!"

"No," she says. She is calm and firm. "Not until I know that you are safe, Aurora. Let me talk to you."

Pop catches up to us. "For the love of Pete, Aurora!" He leans over his knees and takes big breaths. "Listen to your mom." I look her in the eye.

"The edge is steep," Mom says. "Loose rocks and ledges. So, no more running, no rushing forward. Understand?"

"Promise." I nod. I let her see me take a deep breath. I relax my shoulders. She eases her grip on me.

"Frenchie is down below beside the water. He seems okay. It's so lucky." She smiles her really big Mom smile. "Mr. Menkis is with him. He's been looking him over and talking to an emergency medic here at the top. His friends and the fire chief are deciding about the best way to bring Frenchie out."

"Can I see him?"

"Yes. Come slowly. Gracia has a clear view from a little overlook. This way. She wants to see you."

Mom leads us along the ledge. We step down a little

way and to one side. Gracia gathers me in her arms. "How do you feel about heights?" she asks. She smiles a real smile, and her eyebrows arch up, almost like she's playing. "Here, here. Hug the tree trunk. One leg on each side for safety." She keeps her hands on my shoulders. Mom and Pop are close by. "That's it. Hang on tight. Look down," she says.

The first thing I notice is a flash of red. "His needlepoint purse! His birds!" I say, and Gracia nods. It's dangling by its strap on a bony old branch in the face of the rock.

"Look way below, beside the water," Gracia tells me.

Then I see Frenchie huddled there—but not shutting down. Mr. Menkis is close beside him. I let out a little gasp. I look at Gracia. "How?" I whisper. "I can't believe it."

"Nor can I," she says. We crouch down together, because lower feels safer, even if you are clamped tight to a very good tree. The lower I can be on this high piece of ground, the closer I am to Frenchie.

Mr. Menkis helps Frenchie to his feet—very slowly. I wonder how Frenchie feels about squeezing onto that patch of granite with Mr. Menkis. He never chooses to be so close.

"Frenchie's showing a lot of trust," Gracia says.

"Yes, and it's good to see that he can stand without support," says Mom.

They're right. But for me it's surprising to see my friend with his shirt tails hanging down his thighs. No tucked-in mushroom look. I wonder a lot of things: Did he take a swim and leave his pants somewhere? And is he hurting? His body looks hunched and stiff.

I'm dying to call down to him, but I press my lips together.

I take a second to look around. I know exactly where we are. We're high above Ezelda Trink's deepwater quarry. In the distance there's the bank of broken stone. Grout, she called it. I see the shallow swimming ponds and the picnic spot. I see Ezelda's clay studio, the old backhoe she calls Gorgeous, and her megaliths, which look not so mega from here. This is a big bowl in the earth, and we are up on the rim. There are a lot of us.

I see Anzie Maylord, and Mrs. Whilmer, our principal. Mr. Gessup is here. There are teachers and parents from town. There's a whole bunch of fire and rescue team members, and Mr. Menkis's friends, Dave and Jordanna.

Back beneath the trees, I see Cedar sitting on Jewell's hip—and Mrs. Thrift and her husband are playing with him. Mrs. Thrift has a wicked bandaged-up finger. She wiggles it to make Cedar laugh.

I lean toward Gracia, still sitting tight. "So many people," I say.

"So many helpers who want to see him safe." She shows me a wide smile.

Pop goes back and forth between our overlook and the spot where the fire and rescue team is gathered. "They're discussing two options," he says. "Either take him across the quarry or raise him up and out."

Just get him, already!

I let out a growl. Things are moving too slowly. I squeeze Gracia's hand. "How can you stand this?" I ask.

"I'm okay." Her voice is bright. "I can see my son, and he seems surprisingly well." We look down at him. I'm not sure if Frenchie has seen us. He's not that big on greetings, and besides, he's been keeping his head low. He touches the ropes Mr. Menkis is hitched to and gives the fat knots a close look the same way he studies his bird prints.

Mr. Menkis's friends come down around behind us. Chief Nash is with them, and some of the fire and rescue team members too. Dave sees me and gives me a quick wave and a fist pump. Turns out they want to borrow our view. We lean out of their way. But I'm not giving up this tree unless they make me.

They talk on speakerphone with Mr. Menkis, who looks up from below. They ask him what he sees. Is there a way to walk out? Does he think Frenchie could cross the quarry strapped to a backboard?

Uhh . . . No . . .

It's all I can do to keep quiet. Gracia rises to half standing. "He's hypersensitive to anything restraining or confining," she says. "That would not be the best . . ."

"Heard that." Mr. Menkis's voice comes through. "I agree, with Mrs. Livernois. Besides, crossing appears not optimal. We'd need equipment. An inflatable. There's an unstable-looking hill of jagged stone. And a fair amount of terrain to cross on foot. Going up is a fraction of the distance. Frenchie is already interested in my ropes and harnesses. . . ."

That makes me think about Frenchie—the way he is.

"It has to be *up* . . . ," I whisper.

Then, because I am Aurora Pauline Petrequin, I blurt, "Pull him *up*!" My voice echoes off rock and water. "He loves *up*!"

I think that blurt was a good one. But then everyone starts talking at once again. Suddenly, a sharp whistle slices the air—the kind of whistle that comes zinging through someone's teeth and makes everyone go silent.

But who was it?

He's almost invisible, at first, leaning back against a tall pine, but there's Carney Huggins. He peels himself forward, uncrosses his arms.

"Listen to the girl," he says. He nods in my direction. "She knows that boy as well as anyone."

I give him a side smile.

He says, "Speak your piece, Aurora."

"Uh . . . okay. Well, I say *up* because that's Frenchie Livernois, all the way. He loves birds. And trees and leaves and sunshine and rain. If it was nighttime right now, he'd be staring at the stars or the moon, or even the way the clouds blow across the moon." I take a breath. "Up is perfect for Frenchie."

"I agree!" Gracia says. She waves her arm to be counted.

"And me!" says Mom. "*Up* makes sense."

Pop taps a knuckle on my head. "Well done."

Chief Nash is silent as he paces about. He strokes his chin. I know he doesn't want to make a mistake. He only wants to bring Frenchie out safely.

Meanwhile, Carney shows me a thumbs-up, and I give him one in return.

Finally, the fire chief says, "Okay. Bottom line, we have fewer obstacles if we bring him up. It's a go." He nods at Dave and Jordanna.

Yes!

"Let's do it!" says Dave. He speaks into his phone. "Tandem lift, Menkis. That's why we sent you down there in the first place, hey?" He turns to the Chief Nash. "Menkis is the lightest of the three of us, strong as heck, and he knows the kid."

"Spot-on," says Jordanna.

She tells the fire chief, "We spent the summer pulling each other out of ravines and up rock faces. Promise you, we can do this."

They send a harness and a helmet down for Frenchie, then begin to assemble the ropes up top. They are quiet and serious as they work, tying double figure-eight knots and hitching them to carabiners. When one of them finishes a knot, the other one checks it. They strap a pulley to a broad tree trunk and thread a line through it. They talk through the plan with the fire and rescue team.

We hear Jordanna call out, "Ready at the top!"

But, it's not so easy to get a kid like Frenchie into a rescue harness and a helmet. Those aren't the sorts of things he wants on him. Mr. Menkis takes his time. He shows Frenchie how to step into the harness. Frenchie leans away, like he doesn't like the idea—the webbing could pinch or feel scratchy.

I cup my hands around my mouth and call down loud enough that I think Frenchie might hear me. "It's like putting on your orange vest. But tighter. I know you don't like that. But the harness will keep you safe. We want you up here."

Finally, Frenchie picks up one bare foot at a time and steps them inside the leg loops. Mr. Menkis pulls the harness up. Frenchie slips his arms through the top straps.

"He gets it," I say. "He gets so much."

Mr. Menkis brings the straps over Frenchie's shoulders and clips the buckle at his chest. He connects the ropes from up top, lots of slow, careful checking. He settles a helmet on Frenchie's head and buckles the chin strap. The last thing he does is pull Frenchie close to him—like he's holding him in his lap. He lets his feet come off the ground, and Frenchie's come off too. They're dangling, and Frenchie begins to squirm. He grips the rope in the front of him like he'd rather cling there than sit back in the harness. Gracia worries that something is hurting him. She bites the tip of her thumb.

Mr. Menkis talks to Frenchie, right beside his ear. He takes a small square of paper from his pocket. I know it's the Bird of the Day, the one he would've given to him yesterday if Frenchie had made it to class. Frenchie holds the bird. He lets himself settle back a little, but he still grips the rope hard with one hand.

Mr. Menkis calls, "Ready!"

The lines tense, and they begin to inch up.

"Go, go, go, *stop*," Mr. Menkis calls. He cradles Frenchie and steers around a jutting piece of ledge with a touch of his boot.

"Go, go, go . . . and slow, slow . . ."

Dave and Jordanna pull the ropes on his command, with help from the rescue team. Steady-eddy, no scary catches or drops. It's like a dance that they have practiced.

Except for one thing: Frenchie grunts—not like he's afraid. More like he's uncomfortable.

"Easy," Mr. Menkis tells him. "Look up and see. We don't have far to go. Nice and easy."

"It's okay!" I call. "You're coming *up*, Frenchie! BE THE BIRD!" I stand and start flapping my hands. Pop grabs my shirt and pulls me back from the edge. I keep flapping, and I try to tweet the way Frenchie does. One by one, around the top of the rim of this big bowl in the earth, others start to do the same. Mom and Pop and Gracia, Anzie and Carney, Jewell, and Mrs. Thrift, and folks we don't even know, are all flapping. They're tweeting the best tweets they can. It's a chorus! Frenchie must be loving it.

Closer and closer they come. When they pass us, we leave our overlook and scramble up and catch a very good view of Frenchie as he touches back on earth, safe and sound.

Frenchie

Up to the High Place

The harness pressed on all the most hurting spots Frenchie had.

But he heard Aurora's voice. Single. Clear.

BE THE BIRD!

So he flew up with Mr. Menkis, right past the needlepoint purse, and into a circle of birdsongs, at the top.

Frenchie and Mr. Menkis did not stay at the edge of the high place.

Edge is not a good place to stand.

Frenchie saw all the ones he knew best, and when he saw Aurora, he remembered about the piebald deer. She would want to see it. He looked past all the people and into the dark and sunny woods around him.

The deer was still lost.

Mr. Menkis let Frenchie go. Unhitched. Frenchie stepped out of the harness. Both arms. Foot, foot.

He stood still while Gracia put soft arms around him. She spoke into his neck and said what she always said when her eyes turned wet and shone.

"Sun. My. Sun. Love. You. So. Much. My. Sun."

The bright sideways light made Frenchie's eyelids flutter.

SUN SUN SUN.

Aurora

Our Huddle

Gracia hugs Frenchie. Then she hugs us. She grasps every hand of every person she can reach. "Thank you. Thank you for everything." She must say it fifty times, and I know she means it more than a hundred.

There's an ATV waiting to take Frenchie and Gracia out of the woods. Frenchie's walk is stiff—not the normal Frenchie walk. But he goes right to the ATV without help. Gracia climbs in and pats the spot beside her. He creeps onto the mat, hands and knees. But he won't sit down. He curls onto his side next to Gracia's hip and closes his eyes.

"Ed and Rene . . . , I'll call you shortly," Gracia promises. "Aurora, we'll see you very soon. Okay?"

I nod back. I take a tough breath in. I wish we could

take Frenchie home. Right now. But I get it. He has to be checked by a doctor.

Word is, there's already an ambulance waiting out on Bert Gray Road to take him to the emergency clinic in Ellsworth.

The fire and rescue team tuck a blanket around Frenchie.

"All good," says Chief Nash. He hops in beside the driver. I stand with Mom and Pop and Cedar—family huddle. We watch them roll away.

Aurora

Pack Out

The searchers and helpers begin to pack out in groups along the trail.

"I'm about ready for some supper." Someone chuckles.

"Hot shower for me," says another.

"Sure will sleep better tonight knowing the boy is safe."

Sleep. That'll be nice. Hardly ever happens to me but today, right now, I am bone-tired. I know I'm not the only one.

Mom and Pop stay and thank everyone, and so does Jewell. I'm keeping Cedar busy now. We pick up pine cones and make slings of our orange vests to carry them.

"Bye-coes," he says.

"P-p-pine cones," I tell him. I think about him saying bye-baw dee-yah. Piebald deer. But I still don't know why he said it and with such a serious look on his little face.

Anzie is saying goodbye to Mom and Pop now. Carney hangs off to one side. I'm looking at him and thinking about everything that happened yesterday. Suddenly, I realize, I have a question for Carney. I walk up to him.

"Hey," I say. I keep my voice low, and I get him to turn toward me so it's just us talking. "Remember when you saw that flash of plaid down on Punkinville Road yesterday morning?"

"Yep."

"Did I hear someone say you stopped your truck to let a deer cross the road?"

"Yeah. Well, I slammed on my brake because the deer jumped into the road."

"Well, did you get a good look at that deer?" I ask.

Carney raises his eyebrows.

"Did it have a spotted coat? And did it look like no other deer you have seen in your whole life?"

"That's the one." Carney nods.

"Which came first, the deer, or the flash of plaid?"

"The deer."

"Thanks," I say. "That's all I wanted to know."

Anzie has a quick side-hug for me. "Aurora, *you* were so strong today, and so important to this positive outcome. We are so happy! I know blueberry season is over, but we still want to see you at the farm. Promise you'll bring Frenchie and Cedar and all your friends up in the next couple of weeks for pumpkin picking. Okay?"

"Yeah," says Carney. He smiles a sly smile. "All you can carry home in your arms—for free!"

"Uhh . . . but pumpkins are heavy," I say.

"That's right!" He laughs, and Anzie thumps his arm with her knuckle.

"Then just wait!" I call after them. "I'll bring a big burlap sack!"

"I'll count on that!" Carney calls back.

Mrs. Thrift and her husband come to say goodbye, and I find out that she does have a *real* name: Maxine Grindel.

"Rest assured," Maxine tells us, "the emergency clinic will take great care of your friend. I was there myself, yesterday morning." She holds up her wrapped finger. "Say hello to Miss Mummy."

"S-so sorry," I say, trying not to laugh. Getting hurt isn't funny. But she's making a joke about it. I fake a little throat clearing. "Hey, do you think *Mrs. Thrift* can find a new needlepoint purse for Frenchie? Something a lot like the last one? I've got some allowance—"

"Save your money, Aurora!" Mr. Menkis jogs up. Frenchie's purse is swinging from his hand.

"You got it back! Woo-hoo!" I jump up, pop my vest, and send all my pine cones flying.

"Oh! It's been retrieved!" Maxine Grindel tries to clap, then remembers about her finger. Jewell is standing by, and she claps extra hard.

"Yep, went back down and unsnagged it. Piece of cake," Mr. Menkis says. He loops the purse toward me, and I catch it on the upswing. I hug it to my chest, but not too hard. I don't want to smash up Frenchie's birds. They've been through a lot.

"That's going to mean so much to Frenchie," Mom says. "And Gracia too."

"Aurora, you're in charge of making sure he gets it back, okay?" says Mr. Menkis.

"Promise," I say. I hang the purse across my body, over the top of my orange vest, like Frenchie would wear it.

We stay, and Jewell stays, until all the climbing ropes have been recoiled and packed up. We all thank Mr. Menkis, Dave, and Jordanna.

"I'll see you *right at your classroom door* on Monday morning," I say.

"You bet!" Mr. Menkis replies.

"Ready?" Jordanna hoists her pack. "We still have half a weekend, and guess what? We're going climbing!"

"After we sleep," says Dave.

"Oh, come on. Who needs sleep?" Jordanna wants to know. "Hup, two, three, four!"

We are laughing as they head off.

Now it's just Jewell and us. We sit on stumps and rocks

310

and look over the quarry, where the sun has turned into a glowing ball of hot pink again.

"Ahh . . . September sunsets," says Jewell. "Aren't they grand?"

For the next minute or so, we drink in the peace. Even Cedar settles against Mom's legs, with his belly out and his vest lumpy with pine cones. We watch the sun touch the horizon.

Soon, Jewell stands and stretches and sighs a noisy sigh. "Time for me to take my leave. Best be out of the wilds before sundown," she adds.

"We're right behind you. So long, Jewell." Mom and Pop thank her for meeting us on the road, and for taking care of Cedar. She has been a good friend.

We stay a few more minutes. I feel like my feet are planted in this place. Maybe it's because we're standing here where things went wicked wrong, and then got so much better, and now we want to keep everything like it is for as long as we can. Or maybe it's taking these few more minutes for us to believe that it's really over.

We lift our tired selves onto our feet and start down the trail, with the rosy glow of the low sun at our backs.

Aurora

The Spotted Woods

Mom and Pop and Cedar and I are quiet as we take the trail away from the quarry overlook. The steps we take seem easy. Our breaths are small sighs. Soft sounds. They remind me that all is well; Frenchie has been found.

We are yards away from our car when I hear a branch snap, then a muffled whicker in the woods. I look, and my breath catches.

The piebald deer.

He is standing knee-deep in the soft brush, just off the dirt road. Head up, he sees us. He watches. His white patches seem bright as sunlight in the darkening woods.

"Stop," I whisper. Since I am in the lead, Mom and

Pop and Cedar freeze behind me. "On your left. See the deer?"

I hear my parents gasp.

"It's a piebald," I whisper. I turn slowly, look at Cedar and put my fingers to my lips. He smiles at me.

He whispers, "Bye-baw dee-yah."

We watch, still as stones. The piebald reaches up and snaps a clump of leaves off a striped maple. His antlers have grown out, pale and curled. He chomps, but he keeps looking at us. Like all the other times I've seen him, he doesn't spring—not right away—and I know we could get closer. I look for a way in. Suddenly, I see that we not alone. My heart starts pounding.

It's Jewell Laramie.

Hunter.

I see her orange vest, her rounded back. She is crouched and inching closer to the piebald deer. My brain makes a mad leap back to the day in our kitchen when she said the words, *clean double-lung shot.*

"No!" I run at her—fast as I can—knees high, needle-point purse flapping. I push my hand deep into my pocket. I close my fingers around my geode. I draw back my arm. Got my sights on a spot on the ground between Jewell and the deer.

"Ru-u-n!" I scream. I let the geode fly.

I trip and roll. I lead over heels and finish flat on my back. There's a dizzying spin of light sky and black branches above me. Frenchie's purse is twisted around me. I close my eyes and cross my arms over my face. In seconds, Mom and Pop are beside me.

"Aurora! Oh, poor girl!"

And in the distance, I hear Jewell calling, "Aurora! Why, Aurora P.!"

Mom cups my forehead with her hand. "Are you all right? Open your eyes." But I can't, or I won't.

"D-did she hit him?" My voice shakes. "The piebald? Is he okay? Please, please . . ."

"He's gone," Jewell answers. I know she's right beside me now.

"Gone?" I think my heart will split.

"Well, you spooked him now, didn't you?" she says.

"So . . . you didn't shoot? With your bow?"

"Not on your life!" she says.

I open my eyes. Jewell is standing above me.

I roll onto my side and let out a moan. I press my face into my arm and rub my eyes. A few seconds later, I start to laugh—just a little. Then cry. Then laugh again. I don't know what to do with myself.

"I'm sorry, Jewell." I pull myself up to sitting. "But I thought you were going to shoot him, so I am *not* sorry too!"

"How about hurt?" Pop wants to know. "Are you hurt?" He pulls me to my feet and dusts a few forest crumbs off me.

"Yeah, that was an impressive tumble," Mom says.

"I'm fine," I say. "I didn't even feel it." I let out a laugh and smooth the needlepoint purse against my side.

"Jewell," I say, "are you okay?"

"I'm right as rain," she says. "May I say it? I appreciate that you didn't take me out with that pitch. I know you could have, kiddo. You, with your spectacular accuracy." She makes wide eyes at me.

"I figured I'd scare the deer away instead."

"Oh, so you thought about it?" Jewell teases. "Meanwhile, I hope you all got a good look at that magnificent creature. Whew! I have never seen anything like him, not with my own eyes, and I have spent my life in the woods. Dream come true for a woodswoman."

"For us as well," Mom says. "That spotted, speckled coat, and the way he looked back at us . . . leaves you with a sense of awe, doesn't it?"

"Rare treat on a rare evening," says Pop.

Then I tell them. "I've seen it before. More than once. So has Frenchie, and Cedar too. And I'll tell you something else, I think that's where Frenchie's been all this time, following that deer—and I know that sounds impossible. But the piebald doesn't scare as easy as most deer. I think the deer is the reason Frenchie walked away from school and why he never went home. Well, before he got trapped in the quarry, whenever that was."

"Why do you say so? What do you know?"

"I don't know anything for sure. But I've got a hunch,

and it's all because of Cedar." I look for my little brother, but he's making his way to the spot where the deer stood minutes ago.

"Because of Cedar?" Pop asks.

"Yep. He told me. No joking. In fact, he tried to tell us all. He's been saying *bye-baw* ever since yesterday morning. Today on the beach, I finally understood. Right before you came out to get us, Pop. Just before you told us Frenchie had been found. Cedar said, 'Enchie en bye-baw dee-yah.' Can you hear it?"

"Frenchie and piebald deer," Mom says with a nod.

"Beautiful!" Pop says.

"From the mouth of the babe!" says Jewell. "Why, little Cedar P.!"

"And . . . ," I say, "I even asked Carney Huggins if there was anything special about that deer he stopped for on Punkinville Road, and guess what?"

"The piebald." We say it together.

Cedar

What Cedar Petrequin Knew

Frenchie doesn't talk. He looks.

On Friday morning at the school, Cedar saw Frenchie looking out the car window. So he looked too. That's when he saw the piebald deer. The school was busy. Nobody was looking at the deer. Nobody but Cedar and Frenchie.

Cedar tried to tell Aurora. "Bye-baw! Bye-baw!" It sounded just right to him.

But she went along to meet her friends. Frenchie followed them into the school. Pop drove the car around the loop: stop and go, stop and go.

Cedar stuck one finger inside his ear where it ached. He twisted in his car seat so he could keep seeing the deer.

"Bye-baw!" He let out a cry.

"What's that you say, little buddy?" Up in the mirror, Cedar saw Pop's eyes.

"Bye-baw!" Cedar kicked and he cried and he pointed right at that piebald deer.

When Frenchie came out, Cedar saw him. Frenchie stood still. But when the deer walked away, Frenchie walked away with it.

Cedar tried to tell Pop. He tried so hard he cried. He caught a salty tear with the tip of his tongue.

Pop sang the railroad song.

So Cedar sang too. "Yidee yidee yidee-YAY-yo . . . ahh-dah yah-yah-YAY . . .." (It sounded right to him.) Singing made his ear feel better.

All along, Cedar Petrequin knew. Frenchie had followed the bye-baw dee-yah.

Aurora

Up Sundrop Meadow

I'm leading everyone up to Sundrop Meadow. Anzie Maylord invited us to come pick pumpkins, and we're taking her up on the offer. Cedar holds my hand, and we swing our arms. Leena and Joanie come along shoulder to shoulder. Frenchie keeps up fine, a few feet away.

Mom and Pop and Gracia are following. Close, but not too close. You can bet it'll be a while before any of us lets Frenchie out of our sight.

It's been two weeks since Mr. Menkis brought him up from that little ledge beside the quarry. He's looking like the same old Frenchie again: plaid shirt, khaki pants, belt tight. Needlepoint purse, full of bird prints, of course.

But I can tell you this: when Gracia brought him over

for breakfast the morning after the rescue, she told us, "He'll be all right, but he is very bruised." Saying it made her cry.

Mom hugged her around the shoulders for a long time.

Frenchie ate his pancakes standing up. Then he lay on his belly and studied his bird prints on our living room rug. It was four days before I saw him sit in a chair again. He's done a lot of healing. I've been watching. He doesn't look sore anymore. He walks the old Frenchie walk.

Today is a great day for a hike along the edge of the barrens. The little leaves on the blueberry bushes are a blaze of red, pink, and orange now. At Anzie's gate, we let ourselves in. We stand in front of the poem barn. This is new for Leena and Joanie. But Frenchie is ready. I can tell.

I begin to read—at the top of my lungs, of course.

SUN RAIN WIND SWEPT

BUD BLOSSOM BERRY

Leena and Joanie join in. The three of us shout the lines.

SWEET EARTH ROOTS KEPT

MAKE A SOUL MERRY

We're on a second chorus, and getting the giggles, when Carney Huggins comes out of the barn. He has both thumbs stuck into his ears. He waggles his fingers at us, sticks out his tongue, which makes us laugh even more. He tries to hide a grin but he can't, so he turns and runs back into the barn.

We try to get through the poem one last time. But one by one we drop to the ground because we're laughing so hard—and because we want to. Cedar lands beside me, legs in the air.

Only Frenchie is still standing. He's looking up, face to the sun. I prop on one elbow and wonder what he's thinking. But I don't have to know. I'll just keep on being here with him.

When he's ready he'll start heading home. He knows the way. That's Frenchie Livernois, my bird-loving, no-talk, very best friend.

Frenchie

That Same Day

Frenchie stood looking at the big white letters on the side of the barn, and he thought what he always thought when Aurora read them to him.

SUN SUN SUN.

Acknowledgments

I brim with gratitude every time my work goes to publication, never more than now. The world's challenges have been many; our strides have been necessarily long ones. We have adjusted and adapted. And I have never been more aware of how fortunate I am to be doing this work.

To my extraordinary editor, Katherine Tegen: thank you for the clarity you bring to our projects and, in this case, for helping me find the order of things. (The path through the puckabrush!)

Thanks to every good soul at Katherine Tegen Books and HarperCollins Children's Books for your hard work, dedication, and resilience in recent months, and for continuing to support me as you do. You are all deeply appreciated.

Thanks to Sara Schonfeld for good shepherding, and for helping me get the ever-changing-tree mural right. Thanks to your dad, the *near and dear* resource.

Miriam Altshuler, I am so proud that you are my agent. Your suggestion that the piebald deer belonged in a book took hold! Thanks for constantly doing your best by me.

Ramona Kaulitzki, thank for creating the lush and evocative cover art for this book as well as the gorgeous hand-drawn map on its interior. I love them both.

I have a bounty of good friends and family, who never let me stay lost on life's long, winding trail.

So, to my dear mom and dad, my siblings, my cousins and uncles and aunties, and the friends who are as close as family (all of whom seem to think I am way cooler than I really am), thanks for your endless love and encouragement.

To my critique group, *sheeshy-sheesh*, you are my rocks, my gemstones, my geodes, and my tourmaline! Thank you for always covering every detail with me.

To dear friend and writer, Sandi Shelton, another shining source of strength; my love and thanks for endless plot talks and plates of avocado toast.

I am ever grateful to prepublication readers Cammie McGovern and Eliza Factor (and Miranda too!) for their generosity and honesty. (See author's note.)

Mark Mendel, thank you for your poem barns and environmental art projects. For me, the Penobscot barn has served as the gateway to my annual summer writing retreat for twenty-five years. Always, it signals a beginning. (See author's note.)

Thanks to Obadiah Buell and Kelly Dean, for inviting me (and all visitors) to roam the stunning quarry and Granite Garden Gallery up on Whales Back Road in Sullivan, Maine.

To the piebald deer, thank you for showing yourself and staying a while. (See author's note.)

A mountain of thanks to you, my readers. Fact: there is no story without you. Doubt me? Well, consider that eternal question: If a tree falls in the woods and there's no one there to hear it, does it make a sound? The same applies to story.

Finally, to Jonathan and my kids, Sam, Kristy, Marley, and Ian: thank you for the love we share and the ways we celebrate it. (Dang, we are lucky ones!)

Author's Note

Anybody Here Seen Frenchie began with an unexplain-
able little seed that planted itself late at night. I was
almost asleep when I sat up and reached for the pack of
3" x 5" cards I keep on my night stand. I wrote down two
fragments:

flapping and tweeting

a bowl in the earth

When I looked back at my jottings in the morning
light, I remembered what I'd seen in my mind's eye. It
struck me that I'd found an ending. I felt a longing for the
journey.

I had been thinking about a pair of middle graders who
find in each other something both of them desperately

need: friendship. In this case, it is a friendship nuanced by neurodiversity and the vastness of the autism spectrum.

I was determined to get these characters right, particularly Frenchie, who does not speak. With an early draft in hand, I turned to Cammie McGovern and Eliza Factor for comments based on their personal experiences raising autistic sons. Their firsthand insights were invaluable; they helped me to consider the complexity of loving an autistic person. (Eliza's daughter, Miranda, offered the sibling perspective as well.) I gave their reflections my full attention, and I believe with all my heart that Cammie and Eliza added depth, nuance, and authenticity to *all* my characters. If I've been successful, it's because of them; if I've failed, it's entirely my responsibility.

About the Poem Barn: This structure provided the inspiration for Anzie Maylord's poem barn. Created by artist and poet Mark Mendel in 1975, the barn with its

30' x 40' stenciled poem sits atop a favorite meadow of mine in Penobscot, Maine. Mr. Mendel's poem doesn't rhyme, whereas the one in the story does. I needed a poem that could also be a marching song for Aurora. Rhyme worked best. (Apologies to Mr. Mendel.) To learn more about Mark Mendel and his poem barns (there are more, but not enough in my opinion), please visit www.markmendel.com.

About the piebald deer: over a period of two years, my family and I delighted in repeated sightings of this pie-bald deer on the wooded land trust property adjacent to our house (part of his home range) in southern Connecti-cut. He is unforgettable. He stole my whole heart.

—Leslie Connor

THE
CONTEST
OF THE
CENTURY

THE
CONTEST
OF THE
CENTURY

The New Era of
Competition with China—
and How America Can Win

Geoff Dyer

ALFRED A. KNOPF   NEW YORK   2014

THIS IS A BORZOI BOOK
PUBLISHED BY ALFRED A. KNOPF

Copyright © 2014 by Geoff Dyer

All rights reserved. Published in the United States by Alfred A. Knopf, a
division of Random House LLC, New York, and in Canada by Random
House of Canada Limited, Toronto, Penguin Random House Companies.

www.aaknopf.com

Cataloging-in-Publication Data is available
from the Library of Congress.
ISBN 978-0-307-96075-7

Jacket design by Chip Kidd

Manufactured in the United States of America
First Edition

For Angelica and Jack

CONTENTS

Introduction   3

Section I   MILITARY IN ASIA

1 China Takes to the Near Seas   19
2 The Lure of the Indian Ocean   50
3 The Asian Backlash—Tone-Deaf in Hanoi   69
4 America's Choice   110

Section II   POLITICS AND NATIONALISM

5 China's Brittle Nationalism   141
6 Soft Power   175
7 "We Are Not the World's Savior"—   199
   Humanitarian Intervention and the UN

Section III   ECONOMICS

8 Taking On the Dollar   227
9 Post-American Globalization   249
   Conclusion   276

   Acknowledgments   281
   Notes   283
   Bibliographic Essay   291
   Index   293

When China Looks Out to Sea

jing

Dalian

NORTH
KOREA

SOUTH
KOREA

JAPAN

Nanjing

Shanghai

*East
China
Sea*

PACIFIC OCEAN

Okinawa

Senkaku Islands

TAIWAN

*South
China
Sea*

acel
nds

*y
ls*

"Nine Dash Line"

First Island Chain

Second Island Chain

Guam

PHILIPPINES

O N E S I A

THE
CONTEST
OF THE
CENTURY

Introduction

B EIJING WAS IN a state of heightened anxiety and had been for weeks. Each day in the run-up to the National Day parade, the security measures seemed to get a little bit tighter. Our apartment building had a distant view of Jianguomen, which is the main east-west avenue that runs through the center of Beijing, traversing Tiananmen Square along the way, and which was to be the main parade route. During rehearsal the Sunday before, we were told not to go onto our balconies. "What happens if we do? Will we be shot?" a neighbor jokingly asked. The building manager replied in a deadpan manner, "Maybe; who knows?" All the pigeons in the city were locked up and kite flying was banned, presumably to prevent undesirable threats to the safety of airspace. On the day itself, the two blocks on either side of the route were closed off to passersby. The 2009 event was to be the sixtieth anniversary of the foundation of the People's Republic of China, the first parade in a decade, and only the fifth time since the 1950s that such an event had been held. But, unlike in previous October 1 parades, no ordinary people were allowed to line the route and watch the festivities. The center of Beijing was hermetically sealed off from the city's residents. For everyone but the invited crowd of VIPs and journalists, this was a television-only spectacle. Despite the country's booming wealth, China's rulers can often seem insecure, looking anxiously over their shoulders at the people they govern. In the weeks leading up to the parade, they had conducted a crackdown on human-rights lawyers, and three months later they ordered an eleven-year jail sentence for Liu Xiaobo, the democracy activist who would later win the Nobel Peace Prize. The heavy-handed security was fruit of this nervy mindset.

A few hours before the parade was to start, I watched a stream of maybe fifty, maybe one hundred buses pass by, all with a regulation thirty meters in between them. The first group stood out because of the bright clothes of the excited young people inside—this bus orange, that one green, another blue. The next group were filled with soldiers in dress uniform, some trying to catch a last-minute nap, their heads pressed against the glass. With precision timing, they were being ferried to their starting places for a three-hour-long spectacle which was at times intimidating, at times impressive, and at times folksy, but never anything but meticulous. Like the morning mist, which lifted to make way for bright sunshine, the pre-parade paranoia quickly evaporated. By midday, two hundred thousand soldiers and civilians had taken part in the procession, and I did not see a single foot put wrong. It was a display that mixed North Korean mass choreography with the sort of swagger the Soviets used to muster for May Day. The kids in colored T-shirts that I had seen on the buses filled the vast expanse of Tiananmen Square to hold up cards that formed gigantic phrases: "Obey the Party's Command," "Be Loyal to the Party," and "Long Live the Motherland." For an hour, the military showed off the very latest of its hardware, the product of two decades of double-digit spending increases. There were the J-10 fighter jets, China's first homegrown jets, and a long line of DF-31A intercontinental ballistic missiles, which have the range to hit Los Angeles, and which the Xinhua News Agency later described as "remarkable symbols of China's defense muscle." A decade before, much of the weaponry on display had been bought from Russia; this time it was all developed at home.

Military parades have been a feature of Chinese statecraft for centuries. During the Qing dynasty (1644 to 1912), victory ceremonies were often organized for the emperor to demonstrate his authority, and under the Communists they have been revamped for television. Geremie Barmé, an Australian expert on Chinese culture, recalls that in 1984, which also happened to be the year of Deng Xiaoping's eightieth birthday, a group of students from Peking University held up an impromptu sign during the parade that said "Hello Xiaoping." As this was not in the script, the television cameras missed it. Once the event had finished, the spontaneous greeting was restaged and edited into the official broadcast. In 2009, the television highlight was the contingent from the Beijing Women's Militia, who marched in precise fashion past the podium in red miniskirts and knee-high white boots, and who, Chinese media later revealed, were all models specially chosen for their uniform height. The main audience for the parades was the domestic one, which was to be both entertained and cowed by the organizational capacity of the Chinese state. But China is too big and too important for such an event to go unnoticed overseas. China's leaders knew that images of its bristling military display would be beamed around the planet and seemed untroubled if the outside world was also a little intimidated. "It represents the realization of the great revival of the Chinese nation as a result of tireless struggle," as the army described the event.

Before the military parade reached Tiananmen Square, the soldiers stopped in a long column along the main avenue to be reviewed by then President Hu Jintao. He was standing in the back of a Red Flag, China's homegrown limousine, his head and upper body visible through the sunroof as it drove past the troops. Hu, a gray bureaucrat skilled at the inner workings of the party, went out of his way to cut a dour public profile, an almost deliberate anti–cult of personality. Dressed in a Mao tunic buttoned to the top, and with his dyed black hair immaculately coiffed, he seemed at first to have a slightly comic air, and I chuckled when a colleague quipped about his resembling an Austin Powers villain. Yet, as he boomed into the microphone in front of him *"Tongzhimen hao"* ("Greetings, comrades") and *"Tongzhimen xinku le"* ("Thanks for all the suffering, comrades"), his voice, echoing all around the vast square, was a little chilling. Stern-faced, he returned to the podium at the gate of the Forbidden City, right above the giant oil portrait of Mao Zedong, and stood on the same spot where sixty years earlier Mao had declared that the "Chinese people have stood up." Flanked on both sides by the other eight members of the Communist Party's Standing Committee, the body that really runs the country, all dressed in dark business suits with red ties, Hu addressed the crowd. "Today a socialist China, geared toward modernization, the world, and the future, stands rock-firm in the East," he declared. It was his biggest applause line.

Just over two decades before, the same square had been the scene of bloodshed. In the streets surrounding Tiananmen, Chinese soldiers massacred hundreds—maybe thousands—of Beijing residents as they tried to clear the student-led protests. Realizing their legitimacy had been called into question, Chinese leaders would sit somewhat meekly for years afterward as foreigners lectured them on the need to change their political system. Bill Clinton once told his counterpart, Jiang Zemin, that the Chinese Communist Party was "on the wrong side of history." The scars from those events contributed to a desire among China's leaders to maintain a low profile overseas and to focus on development at home. Shortly after the massacre, Deng Xiaoping devised his famous slogan to define Chinese foreign policy, advising his colleagues to *taoguang yanhui*—literally, "hide the brightness and nourish obscurity." Deng knew that the resurgence of China's economy would stir anxieties in the U.S. and across Asia, where many festering rivalries remain—even more so after the 1989 display of authoritarian muscle in Tiananmen. Deng realized that only by emphasizing humility and a willingness to cooperate could China develop its economy without provoking a regional and international backlash. For two decades, China looked inward and focused on rebuilding.

Yet, sitting under the baking sun in Tiananmen Square that morning, I felt Hu Jintao was delivering a very different message—the words of a risen China, not a rising China. He was telling the country and the world not only that the Communist Party was still very much in charge, but that it was also pursuing a path that was moral and right. China, he suggested, was now an important nation with legitimate interests, and it would not be afraid to defend them. Nations do not change tack overnight, of course, but the parade brought to the surface powerful forces that had been building for some time. It represented a symbolic turning point in modern Chinese history, when it became hard to ignore the way the Deng Xiaoping formula of self-restraint was crumbling and the new era of geopolitical competition with the United States that was emerging. The socialist rock in the East wanted to escape from the shadow of the West.

This is a book about the new age of rivalry. It is about why China now wants to start exerting influence around the world and about the growing competition with the U.S. that will be the single most important factor in world politics over the coming decades. If globalization has been the driving force over the last few decades—in fact, since China embarked on its economic reforms in the late 1970s, after the death of Mao—then there is now a powerful force pulling in the opposite direction, an old-fashioned struggle for influence and power between China and the U.S., the two most important nations in the world.

The Contest of the Century revolves around three central points.

The first is that China has started to make the crucial shift from a government that accepts the existing rules to one that seeks to shape the world according to its own national interests, from rule taker to rule maker. Beijing is starting to channel its inner great power. The book provides a portrait of the new Chinese mentality, the energies, ambitions, and tensions that are pushing China in this direction. Much of the discussion of modern China focuses on the nature of the Communist Party and its hold on power, and, indeed, it is impossible to detach ideology from the way China relates to the rest of the world. But China is also responding forcefully to the same sort of instincts that have animated new great powers in the past, with particularly strong echoes from both the U.S. and late-nineteenth-century Germany. "History does not repeat itself, but it does rhyme," as Mark Twain is often quoted as saying—even though it is not clear that he ever did.

Second, to pursue those goals, China is inevitably finding itself pulled into a geopolitical competition with the U.S., the country in whose image much of the global order is fashioned. China and the U.S. are starting to contest the high ground of international politics, from control of the oceans in Asia to the currency that is used in international business. Forget their bland rhetoric: China's leaders think very much in geopolitical terms and would like to gradually erode the bases of American power. Almost every important global issue will find itself colored by this rivalry. Yet it will not be the win-at-all-costs ideological struggle of the Cold War. Instead, this will be an older, more fluid form of rivalry that is based on balance of power and building coalitions of support.

Finally, I will argue that the U.S. is in a strong position to deflect this new Chinese challenge to its position in the world. Whether they have come to praise or to warn about China's rise, most authors on China subscribe to an almost linear transfer of wealth and influence from West to East, from a U.S. in decline to an irrepressible China. There is an air of inevitability in the way China is presented. Yet the roots of American power are deeper than they seem and hard to overturn. If the U.S. can clean its own financial house and avoid the temptations of either confrontation or isolation, it will still hold many of the best cards in the twenty-first century.

———

"Great power" is a phrase with an old-fashioned, dusty feel to it, something from the history textbooks to do with the Schleswig-Holstein Question or the assassination of Archduke Franz Ferdinand. The age of the great power seemed to have passed with the Cold War and America's unipolar dominance that followed the fall of the Berlin Wall. Yet the rise of China strikes many notes from a very different era. "No nation has ever experienced such an increase in its power without seeking to translate it into global influence," Henry Kissinger once wrote about the U.S. in the late nineteenth century. Today's China is animated by the same energies that stirred in the U.S. from the 1890s, when it announced itself to the world. At home, new great powers are possessed by an economic dynamism and a zeal for grand engineering, by the construction of modern cities and the laying of vast railway networks across continents. Before long, that energy takes them overseas, where their companies develop trading posts and factories across the globe. They feel the need to use their new economic power to strengthen their own security, to fend off potential rivals, and to protect their overseas interests— a mixture of pride and fear that leads them to build grand navies. As their standing grows, they try to mold the political, military, and economic rules that govern the international system. Rising wealth creates rising expectations among a new middle class that wants its rulers to stand up for their country. The material benefits of a growing economy are never enough for aspiring great powers—they also want respect, recognition, and influence. Power changes countries, just as it changes people.

When America started staking its claim in the world in the 1890s, it was propelled in part by a growing centralization of power in the presidency. The horrors of the Civil War had given way to a fragmented political environment in the 1870s and 1880s, with neither the executive nor Congress able to establish control of foreign policy. America's international role only started to be transformed when the White House began to exert more decisive influence in the 1890s. In China, something close to the opposite has happened. The last decade has seen what might be described as a fracturing of power in China in ways that have begun to have a decisive influence over the country's foreign policy. China's leaders have not abandoned Deng Xiaoping's advice to keep a low profile—on the contrary, they regularly insist that it remains their guiding principle. Instead, the Deng consensus is being gradually overwhelmed by the reality of modern-day China and its society. Deng's cautious strategy is slowly fraying. Fragmentation of power is not the same as political liberalization, of course, but, rather, a dispersal of influence within the elite. It means that China's senior leaders do not enjoy the almost untrammeled authority that Deng once enjoyed. They face powerful vested interests within the party-state, and an officer class that has its own hawkish take on global affairs. They also have to keep an anxious eye on the nationalist views of a rising middle class. On airport bookshelves in China these days, alongside the Jack Welch and Bill Gates biographies, you can now find titles such as Xue Yong's *How to Be a Great Power*, a sort of Cliff Notes for modern geopolitics. All these voices are pushing China to be more ambitious overseas. China remains resolutely authoritarian, but these days, it also has a lot more politics.

To think about China as a great power might seem obvious to readers who have watched the swagger and military buildup of recent years, but it goes against the two most dominant interpretations of what really drives modern China.

The first is what one might call the Davos view, after the home of the World Economic Forum, the contention that China's leaders are so obsessed with economic development at home that they have little time for or real interest in getting too involved in the affairs of the world. Even if they did want to push harder against the U.S., so the argument goes, they would soon be confronted with the reality of the enormous economic interdependence between the two countries. It is easy to see why such a view would take hold. Achieving high rates of growth has been the singular achievement of China's Communist leaders over the last two decades and their principal justification for maintaining an iron grip on power. And for Davos optimists, globalization has transformed international politics, creating a web of economic connections and dependencies that prevent any country from rocking the boat. Geopolitics, with its emphasis on competition and struggle between nations, has been rendered unnecessary by the multinational global economy. In China, there is a cottage industry of scribes developing slogans to impress the rest of the world with how unthreatening its rise really is—from the "Shanghai smile" and "win-win" economic cooperation to "peaceful development." ("Peaceful rise" was taken up at one stage, but then dropped when it was deemed to be too threatening.) In *The Post-American World,* which is in some ways the most influential international-relations book of recent years in the West, Fareed Zakaria writes that the Chinese are too pragmatic to let the vanities of power politics damage their economic interests. "The veneration of an abstract idea is somewhat alien to China's practical mind-set," he writes.

Yet, when even the most materialistic countries arrive at a certain scale and economic reach, they feel they have no choice but to try and influence events beyond their shores. China's epic urbanization push is being fueled by goods from the four corners of the earth—by oil from Saudi Arabia, by coal from Indonesia, by iron ore from Brazil, and by copper from the Congo. For the first time in its millennial history, China's economic interests are genuinely global, and it needs a foreign policy to match them. Deng Xiaoping's "hiding the brightness" is no longer sufficient. To keep its economy humming, China feels it needs to start molding the world it is operating in. China's economy relies on the continued safety of seaborne trade—something which has been guaranteed since the end of the Second World War by the navy of the United States, the country which the Chinese elite mistrusts the most (with the possible exception of Japan). Like other great powers before it, China is building a navy to take to the high seas because it does not want to outsource the security of its economic lifelines to someone else. The problem-solving China so heralded at Davos is being replaced by something with much harder edges. In short, geopolitics is back.

The second brand of conventional wisdom holds that the regime in Beijing is too insecure about its hold on power at home to think seriously about challenging the U.S. The brittleness is everywhere to be seen, from the heavy-handed security at the 2009 National Day parade to the periodic arrests of dissidents to the opacity of the political process. One of the most commonly cited factoids about modern China is that Beijing actually spends more money on internal security than it does on its defense budget, even though military spending has been rising sharply. But what this explanation misses is that domestic insecurity is feeding, not inhibiting, the desire to stand tall overseas. In one way or another, the Chinese Communist Party has been suffering a legitimacy crisis since it abandoned Marx and embraced the market in the late 1970s, and that crisis has been more acute since the Tiananmen Square Massacre in 1989. The party has tried to fill this gap in all sorts of ways. Economic growth and a reputation for competent governance have been the main props. But China's leaders have also buttressed their legitimacy with an appeal to a nationalism that is tinged with a sense of victimhood. Brittle politics at home are stimulating a more assertive voice abroad.

In the end, thinking of China as an aspiring great power is the best way to demystify the country, to resist the temptation to either demonize or exoticize. China is neither an anti-democratic hegemon launching a new Cold War, as its more conservative critics suggest, nor the postmodern, Confucian meritocracy that some supporters imagine. China is, instead, a state which is behaving in many of the same ways that other states have behaved when they started to become very powerful.

It is an indication of the influence of Deng Xiaoping's *taoguang yanhui* formula that it has simultaneously been attacked by hard-liners at home and inspired fear abroad. The advice was kept secret at first, and to this day, there are differing accounts of the full text that he wrote. In the 1990s, the phrase was heavily criticized by Chinese leftists who thought it a sop to the U.S. Yet for many foreign audiences, it had a different feel. The official translation in China is "hide the brightness and nourish obscurity"; however, in the U.S., the same words have often been translated as "bide one's time," a phrase that contains a certain menace about future intentions. For Deng, the ambiguity was a way of keeping different groups happy. He always knew that a powerful China would start competing for power and influence with the U.S. He just wanted to put off the rivalry for as long as possible.

Such self-restraint has become harder to sell since 2008. A year before Hu Jintao stood up to speak in Tiananmen at the parade, Lehman Brothers had collapsed. The psychological fallout from the global financial crisis was particularly important in China, where predictions about inevitable American decline have taken deep root. Within the Chinese elite, there has been a long-standing argument about how China should behave toward the U.S. when China became a powerful nation: the doves said that China would be best served by playing along with the U.S.-led international system, while the hawks said China would need to stand up to the U.S. Yet it was a debate held in suspended animation. Everyone knew that Beijing would have to answer this question one day, but the priority for the time being was to focus on the building up of what Chinese officials call "Comprehensive National Power." Just as 9/11 empowered American neoconservatives, the financial crisis ended the shadow boxing in Beijing and unleashed powerful demands within parts of the elite to begin taking on the U.S. The time to answer the question, the hawks demanded, was now.

To warn about growing competition, however, is not to predict conflict, especially in an era when nuclear deterrence provides a powerful brake on both nations. There are no Chinese plans for the sort of territorial expansion that scarred Europe in the late nineteenth century, or for a project of global domination. Instead, Beijing has more subtle, long-term instincts about gradually undermining the foundations of American power and influence, starting in Asia and moving outward. International-relations scholars like to ask whether new powers will rise within the existing order or try to overthrow it. But neither explanation captures China's behavior. Instead, Beijing is beginning a process of gradually trying to mold the system in its own direction, to shape rather than tear down. Chinese leaders understand the limitations that globalization places on them, and the benefits that thirty years of trading with the U.S. have brought, but they are also far more skeptical and resentful about American influence than most in Washington realize. There is nothing surprising about what China is now doing. If anything, the surprise is that it did not start sooner.

Competition between the U.S. and China is usually thought of in terms of the location of a factory or the value of exchange rates, but that is rivalry at the retail level. The real contest for power and influence is over the geopolitical high ground: the rules, institutions, and power dynamics which dictate how the world really works. The core of this book will be about the three different fronts on which the competition will take place—military, political, and economic.

The first section focuses on the military contest in Asia, where China's new navy is beginning to challenge the dominance of the U.S. in the western Pacific, setting up one of the defining stories of the coming decades. The tussle that is developing for control of the seas surrounding China is in some ways the central contest, because naval power can create the conditions to shape political and economic realities. Chapter 1 will look at the reasons behind China's naval modernization, the historical and geopolitical anxieties together with the changing role that the military occupies within the Chinese system. Chapter 2 looks at whether China will seek to strike out as a naval power into the Indian Ocean, and Chapter 3 examines the deep backlash that China has provoked in Asia. Chapter 4 analyzes America's response to China's Asian ambitions.

The second section examines the political challenge that China is now presenting. One chapter looks at China's huge investments in soft power; other explores the impact that China's rigid ideas about state sovereignty are having on the way human rights are treated by the international community. Before that, Chapter 5 provides a slight detour into the psychology of China's new assertiveness, looking at the particular form of nationalism which has sprung up over the last two decades and which is the emotional crutch for the desire to challenge the West.

The final section focuses on two different ways in which China is threatening to rewrite the rules of the global economy, first through its plans to challenge the U.S. dollar, and second through the coming boom in Chinese finance and investment, which has the potential to reshape globalization.

———

Of course, Beijing is not the only capital gripped by talk of American decline. Washington, too, is full of fin-de-siècle anxiety, the result of the global financial crisis which laid bare a wealth of much deeper, unresolved problems in the economy and a political system that seems allergic to addressing long-term problems. "The Desperate States of America," as the German magazine *Der Spiegel* calls the U.S.; or, as the former Morgan Stanley analyst David Roche puts it, "Wall Street's crack-up presages a global tectonic shift: the beginning of the decline of American power." America's huge budget deficits and debt levels mean that the risk of a much deeper crisis and a collapse in the credibility of the U.S. dollar is a very real one. And all this is taking place while Washington watches the seemingly unstoppable rise of China. It has become a favorite parlor game among economic pundits to predict the year when the Chinese economy will overtake the U.S. to become the biggest in the world. Some believe it could happen within a decade.

The declinists are correct about two things. America's ability to project power will depend on bringing its long-term debt under control and restoring its reputation as the most innovative large economy in the world. A decade of economic stagnation would derail many aspects of its foreign policy. It is also clearly true that the world has changed in important ways. China's rise is only the most visible example of a diffusion of economic power toward the developing world, which includes India, Brazil, Indonesia, and a host of other nations. The unipolar era that the U.S. enjoyed after the end of the Cold War was always an aberration, and it is quickly coming to an end. If the U.S. strives to maintain the kind of military dominance it has enjoyed for the last two decades, installing China as the new enemy to scare up budgets, it will be in big trouble. Yet the obsession with the *sorpasso* moment, when China's economy becomes the world's biggest, confuses the way power is wielded in international politics. There will be no new military parade in Beijing on the day when China's economy overtakes that of the U.S., no handover ceremony to usher in a new leader. Power and influence are not transferred, like a property title: they have to be earned.

When you start looking at the world through Chinese eyes, it is striking how deeply entrenched American influence begins to appear, and how difficult it will be for China to overturn it. America's alliances are solid and its core political values still widely shared. At the same time, with a political system that strangles creativity, China lacks the tools to project around the world its own ideas about good governance and the good life. The market for Chinese military and diplomatic power is also much smaller than many in Beijing realize, especially in Asia. The harder China pushes, the more likely it is that a coalition of neighbors will emerge, with the U.S. at the helm, to restrain its ambitions. China risks becoming a very lonely great power.

Instead of American decline, the bigger question is whether Washington can sustain broad international support for the system of free trade, freedom of navigation, and international rules it put in place after the Second World War. The rise of China and the other new powers means a return to a world where a balance of power is the natural state of affairs, with the U.S. still the most important nation but unable to dictate terms. Instead of rigid alliances, there will be fluid coalitions that shift depending on the issue. On occasion, China and the U.S. will be on the same side, but more often than not they will be opposed and Washington should have no illusions about China's willingness to push back against American leadership. The most influential state will be the one that is best at setting agendas, mobilizing support, and which comes across as the more reasonable. This should be an environment that suits the U.S., which for decades has shown a flair for the patient work of sustaining alliances and coalitions. But Washington will have to find new ways to work together with Europe, which will remain a natural partner, and to establish stronger ties with India, Brazil, and some of the other new swing voters of international politics. If the U.S. wants to retain its role at the center of international affairs, it will have to convince enough countries that its ideas still work. A quest for continued military dominance will not do the trick: Washington needs to enlist new partners. This is the real challenge that China laid down at its National Day parade in Tiananmen Square.

Section I

MILITARY IN ASIA

————— ∎ —————

China Takes to the Near Seas

To the list of industries now dominated by China, there is one surprising new entry: Miss World. Beauty contests were banned in China by Mao Zedong as one of the worst forms of Western decadence, but their bland internationalism appeals to modern China's desire to be included. Of the last nine Miss World pageants, five have been held in China, all at the seaside resort of Sanya, on subtropical Hainan Island, off China's south coast. Sensing a great way to boost tourism, the local government spent $30 million to build a special venue for the contest, the Beauty Crown Theater, a huge arena near a man-made beach which is shaped like, well, a crown. When it opened in 2003, the winner was Rosanna Davison, a nutritional therapist from Dublin whose father, Chris de Burgh, wrote the syrupy global smash hit "Lady in Red." Qi Guan, a Chinese model who wore a flowing red ball-gown for the evening's finale, was the second runner-up. Her compatriot Zhang Zilin went one better in 2007, winning China's first Miss World title.

When the Miss World show is in town, the swimsuit photo shoots take place across the road, at the Sanya Sheraton Hotel, which looks out onto the white sands of Yalong Bay, a crescent-shaped cove lined with palm trees. With a Ritz-Carlton on one side and a Marriott on the other, Yalong Bay is a transplant of multinational tourism on China's southernmost point. The resort has become hugely popular with prosperous

Chinese families, who escape the urban grind for a few days of sun that before would have required a trip to Thailand. On the beach, I met one couple from Jiangxi Province who were sporting his and hers Hawaiian shirts and shorts. On the winter day when I traveled, it was minus nine degrees Celsius (not quite sixteen degrees Fahrenheit) when the plane left Beijing, and a balmy twenty-three degrees Celsius when we arrived three hours later in Sanya, a reminder of the continental size of China. The Sheraton is also a popular escape for well-to-do Russians living in eastern Siberia. On the menu at the Lotus Café, which is surrounded by a landscaped Japanese-style koi pond, the Sheraton Club Sandwich is offered in English, Mandarin, and Russian.

That day, the hotel was hosting a corporate retreat for the Chinese subsidiary of Syngenta, a multinational based in Switzerland which sells genetically modified seeds. The hundred or so employees spent the afternoon playing games on the beach, including the confidence-building drills in which one person falls back into the arms of a colleague. "Trust your partner, trust your partner," the master of ceremonies shouted. Having fun on the beach, they barely looked up when a Chinese Type 054 frigate sailed casually across the bay, in plain view of the tourists. Yalong Bay, it turns out, has a double life. The brand-name hotels occupy only one half of the beach; at the other end lies China's newest and most sophisticated naval base.

Yalong Bay is where the two sides of China's rise now intersect, its deeply connected economy and its deep-seated instinct to challenge America—globalization China and great-power China vying for a spot on the beach. Celebrating their success in the China market, the Syngenta employees at the Sheraton all wore T-shirts emblazoned with the English-language slogan for their event: "Step Up Together." Yet right next door to their party was one of the most striking symbols of China's great-power ambitions. Ideally situated for quick access to the busy sea-lanes of the South China Sea, the base in Hainan is one of the principal platforms for an old-fashioned form of projecting national power, a navy that can operate well beyond a country's coastal waters. For the last couple of decades, such power politics seemed to have been made irrelevant by the frictionless, flat world of globalization. Yet Yalong Bay demonstrates a different reality. It is one of the launchpads for what will

be one of the central geopolitical tussles of the twenty-first century—
the new era of military competition in the Pacific between China
and the U.S.

———

The Asia-Pacific region is now the most dynamic economy in the world
and accounts for around half of all output, an intricate network that
takes software and design from California, tiny microchips from Japan,
and sophisticated screen technology from South Korea, and assem-
bles them into iPads in a factory in southern China. Given that nearly
90 percent of intercontinental commerce travels by ship, Asia's seas have
become the principal arteries of the global economy. If there is a symbol
that defines the era of globalization, it is the container ship. Traveling
the long sea-lanes west from Asia toward Europe and east toward the
U.S., the biggest ships now carry as many as seven thousand containers,
stacked eight rows high. The enormous economies of scale that container ships offer have made it possible to manufacture socks and televisions in Asia and then sell them at low cost in Walmart or Primark.
The ease and safety with which these hulking ships, the length of four
football fields, travel safely across the world's oceans is what makes the
global economy tick. Freedom of navigation is the unwritten label on
the modern consumer economy.

Two very different visions of Asia's future are now in play. Since the
defeat of Japan in 1945—and especially since the end of the Cold War—
the United States Navy has treated the Pacific Ocean as almost a private
lake. It has used that power to implement an international system in
its own image, a rules-based order of free trade, freedom of navigation,
and, when possible, democratic government. That Pax Americana was
cemented in June 1971, when Henry Kissinger pulled Richard Nixon
away from a state dinner for the president of Nicaragua and showed him
a secret cable from Chinese Premier Zhou Enlai in which Beijing agreed
to a face-to-face meeting between the leaders of the two countries. "This
is the most important communication that has come to an American
president since the end of World War Two," Kissinger told Nixon, with
his customary mixture of grandiloquence and flattery. The four decades
since Nixon met Mao Zedong have been the most stable and prosper-

ous in Asia's modern history. Under the agreement, the U.S. endorsed China's return to the family of nations, and China implicitly accepted American military dominance in Asia.

In many ways, China has been the biggest beneficiary of this system. History is full of examples of rising powers which have complained that the existing rules were rigged against them. In the first decades of the last century, Germany and Japan found themselves squeezed out of important aspects of the global economy as the major powers used their imperial networks to guarantee the essential raw-material supplies they needed for their economies. The roots of both world wars lay partly in this friction. However, since the late 1970s, China has been able to use the very openness of the U.S.-led order to promote its extraordinary growth. China has been allowed to insert itself into an international trading system which has clear and established rules, and it has been able to buy the oil, copper, and iron ore that it needs on global markets. Now the world's biggest exporter of manufactured goods, China has a vast seaborne trade that is underpinned by the calming influence of American naval dominance.

Never written down or officially announced, this understanding between Beijing and Washington on America's role in Asia is crumbling. China now wishes to recast the military and political dynamic in the region to reflect its own traditional centrality. Great powers are driven by a mixture of confidence and insecurity. China wants a return to the leadership position it has enjoyed so often in Asian history. It also frets about the security of its seaborne commerce, especially in the area it calls the "Near Seas"—the coastal waters that include the Yellow, East China, and South China Seas. The Yalong Bay naval base on Hainan Island is one part of the strategy that China is starting to put in place to exert control over the Near Seas, an effort to push the U.S. Navy ever farther out into the western Pacific. In the process, it is launching a profound challenge to the U.S.-led order that has been the backbone of the Asian economic miracle.

Although the Chinese navy's name—the People's Liberation Army Navy, or PLAN—betrays the fact that it was once the poor cousin of the army, for the last twenty years China has been undergoing a rapid military buildup, and the navy has been given pride of place. More important, China has been investing in its navy in a very specific way. China's naval planners have focused on the warships, silent submarines, and rapid small boats which form the basis of what the U.S. Navy calls "access denial." The clear implication of the investment plan is that China is trying to prevent the U.S. Navy from operating in large areas of the western Pacific. China's new navy is both an expression of power and a means to a diplomatic end. By weakening the U.S. naval presence in the western Pacific, China hopes to gradually undermine America's alliances with other Asian countries, notably South Korea, the Philippines, and maybe even Japan. As American influence declines, China would be in a position to quietly assume a leadership position in Asia, giving it much greater influence over the rules and practices in the principal arena of the global economy. Through its navy, China hopes to reshape the balance of power in Asia.

Countries compete for influence in all sorts of ways, over economic rules and political philosophies, but the military arena is the most important. If allowed to blossom, military rivalries have the capacity to calcify all other interactions between the countries. Compromise is hard for political leaders when senior generals are muttering dark warnings in their ears. That makes the emerging contest in the western Pacific one of the central global issues over the coming decades. It will be a crucial test for how the U.S. and China manage their emerging great-power rivalry. It will also be a laboratory for many of the questions about China's rise—how Beijing intends to pursue its leadership aspirations in the region, and whether, in an era of fiscal retrenchment and political polarization, U.S. global influence still has staying power. The naval competition in the western Pacific will set the tone for a large part of global politics.

———

Aspiring great powers have often taken to the high seas as a route to expanded influence. The U.S., U.K., Spain, Venice, and even ancient Athens all built powerful navies to defend their far-flung interests. In the late nineteenth century, Germany was gripped by the allure of constructing a grand navy, prompting Kaiser Wilhelm II to establish the special rank for himself of *Großadmiral* (great admiral). Sea power is not just about control of the seas; it is also a tool to influence other countries and to shape events. Superior sea power allowed the Europeans to begin asserting control over Asia in the fifteenth century, led first by the Portuguese, and it has enabled outside countries to dictate terms in the region ever since. It was through sea power that a small country like Britain, with only a modest army, could command an empire that covered a quarter of the globe. More recently, domination of the Pacific and Indian Oceans since the end of the Second World War has allowed America to be the preeminent power in Asia. American naval power, combined with the air superiority that comes from a large fleet of aircraft carriers, has been the backbone of its effort to spread free trade and democratic values throughout the region.

Navy building can explain a lot about a nation's intentions, its ambitions, and its anxieties. Long lead times mean that naval planners are not thinking about tomorrow; they are placing bets on how the world will look in one, two, or three decades' time. Navies can also provide a grandeur that beguiles some countries. Hu Jintao defined the development of Chinese naval power in 2006 as a "glorious task"; Rear Admiral Wu Shengli, commander of the Chinese navy, described the quest for a strong fleet as part of "the great revitalization of the Chinese nation." The same sentiments are echoed by popular military commentators. "When we look at history, we can see [that] whether a country is powerful or not is closely related with its naval forces," writes Major General Luo Yuan of the China Military Science Society. "When its naval forces are powerful, then the country is strong; when its naval forces are weak, then the country is also fragile." In 2009, the year when the Chinese Communist Party celebrated its sixtieth anniversary with the grand military parade in Beijing, the navy had their own parade earlier in the year. Fifty-two vessels took part in special review at the east-coast port of Qingdao, including previously unseen nuclear submarines. In many ways, it was a coming-out party for China's new navy.

For anyone who grew up during the Cold War, it can be tempting to see all this as an ideological contest. There is a deep chasm in political values between Washington and Beijing that heightens the sense of competition between the two governments. The U.S. believes the Chinese political system is in some sense illegitimate, while the Chinese insist—not without some justification—that the U.S. would like to see a form of regime change in China. Yet one of the striking aspects of China's turn to the seas is that it is rooted in history and geography in a manner that transcends its current political system. It was from the sea that China was harassed during its "century of humiliation" at the hands of the West. China was one of the most prominent victims of nineteenth-century gunboat diplomacy, when Britain, France, and other colonial powers used their naval supremacy to exercise control over Shanghai and a dozen other ports around the country. The Opium Wars were principally a naval exercise: During the first war, in 1840, the British navy was able to deploy the *Nemesis,* a steamship made of iron whose large guns bombarded Chinese defenses. China learned the hard way that having a weak navy leaves a country vulnerable to pressure and bullying by others. The instinct to control the surrounding seas is partly rooted in the widespread desire never to leave China so vulnerable again. "Ignoring the oceans is a historical error we committed," says Yang Yong, a Chinese historian. "And now even in the future we will pay a price for this error."

This sense that China is under siege is aggravated by looking at a map. Chinese talk about the "first island chain," a perimeter that stretches around the western Pacific from Japan in the northeast, through Taiwan, to the Philippines in the south, all allies or friends of the U.S. This is both a geographical barrier, in that it creates a series of channels that a superior opponent could block in order to bottle up the Chinese navy, and a political barrier controlled by governments close to Washington. For a country that wants to start flexing a few of its muscles, this map makes China deeply uncomfortable; it is almost hemmed in from the sea. Chinese strategists talk about "breaking through the thistles," the development of a naval capability that will allow it to operate outside the barrier of the first island chain they think the U.S. has constructed to keep China contained. *The Science of Military Strategy,* a 2005 statement of the PLA's military doctrine, says that if the navy is kept within the first island chain, "the essential strategic space for China's rejuvenation will be lost." Zhang Wenmu, a well-known and hawkish writer on naval issues, argues, "Restricting China to the shallow seas west of the first island chain is both unfair and impossible and China simply cannot accept it."

When China looks out to sea, it also quickly sees the U.S. According to Chu Shulong, an academic at Peking University, this grudge with the U.S. has grown stronger in recent years, as the Chinese navy has expanded. In the decades when China had little more than a coast guard, it was largely unaware that the U.S. Navy was patrolling waters near its shores. But now that its capabilities are more advanced, it witnesses on a daily basis that the American navy is superior, and operating only a few miles from many of China's major cities. "For them, this is a major humiliation that they experience every single day," says Chu. "It is humiliating that another country can exercise so close to China's coasts, so close to the base in Hainan. That is the reason the navy wants to do something to challenge the U.S."

Anxieties about history and geography have meshed with broader concerns about economic security. One of the key turning points in China's push to the high seas took place when China became a net importer of oil for the first time, in 1993. By 2010, China had become the biggest consumer of energy in the world and the second-biggest consumer of oil, half of which is now imported. A Chinese company has built the largest oil tanker in the world, a 333-meter-long vessel called the *Xin Buyang*, which carries three hundred thousand tons of oil each time it travels from the Middle East. New great powers often fret that rivals could damage their economy with a blockade. Such warnings have become common in China over the last decade. For every ten barrels of oil that China imports, more than eight travel by ship through the Strait of Malacca, the narrow sea channel between Indonesia, Malaysia, and Singapore, which is patrolled by U.S. ships. Fifteenth-century Venetians used to warn, "Whoever is the Lord of Malacca has his hand on the throat of Venice." Hu Jintao echoed similar sentiments when he warned in a 2003 speech that "certain major powers" are bent on controlling this crucial sea-lane. Until now, China's maritime security has been guaranteed largely by the U.S. Navy. But, like aspiring great powers before it, China has been forced to confront a central geopolitical dilemma: can it rely on a rival to protect the country's economic lifeline?

––––––

China's naval buildup may be directed at the U.S., but in lots of ways it has also been modeled on the U.S. At the very least, it should come as no surprise to the U.S. that an aspiring great power should seek to exert greater control over its regional waters. From the early days of the American republic, strategists in Washington fretted about the presence of the old European powers in the Americas. In 1823, these anxieties were given an official stamp when President James Monroe declared that the American continents were "henceforth not to be considered as subjects for future colonization by any European powers." In effect, America put up a large "Stay Out" sign over the hemisphere. It is a natural instinct of rising powers to try and establish a buffer that prevents the more established powers from threatening their security. Like China today, America then worried about the risk of a blockade of its economy, or that a European power might organize a coalition among its neighbors to contain its rise. Like Chinese leaders today, American politicians in the nineteenth century took geopolitics very seriously while all the time professing disdain for the old European games of power politics. And, like China today, America was planning for the long term. The Monroe Doctrine was more bluff than fact for over half a century after it was announced. Britain continued to interfere in and occasionally colonize parts of the Americas for much of the nineteenth century. Even by the 1880s, Chile, Brazil, and Argentina all had larger navies than the U.S. It was not until the 1890s, when America started to establish a world-class navy, that it was able to genuinely enforce the Monroe Doctrine—a crucial point not lost on the Chinese today.

Indeed, China's naval push is drawing heavily on American influences. In 1890s America, one of the most important evangelists of naval power was Alfred Thayer Mahan, an undistinguished naval captain who had started to plot a maritime history while whiling away some days at the English Club in Lima, Peru. The book he eventually wrote, *The Influence of Sea Power upon History, 1680–1783*, turned out to be one of the most influential of his generation when it was published in 1890, with the aid of a $200 personal loan from J. P. Morgan, and helped convince Washington of the need for a big navy. Mahan had two major themes. The first was about the virtues of building a naval force that could fight "decisive battles" against prospective rivals, thereby ensuring the command of the seas that can guarantee national greatness. The second was a more nuanced geopolitical theory about the importance of controlling the sea-lanes that are vital to a nation's commercial life.

In the West, if Mahan is remembered at all today, it is largely for the first set of ideas, which have cast him as one of the warmongers of his age. The notion of applying "overbearing naval power" was taken seriously not only in the U.S. but also in Germany, where Kaiser Wilhelm was a big fan and ordered a copy of his great work placed in every battleship. ("I am . . . devouring Captain Mahan's book and am trying to learn it by heart," he once said.) When the Kaiser met with his naval officers for drinks, they would make toasts to "The Day," the chance they craved to show off their newfound naval strength in one do-or-die battle with the dominant maritime power of the age, the British navy. Mahan died just after the outbreak of the First World War, and his obituary in the *New York Times* said that his writings were "really responsible for the German Navy as it exists today." Sir Charles Webster, the British historian and wartime diplomat, once claimed, "Mahan was one of the causes of the First World War"—a charge from which his name has never completely recovered.

But in today's China, it is the geopolitical aspects of Mahan's writing that are greatly admired, the relationship between expanding commercial interests and naval power. Just as China worries about the Strait of Malacca and the first island chain, Mahan obsessed about building a canal across the Isthmus of Panama and about having naval capabilities in both the Caribbean and the Pacific to defend America's new commercial arteries. He pushed for the U.S. to acquire bases in the Caribbean, to allow U.S. ships to control access to the Panama Canal. For Mahan, sea power was a crucial aspect of economic development. The ability to secure sea-lanes and the critical geographical locations that facilitate commercial traffic "affects the very root of a nation's vigor." Mahan's ideas from the 1890s echo many of the challenges the Chinese see today, the mixture of a quest for national greatness and insecurity about economic lifelines at sea. The "Near Seas" is a formulation that has a strong Sinocentric ring to it, with its implication of a form of Chinese historical ownership, but it also embodies Mahan's vision for a country to secure its vital maritime frontiers.

Neglected at home, Mahan has become deeply fashionable over the last decade in Chinese intellectual circles, including translations of his books, academic articles on their importance, and conferences on his ideas. He has inspired a generation of Chinese navalists. "A big country that builds its prosperity on foreign trade cannot put the safety of its ocean fleet in the hands of other countries," writes Ye Hailin, of the Chinese Academy of Social Sciences. "Doing so would be the equivalent of putting its throat under another's dagger and marking its blood vessels in red ink."

One publisher released an edition of Mahan's *The Influence of Sea Power* with a fold-out map of the Asia-Pacific that included all the U.S. naval facilities in the region. James Holmes and Toshi Yoshihara, two American historians who have tracked Mahan's influence in China, write: "His sea power philosophy remains hypnotic. . . . The Mahanian conceit that national greatness derives from sea power beguiles many Chinese strategists." As a result, they conclude: "We should therefore expect China to attach extraordinary value to fighting and winning in the waters that fall within the near-seas."

The U.S. and China have already indulged in some potentially dangerous sparring in the Near Seas—the sort of thing that in the Cold War was known as "nautical chicken." In March 2009, the USNS *Impeccable*, a surveillance ship, was on an operation around seventy nautical miles from the new submarine base in Hainan when it was confronted by a flotilla of ten different Chinese ships. The Chinese crew dropped planks into the water to obstruct the American ship's movements. When it braked, the Chinese sailors then used long poles to smash the surveillance instruments it was towing behind the ship. As the American ship retreated from the area, it was shadowed and harassed for some time. When the Chinese ships decided to take their leave, the crew of one boat dropped their pants and waved their bare bottoms in the direction of the Americans.

The confrontation was significant not just because of the risk that it might have escalated, but because it amplified one of the big underlying political issues in the western Pacific. China's new naval capabilities are interlaced with a broader political strategy designed to exert more control over its maritime reaches. Beijing's most extravagant claim is in the South China Sea, where a series of islets, reefs, and rocks are disputed by a number of countries, including Vietnam, the Philippines, and China. Beijing argues it has a historical right to be the dominant power in the area, a claim expressed in China's now famous "nine-dash-line" map, which assumes ownership of 80 to 90 percent of the South China Sea. (Chapter 3 will have a more detailed discussion of some of these disputes.) At the same time, China is pushing a version of international law which would potentially give it the right to exclude foreign militaries from large sections of the seas that surround it. A United Nations convention called the Law of the Sea tries to codify rules for national ownership of the world's oceans. The law gives countries an "exclusive economic zone"—or EEZ—that runs two hundred nautical miles from their coastline, where they have the rights to resources in the water or under the seabed. According to the U.S.—and a majority of other governments—there is a right to freedom of navigation in this zone that includes military vessels. However, China is the leading member of a smaller but significant group of countries which think that foreign militaries should be excluded from their EEZ unless they have permission. In particular, China objects to surveillance vessels operating too near to its coast, just as the U.S.'s *Impeccable* was doing.

Taken together, the two claims have huge implications. China argues that many of the islands in the South China Sea qualify to have their own exclusive economic zones, even though some are no more than largely submerged rocks and many are administered by other countries. As a result, China argues that most of the South China Sea is part of its exclusive economic zone. If it takes control of all the islands, and if its legal interpretation of the Law of the Sea stands, China would be giving itself the political case to turn away the vessels of foreign navies from most of the South China Sea. Given the centrality of the sea to the global economy, this is a far-reaching claim that has enormous implications for everyone in the region—and especially for the United States. Although China's ultimate aims are still not entirely clear, the evidence of growing ambitions is unnerving the U.S. military. "China is knowingly, operationally and incrementally seizing maritime rights of its neighbors under the rubric of a maritime history that is not only contested in the international community but has largely been fabricated," Captain James Fanell, deputy chief of staff for intelligence for the U.S. Pacific Fleet told a conference in 2013. He described an intelligence briefing he attends every morning at 6 a.m. which brings together the U.S. military's leading Asia-Pacific analysts. "Every day it is about China," he said, adding: "They are taking control of maritime areas that have never before been administered or controlled in the last 5,000 years by any regime called 'China.' . . . China's conduct is destabilizing the Asian maritime environment."

Even with these claims, it might seem improbable that China would seek to tamper with the right to freedom of navigation. China has been an enormous beneficiary of open seas; its economy is based on the free flow of imported raw materials into the country and the export of manufactured products. The assumption among many governments in the region had always been that, even if China would defend its territorial claims fiercely, it would not let those political disputes contaminate its booming commercial links with the rest of the region. Few worried that China would use its growing power to act as a toll keeper of naval traffic in the western Pacific.

Yet confidence in such an assumption is gradually beginning to weaken. Over the last few years, China has shown a willingness to use a form of economic blackmail and bullying during political disputes that raises real questions about how it would behave if it were ever to control the sea-lanes through the South China Sea. During a standoff with Tokyo in 2010, after the Japanese coast guard arrested a Chinese fisherman who had rammed one of its vessels in disputed waters, China limited exports to Japan of rare earths—a group of commodities which China controls and which are central to the manufacture of many products, such as cell phones. When ships from China and the Philippines clashed in 2012 over control of a small island in the South China Sea, Beijing refused to accept imports of bananas from the Philippines, leaving large shipments to rot in a harbor. The local government on Hainan Island has declared it has the power to board vessels which "illegally enter" Chinese waters—one in a string of announcements that have added to the sense of uncertainty about how China will use its growing power. The expansive and ambiguous claims China has made in the South China Sea, combined with its willingness to hold trade hostage to political arguments, have, at the very least, raised questions about freedom of navigation in the region. As Peter Dutton, a U.S. expert on maritime law, argues, China's approach to the Near Seas has already created "hairline fractures in the global order."

Shortly before he retired as head of the U.S. Pacific Command in 2009, Admiral Timothy Keating revealed a conversation he had had with a senior Chinese naval officer, who effectively offered to split the Pacific with the U.S. "You, the US, take Hawaii East and we, China, will take Hawaii West and the Indian Ocean," Keating recalled the officer, whom he refused to name, as saying. "Then you will not need to come to the western Pacific and the Indian Ocean and we will not need to go to the eastern Pacific. If anything happens there, you can let us know and if something happens here, we will let you know." Keating admitted that the offer was perhaps made "tongue-in-cheek," but it was revealing. One reason that tensions in the region are rising is the substantial gap between U.S. and Chinese views of America's natural role in Asia. For many in China, a U.S. retreat from the region is an inevitable response to the revival of Asia. Yet the view is very different from Washington. Since the early years of the republic, the western Pacific has played a large role in America's sense of its own security.

America's first Pacific alliance was signed as far back as 1833, a full two decades before Commodore Matthew Perry more famously first set anchor in Japan. President Andrew Jackson sent a sloop-of-war called the USS *Peacock* on a mission around parts of the South China Sea, including a stop at the kingdom of Siam, modern-day Thailand. During the visit, his envoy, Edmund Roberts, signed the Siamese-American Treaty of Amity and Commerce with a representative of King Rama III. Jackson sent as a present a sword whose gold handle had an elephant and an eagle emblazoned on it. The pool of people at the time in either country who spoke both Siamese and English was almost nonexistent, so, in order to make sure the treaty would not be questioned, it was also translated into Chinese and Portuguese.

The prominence of the Pacific in the American mind accelerated sharply in the 1890s, in the era of Mahan and another of his disciples, Theodore Roosevelt, who a century before Barack Obama was really America's first Pacific president. Roosevelt was the first to predict that Asia would become a center of global power, initially as a result of the rise of Japan, but later as China and India caught up. And he placed the maintenance of a favorable balance of power in Asia at the center of America's priorities. "The commerce and command of the Pacific will be factors of incalculable moment in the world's history," Roosevelt predicted.

America's Pacific role did not fall temporarily into its lap at the end of the Second World War and the decline of the British Empire, nor is it a product of the Cold War. Instead, it is much more deeply rooted in the U.S.'s own history and vision of the world. Over the last century, America has defined its vital interest as preventing any one power from dominating the other main regions of the world and turning them into a private sphere of influence, whether in Europe or in Asia. The U.S. eventually fought the First and Second World Wars because it did not want Germany to dominate Europe—and, in the second war, also to stop Japan from controlling Asia. Washington's ultimate goal in the Cold War was to prevent the Soviet Union from exercising control across the whole of Eurasia.

It should come as no surprise that the rise of China is beginning to stir something deep in the American psyche. Relative decline or not, Washington will be determined to prevent any other country from dominating such a central part of the world. China's naval push strikes to the core of how America understands both its security and its prosperity. The Obama administration's desire to "pivot" toward Asia, as the wars in Iraq and Afghanistan end, might seem like a new departure to address the rise of China, but it is also a very traditional American response to a shifting balance of power in Asia. Unless America suffers a much deeper economic collapse, it is difficult to imagine the U.S.'s not wanting to play a significant role in Asia in the coming decades. Washington was never going to acquiesce in a proposal to split the Pacific. "If the U.S. does not hold its ground in the Pacific, it cannot be a world leader," as Lee Kuan Yew, the former Singaporean leader, puts it in a cold assessment of the political stakes. "The 21st century will be a contest for supremacy in the Pacific because that is where the growth will be."

WEAK PARTY, STRONG MILITARY

Robert Gates was about to go into a meeting with President Hu Jintao when one of his aides showed him some images that had just appeared on a Chinese Web site that specializes in military gossip. It was January 2011, and the U.S. defense secretary had traveled to Beijing to try and mend fences after China had suspended military contacts between the two countries' militaries in protest of U.S. arms sales to Taiwan. The photos purported to show a test flight for the J-20, China's attempt to develop a "fifth generation" stealth bomber that can evade conventional radar. "It's flying!" wrote an Internet user with the name Little Bird King in one of the chat rooms for military issues run by the *People's Daily* group, publisher of the party's mouthpiece newspaper. A large crowd of onlookers watched the test run from outside the fence at a military airfield in Chengdu, some standing on the back of a white pickup truck to get a better view. For Gates, the timing seemed a deliberate insult: the Chinese military were rubbing his nose in one of their new high-tech capabilities.

The photos were a particular embarrassment to Gates, who had publicly dismissed the idea of a Chinese stealth bomber only two years earlier. China would have "no fifth-generation aircraft by 2020," he had told an audience in Chicago. Most American observers thought that China's jets were mediocre copies of old Russian models. A month earlier some grainy photos had appeared on another Chinese military-fan Web site showing the J-20 being pulled out on the Chengdu airfield. Soon after, the photos reappeared on the Aviation Week Web site in the U.S., after blogger Bill Sweetman posted them at 7:30 a.m. on Christmas Day and talked about rumors of a test flight. Yet the Pentagon did not believe the new Chinese jet fighter was ready to fly.

Gates was so angry that he suggested canceling the meeting with Hu Jintao, only to be persuaded to attend by Jon Huntsman, then the U.S. ambassador to Beijing. When Gates asked Hu about the test flight, he was greeted with a nervous silence. The president appeared to know nothing about it. They were seated in one of those U-shaped Chinese meeting rooms, with the principals at the top and a line of their aides on either side. Hu asked his defense minister, Liang Guanglie, who in turn asked the PLA's deputy chief of staff, Ma Xiaotian. No one seemed to know what had actually happened. Eventually, an air-force officer explained that the test flight of the stealth bomber had taken place by coincidence on that day. "I take President Hu at his word that the test had nothing to do with my visit," Gates said rather curtly after the meeting.

Sometimes an uncomfortable silence can tell you as much about a political system as a library full of theses. At the very least, Hu's reticence showed a lack of day-to-day coordination between the PLA and its political masters. Whenever a major U.S. naval vessel passes into the Asia-Pacific Region, the Asia director at the National Security Council receives a written note, so that the White House is not blindsided by activities of the Pentagon. China lacks such a coordinating mechanism. Yet it is equally possible that elements of the PLA were intending to send Gates precisely the message that he had imagined, and that the test flight was held on that day as a deliberate provocation. The Chengdu airfield has two landing strips—one far away from view and one visible from a public road. The test flight used the second runway, and when it was completed, the aircraft was parked beside the road, so that local military enthusiasts could take more pictures. In the past, China's pervasive Internet censors have taken down images of new military technologies they do not want the world to see. This time, they let the photos remain. Andrew Scobell, an analyst with the Rand Corporation, later told a congressional hearing that the message from the test flight was: "America, take heed. The capabilities of our weaponry are ever improving, and we are not intimidated by your technologically superior military might." If sending such a signal to the U.S. also caused a moment of acute diplomatic embarrassment for the country's president, then so be it.

———

One of the ironies about Deng Xiaoping's advice to "hide the brightness and nourish obscurity" is that it requires a decisive figure like Deng to implement. Playing nice with the neighbors involves making the sorts of concessions that can gall nationalists. It needs a strong leader who has the credibility to take a few blows on the chin, and who can face down the more ambitious and nationalistic of his colleagues, especially from the military. Yet Deng also made sure that China would never have such a strongman again. After the quixotic disasters of the Mao era, the Communist Party has gone out of its way to reduce the space for another all-powerful leader. The party now has a fixed retirement age, and an entrenched process of leadership transitions that take place every decade (with some housecleaning every five years). The upside is that the party is much more predictable and professional. The downside is that it is now governed by committee, which can slow decision making and can make it much harder for the leadership to stand up to more strident voices. Over the last decade, China has seen a fracturing of power among the elite, with different vested interests from within the party-state starting to push their own foreign-policy agendas more openly and more aggressively. Cheng Li, a Chinese political scientist now at the Brookings Institution in Washington, uses three couplets to capture the new dynamic of power in China. "Weak leaders, strong factions; weak government, strong interest groups; weak party, strong country," as he puts it.

China's determined push to the seas is a product of its history and geography, to be sure, but it is also being driven by these shifts within the Chinese political system as more voices start to be heard. China's leaders no longer enjoy the unquestioned authority over foreign policy that Deng was able to command. The cautious elite consensus on how to manage the country's rise is gradually being undermined in favor of a more strident defense of national interests and a greater willingness to ruffle international feathers. The Foreign Ministry should be in charge of international relations but is actually the weakest ministry in Beijing, outgunned and out-politicked by other influential groups. Not one foreign-policy official is a member of the twenty-five-strong Communist Party Politburo. Like new great powers before it, China is finding that success creates its own expectations. China's leaders now have to deal with the often raucous Internet nationalism of the urban middle class, which has been reared on stories about the "hundred years of humiliation." The wealthier these urban professionals become, the more impatient they are for China's leaders to assert a bigger role. Local governments and powerful state-owned companies want to have a say on important foreign-policy issues. And the civilian leaders also have to deal with a more restless and powerful military.

If there is one subject that is the hardest for foreign China-watchers to get a handle on, it is the relationship between the Communist Party and the military. Despite the breathtaking changes in Chinese society over the last three decades, high-level politics are still a black box, and that is even more the case for the People's Liberation Army. The military is formally under control of the Communist Party rather than the state, which adds to its sense of mystery and autonomy. To most outside observers, and to many Chinese, the PLA seems like a separate world walled off from the rest of the party-state. The very brief glimpses into the PLA afforded to the foreign media confirm that sense of an institution following its own rules. In 2008, one of my colleagues managed to organize an interview with a senior PLA official. We were instructed to come to the PLA's foreign-affairs office, north of the city center, an airy, palatial building with marble floors and long, empty corridors. As a journalist in China, you can tell a lot about a government official by the way he or she conducts an interview. Most government departments insist that you send over half a dozen sample questions beforehand, and they will reject an interview request if the topics are too controversial. The less secure the cadre, the longer they spend on the initial softball questions. I have conducted interviews in which the official in question proceeded to read out a twenty-five-page prepared answer to these questions, leaving only a few minutes for a real interview at the end. Major General Qian Lihua, director of the defense ministry's foreign-affairs office, walked into the conference room where my colleagues and I were waiting and shook our hands. He picked up a paper that one of his aides had prepared and handed it to us. "This is a written response for the questions you sent over," he said. "Now, what do you really want to ask me?" He went on to give the strongest indication yet that China was building an aircraft carrier. "The navy of any great power . . . has the dream to have one or more aircraft carriers," he said.

Like many of the party leaders of his generation, Deng was himself a veteran of the Communist Party's war against the Nationalists and the Long March. Not only did he have strong personal relationships with the military top brass when he assumed power, but they also had a sense of shared sacrifice in defense of the party. Over the last couple of decades, however, the party and the military have taken different paths. The party has become dominated by trained bureaucrats who have worked their way up the system, spending decades in provincial jobs learning the ropes. The new military leaders are also cut from a different cloth. Rather than party ideologues well schooled in the texts of Marxism-Leninism, they are now professional soldiers who are focused on honing their new skills. The PLA has less influence over domestic politics than it used to enjoy but, at the same time, the party is much less directly involved in the PLA than it once was. The PLA political commissars, who once enforced political orthodoxy among the rank and file, are now much more focused on boosting morale—one Chinese observer likens them to the equivalent of chaplains in a Western army. As Marxism has withered as a guiding force, the military has also developed a stronger sense of its role as a defender of the national interest. China now has a professional officer class with a slightly Prussian air, which is proud of the new capabilities at its disposal and was reared on a worldview that sees China as a powerful and strong nation.

The most dangerous situation would be if a few "rogue generals" started to freelance, using the perceived weakness of civilian leaders to push their own agenda outside of the formal policy process. That would be a large red-flag warning about looming future instability in China's relations with the rest of the world. Most informed observers of China's military believe that this is far from the case, and that the Communist Party leadership still remains firmly in control of the military. But every now and then, there are tantalizing glimpses of a restless military that is occasionally willing to push the boundaries. The test flight of the J-20 on the day Robert Gates was in town was one such case. Another incident happened in 2007, when China used a land-based missile to blow a weather satellite out of space. The test was a wake-up call for foreign militaries, a warning shot about China's cyberwar capabilities. Just as illuminating was the way the test was discovered. With no word coming from the Chinese government, the story first appeared in a U.S. magazine, which was probably tipped off by U.S. or other Western intelligence agencies. And even when the news did break, the Foreign Ministry gave the impression that it had been left completely in the dark by the military.

These little glimpses of the interactions between the PLA and the party suggest an occasionally confrontational streak, but they do not indicate a stark split. The real influence that the PLA is starting to have is more subtle, the result not of open lobbying but from the drip-feed effect of a military worldview that is both intensely proud of China and deeply skeptical about the U.S. military. It is this tide of hawkish views that is helping to gradually chip away at Deng's call for self-restraint. By exposing big shifts in relative power that have taken place between the U.S. and China, the financial crisis encouraged some in China to believe that the time was theirs. Hu Jintao had few connections with the military before he became president in 2002, and Chinese academics and officials who attend regular foreign-policy gatherings with military officials would describe the openness with which Hu was criticized— something that would have been unthinkable only a few years earlier. One leading academic told me of a discussion with some of his military counterparts in which Hu had been attacked by name for being soft on Japan. "Arrogant people with a lot of ego," the academic described them.

I got the full force of this worldview when I went to visit Senior Colonel Liu Mingfu. I wanted to meet Liu because a few months earlier he had caused something of a sensation when he published his first book, *China Dream*, a nationalist tract that called for the country to build a military force to rival and compete with the U.S. In his book he argued that the U.S. and China were embarking on a "marathon contest" for global leadership. Having spared no efforts to contain the rise of the Soviet Union and Japan, Liu argued that the U.S. would "fight a third battle to retain its title" against China. His book became a best seller both on the mainland and in Hong Kong. One large Chinese newspaper ran serializations of *China Dream* for a whole month. Yanghe, a company which makes one of the country's best-known brands of liquor, ordered ten thousand copies to give to its clients. "The chairman described it as a textbook for patriotism," Liu told me, not a little immodestly.

Liu lives in a complex of residential buildings reserved for military personnel, just along the road from the Defense Ministry's huge build-ing in central Beijing. Foreigners are not supposed to enter the com-pound, he said on the phone, so I should wear a woolly hat and keep my head down when passing through the gate. In the end, the car drove in without any problems at all, the guard airily waving us through. Inside the compound, there were few signs of insecurity, but plenty of esprit de corps. There was a well-tended running track, and a theater that put on shows of revolutionary songs at the weekends. It was midmorning, and the exercise area was full of pensioners doing stretches on a series of yellow machines. A lithe fifty-year-old with dyed black hair and the rank of a senior colonel, Liu now teaches at the National Defense University, where he gives lectures on Marxist theory and U.S.-China relations. Liu said that on the very day he launched his book, in 2010, Barack Obama gave a speech saying that the U.S. would never be number two in the world. "It was such a coincidence. As an ordinary military man, I argue loudly that China should try to be the number one, should race to be the champion country," Liu said.

A few months before we talked, a Chinese admiral called Yuan Youfei had caused a good deal of consternation at a high-profile U.S.-China summit when he launched into a long diatribe attacking the "hegemonic" U.S. According to American officials present, Yuan accused Washington of plotting to encircle China and treating Beijing as an enemy. Liu Mingfu said he agreed entirely with Yuan's analysis. For Liu, the Chinese leadership faces a stark choice: either China develops the military capacity to challenge the U.S., or it will be forever bullied by its larger rival. "For China, a runner-up who does not want to be a champion is not a good runner-up," he told me. "But the U.S. wants a mini-NATO to contain China." As we talked in his flat, his wife sat next to him, eating sunflower seeds from a plastic bag and nodding vigorously every time he made a forceful point. A few weeks before, Bill Gates and Warren Buffett had visited Beijing to encourage Chinese entrepreneurs to do more for charity. "Chinese people enjoyed seeing the civilization of Gates and Buffett. America should send more cultural and peaceful ambassadors like that," Liu told me. "But, instead, the American aircraft carriers make 1.3 billion Chinese people see America's hegemony and barbarism." As I was leaving, he gripped my hand firmly. "You British are reasonable people; Germans are very reasonable," he said. "But the Americans?"

Since the first Gulf War, in the early nineties, America has developed a battalion of "TV generals," retired members of the military who provide expert commentary on military operations and, every now and then, slip in a hawkish criticism of the commander-in-chief. In the last few years, something similar has started to happen in China. A small group of media-friendly members of the armed forces have begun to talk openly about their views on military matters, including their mistrust of and distaste for the U.S. military and its policies in Asia. Dai Xu, a colonel in the air force, writes regular articles and appears on television to criticize U.S. efforts to contain China. "If the U.S. can light a fire in China's backyard, we can also light a fire in their backyard," he wrote in 2010. In some ways, Senior Colonel Liu Mingfu is the latest addition to their numbers. The question that remained unanswered during our conversation was whether Liu's brand of saber rattling was a minority position, or if he was reflecting broader views about the U.S. among the armed services that are starting to influence the politicians. Liu is not in active service and is not involved in developing Chinese military strategy. The sort of crude and hard-line views that he puts forward are, therefore, by no means official policy, although *China Dream* did have a foreword written by Lieutenant General Liu Yazhou, the son-in-law of a former Chinese president and a close adviser of Xi Jinping, China's new president.

Many experts on China's military warn against seeing the PLA as a unified bastion of anti-Americanism. They say that the PLA, like so many institutions in China these days, is full of people who have substantial direct experience of the U.S. Indeed, the children of a few senior military figures are believed to have attended university in the U.S. They also have huge admiration for the operational skills and technology of the U.S. military. Others are less sanguine. A few days after I met Liu, I asked Chu Shulong what to make of Liu Mingfu and the other hawkish, military pundits. Chu spent eight years in the PLA before becoming an academic at Peking University, and so speaks from some experience. "These scholars at military institutions have little contact with the real military leaders. They are giving their personal opinions, but they in no way represent the Central Military Commission [the body that runs the armed forces]," he told me. "The real military are much more hard-line than these scholars. They are even more hostile and suspicious of the U.S."

Every now and again, that resentment toward the U.S. leaks out into the open. In 2010, recently retired admiral Hu Yanlin, who had been the navy's chief political commissar and a close adviser to the top commander Wu Shengli, described the U.S. as "the fundamental anti-Chinese force." Talking about the South China Sea, he added that the U.S. "may seek to precipitate a crisis, hoping the internal difficulties would facilitate foreign aggression or that foreign aggression could cause internal anxiety."

The PLA does not dictate policy to its civilian masters, but it does help shape the atmosphere in which policy is made. The nationalist rhetoric and skepticism of the U.S. that are central to the PLA's worldview are slowly leaking into the policy process. Over the last decade, a weaker civilian leadership has found it harder to push back against hawkish voices in the military. All of which makes the personality and background of China's new president so interesting and important. Unlike his predecessor, Xi Jinping is steeped in Chinese military tradition. His father, Xi Zhongxun, was a central figure in the Communist Party war with the Nationalists in the 1930s, organizing a guerrilla base in Yan'an, in northeast central China, that later provided refuge for Mao Zedong. When the younger Xi left university in the late 1970s, his first job was as *mishu*, a sort of personal assistant, to Defense Minister Geng Biao, who was a friend of his father's. Xi proudly wore a military uniform to the office every day. His wife, Peng Liyuan, is a popular folksinger who is attached to the army's song-and-dance troupe. She holds the rank of major general, and until her husband became a senior leader, she was a regular in the huge television spectacle that airs every year on the eve of the New Year holiday. More recently, a photo has reappeared showing her singing to soldiers in Tiananmen Square in the days following the bloody suppression of the 1989 democracy protests.

In some ways, the military is part of his political support base. In two decades as a provincial official, Xi was known as a "military hugger" for his efforts to help the troops stationed in his area, giving them privileged access to amusement parks and festivals, and appearing regularly at military parades. Such a background could give Xi more credibility to stand up to some of the more restive generals. He will have a personal authority in their company that Hu Jintao always lacked. But it could also make him more sympathetic to their nationalist worldview.

In the years during which he was preparing to take the top job, his most famous comments were a rant he gave at a 2009 dinner of Chinese expatriates in Mexico City, in which he warned, "There are a few foreigners, with full bellies, who have nothing better to do than try to point fingers at our country." One of the central questions in China over the next decade will be whether Xi's core instinct is to control the military, or to channel its views. A more natural leader than his predecessor, Xi could be less intimidated by hawkish voices. Yet his early statements have been full of nationalist echoes, and some analysts believe he is relying on the military to consolidate its position. In a speech he gave aboard the destroyer *Haikou,* which patrols the South China Sea, shortly after assuming power, he expanded on his new slogan about promoting a "Chinese dream." "The dream can be said to be the dream of a strong nation and for the military, it is the dream of a strong military," he said. "We must achieve the great revival of the Chinese nation and we must ensure there is unison between a prosperous country and a strong military."

ASSASSIN'S MACE

Long before *Diamonds Are Forever* started playing on my China Southern flight back to Beijing, it had been hard to shake the slightly James Bond feel about Yalong Bay. If you stand on the beach at the Sanya Sheraton and look out to sea, and if the light is not too hazy, you can just about make out a headland to the southeast of the bay. What the eye cannot detect is the large underground submarine base that lies on the other side of the headland. First revealed in satellite photos published in 2008 by U.S. scientists, the images showed the cavelike holes which are the entrances for the submarines. The tunnels give way to a large harbor carved deep into the rock to protect the subs from bombing raids. The underwater base has the Chinese navy's only demagnetizing facility, which makes it much harder for the submarines to be detected. The disclosures about the Sanya submarine base form part of a relentless trend over the last decade, during which observers have been continuously surprised by the technical sophistication of China's military modernization. China has managed to catch a lot of people by surprise.

After touring the U.S. in 1890, Oscar Wilde had one of his characters react with surprise at being told that the U.S. had no ruins or curiosities. "No ruins, no curiosities!" the Canterville Ghost replied. "You have your navy and your manners." For sophisticated subjects of the British Empire, the American navy was an obvious punch line at that time. Yet, by the end of the decade, one in which the U.S. invested heavily in its navy under the influence of Teddy Roosevelt and Captain Mahan, the U.S. had roundly defeated Spain in battles in Cuba and the Philippines, sending an unambiguous message to the world about its new maritime power. As recently as a decade ago, China's navy suffered the same sort of condescension. The 1990 edition of *Jane's Fighting Ships*, a sort of annual bible of the world's navies, described the PLAN as "technically backward and operationally immature." In 1996, three Chinese warships made a goodwill port call in San Diego. American officials who visited the ships noticed that the interior walls were made of plywood, which made them not only flimsy but also a fire risk. The Chinese military was considered so primitive that some American strategists joked that its battle plan for taking control of Taiwan was "a million-man swim."

No one in Washington or any other Asian capital is making the same jokes now. If China's newfound instinct to challenge the U.S. in the Near Seas is rooted in its history, its expanding economic interests, and the restlessness of some of its officer corps, there is also one final and equally important component—it now has the military capabilities to start making a difference. China is starting to push back against the U.S. in part because it can. After two decades of double-digit increases in military spending, China now has the second-largest defense budget in the world, after the U.S. While the U.S. has been fighting a losing battle in Afghanistan for over a decade and pouring more than a trillion dollars into the debacle in Iraq, China has been carefully conducting the biggest military expansion in the world. Of course, China's budget is still much smaller than that of the U.S., which spends almost as much as the rest of the world combined on defense, and which will remain the most sophisticated military power for some time. But China has no intention of challenging the U.S. around the globe over the coming decades. It has no interest in establishing a serious naval presence in the Caribbean, for instance, or posting soldiers in continental Europe. Instead, it is focused on Asia.

With these more limited aims, China is catching up quickly with the U.S. By some estimates, China will have a bigger fleet than the U.S. by the end of this decade, and it already has more submarines. Although it is always dangerous to make straight-line predictions based on existing reality, if China continues with its current rate of increase in military spending, it will have a bigger defense budget than the U.S. by 2025, according to the International Institute for Strategic Studies. Yet China does not need to match the U.S. dollar for dollar in order to achieve its goals: it only needs to spend enough to change the strategic balance in the western Pacific. Chinese strategists talk about "asymmetric" warfare, tactics and tools that can allow a weaker and smaller country to inflict huge damage on a bigger rival. China is not preparing for a war with the U.S. Indeed, the goal is to secure Beijing's political aims without ever firing in anger. Instead, its military buildup is designed to gradually change the calculations of American commanders, to dissuade them from considering military operations anywhere near China's coast, and to push them slowly farther out into the Pacific.

"We do not need to be in such a hurry," Deng Xiaoping told a Central Military Commission meeting in March 1979. Deng was responding to pressure from his military colleagues for a big increase in spending on new weapons. It was a message he found himself repeating for the next decade, at meeting after meeting. China's economic boom did not immediately lead to a rapid military buildup. Though the PLA wanted to invest, Deng insisted that building up the domestic economy would come first; the military would need to show some patience. During the 1980s, the Chinese government actually decreased the proportion of the budget that was destined for military spending. "Deng had to explain over and over again to disappointed officers why it was in the national interest first to develop the civilian economy and then to modernize the military," notes Ezra Vogel, author of an authoritative biography on the Chinese leader. "Deng was probably the only leader of his time with the authority, determination and political skill to keep these officers from launching serious protests against this policy."

But over time, patience wore thin, and the military has started to receive the sorts of resources that it had long been clamoring for. After Deng was forced to call up units of the PLA from outside of Beijing to fire on the Tiananmen protesters in 1989, spending on the military started to increase, including salaries and housing. If Tiananmen was a key turning point, another was the first Gulf War, in 1990–91. The campaign to push Iraq from Kuwait had a profound psychological impact among the Chinese leadership. Watching the images of destruction on their televisions, Chinese military officials were acutely aware of both their own limitations and the vast technological superiority of the U.S.

At the start of the naval buildup, Taiwan was the primary focus. China wanted to have sufficient forces to take control of the island if it ever tried to declare independence formally, and to prevent any other power from intervening in a conflict if it did break out. In the early days of the People's Republic, almost all the viable ships were given to the northern and eastern fleets, which operate near Taiwan, while the southern fleet was considered a poor cousin. Taiwan remains a priority, but over time, the scope of China's naval ambitions has expanded. One of the reasons the opening of the new naval base on Hainan Island was so significant was that it demonstrated the new priorities of China's naval push, the ability to project power not just east, toward Taiwan, but also down into the South China Sea and beyond.

"Since no nation threatens China, one wonders: Why this growing investment? Why these continuing large and expanding arms purchases? Why these continuing robust deployments?" The questions were raised by Donald Rumsfeld in 2005, when the then defense secretary was visiting Singapore for a conference. Iraq was still engulfed with violence at that time, and his comments seemed another exercise in neocon scaremongering. But nearly a decade later, the questions have not gone away. The uncomfortable truth is that China's military investments are focused largely on the United States' presence in the region. There should be little surprise that an aspiring great power would choose to invest more in its military as its interests and power expands. Yet China is not investing in the sort of navy that could be used for policing the world's sea-lanes for pirates and terrorists. Instead, its principal target is the U.S. Navy. According to Dennis Blair, the retired admiral who was head of the U.S. intelligence services early in the Obama administration: "Ninety percent of their time is spent on thinking about new and interesting ways to sink our ships and shoot down our planes."

American strategists sometimes talk about a Chinese "anti-navy"— a series of weapons, some based on land, some at sea, which are specifically designed to keep an opposing navy as far away as possible from the mainland. China has a large and growing fleet of submarines, including nuclear-powered vessels and a group of Russia-supplied diesel submarines which are quiet and hard to detect. It is developing two different versions of stealth fighter jets (including the airplane that was tested the day Robert Gates was in Beijing), as well as its own unmanned drones that can deploy missiles. The navy is developing a new type of destroyer battleship which will have some of the missile defense capabilities of American Aegis ships.

Pride of place in the anti-navy, however, goes to the Second Artillery Force, which operates most of the more than one thousand missiles that China has built up over the last two decades. There are missiles that can take out facilities on land, missiles for targeting satellites, and missiles for attacking ships. One technology in particular has attracted a lot of attention. China has invested heavily in a new generation of so-called carrier-killer missiles, designed to destroy aircraft carriers at sea. Larry Wortzel, a former American military attaché in Beijing, recalls a jocular warning he once received at a diplomatic reception. A Chinese officer put his arm around Wortzel's shoulder and said, "We are going to sink your carriers with ballistic missiles." The missiles, which supposedly cannot be detected by radar, have a range of fifteen hundred to two thousand kilometers. They are the modern equivalent of an "assassin's mace," the weapons used in Chinese historical novels that can undermine a technologically superior enemy. The implicit threat is that commanders of American aircraft carriers would have to think carefully about operating anywhere within that radius from the Chinese coast—a fundamental challenge to the way America projects military power in the region. It is the first weapons system since the end of the Cold War that both is potentially capable of stopping American naval-power projection and was specifically designed for that purpose. The strategy also represents good economics. Each of its carrier-killer missiles cost around $11 million; a new aircraft carrier now costs $13.5 billion.

With any new, untried weapons, there is always an open question as to whether it will actually work. The carrier-killer missile is no exception. Hitting a moving ship at long distance is an incredibly difficult task. The U.S. Navy would have plenty of options to defend its carriers, such as shooting the missile down with Aegis missile-defense cruisers, or trying to jam the "seeker" technology that missiles deploy when they get near a target. Yet American commanders cannot guarantee that their defenses will work. "We want to spoof them, preclude detection, jam them, shoot them down if possible, get them to termination, confuse them," Admiral Jonathan Greenert, chief of U.S. naval operations, once said on being asked about the Chinese carrier-killer missiles. Can they be jammed? "Yes, no, maybe so?" he said.

The carrier killer is a technology whose potency will become apparent over the next decade. A more immediate threat comes from another innovation that has started to attract a lot of attention in Washington—China's growing fleet of fast, mobile patrol craft that carry cruise missiles designed to attack ships. This is another technology that fits the pattern of fighting "asymmetric" warfare against U.S. carrier groups operating near the Chinese coast. These patrol craft use a catamaran hull that was initially designed in Australia for passenger ferries, but which allows the attack craft to skim across waves at high speed. The Houbei-class vessels, as they are called, also copy many of the same features as stealth fighter jets, such as windows with jagged edges and a sloped hull, which help it avoid detection by radar. The Chinese fleet now has around sixty of these catamaran craft, and each vessel carries eight anti-ship missiles. Chinese strategists describe them being used in "wolf pack" operations, in which they can swarm a target group of vessels, attacking in numbers from different directions. Their limited fuel tanks mean that they cannot operate at long distances from the mainland, but they could be very effective in any exchange nearer to the Chinese coast.

The other string of China's "asymmetric" fighting capabilities is cyber- and space warfare. Whereas Chinese hacking of commercial secrets has won a huge amount of attention in the U.S., the potential use of cyberattacks during a conflict is less discussed. This could include attacks on infrastructure in the U.S., designed to inflict damage on the economy, but it could also involve attacking the information systems that the U.S. Air Force and Navy rely on. By taking out U.S. satellites, China could hamper the ability of U.S. fighter jets to operate effectively.

China's navy still has many weaknesses, including the inexperience of its sailors in combat conditions. But the era of the "million-man swim" is long gone. China is quickly acquiring the capabilities to start challenging U.S. power projection in the western Pacific. In the process, the U.S. and China are embarking on an epic tussle for who will have the upper hand in the Near Seas. How that contest plays out will depend on three factors, which we will see in the next chapters. It will depend on how the rest of Asia reacts to China's new ambitions, and on how America responds to the challenge, too. But it will also be heavily influenced by what China tries to do with its new navy in areas far away from its coastal waters. The rivalry between the U.S. and China in the western Pacific will be shaped partly by how China decides to approach the Indian Ocean.

2

The Lure of the Indian Ocean

YOU DID NOT BRING any hundred-dollar notes?" the Yangon bank teller asked. There are all sorts of signs of just how detached Burma has become from the modern world after decades of sanctions and military-led incompetence, but the simple things are the most striking. Burma is one of the few countries in the world where visitors need to take large wads of dollar bills if they want to buy local currency. Forget ATMs; even travelers' checks have passed it by. I handed the teller a collection of $20 notes I had withdrawn shortly before leaving the U.S. She scoured each note carefully, sometimes taking several seconds at a time, handing back any that were marked or even slightly frayed with a polite "tut," as if I had been trying to cheat her. A few days later, as we were driving along rickety back roads on Burma's Indian Ocean coast, the sense of stagnation was even harder to ignore. The poorer houses still had thatched roofs, and in some cases the walls were thatched, too. In many of the villages we passed through, the market consisted of a few piles of bananas and coconuts laid out on plastic sheets on the ground, alongside a few consumer basics. There were very few other cars and only a handful of motorbikes, the road being mostly occupied by bicycles and bike-rickshaws. The buzzing metropolis of Bangkok was just one hour's flight away, and within three hours you could be in Singapore, whose vapid but impressive modernity is an unforgiving benchmark for just how far Burma has fallen behind.

Such a powerful sense of being stuck in time can also have its own allure, of course. The main road threaded through dense forest, but after a while weaved back to the coast. We passed golden beaches backed by palm trees and bougainvillea, empty but for the driftwood left by the tide. The monsoon had already passed through this part of the country, and there was a cool breeze off the Bay of Bengal. A century earlier, Rudyard Kipling wrote part of *The Jungle Book* at a resort just a bit farther south. At the time, both India and Burma were part of the British Empire, and the coast was a popular vacation spot for the Calcutta imperial class, just across the other side of the Bay of Bengal. It probably had not changed much since then.

After several hours of driving north, we came to a vast clearing that had been cut out of undulating forest and vegetation. The sense of timelessness ended with an abrupt shock. An area of several square kilometers had been surrounded by high fences, but there were plenty of telltale signs about what lay behind the locked gates. In the distance were a series of large tubular metal tanks suitable for storing oil. I counted three large red cranes of the type that I had seen on countless construction sites in China. The real clincher was in one corner of the site, where there were several long lines of portable buildings, their white walls and blue roofs marking them out as the dormitories for construction workers, some of whom I could make out in the distance by their orange hard hats. For anyone who had spent time on mainland China, these were the unmistakable sights and sounds of industrial development with Chinese characteristics.

We had arrived at Ramree Island, an isolated peninsula on the north of Burma's Indian Ocean coast, which is quietly becoming one of the geopolitical hot spots of the twenty-first century. The fenced-off construction site I was able to glimpse is part of the single most ambitious overseas project that China has yet undertaken. Ramree boasts a natural deep-water port that looks onto the Bay of Bengal. It is also the starting point for a 2,806-kilometer oil-and-gas pipeline that stretches all the way across northern Burma, over mountain ranges and through tropical jungles, until it arrives at Kunming, one of the main cities in the southwest of China. The plans include a port, a railway line, and a major oil storage-and-treatment facility. A video presentation about the project adopts the kind of breezy management-speak that often accompanies Chinese investments, gushing about "a concept of one development zone, three clusters, and six bases." The presentation includes a designer's drawing for a high-rise housing project and a shopping mall, identical to the sort of development you can now find in the suburbs of a thousand Chinese cities.

Ramree was the site of an important battle in the later stages of World War II: the Allies battled for six weeks in early 1945 to defeat the Japanese forces stationed there, with Indian soldiers doing most of the fighting. The Battle of Ramree Island is better known for the fate of the retreating Japanese soldiers, who tried to escape at night across a mangrove swamp; many of them ended up eaten by saltwater crocodiles. The reported deaths of nearly a thousand soldiers is listed in the *Guinness Book of World Records* as the greatest-ever loss of human life to animals. Ramree was strategically important for the Allies, because it was easily accessible by sea and because it provided an ideal airbase to support the rest of the Burma campaign. In the early twenty-first century, Ramree has again become a crucial geographical node, a place where commercial ambition and geopolitical calculation are colliding. By building a pipeline all the way through Burma, China is attempting to subvert the realities of its geography and to gain direct access to the Indian Ocean.

The basic idea is simple: As a result of the pipeline, some of the oil and gas that China buys from the Middle East will no longer need to travel through the chokehold of the Strait of Malacca. Instead, it can be transported overland from Ramree to China's urban centers. The pipeline gives China a direct outlet to the Indian Ocean that it has never enjoyed before. It is a way of avoiding all that complicated geography at the mouth of the South China Sea, an engineering solution to the "Malacca Dilemma." Why worry about sending ships down those narrow sea-lanes to the South China Sea, which can be blocked by opponents, when China can use a pipeline that starts at the Bay of Bengal?

That, at least, was the strategic thinking that helped win approval for the $2.5-billion pipeline project. But the law of unintended consequences has a way of turning such plans on their heads. The project was sold as a way of reducing risks to China's supply routes. Yet, by avoiding the Strait of Malacca, China has created a new problem for itself in the

Indian Ocean. "If we are going to have a big port and a terminal and a pipeline all on the west coast of Burma, then we are going to need some military protection there," as one Chinese academic, who was deeply skeptical about the pipeline project, told me. "The result is the opposite of what people thought. It means that we are going to need a navy that can operate effectively in the Indian Ocean."

The contest with the U.S. over the Near Seas is already a reality. But as China's power and ambitions expand, it is only natural that its gaze will start to stretch farther afield, toward the Indian Ocean. Ramree Island is potentially the herald of a very different, long-term project to develop the sort of navy that can operate in the Indian Ocean and beyond. China is already the biggest consumer of oil in the Middle East and is tentatively starting to build political relationships in the region— just as the U.S. did a century before when Britain and France were the dominant outside powers. If China is really serious about securing the sea-lanes on which its economy depends, it will need the sort of "blue water" navy that can contest seas all the way from the Strait of Malacca up through the entire Indian Ocean and into the Persian Gulf, home of America's Fifth Fleet. If China decides to go that route over the next two decades, it has the potential to alter fundamentally the nature of competition with the U.S. The challenge that China currently presents to the U.S. is intense but localized, restricted to China's immediate maritime periphery. China's immediate ambitions are regional, not global. But as it casts its sights across the Indian Ocean, the stakes become much higher, raising the prospect that China could pursue a much more sustained and broader challenge to the U.S.

Yet it is far from inevitable that the U.S. and China will end up as competitors in the Indian Ocean. China's approach will depend in part on a number of key decisions that China's leaders will need to take over the next decade, which will involve massive investments and will be crucial barometers of their long-term intentions. Distance from home drastically changes the military calculation for China. In the Near Seas, the geography is on China's side: it has missile sites along its coast, which it can use to exert control over sea-lanes. But in the Indian Ocean, those advantages disappear. If China wants to have the ability to contest the seas well beyond its periphery, and to project power in the Indian

Ocean, it needs to invest heavily in two areas. It will need to have bases in and agreements with friendly countries that will allow it to use their ports and airfields to support its forces. And it will need the sorts of warships that can provide some form of air cover across wide expanses of ocean. In other words, it will need aircraft carriers. The bad news for China is that, although both projects are superficially attractive, they will be politically difficult and economically costly to implement.

THE "STARTER CARRIER"

"Without an aircraft carrier, I will die with my eyelids open," Liu Hua-qing, the former commander of the Chinese fleet, said in 1987—a Chinese phrase that implies a deep, unfulfilled desire. In the modern era, Liu was the first official to push the case for a bigger fleet; he is often referred to as "the father of the modern Chinese navy." It was Liu who introduced the concept of "Near Seas" and "Far Seas" into Chinese strategic thought, and also he who, in the 1980s, led the navy's transformation from a glorified coast guard into a modern fleet. China, he argued, needed to stake its claim as a great power, and an aircraft carrier was the vital platform for projecting naval power over long distances. When he outlined these ideas in the 1970s and 1980s, at a time when most Chinese were not able to eat meat regularly, his plans seemed quixotic. But by the time he died, in early 2011, they had become mainstream: a few weeks before his death, Chinese officials acknowledged for the first time that the country was building its own carrier. All nine members of the Communist Party Standing Committee turned out for Liu Huaqing's memorial service, the only time in recent memory that this has happened for a military leader. A distraught-looking Hu Jintao presented a bouquet of white carnations to his widow. Xi Jinping gave a speech saying that China had to step up the development of its naval capabilities to match its new position in the world.

China's route to a modern carrier has been a tortuous one. In 1998, an obscure Chinese travel agency, whose directors had connections with the navy, purchased the hull of a former Soviet carrier called the *Varyag* from Ukraine. They paid $20 million and said that the ship would be used as a casino. It took them three years to get the vessel back to China.

The *Varyag* was held up in Istanbul for eighteen months while a dispute with the Turkish authorities was resolved, and then it hit bad weather on its way around the Cape of Good Hope, before it was eventually tugged into Dalian, a port in the northeast of China. But by 2012, the newly rechristened *Liaoning* carrier was ready to enter formal service for the first time. The relaunch was accompanied with much fanfare and national pride. The commander of the carrier, Senior Captain Zhang Zheng, gave an interview on the ship's deck to CCTV, the Chinese state broadcaster. Zhang talked rather modestly about all the training the crew would need and the heavy responsibility they faced, but the interviewer could not contain himself. "Captain Zhang, you give me a very deep impression of being open-minded and energetic," he beamed. "The navy also has very high hopes for you."

The battle to build the *Liaoning* carrier tells a lot about the shifting political sands and rising ambitions in China over recent years. As far back as 1928, Chen Shaokuan, the British-trained head of the Chinese navy at the time, first put forward the idea of building a carrier. In the 1980s, when he was head of the navy, Liu Huaqing started to lobby openly for the idea of a Chinese carrier, yet his civilian masters were not convinced. Deng Xiaoping pushed back against the expensive idea. In the early 1990s, Jiang Zemin, who had taken power after Tiananmen, also rejected the proposal. He was afraid that it would unnerve the U.S. too much to see China investing in such a striking symbol of great-power ambition. The early years of naval modernization focused mostly on the submarines and missiles that could help China exert more control over the Near Seas. The quest for an aircraft carrier became yet another of those ideas that were put on hold in the interests of "hiding the brightness."

But from the early 1990s, the idea of a carrier was taken up by China's version of the military-industrial complex. The drumbeat started first in universities and think tanks and soon included mayors who wanted the carriers to be built in their towns, and the shipbuilders who were desperate for the contract. Supporters emphasized the unique place that aircraft carriers held for realizing China's national destiny. Li Jie, a senior captain at the Naval Research Institute, claimed, "No great power that has become a strong power has achieved this without developing carriers." Zhang Wenmu, one of the most vocal champions, argues that in the twenty-first century naval power will be a decisive factor in competition between states. Aircraft carriers are "a concentrated expression of a country's comprehensive national power," he writes.

Kaiser Wilhelm was so fascinated with the navy that he once wore a naval uniform to a performance of Wagner's *Flying Dutchman*, with his sons also decked out in sailor suits. Bismarck had invested only in smaller, less expensive vessels, fearing that the real threats to Germany would come by land. However, under Wilhelm's and Admiral Tirpitz's direction, Germany invested in a huge fleet of battleships, the aircraft carriers of their day. "The Greeks and Romans each had their time, the Spaniards had theirs, the French also," Wilhelm argued to justify the huge investments. The historian Robert Ross argues that China is witnessing the same sort of "naval nationalism" that has infected many aspiring great powers before, in which the natural desire to build up the military becomes distorted by a demand for prestige projects that have a strong nationalist appeal, even if their strategic worth is not so clear-cut. Unlike any other aspect of the country's military modernization, the idea of a Chinese aircraft carrier became part of the popular imagination. As Ross puts it, "Chinese nationalists maintain that the realization of China's historical destiny depends on the possession of a carrier-based navy." Around the same time that China bought the *Varyag*, it purchased another former Soviet carrier from Ukraine, the *Kiev*. In this case, the vessel really was destined for tourism. It is now the centerpiece of a popular aircraft-carrier theme park in Tianjin, the large coastal city near Beijing. San Diego has a museum in a disused aircraft carrier, so the idea is hardly novel, but whereas the USS *Midway* Museum celebrates achievements from the past, the Tianjin museum is aspirational, a bid to capture the public enthusiasm for future naval grandeur. When I visited a couple of years ago, the insides of the *Kiev* were lined with worthy exhibits about the history of aircraft carriers. More recently, it has gone upmarket—part of the vessel is now taken up by a luxury hotel, a response to constant requests from people wanting to spend a night on board. The hotel photos indicate a preference for gaudy baroque, the low-ceilinged suites boasting white leather sofas and opulent chandeliers. Overnight guests have been promised an additional treat: the park intends to put on a mock naval battle every evening.

The launch of the *Liaoning* was a moment full of symbolism, to be sure, but Senior Captain Zhang was right: there is still a lot of work to do. China's "starter carrier," as some analysts have dubbed it, still faces a host of difficult challenges. The television images gave away one of those problems: there were no aircraft on the deck. China bought some fighter jets that can be used on carriers from Ukraine and is believed to have got hold of a similar Russian jet. There is even speculation that one of the models of its new stealth fighter jet could eventually be equipped to land on carriers. But developing its own jets for use on carriers—and training a team of pilots to use them—is another project whose time frame can be measured in decades rather than years. In 1954, the U.S. Air Force lost 776 aircraft and 535 aviators as it tried to develop its fighter jets. Carrier groups need a whole host of supporting ships, including submarines and destroyers that can provide modern defenses against missiles, some of which are still under development. In addition, the Chinese navy will also have to learn how to actually operate a carrier group, which requires the sort of detailed coordination and training that the U.S. has perfected over a century and through several wars. Again, developing this sort of seamanship is another decades-long enterprise.

It may well be that China's leaders will decide over the next decade to go all in and order a sizable fleet of carriers, but before then, they will have to overcome some powerful opposition to such an ambitious spending spree. According to naval planners, you need three carriers to ensure that one group is always operating, because at any single time one carrier is undergoing repairs and the other is preparing for the next mission. Now that China has launched its first carrier, the question is how many it will build. The Pentagon believes that another couple of domestically built carriers will be in operation by 2015. Chinese state media have talked about plans for three carriers, but other Chinese officials have privately talked about building five. The eventual numbers will make all the difference. If China develops a fleet that allows it to have two carrier groups operating at any one time, that will focus the minds of a lot of other countries in the region. But one carrier on its own does little to change the military balance in Asia. And as the Pentagon can attest, operating carrier groups is an extremely expensive business.

Ever since Liu Huaqing first proposed building a Chinese carrier, the project has been tied up in budgetary battles, and the fight for resources is likely to get still more intense. Some estimates suggest that a new carrier in China would cost $10 billion, around 10 percent of the yearly official Chinese military budget. Even with a growing budget, China does not have the resources for everything. If China invests in a big carrier fleet, it will have fewer resources to invest in the "anti-navy" weapons designed to exert greater control over the Near Seas.

For all the prestige that might come from having several carrier groups, plenty of hardheaded Chinese strategists believe they are of little actual military use once they leave China's immediate maritime surrounds. If Chinese military officials hope that they can take out American carriers in the Near Seas, then the U.S., with its far superior air power, would have the same advantage if Chinese carrier groups started operating in the Indian Ocean. "We would be sitting ducks," as You Ji, a Chinese analyst based in Singapore, puts it. The lure of a "blue water" navy is strong, and the vested interests behind a push to build more carriers will be hard to ignore. Yet it is not at all clear that China will have the skills or money over the next couple of decades to construct the sort of navy that would present a serious challenge to the U.S. in the Indian Ocean. And that is before China's leaders tackle the trickiest issue of all—how to supply and protect a new fleet of aircraft carriers operating far from home.

CHINA'S GUANTÁNAMO

In 2004, the Washington office of the consulting firm Booz Allen Hamilton produced a research paper for the Pentagon which put forward the idea that China was trying to establish a permanent military presence in the Indian Ocean. It analyzed a series of commercial ports across the region being built with Chinese help and money and concluded that they formed a "String of Pearls," facilities with potential military use that could help China project military power all the way across the Indian Ocean and into the Persian Gulf. Initially classified, the paper was leaked to the *Washington Times* in 2005. Before long, it started to capture the imagination of the more hawkish observers of China's military buildup, including in India, where there are persistent fears that a rising China will try to encircle it.

If there is one issue that will define what sort of military power China becomes over the next couple of decades, it will be the question of overseas military bases. To build a network of bases would be a decisive statement about Chinese ambitions to project power and to build its own coalition of supporters. China's navalists are gradually becoming more open about pushing the idea. The topic has long been discussed in military circles, but over the last few years it has also started to spill over into public debate about the country's long-term military strategy. It plays into the nationalist sense in China that now is their time. "It is our right" to have bases that can be used to defend the country's new economic interests, says Shen Dingli, a respected academic at Fudan University in Shanghai. "We should be able to conduct retaliatory attacks within other countries or at the neighboring area of our potential enemies."

Proponents of the "String of Pearls" theory argue that China is effectively creating a network of bases in the Indian Ocean by stealth. In Sri Lanka, the island nation with a strategic position at the meeting of the Bay of Bengal and the Arabian Sea, China Harbour Engineering Company is building a mega-port which will be able to house large oil tankers and will have a major refueling facility. The port is in Hambantota, the hometown of Sri Lankan President Mahinda Rajapaksa, allowing China to mix commerce with more personal diplomacy. Just down the road from the port, the same Chinese company also built the thirty-thousand-capacity cricket stadium which was one of the venues for the 2011 World Cup, another propaganda coup for the president. The relationship with Rajapaksa goes well beyond infrastructure, however. With the help of $1 billion in military aid from Beijing every year, and a Chinese veto against criticism at the United Nations, Rajapaksa ended the country's long-running civil war in 2009 after a brutal final showdown. Given such complicit ties, there are plenty of suggestions that, over time, Hambantota could become the sort of place where Chinese vessels regularly dock to refuel and get supplies.

Something similar has been happening in Gwadar, a deep-water Pakistani port on the Arabian Sea, close to the entrance to the Strait of Hormuz—the strategic chokehold for a large slice of the world's oil supply. China helped build a commercial port at Gwadar, which was initially leased to a Singapore company, PSA International. But after a series of problems, the Singapore group dropped out and a Chinese company took over management control of the port. More important, a senior Pakistani official told one of my colleagues in 2011 that the government had asked China to build a naval base next to the commercial port, and that China would have access to the base, potentially allowing Beijing to station some of its ships and submarines in Gwadar. The Chinese have played down the suggestion, but a clear marker has been laid down.

The "String of Pearls" is, of course, an idea straight from the Mahan playbook for aspiring great powers. Mahan urged the U.S. to find strategic locations in the Caribbean and the Pacific that could help the navy patrol the key maritime supply lines and the Panama Canal. A peacetime naval strategy "may gain its most decisive victories by occupying in a country, either by purchase or treaty, excellent positions which would perhaps hardly be got by war," he wrote. Around the same time that America embarked on a burst of navy building in the 1890s, it also launched a drive to acquire overseas bases for its new ships. In the Pacific, it was supporters of the new navy who made the strongest case for incorporating Hawaii into the union. Secretary of State Hamilton Fish described Hawaii as an attractive "resting spot in the mid-ocean, between the Pacific coast and the vast domains of Asia, which are now opening to commerce," as well as being a useful platform for curbing the rise of Japan. Earlier, the U.S. had taken control of the Midway archipelago, which was named because of its location directly midway between Los Angeles and Shanghai. Mahan was particularly obsessed with the Caribbean, where the British navy still had a large presence, and which he thought of in terms not dissimilar to the way the Chinese think today about the first island chain. In 1903, the U.S. Navy leased a new base in the Caribbean, which gave it the perfect launchpad to protect the eastern entrances to the Panama Canal, but which has become famous in modern times for very different reasons—Guantánamo Bay in Cuba.

The "String of Pearls" concept appeals to a certain conspiratorial view of how China works, the image of a small group of Communist Party officials calmly hatching plans for global domination. It suggests that China already has a coherent and thought-out long-term strategy, a series of five-year plans that will eventually afford China a broad network of bases across the region. Given how utterly opaque China's top-level politics remains, it is easy to imagine that the top leadership might have such a disciplined view of its future. But the reality of modern China is much more improvised and reactive than this cliché recognizes. It is certainly true that China's interests are drawing it into the Indian Ocean. Yet Ramree Island tells a very different story about China's overseas expansion, and one which corresponds more closely to how decisions really get made. In a system in which the authority of the leaders is fraying, the driving force is often pressure from below. The Burma pipeline is part of a dynamic whereby business moves first, to create a new reality of its own, and then foreign and military policies are forced to come from behind to fill in the gaps.

The idea for the pipeline was first put forward by a history professor at an unglamorous provincial university. Li Chenyang, an expert on Southeast Asia at Yunnan University, in the southwest of China, started writing newspaper articles in 2004 suggesting that a pipeline could allow China to avoid bringing oil through the Strait of Malacca. In the long corridors outside Li's office, there are large framed maps of the region, detailing Yunnan's long borders with Vietnam, Laos, and Burma. By driving a pipeline from Kunming, Yunnan's capital, down through Burma, Li proposed China could gain access to the Indian Ocean. "The reality is the Americans want to control the Strait of Malacca," as Professor Li put it. "For China to fall under American control is a very risky thing." The idea was immediately taken up by the local government in Yunnan. But whereas Li and his academic colleagues were worried about energy and geopolitics, the local officials had a more prosaic motivation: jobs. Each year, Chinese officials receive a formal performance evaluation, and no matter whether they are running a village of a hundred people or a province of a hundred million, they are judged primarily on their ability to generate growth in their part of the economy. Their careers depend on the local GDP numbers. As a result, local officials are on the constant lookout for new investment projects that will boost growth. Although it has a rich cultural heritage, Yunnan is one of the poorer provinces of China, and its leaders have often complained that the industrial boom in other parts of the country has passed it by. They saw the pipeline as a perfect way to kick-start an oil industry in the province. The construction would bring a lot of jobs and funds, and a refinery would be needed at the end of the pipeline. A lot of the dynamism in China's economy in recent decades is derived from this basic equation, the ceaseless drive at all levels of government for the latest new opportunity. For Yunnan officials, the pipeline is not about geopolitics, it is about GDP.

The proposal also won support from the politically powerful oil industry. China National Petroleum Corporation is the biggest oil company in the country, but in the southwest of the country, it was coming second to its main rival, Sinopec. The new pipeline was a way into that market. Before long, CNPC was on board with the idea. Together with CNPC, the Yunnan authorities started lobbying Beijing hard to win approval. Initially, there was a good deal of resistance. But after several years of pressure by big-oil and provincial government officials, Beijing finally agreed to promote the idea. As Zha Daojiong, a Chinese academic who has followed these sorts of internal debates closely, told me: "From the outside, it can look like China has a coherent energy strategy, but in reality it often comes down to who shouts the loudest."

Europe's empires were not created overnight by grand design. Instead, they evolved through a gradual creeping process that started with trade and investment and ended with the use of military power to protect those business interests. The British Raj had its roots in the perceived need to protect the operations of the East India Company, and it was to defend those very same interests that the British invaded Burma in 1824. After defeating the Burmese forces—and ending Burmese independence for much of the next century—the British briefly moved the country's capital to Sittwe, on the northwest coast, just north of Ramree Island. It is facile to suggest, as some do, that China is trying to re-create an old-fashioned empire, but it is fair to say that China's overseas investments are repeating elements of the same imperial dynamic, the old story of the flag following the trade. In a political system in which some of the lines of control have eroded, ambitious local governments and connected state-owned corporations are pushing projects that involve substantial international commitments, the local economic tail wagging the Beijing diplomatic dog. In the case of the Burma pipeline, the project won the backing of Beijing even though its strategic benefits are really something of a mirage. If there ever were some form of conflict between the U.S. and China, then the pipeline would be much more vulnerable than the sea-lanes through the Strait of Malacca. It would take the permanent presence of a significant fleet to enforce a blockade of the strait, but only one bombing run to destroy the pipeline. The Ramree Island investment brings no actual security for China.

On Ramree Island itself, there is widespread suspicion about China's eventual plans for the area. Common among locals I talked to was the assumption that China would eventually want to have a naval base there, to help secure its interests and protect the commercial traffic to the port. In Yangon, I heard the same story, a constant refrain that the pipeline is some sort of Trojan Horse that will justify a Chinese military presence. There is no evidence that this is happening—and such an idea would likely spark considerable resistance in Burma, including from the new civilian government. But the reality is that China is now building a huge oil facility looking onto the Bay of Bengal, which it needs to protect. Its commercial interests are pulling it into the Indian Ocean in ways that were not originally anticipated.

————

Whether by secret design or by the inertia of its advancing business interests, China is likely to push for a much stronger presence in the Indian Ocean. But just as there are enormous operational challenges ahead if China wants to construct a navy that can contend in the Indian Ocean, so there are huge political obstacles if it tries to establish the sort of military basing rights that would allow it to project power far from its home base. If China really aspires to a stealth "String of Pearls" strategy, it will be very difficult to turn this into reality, because few countries will want to be seen taking sides. Every government in the region knows that, even with the huge investments China is making in its navy, the U.S. will have a superior fighting ability in the Indian Ocean for several decades to come. This means that a Chinese base on their territory would turn them into a highly vulnerable target in the first days of a conflict. Burma's new government has tilted away from China in a way that makes it very hard to imagine its accepting a Chinese base, despite the incessant rumor mill in the country. Sri Lanka, too, knows how vulnerable it would be if Chinese vessels were permanently based at Hambantota. "There may or may not be a Chinese string in the region, but we will not be one of their pearls," as one Sri Lankan official puts it.

Pakistan is the one country that has expressed some interest in hosting a Chinese base. But the idea is a lot less attractive than it seems. Gwadar is occasionally referred to in the press as "the most important place you have never heard of," given its closeness to the Persian Gulf. But on closer inspection, it is of much less strategic use than it seems. Gwadar is an isolated city in the southwestern province of Baluchistan, squeezed in between Iran and Afghanistan, where an insurgency against the state has been running for decades, becoming particularly ugly in recent years. The roads and rail links to the more prosperous parts of Pakistan, around Karachi and Lahore, are, at best, precarious. The port itself is also vulnerable, as it is on a small island, connected to the mainland by one bridge. In the event of a conflict, a single bomb could take it out of action.

Just as the U.S. did in an earlier era, China has long shunned the idea of foreign "entanglements." Beijing has persistently denounced alliance building as a destabilizing form of power politics. We are not that sort of government, Chinese leaders insist. As a result, the establishment of an overseas base would be a Rubicon moment for China, one that cuts to the core of the question about how China really interprets its future role. Foreign bases are not just an exercise in logistics; they are sovereign territory within another nation. A base is the bridgehead to a very different relationship, the sort of defense alliance whereby the bigger nation offers to provide security in return for access and support. In other words, China would need formal allies. But the question every government would ask Beijing is, whom are we defending ourselves from? If China moves down this path, it could start a process of dividing the region between countries that rely on the U.S. for their security, and those that lean toward China. Asian governments would increasingly find themselves asked to take sides, the outcome they fear the most. For that very reason, some in China view it as an extremely dangerous step, one that would lead to greater isolation for China. "It is a self-fulfilling, delusionary idea to build our own bases and our own alliances," Zhu Feng, an international-relations professor at Peking University, told me. "I totally disagree with the idea. We would create a geographic split in the region. It really would be the start of a new Cold War."

———

Of course, the Indian Ocean already has a billion-person-plus rising power, with a growing navy and a strong sense of its own role in the modern world. India is another important reason why China will have to tread very carefully in the Indian Ocean. Washington is by no means the only capital where the rapid expansion in China's navy has provoked anxiety; New Delhi has also been watching the developments with some alarm. India and China share a tradition of fraternal ties rooted in the language of anti-colonialism and the Non-Aligned Movement. In 1927, two decades before he became the leader of a newly independent India, Jawaharlal Nehru signed a joint manifesto with delegates from the Chinese Communist Party at an anti-imperialist congress in Brussels. In 1962, however, the two countries fought a brief but fierce war over a border in the Himalayas that is still under dispute, and since then have viewed each other warily. Now that sense of competition is shifting to the Indian Ocean. "Rivalry has been a defining element of India's relations with China for 60 years," says Raja Mohan, one of India's leading foreign-policy analysts. "But it is now beginning to move from the Himalayas to the waters of the Indo-Pacific."

Just like China, India is also turning to the seas, and for many of the same reasons. As India has morphed since the early 1990s from an inward-looking and highly regulated economy to a more open, trading nation, it, too, has begun to fret about the safety of the sea-lanes that its new wealth depends upon. (Alfred Thayer Mahan is now the subject of great interest in India, too.) Having acquired its first aircraft carrier as far back as the 1950s, India now has three, and another which is a museum in Mumbai. Yet India's naval buildup has had a different quality. Although New Delhi considers the Indian Ocean to be its natural backyard, it does not have the same sort of sweeping ownership claim that China presents. India is neither as suspicious of the U.S. as is China, nor is it building a navy specifically designed to challenge the U.S. The Indian navy has also been much more willing to take part in joint exercises with the U.S., signaling its willingness to carry some of the security burdens in the existing U.S.-led system.

In 2005, the U.S. and India signed a nuclear deal which, at first sight, appeared to herald an exciting era of close relations. In return for Washington's turning a blind eye to India's new nuclear weapons, the U.S. hoped that New Delhi would become an important partner in its regional diplomacy. Commentators in the U.S. gushed about the meeting of minds between the two biggest democracies in the world, multicultural U.S. and opinionated, querulous India. Since then, those high hopes have been dashed. Washington has become frustrated at India's willingness to trade with Iran and to side with China at the Copenhagen climate-change conference. The more enthusiastic U.S. supporters of the deal were surprised to find that India still wants to conduct an independent foreign policy. India remains intensely proud of its hard-won autonomy and history of neutrality. The last thing it wants to be is a full-fledged American ally, to play the sort of loyal lieutenant role that Britain does. Nevertheless, New Delhi remains deeply suspicious about the nature of a rising China, and its relationship with Beijing will be shaped by how China decides to pursue its interests in its Indian Ocean backyard. The "String of Pearls" has had more resonance in India than in the U.S., because the idea anticipates India's fear that China will attempt to encircle it. The prospect of a Chinese naval base on its eastern flank (Burma) or its southern tip (Sri Lanka) plays into those fears. And nothing could exacerbate India's anxieties more than a permanent Chinese presence in Pakistan, which would be interpreted in New Delhi as a deliberate move against India. If China makes a concerted push to establish a permanent presence in the Indian Ocean, India will be pushed closer to the U.S.

AMERICAN PARTNERS?

As China's interests and ambitions expand, it is only natural that it will start to think about how to project naval power in the Indian Ocean, yet at every stage it finds itself facing obstacles that will not be easily over-come. It is years away from a naval fleet that could genuinely challenge the U.S., and it will be very hard to establish the sort of permanent naval bases that would undergird a real military presence. And if it does make a big push into the Indian Ocean, it is likely to pour oil on the slow-burning rivalry with India. Given such formidable obstacles, it is pos-sible to imagine that China will take a very different path in the Indian Ocean, and that it will look to collaborate more with the U.S. Navy. Washington has an opportunity to build a different sort of relationship with Beijing in the Indian Ocean, one that is much less inherently con-frontational. Admiral Michael Mullen, the former chairman of the Joint Chiefs of Staff, used to talk about a thousand-ship navy, a global mari-time network that would share the tasks of policing the oceans and of responding to disasters like the 2004 Asian tsunami. There is a chance China could be gradually drawn into the framework of burden shar-ing in the Indian Ocean that already exists. These exercises would be naval confidence-building measures, a way for the two navies to get to know each other and to learn how to rub up against each other. The rivalry in the Near Seas will not disappear, of course, but it is possible that collaboration in the Indian Ocean could take some of the edge off that competition. Or, as retired U.S. Admiral Eric McVadon once put it: "One can readily imagine a scenario in which U.S. Navy F-18s from car-riers are in air-to-air combat with Chinese planes over Taiwan. One can just as readily imagine those same planes . . . protecting sea-lanes from pirates and terrorists."

In small ways, this is already happening. For the last two decades, the most dangerous place in the world for commercial shipping has been the coast off Somalia, including the Gulf of Aden, where pirates have been able to operate freely. Chinese ships have been among those kidnapped. As a result, since 2009, China has been taking part in the international anti-piracy operations in the region. With the U.S. Seventh Fleet based in Bahrain often in the lead, the operations are an organized show of force by more than twenty of the world's largest navies, which escort commercial vessels through the most vulnerable waters. The contribut-ing countries include Denmark, the U.K., Netherlands, Pakistan, and South Korea—in other words, a broad cross-section of the international community. Chinese naval officials now attend the meetings in Bahrain of the international anti-piracy coalition, which goes by the name Shared Awareness and Deconfliction Group (SHADE), a ghoulish acronym that bears the fingerprints of Pentagon bureaucrats. From 2009 to 2012, Chinese warships escorted more than five thousand commercial ships, most of them not Chinese, through the Gulf of Aden. In the larger anti-piracy operations, a convoy of ships from various countries travels up and down the East African coast in a carefully organized pattern, usually with a U.S. destroyer at the helm. The Chinese ships have never operated under U.S. command, but on occasion they have tagged along on these larger drills. The Chinese captains sail five nautical miles to the north or south of the convoy, maintaining a discreet and wary distance—a powerful metaphor for a country that is still not quite sure whether it wants to collaborate with, or challenge, the U.S. maritime order.

3

The Asian Backlash

Tone-Deaf in Hanoi

WHEN YANG JIECHI STOOD to speak, he was almost shaking with anger. China's foreign minister launched into a twenty-five-minute diatribe aimed at most of the other governments at the 2010 Asia-Pacific Summit. "China is a big country," he fumed. "And you are all small countries. And that is a fact." The other ministers were arranged in a square at the Hanoi Convention Center and seated in large leather armchairs, which made it look as if they were slouching, even recoiling. But their mood was very different. A group of Asian ministers had just demonstrated a rare and powerful act of solidarity in defiance of Beijing. U.S. Secretary of State Hillary Clinton had declared that the U.S. viewed the stability of the South China Sea as a fundamental U.S. interest—a pointed rebuke to China, which argues that the disputes in the area have nothing to do with Washington. After she sat down, representatives of twelve other nations, including the host, Vietnam, stood to issue similar statements, some of them with even more direct criticisms of China.

Yang, who started out as an English translator, built his career in part on strong personal connections with the U.S. Back in the late 1970s, he translated for George H. W. Bush and James Baker on a trip to Tibet and became close enough to the Bush family to earn the nickname "Tiger" Yang. After Tiananmen, when Beijing wanted to mend fences with Washington, it was Yang who was dispatched to talk to then president Bush. It is an indication of how far the mood has changed in Beijing that by 2010 Yang felt the need to deliver such a public smack-down; to make sure he got the message right, he was overheard by some diplomats in the corridor beforehand rehearsing lines. Looking directly at Hillary Clinton, Yang told her that "outside powers" should not get involved in the South China Sea. He lectured the nations from Southeast Asia not to become a cabal organized by an outside power. And then he turned to his Vietnamese hosts, the only other government present run by a Communist party. Yang told them they were behaving like a "capitalist sinner." "As a fellow socialist country, you should be fraternal. Don't let yourself be used by an ideological enemy," he said. In the words of one of the diplomats present, it was a "bullying, eloquent, intimidating" speech. But the effect was disastrous. In less than half an hour, Yang managed to tear up more than a decade of subtle, diligent, and highly effective Chinese diplomacy.

More often than not, ministerial summits are all about the smiling photo, especially in Asia, where great emphasis is placed on presenting a unified front. The July 2010 ASEAN Regional Forum in Hanoi has often been cited as the start of the Obama administration's "pivot" to Asia, a broader shift in strategic priorities away from the Middle East and toward addressing the rise of China. But the real significance was elsewhere, in the mini–Asian revolt that prompted Yang's outburst. The summit lifted the lid on the profound anxieties that China's rise has started to prompt across Asia. From Vietnam to Mongolia, from Japan to Australia, China's expanding military might and political confidence are now producing an existential crisis, the perennial angst of "small countries" living alongside a "big country" they do not quite trust.

The central geopolitical assumption about China's rise is that economic heft will bring with it political influence, starting in Asia. During the last ten years, China has become the biggest trading partner of almost every Asian economy, in lots of cases pushing the U.S. out of that position. Yet Asian leaders have started to turn that logic on its head. The dozen governments which lined up behind Hillary Clinton in Hanoi were setting out a new dynamic of Asian diplomacy. Rather than acquiesce to China, most Asian governments will look to counter its influence if it tries to throw its weight around, enlisting the help of the U.S. There is no natural Chinese sphere of influence in Asia. The defining story in Asia in recent years is not the U.S. "pivot"; it is the Asian backlash.

During the Mao period, China supported Communist insurrections across the region in a bid to destabilize unfriendly governments, and during his first few years in power, Deng Xiaoping was equally careless of the opinions of his neighbors. In 1979, he ordered an invasion of Vietnam, and China fought a short skirmish with Vietnam in the South China Sea in 1988. Over time, however, Deng started to take the advice of Lee Kuan Yew, the Singaporean leader, who has at times been an unofficial mentor to China's leaders, and who warned him of the need to mend fences with the rest of the region. Deng's "hiding the brightness" strategy came to have as one of its central priorities establishing good relations with the rest of Asia; if China was going to be accepted as a participant in the global economy, diplomacy in Asia would be an essential task. In particular, Deng wanted Chinese exporters to be plugged into the network of Asian manufacturing that had sprung up since the 1960s in Japan, Taiwan, and South Korea. As China's economy started to take off, Deng instructed his colleagues to be careful about antagonizing their neighbors. For much of the 1990s and 2000s, China went out of its way to ease the concerns of the rest of Asia about its expanding power and wealth, a strategy that came to be known as its "charm offensive." It settled the outstanding land-border disputes with almost all of its neighbors, including Russia, Mongolia, Vietnam, and Burma, often with significant concessions (Burma, for instance, got 82 percent of the disputed land).

The Asian financial crisis in 1997 provided a huge tactical opening. From Bangkok to Seoul, Asian capitals were incensed at the high-handed and dogmatic way they were treated by the U.S. Treasury Department and the International Monetary Fund. Leaders complained loudly that Washington paid no attention to the particular conditions of their countries, opting instead to push the same cookie-cutter solution for everyone's problems. At the same time, China won respect for resisting the urge to devalue its currency and for its calm stewardship during the crisis. China also started to offer cheap loans and aid packages across the region. Anyone traveling through Southeast Asia these days can hardly miss the Chinese-made schools, government buildings, or football stadiums. The mood toward China shifted dramatically. Asian students started to come in large numbers to Chinese universities. Anti-Chinese sentiment had been so intense in Indonesia in the 1970s that Suharto banned the use of Chinese characters in newspapers for the country's large ethnic Chinese population. Yet, when my wife, Angelica, enrolled at a Chinese-language course in 2005 at Shanghai Jiao Tong University, almost half her classmates were Indonesians.

Chinese diplomats even had a poetic phrase to frame the policy— *"mulin, fulin, anlin,"* "establish good neighbors, make them feel prosperous, and make them feel secure." Diplomats from other countries would marvel at the patience and long-term strategy they witnessed in their Chinese counterparts. After 9/11, when the U.S. became obsessed with the threat from terrorism and embroiled in wars in Afghanistan and Iraq, the Chinese stepped up their efforts to present themselves to the rest of Asia as a reliable and trustworthy regional leader. Beijing also promoted regional organizations that excluded the U.S.—with some success, given that senior Bush-administration officials did not even bother to attend a handful of the regional summits. (President George W. Bush annoyed some of his colleagues by pushing to have Islamist terrorism on the agenda at Asia-Pacific summits.) Across the region, America's friends and allies started to doubt its commitment, providing an opening for China to cultivate its own supporters. During much of the 2000s, it was easy to imagine that Asia was gradually slipping into a Chinese sphere of influence, and it became fashionable to write obituaries for American influence in the region. "We are happy to have China as our big brother," Gloria Arroyo, the president of the Philippines—once a U.S. colony and still a treaty ally—said in 2007.

In many ways, Deng's strategy mimicked Bismarck's approach for managing the rise of a unified Germany in the nineteenth century. Bismarck also knew that the country's economy could be stifled if its neighbors formed a coalition to oppose it, and he set about trying to smooth historical enmities, forging strong ties with any country that might potentially become an adversary. As the American writer Walter Russell Mead once put it, this intricate and exhausting policy "sometimes looked like a French bedroom farce as Bismarck hid Austria in the closet when Russia stormed into the bedroom." But Bismarck's diplomacy worked, and Germany's economy overtook Britain's amid relative geopolitical calm. Adopting a similar approach, China has also boomed amid regional stability, its economy overtaking third-place Germany in 2007 and then Japan in 2010 to become the second-largest in the world.

Yet Bismarck's conciliatory approach did not outlast his own downfall from power. When Germany started trying to throw its weight around more in the 1890s, building up its navy and grumbling about territorial disputes, it soon found that republican France and conservative Russia had developed a firm alliance to oppose it. In one symbolic gesture, the Russian tsar stood for "The Marseillaise," the blood-curdling anthem of French republicanism, whose ideas his predecessors had spent much of the previous century fighting. The Hanoi summit in 2010 was also a symbolic turning point, one of those moments when the ground in Asian politics started to shift. As China has become more powerful, it has shown itself to be remarkably tone-deaf about its neighbors. For all the focus on the rivalry between China and the U.S., the most important shift in the region in recent years has been the rise in Asian anxiety about China. For many of the Asian governments in the room, Yang's diatribe lifted away the veil on how China would really behave when it decided that the period of "nourishing obscurity" was over. "It was a revelatory moment," one Asian diplomat present told me.

For two decades, academics have speculated whether the rest of Asia would "balance" or "bandwagon" with China. The Hanoi summit demonstrated that the new dynamic in Asia will involve a form of balancing, a sign that many of the other Asian powers will come together to block China if it pushes hard to assume a dominant role in the region. This will not be the sort of brittle balance-of-power dynamic that plagued Europe in the late nineteenth century, when countries made rigid military commitments to defend one another. Instead, it will be a more fluid and looser arrangement which seeks to marry greater emphasis on security with continued economic integration. Asia has its own built-in balance of power, which will be used to restrain Beijing's worst instincts.

Of course, the backlash did not occur in a vacuum. It is important to understand some of the historical baggage that Asian governments bring to the current situation. Yang Jiechi's implicit threat about big countries and small countries was so powerful because it carried deep memories of a historical relationship many Asian nations once had with China, one they do not want to return to. China may be the new great power of today's global politics, but in Asia it is also very much the traditional power.

THE ORIGINAL MALACCA DILEMMA

The observation tower in Malacca is not for the squeamish. Visitors enter into a circular glass booth, which is then pulled up a white pole to the top, like one of those hotel elevators with glass walls on three sides, but much, much higher. The top is 110 meters into the sky and gives tourists a spectacular 360-degree view of the Malaysian city. The real interest, however, is the extraordinary vista of the narrow sea channel that shares its name with the city. Look southeast and the Strait of Malacca stretches all the way down to Singapore and the entrance to the South China Sea, where, at its narrowest point, it is 2.8 miles wide. To the northwest, the channel eventually gives way to the Indian Ocean. On a clear day, the Indonesian island of Sumatra is visible on the other side, around thirty miles away. It was a Saturday when I visited, but global commerce has no respect for weekends, and, despite the haze, I could make out a large tanker as it was gliding slowly past the city. On any given week, four times more oil tankers pass along this narrow strip of water than go through the Suez Canal, making it perhaps the single most important conduit of globalization. This is the same Strait of Malacca that Hu Jintao fears could be shut down by "certain major powers" in order to asphyxiate the Chinese economy slowly.

Hu's warning, it turns out, is not an entirely new Chinese preoccupation. Not too far from Malacca's observation tower, past the replica of a Portuguese battleship, past the churches painted in red with large white crosses, and next to the old Dutch town hall, there is a small park which almost has a view of the strait. The park boasts a large, imposing statue of Zheng He, the commander of a Chinese fleet that made several visits to Malacca in the early fifteenth century—the last time China had an impressive navy. Nearby is the newly opened museum about Zheng He, which celebrates his presence in the city and tells the story of an earlier era of Chinese naval expeditions.

In the long arc of Chinese history, Zheng He is one of the most intriguing figures. A Muslim with the surname Ma, he was captured during a Ming dynasty army's invasion of what is now China's Yunnan Province. Castrated by his captors, he was sent to serve in Beijing as a palace eunuch; here he became a close confidant of Zhu Di, son of the Ming founder. (It was Zhu Di who gave him the name Zheng He.) Overlooked in the imperial succession by his father, Zhu Di staged a coup and imposed himself as the new emperor, assuming the name Yongle, meaning "perpetual happiness." One of Yongle's most important initiatives was to order a massive expansion in shipbuilding, and when he needed a commander to take charge of the new fleet, he turned to his loyal confidant Zheng He. Between 1405 and 1433, Zheng He led seven different voyages that explored the littorals of Southeast Asia and the Indian Ocean, even making it as far as Kenya, from where he brought back a giraffe to an astonished Chinese court.

His ships were known as "treasure boats." The biggest of them boasted nine masts and were four hundred feet long—making them four times the size of the Portuguese vessels of the age. When Zheng He's fleet set out on one of its voyages, there could be as many as a hundred other ships alongside, some carrying the porcelain, silks, and lacquerware that the Chinese commanders took with them to dazzle their hosts. There were boats to carry cavalry horses, and others that were essentially gunships, with gunpowder catapults. Including the traveling soldiers, the total crew on each trip numbered nearly thirty thousand. Zheng He and his vast fleets traveled freely around the South China Sea and the Indian Ocean, all this almost a century before Vasco da Gama's much smaller fleet arrived in the region.

The city of Malacca became a crucial staging post on his voyages, a place where goods could be stored while the fleet continued its travels around the region. Zheng He built a stockade with towers and four gates near the harbor, and inside it there were granaries and warehouses. As Louise Levathes, author of the excellent history on the voyages *When*

China Ruled the Seas, puts it, Zheng He's fifteenth-century armadas were so vast that they were "not to be surpassed until the invasion fleets of the First World War sailed the seas." Such was their scope and power that they threatened to reshape the map of the region completely. "China extended its sphere of political power and influence throughout the Indian Ocean," she writes. "Half the world was in China's grasp."

And then they stopped. Yongle's successor had no interest in the expensive voyages. Some of the ships rotted away in the harbor; others were burned. Many of the records were destroyed, and laws were passed banning future adventures. For a long time, the voyages of Zheng He's treasure fleet attracted more attention for why they were canceled than for what they actually did. Some historians put it down to new security threats from Mongol invaders in the north, others to the overwhelming cost of running such a large fleet. Confucian scholars resented the influence at court of the eunuchs, many of whom were involved in the naval adventures. Whatever the reason, it was a crucial turning point. China looked inward—just as Europe was catapulting to global dominance, led by its own naval adventurers. The burning of the "treasure fleet" became a symbol for the introspection and stagnation that eventually brought down imperial China in the early twentieth century.

Over the last decade, there has been a dramatic revival of interest in the story of Zheng He. A new museum has opened in Nanjing, and the six hundredth anniversary of his first voyage was celebrated with great fanfare in 2005, including a flurry of books and lavish television shows. The museum in Malacca is another example of the burgeoning interest. It is no coincidence that the revival of the Zheng He legend came at the very moment when China's naval modernization was beginning to take shape. The travels of the "eunuch commander" have been recast to provide a compelling and coherent story that knits together China's past maritime adventures with its new age of naval expansion. After an era when naval power was almost a taboo in China, the Zheng He story is a way of legitimizing the topic.

The legend has different messages for different audiences. For the domestic audience, Zheng He is a figure whom Chinese can take pride in, helping to build support for the new tilt toward the oceans. For China's neighbors, the messages Beijing hopes to send are equally important. The magnanimous nature of Zheng He's treasure voyages is a sign that China can be trusted as a benevolent guarantor of the regional order, and that the region need not fear China's new navy. It is also an appeal to a certain spirit of Asian pride. The arrival of Vasco da Gama to the region in the late fifteenth century ushered in an era of five hundred years of colonialism and outside control. After the Portuguese came fleets from the Netherlands, then the British and the French, followed eventually by America and its hulking aircraft carriers. The Zheng He story is a way of saying that Asia can reclaim control over its own destiny, with China's new navy at the helm.

"During the overall course of the seven voyages to the Western Ocean, Zheng He did not occupy a single piece of land, establish any fortress, or seize any wealth from other countries," as Xu Zuyuan, a vice minister of communications, put it in 2004. "He adopted the practice of giving more than he received, and thus he was welcomed and lauded by the people of the various countries along his routes." He added: "The essence of Zheng He's voyages does not lie in how strong the Chinese navy once was, but that China adhered to peaceful diplomacy."

China's most senior leaders have tried to promote the message of Zheng He. During a visit to the U.S., Premier Wen Jiabao used the Zheng He legend to launch a quiet dig at American interventionism in the Bush years. Zheng He "brought silk, tea, and the Chinese culture" to foreign peoples, he said, "but not one inch of land was occupied." Hu Jintao was even more audacious. In a 2003 speech in Australia, he told a Zheng He–inspired story about Chinese links to Australia that well predate Britain, a tale that historians consider far-fetched, but which is rich in symbolism. "The Chinese people have all along cherished amicable feelings about the Australian people," Hu said. "Back in the 1420s, the expeditionary fleets of China's Ming dynasty reached Australian shores. For centuries, the Chinese sailed across vast seas and settled down in what they called Southern Land, or today's Australia. They brought Chinese culture to this land and lived harmoniously with the local people, contributing their proud share to Australia's economy, society, and its thriving pluralistic culture." Why would anyone in Asia seek to balance against a nation, Hu suggested, that only wants such "harmonious" ties with its neighbors? And after five hundred years of outside domination and colonialism, why would Asia need foreigners interfering in its affairs?

At the same time that Beijing was reviving the Zheng He legend, some of the main themes behind the story were beginning to gain currency in Western academic circles. A number of scholars started to suggest that East Asia had sustained a much more stable system of interstate relations in the era before Western colonialists arrived, with China at the helm. Wars and territorial conflicts were much less common than in Europe, the argument went, and diplomatic interactions were more sophisticated. At the heart of this arrangement was a broad acceptance of Chinese leadership, in the form of the "tributary" system. Rulers who paid a level of tribute to China, both political and symbolic, were left to govern their own affairs, untroubled by too much interference from China, which was the principal cultural and intellectual influence in the region.

Such views permeated both the academia and journalism. The American scholar David Kang wrote a well-received 2007 book called *China Rising*, which essentially argued that East Asia was quite content to return to a similar pattern of relations, whereby most countries in the region accepted a degree of Chinese leadership as a natural and stabilizing influence. "China's neighbors recognized the preponderance of Chinese power and accepted it, rather than trying to balance against it," he said of the old regional system. Turning to the present, he added: "Most East Asian states view China's return to being the gravitational center of East Asia as inevitable." In *The Second World*, writer Parag Khanna argued in 2008 that while the U.S. was invading Iraq, China had been binding Asia together into a Greater East Asian Co-Prosperity Sphere, a reference to Japan's 1930s project for an Asian economic bloc, through the force of its economy and the attraction of its culture. He quoted a Malaysian diplomat who claimed, "Creating a community is easy among the yellow and the brown—but not the white."

One of the problems of the Zheng He story is that so few records exist to explain what really happened on his voyages, and the fragments that do remain are open to lots of different interpretations. It may well be that Chinese power and the tributary system acted as a soothing balm over the region long before the West arrived, and that Zheng He organized "voyages of friendship." But there are lots of other ways that his story can be told, many of which cast a very different light on Chinese power and the way it is remembered across the rest of the region. By some accounts, the Zheng He voyages were less about mutual respect and more about inspiring fear in China's neighbors through naval superiority.

The treasure fleet was an impressive sight, to be sure, but there is also some evidence that the voyages were accompanied by substantial violence. Geoffrey Wade, an Australian historian of the Ming period, describes the fleets as an exercise in "shock and awe," an "early form of maritime colonialism," or, more provocatively, as "gunboat diplomacy." Christopher Columbus set out across the oceans with three ships, Vasco da Gama with four, and Magellan with five; Zheng He's fleets had two to three hundred different boats. These huge armadas enjoyed "the best and most advanced firearms in the world," as Wade puts it. Zheng He projected political influence across Southeast Asia not through the inventiveness of Chinese products or the benevolence of Chinese rule, but through a show of naval power that could not be matched. His forces became involved in a civil war in northern Sumatra and in another conflict in Java. In one incident, Zheng He intervened in a conflict in Ceylon (modern-day Sri Lanka), destroying its military before capturing the king and his family members and bringing them back to Nanjing. The military nature of his voyages also left its mark on Malacca. The Chinese used Malacca not just as a place to store goods, Wade argues, but as the site of a semi-permanent military garrison, which Zheng He used to control the traffic along the Strait of Malacca. Even then, policing the strait was an important way of imposing the will of the Ming Empire on the states in the region that relied on maritime commerce. If Wade is correct, that would make Malacca China's first overseas naval base.

One of the problems with the official Chinese story about Zheng He is that it contrasts so dramatically with how China treated other parts of the region in the same era. In 1406, at the same time that Zheng He was on one of his seven voyages, supposedly bringing the marvels of Chinese culture to Southeast Asia, Ming China launched an invasion of what is today northern Vietnam. The Chinese forces disguised their horses with images of lions in order to frighten the elephants that led the Vietnamese forces. A year later, they declared victory after a conflict which by some accounts had killed several hundred thousand Vietnamese. It was a full-blown colonial occupation: China levied taxes on gold and salt, as well as lacquer, sappan wood, kingfisher feathers, fans, and aromatics. In this broader context, Zheng He's voyages seem less like an exercise in benevolent exploration than a crude expression of Ming power. As Zheng He has been quoted as saying, "When we reached foreign countries, we captured barbarian kings who were disrespectful and resisted Chinese civilization."

The competing myths about Zheng He are more than just historical curiosity; they are also hugely important for present-day discussions of Asia. They lay bare some of the fault lines in the region's politics, which are becoming ever more apparent. Behind Beijing's revival of Zheng He, there is a curious disconnect between how China views itself and the way others in the region often view it. Chinese elite and popular views are laced with the sort of sentiments contained in the official Zheng He story, that China's imperial record was benevolent and that it was widely appreciated across the region. Chinese accounts stress that the country was a benign great power, which never sought hegemony, and which attracted others only through the sophistication of its culture and the innovation of its economy. A sense of entitlement lies behind Chinese descriptions of its past "greatness," a feeling that China's centrality and superiority are preordained. "The rise of China is granted by nature," as the Tsinghua University scholar Yan Xuetong once put it. With such a narrow view of the past, there is little understanding of the violence and interference that sometimes accompanied the dominant role China historically played in East Asian affairs. Beijing had hoped the new interest in Zheng He would help make the case for revived Chinese leadership in the region. Yet the same events also serve as a reminder of the subservient position in which other Asian nations were once placed.

Whether the legend is accurate or not, China's revival of it misses the broader point about modern Asia. Countries such as Indonesia, South Korea, and Vietnam do not see themselves as "small nations" alongside a naturally dominant bigger power. They are proud, modern nation-states, which believe that they should be treated on the international stage as equals. In many cases, they have emerged from their own experiences of colonialism to construct resilient states with a strong taste for their own independence. They are not looking for a new era of Chinese protection, benevolent or otherwise. Zheng He is a figure from a world of hierarchy and deference that they do not wish to return to.

THE YEAR IT ALL WENT WRONG

"If Bismarck were in Beijing today, he would say this was our worst nightmare," Shi Yinhong, a scholar at Renmin University in Beijing, once told me. We were talking toward the end of 2010, the year when Beijing managed to alienate pretty much every one of its neighbors in ways that will be very hard to repair over the next decade. Every step China took to pursue its interests or to push back against American influence caused Asian anxieties to rise further. In 2010, Asia's fear of creeping Chinese domination became one of the dominant driving forces in regional politics. Shi Yinhong is one of the cooler-headed realist voices among the foreign-policy community in Beijing, a keen observer of the balance-of-power dynamics that were at the heart of Deng's strategy. He believes China should be doing everything it can to avoid encouraging a coalition of neighboring states that will club together against it. But as he looked around the region in 2010, he could sense that the tide might be starting to turn against China. "Bismarck's advice was always that, if you have five neighbors, you need to be on good terms with at least three," Shi said. "That is not our case."

The Bismarck playbook for China in Asia is pretty straightforward: chip away at America's alliances in the region. The U.S. overcomes the huge distances that separate San Diego and Hawaii from the western Pacific by maintaining a substantial presence in Northeast Asia. That presence is anchored in its decades-old alliances with Japan, where around fifty thousand U.S. soldiers are based, and South Korea, where there are around twenty-eight thousand. For China to assume quietly a much stronger role in the region, one of the quickest routes would be to engineer the gradual erosion of support for America in Japan and South Korea. Throughout the 2000s, there were plenty of warning signs that these alliances were coming under pressure, in part because of the allure of the growing Chinese economy, and in part because of American missteps. Beijing had a game-changing opening to weaken American standing in the region. But, rather than driving a wedge between the U.S. and its most important allies, China has managed to push them much closer together. In its effort to start throwing its weight around, China has reinforced the balance of power in the region in America's direction.

In Japan, the immediate bone of contention was the relocation of the U.S. base Futenma in Okinawa, a long-running and poisonous political argument that has been raging ever since three U.S. servicemen raped a twelve-year-old Japanese girl in Okinawa in 1995. But the Futenma issue reflected a broader unease about the alliance with the U.S. In 2009, voters threw out the Liberal Democratic Party, which had been in power for fifty years, and installed the Democratic Party of Japan, many of whose leaders had grown up in the era of anti–Vietnam War campaigns. The new prime minister, Yukio Hatoyama, openly flirted with the idea of a new East Asian cooperation forum that would bring Japan much closer to China and would cut out the U.S. The U.S.-Japan alliance had never looked so rocky, even during the intense economic disputes of the 1980s. In early 2010, Ichiro Ozawa, the power-behind-the-throne of the new government, took a group of 143 lawmakers to Beijing on a visit that had a deferential air. A smiling Hu Jintao posed for photos and shook the hands of every single member of the Japanese delegation.

Yet Japan was jolted out of its drift away from the U.S. by Beijing's behavior. In August, the two governments found themselves at loggerheads after the Japanese coast guard arrested a Chinese fishing-boat captain who had barged their vessels close to a group of disputed islands, which the Japanese call the Senkaku and in China are called the Diaoyu. (Japan has had administrative control of the islands since the end of the Second World War, though the actual land title was owned by private citizens.) The Chinese response stunned Japan. While the government launched an aggressive diplomatic campaign to get the captain released, large anti-Japanese demonstrations broke out across China. At one stage, the Japanese ambassador was hauled in to receive a formal complaint in what the Xinhua News Agency gleefully described as "the wee hours"—the fourth such dressing-down he had received.

At the same time, China also started to block some exports to Japan of rare earths, metals which are widely used in high-tech manufacturing; this was one of the first times Beijing had so blatantly used economic coercion in a dispute.

China insisted that Japan was using the legal process of the arrest to advance its claim over the islands. But the aggressiveness of the Chinese reaction sent a deep chill through Japanese politics. Support in Tokyo for the idea that Japan should seek greater rapprochement with China and should start to distance itself from the U.S. has withered. Yoichi Funabashi, the editor-in-chief of the *Asahi Shimbun,* one of Japan's leading newspapers, likened the Chinese reaction to a "shock-and-awe campaign." Funabashi had once worked actively to encourage student exchanges between the two countries and had been one of the more liberal voices calling on Japan to make amends with China for its wartime crimes. But in a letter shortly after the dispute, he revealed the sense of disillusionment. "Japan and China now stand at ground zero, and the landscape is a bleak, vast nothingness," he wrote. In an interview shortly afterward, he warned that Asia risked regressing to a "rule of the jungle."

The situation deteriorated further in 2012 over a new argument about the Senkaku/Diaoyu Islands. Japan opened the new dispute. When the nationalist firebrand governor of Tokyo, Shintaro Ishihara, suggested he would buy the islands, the national government intervened and purchased some of the land. Japan thought this less provocative than Ishihara's acquiring the islands, but China's reaction was even more furious than two years before. Beijing accused Tokyo of trying to change the informal status quo surrounding the islands and has maintained a constant stream of patrol vessels around the islands to reinforce its sovereignty claim. At the time of writing, tensions have escalated to such an extent that there is a genuine risk that a mistake or miscalculation between vessels or aircraft of either country could start a broader conflict.

Whatever the rights and wrongs of the immediate dispute, Beijing's reaction has helped consolidate the anti-Chinese shift in Japanese politics. At the end of 2012, the LDP was returned to power, with longtime China skeptic Shinzo Abe as prime minister. Prime ministers may come and go in Japan, but public opinion is now deeply suspicious of China. There is a broad consensus in Japan to shift its military from the north, which was its Cold War focus, to its maritime reaches in the southwest, a direct response to China. Tokyo is now pushing the limits of its espoused pacifism, talking about "dynamic defense cooperation." China's chance to slowly dislodge Japan from its U.S. alliance has been lost.

———

In South Korea, Beijing was presented a similar opening to peel the country away from the U.S. In 2002, riots broke out in Seoul after two middle-school-aged girls were run over by a U.S. armored vehicle, a signal of long-festering resentments about the heavy U.S. military presence in the country. Popular campaigns sprouted over the next decade calling for an end to the American bases. Among younger South Koreans, who had no memory of the war, it became common to suggest that the U.S. soldiers were a greater threat to the country than the North Koreans, whose vast armory of missiles is aimed directly at Seoul. Psy, the South Korean rapper, had the most-watched-ever YouTube video in 2012 with "Gangnam Style." But a decade earlier, his music captured the anti-American mood of his generation of South Koreans. The lyrics to his song "Dear American" included the lines "Kill those fucking Yankees who have been torturing Iraqi captives, Kill those fucking Yankees who ordered them to torture." In one 2002 performance, he smashed a model U.S. tank on the stage.

This popular sentiment found political expression in the "sunshine" policy, introduced in 1998 by President Kim Dae-jung, who had been a dissident while South Korea was a dictatorship. He sought to engage North Korea and to coax it toward Chinese-style reforms. For nearly a decade, Seoul played down human-rights abuses and did everything it could to assuage the hypersensitivity of the North Korean dictator Kim Jong-il. At the same time that George W. Bush was including North Korea in his "axis of evil," the South Korean government was sending Pyongyang hundreds of millions of dollars in bribes—delivered, it was later revealed, by the Hyundai Corporation.

Yet, through its close support of North Korea, China has lost its chance to weaken South Korea's ties to Washington. Beijing's indulgence of Pyongyang has become self-defeating, a triumph of ideology and anti-American paranoia over the country's long-term strategic interests. One of the key turning points was in March 2010, when a South Korean warship called the *Cheonan* was sunk by a torpedo, killing forty-six sailors. An investigation team, which included experts from Sweden and Australia, concluded that the *Cheonan* had been attacked by North Korea. International condemnation quickly followed, yet China demurred. While diplomats from the countries involved in the inquiry toured the world to show other governments their findings, Beijing declined a chance to survey the evidence. The cause of the *Cheonan*'s sinking was unclear, it said. The Chinese government also took five weeks to express condolences to South Korea for the loss of so many soldiers, causing deep offense in Seoul. Nuclear-armed and miserably poor, the Stalinist regime in North Korea relies on Chinese aid to fend off complete collapse. It is also the one country in the region that might plausibly be called an ally of China. The implication seemed clear: Beijing was simply unwilling to criticize its North Korean ally, no matter how dangerous that ally's behavior.

To outsiders, the Chinese position appeared rigid and dogmatic. On the inside, however, China's links with North Korea had been the subject of intense discussion, with many senior officials calling for the government to distance itself from Pyongyang. The alliance had been forged during the Korean War, when China fought alongside Kim Il-sung's army to push back the Americans. Several hundred thousand Chinese died in brutal fighting, including one of Mao Zedong's sons, who was buried there. From that day, Chinese propagandists described the relationship with Pyongyang as being as close as "lips and teeth."

By the early 2000s, however, the sense of comradeship had been replaced by a gnawing embarrassment. Millions were starving in North Korea while cronies of the vulgar, despotic regime of Kim Jong-il nipped across the Chinese border to buy Louis Vuitton goods at the new luxury malls in Shenyang, in the northeast of China. For many Chinese, it was an uncomfortable reminder of the worst days of China under Mao— the mixture of power worship and public misery from which modern China had escaped under Deng. The few scholars I knew who had been allowed contact with North Korea would quietly hint at a sort of shame that China was propping up such a regime. Popular views ran in a similar direction. The Internet in China almost never misses a chance to denounce American policy in the region, but in the case of North Korea, comments would often sympathize with the U.S. and openly mock China's ally.

The booming economic relationship with South Korea also pushed China to question its ties with Pyongyang. Tens of thousands of South Korean companies have invested in China, many of them around the east-coast city of Qingdao, and the flows of goods and people between the two countries have become one of the brightest constellations in the Asian manufacturing network. Two decades ago, there was one flight a week between South Korea and mainland China: by 2010, there were 642. In economic terms, South Korea will be a big part of China's future, not the sclerotic North. Courtesy of WikiLeaks, we know that this frustration occasionally spilled over into the conversations Chinese officials had with other governments. In 2009, Chinese Vice Foreign Minister He Yafei told an American diplomat that North Korea behaves like a "spoiled child." In another cable, a South Korean minister described two conversations with senior Chinese officials who said that they supported the idea of a unified Korea, rather than continuing to prop up Pyongyang. Of course, the Chinese diplomats were doing what good diplomats are supposed to do, presenting a version of events that the South Koreans wanted to hear. But the comments also seem to have reflected the view of significant parts of the foreign-policy establishment. According to Peking University Professor Zhu Feng, no question in Chinese foreign policy has been more hotly debated than the ties with North Korea.

Yet, by the time the *Cheonan* was sunk in early 2010, the party leadership had already ended the debate. China's leaders were given a mortal scare by two developments in North Korea. Kim Jong-il's stroke in 2008 reminded them of the political frailties of the regime. At the same time, a failed currency revaluation in late 2009 underlined the ever-present potential for economic implosion. Faced with the actual prospect of the regime's collapsing, China decided this was something it could not tolerate. Ever since Mao ordered his troops to fight in the Korean War,

China has seen North Korea as a sort of buffer, a placeholder that keeps the U.S. military presence at a distance from its borders. The passage of time and the decrepitude of the Pyongyang regime have not changed that fundamental reality. During a period when China was looking to try and push back against U.S. influence in the region, the last thing Beijing wanted was the end of the North Korean regime and its replacement by an America-friendly, united Korea. Beijing decided to double down on its support for the Kim family regime. Xi Jinping, then China's vice president, gave an extraordinary speech in October 2010, six months after the *Cheonan* sinking, describing the Korean War as "great and just"—a retreat to the 1950s orthodoxy that the U.S. had started the war, and a signal that the fraternal Communist links with the North would trump the economic pull of the modern South. When Kim Jong-il eventually died in 2011, Beijing had already given its support for the dynastic succession plan to hand over North Korea's nuclear keys to his twenty-something son, Kim Jong-un. China, in effect, has pledged to underwrite the North Korean regime for another generation.

The sinking of the *Cheonan* was the moment when South Korea's worst suspicions about China were confirmed. By then, South Korea had a different government, which was much more skeptical about the North and more supportive of Washington. Not only was Seoul outraged at the length of time it took for Beijing to send condolences, but China's continued tolerance for Pyongyang's truculence seemed to suggest to many in the South that it could not be trusted to uphold basic rules of international behavior if they conflicted with its interests. Beijing managed to make things worse with some ham-fisted diplomacy. In November 2010, North Korea shelled the small island of Yeonpyeong, near the sea frontier between the two countries, killing four South Koreans and causing an even more anguished reaction in Seoul. Under pressure to rein in its ally, Beijing decided to call for a meeting of the so-called six-party talks—the diplomatic forum that had been operating for the previous decade to resolve the North Korean nuclear issue. The Chinese government knew that Seoul would not accept talks until it received a public apology from North Korea, but it calculated that the gesture might help deflect some of the blame for the standoff onto South Korea. With no formal warning, Dai Bingguo, the senior Chinese foreign-policy official, turned up in Seoul to discuss the proposal. He did not have a visa, so South Korean Foreign Ministry officials had to rush out to the airport to get him into the country. Dai insisted on meeting with President Lee Myung-bak that evening, even though he did not have an appointment. And even though he asked that the meeting be off the record, he brought a group of Chinese journalists along with him. Lee told him that Seoul would not agree to a meeting involving the North Koreans, but Dai went out and announced the proposed summit anyway. The ill-feeling that Dai generated in Seoul summed up the broader setback to China's long-term interests. By giving so much support to Pyongyang, Beijing was actually doing some of Washington's own diplomatic work. South Korea's unease about the American military presence has not ended, but the alliance between the two countries has been reinforced.

A LINE WITH NINE DASHES

If it was the sinking of the *Cheonan* that prompted a lot of soul-searching in Northeast Asia about China, then the moment of clarity in Southeast Asia came from a more mundane source: the United Nations Commission on the Limits of the Continental Shelf.

In 2009, this largely obscure UN body set a deadline for countries in the region to deliver submissions of their claims in the South China Sea and its myriad of disputed rocks, islets, and coral reefs. The South China Sea has a large and complicated list of claimants. China, Taiwan, and Vietnam claim most of the area and its islands, but the Philippines, Brunei, and Malaysia also claim part. The UN Law of the Sea Treaty provides a framework of international legislation to adjudicate such disputes, a process of case law and precise legal language which is designed to take the heat out of emotionally charged arguments. In the case of the South China Sea, however, the result was the exact opposite. After Vietnam and Malaysia submitted a joint written claim to the panel, China was incensed. Beijing released its own note, which stated: "China has indisputable sovereignty over the islands of the South China Sea and the adjacent waters." Alongside this diplomatic *note verbale,* Beijing attached a map of the area, in which China's claims are demarcated by a line made up of nine dashes.

The "nine-dash line" map was not new: it was first drawn by Chinese cartographers in the 1920s and was adopted as a semi-official map in 1947 under the Nationalist leader Chiang Kai-shek, before the Communists had even taken power. But this was the first time it had been used as part of an official Chinese claim in an international forum. And for many in Southeast Asia, it was a symbol of a certain kind of new Chinese arrogance. Shaped like a large U, the "nine-dash line" starts from China's southwest coast, snakes down adjacent to Vietnam's coastline, curves round along the littorals of Malaysia and Brunei, and then returns to the Chinese mainland after skirting close to the Philippines' coastline. In effect, it marks out almost the entire area of the South China Sea, except a narrow strip beside the coast of the other countries in the region. China says the map is a reflection of its "historical rights" that come from having controlled the different islands for centuries. The Chinese sometimes say the map's U-shape resembles a "cow's tongue"; one acquaintance describes it, slightly less flatteringly, as "a distended testicle."

"We will never seek hegemony," declares China's latest defense White Paper—a stock phrase that is one of the mottoes of official Chinese policy. But in many other Asian capitals, where claims to such "historical rights" inevitably remind them of the subservient position that they were placed in during previous eras of Chinese power, the sheer, jaw-dropping breadth of the Chinese map felt a lot like a push for hegemony. "We maybe should not have been so surprised," a Thai diplomat confided about the introduction of the Chinese map with the "nine-dash line." "But to see with your own eyes that they were actually trying to claim pretty much everything—well, it was quite a jolt."

One legacy of five hundred years of Western naval ascendancy in Asia is the names that are commonly used for many of the island features in the South China Sea—there is Mischief Reef, Macclesfield Bank, Woody Island, and Scarborough Shoal. The sixty or so rocks in the South China Sea are mostly divided into two groups: the Paracel Islands in the northern section of the sea and the Spratlys farther to the south. For decades, the disputes over who owns the land features were a somewhat obscure sideshow, even if China and South Vietnam did briefly fight over some of the islands in 1974, when China took control of the Paracels, and again in 1988. But over the last five years, they have rapidly become a perfect storm of modern geopolitics. The South China Sea has been the place where American and Southeast Asian concerns about China's military buildup have started to overlap. For the U.S., China's claims set off alarm bells about the long-term threat to the U.S. maritime order. But for the Asian claimants, the dispute also brings together oil, fish, and potent nationalism.

For what might appear a few insignificant specks of land, the economic stakes over the disputed South China Sea islands are enormous. In China, the South China Sea is sometimes referred to as a "maritime Daqing"—the oilfield in the northeast of China which was discovered in the 1950s, a lifeline to the Maoist economy in an era of economic isolation, as well as a staple of Communist propaganda about hardworking self-reliance. Chinese estimates suggest there could be as much as 213 billion barrels of oil in the South China Sea, not far short of Saudi Arabia's reserves. Another Chinese estimate suggests there is enough natural gas to meet demand for four hundred years, at current levels of consumption. (Some private estimates are much less optimistic, partly because much of the oil is incredibly hard to recover, indicating reserves closer to 2.5 billion barrels.) If a potential oil boom were not enough, the seas are also rich in fish, making them increasingly attractive to fleets in China and Vietnam, which have seen the stocks in their more traditional catchment areas near the coasts decline through overfishing, pushing them ever farther afield, into contested waters. China is the biggest consumer (and exporter) of seafood in the world, and seafood provides half of the protein intake in the average Vietnamese diet. For both countries, fishing is an industry whose importance is hugely underappreciated.

As tensions have escalated in recent years, China has insisted that the other countries are principally to blame, and it has plenty of evidence to support this claim. Beijing was outraged that Malaysia and Vietnam put forward a joint submission to the UN panel, which the Chinese saw as evidence of other countries' ganging up against them. Chinese officials complain loudly that China is the only country not to have exploited oil resources in the South China Sea. "There are seven hundred wells already in areas that we believe are ours," a Chinese official told me. "And yet people accuse us of being assertive." They point to the buildup of infrastructure on island features controlled by other countries, notably Vietnam in the Spratlys, where it controls twenty-nine of the land features. Beijing is also adamant that Washington's attempt to involve itself in the dispute has emboldened Vietnam and the Philippines to take a more confrontational stance toward China. Many in China are convinced that the U.S. is conspiring against it in the South China Sea. "China is not the maker of these problems and still less the perpetrator of harm," says Cui Tiankai, a former vice foreign minister who became ambassador to the U.S. in 2013. "Rather, China is a victim on which harm has been imposed."

The other claimants tell a very different story. They describe a gradual but decisive increase in China's naval presence in the region over the last decade, as well as a deliberate buildup of military installations on some of the islands that it controls, part of a creeping process in asserting sovereignty. Satellite images from Woody Island (Yongxing in Chinese) in the Paracels bear this out. The small island is around two hundred miles south of the submarine base on Hainan. It has no indigenous population or natural water supply, but over the last few years it has become a fortified military stronghold. A major port has been built from an area that was dredged. At the same time, the landmass has been extended to build a runway for military planes: the satellite images show a thin strip of land almost twice the length of the island. Another thin strip denotes a mile-long road between the island and a small islet, which is now used as a monitoring center for naval activity in the region. In 2012, Beijing declared the island's main town, Sansha, to be a formal municipality. There is a local government building, which, with its painted white walls, long neoclassical columns, and a large dome, looks like a small version of the U.S. Capitol. On the day it was declared a municipality, a local agriculture official from Hainan called Xiao Jie was dispatched on a twenty-hour boat trip to become the mayor. "There is no arable land here," he said of his new job. "The main objective is to protect our nation's maritime sovereignty."

———

Southeast Asian governments accuse Beijing of adopting a strategy of "talk and take." Given the chance, Vietnam and the Philippines can reel off long lists of behaviors by the Chinese they consider to be bullying. The Vietnamese point out that two of the nine lines on the famous Chinese map are in territory which under international law is considered Vietnam's exclusive economic zone, the two-hundred-mile area beyond a country's coast that is recognized by international law. In 2007, Beijing pressured Exxon Mobil and several other foreign oil and gas companies into abandoning drilling operations off the Vietnamese coast—an event that some cite as the start in the current period of tensions. In 2011, Chinese government vessels cut the cables of two ships that were conducting oil and gas surveillance for PetroVietnam. Two months earlier, a Philippine vessel doing a seismological study in a disputed area was forced to leave by two Chinese government ships. Every year, the Chinese authorities enforce a fishing moratorium in parts of the South China Sea, which they say is to preserve stocks, but the decision is not taken with other governments. And each year, they arrest dozens of fishermen who break the moratorium.

It is tempting to think of this activity as a calculated, long-term plan to gradually assert control over the region. Yet, like so many incidents in which China's inner great power has started to be unleashed, there is another side to China's new assertiveness in the South China Sea, a simmering pressure from below to take more action. China's approach to the South China Sea has been one of the clearest examples of how competing vested interests are helping to drive parts of foreign policy— the fracturing in power that the Chinese establishment has witnessed. A whole series of different government bureaucracies have overlapping responsibility for elements of the government's presence in the South China Sea, and sometimes they tussle with one another to make their presence felt. The Chinese are acutely aware of this, labeling the different groups as "the nine dragons," a reference to the ancient legend of a dragon king whose nine sons can be seen in countless murals "stirring up the sea."

Some of that pressure has come from local governments. The government of Hainan Island, where the new naval base is, has administrative responsibility for the Spratlys and Paracels, and for the last two decades has been trying to launch high-end tourism on the islands as part of its own development plan. In recent years, it has gradually worn down the resistance of the central authorities to these initiatives. Travel agencies on Hainan offer luxury diving trips to customers in the Paracels, and there is now a sailing contest between Hainan and the Paracels. The big oil companies, which are among the most connected and powerful sections of state-owned industry, have also lobbied hard for the government to push its claims in the region more aggressively. In 2012, CNOOC, one of the big three oil companies, invited foreign oil groups to exploit jointly nine blocks in disputed areas—several of which are in Vietnam's exclusive economic zone.

Even among the Chinese government departments which enforce activities in the region, there are competing interests. The Bureau of Fisheries Administration is responsible for policing fishing in Chinese waters, but China Marine Surveillance also conducts law-enforcement activities in the region. Like any good bureaucracy, they are both keen to show their worth in order to boost their budgets, which have grown rapidly in recent years. They even have a phrase to justify their sometimes vague and overlapping roles: "Grab what you can on the sea and then afterwards divide responsibility between the agencies." The Agriculture Ministry, which is responsible for the fisheries bureau, operates a reward system for individuals who have been "tough and brave in defending China's sovereignty": officials get a bonus for evicting a large number of foreign boats from waters that China claims as its own. With dozens of armed vessels and aircraft at their disposal, these agencies have also played a role in pushing the boundaries of China's sovereignty claims. While sending the navy could be seen as a highly provocative move, these law-enforcement vessels can stake China's claim in a less confrontational fashion.

There are two other factors behind the deep sense of unease in Southeast Asia. It is not only the extent of China's claim that has rattled the region, but also the ambiguity of it. No one quite knows what they are dealing with. Even though the "nine-dash line" map has been in circulation for several decades, China has never actually defined the territory that is included in its map. At times, Foreign Ministry officials have attempted to calm nerves by indicating that China claims only the islands and land features within the line. Such a claim would still involve a series of difficult disputes but is much less expansive than claiming the entire area on the map. Yet, at other times, Chinese officials and analysts have indicated that their historic "title" to the South China Sea gives them exclusive rights to everything inside the line. Others have suggested that the area is part of China's "sovereign waters." Peng Guangqian, a hawkish major general in the PLA, has described the waters inside the "nine-dash line" as "China's . . . 'blue-colored land'" and as a region "owned" by China. CNOOC's attempt to sell oil leases within disputed waters and the fishing bans imposed by China indicate an official position that is very different from the one outlined by the Foreign Ministry. Such ambiguity could mean several things. It could suggest that there is flexibility in China's position, which could be exploited in negotiations. But it could also mean that China is trying to have it both ways, its diplomats sticking to a narrower claim while its actual behavior pushes for a much more expansive version.

There is also a question of size. In dealing with China, the other countries feel less like sovereign equals and more as if they are trapped next to a large elephant that could swat them aside. That very size difference makes Chinese moves seem much more threatening to its neighbors than Beijing realizes. The Southeast Asian claimants want a multilateral discussion of the different claims, believing that only this will allow them to talk as equals. Fearing the others will gang up on it, China insists that each country should deal with it on a one-on-one basis. For the smaller countries, Beijing's insistence on bilateral negotiations feels like a form of bullying. "China's attitude," says a senior politician from one Southeast Asian nation, "is, 'It does not matter what the precise nature of our ultimate claim is; if we say it is ours, then that means it is ours.'"

————

To be fair to the Chinese, the regional backlash against its behavior in the South China Sea appears to have been given a gentle push by some clever American spin. If there is one area where Washington still holds a decisive advantage over Beijing, it is in the dark arts of the background media briefing. In March 2009, Jeff Bader, the Asia director at the National Security Council, and James Steinberg, the deputy secretary of state, traveled to Beijing for a series of meetings with their Chinese counterparts. The South China Sea was one of the topics that featured heavily in the meetings. A few weeks later, the *New York Times* ran a story saying that China now referred to the South China Sea as a "core interest."

In diplomacy, small phrases can carry immense power. In the code language of Chinese diplomacy, these two words are enormously important. The other "core interests" are Taiwan and Tibet, issues on which the party will move mountains to prevail. To describe the South China Sea in such terms would indeed represent a substantial escalation, a sign that China saw absolutely no room for compromise or negotiation. The Chinese officials had in fact been in an uncompromising mood during the meetings, delivering several lectures on their rights in the South China Sea. Yet Bader and Steinberg insist that the explosive "core interests" formula was never actually used in their meetings. Hillary Clinton later said that Dai Bingguo, the leading Chinese foreign-policy official, used the phrase with her at a U.S.-China summit two months after Bader and Steinberg's meetings, although this, too, is disputed, both by Dai's underlings and by some of the American delegation. ("Hillary appears to have refreshed her memory," as one American official acidly puts it.) Whatever the origin of the phrase, however, China had been snookered. The government could not confirm the statement without provoking outrage in Southeast Asia. But neither could it officially deny the story, for fear that it would be accused by nationalists at home of being weak. Instead, Beijing suffered in silence.

If the "core interest" story was spin, it was the sort of exaggeration that was instantly believed around the region, because it seemed to tally with the reality of Chinese behavior. Washington's rhetoric since 2010 has sometimes leaned on clumsy slogans along the lines of "America is back" in Asia, but the real story was the open door that was waiting for Washington in a region where anxiety about China was soaring. In the Philippines, for instance, there had been popular rejoicing when the U.S. Navy was forced out of its base in Subic Bay in 1992, and leaders like Gloria Arroyo welcomed China as a "big brother." But U.S. warships are now returning with ever-greater frequency, and the country's new president, Benito Aquino, declared in 2012: "We need to take a united stand against the recent aggressive actions from China."

In essence, China has started to suffer from the fundamental contradiction of its strategy. For the best part of two decades, Beijing had been pursuing two separate goals. It has a military strategy of trying to gradually push the U.S. back into the Pacific Ocean and exerting greater control over the Near Seas. At the same time, it has a diplomatic imperative of preventing its neighbors from forming a coalition to block it. Yet it turns out the two goals are not compatible. The harder it pushes back against the U.S. and in favor of its territorial claims, the more it rallies the region to embrace Washington. China has suffered one strategic setback after another. It has ended up strengthening the cornerstone U.S. alliances in Northeast Asia. At the same time, China's behavior in the South China Sea has allowed the U.S. to become much more engaged with the nations of Southeast Asia. As Shi Yinhong, the Chinese academic and Bismarck fan, put it rather mournfully: "We have achieved the very opposite of what we had hoped for."

America's own experience in the nineteenth century demonstrates the extent to which China's strategy has misfired. For almost two centuries, the U.S. has claimed a form of regional ownership and has worked to exclude other great powers from exercising decisive influence in the Western Hemisphere. "Why should we not have our own Monroe Doctrine?" a Chinese diplomat once quietly suggested. He quickly checked himself, because China denies it has any such pretensions, but it is not hard to understand the sense of frustration behind the question. To some Chinese ears, the U.S. operates a double standard by working so hard to prevent China from exerting the same sort of influence that it enjoys in its own backyard. It used to be considered somewhat glib to compare China's attitude toward the Near Seas to the Monroe Doctrine. But as China's claims have hardened, the comparison has started to seem more valid. What are the "nine-dash line" and claims to "historical rights" if not an assertion of a certain sense of ownership and entitlement to regional dominance? Yet the very different history behind the Monroe Doctrine underlines the substantial disconnect between how China sees itself and the way much of Asia experiences China. American naval power from the 1890s was certainly one factor in allowing Washington to expand its writ, but it was not the only one. Just as important was the generous reception that the U.S. received in large parts of Latin America at the time. The Monroe Doctrine was not imposed on an unwilling hemisphere: in much of the region, it was welcomed.

When Brazil hosted the Third Pan-American Conference in 1906, the star turn was Elihu Root, Teddy Roosevelt's secretary of state, who was touring the region to explain the implications of the Monroe Doctrine. Root was given a rapturous reception, because many South American governments saw the Monroe Doctrine not as the imposition of American power but as a guarantee of their independence from European colonial rule. Confidence in Washington was so high that the Brazilians renamed the building that hosted the conference the Palacio Monroe—a name it retained when it became the permanent home for the Senate. Joaquim Nabuco, one of the most influential Brazilians of the era for his role in the abolition of slavery, was happy to publicly declare himself a "Monroista." "For me the Monroe Doctrine means that we have separated ourselves from Europe as completely and definitively as the earth from the moon," he said. Of course, in the decades after the Second World War, during which the U.S. helped overturn elected governments in Guatemala in the 1950s, Brazil in the 1960s, and Chile in the 1970s, the region's view of U.S. primacy shifted dramatically. Anti-Americanism quickly became part of the Latin American political DNA. Since then, many governments have tried to push back against Washington in just the same way that Asians are doing today against China. But the fact that the Brazilian Senate building was named after Monroe underlines the way his doctrine was understood in the region at the time.

The Asian backlash that started to take shape in 2010 will not be easily reversed by China, even if it tries to return to another bout of "smile diplomacy." The year was not a flash in the pan, but instead represented a long-term realignment in Asian politics, one in which many governments concluded that their interests overlapped with those of Washington. One way to demonstrate that this is no temporary setback for China is to look more closely at two pivotal countries in the Asia-Pacific Region, which could not be more different in terms of politics, culture, and history, but which are exhibiting similar instincts about a rising China: Australia and Vietnam.

THE WEATHER VANE

"You could not get much closer to China than we are," Geoff Raby, the former Australian ambassador in Beijing, likes to joke. "But we will." Australia figures in very few accounts of international politics, an isolated if enormous island perched on the bottom edge of the Asia-Pacific with a modest population of twenty-two million. But such neglect is misplaced. For the last three decades, Australia has been an important weather vane for China's rise, a sort of early-warning center for the opportunities and risks. If you want to find out how the world will react to a more powerful China, Australia is a good place to start.

Australia was one of the first countries to wake up to the economic potential of the Chinese boom. The signature breakthrough came in 1985, when the then Chinese leader Hu Yaobang decided to visit Australia. Bob Hawke, Australia's prime minister, threw out the protocol of a formal visit and instead took him on a tour of the Pilbara, a distant region of Western Australia more than three thousand kilometers from Canberra that is rich in minerals. There is a famous photo of the two of them, both in white shirts without ties, standing on top of a mountain and looking across acres of red earth that have since become one of the biggest iron-ore mines in the world. In many ways, the photo was the start of the current commodities boom.

Fast-forward more than two decades, and one-quarter of Australia's exports now go to China, its biggest market. Chinese demand not only soaks up Australian resources, but has caused the prices of those commodities to soar, too. Australia has been one of the biggest beneficiaries of China's growth. The economy has grown every year for the last two decades, even during the financial crisis—the first time this has happened in the country's history, and a record that no other developed economy has matched over the same period. The China market has also created pockets of huge wealth. The average price of a home in Peppermint Grove, the smart suburb of Perth in Western Australia, the heart of the mining boom, is now $5.1 million. With the possible exception of South Korea, no country is now more dependent on the Chinese economy. In Kevin Rudd—or Lu Kewen, as he is known in China—Australia became the first Western country in 2007 to have a prime minister who speaks Chinese. Immigration has also forged a powerful personal link with China, of the sort that can start to mold self-perceptions. Mandarin Chinese has now overtaken Italian as the second-most-spoken language in Australia. Chinese tourists spend more money in Australia than do visitors from any other country.

The extent and velocity of these economic links with China are prompting some profound questions for Australia. Australia has been a loyal ally of the U.S. since the end of the Second World War, and, more than any other country in the Asia-Pacific, Australia is extremely comfortable with U.S. military dominance in the region. The last few decades have been the best in Australia's history. It is free to trade with anyone it wants in Asia, while enjoying the political and military protection of a country with very similar political and cultural traditions. Australians, however, are starting to wonder if they can afford to remain so close to America when they do so much business with China. "Australia is having to ask itself how to reconcile its two core interests," says Michael Wesley, former head of the Lowy Institute, the Sydney-based think tank that is one of the best sources of analysis on China. "Its security, which is tied to the United States, and its prosperity, which is ever more closely tied to China."

Politics will follow economics—that is the core insight behind the predictions of inevitable Chinese leadership in Asia, the idea that the countries which depend on Chinese economic dynamism for their livelihood will start to bend to the political prerogatives of Beijing. If that idea is true, then one might expect to see Australia looking for some sort of middle ground. Indeed, if the Asia-Pacific region was comfortable with the prospect of China's assuming a central leadership role, one of the early signs would be a decision by Australia to drift gradually away from its close defense relationship with the U.S.

Through one of the quirks of presidential scheduling, Presidents George W. Bush and Hu Jintao happened to visit Canberra on consecutive days in 2005, and both leaders were invited to give speeches to Parliament. These were during some of the darkest days of the Iraq War, which Australian troops were helping to fight. Bush, who lectured the audience on the fight against terror, received a reception that might be described as cordial. Hu came to Parliament the next day and gave a very different speech, about respecting differences. "Our world is a diverse place, like a rainbow of many colors," he said. "Civilizations, social systems, and development models, different as they may be, should respect one another, should learn from each other's strong points." The *Australian Financial Review* summed up the visit with the headline "Bush Came, Hu Conquered."

The reaction to the visits was one of the signals of a deeper bout of uncertainty in Australia. At one stage, Australia's foreign minister, Alexander Downer, referred to the alliance treaty with the U.S. as "symbolic." The reality was very different—a treaty imposes legal obligations on both parties—but his comments caused consternation in Washington. The Chinese sought to apply subtle pressure. According to Chen Yonglin, a Chinese defector who had worked at the consulate in Sydney, senior officials in Beijing were openly suggesting that Australia could come to play a role somewhat similar to France's—still part of the Western alliance, but detached from America and willing to take its own path on important issues.

Yet, in the end, the very opposite has happened. Trade with China has boomed, investment from China has boomed, the Australian economy has boomed, yet Australia has not only decided to maintain its ties with the U.S., it has actually strengthened them. In late 2011, Barack Obama visited Australia to announce that up to twenty-five hundred U.S. marines would be deployed to the country, part of an expanded defense alliance between the two countries. "Our enduring interests in the region demand our enduring presence in this region. The United States is a Pacific power, and we are here to stay," he said in a speech to the Australian Parliament, which received a standing ovation.

Of course, a couple of thousand marines will not alter the strategic balance in Asia, but the politics are very important. Australia is defying the apparent logic that China's economic size will give it political influence. Canberra sees that China's military buildup could undermine the stability of the region's economy and believes a robust American military presence is the best way to fend off that prospect, a bulwark against the worst instincts of a more powerful China. As Kevin Rudd told Hillary Clinton, the goal should be to integrate China into the international community "while also preparing to deploy force if everything goes wrong." The U.S. marines are an insurance policy for an uncertain future.

Australia has also been one of the first Western countries to start thinking long and hard about what it means for a democracy to be so economically close to the authoritarian Chinese state. In 2009, Stern Hu, a China-born Australian citizen working for the mining multinational Rio Tinto in Shanghai, was arrested on charges of stealing state secrets. At the time, Rio Tinto was also involved in a tense commercial dispute with Beijing over iron prices, lending a heavy political hue to the arrests. The charges were later reduced to stealing commercial secrets, and Hu received a ten-year jail sentence. Hu admitted to taking bribes, but few in Australia believed he would have been prosecuted had his company not been involved in a difficult argument with the government. A month later, Beijing launched a fierce lobbying campaign to change the program of the Melbourne Film Festival to exclude a film about Rebiya Kadeer, an exiled activist from the heavily Muslim province of Xinjiang in northwestern China whom Beijing accuses of sowing ethnic unrest. When that pressure was ignored, four Chinese films were withdrawn from the festival. The dispute sent a chill through parts of Australia about the implications of growing Chinese influence. "The Chinese embassy told me I had to justify my actions including the [Xinjiang] film in our programme," Richard Moore, the head of the festival, complained. "But, hey, we are just an independent arts organisation and it is our programme!"

Australia will continue to be an important weather vane. Although the beefed-up alliance with the U.S. has broad political support, there are also important and influential critics. Former prime minister Malcolm Fraser has denounced the U.S. approach to China as a rerun of Cold War–style "containment." He derides Washington for thinking of Australia as a "strategic colony, taken for granted, total support for whatever the United States may do." The most articulate criticism of U.S. policy in the region has come from Australia, by the former government adviser-turned-academic Hugh White. In a 2010 essay "Power Shift," he argues that if the U.S. does not find a way to accommodate China's interests in the region, it will slip into an open confrontation with Beijing. "As China grows, America faces a choice of Euclidian clarity," he writes. "If it will not withdraw from Asia and if it will not share power with China, America must contest China's challenge to its leadership." Canberra's role in all this, White says, is to help persuade Washington that it must accommodate China. Australia's debate on how to deal with China is not for the fainthearted. Greg Sheridan, the foreign editor of the newspaper *The Australian,* called White's essay "the single, stupidest strategic document ever prepared in Australian history" and an exercise in "appeasement." Discussions about the relationship with the U.S. will long reverberate, but that does not detract from the basic message behind the new deployment of marines. Australia has decided that, for the next generation at least, it will continue to bet on the U.S.

SWORD LAKE

The first time I visited Vietnam was as a tourist, and for a day or two my wife and I went to what seemed to us the obvious sites in Hanoi. We strolled along wide avenues still lined with trees the French had planted when they were the colonial power, and whiled away an afternoon in street-side cafés. Our hotel, the Metropole, was an imposing colonial building with a white façade, green shutters, and wood paneling that had been the focal point of French society in the city in the 1920s and 1930s. It was very proud of the fresh croissants it baked for breakfast. The next day, we went to the "Hanoi Hilton," the Hoa Loa Prison, where John McCain spent some of his five and a half years as a prisoner of war after his plane was shot down during the Vietnam War. It was built originally by the French, but the North Vietnamese used it as one of the main places for detaining captured American servicemen. Now it is a museum, its walls covered with photos of McCain, whose hair turned prematurely white in captivity.

It took a day or so for us to pick up on something that we would have known if we had been a bit more curious before arriving. However much the Vietnamese detested French colonialism, and however many millions had died in the war with the U.S., these had in many ways been but passing episodes in a much longer history of defending the country's sovereignty. In that longer story, the principal antagonist was China. Half a mile from our hotel was the Hoan Kiem Lake, a shimmering pond filled with water lilies that forms the focal point of the city center. It is also a somewhat mawkish memorial to the struggle against China. The name means "Lake of the Restored Sword," a reference to the legend that Emperor Le Loi was handed a magic sword which he used to fend off the Chinese invasion during the Ming dynasty in the early fifteenth century. Near the shore on the east side, there is a small island accessible by a red bridge. It houses the Ngoc Son Temple, built a couple of hundred years ago to honor a thirteenth-century general who helped defeat the Chinese Yuan dynasty. A couple of miles away, the Hai Ba Trung neighborhood in central Hanoi is named after two sisters who led a three-year-long rebellion against Chinese rule in the first century A.D. When we mentioned that we lived in China, several people immediately informed us how many times China had invaded Vietnam over the years, even if they sometimes offered different numbers.

In the annals of China's imperial history, Vietnam is the one that got away. The Han dynasty occupied a large part of what is today's Vietnam in the second century B.C., and China retained control of the country for most of the next thousand years. Vietnam eventually prized itself free from the Chinese embrace, but that long history has left traces of a sense of entitlement in China. A caption at the Shaanxi History Museum in Xian, one of China's premier collections of antiquity, reads: "Until 200 years ago, Vietnam was part of China, and even today in the homes of Vietnam people you can see Chinese characters." Like all such histories, Vietnam's links with China are full of complexities and discontinuities. Although it was Le Loi's victory in the fifteenth century over Ming invaders that cemented the independence of Vietnam, the decades that followed his triumph were the high point of Confucian cultural influence in Vietnam. But the Hanoi tourist sites underline the broader point; a significant slice of modern Vietnamese identity is rooted in the struggles to maintain autonomy from China. The anxieties stirred in Vietnam by the rise of China are in one sense the direct opposite of the response in Australia. Whereas Australia fears the end of a historical era it has been comfortable with, Vietnam fears a return to an older historical pattern it wants to avoid.

Vietnam is, therefore, one of the most interesting fault lines along the rise of China. More than any other country in the world, Vietnam has a political system that looks very similar to China's—an all-powerful party that is still run on Leninist principles but which has dumped Marx and embraced the market in a bid to modernize its economy and society. The Communist Party ties run deep. In his somewhat intimidating way, it was this spirit of fraternal political unity that Chinese Foreign Minister Yang Jiechi was trying to appeal to in his diatribe in Hanoi. Vietnam also knows that China's economy is one of the main potential growth engines that can drive its own prosperity. Huge public investments in the southwest of China are driving new road and rail links down into northern Vietnam, cementing the economic connections even further. A new high-speed train will soon link Hanoi to Nanning, the capital of the border province of Guangxi. Yet Vietnam is the country where China's great-power posturing is provoking deeper existential angst than almost anywhere else, as a new era of geopolitics collides with some very old Asian histories. Vietnam is thus an important barometer for both the mounting Asian backlash against China and the intricate balance of power that is taking shape in Asia. Hanoi believes it can both integrate its economy with China and seek new friends to help restrain China. Vietnam is working to have it both ways.

———

China looms large over every issue in Vietnam. Like China, Vietnam has a substantial claim over the South China Sea, including both the Paracel and Spratly Islands, and Hanoi has watched the expansion of China's navy with increasing unease. For Vietnam, the territorial disputes in the South China Sea are about much more than just control of some islands. With the exception of Chile, Vietnam is more dominated than any other country by its coastline, which stretches 3,260 kilometers— "a balcony looking onto the Pacific Ocean," as some Vietnamese describe its location. Vietnam's long-term economic plans talk about deriving 50 percent of its GDP from maritime activities, including fishing and exploiting natural resources in areas it claims as its own. The fate of the small group of rocks and islets in the South China Sea cuts to the core of Vietnam's vision of its own economic future.

Leaders in Vietnam run the constant risk of being accused of selling out to China. After Chinese ships cut the cables of the two Vietnamese oil-survey ships in mid-2011, large anti-Chinese demonstrations broke out in both Hanoi and Ho Chi Minh City. Afraid of being accused of appeasement, the Vietnamese authorities allowed the protests to continue every Sunday for twelve weeks—an eternity for protest movements in a one-party state. The protesters wore T-shirts and caps with the symbol for "No-U"—in reference to the Chinese map for the South China Sea. Others sported the slogan "Say No to the Ox-Tongue Line." Once the protests were eventually shut down by the authorities, some formed a "No-U" football club to play on Sundays.

The fissures of anti-China nationalism cut right across the Vietnamese establishment. In 2011, twenty prominent figures in Vietnamese society—terming themselves "patriotic personalities"—submitted a letter to the Vietnamese Politburo suggesting that Hanoi had been "too soft" on China. Their number included Major General Nguyen Trong Vinh, who had been the country's ambassador to China. Trong Vinh has also been a public critic of a controversial Chinese mining project in the Central Highlands region, which has proved to be a lightning rod for fears about Chinese economic domination. Trong Vinh was joined in that protest by an even more illustrious figure, General Vo Nguyen Giap, whose role as chief military planner in the victory over the French at Dien Bien Phu in 1954 and in the war against the U.S. makes him one of the nation's most celebrated military figures. Vietnam's leadership also has its pro-China faction, and some of the most senior leaders in the country are considered more sympathetic to Beijing. Yet, in both the Vietnamese Communist Party and in the military, analysts say that younger members tend to support closer ties with the U.S. Anti-Chinese sentiment is even stronger among Vietnam's large overseas diaspora, especially the population in the U.S. In some ways, one of the nightmare scenarios for the Vietnamese leaders would be for these different forces to be brought together by a dispute with China—popular nationalism, the anti-Chinese faction among the elite, and a significant section of the diaspora. A serious crisis with China could deal a potentially fatal challenge to the legitimacy of the Vietnamese Communist Party.

Vietnam's response to China's behavior should come as no surprise: it, too, is turning to the seas. Hanoi does not have the resources to mount a significant navy, even though the defense budget is rising sharply, but it can buy the sort of hardware that might allow it to conduct its own "asymmetric" challenge to China. In 2009, Vietnam placed an order for six Kilo-class submarines from Russia—a type dubbed a "black hole" by the U.S. Navy because special rubber tiles allow them to evade detection by sonar. The submarines will help Vietnam to monitor the movements of Chinese vessels in contested areas and to deter any Chinese attempt to grab islands currently occupied by Vietnam. To get a sense of just how seriously Vietnam takes the military challenge from China, it is worth considering that the order for the submarines was placed during the heart of the financial crisis, when the country's export industry was being decimated. And for a country of Vietnam's size, such a number of submarines does not come cheap—the $3.2-billion price tag is equivalent to a year of the entire defense budget.

In the summer of 2010, a U.S. Navy destroyer called the USS *John S. McCain* docked at the Vietnamese port of Danang. The vessel is named after both the father and grandfather of Senator McCain, both of whom were four-star admirals: the eldest McCain captained aircraft carriers in the Pacific War, and his son was commander of the U.S. Navy in the Pacific. Vietnam has not only been investing in its navy, it has also been assiduously making friends with other important naval powers, none more so than the U.S. The visit by the USS *McCain* capped one of the more remarkable turnarounds in Asian politics in recent years. Large tracts of land in Vietnam are still unusable because of unexploded bombs dropped by American planes. Yet, just over three decades after the Americans abandoned their embassy in Saigon, Vietnam has turned to the U.S. for support. The contacts began tentatively in the late 1990s but have gathered pace as concerns about China have risen. In 2009, Vietnam took one important step when several of its senior officers flew out to spend some time on the USS *John C. Stennis,* an aircraft carrier, to view its operations in the South China Sea. The appearance of the USS *McCain* marked the first time the two countries have conducted joint naval activities, in this case a training exercise and a search-and-rescue drill. (They also swapped tips about cooking on board a naval vessel.) If the substance seems a bit trivial, the message to China was not: it was a powerful statement that Vietnam sees the U.S. naval presence in the region as both legitimate and important. "China complains that the

U.S. is stirring up trouble," a senior Vietnamese diplomat told me, "but we think the increased U.S. presence in the region is important to help stabilize the situation."

China routinely denounces any exercise of U.S. military power in the region as evidence of a "Cold War mentality" and of a strategy to "contain" China, just as it once did with the Soviet Union. Washington's new friendship with Vietnam is further evidence to many Chinese that Washington is determined to maintain its hegemony. But China's anger misses the two most important points about Vietnam's rapprochement with the U.S.—both why it is taking place and the actual nature of their military cooperation. The uncomfortable truth for China is that collaboration with the U.S. is not being pushed on Vietnam; it is being solicited. Beijing also ignores the enormous subtlety with which Vietnam deals with China. Rather than shun its neighbor, Hanoi goes out of its way to try and engage Beijing, a delicate dance in which deterrence is mixed carefully with dialogue. Vietnam's suffocating history with China is, of course, an extreme example, but the pattern also fits many other countries in the region. Asia is now a continent of confident nation-states who cherish the autonomy they have won in the postcolonial era, and who want to make the most of the opportunities that globalization is bringing, including the rise of China. But they want to navigate this new era on their own terms, not as someone's "little brother." For Hanoi, setting aside wartime resentments of the U.S. is a price worth paying so it can establish its own path. This is not containment: Vietnam sees the U.S. presence as a way of getting its relationship with China on the right footing.

Hanoi takes elaborate care not to provoke China too far. Whenever Vietnam conducts some sort of exercise with the U.S. military, it usually does something similar with the Chinese shortly before or after. Vietnam and China have a defense hotline that they can use during periods of tension. The two Communist parties have also established a joint steering committee that allows officials from both countries to meet regularly and discuss ways to defuse problems. The party-to-party ties allow for a frankness of conversation that few other countries can achieve with China. Delegations of earnest experts in socialism and Marxism shuttle between the two capitals, glad for the rare chance to exchange ideas in another country. Even with the high level of anti-Chinese sentiment in the country, Vietnam exudes a certain confidence in its ability to cope with a rising China, the sort of self-assurance that comes from experience. In 2012, when China and the Philippines were locked in a tense standoff over the Scarborough Shoal, another disputed section of the South China Sea, a Vietnamese official commented to me, with a slightly world-weary air, "We have been coping with the Chinese for two thousand years. We know exactly how to deal with them." The comments were partly aimed at the Philippines, which was viewed in many quarters as having provoked a fight with Beijing it could not win, but it was also partly aimed at the U.S. This is the great paradox of modern Vietnam. Hanoi is the government that has the most sophisticated channels to talk with Beijing, but its combustible politics and deep-seated historical resentment make Vietnam the country one can most easily imagine fighting a war with China.

———

This complexity places considerable limits on the U.S. Into such waters, Washington should proceed carefully, fully aware of the way its rapprochement with Vietnam might be viewed in China. One of the surest ways for the U.S. to turn a budding rivalry with China into sullen hostility would be to make a big push to expand military ties rapidly with Vietnam. If the U.S. were to start stationing substantial military assets there, for instance, China would begin to think of this as a potential staging point for aggression against its territory. "Vietnam is to China what Cuba is to us," as one former senior U.S. official puts it. "When the Soviets flipped Cuba, we decided that it had profound national security implications. It almost caused the end of the world."

Pushing too hard would also alienate Hanoi. "We do not want to be owned by anyone," the Vietnamese diplomat told me. Closer ties with the U.S. give Vietnam a wedge to avoid being sucked further into a Chinese orbit, but Hanoi has no interest in becoming a new U.S. client state in the region. It wants enough, but not too much U.S. help. Hanoi is still hugely sensitive about allowing a U.S. military presence in the country: the American soldiers taking part in searches for missing personnel from the Vietnam War have to wear civilian clothes when they are outside of U.S. diplomatic compounds. Only once they are inside are they allowed to change back into uniform. Hanoi is also very particular about the use of the Cam Ranh naval base, a natural deep-water harbor near the strategic chokeholds of the South China Sea. Vietnam allows foreign logistics and survey ships to visit the port, but not battleships. Leon Panetta, the former U.S. defense secretary, went to Cam Ranh in 2012 in a high-profile visit that seemed like a major advance in military ties between the two countries. But the U.S. vessel he visited in the harbor was the USNS *Richard E. Byrd,* a cargo ship. For Vietnam, these little details matter a great deal.

Vietnam's relations with China may be unique in their historical complexity and intensity, but they set out the bigger patterns that are starting to shape Asian politics. Behind Vietnam's fervent diplomacy is a fierce desire to avoid being pulled into a Chinese sphere of influence. Yet the Vietnamese regard the U.S. purely as a balancing power, not as an ally, or as a nation they want to see dominate the region, or as a partner in containing China. For both Vietnam and Australia, the endgame is not to circumvent China and its booming economy, but to find ways to deal with China on their own terms. Military cooperation with the U.S. is not a new exercise in containment; it is a way of feeling comfortable about getting closer to China.

4

_____

America's Choice

THERE ARE so many powerful nineteenth-century echoes in China's rise that it is easy to miss the most important exception. When the U.S. and Germany were establishing themselves as great powers, they had the luxury of a relatively benign regional environment. For the U.S. in the 1890s, the European empires which had once dominated its hemisphere, Spain and Portugal, were weak or crumbling, while its neighbors, Canada and Mexico, presented little security threat. "The Americans are a very lucky people," Bismarck liked to joke. "They are bordered to the north and south by weak neighbors and to the east and west by fish." Germany had to deal with a much more complicated set of neighbors, but it also enjoyed the good fortune that its rise was accompanied by decaying empires on its frontiers, from the Austro-Hungarians next door to the Ottomans to the southeast, or the Russian monarchy to the east. China faces a completely different backdrop, a region that is full of successful and ambitious states who also believe this is their time. From South Korea round to Indonesia and then to India, China is encircled, which places significant limits on its ability to get its own way. Japan, even after two decades of stagnation, is still the third-largest economy in the world, and has arguably the most capable navy after that of the U.S. China is not rising in isolation, but into a region of proud nation-states that want to stake their own claims in the modern world.

As a result, there is an iron rule to the new era of geopolitical competition in Asia, which Washington and Beijing ignore at their peril: do not ask the other Asians to choose sides. The government that pushes Asians to pick one power over the other will lose. Modern Asia has its own internal balance of power, which will make it hard for either the U.S. or China to dominate the region. Asians believe they can trade with China and at the same time encourage an active U.S. presence, and they will push back against anyone who tries to force their hands. Everything else follows from this simple understanding.

China's behavior over the last few years has been so counterproductive because it has run up against this iron rule. Beijing was in effect trying to suggest that America is the region's past and China the future, so Asian governments should fall in line with its wishes. Leaders in the Asia-Pacific responded by doubling up on their ties with Washington. The harder China pushes, the more the region's governments will band together into a loose coalition to deter a Chinese push for dominance.

Yet the new Asian reality also poses difficult questions for the U.S. American officials like to say that they have always been attentive to the regional balance of power, but the reality is that the U.S.'s unrivaled military superiority meant that it did not have to think too hard about diplomacy. The difficult process of coalition building seemed less pressing when most challenges could be addressed by sending in an aircraft carrier group. All this is now changing. Even those who are skeptical about China's current capabilities do not doubt that, over the next two decades, American control of the western Pacific will be substantially loosened. That means the U.S. will have to develop different ways to maintain a favorable balance of power. The U.S. needs to rethink the way it exerts influence in Asia.

An Asia strategy first, not a China strategy. By focusing too closely on China, America tends to overreact to the country, a tunnel vision that leads to the assumption that the U.S. and China are the only central players. The result is a division into two different camps that favor either accommodating China or confronting it, neither of which is wholly realistic.

The hawkish response to China's military buildup is to call for a renewed effort to reassert American supremacy in the region. Pressure is building, especially on the right, for a decisive military response to push back against Chinese assertiveness. Yet down that path lies the potential for a permanent cycle of escalating tensions, of provocations and counter-moves and rising defense budgets. It is a recipe for a contest that would feel a lot like a new Cold War. It would also damage America's ties to the region. If the U.S. takes too confrontational an approach to China, it will lose support of some of its friends and allies, who will accuse Washington of pushing the region toward conflict. A strategy to contain China could not work. Asians want the support of the American military so they can feel comfortable engaging with China, not so they can isolate it.

At the same time, an excessive focus on China can lead America to lean too far in the opposite direction in an effort to accommodate Beijing, to search prematurely for a formula for sharing power between the two giants. The early years of the first Obama administration were full of talk of a G-2 between the U.S. and China to tackle global issues together. Such an effort would also fail the new Asian rule on several fronts. By transmitting a sense of weakness to China, it might actually embolden the more hawkish elements in Beijing, who would sense decline. And it would also terrify many Asian nations who dislike the idea of Asia's becoming a Chinese sphere of influence and who would feel abandoned by the U.S. If such fears took hold, Japan could seek its own nuclear weapons, maybe South Korea, too; Vietnam's existential crisis would deepen. Conflicts could become more likely, not less. Asians do not want the U.S. to confront China, but they also do not want the two governments to conspire to set the regional agenda. Even if Washington wanted to appoint China as a co-leader in Asia, that role is not America's to give.

Instead, it makes more sense to start not with China, but with Asia as a whole. If the U.S. is going with the grain of what most of a rising Asia wants, it will become much easier to fend off any Chinese efforts to alter the status quo. The good news for Washington is that ideas that it says it wants to promote in Asia—free trade, open navigation, legal protections for investment, economic integration across the Pacific, and an emphasis on human rights—are all things that most Asian governments also support. As its military dominance starts to wane, Washington's objective is to help build an Asian regional order based on these principles, which China could not overturn even if it wanted to. All this will require a delicate balancing act. As the iron rule dictates, the U.S. will need to avoid turning China into an implacable enemy. But it also needs to demonstrate to both China and its allies that it has staying power, and that, despite Chinese predictions, it is not about to retreat back across the Pacific for evening cocktails in Hawaii. China and the U.S. will eventually have to learn to live with each other, to find a way to respect each other's interests in the western Pacific, if they are to avoid a rivalry that feels like the Cold War. But that accommodation will be more favorable to the U.S. and more stable for the region if China believes any bid for regional dominance would come at enormous costs and regional isolation.

Elements of this approach are already being developed in what is now called the Obama administration's "pivot" to Asia. The president has left no doubt that he sees the Asia-Pacific as a central long-term priority for U.S. national security. But many of the details are not clear. As things stand, the U.S. economic agenda in the region is shaky, and the hints Washington has given of its new military strategy are downright alarming. This chapter will look at the four pillars of the U.S.'s approach to Asia—military, diplomatic, economic, and political.

HOW NOT TO FIGHT CHINA

In 1992, a young deputy air-force attaché at the U.S. Embassy in Beijing called Mark Stokes started to tour quietly around various parts of the country, looking for clues about what the Chinese military were up to. In those days, there were not nearly as many foreigners living in China as there are today, and in most cities a Western face soon attracted a lot of attention. But by hanging around cities with large military bases, such as Leping in the southern province of Jiangxi, and comparing impressions with what was being written in Chinese military literature, Stokes was able to gain some insights into what the PLA was actually planning. He started to accumulate evidence about what appeared to be the start of a major strategic bet by the Chinese military on medium-range and long-range missiles. It was the first sign that China was building a military that one day might seek to exert greater control over the western Pacific. "In many ways, we are still in the same position we were in then of underestimating China's ability for important breakthroughs in areas that directly challenge the U.S.," says Stokes, who now helps run a consultancy that monitors the Chinese military.

For much of the last two decades, the Pentagon has held an anguished internal debate about the nature of China's military modernization. Back in 1992, plenty of people in the Pentagon dismissed the analysis of people such as Stokes, rejecting the idea that a country as poor as China would have such clear-cut military ambitions. Others argued that China's ability to contest Asia's seas with the U.S. was heavily constrained by its dependency on the global economy. China could not afford to upset the apple cart, they said. In the 1990s, the debate was largely academic, because the U.S. still had a dramatic superiority, which it had coolly demonstrated in the 1995–96 standoff over Taiwan's election. After China launched several missiles into Taiwanese waters in order to intimidate voters, the U.S. sent two aircraft-carrier groups into the region as a demonstration of force. Beijing was furious, but it could not do anything, and Taiwan held its election without further threats. Yet, over the years, the Pentagon has consistently been surprised at the pace of China's military buildup, from its ability to take out satellites to the stealth fighter jet it tested while Bob Gates was in the country. Today, if you ask the question about how the U.S. would respond to a similar crisis, the answer from U.S. military officials often involves a lot of nervous fidgeting.

One of the jobs of a military is to plan for worst-case scenarios. The U.S. military conducts regular war games to test how conflicts with potential adversaries such as China might play out, and in recent years these have delivered some disturbing conclusions. In several of the simulations, the U.S. participants found that Chinese missiles quickly overwhelmed many American bases in the region, as well as sinking some of the aircraft carriers that the U.S. sent into the western Pacific. It is a measure of the rapid advance in China's air force and navy in the last two decades that, if a conflict did break out over Taiwan, it is now not at all clear that the U.S. would be able to intervene decisively in the Taiwan Strait.

The U.S. has not lost an aircraft carrier since the Japanese sank the *Hornet* in 1942. In both practical and symbolic ways, the aircraft carrier has been the symbol of American power projection over the six decades during which it has dominated the Pacific. The credibility of U.S. defense guarantees for the region has been carried on the backs of America's eleven carriers, with their decks each the size of three football fields filled with dozens of fighter aircraft. But it is those same vessels that are now potentially under threat by China's vast new array of missiles. The loss of a carrier would be a massive psychological blow to American prestige and credibility, a naval 9/11. The mere prospect that carriers might be vulnerable could be enough to restrict their use. Even if the U.S. Navy commanders thought their carriers would probably survive in a conflict, they might be reluctant to take the risk. As a result, the U.S. needs a Plan B.

Deep in the bowels of the Pentagon, that new plan is taking shape. It is not actually described as a plan—instead, Pentagon officials call it a new "concept" for fighting wars. But it does have a name, AirSea Battle, which echoes the war-fighting doctrine from the later stages of the Cold War called AirLand Battle, when the massive buildup in Soviet troops appeared to give the U.S.S.R. the capacity to overrun Western Europe. Many of the details about AirSea Battle remain vague. But the few indications that have been made public suggest an approach that, if pushed too far, could be a manifesto for a new Cold War.

————

In 2005, the American writer Robert Kaplan did a cover story for *The Atlantic* entitled "How We Would Fight China." I can remember receiving a copy in my office in Shanghai and tossing it angrily onto a pile of papers, the plastic wrapper still on the magazine. This was the high point of the debacle in Iraq, and the idea of talking up a war with China at that very moment seemed the height of neoconservative conceit. It made me uncomfortable for all sorts of other reasons. When you have recently moved to a country, are learning its language, making friends, and exploring its mysteries, it is unsettling to be asked to start thinking about how it might be defeated militarily. When I did eventually read Kaplan's article a few years later, it was not as hawkish as the title suggested and contained sensible recommendations about getting on better with the rest of Asia and dispersing U.S. military assets across the region. But I also began to realize that the question he raised was a crucial one. China does not have a grand imperial plan to invade its neighbors, in the way the Soviets did. But in any country with a rapidly growing military—one that is feeling its national oats and is involved in a score of unresolved territorial disputes—there is always the risk that its leaders might be tempted by some sort of military solution, the lure of a quick win that would reorder the regional balance. If China and its neighbors all believe that the U.S. has a credible plan for a conflict, this both acts as deterrence against any eventual Chinese adventurism and reduces the risk that anxious Asians will start their own arms races with Beijing. Or, as T. X. Hammes, the American military historian, puts it: "We need to make sure no one in the Chinese military is whispering in their leaders' ears: If you listen to me, we can be in Paris in just two weeks."

Alarming as it may sound, the question of how to fight China also forces Washington to reflect on its deeper objectives in Asia. Bob Gates, the former defense secretary, used to remark that the Pacific had "for all practical purposes been an American lake for our navy since the end of World War II." But relative decline means finding different ways to achieve U.S. goals. With its superiority now under challenge, Washington faces a choice: it can try to retain its primacy, or it can shift to a more defensive approach that is geared toward preventing another power from ever turning the region into a sphere of influence. Deterrence is not always the same as domination. Washington's answer to this question remains muddled. When asked to define their military objectives, American officials will say that deterrence is their principal goal, but they also give plenty of indications that they still aspire to a more maximalist role, to try and hang on to their unquestioned superiority. Shortly after he became head of the U.S. Navy in 2011, Admiral Jonathan Greenert issued a set of "Sailing Directions," which set out the navy's mission and made the claim that "we own the sea." When I asked another senior U.S. official about the objectives of AirSea Battle, he said, a little awkwardly, "It is part of a conversation we are having about the different forms we expect our pre-eminence to take."

AirSea Battle is a direct response to the war-game simulations that showed Chinese missiles taking out American carriers. Its target is the buildup by other nations of what in Pentagon-speak is known as "anti-access/area-denial," or A2AD for short, the weapons and ships that are designed to prevent an opponent from getting into the seas around its coasts in the event of a conflict. "We need to make sure that we can actually get to the fight," an air-force official explained. In public, Pentagon officials claim AirSea Battle is not aimed at China. One senior Pentagon official insisted to me, "This is not an anti-China battle plan." But when the Pentagon starts to describe the new threats it is facing—long-range, precision-strike missiles that can restrict the movements of its ships, advanced submarines, and skills in cyberwar—it becomes clear that AirSea Battle is primarily about China. The hypothetical threat that the Pentagon planners outline describes accurately the precise strategy that China has been developing to restrict U.S. access to the western Pacific. No wonder U.S. military officers sometimes refer to China as "Voldemort"—in the Pentagon's new battle plan, China is the enemy whose name they dare not speak.

Amid the military jargon there lies an idea that—if taken to its logical conclusion—is fraught with peril. The first time AirSea Battle was described in public was in a paper by an independent Washington think tank called the Center for Strategic and Budgetary Assessments. The paper said that if the U.S. and China ever came to blows, the U.S. should direct a "blinding campaign" at China's missiles and sophisticated radars. In early 2012, the Pentagon released a document called "Joint Operational Access Concept" (known in the building as JOAC), a 75-page paper which has a couple of recommendations that stand out. In the event of a conflict, the paper says, the U.S. should "attack the enemy's cyber and space" capabilities. At the same time, the U.S. should attack the enemy's anti-access forces "in depth."

The clear implication of this advice is that, if war ever were to break out, the U.S. should plan to launch extensive bombing raids across mainland China. To neutralize China's weapons that might prevent the U.S. from "getting to the fight," the U.S. would need to take out the missile bases and the surveillance equipment that they rely on, including land-based radar. These facilities are spread across the country, including many highly built-up areas. The basic idea behind AirSea Battle leads to a fairly uncompromising conclusion that, in the early stages of a conflict with Beijing, the U.S. should destroy dozens of military sites across mainland China.

There are several reasons why this would be a dangerous way to think about a conflict with China. For a start, it is a recipe for rapid escalation. Given that two nuclear powers are involved, there should be big incentives to leave room for diplomats to try and find a way to resolve the situation. Yet, in calling for U.S. forces to take out China's missile batteries as a first step, AirSea Battle is a formula to intensify any conflict quickly. It is not at all clear how China would interpret such a bombing attack. American commanders might rationalize their actions by saying that they were only going after the Chinese missiles that could hit their ships and satellites. But the Chinese might well conclude that the U.S. was also targeting its nuclear weapons. The fact that Washington knows so little about the Chinese decision-making process on nuclear war makes this even more risky.

Using AirSea Battle's ideas against China is an all-or-nothing battle plan. Military strategists talk about devising a "theory of victory," a war-fighting plan which will also create the sort of victory that can be translated into a realistic political settlement. But if AirSea Battle means swiftly ordering bombing raids across China, it does not provide any off-ramps that would create space for diplomacy. Short of complete Chinese capitulation, it is difficult to see how such a war would end.

As an approach to fighting, AirSea Battle would likely be very expensive, too. It would require the Pentagon to fast-track a lot of weapons projects, such as a new generation of stealth bomber, at a time when budgets are coming under pressure. It is not only the usual critics of the military-industrial complex who fear this is part of the hidden agenda of AirSea Battle. An analysis by the Marine Corps concluded that the plan would be "preposterously expensive." At the same time, Chinese hawks pushing for more aggressive defense spending would use the American investments as powerful evidence to push their own budget demands. The U.S. military objective should be to deter China, not provoke its hard-liners. Toward the end of the Cold War, the arms race ultimately bankrupted the Soviet Union before the pressures of high defense spending began to seriously undermine the U.S. But if a deeper arms race were to develop between China and the U.S., it is not at all clear that Washington would be starting from a stronger financial footing.

Then there are the allies. The iron rule of Asian geopolitics is to avoid forcing countries to choose, yet it is possible that AirSea Battle would oblige Washington to make some fairly hefty demands of its allies. Asian governments are keen on a U.S. military that can push back against Chinese aggression and are eager to enlist U.S. help in this regard. But some allies might balk at the prospect of a plan to attack deep into mainland China, especially if it involved launching bombing raids from their territory. Ben Schreer, an Australian military strategist, says AirSea Battle is suited to "a future Asian Cold War scenario." Winning the support of allies is even harder when the U.S. cannot tell them much about the plan. Given the high secrecy around AirSea Battle, I have met Japanese and South Korean officials who insist they have been forced to talk with the Center for Strategic and Budgetary Assessments—a think tank—in order to find out what it really means. Rather than providing assurance to its friends and allies, Washington's new battle plan could easily rattle some of them.

All these objections combine to create one final problem with AirSea Battle: Is such an approach politically viable? Whatever the level of international support the U.S. might enjoy at the beginning of a conflict would be sorely tested if the Pentagon were to escalate the dispute quickly into bombing runs on mainland China. Washington would likely face enormous international pressure to desist, putting it immediately on the back foot. Given all the risks, especially the chance of nuclear escalation, it is not at all clear that an American president would ever actually endorse a war plan that involves such a rolling bombing campaign. Successful deterrence relies on being able to demonstrate a military threat that is credible and realistic. Pentagon planners hope the Chinese military will be cowed by the mere thought of an American military strategy based on AirSea Battle. But, equally, the Chinese might come to see it as a one great big bluff.

———

At the very least, AirSea Battle concentrates the mind. It is prompting a much broader debate in the U.S. about how to construct credible deterrence. If the basic objective is to convince Chinese hard-liners that there is no path to a quick win in the western Pacific and to defend its allies, then U.S. strategy should be built around finding ways to raise the costs so that China's leaders would never be tempted even to consider such a proposal—and to do so in ways that are politically and economically realistic and which are not hugely provocative toward China. In its effort to force U.S. carrier groups into the seas around China's coasts, AirSea Battle fights the very war that Beijing has long been planning for. Instead, the U.S. and its allies will have to think about ways to invert that logic—to draw China's untested navy out of its comfort zone, using the region's geography against it and imposing high penalties that would give Chinese military commanders pause for thought.

The American naval historians Toshi Yoshihara and James Holmes suggest that the U.S. partly focus on what they call "war limited by contingent," smaller-scale operations which provide support to allies, preventing dramatic escalation but making life extremely difficult for the Chinese navy. They draw the analogy of the duke of Wellington's campaign in Spain and Portugal in 1807–14, which was in military terms a mere sideshow to the broader conflict with France, but which Napoleon complained gave him "an ulcer." The geography along different parts of the first island chain provides many strategic locations which can be used to construct a series of small-scale facilities with missile batteries, tunnels, and decoys that could create havoc for another navy in the vicinity. These facilities would be purely defensive and would present no direct threat to the Chinese mainland, but they could be used to make it extremely costly and difficult for China to exert control over the nearby seas. Under such an approach, the U.S. could also enhance the sense of deterrence by increasing the number of submarines it has operating in the region. "The ideas that China is pursuing about denying access can work both ways," Holmes told me. "There are many ways to give China an ulcer, which could be one of the best ways of deterring aggression before it ever happens."

In the event of a broader conflict, another option might be to reach back into the Pacific War playbook. During the Second World War, the United States imposed a blockade on Japan that cut it off from the rest of the world for four years, and the same approach could potentially be used again. Rather than seeking to smash China's mainland missile defenses quickly, the military objective would be to impose enough strain on the Chinese economy that China's leaders would be forced to the negotiating table. At first glance, such an approach might sound like an implausible suggestion, given the high degree of dependency between the two economies. But this would be a situation in which the two countries were already involved in a war that had devastated the global economy. The only question is how the U.S. would wish to conduct that war.

The region's maritime geography would help a blockade. Given that so much of China's energy comes from the Middle East, a blockade could be enforced by controlling only five strategic chokepoints—the Straits of Malacca, Sunda, and Lombok, which are the gateways from the Indian Ocean to the Pacific, and the routes to the north and south of Australia. A blockade forces the Chinese navy to come out: rather than operating from the protective confines of its coastal waters, the Chinese would have to launch operations far away from base. China's naval strategy is based on the "asymmetry" of not having to match the U.S. ship for ship, sub for sub. But the farther from China that its forces are required to operate, the greater demands are made on China's more inexperienced commanders.

There are plenty of strategic difficulties with a blockade. Without Russian support for the plan, China would have an overland route. Such a plan is also likely to enhance China's feeling of being under siege: this is, of course, the very "Malacca Dilemma" that China has long fretted about. However, a blockade would afford lots of ways that the leaders of both countries could bring the conflict to an end while saving some face. A slow process, it provides opportunities for both sides to back down while claiming some sort of victory. Such an outcome would be politically messy, with both nations claiming to have prevailed and nationalist tensions soaring. But the result could open the way to a return to the status quo of freedom of navigation in peacetime. In the disastrous scenario of a U.S.-China war, it is at least possible to imagine how such a conflict might end.

Even the proponents of these ideas acknowledge that they are at best half-answers, but they are kick-starting a broader discussion about strategies for deterrence. The debate is also raising difficult questions about how the navy should focus its investment in the coming years. Many of the possible options for a conflict in the western Pacific would require the U.S. to substantially rethink the sort of navy it needs. During one of their presidential debates, Barack Obama mocked Mitt Romney's defense-spending plans by telling him, "We have these things called aircraft carriers, where planes land on them." For almost a century, aircraft carriers have been essential platforms during conflict and powerful diplomatic statements during peacetime, as they roam the world from one harbor to another. But in areas like the western Pacific, their effectiveness could be coming to an end. As Henry Hendrix, a U.S. Navy captain and historian, puts it, aircraft carriers are "big, expensive, vulnerable—and surprisingly irrelevant to the conflicts of the time."

Some parts of the American navy believe that the U.S. should invest in a larger fleet of smaller and faster warships, which would increase the number of targets an opponent's missiles needed to take out but dramatically reduce the political and economic costs if one were hit. Other strategists propose much bigger investments in quiet, stealthy submarines, which would be harder for China's new surveillance technologies to pick up when they operate in the western Pacific. In a more defensive strategy that is designed to prevent another country from exerting sea control over the region, submarines are likely to be one of the main tools. And there are also strong proponents of weaponized drones— unmanned aircraft—which in the future might have the ability to operate at much greater distances from a base or a ship than fighter jets can. All three of these technologies could potentially give American commanders better options than sending in aircraft carriers. Yet downgrading the role of aircraft carriers is a decision fraught with difficulties. The fleet of carriers has become a symbol of American commitment to helping police the oceans. Any significant cut in their numbers would be viewed as a signal of retreat by some U.S. allies in Asia—precisely the people whom the new strategy is designed to reassure. Either way, there are no straightforward answers to the headaches China will cause the Pentagon in the coming years.

LEADING FROM BEHIND

The quest for a military Plan B dovetails with the second leg of American strategy, how to engage with the rest of Asia. As Chapter 3 indicated, the U.S. has the wind in its sails: China's behavior has provoked a powerful backlash in the region, mobilizing Asia's internal balance of power and pushing many of Asia's other rising powers much closer to the U.S. If constructed in the right way, Washington's web of friends and allies in the region could provide a parallel layer of deterrence against a Chinese push to dominate the region.

Yet, despite this fertile territory, the business of managing a coalition in Asia will be an extremely complex and delicate task. Even if it wanted to, the U.S. could not construct an Asian version of NATO. The potential partners are too diverse. They include a solid treaty ally, like Japan, but also a country like India, which would never sign up for anything that looked like a formal alliance, no matter how worried it became about Chinese naval power. Unlike Western Europe during the Cold War, these Asian powers have much less sense of a collective threat. Many countries have individual disputes with China, but they are less likely to intervene in one another's quarrels. Any effort to construct an Asian NATO against China would also break the iron rule: it would come across as the sort of confrontational step that could erode broader support for the U.S. in the region. A rigid alliance would feel a lot like an exercise in containment.

The U.S. also has to avoid being sucked into traps by its allies. Washington's objectives should be to maintain a favorable balance of power and to provide clear defensive arrangements against any potential aggressors. The big risk, however, is that allies will feel emboldened to pick fights with China because they think that the U.S. will bail them out if things get out of hand. Low-level standoffs such as the Scarborough Shoal incident in 2012 will provide dilemmas for Washington about whether or not to intervene. There will also be persistent pressure for the U.S. to pick up the bill for things that its allies are perfectly capable of paying for themselves.

One way to deal with these tensions is for the U.S. to take more of a backseat as new Asian political arrangements emerge. The default instinct in Washington is to try to organize everything, to put itself at the center of the conversation. However, it is also in America's interest to see the creation of robust regional organizations. Asia is a long way from replicating the sort of integration that Europe witnessed after the end of the Second World War, but there is a genuine move toward closer cooperation that, if successful, would help build a more predictable and stable environment. Stronger regional institutions can restrain bigger countries from throwing their weight around too much, and can act as shock absorbers during disputes.

In truth, both the U.S. and China have been lukewarm in the past about Asian regionalism. During the George W. Bush years, the U.S. was somewhat dismissive of the alphabet soup of different Asian organizations that have sprung up over the last three decades, many of which have thus far been ineffectual talking-shops. China, over the last few years, has openly played divide-and-rule at several summits of ASEAN, which brings together Southeast Asian countries, to prevent it from taking a common position over the territorial disputes in the South China Sea. At the July 2012 summit of ASEAN in Cambodia, China used its influence with the Cambodian government, which leans heavily on aid from Beijing, to block the joint statement that some of the members wanted ASEAN to issue. Chinese diplomats were sitting in a room next door to the main session, and the other delegations watched aghast as Cambodian officials shuttled between the official meeting and the Chinese to show them different drafts of the text. Yet, even as ASEAN has struggled to articulate strong positions, its more important members are quietly trying to create a more coherent organization. Indonesia, the potential anchor power in Southeast Asia, is starting to take a more active role in building a regional consensus, as is Singapore.

The same efforts at regionalism are beginning to take shape in the security field. One of the best ways to establish enduring deterrence is to encourage more security cooperation between Asia's other powers, independent of the U.S. China's hard-liners may always think that American presence in the region will be hostage to the next budget crisis in Washington, but its neighbors are not so easy to dismiss. There are already all sorts of signs that this kind of balancing behavior is starting to happen. In addition to its new efforts to collaborate with the U.S.

Navy, Vietnam has signed defense pacts with nine other countries in Asia. Hanoi is restoring its ties with Russia and increasing naval cooperation with India, which has started sending warships through the South China Sea. At the same time, South Korea is cooperating with Indonesia, the Philippines, and Australia. Perhaps the most important potential new axis is between Japan and India, where powerful voices in both countries are pushing the idea of a long-term strategic pact. India and Japan do not share the same disputes with China, but they do have one common interest: just as Japan does not want China to dominate the western Pacific, India does not want China to become a powerful force in the Indian Ocean. Both India and Japan also have burgeoning defense ties with Australia. It is early yet, but these initiatives have the potential to become an important means of balancing Chinese power in the region.

The difficulty for the U.S. will be to avoid getting in the way. Such agreements work in the same direction as American interests, but they run very much counter to the swashbuckling political style of the U.S. The Obama administration found itself on the sharp end of intense criticism when a White House official described the 2011 Libya operation as "leading from behind." Political opponents were quick to slam the idea as a failure of American leadership and of managing decline. Yet, in a future in which its military dominance is challenged and careful diplomacy becomes more important, leading from behind will sometimes be exactly what the U.S. needs to achieve. As Raja Mohan, the Indian analyst, puts it: "The U.S. needs to do less working 'on' Asia and more working with."

The eventual U.S. goal will be to help fashion a loose, informal web of collaboration across the region which is based on shared interests, and which makes it harder for any one country to try and overturn the status quo. Rather than an organized alliance structure, it will be more of a latent coalition, ready in the wings if needed. The central selling point is that it shifts the burden onto China. If Beijing behaves in ways that do not alarm its neighbors, the efforts to balance against it will be only modest. But if China continues to push hard and fans anxieties across the region, then a more robust coalition will take shape against it.

If Washington has the right military strategy and diplomatic arrangements in place, it will then be in a much stronger position to have a conversation with China about the long-term future of the region. The U.S. and China will eventually have to accommodate each other, but this will not be some diplomatic grand bargain, an Asian Treaty of Versailles for the twenty-first century. Instead, it will be a more mundane and long-term set of conversations about establishing rules of the road that allow both countries to live with each other. It will involve establishing limits on the sort of surveillance activities that navies can do, where China has some legitimate complaints. At the same time, the only way to find a way out of the myriad territorial disputes will be negotiations about joint development of energy resources, which the U.S. could conceivably help foster.

To help that process, the U.S. will need to try and establish as good a relationship as possible with the PLA, even while it is building its ties with other Asian countries. At present, the two biggest militaries in the world barely talk. "When we do meet, it hardly rises above the schoolyard," says one former senior officer in the U.S. Pacific Command. The U.S. is partly to blame. Particularly under Donald Rumsfeld, the Pentagon was deeply suspicious of having a closer relationship with China. More recently, it has been China that has put up the barriers, despite encouragement from the U.S. Some Chinese military officers worry about giving away secrets and suspect that U.S. insistence on closer ties is a sign that Washington sees the military balance moving against it. Yet the piracy operations off the coast of Somalia have shown that there is a potential opening for greater cooperation. Further efforts to build confidence should include inviting China to observe some of the naval exercises the U.S. Navy organizes in the region. If their navies work together more on issues such as humanitarian assistance, this could take some of the edge off the inevitable competition. Little will be lost and much potentially gained by being on better speaking terms with the PLA.

IT'S THE ECONOMY, STUPID

America's military presence alone is a thin reed on which to hang an entire Asian strategy. Trade is the lifeblood of the Asian economy, the source of its dynamism and decades of high growth. And it is through trade policy that many in Asia will ultimately judge American seriousness about the region.

During the last election, Asia was barely mentioned, and when it was, the tone of scorn was not hard to detect. China came in for particular criticism—Mitt Romney ran TV ads in Ohio on a constant loop about "Chinese cheaters"—but trading with Asia in general was often presented as a persistent threat to American jobs. As a senior politician in one Southeast Asian country puts it: "No one ever stood up and made the case in favor of globalization, saying that this is why Americans can buy so many cheap goods at Walmart." If Washington wants to remain central to the conversation about Asia's future, then it will need to tell a story about economic engagement with the region that is very different from election-time rhetoric. Asian politicians want to hear American leaders making the case for placing Asia at the center of the country's economic future. And they want to hear that case made in Ohio—and not just when American politicians are visiting the region. Nothing would demonstrate staying power more than long-term American commitments to reduce trade barriers with Asia.

Trade policy is another area in which the U.S. and China are quietly competing to construct the future path of Asia. Washington does actually have an ambitious trade strategy for Asia. The U.S. is now one of the leading proponents of the Trans-Pacific Partnership, a trade agreement that is being negotiated between a group of nations on both sides of the Pacific, including Singapore, South Korea, Australia, Chile, and Mexico. Japan is also hoping to join. The core idea is to establish rules on a series of issues that are not properly covered in existing trade agreements, and which will be at the center of economic governance in the twenty-first century—things like the protection of intellectual property, stronger protection for investment, and restrictions on the generous subsidies that some governments give to their industries. It aims to set high standards which would be binding on all its participants. Trade agreements are slow-burning exercises: TPP has been under negotiation since 2002. But American officials hope TPP can eventually become a template for broader trade integration for the Asia-Pacific Region.

China is pursuing a different path through an initiative called the

Regional Comprehensive Economic Partnership (RCEP). The goals are much less ambitious: a modest reduction in tariffs on some industries, leaving out more politically sensitive areas. It offers an easier but shallower form of trade integration. And from the U.S. point of view, it has the added disadvantage that it seeks to lower barriers only within Asia, not across the Pacific. The stakes are high. If the Chinese approach ends up prevailing, U.S. companies could find themselves at a big disadvantage in some of the world's fastest-growing markets.

America has some big advantages in this competition. Most Asian governments would prefer a model for trade integration that spans the Pacific rather than closing off the region. Yet there are two big sets of problems facing the U.S. trade agenda in Asia. The first is that it excludes so much of the region. Not only is China, the biggest Asian economy, absent from the negotiation, but so is India and nearly half of the members of ASEAN, the Southeast Asian group. It is hard to make the case that the U.S. is pushing regional trade integration when such a large part of the Asian economy is not at the table. Over the coming years, Washington will likely need to develop a second string to its trade agenda, one that complements TPP by finding ways to promote trade integration between the U.S. and other parts of the region. One idea would be a deeper trade partnership with ASEAN. Whatever the approach, however, the U.S. will need a trade strategy that does not give the impression that it is dividing up the region.

There are also lots of questions about TPP itself. Many in Asia question whether the U.S. really has the stomach to push through an important trade deal at a time when unemployment is so high and large sections of the electorate appear to be souring on the benefits to the U.S. of globalization. The success of TPP will also partly hinge on bringing Japan on board, the third-largest economy in the world, despite likely strong opposition from its agriculture lobby. That leaves the U.S. uncomfortably dependent on Japanese politics. If TPP does not progress, it would be an enormous setback to the U.S.'s efforts to demonstrate that it has more to offer Asia than just its navy. "If the U.S. rhetoric on trade is not matched by some action, it is hard to exaggerate the sense of disappointment this will cause," says another senior Asian politician.

BURMA AND HUMAN RIGHTS

On the day I arrived in Yangon, a large crowd was lining the streets of one of the main avenues near the center of town. They were there to greet the country's president, Thein Sein, who had just returned from an overseas trip. Only a couple of years beforehand, such a stage-managed stunt of support for the leader would have been evidence of the corrosive weakness of the Burmese military regime. But this was the autumn of 2012, and there actually was reason to celebrate. Thein Sein, the former general-turned-civilian-politician, had just become the first Burmese leader in four decades to visit the U.S., a political prize for the surprisingly brisk burst of political and economic reforms he had introduced since taking power in 2011. And while he was on American soil, he received an even bigger reward from his new American friends: the Obama administration announced that it would start lifting the sanctions which for most of the previous two decades had smothered its economy. Burma was being welcomed back into the modern world.

The trip was even more remarkable for the odd-couple act that Thein Sein put on with Burma's most famous resident. At the same time that the president visited the U.S., Aung San Suu Kyi was also making her first trip to the country since being released from house arrest in late 2010. For part of her fifteen years of isolation, Thein Sein had been the number-four leader in the Burmese regime that incarcerated her. Yet, as both of them toured the U.S.—he at polite diplomatic engagements at the United Nations, she at a series of rapturous rallies where she was greeted like a rock star—they went out of their way to say glowing things about each other. Whenever he was given the chance, Thein Sein praised her for the responsible role she was playing as the main opposition leader in Parliament. After she was presented with the Congressional Gold Medal, an honor which she had actually been awarded during her period of house arrest, Thein Sein said, "We are proud of her." For her part, Aung San Suu Kyi told audiences that Thein Sein was sincere in his efforts to promote reform, and that he needed all the help he could get from Burma's American friends. For several decades, he had been banned from visiting the U.S. and she had been prevented from trying, but here was the former dissident and her onetime jailer making the case for each other to American audiences. When they met at the Waldorf Astoria in New York, Thein Sein, wearing a V-neck sweater and comfortable shoes, came across as her kindly uncle.

Shortly before he left for the U.S., Thein Sein made another trip, this time to Beijing. In a meeting with Xi Jinping, he insisted that Burma's embrace of democracy would not affect its friendship with its "traditional neighbor" China. But the statement was not really true. The voyage that took Thein Sein to New York was also, in many ways, a journey away from Beijing. The powerful backstory to Burma's perestroika has been a desire to break free from overweening Chinese influence.

There are, of course, many reasons why the new civilian government in Burma has decided to change course after five decades of brutal military rule. There was the gnawing shame of isolation that kept its leaders from traveling to many parts of the world and left its economy hamstrung. In the 1960s, Yangon had been a thriving Asian hub, the sort of place where PanAm flights to the region stopped, but four decades later, the sense of stagnation was overwhelming. Zarganar, the country's best-known comedian, who was jailed four times by the military, described his disbelief when he was allowed to leave the country for the first time and visit Thailand in 2011. "When I saw the airport, I got a shock," he said. "When I saw a good road and big bridge, I got a shock. And seeing the big buildings, I got a shock." Yet, on top of the desire to modernize the country, the new government also wanted to escape from China's suffocating embrace. Burma's political revolution really began in earnest with an act of defiance toward Beijing, the decision to block a plan for a Chinese company to build a huge dam in the northeast of the country. At the time Aung San Suu Kyi was released from house arrest in late 2010, the political direction was still unclear: it could easily have been one more in the series of head feints the military had pulled in the past. The signal that this time things really were different came with the decision to stop the Myitsone Dam (pronounced *Mitso*), which had become the subject of an unprecedented political campaign within Burma. "It was a very significant step," U Han Thar Myint, one of the central committee members of Aung San Suu Kyi's National League for Democracy, told me. "It was the first time that the government had made a major decision based on the opinion of the people in fifty years."

Burma's tilt away from China is yet more evidence of the backlash against Beijing that has seeped across Asia in recent years. But it is significant in another important way. Burma has become a trial run for how much importance the U.S. will place on human rights and political reform in this new era of geopolitical competition in Asia. Burma's opening is raising some fairly fundamental questions about Washington's objectives in Asia. Thein Sein's visit to the U.S. has lent the impression that Burma is in the process of being "flipped," from a nation that sought patronage from China to one that takes direction from the U.S. As the U.S. seeks to shore up its diplomatic presence in the region in response to China, the temptation to try and draw Burma into the American camp is very strong. In a region where a new balance of power is taking shape, there is a certain cold, realistic logic to the idea of downplaying concerns about human rights in order to win new friends. That would be a big mistake. If Washington's objective were to contain China, then it would need the support of as many regimes in the region as it could muster. But if its goal is to foster an Asia of strong, independent states, then political reform and human rights will be a central objective. The endgame in Asia for Washington is not to have a bigger club of sometimes embarrassing friends than China; it is to forge a robust and stable set of rules and institutions laced with American values of openness and political pluralism which will be resistant to Chinese pressure. That is the real prize. And Burma is now the test case.

When Western governments imposed sanctions on Burma in the late 1980s, China was far from alone in filling Burma's gap. India has major interests in the country, and there has been a huge amount of Thai investment, including in controversial areas like teak and jewels. But, particularly during the late 2000s, the Chinese presence expanded rapidly. Some of those investments are quirky. Not far from the Shwedagon Pagoda, the gold-domed temple that rises from the center of Yangon, there is a Chinese-run entertainment center called Ice Wonderland, where you can pose beside ice statues of Mickey Mouse and descend slides made from ice. Residents of subtropical Yangon borrow long thermal coats to survive the minus five degrees Celsius. But there are also investments like the Myitsone Dam. The project is one of those jaw-dropping Chinese development schemes that speak to an almost mythical confidence in the power of engineering. The Myitsone Dam was planned to be one of seven in the mountains at the start of the Irrawaddy River that would in total have generated twenty gigawatts—more than the Three Gorges Dam itself. The Chinese group behind the project was CPI, part of one of China's most important energy groups, and run by the daughter of a former Chinese premier.

Right from the start, however, the project encountered resistance. Myitsone is in Kachin State, in one of the areas of the country that have been ravaged for decades by fighting between the government and the Kachin ethnic minority. As Ko Maw Tun Aung, an environmental activist originally from Kachin, told me, Myitsone is an almost sacred place in Kachin culture, considered to be a spiritual birthplace. "It is the sort of mystical place we hear about in bedtime stories," he said. The Chinese also found themselves in bed with some of the least savory elements of the former regime. Their partner was a Burmese company called Asia World, which is the subject of U.S. sanctions and has been accused of being involved in heroin smuggling. The U.S. Treasury Department describes the company's owners as "regime henchmen" and "junta cronies."

In a country where, until recently, politics had been tightly controlled, the dam quickly became a catalyst for an intense burst of campaigning. The well-known writer Ju began to hold events decrying the damage to the river valley. She was joined by cartoonists, artists, composers, and poets. "It is a different country now; it is not good enough for the Chinese just to do a deal with the regime," said the writer Ko Tar. The media also began to campaign aggressively against the dam—led by the Eleven Media Group, which started out publishing a sports weekly but now publishes the most dynamic newspaper in the country. The movement quickly took on a life of its own, largely bypassing the National League for Democracy, Aung San Suu Kyi's party, which was the nominal opposition. Sensing the shifting tide, "the Lady" lent her support. She released a public letter calling for an "amicable" resolution to the issue and made an appearance at a Yangon art gallery that was showing an exhibition about the dam.

Not only did the campaign against the dam open unprecedented space for political activism, it was also notable for the stridently anti-Chinese sentiments that it exposed. The project struck a chord across many sections of society that felt that China had become far too influential during the years of isolation and that it was time to take a stand. U Tin Oo, one of the leading figures in the NLD, described the broader issue as being whether Burma becomes "not just China's satellite state, but China's vassal state." The media coverage of the campaign played up the anti-China angle. Than Htut Aung, chairman and CEO of the Eleven Media Group, said in one interview: "I informed the government and the opposition of the real situation in our country. In the 19th century, the superpowers were the British and the French. They colonised India and us. In the 20th century, the superpower was the US and they took Vietnam, Korea and Germany. In the 21st century, it's China and we cannot sacrifice our country to China. I told the generals and Aung San and she knows." Even among the military, some of whose members have become very rich doing business with China, there was resentment about the regime's closeness to Beijing, which in the 1960s had backed a Communist insurgency and had denounced the Burmese military as "fascist." Thein Sein had himself commanded a unit of the army which fought against the China-backed Burmese Communist Party.

––––––

Yangon has some of the buzz of the cool, new thing these days, the best hotels packed with Westerners who have decided to take the chance of looking around. When I met one of the anti-dam activists in a café called Coffee Circles, we were surrounded by hip, young Americans and Europeans, typing on their MacBooks and talking enthusiastically into headphone sets, the sort of frontier atmosphere that you could see in Shanghai a decade ago. Burma is also the exciting new topic in American foreign policy. The dramatic political opening has presented a big strategic opportunity for the U.S., which it has grabbed with both hands. The then secretary of state Hillary Clinton visited the country in late 2011, and Barack Obama followed suit in 2012. But just how the U.S. chooses to engage with Burma's government—and how quickly it withdraws remaining sanctions—will have a big influence on the sort of society that emerges. Plenty of pitfalls lie ahead. The reforms that have been introduced so far to open the economy are only partial, and their success is not assured. Cronyism is easy to catch, but difficult to get rid of. Lots of members of the old regime and the business interests connected to them would be happy to see the government give the impression of reform, allowing sanctions to disappear, while changing little in the way the country is really run. Momentum could easily be lost. The U.S., therefore, faces a lot of difficult decisions. If Washington lets its companies rush in quickly to Burma with few questions asked, it could retard the pace of reform. But if it puts a lot of pressure on the government, some leading figures might seek to tilt back toward China.

In his latest book, *On China,* Henry Kissinger warns that "an explicit American project to . . . create a bloc of democratic states for an ideological crusade is unlikely to succeed." Kissinger has long criticized the Wilsonian tradition in American foreign policy for its missionary, evangelical quality, which he argues alienates potential partners and allies and frustrates national interests. In Asia, he believes that the American promotion of human rights as a central goal is bound to complicate the cool-headed negotiations that Washington will need to have with China in the coming years. The Chinese, he argues, will view this as a threat to their own legitimacy, creating even more competition between the two great powers. Kissinger believes there is too much at stake for the U.S. to indulge in an emotionally satisfying but counterproductive campaign for democracy.

This brand of realism holds strong appeal for many in Washington who are less optimistic than Kissinger about the prospects of doing diplomatic business with China. If the goal is to push back against Chinese adventurism, some argue, that exercise will be made much harder if human rights are treated as a central issue. It will be more difficult, for instance, to improve relations with Vietnam or Cambodia if Washington is constantly harping on their political failings. If the U.S. pushes too hard on human-rights issues, so the argument goes, it could help carve the region into rigid camps, authoritarian and democratic. No one in Asia likes the U.S. when it is delivering shrill lectures about political values that it has been happy to ignore in many other parts of the world. The Obama administration has at times appeared to support parts of this view, especially when dealing directly with China. "Successive administrations and Chinese governments have been poised back and forth on these issues, and we have to continue to press them," Hillary Clinton said before her first visit to Beijing as secretary of state in 2009. "But our pressing on those issues can't interfere with the global economic crisis, the global climate change crisis, and the security crisis."

Yet, in the long run, it would be a mistake to downplay human rights. It is obviously important to get the tone right and to avoid hectoring, but political reform should still be a central plank of U.S. strategy. In some cases, close attention to human-rights issues could aggravate rivalry with China, but the bigger risk for the region is that Washington and Beijing get drawn into a contest for influence in which they are constantly lowering the common denominator in order to avoid "losing" a country to the other side, the cynical logic attributed to Franklin Roosevelt of "he may be a son of a bitch, but he is *our* son of a bitch." In the end, promoting good governance is a way of keeping U.S. policy makers honest. If Washington starts backpedaling on the need for reform in places like Burma, those countries could find themselves pawns in a great-power confrontation between China and the U.S. Elements of the old regime in Burma would be delighted to play Beijing and Washington against each other, allowing them to fend off the pressure for further reforms while maintaining a hold on power. Indeed, some of the activists who helped stop the Myitsone Dam worry that this is already happening. "We are already being used," says Ko Maw Tun Aung. "It feels that we are being played with, that we are slowly being dragged into these regional games."

This debate is already being played out in Washington as the Pentagon tries to revive contacts with a host of militaries around Southeast Asia as part of the Obama administration's "pivot." The U.S. military has reopened links with Indonesia's armed forces, which had been put on hold because of human-rights abuses in East Timor, and it has paid for the sons of Hun Sen, the authoritarian leader of Cambodia, to attend the West Point military academy. Washington is also reviving military-to-military ties with its Burmese counterpart, which over the last two decades has been responsible for a host of crimes against humanity. The Pentagon is confident that, through these sorts of relationships, it can help mold the culture of the military in Burma and boost the careers of younger officers who want to make a break from the past. But it is treacherous terrain, where it is easy to fall back onto the habit of turning a blind eye on abuses in return for political support.

Washington has played this game with Burma before. In the Cold War 1960s, when the U.S. was worried about both Soviet and Chinese influence in Southeast Asia, the U.S. saw the Burmese military as an important counterweight against the spread of communism. The last Burmese president to visit the White House was Ne Win, the very man who ushered in the country's five decades of military rule with the coup he launched in 1962. In 1966, he visited Washington at the invitation of the Johnson administration, which had arranged for him to play golf in Maui for four days on the way. Ne Win was given the keys to the city of Washington, and he and his wife had a private dinner with the Johnsons at the White House. Over the years, Ne Win proved adept at navigating between the U.S. and China as he cemented his hold on power; the Burmese military eventually secured weapons purchases and training from both countries.

———

Burma is an important test in another way. The sort of politics that emerges in countries like Burma will influence the kind of Asian regionalism that develops. Asia will be much more immune to the machinations of great powers if the region is dominated by well-run, independent, and stable states that are free from the sort of crony-vested interests that outsiders can manipulate. States with strong institutions are better able to stand up for themselves. A strong consensus behind transparency and good governance can place limits on the worst elements of the Chinese system—the more ruthless, cash-rich state-owned companies, which support extravagant projects that appeal to some elite interests but have little popular support. Through the remaining sanctions, the U.S. still has the leverage to nudge Burma toward introducing stronger rules for monitoring huge investment projects, such as large dams. In the process, Washington might lose some of its new friends in the Burmese elite, but in the long run it will help Burmese society. If the U.S. appeared to be trying to impose democratic reforms on a reluctant

region, it would be breaking the Asian iron rule and creating problems
for itself. But the reality is that, across the region, there is strong popular pressure for more transparent and less abusive government. Indeed,
if China tries to push back against this trend, it will only intensify the
backlash against its influence. Even from a realist's point of view, promoting good governance is also good politics for the U.S. It plays to
American strengths and Chinese weaknesses.

If Washington really wanted to "flip" Burma to its side against
China, it would fail, if for no other reason than geography. The U.S.
is thousands of miles away, but China is right next door—a consumer
market of 1.3 billion that is still growing fast. Burma's leaders do not
want the Chinese breathing down their necks, but they also realize
that China's economy is one of the main keys to Burma's own future
prosperity. The controversial Myitsone Dam is only one of a string of
major investments that China is conducting in the north of the country,
including the twenty-eight-hundred-kilometer rail-and-pipeline project
to Burma's Bay of Bengal coast. The government has been eager to gain
the good graces of Washington to help dismantle the sanctions that have
strangled parts of its economy, but Burma cannot and will not close the
door on China. As Aung San Suu Kyi put it: "You must not forget that
China is next door and the U.S. is some way away."

The real irony is that the foreign government with the biggest stake
in seeing improved human rights in Burma is China. Even though the
political opening in Burma has allowed an outburst of anti-Chinese
sentiment, there are actually good reasons why China would want a
more representative and liberal government in Burma. China's investments in the country have given it a direct stake in several of the uprisings and conflicts between the government and ethnic minorities that
have scarred Burma for decades, including the pipeline that runs right
across several areas of unrest. Geography also makes China a party to
some of these disputes, given both its long, loosely policed border with
Burma and the fact that some of its own ethnic minorities in southwestern China are related to groups within Burma. In early 2012, tens
of thousands of refugees from Burma fled across the border into China
after fighting escalated between the military and the Kachin Independence Army. If a civilian and more representative government can bring

some stability to these regions and begin to draw the poison out of long-standing ethnic conflicts, China would stand to gain enormously.

More than any other issue, the promotion of human rights and democracy has to be done with a light touch. Preachy rhetoric does little to change minds, in China or anywhere else. But in the long run, the promotion of more transparent and open government is a central U.S. interest. The more well-governed states there are in Asia, the more resilient and stable the region will be.

Section II

POLITICS AND NATIONALISM

5

China's Brittle Nationalism

A s MIDNIGHT STRUCK to usher in the Chinese New Year, the firecrackers were almost deafening, but Li Yang continued to teach his English class as if nothing were going on. Outside the school gymnasium, the local residents were celebrating the most important holiday of the year, the one day when Chinese families make a special effort to be together. As many as 150 million people return to their hometowns, making the Chinese New Year the biggest annual human migration on the planet. It is also the largest spontaneous fireworks display; the next morning's streets are lined with ash and debris. The roar did not prevent Li Yang from holding his three hundred students in thrall. Standing below a basketball net on an impromptu stage, he shouted out English words in his raspy voice, which they then repeated. "Success!" he called. *"Success!"* they called back. "Sux—sess," he boomed, pausing between the two syllables. *"Sux-sess,"* the enthusiastic audience replied. Li uses a method of language teaching that involves shouting the words—"exercising the tongue muscle," as he calls it—which he believes is essential to overcoming the awkwardness of learning a foreign language.

"Opportunity!" Li shouted. *"OPPORTUNITY!"*

"All right, *bu cuo da jia*. Well done, everybody." He joined them in a loud round of group applause.

Li is at the forefront of the "English fever" that has been sweeping China for the last decade. Learning English has become one of the main paths to social mobility—the key to getting a good job, getting married, and getting on. Researchers estimate that there are between two and three hundred million people studying English throughout China, not far short of the population of the entire U.S. The British Council has calculated that there may be more English speakers in China than there are in India, even though English is the secondary official language of India. English has become the touchstone for the ambitions of China's aspiring middle class. Li Yang, who speaks with an almost pitch-perfect American accent, is the best-known popular English teacher in the country, a cult figure who is treated like a film star, stopping to give autographs to young fans in airport lounges.

The class was taking place in a suburb of Guangzhou, the main city in the south of the country, where the students were attending a week-long "boot camp" that Li runs over the Chinese New Year. Some had traveled from as far away as Xinjiang in the west and Inner Mongolia in the north, a four- or five-hour flight. Throughout the year, Li tours schools across the country to give seminars, visiting as many as two hundred cities each year. His blog was the most popular education-related Web site in the country before he lost interest in daily postings. In the past he has filled entire sports stadiums with his classes, an improvised performance of jokes, advice, and interactive shouting—part teasing and part scolding his students. Beside the stage, one of the teachers wrote a series of inspirational slogans that were projected onto a screen, and Li then used these as the basis for his classes. "Education is the secret to success!" the teacher wrote.

Li has won a broader fame in China for two reasons. His unorthodox teaching methods have attracted a good deal of attention, especially during China's pre-Olympics burst of learning English. More recently, he gained a different kind of notoriety when his estranged American wife won damages in a Chinese court for assault, a 2012 case that broke new ground in the prosecution and discussion of domestic violence in China. Kim Lee, originally from Florida, had helped Li build up his teaching business. She posted pictures on the Internet of her damaged face and ear and described in detail how he "beat me" and then "slammed my head into the floor ten more times." But when I met Li, he had yet to be accused of wife beating, and I was curious about a different aspect of his teaching style. Along the wall in the main classroom were a series of large photographs of soldiers in uniform with slogans such as "Integrity!" and "Duty—It is our Duty to give something back to our great country." The schools are called "boot camps" for a reason. The group of three hundred students is divided into classes of around twenty, each of which is assigned a monitor dressed in army fatigues. The monitor wakes the kids at 6:30 a.m. and brings them downstairs for their first, pre-breakfast shouting exercise. For the large sessions in the main hall with Li Yang, the monitors march the different classes of students in at precise times, with a military anthem blaring, and each monitor carrying a red flag. The cosmopolitanism of "Crazy English" is laced with a harder-edged nationalism.

Li peppers his talks with casual put-downs of America and the English-speaking world. "We Chinese are victims of English—so difficult, but we have to learn it," he tells the audience. He is obsessed with what he sees as the growing softness of young Chinese. Over the New Year holiday his company ran two boot camps—a cheaper version in downtown Guangzhou, and a more expensive, "platinum" camp at a private school in a distant suburb. While driving between the two campuses, he told me that he much prefers the students at the cheaper program, because they work harder. "Chinese kids are becoming spoiled," he says. "We cannot become like the West." Li exhorts his classes to improve their English not just as a means to self-improvement but as a form of patriotic duty. He wants to use language training to stiffen the national backbone. Every one of the students in his courses wears a red windbreaker with Li Yang's signature motto on the back: "Conquer English to Make China Stronger!"

The literary quote most often repeated to me by Chinese friends and acquaintances is not from Mao or Confucius, but from the novelist Lu Xun. "Throughout the ages Chinese have had only one way of looking at foreigners," Lu wrote in the 1930s. "We either look up to them as gods or down on them as wild animals." One of the most interesting, perplexing, and important aspects of the rivalry between Washington and Beijing is modern China's simultaneous admiration for and resentment of America. The three decades of economic reforms have created a tidal wave of Western influences in Chinese cities, from the cars that people drive, to the supermarkets they shop in and the suburbs they now flock to, with their wide roads and neatly spaced uniform houses. The "English fervor" is one part of that mindset. There is no prouder parent in China today than one whose child is studying at a brand-name American university. But there is a parallel instinct that is equally powerful, a desire to stand up to the West, to make up for past injustices, and to restore China to its natural position of superiority.

Every nation's nationalism has a blind spot, a raw nerve that is all too easily tweaked, which reveals a deeper angst. Post-colonial societies have an obvious and natural sense of injustice that colors their view of the West. And rising powers are often particularly touchy, hypersensitive about condescension from the established players. But none of this really captures the potentially toxic quality of modern Chinese nationalism, the nervous energy that is constantly just beneath the surface. China's worldview is being nurtured by an often abrasive brand of nationalism that is informed by deep historical wounds, and which is infused with a desire for payback. "A weak country will be bullied and humiliated," warns one popular Chinese history textbook. China's sense of itself as a great power is closely wound up in this parallel feeling of victimhood. This brittle nationalism provides the emotional underpinning for the emerging contest with the U.S., a constant psychological tension which is shaping many of China's interactions with the world. As Peter Hays Gries, author of a book on modern Chinese nationalism, puts it: "The West is central to the construction of China's identity today: it has become China's alter ego."

Li Yang has positioned himself exactly at the sweet point of this identity crisis, the on-off romance with American-style modernity. The first day I visited the school, Li was wearing a brown suede jacket over a mauve turtleneck sweater, smart jeans, and brown lace-up boots. Along with the designer glasses he was sporting, it was the sort of moneyed, smart casual you see more often in Santa Monica than in mainland China. His classes can sometimes feel like an American civics lesson. Before one of Li's teaching sessions, the screen on the stage was filled by a large video of Barack Obama giving his first election victory speech at Grant Park in Chicago. "If there is anyone out there who still doubts that America is a place where all things are possible . . ." Obama pronounced. Li provided the simultaneous translation when Tony Robbins, the American "life coach," came to China, and there is a strong element of self-help philosophy in his teaching. The students carry around marker pens and ask teachers to write a comment on their "Crazy English" windbreakers. On the shoulder of one of the students, a teacher had written: "Don't forget me when you become President!"

Yet Li delights his students by taking potshots at the foreign teachers in his school, who sat in a circle behind him onstage when he was giving his lectures. He called on one of the teachers to stand up, an American named Shawn who was considerably overweight. "America is a ridiculous country," he boomed. "Why do you people get so fat? Why do you eat so much?" The audience roared with laughter. "Are you offended, Shawn?" he asked. Shawn smiled gamely—a slice of humiliation is clearly part of the contract for teaching at Li's schools. "I hate going to America," Li later told me in his car, a black Buick sedan. "I mostly stay at home and watch TV. What is there to do apart from going to Sam's Club? I find America boring." As the car pulled up to the second school, the driver nearly knocked over one of the teachers by accident. "These foreign teachers, they are so lazy," Li muttered. "They become language teachers because they are too lazy to do anything else. I always tell them this."

NEVER FORGET OUR NATIONAL HUMILIATION

Blame it all, if you like, on Lord Elgin.

China and Greece have one powerful thing in common—a deeply held grievance over the cultural vandalism of the British Empire. In both cases, their resentment is focused on the Bruce family from Fife in Scotland, inheritors of the earldoms of Elgin and Kincardine, and colonial adventurers of the most notorious brand. For Greece, it is the seventh earl, Thomas Bruce, who dominates the family's share of historical infamy. It was he who in 1801 removed the marble sculptures from the Parthenon that are still housed in the British Museum. For the last few decades, Greece has viewed Britain's refusal to return the marbles as an acute form of post-colonial condescension. For modern China, it is his son, the eighth earl, James Bruce, who has a central place in the gallery of foreign villains. It was this Lord Elgin who gave the order in 1860 to set fire to the Yuanming Yuan, the Garden of Perfect Brightness, a vast complex of Qing dynasty gardens and buildings to the northwest of Beijing which were known in English as the Summer Palace.

James Bruce has received much less attention than his father in the U.K. over the years. When Britons reflect on the history of empire, we focus heavily on India and to a lesser extent on East Africa, but we rarely discuss the episodes in China. At my school, we only learned about the Second Opium War, 1856–60, in which Elgin was a central figure, because of the way Lord Palmerston used it for domestic political gain in a general election. When Elgin sailed in 1856 on board the *Furious*, he almost did not make it to China: when they stopped on the way in India, the Sepoy Mutiny, one of the biggest uprisings against colonial rule, broke out, and the governor of Calcutta pleaded with him to use his seventeen hundred troops to help put down the uprising. They were delayed for several months. But their voyage to China culminated in an incident of imperial arrogance that still reverberates a century and a half later, even if it is largely forgotten at home.

Uncomfortable in the claustrophobic confines of the Forbidden City, which had been the focus of power under the Ming dynasty, the Qing dynasty rulers constructed a new compound to the northwest of Beijing on an area of eight hundred acres. Amid the palaces and pavilions, there were opera houses, fountains, waterways, and intricate gardens. The complex also boasted extensive hunting grounds and riding trails, which were among the favorite haunts of Xianfeng, who became the seventh Qing emperor in 1850. He was born at the Summer Palace, by which time it had already become the main seat of power.

Elgin had been dispatched to China after a dispute over a ship called the *Arrow*, which had been impounded by the Chinese authorities. The British used the incident as a pretext to push for greater opening of China to European trade. By September 1860, a British and French force was on the outskirts of Beijing and threatening to invade if Xianfeng did not grant their demands. Elgin sent a small team to conclude an agreement with Xianfeng's envoys, which included a senior British official, Harry

Parkes; Elgin's secretary, Henry Loch; a group of Sikh cavalry; and a journalist from *The Times* called Thomas Bowlby. Instead of reaching a deal, they were imprisoned and tortured. Parkes and Loch were later released, but fifteen of the twenty-six taken prisoner were killed, including Bowlby. According to one of the Sikh soldiers imprisoned with him, Bowlby's dead body was eventually fed to dogs and pigs.

The British and French armies decided they needed to extract symbolic revenge. Elgin later said that he wanted to find a way to punish Xianfeng personally without hurting the residents of Beijing. His solution was to burn the Summer Palace. Xianfeng had already fled, and the compound was unguarded when the French and British troops arrived. At first, the soldiers went on a spree of frenzied looting and plundering, smashing porcelain vases and jade ornaments. After a day, the officers reasserted control over the troops and organized them to complete the main mission: to methodically destroy the elaborate Summer Palace complex.

Outraged at the death of its correspondent, *The Times* supported Elgin's actions, but even at the time, at the height of empire, the Anglo-French force was denounced at home. Victor Hugo said that Elgin was worse than his father and famously warned that the incident would come back to haunt the British and French. The marquess of Bath described it as an act of "vandalism" that was comparable to the sacking of Rome or the burning of the Alexandria Library. On his way to China three years earlier, Elgin had written, "We have often acted towards the Chinese in a manner which is very difficult to justify." But although he later regretted burning the Summer Palace, he defended the decision on the grounds that it was necessary to set an example, so that other Europeans in China would remain safe. It had been a "painful duty," said Elgin, who went on to become viceroy of India. Some of the soldiers he commanded realized the consequences. "The people are very civil, but I think the grandees hate us, as they must after what we did to the palace," Charles George Gordon, who was then a young army captain, later wrote. "You can scarcely imagine the beauty and magnificence of the places we burnt. It made one's heart sore to burn them. . . . It was wretchedly demoralising work for an army."

China's rulers tried to restore many of the buildings that had been destroyed, even if a shortage of funds meant they had not quite completed the job by the time the Boxer Rebellion broke out in 1898. Called I Ho Ch'uan in Chinese or Righteous Harmonious Fists, the Boxers—as they were known in English—were a secret society that called for the expulsion of "foreign devils." The initial target was Chinese Christians, but some British missionaries were also killed. By 1900, the violence against foreigners was so intense that hundreds took refuge in the Legation Quarter in Beijing, where foreign diplomats resided. To relieve the siege, a twenty-thousand-strong army from eight countries made its way to Beijing—six European countries, Japan, and this time the U.S., which had troops in the region following the conquest of the Philippines. After they relieved the Legation Quarter, the foreign armies embarked on what one American marine called an "orgy" of looting, so extensive that the troops later held open-air markets to trade the gold, silver, and silks they had stolen. (Again, the actions of the foreign armies were denounced in their home countries, this time with Mark Twain to the fore.) Before they left Beijing, the armies decided they needed to perform one last act to rub in their victory. They looted, ransacked, and burned down the Summer Palace again.

In some ways, it is surprising that the Summer Palace has been turned into a symbol of the wonders of Han Chinese civilization. The Qing rulers were Manchus, who were considered by many of their Chinese subjects to be foreign barbarians, and the ravishing complex they built was full of overseas influences. A series of marble pavilions in the northeast of the complex, including one known as View of Distant Seas, were actually designed by Jesuit missionaries. The destruction continued for many decades after the foreign armies had left, this time at the hands of ordinary Chinese people, who quietly took away many of the remaining treasures. During the Cultural Revolution, the Summer Palace continued to be thoroughly ransacked. The Zhengjue Temple, one of the few buildings that remained intact, became a boiler factory. But in the late 1970s, as China started to breathe again after the nightmare of the Cultural Revolution, historical interest in the Yuanming Yuan site picked up.

A petition was circulated in 1980 to get funds for its protection—120 years after the duke of Elgin's fateful order. The Chinese historian Wu

Hung described the pavilions of the View of Distant Seas, by then crumbling and smashed columns, as China's "national ruin." A picture of the destroyed pavilions became a regular fixture in popular culture, reproduced on playing cards and cake tins. As interest in the stories of Elgin and the anti-Boxer armies spiked, the Summer Palace site gradually evolved into an emotional symbol of both cultural unity and patriotic outrage. So it was not a complete surprise that, when the G-7 imposed sanctions on China after the 1989 Tiananmen Square Massacre, Deng Xiaoping reached into this collective memory of anti-imperial anger to frame his response. "I am familiar with the history of foreign aggression against China. When I heard the seven Western countries had at their summit decided to impose sanctions on China, my immediate association was to 1900, when the allied forces of the eight powers invaded China," he said.

The stories that a country tells about itself say a lot about how it views the rest of the world. Tiananmen was a fundamental break in the way Communist China has decided to describe its own history. During the Mao years, China was the proud winner in a revolutionary struggle against imperialism and its internal class enemies. The Chinese people had stood up, as Mao declared in 1949. There was plenty of anti-foreigner sentiment—during the Cultural Revolution, Red Guards burned down the British embassy—but China presented itself as victor, not one of history's injured parties. After Tiananmen, however, Chinese history-writing started to reflect a very different self-image, a form of anti-Western nationalism that adopted the tone of an aggrieved victim. Jiang Zemin, who took over from the ousted Zhao Ziyang as party secretary-general after the massacre, announced that the education system "must prevent the rise of the worship of the West." In a speech entitled "Patriotism and the Mission of the Chinese Intellectual," he thundered that the U.S. and its allies were "trying to turn China into a vassal state dependent on the Western superpowers." Deng, who continued to pull the strings behind the scenes, gave a speech to the PLA in which he blamed the protests on the way history had been taught to young people. "During the last ten years, our biggest mistake was made in the field of education, primarily ideological and political education," he said. The students had occupied Tiananmen Square and had called into question the very legitimacy of the Communist Party for one simple reason: they had not been taught how to be sufficiently patriotic.

The new patriotic education had a name: National Humiliation History. *Wuwang guochi*—or "Never forget our national humiliation"—had been a popular phrase in the 1920s, after Germany's colonial possessions in China had been handed to Japan at the 1919 Versailles Conference. With their backs to the wall after 1989, the Communist authorities started to lean on the same emotional memory of national humiliation. The school curriculum began to emphasize the "Century of National Humiliation," which started in 1840 with the First Opium War and ended with the Communist takeover in 1949. This time frame knits together the different invasions, unfair treaties, economic exploitation, and other indignities that a weakened China suffered at the hands of the Western powers. The destruction of the Summer Palace, first by Elgin, then by the anti-Boxer armies, became a central episode in the narrative.

The bullying, war crimes, and injustice were real, of course, the genuine story of a proud civilization humbled by foreigners who had become more powerful without anyone in China realizing it. Yet it is also a version of history that leaves out as much as it includes. Qing China (1644–1912) ruled a country twice the size of the one controlled by the Ming dynasty that preceded it (1368–1644). Long before British warships ever sailed up the Yangtze, China's frontiers had been a constantly shifting map that contained their own stories of expansion and aggression. One of the foundational myths of modern Chinese identity is the benevolence of imperial rule, the belief that China expanded as a result of the superiority of its culture rather than the strength of its armed forces. Today's official histories also have little to say about the Taiping Rebellion, a civil war in the 1850s which Elgin stumbled into, and which took as many as twenty million Chinese lives, making it one of the most brutal episodes in China's or any country's history. In the "national humiliation" canon, Qing China was neither an expansionary empire nor a dynasty whose writ was crumbling, but a victim of history— a defenseless and naïve innocent plundered by a warmongering West.

To mark the 150th anniversary of the First Opium War, a book entitled *The Indignation of National Humiliation* was published in 1990, the first in a series of new textbooks that aimed to provide the patriotic lessons Deng thought China's youth needed. The 1998 text *Never Forget National Humiliation* set as its goal the rejuvenation of a Chinese nation that would "rise again to be an awesome and gracious great power like in the past that will stand lofty and firm in the Eastern part of the World." Another school textbook implored its student readers: "In modern Chinese history since the Opium War, foreign powers have launched invasion after invasion, act after bloody act of coercive pillage, occupying Chinese sovereign territory, slaughtering the Chinese masses, looting China's wealth, and stealing China's cultural artefacts. All this stained China with blood and tears." Jiang Zemin ordered that the curriculum start in kindergarten.

The new emphasis on National Humiliation History proved hugely popular; its themes were used to frame major political events. During the 1997 handover of Hong Kong from British rule, Jiang Zemin described the occupation of Hong Kong as "the epitome of the humiliation that China suffered." Speaking to a huge crowd in Beijing two days after the handover, he announced: "The return of Hong Kong marks an end to the 100-year national humiliation." When a NATO bomb hit the Chinese Embassy in Belgrade, a *People's Daily* article thundered: "It is 1999, not 1899. . . . This is not the age when Western powers plundered the imperial palace at will. . . . The Chinese people are not to be bullied. . . . In the veins of the Chinese people circulate the blood of the anti-imperialist patriots over a period of 150-plus years." The slogan "Never Forget National Humiliation, Rejuvenate China" started to appear on signs in parks. An aerial photo shows a group of Chinese police forming the phrase with their bodies as part of a parade-ground drill. In the aftermath of a 2001 diplomatic standoff between China and the U.S. after China shot down a U.S. spy plane, the government declared a National Humiliation Day in mid-September. Thousands of students turned out to celebrate the occasion at the Summer Palace. "This is the national phrase of China," says the historian Zheng Wang. "It is the key to [the] cultural and historic formation of Chinese nationalism."

At first sight, it seems an odd sort of political project, to encourage national regeneration by constantly harping on past suffering. Not only is history written by the victors, but it usually dwells on the victories. Instead, China has developed a form of hair-shirt nationalism, the manipulation of the authority that comes from past suffering to forge a permanent sense of victimhood. The Communist Party has faced a slow-burning threat to its legitimacy ever since it dumped Marx for the market and dropped the Mao cult of personality, a threat that was only exacerbated after it turned the army on its own people in Tiananmen. Chinese sometimes talk about their *xinyang weiji,* a crisis of faith which has eaten away at society as the old Confucian or socialist sense of order has eroded. The emphasis on humiliation has helped the Communist Party create a sense of unity that had been fracturing, and to define a Chinese identity fundamentally at odds with American modernity. This strand of nationalism has become an important part of its claim to maintaining a monopoly of political power, a deliberate project to mold the historical instincts of young Chinese.

The crude version of history that is portrayed in Chinese textbooks is scorned in private by Chinese academics, but it is a dangerous orthodoxy to oppose. One of the most dramatic acts of censorship in recent times involved the writing of history—and not just any history, but the story behind the burning of the Summer Palace. In 2006, the authorities closed a magazine called *Freezing Point* after it published an article by Zhongshan University historian Yuan Weishi which took issue with what he saw as the blind nationalism and anti-foreigner sentiment of school textbooks. The official Chinese histories, he said, completely glossed over the mistakes made in the later years of the Qing dynasty. Professor Yuan did not doubt the official version of how the palaces and gardens at the Summer Palace had been destroyed. But he suggested that China broke its word by arresting the diplomats and killing the soldiers. The Qing rulers, he said, had been asking for trouble. He also objected to the way the Boxer Rebellion was constantly praised as "a magnificent feat of patriotism," while the violence against foreigners was ignored. "Our youth are still drinking wolf's milk," Yuan wrote, a reference to the excuse people gave during the Cultural Revolution for violent excesses. The new generation of textbooks "suggest that the current Chinese culture is superior and unmatched and that outside culture is evil and corrodes the purity of existing culture. . . . To use this kind of logic to quietly exert a subtle influence on our children is an unforgivable harm."

For daring to criticize the official verdict, Yuan Weishi was vilified. He had "attempted to vindicate the criminal acts of the invading powers," as the propaganda authorities put it. Li Datong, managing editor of the magazine, was fired. *Freezing Point* was later re-opened under new editors, but only on condition that its first issue carry an article entitled "The Main Theme of Modern Chinese History Is Anti-Imperialism and Anti-Feudalism." Sipping Coca-Cola in a café next to his apartment a couple of years later, Li Datong described to me how control of history had been so central to the party's hold on power and its legitimacy. He went through a long list of historical subjects, from the decline of science in the Qing and Ming dynasties to the Korean War, about which it was impossible to have an honest debate. "The legacy of a ruling party is the right to define history—they use history to brainwash people," he said. "The textbooks say that history proved that such-and-such happened, that history chose the CCP to be the ruling party. They think this can convince people how great the CCP is."

———

Totalitarian regimes are able to completely invent their own histories. North Korea can get away with claiming that Kim Jong-il wrote fifteen hundred books and composed six operas because no one can say otherwise. But China is no longer that sort of regime. Though dictatorships censor their histories, they cannot create them in a vacuum. The CCP may have manipulated the idea of "national humiliation" after Tiananmen for its own ends, but it did not make it up. To understand the force of modern Chinese nationalism, it is important to recognize that the CCP has helped revive an older intellectual tradition that had its roots in the early years of the Chinese republic and the attempt to forge a modern nation-state after the collapse of the Qing dynasty in 1912. The patriotic-education campaign has been so influential in part because it taps into a long-standing emotional reflex about what it means to be Chinese. As the historian William Callahan puts it: "It would not be an exaggeration to say that when the idea of 'modern history' took shape in China in the 1920s, it was guided by the history of national humiliation.'"

The seminal event in the early years of the republic was the May Fourth Movement, a youthful protest which encapsulated the new country's search for a place in the modern world. The ideas behind May Fourth came to be characterized by the slogan "Mr. Science and Mr. Democracy," but it was also steeped in the nationalism of bruised pride. At the end of the 1919 Versailles Conference, which awarded Germany's possessions in China to Japan, Chinese students who were living in Paris surrounded the hotel of the Chinese delegation to prevent them from leaving to sign such a humiliating treaty. On hearing the news from France, a group of around three thousand students in Beijing met at Tiananmen Gate on May 4 and decided to march on the house of Communications Minister Cao Rulin. According to one of the demonstrators, a student named Luo Jialun, the crowd started cursing Cao as a "traitor to the country" when they arrived at his door. They then proceeded to storm into his house. Cao changed into a policeman's outfit and escaped over the back wall, injuring his leg along the way. Zhang Zongxiang, a former minister to Japan who had been visiting that day, was not so lucky: he was beaten with iron rods torn from an old bed and left nearly dead. Cao's house was then burned to the ground. The historian Rana Mitter summed up the launch of the May Fourth Movement this way: "The combination of these factors—youth, internationalism, and violence—would shape not just the day of the demonstrations, but much of the path taken by twentieth-century China."

As republican China struggled to find its way in the 1920s and 1930s, the feeling of injured national honor was a powerful political reflex among the new urban middle classes being established in cities like Beijing and Shanghai. Political leaders used this aggrieved nationalism as a way to appeal to the new constituencies and social organizations that were developing. When Chiang Kai-shek's Nationalists asserted control over the country in 1927, they decreed a National Humiliation Commemoration Day. It is worth noting that the controversial "nine-dash line" map of the South China Sea was drawn up during this period, one example of the way China's current territorial claims are wrapped up in this mentality of restoring injured pride.

Chiang Kai-shek kept a daily diary for two decades, and at the top right corner of each page he wrote the same words—*xue chi,* "wipe out humiliation." The weaker he got politically, the harder he pushed the humiliation narrative. Shortly before he lost the Civil War to the Communists, he published a book called *China's Destiny,* which blamed much of the country's ills on foreigners. The text was scorned even by the Chinese intellectuals who still supported his regime, but it was priced cheaply and proved a huge hit. "During the past hundred years, the citizens of the entire country, suffering under the yoke of the unequal treaties which gave foreigners special 'concessions' and extra-territorial status in China, were unanimous in their demand that the national humiliation be avenged, and the state be made strong," he wrote. When this nationalist potboiler was released, his wife, Meiling, happened to be in the U.S., trying to raise money for the anti-Communist cause, and Chiang himself was about to be awarded the Legion of Merit. An English-language version of the book was first shelved and then heavily edited to take out the fire-breathing passages. Lest Chiang's views about the West gain too wide a circulation, the State Department classified its copy of the Chinese original as "top secret."

The emphasis on humiliation and suffering in these histories actually has even deeper roots. China celebrates many of the usual sorts of historical heroes—brave generals and great thinkers. But it also reserves a special place for Goujian, the king of the state of Yue in the Warring States period (around the fifth century B.C.), whose story strikes a very different emotional chord. Having been captured by the rival king of Wu, Goujian set about trying to be as submissive as it was possible to be. He slept amid the horse manure of the rival king and even tasted the king's excrement. When he was eventually freed and allowed to return home, he spent the next two decades submitting himself to one humiliation after another in order to keep his desire for revenge intense. The Chinese phrase *woxin changdan* ("sleeping on brushwood and tasting gall") stems from Goujian's nightly exercise in self-flagellation, when he would sleep on a bed of brushwood and lick a gallbladder full of bile. It was this regimen of suffering and self-victimization that gave him the strength finally to defeat the king of Wu. The story of Goujian is "as familiar to Chinese schoolchildren as the biblical stories of Adam and Eve or David and Goliath are to American youngsters," wrote Paul Cohen, the American historian who has brought the mythical story to the attention of a wider Western audience. Perhaps it is no coincidence that the Goujian story was particularly popular in the 1920s and 1930s, when National Humiliation History began to take off. It also gained another lease on life in the 1990s and 2000s.

———

Though it is always tempting to think that everything in China is mapped out by an all-powerful Communist Party, the reality is that modern nationalism is very much a two-way process. The Communist Party has been happy to fan the sense of victimhood to buttress its own legitimacy. Yet the foundational myths that are at the heart of today's nationalism have their origin well before the Communists took power, and will not disappear if they should ever fall. At the same time that the party has been pushing its own "patriotic education," the themes of victimhood and resentment at the U.S. have flourished in their own right among young educated Chinese. The publishing industry has had a series of huge successes with potboiler polemics, in the Ann Coulter style, raging against the West. They started with the 1996 hit *China Can Say No,* written by a group of young intellectuals, which warned that China risked being "culturally strangled" and turned into a "slave" if it did not resist its infatuation with America. Two of the authors had taken part in the 1989 Tiananmen Square protests, but in the book they turned their ire on activists such as Fang Lizhi, the astrophysicist who inspired some of the 1989 protesters and ended up an exile in the U.S. after spending a year in the U.S. Embassy in Beijing.

Chinese intellectual life in the 1980s had been dominated by a fascination with the West and a thirst for political experimentation, but in the years after Tiananmen there has also been a strong counter-reaction, a popular clarion call that China needs to stand up for itself and to find its own path, resisting the temptations of the West. A string of popular anti-American titles have been released in recent years, with titles like *The Plot to Demonize China.* In 2009, the authors of *China Can Say No* published a follow-up, this time called *Unhappy China,* which was just as big a hit. Detailing a long list of tales about continued Western condescension toward the Chinese, the book urges China's leaders to turn the nation into a hegemon, or be cast aside. The writers and audience for these books, mostly young, are not party apparatchiks. They see themselves as loyal to a China that is a great and respected nation, not to the Communist Party.

The most famous megaphone of modern Chinese nationalism is the *Global Times,* the third-most-popular newspaper in the country. With a mix of conspiracy and indignation that has echoes of Fox News, *Global Times* has built a huge successful franchise by fanning the flames of any perceived slight to China and by criticizing the weaknesses of the U.S. and Japan. It has come to dominate the market for full-throated populism. Hu Xijin, the paper's dynamic editor, once described Chinese liberals as "the cancer cells that will lead to the demise of China" and "a key tool in the hands of the Americans who want to topple China." However, it can also be quite critical of the government, especially concerning Beijing's dogged support of North Korea. In a way, *Global Times* is the perfect example of the two-way nature of Chinese nationalism. It is published by the same group that produces the *People's Daily,* the party's mouthpiece and distiller of official truths, which gives it an official stamp of approval. But it is also far more interesting and controversial than the dreary *People's Daily,* projecting its own abrasive worldview and building its own constituency among the public. *Global Times* does not provide the official China line, but it is the Communist Party's nationalist alter ego. That alone makes it essential reading.

MEMORIES OF A HOLOCAUST

When we moved to Shanghai in early 2005, my wife and I rented a flat on Huai Hai Road, one of the main streets running through what in colonial days was known as the French Concession. In a city that has become overrun by skyscrapers, the area is a museum of prewar Western architecture. One block away from our flat was the Normandie Apartments, a wedge-shaped building reminiscent of the Flatiron Building in New York; three blocks in the other direction was a Russian basilica. Its avenues lined with plane trees planted by the French, the area has an unhurried feel that is a welcome break from Shanghai's frenetic pace. It has become a popular neighborhood for foreigners, including the tens of thousands of Japanese who now call Shanghai home. Many of the shops along Huai Hai Road had Japanese writing in the windows to attract customers, including the tailor on our block and the tobacco store run by a couple from Anhui Province.

At about the same time that we arrived in Shanghai, a group of right-wing historians in Japan published a new textbook which downplayed important aspects of the war crimes committed by Japanese soldiers in China. One of the books described the evidence behind the massacre in Nanjing in 1937 as "inconclusive." It was not the first revisionist textbook in Japan to minimize war crimes, and it was only taken up by a small number of schools. But it caused a furor in China. Meetings with Japanese politicians were canceled, official protests lodged. After a few weeks, messages started to circulate on the Internet about a demonstration in Shanghai on the following Saturday. "A lot of people are talking," one of our new Chinese acquaintances told us a couple of days before the demonstration.

At around 10 a.m. that Saturday, we headed out to try and find the protest, only to discover that our section of Huai Hai Road had already been totally closed off to traffic. After walking up the street, we could eventually see the beachhead of a demonstration that looked to be much bigger than the modest protest we had been expecting. The group had started near the Bund and had already halted the traffic in some of the city's busiest shopping and business areas. The demonstrators were all young, mostly university or high-school students. Older residents watched from the sidewalk, a little bemused, not quite knowing what to think. The protest gathered numbers along the way until it had at least ten thousand people by some counts—making it one of the biggest public demonstrations since the 1989 protests in Tiananmen Square. The students carried banners and shouted slogans such as "Down with Little Japan," "Japan Out of Asia," and "We Love Our China, We Hate Your Japan." By the time they reached our stretch of town, they had developed a distinct sense of impunity. When they passed a little sushi restaurant a block away from our flat, they threw eggs and plastic bottles at the windows, as well as red paint. At the cigarette shop with the Japanese script, they smashed the window. There were plenty of police keeping an eye on the protest, and occasionally they would move people along. But mostly they stood back and laughed.

The demonstration carried on three miles farther, through another of the city's busiest areas, before it reached the Japanese consulate in Hongqiao, in a modern office building. By then a couple of Japanese cars had been overturned, and there was a report that a few demonstrators attacked a police car which they believed was protecting a Japanese citizen. Some local shop owners had put up Chinese flags, not as a patriotic act but to try and convince the protesters that their businesses had no Japanese connection. At the consulate, a large contingent of police was waiting, including some from an anti-riot squad in special protective equipment. But although they made sure no one entered the consulate, they, too, stood aside as the demonstrators threw rocks and bottles at the premises.

For a while, I walked alongside a young woman called Wang Hongli, who said she was sixteen and in high school. Her dark hair was cut in a bob, she was carrying a knapsack on her shoulders that was covered in "Hello Kitty" stickers, and she wore round John Lennon–style glasses. "You must think this is all very strange," she said at one stage. She told me how word of the protest had spread rapidly by text message over the previous two days. At first she had not thought about attending, but she kept getting more and more messages. A friend of a friend, who was a student at Fudan University, had said he was going. Eventually, she and a couple of schoolmates had decided to come along, although the friends had given up after a while. When I asked her why she was so keen to stay with the march, her mood darkened and she fixed me with a severe look. "We hate the Japanese, just hate them," she said. Most of the students thought the whole thing was quite fun, and there was a day-out-of-school feel about the event. This was probably the first chance they had ever had in their lives to walk through the streets chanting political slogans, and many reveled in the experience. The good humor could not disguise, however, that this was an exercise in political mob violence.

―――――――

One of the more peculiar aspects of the "national humiliation" mindset is that it allows Chinese officials to decide when the country has been offended. Officials at the Foreign Ministry will announce with a straight face that a particular government has "hurt the feelings of the Chinese people." The phrase often prompts a bemused sneer from foreigners, but makes some sort of sense within the emotional framework of victim nationalism. In 2008, Danwei, a Beijing-based Web site, reported on a fascinating piece of research conducted by a Chinese blogger. He had gone through the archives of the *People's Daily* since 1946 and collected all the instances in which the Chinese government had accused someone else of "hurting the feelings of the Chinese people." In total, nineteen countries and organizations had committed the sin—representing around two-fifths of the world's population. The United States had done so twenty-three times, with another ten from NATO (mostly to do with the 1999 Belgrade bombing), which were really the U.S. as well. Only one country had managed to offend China more—in fact, on a total of forty-seven occasions. That nation was Japan.

Japan is the epicenter of China's victim complex. It is Japan that is most likely to turn young, cosmopolitan, Internet-savvy Chinese into fire-breathing protesters, Japan that is most likely to elicit reactions that mix inferiority and superiority. Japan is also the area of foreign policy where nationalism has its greatest potential impact, a populist anger that is at times encouraged by the government but which is also increasingly tying its hands. Nationalism is becoming a major force in the relationship between the two richest countries in Asia. After the 2005 protests and another round of demonstrations in 2010, the protests reached a new intensity in late 2012, as the dispute over the Senkaku/Diaoyu Islands flared up again. In one incident, a Chinese man was paralyzed after a mob of anti-Japanese protesters in the city of Xian attacked his car. His crime was to drive a Japanese vehicle.

The immediate source of such anger is the catalogue of grotesque war crimes committed by Japanese soldiers during the occupations and wars of the 1930s and 1940s in China. Japan operated labor camps and conducted medical experiments on Chinese prisoners. At one stage, Japanese planes dropped fleas infected with the plague onto a Chinese city. In Nanjing in 1937, the invading Japanese army slaughtered a significant part of the local population. The estimates of casualties range from fifty thousand to three hundred thousand, the latter figure being widely accepted in China. In an era of jaw-dropping, shocking crimes, Nanjing was one of the great crimes. When the Japanese were finally defeated, however, hostility toward Japan remained surprisingly restrained. Mao's China was the victor, not a victim that wanted to linger on war crimes. When Japanese Prime Minister Tanaka Kakuei visited in 1972 to reopen relations with China following the Nixon trip, Mao is reported to have observed that, without the war with Japan, his Communist revolution would not have succeeded. In keeping with that mood, the massacre at Nanjing was deliberately downplayed. In some ways, it is a natural human reaction to avoid thinking about such events when they are still raw. Sometimes, survivors of an atrocity just want to carry on with their own lives: it is often the next generation who feels the urge to guard memories. But by the 1980s, the official tide had started to shift. With economic reformers under pressure by leftists for their diversion from Marxist truths, a spot of Japan-bashing nationalism was a useful crutch. After the 1989 massacre, official attention to Japanese war crimes snowballed as the National Humiliation History canon was launched.

The war crimes from the 1930s would be reason enough for modern China's antagonism toward Japan, but the roots are much deeper, stretching back into the emotionally strained history of the nineteenth century. The Opium Wars with Britain may have been a huge jolt to Chinese self-esteem, but in a sense they were a warm-up act for the real psychic shock that imperial China suffered: the rise of Japan in the second half of the nineteenth century. China had always looked upon Japan as a "little brother" nation, one of the countries which had been brought under the civilizing realm of Confucian culture and Chinese script. Chinese emperors thought of themselves as the center of a world where nations like Japan offered them deferential respect. Defeat in the 1894–95 Sino-Japanese War was a double blow: not only did China lose to one of these junior nations, but Japan had fortified itself precisely by choosing Western over Chinese culture. (It was after this war that Japan took control of the Senkaku Islands.) The Meiji Restoration in Japan, from the 1860s, was a modernization project that deliberately turned its back on Asia and sought to learn from the West, importing everything from military organization and engineering colleges to fashions. The protests after the Versailles Treaty in 1919 were not just about continued imperial interference in China: they were in a pique of rage that Japan was now a member of the club of imperial bullies. Sun Yat-sen and several other senior figures from the early years of the Chinese republic actually spent time in exile in Japan and were inspired by its zeal for modernization, but they also felt the loss of the Sino-Japanese War deeply. One of them, Kang Youwei, described it as "the greatest humiliation in two hundred years." Modern Chinese nationalism began with defeat by Japan in 1895.

China's anti-Japanese tilt has not taken place in a vacuum, of course, but has had its own mirror in Japanese society. For the last couple of decades, Chinese nationalists and right-wing Japanese revisionists have fed off one another. In the decades immediately after the Second World War, Japanese textbooks included an open discussion of events such as the Nanjing Massacre, as Japanese society and its American occupiers sought to erase the vestiges of imperialism. But from the 1970s, with the Cold War in full flight, revisionist versions of Japan's role in the war started to gain some ground both in the academy and in popular culture, including *manga* comics. Japanese efforts to fudge history produced a resentment in China that reached a peak during the prime minister-ship of Junichiro Koizumi—the idiosyncratic Elvis Presley fan—who led Japan from 2001 to 2006. Unlike his predecessors, Koizumi made a habit of visiting Yasukuni, a Shinto shrine not far from the presidential palace in Tokyo, which honors the war dead. Koizumi described his visits as "a matter of the heart," but the Yasukuni Shrine also honors many of the military leaders from the Second World War who were later branded as "war criminals." Among the portraits of kamikaze pilots at the shrine's war museum there is also a portrait of General Tojo Hideki, head of the Imperial Japanese Army. In late 2012, Japan returned to power Shinzo Abe, another leader with strongly nationalist tendencies, whose grand-father was arrested as a war criminal after the Second World War but never charged. Members of his cabinet have resumed visits to Yasukuni.

China saw these visits as a crude insult, and it was not alone in thinking this way. Distaste for revisionism in Japan has also been strong in South Korea, which has its own painful memories of Japanese occu-pation, and which threatened at one stage to break off diplomatic relations with Tokyo because of what it saw as Koizumi's provocations. The deep sense of hurt in South Korea about continued Japanese efforts to massage its wartime past show that these emotions are not merely the product of China's propaganda authorities. Japan's attitude to the war remains a deep sore across Northeast Asia.

China's response has been to gradually turn up the emotional temperature. It was Iris Chang's 1997 book, *The Rape of Nanking*, that first really brought the events of 1937 to the attention of many Americans. As well as documenting the atrocities, the book made a central intellectual claim that was clear from its subtitle: *The Forgotten Holocaust of World War II*. Over the last couple of decades, China has gradually begun to use the idea of a holocaust to frame the memory of the Japanese invasion and the retelling of the Nanjing Massacre. In 1985, the local authorities in Nanjing built a museum to commemorate the massacre, which includes a large display of bones from bodies found at a nearby location which was dubbed "the pit of ten thousand corpses." In the mid-1990s, the museum was expanded, and it now includes a series of powerful sculptures. Qi Kang, who helped design parts of the reformed memorial, says that he was influenced by the Holocaust museums that started to appear in the U.S. in the 1990s, and the Nanjing memorial has a similar bleak and desolate aesthetic. Near the entrance, the figure three hundred thousand—the official estimate of the number of deaths—is carved into a wall. Ian Buruma, who has written extensively on both Japan and the Holocaust, argues that the only real parallel with the way the Chinese Communist Party has started to use this history is in Israel's Likud Party. "The humiliations of the past must act as a spur to national strength and unity," he wrote. "The more people are told about the terrible things inflicted on their people by foreign enemies, the more they will follow their 'patriotic' leaders." There is no higher form of victimhood than a holocaust.

The emotionally charged atmosphere of the Nanjing memorial is even more intense at the September 18 History Museum in Shenyang, established to celebrate the 1931 Mukden incident that was used as a pretext for Japan's invasion of northeastern China. The museum's catalogue calls on visitors "not to forget national humiliation and to invigorate China." The main gate is a huge stone carved with the date September 18 and riddled with bullet holes. There is a picture of a blood-red tear-drop, and beside it an inscription which blames the "criminal Japanese militarists" who invaded "Great China with its five thousand years of history." At the end of the museum, the text reads: "As we are about to leave the exhibition room, everyone's heart is dripping blood, and every drop of blood seems to congeal into a question mark: How could Japanese imperialism dare to lift a butcher's knife against our great and vast China?"

A WOLF IN MONK'S CLOTHING

When we arrived in the center of Lhasa, the air still held the scent of burnt timber. The old Tibetan quarter of the city is little more than a handful of narrow streets lined with two-story stone buildings. On every block there were several black, singed frames where once had been small storefronts. It was ten days since the Tibetan capital city had been shaken by the worst outburst of racial violence since the 1960s, but the old section of the city remained in near lockdown. On every street corner, armed guards looked on, demanding to see the credentials of the few passersby.

Four days before the riot, around three hundred monks from the Drepung Monastery, just outside Lhasa, had staged a march toward the city—the first open political protest in the streets of the city in more than a decade. Fifteen monks were arrested. On March 14, 2008, a Friday, monks from the Ramoche Monastery also started a small protest. Ramoche is located near the center of the city, and this time the protest attracted many followers. With rumors spreading that the monks arrested earlier in the week had been beaten, some members of the crowd started to attack the police. The police initially held back, perhaps because there was no one to give them orders—most senior officials from the province were in Beijing at the time, for the National People's Congress. At some stage, the ethnic Tibetans who were protesting turned their attention from the police to the large population of migrants who have moved to the city in recent years—mostly Han Chinese, but also some Hui Muslims. They used gasoline to burn the shops and businesses of the migrants. By chance, the Beijing correspondent of *The Economist,* James Miles, was in the city at the time. He watched dozens of different businesses being burned, looted, or destroyed. "It was an extraordinary outpouring of ethnic violence," he wrote.

Foreign journalists are only allowed into Tibet on tightly controlled visits, an indication of just how sensitive the political situation is. Miles happened to be on one of those visits—his first reporting trip to Tibet in fifteen years of covering China. Ten days after the riot, I was lucky enough to get one of the four places for Western reporters on another government-organized trip. The Foreign Ministry hoped the visit would help explain to the world its version of events in Tibet. Things did not quite work out that way. Instead, we found ourselves at the center of a firestorm that cast a long shadow over that year's Beijing Olympics and brought out the very worst aspects of China's brittle, anti-Western nationalism. The Beijing Olympics were supposed to be the occasion when China cast off much of the emotional baggage that feeds its nationalism. China had spent the best part of a century trying to secure the chance to host the Olympics. As far back as 1908, Chinese writers saw the Olympics as a perfect vehicle to erase the country's image as the "Sick Man of Asia." By 2008, that moment had come. The Games were the perfect opportunity to showcase the country's many achievements and to cast off any lingering sense of inferiority. But five months before the opening ceremony, in the streets of the Tibetan capital of Lhasa, that dream started to go sour.

In the days after the Lhasa riot, Chinese TV was broadcasting an almost constant loop of images of the "3/14 incident," as it was known, showing how Han Chinese had been victims of the violence. We were taken to one clothes shop that had been set on fire, where five young women—four of them Han and the other Tibetan, according to reports—had been burned alive. The only things left were the charcoal frame of a storefront and bouquets of flowers lined up against what remained of the outside wall. A shopkeeper, who was a Hui Muslim, told me about the horror he had experienced on seeing a mob start to set his business alight, before they decided to go elsewhere. All the shops on his street were still shuttered, but most of the ones that were untouched had white silk scarves tied around the padlocks, a signal to the protesters that they were owned by Tibetans. The narrative that the Chinese authorities wanted us to believe was indeed true: there had been an ugly race riot in Lhasa, and Han Chinese had been the principal victims.

Except that the official story stopped there. For all the gory details about what had happened, no convincing explanation was put forward as to why the protest took place. Government officials simply told us that the rioters were all common criminals and that they would be dealt with according to the law—"*kuai zhua, kuai shen, kuai sha*," as Tibet Party Secretary Zhang Qingli later put it—"quick arrest, quick trial, quick execution." There was no discussion about why such an ugly episode in racial violence had actually taken place, no reflection on why ethnic Tibetans had turned on the other residents of Lhasa in such a brutal manner. With the rioters dismissed as common criminals, there was no need to ask probing questions about how Tibet was governed. Moreover, the obsessive attention given to the "3/14 incident" obscured the reality that the Lhasa riot was not an isolated event. Instead, there had been a wildfire of protests across the Tibetan plateau. According to Robert Barnett at Columbia University, there were at least ninety-six different protests during that month, in which thirty thousand Tibetans took part. "The question that now faces China's leaders, if not the world, is 'Who lost Tibet?'" Barnett wrote shortly afterward.

The official story started to unravel when we were taken to the Jokhang Temple, in the center of the city, one of the centers of Tibetan Buddhism. A senior abbot, portly in his purple robes, met us in an entrance hall and launched into a long explanation about how calm had been restored. "Everything is back to normal," he insisted. As he was speaking, a group of maybe twenty young monks began to swarm around us. It was unclear at first what was happening, but we soon realized that it was an impromptu protest. The monks seemed in a state of extreme distress, some shouting while others cried. The state media at the time had been going out of their way to demonize the Dalai Lama ("a wolf in monk's clothes," Zhang Qingli called him), but the monks wanted to convince us of their undimmed affection for him. They told us that they had been under effective house arrest since the protests began and that the temple was still in lockdown. And then they dropped the real bombshell. The monks told us that everything going on in the temple that day had been arranged for our benefit. At the time, we were standing in a large hall outside the main temple. Through the door, we could see a throng of people who seemed to be going through their daily prayers, many with prayer beads in their hands. It was all a lie, the monks said. The people inside the temple were all Communist Party officials who had been brought in for the day and told to pretend to be regular worshippers.

Our government minders were apoplectic, but with TV cameras running, they could not afford to break up the protest. So they tried to chip away at the edges. On a couple of occasions, I had to fend off attempts to pull me out of the tumult. After the monks had been talking for about fifteen minutes, two large security officials came up behind me, placed their hands on my shoulders, and lifted me away. The image from the temple proved explosive. The official Chinese narrative about Han Chinese being the victims of the Lhasa riot was true as far as it went. But the elaborate deceit at Jokhang exposed just how much effort the government was exerting to prevent any discussion of the simmering political problems that lay behind the rioting across the Tibetan plateau.

———

The Chinese government's response was effectively to go to war against the foreign press. In the days after the Lhasa riot, most foreign journalists reported as best they could on the event, even though they were not allowed to visit the site. But there were also plenty of mistakes. One German newspaper used a picture of a violent clash between protesters and police which had actually taken place in Nepal. CNN was accused of having cut out part of a photo of Chinese armed police that showed rioting Tibetans. The government jumped on the errors as decisive proof that the foreign media were irredeemably biased against China, and most Chinese of my acquaintance believed the authorities. Before long, witch hunts were being conducted against any foreign journalist who had been deemed to offend the honor of the nation. For a few days, the target of the campaign was Jane Macartney, the correspondent of *The Times* of London. (This was particularly unfair as she had not written the article that appeared to cause offense, but it at least had a certain historical irony—she is a direct descendant of Lord Macartney, the British envoy in the late eighteenth century who refused to bow to the Qianlong emperor, a standoff that proved to be a precursor to the Opium Wars.) Geremie Barmé, the Australian academic, correctly described the exercise as "a radical demonisation of the western international press." The four Western reporters who had been on the trip in Tibet also started to come under attack. When I arrived at the office in the morning, I would find abusive messages and a few death threats waiting on the answering machine. My colleague who runs the *Financial Times'* Chinese-language Web site called one day, after reading the volume of hate mail that was coming into the site. He suggested that I maybe start to change the route I took to and from the office, just in case. At the time, I shrugged off the threats, assuming them to be from young men in Internet cafés who were letting off a little steam. But one of the other reporters who had gone to Lhasa received a rather more intimidating threat. Someone got hold of a photo of him, cut off the head, and then posted the two images on a Web site.

Before long, the furor spilled over into the preparations for the Olympics. A few weeks after the Tibet riot, the Olympic torch was due to travel through several European capitals, part of an elaborate global tour. In London, a few pro-Tibetan protesters tried to disrupt the torch relay and were pushed away by Chinese police in track suits who were running alongside. In Paris, the protesters were more aggressive and tried to grab the torch from a young Chinese woman in a wheelchair. Jin Jing, a twenty-seven-year-old from Shanghai who was due to compete in Paralympic fencing, became a national hero after fending off the attack, "an angel in a wheelchair" as the Chinese media dubbed her. "I still feel very angry now, and I think the man was very irrational," she said the next day. "Hosting the Olympics is such a good thing for our country, so why do they want to ruin it?"

Back in China, a new wave of angry popular protests broke out, once again with the urban, educated youth at the forefront. Some of these young Chinese had an idealized view of the foreign media and were deeply upset at what they believed to be the obvious bias of the coverage of the Tibet riots. ("Don't be so CNN" became a popular retort.) The disruption to the torch relay just added to their ire. After a rumor circulated that a Carrefour executive had made a large donation to a radical Tibetan group, a boycott campaign was organized online. Huge demonstrations of young people erupted at some of the chain's Chinese stores. In Hefei, a provincial city three hundred miles inland from Shanghai, ten thousand people congregated one Saturday afternoon in the car park of a Carrefour to demonstrate their displeasure. An Internet video about the history of Tibet which went viral among young Chinese was entitled "Tibet WAS, IS, and ALWAYS WILL BE a part of China."

In some ways, tempers were even more frayed among young Chinese studying at overseas universities—precisely the constituency that some in the West hope will be an eventual bulwark for liberal reform in China. At Duke University in North Carolina, a young Chinese student named Grace Wang attempted to intervene in a fierce debate that had broken out between Han Chinese students at the university and ethnic Tibetans. Her intervention went viral on the Internet, and she was subjected to a vicious hate campaign, in which she was labeled by other Chinese students a "race traitor." After her parents' home address in Qingdao was circulated on the Internet, a photo appeared online which purported to show feces smeared all over the door. They had to go into hiding.

It is hard to understand the intensity of the 2008 events without seeing how deeply rooted Tibet is in the framework of national humiliation. One of the flip sides of modern China's victim mentality is a ferocious defense of its sovereignty, which was impugned by foreign powers in the nineteenth century, the invaders who "carved up China like a melon." In the periods when China has been weak, its ambiguous influence over Tibet has loosened further, including when the British invaded in 1903. Control over Tibet is tightly linked to the urge to restore national pride. It is that mindset that can turn a dispute between Han Chinese and one of the country's ethnic minorities into a struggle against imperialism. Since the early years of the republic, China's leaders have been faced with the dilemma of trying to forge a modern, unified nation-state from the loose, saggy terrain of a multinational empire. The new national identity has leaned heavily on a strong sense of shared suffering, which Beijing has then imposed on all the country's ethnic groups, even those whose historical connections to the Chinese state are full of nuance, complexity, and in some cases conflict. For Beijing to recognize deep political problems in Tibet or among other ethnic groups would be to undermine the narrative of China as a victim of outside interference. When Tibet explodes, the West sees a Beijing government floundering in a very different political culture; official China sees such complaints as a challenge to its core identity.

The Olympics were supposed to provide the catharsis from this psychological burden, to show that China could move from victim to victor. Instead, the buildup to the Games made many Chinese feel that the country was being subject to a series of damning judgments, as if the West did not yet believe China was good enough. After all the changes and successes of the last three decades, many Chinese felt that the country was still not considered truly respectable. This was another reason to be furious at the Tibetans: they had tried to spoil the party. Beneath their bureaucratic exterior, the Tibetan riots exposed a kind of emotional rage among Chinese leaders, who experience such setbacks as a form of personal humiliation. At the same time, the contortions to avoid an open discussion about Tibet led even the more sensible members of the Chinese bureaucracy to take the most addled, paranoid positions. On one occasion, a very senior Chinese official was asked to explain why foreign journalists were banned from visiting Tibet except on carefully organized tours. Journalists could not be trusted, she said, because all the photos of the Dalai Lama hanging on the walls of homes and offices in Tibet had been brought in by foreign reporters. Tapping her finger on the table for emphasis, she repeated: "Every single photo."

SHALLOW AND INTENSE

Li Yang was about halfway through a three-hour teaching session at the English-language boot camp when he started calling attention to me. "We have an important guest, Jiefu, from a British newspaper," he announced, using a Chinese transliteration of my name. I was sitting at the back, and all the students turned round to look at me. They laughed when Li told them, "He has come down here to taste our *jiaozi* [dumplings]." Gradually, more and more of his comments seemed to be aimed in my direction. "The best place to teach English would be in church, but I do not think that Comrade Hu would allow this—don't you think, Jiefu?" he said, smiling.

Li insists that his entire routine is improvised, even when some of the sessions last for hours. To prove it, after a while he decided to summon me to the stage. Several hundred young Chinese students looked around at me with an expectant gaze, perhaps suspecting some sport might be in the offing. It would have been extremely rude to refuse, so, somewhat embarrassed, I wandered onstage. Li started questioning me about my life in China. Then he asked me what I thought to be the most impressive thing about China. I mumbled something, I believe, about the striking ambition and energy of ordinary Chinese people to improve their lives. "*Wow!*" thundered Li. "Listen to this. Jiefu, say that again. Repeat that, please, Jiefu. Everyone, listen closely." My onstage ordeal continued for another ten minutes, during which Li anticipated one of my strongest reactions—and something that has also been a persistent criticism of his school. Looking out at the rapt audience hanging on his every word, with red flags lined up all across the auditorium, and monitors in army fatigues standing in the aisles to watch over the students, Li turned to me and said, "Jiefu, you must think this is a lot like the Cultural Revolution."

Class eventually broke for dinner, a school meal served on metal trays with four different compartments, one each for the meat dish, vegetable, rice, and fruit. The Chinese New Year was only a few hours away, which the students would spend in a class, but there was time for one more entertainment: a torch rally. The students assembled in drill formation on an adjacent sports field to watch some fireworks and to listen to a short speech by Li. Then, with their monitors each carrying a torch, they marched in formation around the campus, chanting slogans in English about "Success" and "Achievement." I watched, unsure what to think. If there had not been so much laughter in the air, if the students had not been so charming and curious, and if these kids had not been sacrificing the most important holiday of the year to learn a foreign language, then there might have been something just a little fascist about the spectacle.

After two days in his company, I still could not decide whether Li Yang was really tapping a deep vein of nationalism, or whether his anti-American shtick was just performance art, a ritual about humiliation and sacrifice that his students understand and laugh at but which they do not really believe. That is the broader challenge in trying to understand Chinese nationalism. The last decade has seen a series of angry fits at the rest of the world, full of bitterness and bile, but these have quickly subsided. Is there a volcano of resentment waiting to explode, or are these just tantrums that will ease, the growing pains of a new great power adjusting to its place in the world? One of the most important questions about modern China is whether the nationalist chorus is relatively small, a rump of 10 percent of the population, who get more attention than they deserve, or whether it is the reflection of a set of attitudes that are ingrained into the national DNA.

Prasenjit Duara, an Indian scholar of China now based in Singapore, described the mood of some of the young Chinese nationalists this way: "Day 1: Eat at McDonald's; Day 2: Throw rocks at McDonald's; Day 3: Eat at McDonald's." There is, he says, "a simultaneous superficiality and depth of nationalist feelings" in modern China. In each of the big nationalist outbursts, the Communist Party has for a moment looked vulnerable, as if the events might spin out of control, but it has then managed quickly to turn off the tap. After a NATO bomb hit the Chinese Embassy in Belgrade in 1999, hundreds of Chinese students spent the next few days protesting outside and vandalizing the U.S. Embassy in Beijing. The atmosphere was feverish. Western residents of the city at the time said that for a couple of days they felt under threat if they stepped outside. And then the protests stopped. A Chinese friend of mine who was at university in Beijing at the time recalls turning up for class one morning to be told by a teacher to get on a bus, which dropped all the students off outside the U.S. Embassy. The next day, the bus was there again to take them to the embassy. On the third day, lectures went on as normal.

The anti-Japan protests in 2005 followed the same path. The week before the big Shanghai demonstration, there was a large protest in Beijing, and the week after, Guangzhou and Shenzhen held demonstrations. Then the movement fizzled, and the students returned to their classes. When we left Shanghai three years later, the cigarette shop on our block still had Japanese characters in the window. Duara's observation also captures the central ambiguity at the heart of the Li Yang phenomenon, the simultaneous fascination with and distaste for the West. The generation of Chinese who have been through "patriotic education" is the same generation that is exposed to the world through the Internet in ways that their parents could never have dreamed of and is attracted to all the same symbols of American consumerism. A year or so before I left Beijing, a new Apple Store opened, which I must have walked past fifty times. But I never once entered, for the simple reason that there was always a queue outside to get in.

Yet, at the same time, each cycle of nationalist spasms seems to get a bit bigger and a little more autonomous, further outside the control mechanisms of the state. Nationalist pressure has been an important factor in some of the disputes in the South China Sea, and has become increasingly influential in the argument with Japan over the Senkaku/Diaoyu Islands. In both cases, the populist online pressure found common cause with the sections of the military that want to take a more confrontational approach. As the protest waves become more intense, the leadership finds its room to maneuver more limited. The events that have produced demonstrations in recent years have been relatively minor—a stray bomb, a handful of textbooks, some unruly protests during an Olympics torch relay—yet each managed to create a paroxysm of angst that left the country temporarily off-balance. It begs the question of what might happen in the event of a major international incident—a 9/11-style terror attack, or a genuine confrontation with the Japanese navy in the East China Sea. The raw, popular nationalism does not dictate Chinese foreign policy, but at the very least it makes it hard for the government to back down or make concessions.

For the U.S. and other Western countries, the broader lesson is that they have to be aware that there will always be this emotional tension in the background of their relations with Beijing, a trauma which has yet to be fully resolved, and which makes its leaders at times hair-trigger sensitive to perceived slights. One of the most difficult tasks for American politicians will be to find a way to engage with the Chinese people over sensitive issues, from political reform to territorial disputes, in a way that does not step on any of these trip wires. At the same time, the U.S. has a responsibility to pressure its ally Japan to, at the very least, refrain from provocative gestures that revive historical tensions. By inflaming South Korea as well as China, such stunts harm not only Japan's influence in the region, but also that of Washington.

Chinese liberals argue that it is the political system that nurtures the particular virulence of today's nationalism. Hard-line views are very much a minority, they suggest, but, because political and historical debate is so curtailed, there is no room for nuance or context, and emotions are easily manipulated. Japan has a nationalist right wing whose views are often toxic, but their impact is diluted and absorbed by a more open political debate. If that liberal view is correct, then it is possible to imagine that, in the long run, political reform might draw some of the poison from Chinese nationalism. The anger of a small minority can multiply in strength under an authoritarian government that does not want to appear weak; but in a more open system, shrill voices find it harder to dominate the debate.

That is the theory, at least. Maybe a democratic China would have a more comfortable sense of its own identity and place in the world, as liberals and many in America hope. But it is equally possible to imagine a very different scenario, in which a loss of control by the Communist Party leads to even stronger nationalist pressures. The students who have taken part in anti-U.S. or anti-Japanese protests know one basic truth, that this is almost the only way they can safely take part in popular demonstrations. The Communist Party's most vulnerable flank is at the nationalist, populist right. A party that loudly claims the mantle of national salvation cannot afford to look weak in the face of perceived slights. If the Communist Party's grip on power ever did start to loosen seriously, it is not too hard to imagine an embattled Chinese leader searching for an anti-America or anti-Japan cause and placing it at the center of his agenda.

6

Soft Power

HARMONIZING THE WORLD

THE LARGE NEON SCREENS on the corner of New York's Broadway and Seventh Avenue are among the most visible and prestigious advertising sites in America. The signs are sixty feet high by forty feet wide and are seen by many of the half-million people who daily pass through Times Square. The spaces have been rented by Coca-Cola and by the Prudential insurance company; HSBC had its name in lights for a decade. The new name on the signs is not quite so familiar to most New York tourists: Xinhua, China's state-run news agency, the propaganda arm of the Chinese Communist Party. As well as renting the neon advertising screen, Xinhua has also taken the top floor of the forty-four-story skyscraper at 1540 Broadway—only a block away from the sumptuous new *New York Times* building designed by Renzo Piano with silver birch trees in the atrium.

The financial pressures that are slowly strangling many of the world's media groups do not appear to be hampering Xinhua. In 2010, the agency opened a new twenty-four-hour English-language news channel called CNC World, which the group's president, Li Congjun, described as an attempt to "present an international vision with a Chinese perspective." Beijing has long complained of unfair treatment from what it calls "the Western media." Officials believe that if the world could just find out more about the reality of China, about its history and progress, then people would think very differently about the country. They want more good news, and if the BBC and CNN will not provide that service for the world, then Xinhua and the other arms of the official Chinese media will.

A decade ago, China was thought of as an inward-looking, developing country with modest international ambitions, whose leaders cared about little other than the next month's GDP figures. But it is hard to think in quite the same way about a country that has such grand global ambitions for its media groups. China wants to crack the Western monopoly on news. According to several informed reports, China spent around $8.7 billion in 2011–12 on the overseas operations of just four news organizations—Xinhua, Chinese Central Television (CCTV), the English-language *China Daily,* and China Radio International. The entire budget for the BBC World Service is around $400 million a year. With big budgets come big goals. Beijing mainly wants to improve China's image in the world, but it also hopes that Chinese news organizations can loosen the grip that American values of democracy, individualism, and human rights have on the international media business. "While our media empires are melting away like the Himalayan glaciers, China's are expanding," Orville Schell, the director of the Asia Society's Center on U.S.-China Relations, was quoted as saying—in the *New York Times.*

Like many of the trappings of modernity, from Maglev trains to the Nobu restaurant chain, soft power has become an obsession in contemporary China. Originally coined by the American academic Joseph Nye, soft power is the idea that the more attractive a country's culture and society, the more influential it will be. America's international dominance, so the theory goes, rests not just on its military power or its economic weight but also on the fact that so many other countries around the world have sought to copy its rules, institutions, and way of life. Nye defined soft power as "the ability to get what you want through attraction rather than coercion or payment." In some ways, China takes the basic idea of soft power more seriously than the U.S. The first academic in China to take up the theme was Wang Huning, a scholar at Fudan

University in Shanghai, who has since become one of China's most senior foreign-policy officials and a member of the party's Politburo. His ideas have been adopted at the top levels of the Chinese leadership. In his keynote speech to the important Communist Party Congress in 2007, Hu Jintao gave the concept his official stamp of approval, telling the audience: "We must enhance culture as part of the soft power of the country." Whole university departments in China are now devoted to soft power, and the Foreign Ministry has opened a special department to improve the country's image. There is even a new museum in Beijing celebrating public diplomacy, the art of national image boosting.

For Beijing, soft power is a tool to present a less threatening image to the world, to massage anxieties caused by the country's rise. But there is also a hard edge to the soft-power fascination. Some Chinese scholars argue that it is also an essential part of a project for challenging America. Shen Jiru, an academic at the Chinese Academy of Social Sciences, argues that soft power was central to the U.S.'s winning the Cold War, the mass appeal of its popular culture helping to curtail international support for the Soviets. The Soviet Union had been equal to the U.S. for a time, he says, but "lost the whole game due to a flaw in its soft power." China, he urges, should not make the same mistake. For many of the officials and academics pushing the promotion of Chinese soft power, this is much more than just a PR campaign, but part of a broader struggle for influence and respect. China is taking on the U.S. at its own game in a global cultural contest.

China's soft-power push is both a window onto its expanding ambitions and an important emotional crux in the emerging rivalry with the U.S. If the feeling takes root in the U.S. that China is presenting a worldview that will be attractive to large parts of the world, this will add real political edge to the competition. The temptation will grow in the U.S. to elevate the rivalry to a form of ideological contest, with echoes of the Cold War. There are already a few hints of this in official American reactions to the investments China is making in its media sector. "During the Cold War we did a great job in getting America's message out. After the Berlin Wall fell we said, 'Okay, fine, enough of that, we are done,' and unfortunately we are paying a big price for it," Hillary Clinton told Congress in 2011. "We are in an information war and we are losing that war. Al Jazeera is winning, the Chinese have opened a global multi-language television network, the Russians have opened up an English-language network. I've seen it in a few countries, and it is quite instructive."

Soft power can come in lots of shapes and sizes. Some academics in China believe that the country should be promoting its model of economic management, particularly to other parts of the developing world, as a way of making the country more influential. A few even suggest that China's political system could be exported. But most of the discussion about soft power in China has focused on culture and the idea that the best way to make the country seem more attractive to the outside world is through the potential magnetism of Chinese civilization. The big media investments are the most visible element of China's soft-power project, but beneath the surface there are, in effect, two central ideas about the attractiveness of Chinese culture: an attempt to establish a sort of modern Chinese aesthetic that the rest of the world might find enticing, and an effort to tap into the wisdom of ancient thinkers to flesh out a non-Western worldview. China wants to present itself to the world as a culture that is both new and old.

When he was sixteen, Yan Xuetong was sent to work on a farm in the northeastern province of Heilongjiang, right near the border with Siberia. It was the height of the Cultural Revolution, and, like many members of his generation of urban youth, he was taken from his home and school and instructed to learn the greater wisdom of a peasant life. It was an unimaginably harsh existence. During the winters, they sometimes had to haul around large sacks through the snow, barefoot. For months, they would go without vegetables. The brutalities of the Cultural Revolution changed young Chinese in different ways. Some never overcame the emotional scars from that time, and suffered an adult life of depression or even suicide. Others developed a toughness and resilience that, in a perverse way, have served them well as society and the economy opened up. For Yan, who was from a family of scholars, the conclusions he drew were more philosophical. Mao Zedong's mad experiment with enforced anarchy, he decided, had destroyed the country's ancient ethical tradition of sincerity and replaced it with lying and hypocrisy.

Nearly four decades later, Yan is one of the most prominent public intellectuals in China and a professor of international relations at Tsinghua University in Beijing. He has written extensively about American foreign policy and Chinese military strategy. In recent years, however, he has turned to a project that has its roots in his disillusionment during the Cultural Revolution. He is trying to find ways to reconnect with what he sees as China's ancient ethical traditions, in particular the idea that China and the world should be governed by what he calls "humane authority." China, he believes, needs to re-establish the sense of morality that used to guide its behavior, both at home and abroad.

If that sounds a little esoteric, Yan has some fairly robust ideas about why it is a subject worth paying attention to. The quest to recover a Chinese ethical tradition, he believes, is a central part of the soft-power contest that a rising China faces with the U.S. The U.S. and China are in, he says, a "race for global supremacy," and an integral part of that competition will be a "battle for the hearts and minds" of people around the world, which will "determine who eventually prevails." The search back into China's philosophical traditions is not just an academic exercise, but part of a broader effort to present a vision of China and Chinese-inspired ideas that can challenge American modernity. "America's ideology is still much more influential around the world than China's," he told me. And he wants that to change.

These are interesting times in China's universities. After three decades during which Chinese society kept its head down and concentrated on getting ahead, it is starting to come up for air. Among some Chinese intellectuals, there is a hankering to generate new ideas about how global society is organized, to provide Chinese solutions to the world's problems. In a similar vein to Yan Xuetong, Zhao Tingyang at the Chinese Academy of Social Sciences has become a star of the Beijing intellectual scene with a series of works about the concept of *tianxia*—literally, "all under heaven"—another idea from the classical philosophy that attempts to define a vision of international harmony. Just as the Chinese authorities have embraced soft power to present a more positive image to the world, some Chinese intellectuals are brimming with optimism about the lessons that Chinese ideas can present to the world.

One of the striking features of the way China has embraced soft power is the suggestion that China now sees its values and culture as exportable. China and the U.S. have one very powerful thing in common, a sense of exceptionalism, the deeply felt belief in the superiority of their cultures and societies. American exceptionalism has an evangelical quality, the idea that its institutions and values are by their nature universal and should be copied by others; in recent times however, Chinese culture has been presented as being more exclusive. Chinese have tended to believe that their strengths were tied up in a history and set of values that are unique to China and which cannot be easily adopted by outsiders—at least by those countries outside the traditional Sino-centric world of East Asia. But the soft-power push indicates the beginning of a very different sort of attitude to Chineseness, a confidence that China now represents something that can be introduced in other countries, that it has things to teach the rest of the world. Amid official rhetoric about the "revival" or the "rejuvenation" of China, which has been given new impetus under Xi Jinping, China is reconnecting with an older tradition when it considered itself a natural cultural magnet for the world that surrounded it. "The Chinese have always prided themselves on being civilized as bearers of universal ideals," Wang Gungwu, the doyen of overseas Chinese historians, has written. China is dabbling with its own ideas of universal values.

"Five years ago, no one talked about this. People said it was crazy to talk about these sorts of things, that only our grandchildren might have to address these sorts of issues," Yan told me. "But when you are the biggest power in the world, you have to provide leadership. The new leaders that are taking over in China now, they will face a debate about future strategy and how we use power that the leaders of the past two decades did not."

During the Cultural Revolution, Red Guards destroyed the temple dedicated to Confucius, whom Mao scorned for his "feudal mentality," but over the last decade the ancient sage has witnessed a remarkable revival. The academic Yu Dan's book *Confucius from the Heart* sold ten million copies. Among party elders, there is still some token resistance to the veneration of Confucius: a statue was unveiled in Tiananmen Square in 2011, outside the reopened National Museum, only to be taken away a few weeks later. But it is another example of the extreme intellectual dexterity of the Chinese Communist Party that, having spent three decades denouncing everything Confucius stood for, it now presents itself as the legitimate inheritor of the millennial cultural tradition he represents. Yan Xuetong is one of the many intellectuals who have tried to tap into this surge in popular enthusiasm for ancient wisdom. He has mined Confucius and Mencius, as well as the less well-known writers from a similar era, such as Xunzi, Laozi, and Hanfeizi, to look for lessons about how a powerful China should behave. The most influential states, he concluded, were not necessarily the ones with the most powerful military, but the ones who won over the most hearts and minds of people at home and abroad. And this ability rested on the "humane authority . . . the superior moral power of the ruler."

The conclusions he draws for China are blunt. "An increase in wealth can raise China's power status but it does not necessarily enable China to become a country respected by others," he writes. "For China to become a superpower modeled on humane authority, it must first become a model from which other states are willing to learn." Some political reforms will be required, he believes, but that does not mean China should copy the U.S. "If China wants to become a state of humane authority, this would be different from the contemporary United States," he writes. "The goal of our strategy must be not only to reduce the power gap with the United States but also to provide a better model for society than that given by the United States."

If Yan is often blunt about his objectives, Zhao Tingyang is more oblique. The title of Zhao's best-known work is *The Tianxia System: A Philosophy for the World Institution*. In his elliptical style, Zhao describes the current international order as one which contains not just the odd "failed state," but a "failed world" that is rendered unworkable by excessive competition between nations and endless wars. Like Yan, he thinks the solution is for one country to provide an impeccable moral and political example. The world institution he envisages would be a voluntary order, based on the attractiveness of that country's "magnanimous" thought and behavior. International harmony would be established not by violence or power, but by the demonstration of virtue and good governance. "Tianxia theory," he writes, "is a theory for transforming enemies into friends where transformation seeks to attract people rather than conquer them."

The sorts of ideas that people like Yan and Zhao have started to discuss come with some very dangerous trip wires. *Tianxia* is an idea with deep roots in two thousand years of Chinese empire that was based on hierarchical relations between China and the other nations and peoples in the region. It reeks of a certain kind of cultural superiority and of a return to hierarchy. Most of the writers now championing ancient thinkers also leave open big questions about how China would be governed. Does "humane authority" require the sort of accountability that only democracies have been able to offer? As a result of these obvious problems, there has been a tendency among China-watchers to dismiss much of the work of the neo-Confucian writers, to see them as willing supporters of government propaganda. But these discussions are important for two reasons. They demonstrate a growing appetite among public intellectuals in China for devising ways of interpreting the world around Chinese precepts and history and forging a Chinese worldview. They are also a serious attempt to mold a language for China to explain its ambitions to influence the world and the role it wants to play. "Ancient Chinese policy will become the basis for much Chinese foreign policy, rather than Western liberalism or Communist ideology, both to justify and to be understood by Chinese people," Yan says. "It is easier to teach common people why they are doing certain things if it is explained in these terms. It makes it different from the U.S."

———

Before the opening ceremony for the 2008 Beijing Olympics, Zhang Jigang, the event's deputy director, made the following prediction: "I really hope that the people of the world can . . . get to know China, to understand China, to love China, to long for China." If trying to revive a Chinese intellectual tradition is one part of the underlying project, the other is an effort to present it as modern and hip, to define China Cool. The emotional high point of China's soft-power push was the ravishing Olympics opening ceremony—another beneficiary of a budget stretching into the hundreds of millions of dollars. Zhang Yimou, the country's most famous film director, was instructed to demonstrate the richness of traditional Chinese culture, the sort of brief that has produced many a tired, bureaucratic show for foreigners. Yet, with the help of fifteen thousand immaculately drilled performers and luminous lighting to tell the story of paper, printing, and the compass, he provided a vision of modernity China-style, with a powerful state rooted in Confucian wisdom yet also married to modern technology. After the ceremony, Zhang admitted that the only other country that could have put on a performance of such scale and discipline was North Korea, and they could not have mastered all the high-tech visual trickery that went along with it. Steven Spielberg, who had withdrawn as an adviser to the ceremony in protest against Chinese policies in Sudan, called it "arguably the grandest spectacle of the new millennium."

When visitors to the Olympics got tired of the sport, they were able to do a side trip to see some of the newest wonders of modern architecture. They would probably have seen the recently opened Norman Foster airport terminal, whose roof is shaped like a dragon. Beside the Great Hall of the People in central Beijing, they could visit the new titanium-domed concert hall, which goes by the name "the Giant Egg." And of course, there was the "Bird's Nest" stadium at the Olympic site, by Swiss architects Herzog and de Meuron, which is encased in twenty-eight thousand strips of structured steel, like a woven basket. But the biggest architectural draw was not even finished: the new China Central Television headquarters in the city's main business district. CCTV is the principal state-run broadcaster in China and, in the eyes of many Chinese, a reliable mouthpiece of stale government propaganda. It has spared neither money nor effort in its quest for a prestige building with the sheen of brand-name modernity. The $800-million project, on which work started in 2004, is the brainchild of the Rotterdam-based Office for Metropolitan Architecture and its principal architect, Rem Koolhaas. It is as much an exercise in engineering as in architecture and might only have been possible in China.

The building is made up of two L-shaped towers made of glass and metal, pieced together to create a cantilevered corridor that seems to hang in the air. Beijingers have bestowed many nicknames on the project, the most popular of which, *da kucha,* means "big shorts." Other, less flattering names include a play on the words for hemorrhoids. The design would have violated the building codes of most developing countries, but the architects managed to convene a meeting of the different

Beijing agencies to talk them through the idea. One of the quirks of modern China is that so many senior officials are qualified engineers, and that allowed them to follow all the technical details as Koolhaas and his thirty-something protégé, Ole Scheeren, walked them through the computer models. The building was approved. Even then, there was still huge anxiety about joining the two towers together, which was done before dawn in case the daytime heat caused the steel to expand slightly. It was a moment of "early-morning intimacy," as Scheeren told me.

A week before the Beijing Olympics, the *New York Times* architecture critic Nicolai Ouroussoff had this to say about the host city: "If Westerners feel dazed and confused upon exiting the plane at the new international airport terminal here, it's understandable. It's not just the grandeur of the space. It's the inescapable feeling that you're passing through a portal to another world, one whose fierce embrace of change has left Western nations in the dust. The sensation is comparable to the epiphany that Adolf Loos, the Viennese architect, experienced when he stepped off a steamship in New York Harbor more than a century ago. He had crossed a threshold into the future; Europe, he realized, was now culturally obsolete." The gushing about Beijing's new architectural triumphs (each one, as it happens, built by a European architect) might be an extreme example, but the article underlined the trepidation and awe that some in the West feel about China's rising cultural attraction. China is now beginning to promote its values and culture abroad just at the time when the West is undergoing a profound crisis of confidence. The financial crisis has not only inflicted huge damage on the economies of the Western world, it has also sapped confidence in the ability of democracies to solve their deepest problems. While China appears to be steaming ahead with its modernization plans, barely missing a beat during the crisis, the U.S. and other democracies are beset with doubts about corrosive political partisanship, about the power of vested interests, and about the inability of politicians to see beyond the latest headline. According to Ian Buruma, one of the most perceptive writers on modern Asia, "China's success story is the most serious challenge that liberal democracy has faced since fascism in the 1930s."

Amid such disillusionment, China's campaign to sell its cultural vitality around the world could not be better timed. Yet it will fall short. China's efforts to mobilize soft power misunderstand the forces that actually make societies attractive. The flaw is nowhere more evident than in the huge amount of money China is spending on taking its media groups overseas.

FOXIFICATION

In forty years in the television news business, Jim Laurie has done just about everything there is to be done. He spent two decades touring the world as a foreign correspondent for NBC and ABC. He was the only American network journalist in Saigon when the Vietnamese Communists took the city in 1975. Laurie has done breaking news and long-form documentaries, taught journalism, and helped set up News Corporation's news channels in India. In his locker, there are two Emmys and a George Peabody Award. It is a CV that any aspiring journalist would die for. And now he has a new challenge. He is one of the senior executives for CCTV America, the recently established U.S. operation of the Chinese state broadcaster.

In China, CCTV's showcase program is the main 7 p.m. news broadcast, which is a template for political power in the country. The broadcast begins with a rundown of the activities that day of the secretary general of the Communist Party, describing his meetings with foreign leaders and regional bosses and noting any comments he might have made. Then it moves to the number two leader in the Communist Party Standing Committee, before describing the day of the number three in the list. The set is gray; the newscasters are unsmiling and stolid. A Chinese friend likes to joke that the broadcast is designed to persuade older Communist officials that nothing has actually changed in the country over the last three decades. CCTV runs a dozen or so channels, and some of its programming has tried to push boundaries. A few of the scandals about shoddy consumer products in China in recent years have actually been first aired on CCTV shows. But it can never escape its principal purpose, as the state's main tool for dictating the national news agenda.

Laurie was teaching journalism to students in Hong Kong when he got the offer to help start CCTV America. "The Chinese want to play catch-up," he says. They saw the global impact of Al Jazeera, the Qatar-based channel that broadcasts in both Arabic and English and which has won any number of accolades in recent years. Russia and Japan also have English-language channels vying for foreign audiences. Al Jazeera's success persuaded Chinese executives that there was a huge potential demand for "non-Western" news. The Chinese took the view that U.S. networks seemed to be shunning more conventional news in favor of Hollywood gossip and stories about celebrity addiction. They also observed what Laurie calls the "Foxification" of news in much of the West, where the once straitlaced presentation of facts has given way to different points of view and much more attitude. "The Chinese want to have their own perspective represented," Laurie says.

When Chinese Communist Party leaders met in October 2011 for their annual plenum, they issued a document with the following title: "Central Committee Decision Concerning the Major Issue of Deepening Cultural System Reforms, Promoting the Great Development and Prosperity of Socialist Culture." It was the most definitive in a series of policy statements over the last few years which have endorsed the promotion of cultural soft power. The document concluded: "Whoever owns the commanding heights of cultural development and soft power will enjoy a competitive edge internationally." Such high-level endorsement helps loosen budget strings. Over the last few years, Beijing has thrown a huge amount of resources at projects aimed at reaching the "commanding heights" of global soft power. There are more than four hundred government-sponsored Confucius Institutes around the world, promoting the Chinese language. When Hu Jintao visited the U.S. in 2011, the government rented another of the huge screens in Times Square to run a series of expensively produced promotional videos to show a more appealing side of China. There were images of "award-winning Chinese talent" such as pianist Lang Lang and "thrilling Chinese athletics," including Yao Ming. Another section of images of successful entrepreneurs was entitled "Chinese wealth," which, in retrospect, was probably not the best message to win over skeptical New Yorkers.

Of all the initiatives that have been launched to support the government's soft-power campaign, the overseas expansion of Chinese media is the biggest and most ambitious. The injection of resources into the international divisions of Chinese media has been striking. *China Daily,* the party's English-language daily, is now sold widely across the U.S. and Europe. Friends have reported that at times it is the only English-language paper available free in certain European hotels. It partners with a host of other papers that allow *China Daily* sections to appear across Asia. Readers of the *Washington Post* also receive a weekly "paid supplement" inside their paper which is written by *China Daily* staff. At the same time, China Radio International provides programming for a number of radio stations in the U.S., having started out with a station in Galveston, Texas. The Xinhua News Agency moved its journalists from a Queens suburb to Times Square. As well as its more traditional print and news-wire services, it is developing a Web-based TV service in foreign languages for a hundred countries. In a number of African countries, for instance, newspapers which in the past used Reuters or Associated Press articles for many of their news pages now lean heavily on Xinhua. CCTV is just as ambitious. It has recently opened a broadcast center in Nairobi, and since early 2012, it has been employing around a hundred people in Washington to put together programming for the U.S. market from a new studio just a few blocks from the White House.

Laurie says that CCTV spent a huge amount of time studying the BBC and CNN, looking at how they present news and trying to establish a "professional look." It also went about hiring journalists with internationally respected credentials. Cutbacks in the West have helped. In Latin America, CCTV picked up the former BBC Brazil and Cuba correspondent Mike Voss, who was laid off in one of the organization's cost-cutting rounds. While in China, I saw Voss giving an interview to the main CCTV channel, explaining his decision to join them. "I have already done more live takes in two months with CCTV than I did in the last year with the BBC," he said. "This shows they are really committed to the news." When Tom Brokaw was booked to appear on one of CCTV America's shows, the conservative *Weekly Standard* made a gibe about how China was "trying to buy good coverage for its Communist regime." Laurie is well aware of the baggage that his new network carries. "We are CCTV—and all that comes with it," he says. But he insists that the new channel is pushing back barriers on what a Chinese network can cover. During the week of their first broadcasts, the Pope happened to be visiting Havana, and Voss pitched a story on the trip.

China's relations with the Vatican are a politically treacherous subject in Beijing, and so a visit by the Pope to another Communist country is delicate territory. But CCTV America broadcast the item.

As well as the look, CCTV America has paid close attention to tone. Russia Today, Moscow's alternative to CNN, takes an aggressively anti-Western point of view and takes pleasure in its potshots at the American networks. One regular feature is about a piece of news that U.S. news channels have chosen not to cover, which usually includes a dig at America's presumed moral authority. In 2012, WikiLeaks founder Julian Assange was given a show on the channel. The Russia Today Web site is even more dismissive. One column about the U.S., by a writer called Robert Bridge, concludes: "What we are left with is an obese, drug-addled Burlesque Empire, bursting at the seams with electronic circuses, cocaine and corn puffs, physically and mentally incapable of finding the remote control when the scenes of war become too unappetizing." Alongside such competition, CCTV America is altogether more straitlaced. On a typical night, the news is heavy on economic themes and avoids sensationalism or gossip. It is straight, professional, maybe a little dull, but not without authority. If there is an implicit criticism of the U.S. and the West, it is not a full-throated one. Instead, the underlying politics are more subtle, an exercise in the sort of relativism that Chinese officials often adopt—an argument along the lines of "Your society has problems, our society has problems, so let's not be too judgmental about each other's political systems."

No one has a monopoly on providing the news, of course, but the identity of the leading broadcasters is still a matter of some importance. Imagine, for a second, if such important international stories as the protests in Cairo's Tahrir Square or the war in Bosnia had been beamed to the world not by the cameras of the BBC and CNN, but by the producers and correspondents of CCTV. Would the events have played out in the same way? Would the pressure on the Egyptian government not to use violence against the protesters have been the same? Would Washington have felt obliged to get involved in Bosnia had the dominant broadcaster in Sarajevo been Chinese? The high-minded goal behind China's overseas media splash is to try and frame the global conversation, to push a news agenda that is not so laced with Western values. Beijing does not want to evangelize the world against democracy, but it does want to shift some of the terms of the global debate. At the same time, lurking behind the project there is a certain animus for what Chinese officials routinely denounce as the "Western media," a term of abuse that lumps together journalists from any democracy, be they American, German, or Japanese. Beijing is trying to counter what it sees as the systematic bias in how foreign reporters portray China and the Communist Party to the rest of the world. The heads of foreign media bureaus in Beijing are summoned to the Foreign Ministry for periodic dressings-down by a senior official, and during one meeting I took notes. "Lots of good things happen in China but they do not interest you," the official complained. "You pick on anyone or anything that seems to support your views, which makes people think you have an agenda. You only seem to see the problems, so that makes people nervous." The lecture went on: "The Chinese people are getting more and more bored with this arrogance. They think it is unfair."

CCTV America's first show aired on February 6, 2012. Two days later, a man named Wang Lijun walked into the U.S. consulate in the Chinese city of Chengdu and set off the biggest political scandal in China since the 1989 Tiananmen Square Massacre. In the process, he also exposed why CCTV America and China's overseas media push will likely fail.

Wang was the police chief in Chongqing, a large city in the center-west of China, a few hundred kilometers from Chengdu. He sought refuge in the U.S. consulate after falling out with Bo Xilai, the local party boss. And he started talking. Wang brought a series of stories about corruption, legal abuses, and power grabs in Chongqing. The most explosive tale involved Bo's wife, Gu Kailai, who he claimed was responsible for the death a few months earlier in a Chongqing hotel room of Neil Heywood, a British businessman. The son of a famous Communist revolutionary, Bo had been considered a shoo-in to be promoted that autumn to the Politburo Standing Committee, the Communist Party body that really runs the country. Instead, Bo was relieved of his duties and expelled from the Communist Party, and his wife was charged with the murder of Heywood. It was the most damaging and open split in the top levels of the party in two decades.

Before long, the revelations were falling thick and fast. Elite-level politics in China is still something of a black box, but for once foreign journalists working in China had a glimpse inside. Within weeks, Bloomberg had revealed the $240-million family fortune that the Bo clan had managed to build up, my colleagues at the *Financial Times* had talked to a Chongqing billionaire who had been tortured and squeezed out of his fortune by rivals friendly with Bo, and the *Wall Street Journal* had detailed the complex relations between Heywood and the Bo clan. It was a tour de force of foreign correspondence. It was also the biggest political story in China in two decades. And yet almost none of it appeared on CCTV America. "There are certain issues that will not be covered by state TV in China," Laurie admits.

A couple of weeks after CCTV America started broadcasting from its new Washington studio, I got to meet Wadah Khanfar, the former director general of Al Jazeera and the man who helped turn it into an internationally recognized network. Al Jazeera demonstrated that there really is a market for non-Western news. Yet, in describing the network's early brushes with the U.S. authorities and its empathy for the stories of ordinary people, Khanfar talked about Al Jazeera in a way that could not have been more different from CCTV. The network first came to prominence during the Iraq War for broadcasting stories that the Western press were unable to. As security deteriorated across Iraq after the invasion, Western reporters found that important parts of the country were simply too dangerous to spend much time in. Al Jazeera filled this gap. While the Bush administration was still insisting that ordinary Iraqis had been liberated, Al Jazeera articulated the mounting rage against the occupation. Its message was implicitly anti-Western, which infuriated the Pentagon. But it was also largely correct.

A decade later, now with its own English-language channel, Al Jazeera hit another journalistic gold mine when the Arab Spring started. The self-immolation of a disgruntled trader in rural Tunisia became the unlikely spark for an astonishing wave of political change from Cairo to Benghazi, fueled by ordinary people standing up to despotic leaders. Al Jazeera was there once again to record their frustrations. Khanfar talked passionately about how grassroots political movements were finally changing a region whose politics had been ossified for so long. And he made no attempt to hide the network's role in pushing their agenda. "We were the voice of the Arab Spring," he proudly declared. Some of that spirit has spilled over into its coverage of China. Over the last decade and a half, the Chinese authorities have expelled only one foreign correspondent working in the country. Hassling and lectures are common, and some journalists have been beaten by local thugs. But only one reporter has actually had a visa rescinded because of official displeasure at the reporting. Her name was Melissa Chan, and she worked for Al Jazeera.

To be sure, the Western media do a partial job in China. Sometimes that is down to our prejudices, which can push some reporters to only see events through a narrow human-rights prism. Sometimes it is down to our personal limitations, in language or education. But mostly it is down to the nature of the political system, which still remains largely impenetrable. There is a global audience that would love to have more information about what is really happening in China—not out of hostility toward the Communist Party, as Beijing officials imagine, but out of genuine curiosity. That means there is endless demand to know more about the thoughts and personalities of the people who lead the second-most-important country in the world. But there is little appetite for insipid propaganda. The best way for a new network or paper to establish itself is to identify a huge story where it has some advantage and to plunge wholeheartedly into that story. Al Jazeera won itself an audience by broadcasting important tales that the Western media could not match. The gap in the international market where CCTV America could really make its name is the real story about China. But that is a story CCTV cannot tell.

VELVET PRISON

On the December day when his close friend Liu Xiaobo was awarded the 2010 Nobel Peace Prize, the Chinese human-rights lawyer Teng Biao found himself staying at the upmarket Shengping Yuan Hotel, just over an hour's drive north of Beijing. At that time, Liu was one year into an eleven-year sentence for "subverting state power," which he was serving at a prison in the bitterly cold northeast. Back in Beijing, the authorities operated on the principle of guilt by association. Liu Xiaobo's wife, Liu

Xia, had prepared a list of 143 friends and family members whom he would like to represent him. Everyone on the list who was still in China was barred from leaving the country. The crackdown on Liu's supposed sympathizers sometimes verged on the surreal. A few days before the ceremony, Mao Yushi, an eighty-one-year-old economist and occasional government critic, was supposed to travel to Singapore to give a speech on the development of rivers in the Himalayan region. He was stopped at Beijing airport and told that his planned trip was a "threat to national security." The climate of intimidation, he said, "reminds me of the Cultural Revolution," when his wife's hair was shaved by Red Guards and he was tortured and imprisoned.

Teng Biao's prison was of the velvet kind. A lecturer at Beijing's University of Politics and Law, Teng had also worked part-time for the previous decade as a lawyer, taking on cases about forced abortions and illegal land seizures. He was also one of the original signatories of Charter 08, the pro-democracy petition that Liu Xiaobo helped write, which was based on Czechoslovakia's Charter 77 and was the real reason for his long prison sentence. The Beijing authorities wanted to prevent Teng, who keeps copies of the political writings of Václav Havel on his bookshelf, from holding any public celebration of the Nobel. They also wanted to stop him from talking with the foreign journalists in Beijing, whose daily dispatches on the prize were a constant embarrassment for the government. So, along with a large number of activists, he was taken on an enforced trip out of Beijing, at the taxpayers' expense. The hotel where he was staying is just north of Badaling Station, on the Great Wall, one of Beijing's most visited places, and right next door is the Longqing Gorge, a beautiful limestone canyon with a fifty-meter-high waterfall.

One of the least understood powers of authoritarian regimes, but one which Havel knew well, is arbitrariness. In their bid to intimidate and punish Liu Xiaobo's friends, the Chinese authorities mixed subtlety with crude thuggery. Hua Ze, an independent journalist who used to make documentaries for state TV, had a black hood thrust over her head by the police, who took her into detention for nearly two months, during which she was also beaten. Yu Jie, another close friend of Liu's who was writing his biography, suffered a similar fate. The day before the prize ceremony, he was taken in a hood by state security agents to a prison, where he was burned with cigarette butts. "Right now, foreigners are awarding Liu Xiaobo the Nobel Peace Prize, humiliating our party and government. We'll pound you to death to avenge this," the leading security official told him. "If the order comes from above, we can dig a pit to bury you alive in half an hour, and no one on earth would know." Yu now lives in exile in Washington.

Yet, like Teng Biao, the poet A'Er had a more luxurious brush with the law. He was kept for several days at a holiday villa to the west of Beijing in Pinggu and wrote a poem about a tree trapped in rock that he could see from his window. When he was released, A'Er fled to Lijiang, his hometown, a popular tourist spot in the southwest much prized for its moderate climate and mountain walks. Eight plainclothes policemen followed him and stayed to keep an eye on him during his three-week stay. Teng Biao was held at his Beijing resort for three days. At first he was allowed to make phone calls, though not to receive them. From his bathroom, he called a friend, gave him the sign-on to his Twitter account, and asked him to write some messages commemorating Liu Xiaobo's award. He got four tweets published before the police discovered the ruse and took away his mobile. "They were incredibly angry," he later told me. "But I was very pleased with myself."

At the heart of Beijing's soft-power drive is the notion that if China somehow had better PR its image would change. If Chinese media only had a higher profile overseas, or if China had an appealing set of values to sell to the world, or if the leaders had a snappier phrase with which to frame China's ambitions, then people would start to think differently about the country. They might start to "love China, to long for China," as the Olympics deputy director had hoped. But the harsh truth is that China's ability to project soft power is hampered by the reality of life in China. The effort to project some form of "humane authority" is constantly undermined by the real-life capriciousness of China's leaders. It is hard to make a society seem attractive when those who disagree with the carefully policed mainstream are persecuted in such a way, when dissent is criminalized, and when those who seek to criticize are brushed aside so ruthlessly. The problem is the messenger, not the message. One of the strategic goals of the soft-power push is to present an unthreatening vision to the world of what a powerful China might portend, but it is persistently undercut by the reality of what a powerful China means for the more awkward members of Chinese society.

Liu Xiaobo and his friends missed a somewhat melancholic ceremony in Oslo. Thorbjorn Jagland, the head of the Nobel Committee, brought in the red binder with gold trim that holds the Nobel citation. He then placed it on an empty chair. What they witnessed at home was an outbreak of paranoia. On the day of the ceremony, the prize was described as a "political farce" by Foreign Ministry spokeswoman Jiang Yu. "Prejudice and lies are untenable and the Cold War mentality has no popular support," she said. Chinese officials warned Norway that business deals were now under threat. Ambassadors in China were called in by the Foreign Ministry and told that their governments should not have anyone present at the ceremony in Oslo. In the end, nineteen of the countries said that their ambassadors would not attend the prize ceremony. Most were obvious bedfellows of an irate Beijing—for instance, Cuba, Russia, and Sudan. But there were a few surprises as well, such as Colombia, the Philippines, and Sri Lanka. Chinese officials claimed that 101 countries in total had expressed opposition toward having the prize awarded to Liu Xiaobo. The *Global Times*, a nationalist tabloid and sister publication of party mouthpiece the *People's Daily*, wrote: "All the applause has come from the West and the citizens of the third-world countries are all now China's allies." Dai Bingguo, China's senior foreign-policy official, told Hillary Clinton that the prize was part of an American conspiracy to weaken China. Speaking a few months later, a senior Chinese official captured the tone of self-pitying victimization that underpinned Beijing's aggressive reaction. "The Nobel Prize was a wake-up call about the existence of a difference over ideology that many here thought had fallen away as a result of the growth of the Chinese economy," the official said. "This prize makes us think that maybe the Cold War is not entirely over. The cloud is still there."

China treats soft power as a problem that can be solved by bureaucrats. Beijing throws money at it, just as it has with high-speed rail or wind power, attracting brand-name international architects with big-ticket commissions. But modernity is not something that can be bought off-the-shelf. Soft power is generated by society from the creativity of its citizens, not created by culture ministries. China hopes its soft-power investments will blunt criticism of its political system, but it is the political system that is holding back its soft power. The cast of people who were harassed during the Nobel ceremony underlines the central dilemma. Among the political activists, there were also poets, writers, journalists, lawyers, and other members of the intellectual elite. (Before he became more involved in politics, Liu Xiaobo was the *enfant terrible* of Chinese literary criticism.) China is fighting a soft-power battle with one hand tied behind its back. It wants to channel the energies of the country's leading thinkers into helping define a vision of a modern China that will appeal to the rest of the world. But it also punishes those who step too far out of line from the official script.

Take the two artists most closely associated with the Beijing Olympics, the film director Zhang Yimou and Ai Weiwei, the sculptor who helped two Swiss architects with the design of the stunning Bird's Nest stadium. These are the sorts of figures with the talent to shape a distinctive and attractive Chinese modernity, to persuade the rest of the world that the future will be shaped by Chinese and not American imaginations. Yet Ai Weiwei spent two months in jail in 2011 because of his criticisms of the government and is now banned from talking to the media. (He was "harmonized," as ironical young Chinese activists say whenever one of their number is harassed by the born-again Confucian authorities.) A few weeks before his arrest, he told me: "Mao used to say that the Communists came to power on the back of the gun and the pen. But the pen is not working anymore." If Ai revels in the status he has now as a leading dissident, Zhang Yimou is still very much in favor with the establishment. He has become the Communist Party's in-house creative director. After his Olympics success, he was asked to put on a grand pageant in Tiananmen Square on the evening of the 2009 military parade. But even this status does not afford him any more real creative space. I once asked Zhang why his recent films had all been period pieces that shunned the fascinating complexities of contemporary China. If he made a film about today's China, he said, he would have so many problems with the censors that it would not be worth his trouble.

Winning a Nobel Prize had long been a Chinese obsession. Delegations were sent to Sweden to investigate what the judges were looking for. Conferences were held and a national literature prize established to seed local talent. The push to win a Nobel Prize "had become a cause of a psychological disorder, a token whose value and authority as imagined in China was inflated out of all proportions to its real importance," the China scholar Julia Lovell wrote in a 2006 essay. In a way, the Nobel obsession demonstrated the way China has got things the wrong way round, a bureaucratic-led push for recognition taking the place of actual creativity. As they did most years, in 2010 the main Chinese news Web sites ran special pages for the Nobel awards, including long profiles of the winners for medicine, chemistry, and economics, as their names were announced. When the award of the peace prize to Liu Xiaobo was unveiled, however, the special Web pages quickly disappeared. Official China craved a Nobel Prize: just not *that* prize. Some disgruntled Chinese took matters into their own hands. A group of academics founded the inaugural Confucius Peace Prize, which was awarded the day before the Nobel ceremony in Oslo and was designed to demonstrate displeasure with the Norwegian committee's decision to honor Liu. According to Qiao Damo, a poet who was one of the prize organizers: "We thought it better to have a prize that suits Eastern values of peace, which are different from Norway and the West"—a sentiment somewhat undermined by the fact that Qiao was also on the short list of winners. The prize brochure put it slightly differently: "Norway is only a small country. With over one billion people, [China] should have a great voice on the issue of world peace." In the end, the event had a farcical air. The aging Taiwanese politician who was given the award, Lien Chan, declined to attend because he did not take it seriously. His place was taken by a surprised-looking six-year-old girl who stepped up to collect the cash award.

Validation of a sort eventually came when the 2012 Nobel Prize for Literature went to the Chinese author Mo Yan. Television programs were interrupted to announce the news, and the *People's Daily* gushed the next day that the prize was "a comfort, a certification and also an affirmation—but even more so, it is a new starting point." Mo is a particularly unusual talent, an internationally respected writer whose work is full of social criticism but who is also a vice chairman of the state-run Chinese Writers Association. It is a testament to his skills, both literary and political, that he has managed to walk this tightrope. But it has not always been easy. His reputation at home was damaged when he took part in the 2009 Frankfurt Book Fair, another one of those events which exposed the limitations of China's soft-power push. As the guest of honor that year, Beijing saw the festival as an opportunity to promote Chinese literature and spent $7.5 million on the event, sending two thousand publishers to Frankfurt to promote the country's authors. Mo gave a speech to the opening session, which was attended by then vice president Xi Jinping. Yet, from the start, the festival was marred by behind-the-scenes fighting between Chinese officials and the organizers over what would be discussed at the events. At a symposium before the festival, the German hosts asked dissident writers Dai Qing and Bei Ling to speak, but then withdrew the invitations after Beijing objected, only to reinstate them following a protest by German journalists. In the end, when the two writers stood to speak, the official Chinese delegation walked out. Mo was among that group.

A similar furor erupted at the closing ceremony, when Dai and Bei said they had initially been invited to speak, only to be barred again after another protest from Beijing. The result was a huge own-goal, with much more attention paid to Chinese political interference than to any of the writers actually present. As long as Beijing tries to control the definition of Chinese culture and to decide who will speak on its behalf, China will continue to punch well below its weight. "I had no choice," Mo said in an interview a year later with a Chinese magazine, when asked to explain why he had walked out on other writers. "A lot of people are now saying about me, 'Mo Yan is a state writer.' It's true, insofar as . . . I get a salary from the Ministry of Culture, and get my social and health insurance from them too." He added: "That's the reality in China. Overseas, people all have their own insurance, but without a position, I can't afford to get sick in China."

It was a Chinese liberal intellectual and diplomat, Hu Shi, who in the 1930s provided the best answer to those afraid of Chinese soft power. He was writing in another era of intense debates in China about how to modernize its society and whether it should follow a Western path. If there was anything really valuable in traditional Chinese culture, Hu Shi told his compatriots, then it would easily survive the entry of

Western ideas into the country. "If our culture really contains priceless treasures that are able to withstand the power of the cleansing foreign attack, this indestructible part of our culture will naturally emerge even more fully after scientific culture washes over it," Hu wrote. The threat to America's soft power does not come from China, but from its own seeming inability to solve basic issues of governance. The U.S. should worry less about the attractiveness of China and more about getting its own house in order.

A few months before he left office in 2012, Hu Jintao gave another speech about soft power, this time with much harder edges. "We must clearly see that international hostile forces are intensifying the strategic plot of Westernizing and dividing China, and ideological and cultural fields are the focal areas of their long-term infiltration," Hu warned. Gone was the confident vision of a proud culture winning its due in the world, replaced instead by an insecure, enemies-under-the-bed nervousness. Hu added: "We should deeply understand the seriousness and complexity of the ideological struggle, always sound the alarms and remain vigilant, and take forceful measures to be on guard and respond." The speech was an appropriate bookend for the hidden agenda behind the soft-power push. As a result of its slow-burning legitimacy crisis, the Communist Party has reached for any number of new props to replace its socialist ideals, from economic managerialism to nationalism. Confucius, the Olympics, and Nobel Prizes are all part of the same search for legitimacy. China is not really selling itself to the world: the party is trying to justify itself to the Chinese people.

7

"We Are Not the World's Savior"

Humanitarian Intervention and the UN

WHEN BARACK OBAMA MADE his first-ever trip to China in November 2009, he got to meet most of the country's top leaders, with one very notable exception. That same week, Zhou Yongkang decided it was the right moment to take a large Chinese delegation to Sudan. A member of the all-powerful nine-man Communist Party Standing Committee, Zhou had the day job of running China's vast security apparatus. It was he who orchestrated the arrest of Liu Xiaobo. But Zhou [pronounced *Jo*] also occasionally dabbled in foreign policy. When the ailing Kim Jong-il unveiled his twenty-something son Kim Jong-un as his successor during a mass rally in Pyongyang in 2010, Zhou was standing right next to him on the platform. Zhou has also been one of the linchpins of China's close ties with Sudan. During his trip to Khartoum, Zhou met with Omar al-Bashir, the Sudanese president, who, partly as a result of U.S. pressure, had been charged four months earlier by the International Criminal Court in the Hague with genocide and crimes against humanity.

Back in Beijing, Obama was enduring a frustrating visit, every stage of which was carefully stage-managed by the government to limit open contact with ordinary Chinese people. At a joint "press conference" in the Great Hall of the People, there were no actual questions allowed from either the American or the Chinese media. Instead, the two presidents read out short statements and walked away in silence, looking as if they had just been to couples counseling. On the same evening, Bashir, who now faces an international arrest warrant, held a banquet for Zhou and the Chinese delegation in Khartoum. "As an old friend of the Sudanese president," Zhou said in an after-dinner speech, "I got a full sense of the profound changes that have taken place in Sudan under your leadership as soon as I stepped on Sudanese soil."

It is not hard to see why some in Washington might feel China is becoming the cheerleader for the world's more authoritarian and anti-Western regimes. In the last few years, Beijing has gone out of its way to protect the Kim regime in North Korea, despite its increasingly dangerous behavior. China provided a financial lifeline to Hugo Chávez in Venezuela, and helped reduce international pressure on the Syrian regime as the country's civil war escalated. China has even become an important backer of Robert Mugabe in Zimbabwe, helping protect him from censure in the United Nations and elsewhere. When Mugabe celebrated his eighty-sixth birthday in February 2010, the Chinese Embassy in Harare put on a party for the president to mark the occasion, with more than a hundred guests invited. Mugabe was presented with a large cake, made from eight different layers. A group of Chinese diplomats sang the Zimbabwean national anthem for him in the Shona language. It was the first time Mugabe had visited an embassy in the capital in the three decades he has been in power.

Among all these relationships, however, the Sudanese connection has been the most controversial. Over the last two decades, China has invested $7 billion in the oil industry in Sudan, making it both the main customer and the biggest investor in Africa's largest nation. With the possible exception of North Korea, Sudan is the nearest thing China has to a client state. Shortly after Omar al-Bashir took power in a coup in 1989, he found himself the subject of international sanctions as a result of his links to terrorism. (During the 1990s, Sudan provided a home for Osama bin Laden for several years.) As Western oil companies pulled out of the country, China stepped into the vacuum. China's oil companies were in the first throes of their "go out" strategy, where Beijing encouraged selected companies to operate overseas, and Sudan provided the perfect opportunity, a country with ample reserves not already tied up by China's Western rivals. Within a few years, the Chinese companies accounted for more than 70 percent of Sudan's entire exports. As it happens, one of the executives at the helm of the oil industry who helped set up the Sudan investments was Zhou Yongkang, the security boss who in the 1990s ran China National Petroleum Corporation, the largest oil group. Relations between the two countries started to go well beyond oil. In its bid to curry favor with Khartoum, China trained Sudanese helicopter pilots and became one of the government's main suppliers of arms. Twice during the Darfur conflict, a UN panel of experts noted that Chinese weapons were being transferred to Darfur by the Khartoum government. When Hu Jintao visited Sudan in 2007, at the height of the international furor over Darfur, he offered an interest-free loan to build a new presidential palace.

At the same time, China has also become the political protector of the Sudanese regime. During the very worst years of the slaughter in Darfur, in 2003 and 2004, China provided crucial political support using its position on the United Nations Security Council to block or water down measures aimed at the regime in Khartoum. At the UN, Darfur was a hugely divisive issue. The conflict exposed the stark difference between the way the U.S. and European nations now understand the world, and the way China does. For many in Washington, the events in Darfur were "genocide," a grotesque series of crimes by the government against its own citizens, which made some sort of outside intervention a moral imperative. Beijing argued that the violence was an internal affair of Sudan and that heavy outside intervention in the country would only destabilize it even further. The rest of the world had no right to override Sudan's sovereignty. China effectively put up a large sign saying: "Keep out."

If the twentieth century saw fierce ideological battles between fascism and liberal democracy and between capitalism and communism, then one of the central dividing lines in this century will be the issue of state sovereignty. As China has become more powerful over the last decade,

Washington and Beijing have started to compete over the basic rules at the heart of the international system, about the duties and responsibilities of what is sometimes called "the international community." In part, it is a battle for the soul of the United Nations, where many of these disputes are played out, but it is also a bigger discussion about the role of human rights in international affairs. In one corner, the U.S. and Europe urge greater outside intervention in states that are conducting massive abuses against their citizens; in the other corner, China and Russia defend a belief that absolute sovereign rights are the bedrock for a stable international system. Sudan was a warm-up act for this clash between two very different philosophical views about the way the world should work. Beijing would like to use its new influence to set the tone for how international politics will be organized and to check what it sees as Western moralizing and meddling.

This tension has been at the heart of the UN ever since it was founded in 1945, created out of the ashes of the Second World War by men scarred by the experience of Nazism. The UN's architects aimed to establish a world free from foreign invasions by territory-hungry great powers. The defense of sovereignty was proclaimed as a core value. Article II, Part 7, of the UN Charter reads: "Nothing contained in the present Charter shall authorize the United Nations to intervene in matters which are essentially within the domestic jurisdiction of any state." Over the next decade, the UN was closely involved in the process of decolonization, which added to its doubts about outside interference in the internal affairs of sovereign nations. The number of member countries has risen from fifty at the start to 194, and the leaders of these new nations had little intention of letting the UN become a rubber stamp for meddling in their politics by former colonial masters. Decolonization, as the Indian writer Pankaj Mishra puts it, was "fueled by an intense desire among humiliated peoples for equality and dignity in a world controlled by a small minority of white men."

Yet, right from the start, the UN was also squarely focused on human rights and the protection of minorities. The same shattering war experiences encouraged world leaders to sign in 1948 the Universal Declaration of Human Rights at a conference in Paris. Having seen the paralysis of the League of Nations, the UN's founders did not intend to create an organization that would be impotent in the face of wide-scale abuses. This debate about sovereignty lay dormant during the Cold War, when the U.S.-Soviet rivalry neutered the effectiveness of the UN. But by the time the Berlin Wall fell, it was clear that many of the greatest humanitarian problems in the world were caused no longer by wars between nations, which had declined, but by abuses taking place within nations—from Uganda to Cambodia. The growing awareness of environmental degradation has only added to the perception that sovereignty has its limits.

The end of the Cold War prompted a wave of optimism about the creation of a new, coherent international community which could put the stale arguments of the previous decades aside, and which would never again be too late to the scene. Yet this confidence was short-lived. The recurring crises in Bosnia, Kosovo, and especially Rwanda, where eight hundred thousand people were massacred, reinforced the uncomfortable reality that the UN lacked the tools to deal with the worst humanitarian crises. Stung by its failure to do anything to stop the bloodshed, then UN secretary general Kofi Annan launched a discussion about when it was right for the international community to intervene to protect vulnerable populations. The negotiations were tortuous, in part because of the objections of those developing countries which did not want to provide an excuse for the U.S. and other Western powers to send in the marines every time there was a crisis. But in the end, a committee led by Gareth Evans, a former Australian foreign minister, and the Algerian diplomat Mohamed Sahnoun, came up with a formula which was approved unanimously at a UN summit in 2005 and which became known as the "Responsibility to Protect."

The end result was a carefully crafted compromise. Military action was held out only as a very last resort; instead, there would first be a whole spectrum of policy options for the UN to take, from pressure and diplomacy to sanctions and referring leaders to the International Criminal Court. But, for all the caveats, the governments of the world committed themselves to take action in cases of genocide or grave crimes against humanity. The combination of the Rwanda disaster and the disappearance of Cold War ideological divisions gave the UN an opening to promote a new international philosophy about the defense of innocent civilians from rapacious governments. Robert Mugabe may have denounced it as a "phony principle," but for its supporters, "Responsibility to Protect" was an attempt to enshrine a series of basic guidelines that would underpin the international community in a new century. Martin Gilbert, the British historian of Winston Churchill and the Holocaust, called it "the most significant adjustment to national sovereignty in 360 years."

China voted in favor of "Responsibility to Protect," but right from the start Beijing was deeply anxious about the whole project. Under Mao, China had been a revolutionary power that occasionally looked to export its model around the world and saw international forums as a stage for occasional tantrums. But since the late 1970s, it has put its firm support behind the old Westphalian notions that sovereign nations should keep out of one another's affairs. The survival instincts of the party demanded as much. During an era when democracy has spread rapidly, this aggressive defense of sovereignty is a way to deflect attention from China's own affairs and to help make the world safe for the Chinese Communist Party. After all, how can Communist China shield itself from overseas criticisms of its own political arrangements if it routinely sticks its nose into the affairs of others? China has worked assiduously to make sure that the UN Human Rights Council, which is supposed to report on abuses around the world, has remained a toothless talking-shop.

Yet there is more to China's position than just opportunism. China has its own arguments for why a policy of strict nonintervention is a strong foundation for the international system. Rather than weakening the international community, China believes it is creating a more equitable world, a "democracy between nations" in which each state is treated equally by the rest of the international community. Beijing sees its friendship with dictatorial regimes as part of an approach that is better for the developing world than the bullying interventionism of the West. Whereas the West values human rights and transparent governance, China places emphasis on stability. Beijing argues that only when a poor country has a solid government, whose sovereignty is respected by other nations, can it then introduce the sorts of coherent, long-term policies needed to promote growth and reduce poverty. Even when the

Western powers have a good point about abuses, Beijing claims, the initial intervention on humanitarian grounds often becomes an excuse for prolonged colonial interference that makes the situation worse. For Beijing, nonintervention is a firewall against destabilizing meddling.

The irony is that, from Beijing's point of view, the U.S. is the radical, revolutionary power trying to change the rules of the game. While the West has become more animated about tackling humanitarian catastrophes since the end of the Cold War, China believes it is defending tried and tested ideas about how states should behave, which took root in Europe four centuries ago and are a better guide for international stability. From Sudan to Zimbabwe, China believes it is defending a status quo the West once established but now wants to tear up.

In conversations and interviews about this subject, Chinese officials would occasionally try to play Europe off against the U.S. "We want the same multipolar world that Europe wants," a senior diplomat once told me. "Europe's view of the world emphasizes system building, rules, dialogue, and discussion, as opposed to a view of the world that stresses confrontation." But mostly I would be on the receiving end of a finely honed series of talking points about how Western or American interference was a big part of the problem in the developing world. "Look at Liberia," a lunch companion from the Foreign Ministry told me. "It has had lots of U.S. help and influence and money, but it is not a mini-America. You cannot govern another country from the outside."

China also has its own list of grievances about American obstruction at the UN, starting with the large number of vetoes that Washington has exercised to protect Israel from criticism about human-rights abuses. And, like many other developing countries' governments, China is quick to point out the double standards in American moral leadership. Washington does not like our support of Mugabe, Chinese officials would say, but it backed Mubarak for so many decades. The U.S. complains when we buy oil from Iran, they ask, but is the situation in that country really much different from Saudi Arabia? Or Equatorial Guinea? Chinese diplomats can play these games all night. Beijing is also not shy about using the anti-colonial card, suggesting that noninterference is a bulwark against the sort of exploitation China itself suffered at the hands of the imperial powers in the nineteenth century. At the United

Nations, China often listens closely to what other developing countries are saying and then, if it does not have big issues of its own at stake, will follow their views. It has become very skilled at channeling anti-colonial resentment in the developing world against America's messianic tendencies. "We are very different from you," a senior official at the Foreign Ministry once told me. "We do not think that we are the world's savior."

China's defense of sovereignty has a lot of support at the UN from developing countries with colonial pasts. There is even sympathy among such big democracies as Brazil and India, on whom the humanitarian evangelism of the West often grates, and who were appalled by the aggressive unilateralism of the Iraq War. Plenty of developing countries, democratic and authoritarian, would like to see limits placed on the moralizing interference of the U.S. in the affairs of others. All of this makes nonintervention an extremely important policy for China. It provides international protection for the Chinese Communist Party. At the same time, it gives the government a powerful anti-colonialist calling card as it seeks to expand its international influence. We will do business with you and not ask any questions about how you run your country, China tells other developing nations. It is not just autocrats who find this extremely appealing.

But then there was Darfur. The fierce debates about Sudan in the early years of the 2000s put China at the center of UN politics in a way it had never been before. China came under intense political pressure because its support of Sudan appeared to be making a mockery of the post-Rwanda "never again" rhetoric at the UN, even as diplomats were drafting the "Responsibility to Protect" doctrine. For all the attractions that China's opposition to outside interference holds for many governments, there is also a powerful downside—in the hands of a veto-holding, permanent member of the Security Council, it can render the UN mute at the very moment when it should be at its most active.

The burden of proof for genocide is a very high one, and for some of the most informed observers of the events in Darfur, that bar was not reached by the Sudanese government. Human Rights Watch, for instance, declined to define what happened as genocide. It is also true that the complex events in Darfur were not a one-sided affair—the government in Khartoum was responding to a rebellion in the province. At the same time, there exists ample documented evidence to show that, between 2003 and 2010, widespread and grotesque human-rights abuses were committed by the Sudanese government or by the local proxy it used, a militia group called the Janjaweed. There is extensive testimony of villages burned to the ground, the men then killed and the women raped. In a country that had seen constant outbreaks of civil unrest since its independence, this was more than the usual burst of violence. A decade after Rwanda, Africa was witnessing again an organized campaign of ethnic cleansing.

Yet the early years of the conflict were also the time when China's oil investments started to bear real fruit, and Beijing did everything it could to shelter its Khartoum ally from international pressure, often with the support of Russia. In 2003 and 2004, when Kofi Annan was trying to draw the world's attention to the emerging catastrophe, China tried to keep the Darfur situation off the agenda at the UN. In 2004, it threatened to veto a resolution which merely raised the prospect of sanctions. A year later, with African Union peacekeepers struggling to control the situation, it blocked the idea of a UN peacekeeping operation. Chinese officials argued that, however bad things were in Sudan, they would become much worse if heavy-handed intervention by outside powers led to the downfall of the Khartoum regime. "The country would have become another Somalia," a Foreign Ministry official told me a few years later, still with a tone of indignation that China had come in for such intense criticism.

In the near-decade since the Darfur crisis, the same debates about outside intervention have continued to rage. The fiercest dispute has been over the civil war in Syria that started in 2011. In this case, Russia took the lead in blocking sanctions on the Assad regime as it waged war on its people, but China moved in lockstep at each stage in the process—both countries vetoing three separate UN Security Council resolutions. The international community remains deadlocked. Almost a decade after the "Responsibility to Protect" was negotiated, the leading powers at the UN are no closer to agreeing on how to respond to these types of crises.

The bruising arguments over Sudan and Syria have prompted anguished discussion in the West about a new "axis of authoritarians," with China and Russia using their vetoes at the UN to protect dictators around the world from outside pressure. There is widespread criticism in the West about the deadening impact that China's noninterference principle is likely to have on international politics. As François Godement of the European Council on Foreign Relations puts it, the effect of China's growing influence is a "hollowing out of the international system." Michael Ignatieff, the Canadian intellectual-turned-politician who was one of the leading voices in the interventionist debates of the 1990s, has also become one of the fiercest critics of the new axis between China and Russia. "Syria tells us that the era of humanitarian intervention, 'responsibility to protect,' is over, because it assumed a historical progression that has turned out to be false," he wrote. "When they look at the world this way, the Russian and Chinese regimes mock our view of history."

This is a powerful view, and one that is deeply pessimistic about the ability of the West to continue to shape the values at the heart of the international community. It fits into the narrative of decline, of a West that is now powerless to turn its ideas and instincts into coherent action in the face of the influence of rising powers. Yet it is also a mistaken view, because it misses two essential features about the emerging international environment, both of which are potential game-changers. It ignores the way in which China's rapidly expanding interests around the world are undermining its reluctance to get involved in crises. And it also downplays the potential for the U.S. to find common ground with some of the other new rising powers, who are likely to have considerable influence in the coming years over the shape of the new global order.

ENTER THE SWING STATES

To the other members of the guerrilla group, she was known as Estela. When the Brazilian military arrested her in 1970, one of the worst years for violence during the two-decade-long dictatorship, she was subjected to a ferocious array of torture techniques. Her head, thighs, and breasts were given electric shocks, and she was suspended naked and upside down on a stick. She eventually suffered a hemorrhage of the uterus, which prevented her from having more children.

Dilma Rousseff is now the first female president of Brazil, having won in a comfortable election in 2010 for the center-left Workers' Party. But her first entry into national political life was as a member of the Palmares Armed Revolutionary Vanguard, a far-left guerrilla group which took up arms to overthrow the military dictators who ran the country from 1964 to 1985. Her predecessor, Luiz Inácio Lula da Silva, was locked up by the military for his political activity against the dictatorship. His predecessor, Fernando Henrique Cardoso, fled to exile in Chile and then France after the military ordered his arrest. The man that both Lula and Dilma defeated to win the presidency, José Serra, was also an exile in Chile. For the last twenty years, Brazil has been run by a generation of leaders who got into political life to oppose the military dictatorship and to fight against the abuses committed against Brazilians by their own government.

Yet, over the last decade, Brazil has been a persistent critic of Western-led efforts at humanitarian intervention in countries where other dictators were conducting grotesque abuses of their populations. Celso Amorim, Lula's foreign minister, once described the idea of the "Responsibility to Protect" as *"droit d'ingérence . . .* in new clothes," a concept dating back to the seventeenth century about interfering in the affairs of another nation. On the occasions when Brazil has been a rotating member of the UN Security Council, it has often used its votes to express skepticism about U.S.-backed pressure or interventions. In 2004, when international outrage at the violence in Darfur was escalating, Brazil joined China in opposing any resolution on Sudan that smacked of new international sanctions. When China and Russia vetoed a UN Security Council resolution in October 2011 which criticized the violent oppression of opposition in Syria, Brazil was again on the Security Council. This time it abstained.

Just as in China, the defense of state sovereignty has been hard-wired into Brazilian elites for several generations. In the early twentieth century, Brazil was opposed to the use of military interventions to collect on the bad debts of countries that had defaulted on bond payments. (Before the IMF, it was the marines that enforced repayment of debts in developing countries.) Suspicions about the great powers hardened in the 1950s, with the era of decolonization. At the end of the Cold

War, Brazil did not see the West's new enthusiasm for humanitarian interventions as part of a welcome, modern activism in defense of the oppressed; instead, it saw this as the old wine of colonial interference, in new bottles.

Among the elites of many other large developing countries, it is pretty easy to find similar sentiments, especially in nations with a recent colonial past. In that high-profile 2011 vote on Syria during which Brazil abstained, South Africa and India also happened to be on the Security Council at the time. They also abstained. In South Africa, the years of struggle against the apartheid regime left the African National Congress deeply cynical about the motives of Western governments in preaching humanitarian intervention. In the six decades since its independence, India's self-image has been intimately linked to the concepts of the Non-Aligned Movement, making it another natural skeptic of Western motives. Susan Rice, who was the U.S. ambassador at the UN during the first Obama administration, chided Brazil, India, and South Africa for taking positions that "one might not have anticipated, given that each of them came out of strong and proud democratic traditions." Yet, on the face of it, Brazil, India, and South Africa appear to have more in common with China about the basic ground rules of how the international system should work—at least more than they do with Washington.

In many ways, the dispute over intervention and sovereignty is one part of a much broader challenge that the U.S. faces as a result of the big shifts in relative power that are taking place around the world. Even those who deny that America is in decline recognize that economic power is becoming more diffuse as a group of populous, developing nations try to turn strong growth rates into a bigger international presence. China is not the only potential challenger to the international order that the U.S. erected after the Second World War. There is now a new generation of powers, not just India, South Africa, and Brazil, but also Turkey, South Korea, and Indonesia, who are in some ways the floating voters of international politics, new entrants to the top table of global governance who have not yet decided how they want to apply the influence that their economic heft is accruing. If, more often than not, these governments were to side with China and Russia, it would represent a much broader threat to Washington's ability to keep setting the international agenda.

Of course, the U.S. has faced a parallel challenge before, in the 1960s and 1970s, when the dominance it enjoyed after the war was put into question by the rise of Western Europe and of Japan. It seems obvious in retrospect that these countries would make common cause with the U.S. and become part of the unified political entity we now call the Western powers. But at the time it was not so clear—think about the Gaullist efforts to distance France from the U.S., or the period of intense economic rivalry with Japan that lasted well into the 1990s. Washington was able to find ways to integrate these new powers into the institutions and rules that it had established. The U.S. is facing another, similar inflection point. Either it finds a way to embrace some of these newer powers, or it will see its influence over the international community gradually slide. That is true for a range of issues, from trade rules to the membership of international institutions, but it is also very much the case with the values at the heart of the international system. It is hard to argue for the moral legitimacy of the U.S. approach to abusive dictators when several of the biggest democracies in the world are openly opposed. Handing out lectures to these countries about their democratic heritage will not do the trick.

It might seem surprising at first, but one long-term U.S. objective should be to try not to alienate Russia. Of course, in many of the most contested votes at the UN in recent years, Russia and China have been very much on the same side. Indeed, Moscow has often been more of an obstacle than Beijing. Many Russia analysts suspect that Vladimir Putin has taken confidence from the success of Chinese authoritarianism as he has cemented his own control of power in Moscow. Some American neoconservatives warn that the Shanghai Co-operation Organisation, a security group that brings together Russia, China, and several Central Asian countries, is becoming an authoritarian anti-NATO. The antipathy in the U.S. toward Russia is particularly pronounced on the right—and was given voice when presidential candidate Mitt Romney called Russia "without doubt, our number one geopolitical foe." Yet the obsession with Russia among some on the American right is itself something of a Cold War hangover that vastly overstates Moscow's influence. Russian power rises and falls these days with the price of oil, not the potency of its political system or its economy. More to the point, it is a major strategic error to overplay the ideological affinity of the two countries. A China that behaves more and more like an ambitious great power is likely to be seen by Russia as being as much a rival as a partner. Moscow is already worried about the political and economic inroads that Beijing is making into Central Asia, about Chinese migration into eastern Siberia, and about Chinese naval intentions in the northern-Pacific Arctic region. As Chinese power grows in the coming decades, Russian anxieties are only likely to expand, too. During the Cold War, Washington was so intent on opposing communism around the globe that it ignored the emerging split in the Sino-Soviet relationship throughout the 1960s, until Richard Nixon finally exploited the opportunity when he met Mao in 1972. Some conservatives would have America make the same mistake again. Russia will never be a close partner to the U.S., but its own competition with Beijing will afford Washington opportunities to peel Russia away from China on the occasional issue. At the very least, the U.S. should be at pains to avoid pushing the two countries together by treating them as a new authoritarian axis.

When it comes to finding more common ground with the large democracies in the developing world, the prospects are actually much better than their voting record at the UN over the last few years would suggest. Beneath the surface, there has been something of a revolution in political attitudes in the developing world toward human rights and outside interference in crises. Two decades ago, the dominant position in Africa and Latin America was an energetic defense of the Westphalian order and its rigid interpretation of sovereignty. There was little appetite for interference, and strong opposition to collective commitments on human rights. The Cold War had only added to the distaste for being manipulated by great powers. In recent years, however, there has been a gradual but important shift in attitude toward the sorts of ideas the U.S. and Europe would like to see at the heart of the international system— not just toward democracy and the rule of law, but also toward regional agreements on human rights. Many developing countries have come to see the maintenance of stable democracies in their region as a bulwark against instability. In 2000, the African Union rejected the idea of nonintervention in favor of a concept it defined as "non-indifference"— a slightly vague formulation, to be sure, but one that leaves open the possibility of intervening in the event of crimes against humanity. Since 1997, no government that has come to power through a coup has been allowed to participate in an African Union summit. The organization's limitations may have been exposed when it was tasked with running the peacekeeping operation in Darfur. But in terms of the political philosophy, the shift has been marked.

In recent years, the Arab League has also sharply changed its approach to outside intervention, eagerly backing the U.S.-led operation in Libya and working energetically to encourage stronger measures against the Syrian regime in the face of opposition from China and Russia. Turkey, another important new swing state, joined forces with the Arab League in its efforts. Something similar has also been happening in South America, with Brazil in the lead. Mercosur, the regional grouping, has twice threatened coup plotters in Paraguay with expulsion, maintaining that only democracies can be members (although its criteria for democracy have been elastic enough to include Venezuela). In 2004, Brazil sent peacekeepers to Haiti under Chapter VII of the UN Charter, which allows for the use of force. Across the developing world, there has been a steady erosion of support for the idea that national sovereignty should be defended at all costs. A political corner has been turned.

The real issue is not U.S. rhetoric: it is U.S. practice. Developing world democracies are not opposed to the idea of outside interference in human-rights disasters, but they are worried about the potential manipulation of these rules by the U.S. to justify the sort of behavior countries like India and Brazil consider to be bullying. Skepticism about American motives did not begin with the invasion of Iraq. But the way the war was conducted—the attempts to railroad the UN, the manipulated intelligence, the character assassinations of those who stood in its way—confirmed the very worst fears that many governments hold about the U.S. UN diplomats from developing countries still talk about the contempt for the institution that they felt they received from John Bolton, when he was George W. Bush's ambassador to the UN. The Libya conflict in 2011 added to their mistrust. Like China and Russia, some of the governments were dismayed by the way the Libya operation in 2011 developed, when the U.S., U.K., and France quickly transformed UN approval for a humanitarian operation in the east of the country into a military campaign to oust Muammar Qaddafi. "We never said it was OK to go for regime change," one Indian diplomat told me. Many of the new swing powers agree on the need to respond to humanitarian crises, but they are loath to underwrite a new set of rules which could become a blank check for further U.S. unilateralism.

If the West wants to establish legitimacy for its new agenda of humanitarian activism, then it needs to find a way to overcome some of these reservations among the new swing states. As it happens, Brazil is the country that has offered up the most interesting olive branch. In late 2011, Dilma Rousseff's government published a little-noticed document it called "Responsibility While Protecting." The basic idea was to try and find a way to regulate and monitor foreign interventions that are approved by the UN. It would establish clearer rules for what sort of military behavior is permitted, and a monitoring mechanism to review interventions as they are conducted. For some U.S. officials, the Brazilians are more interested in grandstanding than in providing constructive leadership. Rousseff's initiative was dismissed by many as the actions of a "spoiler" government with no interest in working with Washington. But in reality, it was a serious attempt to start a debate about ways to make Western intervention work. Brazil was offering itself as a mediator between the West and other sections of the developing world. This is a conversation the U.S. needs to engage in, for the balance of influence in these global debates will depend heavily on where the new swing states position themselves. If the U.S. cannot build a common understanding with the largest democracies in the world, it will be hard work to retain its position at the center of the conversation.

GREAT POWER BURDENS

For a country like South Sudan, which is the newest in the world and one of the very poorest, it probably helps a little to have a leader who is physically imposing and highly recognizable. At six foot four, with a bushy black beard, Salva Kiir towers over most of the other presidents and prime ministers he meets. He also stands out because of the black cowboy hat he always sports, whether addressing the United Nations or having coffee at the White House. His first ten-gallon Stetson was a present from George W. Bush, who played an important role in South Sudan's independence campaign, and Kiir liked it so much he bought a large collection for himself. It is tempting to speculate what the Chinese made of Kiir when he made his first trip to Beijing in 2007. If they thought of him then as a folkloric figure with his black cowboy hat, they certainly do not now. For Kiir's 2007 visit turned out to be a groundbreaking moment in China's relations with the rest of the world.

The Darfur conflict in the 2000s is not the only war that has torn apart Sudan since it gained independence in 1956: the country also suffered a two-decade-long civil war. In 2005, Kiir took over the leadership of the Sudan People's Liberation Movement, the political group from the south of the country that fought the government in Khartoum, when their leader, John Garang, died in a helicopter crash. In the same year, he became vice president of Sudan after a peace agreement was signed ending the war. It was in this capacity that he visited Beijing two years later. Given its huge oil investments in the country, China was delighted by the end of the civil war, but the relief was short-lived. Around three-quarters of Sudan's oil reserves are in the south of the country, and according to the 2005 peace agreement, the south would be given a chance in 2011 to vote on independence. When he was in Beijing, Kiir met with President Hu Jintao and a series of other senior leaders, and at each appointment he presented his Chinese hosts with two documents. One was a copy of the oil map, showing just how many of the wells China had invested in were in the south of the country. The other was a copy of the peace agreement guaranteeing the south's right to secede. "He placed the two documents on the table and said, 'You figure it out,'" a South Sudanese official later explained. Kiir put China on the spot in a way that had never quite happened before. Support our bid for independence, he suggested, or lose your oil. He was calling Beijing's bluff on its principle of never interfering in the politics of another country.

Noninterference is a luxury that great powers sometimes cannot afford. The policy was a perfect adjunct to Deng Xiaoping's advice about keeping a low profile, but it is running up against the reality of China's global footprint and its expanding overseas interests. China's economy is now fed by iron-ore mines in Peru, copper mines in Congo's Katanga

Province, and oil fields in South Sudan. This web of interests is gradually drawing a reluctant China into the life of countries whose affairs it was once completely unconcerned about, a slow-burning but profound shift in China's global role. In a sense, China is beginning to experience its own split between foreign-policy realists and idealists. Chinese idealists push for a rigid policy of noninterference, but the realists suggest that China would be better off letting principles slide and defending the new interests that it is developing. Over the last decade, China's capacity to stand aloof from important events around the world has been slowly compromised.

One element of these new obligations is the way Beijing has been forced to respond to the growing number of Chinese workers who are now overseas. As a result of China's new network of global interests, there are probably around six million Chinese living abroad now, some in the most dangerous and unstable places in the world. There are forty-five thousand Chinese in Nigeria, around twenty-five thousand in Sudan, and ten thousand in the Democratic Republic of the Congo, as well as another ten thousand in Pakistan. In 2007, seven Chinese oil workers were killed during an attack on a Sinopec facility in Ethiopia. In Pakistan, there have been several kidnappings of Chinese workers, including the 2007 abduction of a group of Chinese women in Lahore, an event that led to the siege of the Red Mosque.

In the space of a decade, Beijing's response to such problems has been revolutionized. In 2000, a long-simmering ethnic conflict in the Solomon Islands erupted in Honiara, the country's capital, when the prime minster was seized by an armed gang. Lawlessness broke out, and mild panic ensued. Honiara has a sizable Chinese population, which began to feel itself under considerable threat. Messages were sent to Beijing asking for help. But the Chinese government had few options at its disposal. It did not even have an embassy in Honiara, because the country recognized Taiwan, not the People's Republic. In the end, Chinese diplomats in Papua New Guinea managed to get through to one of the rebel leaders on the telephone to negotiate safe passage for the Chinese residents who wanted to leave. A commercial ship owned by the state-owned group COSCO picked them up. The navy was asked if it could launch a rescue operation, but it was unable to do so. When

China faced a similar dilemma just over a decade later, in February 2011, when the security situation in Libya was becoming precarious as a civil conflict intensified, the Chinese Foreign Ministry made a staggering announcement. There were, it said, thirty thousand Chinese working in Libya, on construction sites and at oil facilities, making them by far the largest group of overseas residents apart from those from Libya's direct neighbors. As law and order broke down across the country, several of the Chinese facilities in Libya were attacked—which some in Beijing suggested was because the assailants did not fear any comeback from the Chinese authorities. This time there was no prevarication in Beijing. China sent the frigate *Xuzhou* to help evacuate its workers—the first time ever that a Chinese warship has been on active operation in the Mediterranean Sea, and a striking example of China's emerging capacity to project naval power.

As well as protecting vulnerable overseas residents, China now also has to deal with volatile, nationalist reactions to such incidents. When the workers in Ethiopia were killed in 2007, the Internet in China exploded with calls for revenge. Chinese officials privately admit that they now feel considerable public pressure to take more decisive action when Chinese workers are at risk, as they were in Libya. China is still a long way from having the capacity or political desire to intervene militarily in such conflicts on its own, but it is not too hard to imagine that in the future it might launch an armed operation to get its people out of a particularly dangerous situation. At the very least, the perils that Chinese workers are now exposed to are forcing Beijing to be less sanguine about the internal politics of some of the places where it is doing business.

The real baptism by fire, however, has been in Sudan, where Chinese ideas about nonintervention have been steadily undermined by its interests. During the Darfur crisis, Sudan had been Exhibit A for those who believe a powerful China will block efforts at humanitarian intervention and defend a strict interpretation of state sovereignty, undercutting Western ideas for a more active international community. Yet it is precisely Sudan where Beijing has been confronted with the contradictions of its expanding global interests, where its investments have suffered a head-on collision with its political principles. Much to its discomfort,

Beijing has found itself thrust into the unfamiliar role of power broker in a distant land.

When China started to invest in Sudan in the early 1990s, the Darfur conflict was still years away, but the country was mired in the fierce civil war between the government in Khartoum and the south of the country. Whereas the north of the country is largely desert and populated by Muslims, including the groups who dominate the government in Khartoum and who consider themselves Arabs, the south is more lush and is populated by Christians and animists. As many as two million people died in the civil war, which lasted for more than two decades and left the south of the country a wasteland.

China was not even a signatory to the 2005 peace treaty, which the Bush administration helped broker, preferring to keep its distance from the whole process. And on the face of it, the cease-fire was good news for Beijing, reducing the risk of attacks on its facilities and opening the prospect of new business opportunities. Yet, as the biggest investor and biggest customer of Sudan's oil, China was caught right in the middle of a new political dilemma. Around 75 percent of Sudan's oil was in the south of the country, but from there it traveled by a Chinese-built pipeline that traverses the border and goes all the way up to Port Sudan, on the northeastern coast. And as Salva Kiir made clear to his Chinese hosts in 2007, the south would be allowed to hold a referendum four years later on outright independence. Every observer who knew the country predicted overwhelming support for secession.

The situation in Sudan presented a series of different diplomatic nightmares for Beijing. Not only does China like to avoid getting involved in internal politics, but it is particularly allergic to any move that endorses the breakup of multiethnic countries. Beijing fears that such campaigns could encourage similar demands from its own ethnic regions, such as Tibet and the heavily Muslim Uighur population in Xinjiang, as well as encouraging an independence push by Taiwan. When Kosovo declared independence from Serbia in 2008, China refused to recognize the new state. In addition, Beijing was intensely suspicious of the role of the U.S. in the Sudan situation. In its early years, the SPLM had adopted a leftish posture and had received support from Cuba, but gradually it began to win heavy backing from conservative groups in the U.S., many of whom were mobilized by the prospect of a group of Christians being oppressed by Muslims. (Some South Sudanese see themselves as the descendants of the Biblical "Kushites," an identity that is embraced by some of their American sympathizers.)

Some Chinese officials and scholars thought that the U.S. was supporting the referendum as a way of trying to engineer a regime change in Khartoum. Others suggested it was part of a plot to slow Chinese progress in Africa. So at first Beijing stuck with its principle and supported the maintenance of a united Sudan. Yet, as the independence vote approached, Beijing began to realize the trap it was facing. If it opposed the referendum, it could face hostility from an independent government in the south that would see China as the principal backer of its enemy. To the South Sudanese, China had never been a neutral political force in their country—on the contrary, Beijing's heavy oil investments and weapons sales to Khartoum made it a partisan supporter of the government side in Sudan's civil war. For them, China had already taken a side.

Salva Kiir's 2007 visit to Beijing turned out to be the start of a process whereby China quietly but decisively changed its policy 180 degrees—from protecting the sovereignty of Sudan, as it did over Darfur, to endorsing the country's breakup. In 2008, China opened a consulate in Juba, the main city in the south. Before long, officials from both countries were exchanging regular visits. China intervened in 2010, when reports surfaced that the Khartoum government might try to delay the referendum. Liu Guijin, Beijing's special envoy for Africa, insisted the vote go ahead on time and called for international help to make sure the process was credible. China itself donated $500,000 to the Southern Sudan Referendum Commission and sent observers for the vote—in which independence was approved by 97 percent of the people voting. In the past, China might have claimed indifference to the internal problems in Sudan and turned a blind eye if Khartoum had used violence to sabotage the referendum. But in this case, Beijing found itself promoting an orderly vote for independence—and on the same side as the U.S. Whatever its initial reservations, China became one of the midwives for the birth of an independent and democratic Southern Sudan. To defend its oil, Beijing decided to tear up its pledge of noninterference. On July 9, 2011, South Sudan declared independence. Wei Zhixin, China's housing-and-infrastructure minister and a close confidant of President Hu Jintao, traveled to Juba to witness the occassion. The highlight of the seven-hour-long ceremony was the moment when the flag of Sudan was electronically lowered at the same time as South Sudan's new flag was raised. Two Chinese engineers were on hand to make sure the remote-control system worked properly.

———

In some ways, the partition of Sudan was only the start of China's political dilemma in the country. Even once Juba had declared independence, many of the main issues between Sudan and South Sudan remained unresolved—including where the actual borders lie, control of some of the oil wells, and the division of oil wealth between the two governments. China was again caught right in the middle of the new disputes. Beijing's first response was to try and retreat back into its shell. Li Zhiguo, China's ambassador to South Sudan, insisted there was no need for China to get involved in mediation: "The issue is an internal affair of the two brothers of Sudan." Events on the ground, however, swiftly undermined Beijing's policy of studied indifference and sucked it back into the toxic politics of the "two brothers." By November, four months after South Sudan declared independence, negotiations between the two governments were floundering, with Khartoum asking for $36 for each barrel crossing its territory and Juba offering $1 (which was closer to international levels). Khartoum halted all exports of oil from South Sudan until the payment situation was resolved, and impounded several shipments of oil. In effect, China's oil imports were being held hostage.

South Sudan responded to this brinkmanship by trying to put pressure on Beijing. Juba felt that China could do more to restrain Khartoum and tried to use its own leverage to force Beijing's hand. Chinese oil executives in South Sudan were summoned to a meeting in Juba, where they were told once again that if China continued to take Khartoum's side passively in the dispute, it could lose its oil contracts in South Sudan. Unsatisfied with China's response and Khartoum's tactics, Juba upped the ante in January 2012 by shutting down its entire oil industry. And a month later, just to make sure that Beijing understood what Juba believed to be its complicity in the dispute, South Sudan also expelled from the country Liu Yingcai, the president of Petrodar, the China-owned company which dominates the industry. The disputes between the government and Petrodar were long-running and complex, but the principal allegation was that the Chinese company had been siding with Khartoum.

At the same time that the oil dispute was heating up, violence in the border areas intensified, with Chinese interests again stuck in the middle. Two of the border provinces contained large numbers of guerrillas who had fought with the SPLM. Bashir had alleged (probably correctly) that Kiir was giving the rebel groups unofficial support and threatened to "chop off their hands." When South Sudan shuttered the oil industry, Bashir stepped up his military activities, sending warplanes to bomb oil fields in the south. At the same time, rebels linked to South Sudan captured a large oil field in Heglig, on the Sudanese side of the border. To make matters worse for the Chinese, twenty-nine Chinese oil workers in South Kordofan were kidnapped by rebel groups, prompting a huge outcry at home. They were released ten days later.

Finding itself squeezed on all sides, China was forced to get involved in crisis mediation. In April, Foreign Minister Yang Jiechi traveled to Addis Ababa to meet with Salva Kiir, while, at the same time, Jia Qinglin, one of the most senior Communist Party officials, visited Khartoum. Chinese leaders were also feeling pressure at home, where different groups wanted the government to take more decisive steps to try and resolve the standoff. As one official told the International Crisis Group, in a comment that perfectly encapsulates the new dilemma of the reluctant great power: "We are bystanders: we cannot just be bystanders, we need to be a player. Can you imagine how any Western country would engage if they had all these interests?"

When various efforts at mediation failed, the only solution was to go to the United Nations. On May 2, 2012, the UN Security Council unanimously approved Resolution 2046, which called for an immediate halt to fighting between Sudan and South Sudan. The resolution was remarkable for a number of reasons.

First, China approved a measure that not only heavily criticized Sudan, a country which for nearly two decades had been almost a client state, but it also threatened to impose sanctions under Chapter VII of

the UN Charter, the sort of meddling punishment that Beijing is usually so reluctant to inflict on other countries. That alone indicates how
China's position on outside interference can bend out of all recognition
when its own interests are at stake.

But the timing was also interesting. Two months before the Sudan
vote, China and Russia had vetoed a resolution that included a much
vaguer threat of possible sanctions on the Syrian regime, a position that
the U.S. ambassador to the UN described as "disgusting." Two months
later, they vetoed a similar resolution on Syria again, prompting Hillary Clinton to denounce Beijing and Moscow as "despicable." The
Syrian vetoes garnered all the attention and seemed ample evidence of
the emerging authoritarian axis. It was these Syria votes at the UN that
prompted Michael Ignatieff to say of China's and Russia's worldview:
"This is not your world, they want us to know, and history is not moving
in your direction. You will have to reckon with us. We shall indeed." Yet,
in between the bitter standoffs over Syria, the UN vote on Sudan was
compelling evidence that the historical forces are also pulling China
in a different direction from the one Ignatieff imagines, one in which
it has little choice but to immerse itself in the messiness, the compro-
mises, and, most of all, the meddling that conflict resolution demands.
The dispute between Khartoum and Juba is far from resolved, but in
the breakup of Sudan, China has found itself the indispensable outside
power in a country whose politics it barely understood but could not
escape.

Just like a new president or prime minister taking office, one of the
luxuries of being the new great power is the chance to promise a break
from the vices of the old order and its addiction to cynical power plays.
For several decades after it started to become a global force, America's
leaders insisted they could help shape the world without behaving like
the old European powers. Fifty years after Rudyard Kipling wrote the
poem "White Man's Burden" in reference to the violent American conquest of the Philippines in the 1890s, President Franklin Roosevelt was
still castigating Europe for its imperial misbehavior. By the same logic,
it will be quite a while before Beijing changes its rhetoric about nonintervention. The policy is just too useful and too central to China's self-
image. Yet, over time, China will find itself compelled to get its hands

dirty on a more regular basis, to play the local power broker, to pick sides, maybe even to send in its military for more than just peacekeeping operations. None of this means that China and the U.S. will always be on the same side, as they ended up in South Sudan. But China's ideological aversion to outside intervention will start to fade.

Section III

ECONOMICS

8

Taking On the Dollar

I N 2009, I had lunch in Hong Kong with a lawyer who was describing to me his many professional woes. We were sitting at the bar of an Italian restaurant in Pacific Place, a complex of tinted-glass office towers in the Admiralty District of the city with a cavernous shopping mall down below. Outside the restaurant, wealthy women flitted between the Chanel and Louis Vuitton stores, their high heels echoing on the marble floors. The set lunch of Caprese salad followed by linguine with crab was perfectly executed, but my lunch companion was not enjoying the meal. He launched into a lengthy whinge about how his business was all disappearing to Shanghai, which the Chinese central government wants to turn into the country's main financial center. Companies were listing their shares in Shanghai, instead of Hong Kong, he complained. Multinationals were shifting their headquarters to Shanghai, and fund managers were also moving up there. Hong Kong was suffering the gradual erosion of its role as China's conduit to the international financial world. "And another thing," he said, almost without pausing for breath. "Our landlord wants to raise our rent by fifty percent."

I have been traveling to Hong Kong regularly for much of the last decade, and on each visit I hear the same foreboding about the future of the city and the same fears about the lethal competition from Shanghai. It is the second-most-common complaint, after the pollution being blown down from the factories in southern China. Admittedly, Hong Kong did suffer two huge body blows, from the 1997 Asian financial crisis and the SARS outbreak in 2003, which possibly colors some of the grumpiness. Yet the soul-searching always seems out of place, a narrative that is rebuked by the constant bustle and progress. More than most other cities, Hong Kong adapts. To the visitor it always seems to be booming, with new high-rises, new malls, and new slivers of land reclaimed from Hong Kong Harbor. And the rents just keep going up.

The next new business opportunity for Hong Kong is already starting to take shape, and it could be a huge one. Beijing is putting in place an ambitious plan to allow the Chinese currency to play a larger role in the global economy, and Hong Kong is the launchpad. It is the first place where the Chinese currency, the renminbi, can be freely traded by Chinese and non-Chinese companies. There is also now a market in Hong Kong for corporate bonds issued in the Chinese currency, known as "dim sum bonds," which allows people to put some of their savings into securities denominated in renminbi. (One of the first issuers was the McDonald's Corporation, which must now sell Big Macs in China to repay the dim sum.) The financial world is abuzz with talk about the start of a momentous shift. HSBC predicts that by 2015 at least half of China's trade with the developing world will be in renminbi, around $2 trillion. "We could be on the verge of a financial revolution of truly epic proportions," says Qu Hongbin, HSBC's China economist. "The world is slowly, but surely, moving from greenbacks to redbacks." The Washington-based economist Arvind Subramanian predicts that the Chinese renminbi could become "the premier reserve currency by the end of this decade, or early next decade." Hong Kong has found a new role. It could be the international hub for the world's new global currency.

This might sound like arcane business-speak, the kind of thing that is of interest to financial professionals but not to anyone else. Yet, in reality, the question of whether the renminbi will supplant the dollar is one of the central contests that will determine the shift of power from West to East over the course of the next few decades, a delicate combination of high finance and geopolitics. The political influence of the U.S. dollar is the often overlooked anchor of American global influence.

Just as the period of British pre-eminence from around 1850 to 1914 was sustained by the central role of sterling, American global reach in the post–World War II era has been underwritten by the pervasiveness of the U.S. dollar, which is used in 85 percent of cross-border business. The dollar's position as the main reserve currency is both cause and effect of American power, a symbol of confidence in the world's most productive economy and a manifestation of America's position at the center of a series of economic, political, and military relationships at the heart of the international system. American politicians sometimes like to talk about the U.S. as the "indispensable" nation, a phrase that never fails to grate on foreign audiences, but in the case of the dollar it is quite apt. The dollar's role in the world is a reflection of continuing trust in Washington as the guardian of the global order.

Washington is drowning in warnings about the end of the dollar era. Edward Luttwak, a hardheaded scholar of military strategy, downplays the military threat from China, but adds: "The real challenge to American and Western strategy is far more subtle: a slow, not uncomfortable slide into subordination in a China-centred world, with the renminbi as its currency." The National Intelligence Council, which publishes the U.S. government's official intelligence estimate, forecasts that "the fall of the dollar as the global reserve currency . . . would be one of the sharpest indications of a loss of U.S. global economic position, strongly undermining Washington's political influence too." If the dollar does start to lose that position to the renminbi, it would indicate that a real power shift was taking place and that China was assuming a central role in the world's political and economic affairs. Since the financial crisis, there has been a lot of talk about a "currency war," a somewhat faux dispute about U.S. and Chinese efforts to weaken the value of their currencies that was coined by the Brazilian finance minister. The real "currency war" for the next few decades is the contest for the title of global reserve currency.

––––––––

The privilege of issuing the main reserve currency is more than just symbolism. The advantages are enormous. All governments borrow money, even in the very best-managed economies, and if a country does not have enough savings at home, the Finance Ministry will have to borrow abroad in someone else's currency. When countries face economic problems, these overseas borrowings often become the weak link. If markets start to lose confidence in a government and its policies, it becomes much harder to roll those debts over, or to issue new bonds. The country's currency also starts to weaken sharply as investors get cold feet. The government then faces a double whammy—it loses access to new international funding, and the cost of its existing debt suddenly shoots up, because its currency is now worth less. Imports also become more expensive, putting further pressure on dwindling sources of foreign currency. Many of the economic crises that developing countries have faced in recent decades have followed this pattern.

Yet America has been shielded from such troubles. The U.S. dollar is overwhelmingly the preferred unit for business and financial transactions around the world. Global trade is lubricated by dollars—99 percent of all foreign-exchange transactions in both South Korea and Chile, two big exporting nations, are sales of local currency for dollars. For the world's central banks—the biggest, most conservative, and most influential investors on the planet—the U.S. dollar remains the principal anchor of their foreign-currency reserves. It is the same in the black market economy. When Somali pirates or Mexican drug lords demand payment, it is U.S. dollars they want to receive. Because the dollar is used so widely in commerce and investment, and because it is such a trusted store of value—it is "as good as gold," as the saying goes—foreigners are only too happy to buy bonds from the American government that are issued in its own currency. As a result, the biggest and most liquid bond market in the world by far is the U.S. Treasury bond market. Even if the dollar suddenly gets weaker, this does not affect the American government in the same way it would affect other countries, because the U.S. repays foreign investors in the same currency it collects in tax revenues. That makes the position of the U.S. dollar a hugely powerful tool. It gives an important competitive advantage to American companies and banks, which get to do business in their own currency and avoid the vagaries of foreign-exchange markets. And it allows the U.S. government to live beyond its means without facing the punishment that other governments inevitably suffer. Washington can finance its global power projection with a credit card that has no limit. "Deficits don't matter," as Dick Cheney liked to say.

Except that, eventually, they do. Even for America, there are limits to the sorts of deficits it can run. At some stage, the credibility of the U.S. dollar will be called into question—and with it the underpinnings of America's global position. To be fair, there have been many dollar scares in the past that proved to be unfounded. When I was studying in Washington in the 1990s, my dissertation supervisor was David Calleo, who was one of the leading voices in the school of thought sometimes called "imperial overstretch." He wrote persuasively about the ructions caused by Lyndon Johnson's budget deficits in the 1960s, which were needed to finance the Vietnam War, and the subsequent stresses the dollar came under in the 1970s, when Nixon eventually abandoned the convertibility of the dollar into gold. Yet the dollar's primacy survived the episode. To Europeans who worried about the risk of inflation, then treasury secretary John Connally retorted: "It is our currency and your problem."

The same pressures returned during the Reagan years and the arms race with the Soviet Union. The Soviets eventually blinked first, their economy imploding under the burden of heavy defense spending, but America's finances also came under intense pressure, prompting a new bout of predictions that American dominance and the dollar era that financed it were coming to an end. Paul Kennedy had a massive publishing success at the time with his *Rise and Fall of the Great Powers*, a tome about imperial overstretch over the centuries which captured the prevailing mood. Again, the pessimism proved short-lived. The end of the Cold War and the supreme confidence of the early years of the George W. Bush administration made these sorts of predictions seem alarmist, almost foolish, and in the boom years of the mid-2000s they were brushed aside as a kind of intellectual defeatism. Yet, after a decade of two expensive wars and the biggest financial crisis since the 1930s, which forced the government to run a deficit of $1.1 trillion in 2012, America's outstanding government debt is now almost as large as the economy itself—something that has not happened since the Second World War. The credibility of the dollar is once again being called into doubt, and the idea of "imperial overstretch" is very much back in vogue. In the financial world, some talk about when rather than if there will be a dollar crisis. It is precisely at this moment of uncertainty in the fate of the U.S. currency that China has chosen to start claiming a bigger role for the renminbi in the global economy.

THE DOLLAR TRAP

"How do you deal toughly with your banker?" Hillary Clinton asked, shortly after she became secretary of state. Since the start of the financial crisis, a new phantom has started to loom over U.S.-China relations: the massive amounts of American government debt that are now in China's hands. China has the largest foreign-exchange reserves in the world, at around $3.3 trillion, and overtook Japan in 2008 to be the largest overseas holder of U.S. debt. Although the exact composition of China's reserves is a state secret, analysts who have sifted through the available information estimate that around two-thirds of those reserves are in U.S. dollar assets. The likely result is that China owns around $2 trillion of U.S. government debt. "Never before has the United States relied on a single country's government for so much financing," as economist (and later White House official) Brad Setser put it. "Political might is often linked to financial might and a debtor's capacity to project military power hinges on the support of its creditors."

The handover of global responsibilities from the U.K. to the U.S. was a long and drawn-out process, but the final blow was delivered because Britain owed too much money to Washington. In 1956, when the U.S. wanted to show its displeasure at the British invasion of the Suez Canal, Eisenhower refused to let the IMF issue an emergency loan which Britain needed to defend its currency. Fearing a complete financial collapse, Britain pulled out its soldiers from the Canal Zone. British influence in the world was never the same again. If China could turn this financial power into real political leverage, it would have dramatic consequences for both America's economic policy and its ability to exert influence around the world. It would give Beijing the hold over Washington that the U.S. once held over its own great-power predecessor.

China is well aware of the potential significance. Every now and then, there have been comments from low-level Chinese officials raising the potential threat. In 2007, Xia Bin, who was then a leading economist at a government think tank called the Development Research Center, caused an international fuss when he suggested that China's dollar holdings should be used as a "bargaining chip." When the U.S. announced it would sell more arms to Taiwan in 2010, three senior PLA officers—Major General Zhu Chenghu, Major General Luo Yan, and Senior Colonel Ke Chunqiao—told the Xinhua News Agency that China should retaliate by selling U.S. government debt, which could lead to a sharp rise in U.S. interest rates. According to American diplomats, the threat to sell dollar assets has also occasionally hung over conversations about the Dalai Lama. The more nationalistic sections of the Chinese press call it "the nuclear option"—threatening to dump dollar bonds in order to change American policy. Or, as Gao Xiqing, the head of China's sovereign-wealth fund, told the American journalist James Fallows: "I won't say *kowtow*, but at least be nice to those countries that lend you money."

In the U.S., this potential threat from China has now been a feature in two presidential elections. When he was running for the 2008 presidential nomination, then senator Joe Biden warned, in a Democratic debate, about the risks of having China finance U.S. debt. We need to "make sure that they no longer own the mortgage on our home." Hillary Clinton, also then a senator and a presidential candidate, piped in: "I want to say 'Amen!' to Joe Biden, because he's 100 percent right." In 2012, the theme returned with a vengeance. In May, there was a standoff in Beijing over the blind activist Chen Guangcheng, who, having escaped house arrest and taken refuge in the U.S. Embassy in Beijing, announced that he wanted to leave China for the U.S. Paul Ryan was asked if the U.S. still had any influence over China in such a dispute. The Republican vice-presidential nominee answered: "When you depend on another country like China for the cash flow in your country and for your debt, there is not a lot you can do when you are asked to stand up to them on a principled matter such as this." Ryan somewhat misread the situation: the next day Chen was given permission to move to New York.

———

Paul Ryan was wrong for a reason. The supposed leverage that China derives from its dollar holdings is something of a myth—and China knows it. The curious thing about this discussion is that, although some Americans complain that the debt gives China excessive influence, China is increasingly angry at how little sway it has. In the years since the financial crisis, there has been a growing frustration in China that its U.S. bond holdings give it almost no leverage whatsoever. When the crisis broke, Beijing started to issue a series of warnings about American economic policy and its obligations to do right by China. "I request the U.S. to maintain its good credit, to honor its promises and to guarantee the safety of China's assets," Premier Wen Jiabao told a 2009 press conference. Beijing worried very loudly about the inflationary risks of the monetary expansion the U.S. Federal Reserve launched in response to the crisis. Chinese officials started to push for guarantees about repayment on their U.S. debt, especially in the troubled mortgage agencies Fannie Mae and Freddie Mac. It is possible that Chinese pressure had something to do with the timing of when the two mortgage agencies were brought under government control. But, by and large, China's attempt to strong-arm the U.S. did not work. Beijing did not receive any formal guarantees, and it exerted no influence over American monetary or fiscal policy. The Fed has continued to do as it wishes. The Tea Party has more influence over the Fed than does the Chinese Communist Party.

Larry Summers, the former U.S. Treasury secretary, once described the situation between the two countries as "mutually assured economic destruction." Beijing has come to realize that it is trapped—trapped by the size of its exposure to the U.S., trapped by the reality of financial markets, and trapped by the logic of its own policies. In any month when China exports more than it imports, this leads to an inflow of foreign currency into the country. In order to prevent the value of the renminbi from rising, which would hurt its exports, the Chinese central bank buys up the dollar excess. China's foreign-currency reserves are the direct product of this policy of keeping its currency artificially cheap, in order to boost exports. This was a choice made by China, not by anyone else. Indeed, large parts of the world have called on China to change its approach and to allow its currency to become more expensive. Having built up such a stockpile, China's official money managers are then faced with limited options. The U.S. Treasury market is by far the largest and most liquid in the world. It is also the only one with the size to absorb the sort of volumes of reserves that China has been accumulating. China therefore has little choice but to recycle a large portion of its surpluses into U.S. government bonds.

The harsh reality for China is that it has too much at stake to turn its back completely on U.S. bond markets. Economic interdependence makes it hard for China to rock the boat. At best, China can gradually scale back the rate at which it buys new American debt. But if China were to try and sell a substantial chunk of its U.S. bond holdings, it would send the market into a tailspin, and bond prices—including China's own investments—would plummet. Such action would also force down the value of the U.S. dollar, making China's exports less competitive and threatening hundreds of thousands of factory jobs. It would be a huge self-inflicted wound. This formula does not make sense for a regime whose legitimacy is tightly wound up in delivering economic results. China's holdings give it theoretical leverage over the U.S., but it is leverage that it is technically difficult and politically suicidal to exploit. Beijing knows as much. "We hate you guys . . ." Luo Ping, a senior Chinese banking official, admitted in 2009. "US Treasuries are the safe haven. For everyone, including China, it is the only option." He continued: "Once you start issuing $1 trillion–$2 trillion . . . we know the dollar is going to depreciate, so we hate you guys but there is nothing much we can do."

———

Luo Ping was only half joking. His mock anger was politically important because that sentiment became one of the starting points for the campaign to take the Chinese currency global. Frustrated at its inability to influence American economic policy, Beijing has started to think much more seriously about finding ways to rein in the influence of the dollar and Washington's ability to run endless deficits. Resentment at the "dollar trap" helped launch a much broader Chinese critique about the place of the U.S. dollar in the international economy. If China could not influence the way the U.S. managed its economy, it would try and reshape the international financial system instead, and make the dollar less indispensable. Hu Jintao called in 2008 for a "new international financial order that is fair, just, inclusive and orderly."

The first sign that something was brewing in Beijing came from the governor of the Chinese central bank, Zhou Xiaochuan. Zhou is a chemical engineer by training but is considered one of the Communist Party's intellectual heavyweights in the field of international economics. With his donnish air, he likes to tease journalists with the sort of delphic pronouncements that once made Alan Greenspan a cult figure—before the financial crisis, that is. In March 2009, six months after Lehman Brothers collapsed, the central bank started to put up on its Web site a series of long and detailed speeches and essays by Zhou that called for substantial reforms of the international financial system. Zhou had himself some fun at the expense of the Western investment banks, which had almost felled the global economy. He criticized the "herding phenomenon" among investors and the "inertia and sloppiness" that stopped executives from "asking tough questions." But his broader message was aimed at the role of the U.S. currency. The international financial system, he said, needs a reserve currency "that is disconnected to individual nations and is able to remain stable in the long run, thus removing the inherent deficiencies caused by using credit-based national currencies." In between the technical language of international financial policy, the message was clear: the world needs to become less reliant on the dollar.

Zhou's speech was the starting gun for China's campaign to develop a more international currency. Since then, China has unveiled a steady series of reforms aimed at forging a bigger role for the renminbi. Using Hong Kong as a trial ground, the government in 2009 started to allow the use of the renminbi to settle international trade—the first stage in a plan to turn it into the main currency for trade in Asia and between developing countries. In 2011, it allowed renminbi bonds to be sold in Hong Kong, letting foreign investors buy assets denominated in the Chinese currency. Since then, Beijing has announced a slew of reform measures that will gradually make it easier to trade and invest in the Chinese currency. By the end of 2012, around 15 percent of China's trade was being conducted in renminbi. The final stage would be to turn the renminbi into the sort of international safe haven that attracts the world's central banks to park a substantial share of their reserves in the currency. That would be the real stamp of approval. In what was largely a symbolic gesture, Malaysia has already taken the first step, acquiring some renminbi bonds.

Chinese policy makers usually couch the project in technical terms, pointing out that it will reduce the costs of doing business for Chinese companies and expand the opportunities for Chinese banks. But they also do little to hide their broader political objective of forging a new international system that is not dominated by the U.S. dollar. Li Ruogu, head of the China Export-Import Bank, argues that "the financial crisis . . . let us clearly see how unreasonable the current international monetary system is." Another official told me: "We have the second-biggest economy in the world, so we should have a currency that enjoys many of the privileges that the U.S. also gains." According to Zha Xiao-gang, a researcher at the Shanghai Institutes for International Studies: "The shortcomings of the current international monetary system pose a big threat to China's economy. With more alternatives, the margin for the U.S. would be greatly narrowed, which will certainly weaken the power basis of the U.S." One Chinese academic even goes so far as to say that ending the dominance of the dollar is as important for Beijing's ability to project power as was "China becoming a nuclear power."

Attacking the power of the U.S. dollar is not a new form of geo-political sparring. In the 1960s, General Charles de Gaulle sought to challenge American leadership of the West and to position himself in the middle ground between Washington and Moscow. One of his tactics was to withdraw France from the military arm of NATO. The other was to take aim at the dollar. Throughout the mid-1960s, as America became bogged down in Vietnam and its public finances came under pressure, de Gaulle gave a series of press conferences in which he called for an end to the primacy of the dollar and urged other countries to convert their holdings of U.S. currency into gold. And it was a French finance minister (and later president), Valéry Giscard d'Estaing, who famously complained in the 1970s that the benefits America derived from the dollar were "an exorbitant privilege." "There was no doubting de Gaulle's intention: to promote his drive to reduce US economic, military and cultural influence," *Time* magazine said of his campaign. (As part of his effort to demonstrate independence from Washington, de Gaulle recognized the People's Republic of China in 1964, a full seven years before Nixon and Kissinger made their celebrated opening to Beijing.) China sees a global role for its currency in a similar light to de Gaulle's, as both good business and good power politics. Even though

Beijing knows it will be a long process that could take several decades, some officials see it as a central part of a broader struggle to place limits on American power and to increase China's own room for maneuver. In their minds, it is a rather nerdy, pointy-headed proxy war for influence.

————

When then U.S. treasury secretary Tim Geithner spoke to a group of students at Peking University in 2009, he was asked if China's holdings of U.S. government debt were safe. Of course they are, he responded. The audience laughed. It is not just the Chinese elite who frets about the dollar. One of the surprising aspects of the Chinese reaction to the financial crisis has been the way in which seemingly technical issues about the international financial system have seeped into public debate. The U.S. dollar has become a flashpoint for some of the broader nationalist tensions that have been boiling up within China. In 2012, the car of the U.S. ambassador to China, Gary Locke, was surrounded by an angry mob of around fifty people who had been protesting at the nearby Japanese Embassy. One demonstrator grabbed the flag off the front of the car. Then the crowd shouted: "Give us back our money."

In Song Hongbing, China's currency nationalists have found an unlikely cheerleader. A few years ago, Song was an unknown economist at a Chinese government think tank. But his 2007 book *Currency Wars* turned him into an unlikely star of the publishing world, selling half a million copies, and making him the spokesman for popular resentment at the dollar-based world. The book aims to be a sort of financial history, but it is really a hodgepodge of dubious stories about financial conspiracies down the ages, arguing that the Rothschild banking dynasty has been pulling the strings in the international financial system ever since the nineteenth century, when it made a fortune speculating on the outcome of the Napoleonic wars. He claims the Rothschild family wealth is now a hundred times greater than that of Bill Gates. One of his main targets is the fact that the regional U.S. Federal Reserve banks are technically owned by the private banks rather than the government. But Song also manages to recycle some ugly myths about the prominence of Jews in the financial sector and their alleged role in events ranging from Waterloo to the Asian financial crisis. Such insinuations did not prevent the book from generating buzz in some surprising places—two different sources told me that Premier Wen Jiabao had asked to read a copy of *Currency Wars.*

Song's background does not make him an obvious critic of American financial excess. While he was living in the U.S., he did some work creating financial-risk models for Fannie Mae and Freddie Mac, the two mortgage finance institutions at the center of the housing bubble. But the book seems to have tapped into popular suspicions that international finance is rigged against China and that the U.S. will debase its currency. His timing was impeccable: *Currency Wars* came out just before a massive financial crisis which was caused in part by the arrogance of a U.S.-based international financial elite. That has helped turn Song into an often quoted authority on the links between finance and politics. In the process, he has also helped popularize a certain strain of victim nationalism that sees the dominance of the dollar as one of the tools used to curtail China's rise. "Before my book, people thought currencies were really an academic issue, but now they see it as a political issue, as a struggle for power," Song told me. "The big power is the one who issues the money, who can define what money is. The currency war is a struggle, a fight for who controls the money and who can issue it."

One of the peculiar aspects of Song's writings is that he shares many of his concerns with a section of the right wing in America. He has not only an intense aversion to the investor George Soros, but also a deep suspicion of the powers of the U.S. Federal Reserve. "Congress should have the power to issue money, not the Fed," he told me. "No one audits the books of the Fed." He added: "Ron Paul has very much the same view. Why is money issued by a small group of unelected people?" When I asked him why he was so obsessed about Jews in finance, such as Soros, he smiled a little uncomfortably and attempted the sort of compliment that runs its own risks of stereotyping. "I personally admire the Jews," said Song. "They were prohibited from doing anything else, they could not own land, so money was the only way to succeed."

A bespectacled forty-something in a starched shirt with personalized cuff links, Song was clearly enjoying his success when I met him. He had opened a new consulting business, called the Global Business and Finance Institute, to give advice on international financial issues. A sequel to his book, *Currency Wars 2*, which describes plans by a small group of bankers to launch a new global currency, had been published, and a third volume is in the works. He had also just rented a suite of offices in Beijing near Dongzhimen Avenue, modern China's new power center, which houses the imposing and slick headquarters of many of China's largest state-owned companies. One side of the office was taken up by a new side business: a group of young computer programmers were designing a video game based on *Currency Wars*. Song described to me the outline for the game. The early stages would involve starting your own business and building up capital. If a gamer managed to reach the final stage, he would get to become a big hedge-fund speculator who could launch an attack on the U.S. dollar. "You can become the sort of financial big guy who has the resources to start a currency war," he said. "Someone like George Soros."

JEKYLL ISLAND

In November 1910, a group of the great and the good from America's financial elite assembled after dark in a railway car at a quiet siding in Hoboken, just across the river from Manhattan. They used only their first names in front of the porters. When they reached Brunswick, Georgia, two days later, they took a boat to Jekyll Island and checked in at the private club partly owned by J. P. Morgan. They told people they were going duck hunting, and one of the party even carried a shotgun onto the train to keep up the pretense, although he had never used one in his life. But their real purpose was to draft legislation to completely shake up the country's banking system. In the process, they also revolutionized the role of the U.S. dollar.

The men at the secret meeting on Jekyll Island included Benjamin Strong, head of Bankers Trust; Henry Davison, who was J. P. Morgan's right-hand man; Paul Warburg of Kuhn, Loeb; and Frank Vanderlip, a former journalist who was by then the boss of what became Citibank. They were joined by Senator Nelson Aldrich of Rhode Island, head of the Senate Finance Committee, whose daughter was married to John Rockefeller, son of the richest man in the country, and Abraham Piatt

Andrew, assistant secretary of the Treasury Department. The most famous consequence of the meeting was the bill that created the Federal Reserve, America's central bank. The 1907 financial crisis had exposed the vulnerabilities of the economy to such an extent that the government effectively had to rely on J. P. Morgan to broker a solution—he called leading bankers to his Manhattan town house and would not let them leave until they had devised a rescue plan. As a result of the legislation they wrote, the Federal Reserve System took over that role of regulating and managing credit conditions in the country. Every modern economy in the world now has a central bank that plays the role of lender of last resort. But, given that sections of the American right believe the Fed is an example of excessive government interference, the Jekyll Island meeting is, to this day, viewed by some as an elite conspiracy against the interests of ordinary Americans. In 2010, the libertarian politician Ron Paul was the headline guest at a conference on Jekyll Island about the misdeeds of the Fed. "People are demanding that we not put up with a secretive organization like the Fed that prints all this money and causes all this mischief," the former presidential candidate told the audience.

Establishing the Fed was only one part of the 1910 Jekyll Island plan, however. The legislation they developed also created the legal instruments for the dollar to become an international currency—as it happens, a plan quite similar to the one China is now pursuing. They started by establishing procedures so that trade could be settled using U.S. dollars. Then they created the legal framework for the issuance of international U.S. dollar bonds. The impact was dramatic. According to the financial historian Barry Eichengreen, just one decade after the bill was passed in 1913, the U.S. dollar already accounted for a larger share of central-bank reserves than the British pound. It was also used in more bond issues and exceeded sterling in loans linked to trade by a factor of two to one. Even before the Jekyll Island plan was implemented, the American economy had the scale for the dollar to play a larger role in the global economy, but lacked the legal instruments and market infrastructure. Within just a decade of its approval, the status of the U.S. dollar had been transformed and sterling's diminished.

Just as Americans should not be surprised by China's urge to build a grand navy, they should also not be blindsided by Beijing's ambitious plans to turn the renminbi into a global currency. After all, this is precisely what America did at a similar stage in its development, when it wanted to start turning its economic scale into greater international influence. Whereas America's plan was written by an elite band of Wall Street and Washington figures, China's global-currency push has been orchestrated by a small group of the Communist Party elite. (The party's senior officials also often plot new strategies at its own beachside retreat, Beidaihe, a few hours east of Beijing.) Given America's current troubles and China's inexorable growth, it is tempting to think that something similar might happen again over the coming decade or two, when it is quite likely that China will become the biggest economy in the world. But for history to repeat itself, and for the renminbi to eclipse the dollar, two very substantial conditions will need to be met. China will have to tear up its economic model, and America will need to let it happen. Both are possible, but neither is inevitable.

GRIDLOCK

As to the second condition, there certainly is no shortage of reasons for thinking that the U.S. could be heading for the sort of crisis that would shake the foundations of the dollar era. The litany is a familiar one—high debt levels, chronic budget deficits, political gridlock, spiraling entitlement spending, and crumbling infrastructure. In some ways, the status of the dollar is actually making things worse. The U.S. government's ability to keep borrowing from abroad allows it to put off taking some of the tough decisions that will eventually need to be taken. Some Americans worry that having a reserve currency is the equivalent of a "resource curse," the sort of natural advantage that leads to indulgent, ineffectual government.

Yet, despite all these problems, the fate of the U.S. dollar still lies largely within the control of the U.S. government. Big shifts in the international monetary system take place rarely, and then usually only in response to dramatic events. Once gained, the position of reserve currency is not easily lost. The system is a reflection of the collective confidence and force of habit of millions of economic agents around the world and only changes from one anchor to another when there is little alternative. The loss of influence suffered by the British pound is one example. The decade starting in 1914, which was the period in which the U.S. dollar began to stake its claim at the heart of the international monetary system, was also the decade that included the First World War, an event which all but bankrupted Great Britain. With the value of sterling plummeting from 1915, all of a sudden Brazilian coffee traders started pricing their goods in dollars, and Dutch tulip-bulb farmers wanted export credits to be issued in dollars. The Second World War finished the job on Britain's finances and completed the process of transition from sterling to the dollar. The ascendance of the dollar required not only the decisive plan that was devised on Jekyll Island, but also a collapse of confidence in sterling.

Now, admittedly, it is not completely out of the question that the U.S. will suffer a similar financial convulsion. In the summer of 2011, some members of the U.S. Congress seemed quite happy to use the threat of default as a short-term political tactic. The subsequent downgrading of U.S. government debt by Standard & Poor's was a stark warning about the potential erosion of confidence in the dollar. Ever since then, Washington has been living from one budget crisis to another. Yet even this 2011 mini-crisis served to demonstrate the unique position that America holds in the international financial system. In such moments of nervousness, investors seek a safe haven, and the place they looked to was, ironically, the U.S. Treasury bond market. In the very week when America's credit rating was downgraded, the price of American debt actually rose by near-record levels. There are huge incumbent advantages to being the principal reserve currency that are not easily dismantled. If the U.S. can muddle through its current troubles and present a coherent long-term plan for bringing its debts under control, the U.S. dollar will retain a central role, if for no other reason than inertia. That is politically easier said than done, of course, but the correct response to the Chinese challenge to the dollar is nothing more and nothing less than good housekeeping. The U.S. holds its fate in its own hands.

STATE CAPITALISM

The China model of economic management had its finest moment in November 2008. Lehman Brothers had collapsed two months earlier, sending the Western economic world into the sort of panic not seen since the 1930s. Over the next few weeks, the brutal consequences for China started to mount. In southern and eastern China, the areas where most of the export factories are concentrated, tens of thousands of migrant workers would line up every day at railway stations to return home to their villages, their jobs having disappeared almost overnight. Seeing a potential threat to its legitimacy, the Chinese party-state snapped into action. In November, Beijing announced a massive economic stimulus plan with a headline figure of $586 billion to backstop the collapsing economy. The Chinese government's main planning agency—the National Reform and Development Commission—is based in the northwest of the city, in a neighborhood that has three or four modest hotels. For several weeks after the government announced the stimulus plan, every conference room in these hotels was booked by local government officials from around the country who came to present their best "shovel-ready" projects. From dawn to dusk, planning officials surveyed the plans for construction and infrastructure, giving a quick yes or no. The state-owned banks then provided the initial financing, and work began as quickly as possible. Roads, bridges, airports, and tunnels were built in record time. It was probably the biggest-ever emergency public-works program.

It turns out that China had the perfect "model" to respond to the sort of economic crisis that seems to happen every eighty years. When foreign analysts talk about Chinese "state capitalism," they are usually referring to the presence of state-owned businesses in many areas of the economy. But the real key to the system is the way the financial system works. China was able to respond so quickly to the crisis because of the control the state has over the big four banks, which are responsible for between a third and a half of new credit in the country. The government was able to use its direct influence over the banks to funnel credit quickly to infrastructure projects. In the U.S., when the crisis hit, bank lending all but seized up as uncertainty took hold of economic decisions. In China, bank lending exploded. In 2009, the country's banks issued twice as many new loans as they had written the year before. These banks had spent the previous five years getting stock-exchange listings, attracting foreign shareholders, and publishing ambitious statements about corporate governance. But, for all the talk that they were becoming more independent, when it came to the crunch they took a political order from the top and opened the credit floodgates. As China rebounded much more quickly from the global financial crisis than any other major economy, the normally disciplined Premier Wen Jiabao let slip a somewhat triumphalist note. China's economic model, he said, allowed the government to "make decisions efficiently, to organize effectively, and to concentrate resources to accomplish a large undertaking."

Yet this same brand of state capitalism is also the main obstacle to China's developing a major global currency. The project to take the renminbi global is actually a pivotal moment in modern China, because it presents the leaders with an almost existential choice. For the renminbi to become an internationally accepted currency and a trusted store of value, China will need to make the sort of root-and-branch economic and financial reforms that would transform the way the economy is run. The scale of the changes that China would need to implement to achieve this goal makes the problems facing the U.S. at the moment look modest in comparison.

At the moment, Beijing is trying to square an economic circle. Although China is now the biggest exporter of manufactured goods in the world, the reason few people use the renminbi to settle trade transactions is that Beijing maintains a high wall of capital controls that protect its economy from the fickleness of international financial markets. As a result, it is still very hard to take Chinese currency in and out of the country, and for foreigners to invest money in China's financial markets. This is where Hong Kong comes in—it is a perfect halfway house, an offshore laboratory where Beijing can experiment with allowing its currency to be widely held without the risk of a destabilizing financial blowback. But the offshore market in Hong Kong can only take the renminbi so far, because the volumes will always be limited. To turn the renminbi into a currency that even the world's deeply conservative and cautious central banks would feel comfortable holding, China would need to tear down some of those barriers, allowing money to move freely in and out of the country. In other words, to boost the credibility of its currency, China would need to open itself up to international capital in just the way that New York does. This would not be a simple technical change: it would mean a revolution in how China runs its economic affairs.

Opening the economy to financial flows would put huge strains on the Chinese economic model. Beijing would have to dismantle many of the tools that allow it to funnel huge volumes of cheap credit to its favored investment projects. One reason the state banks have such a stranglehold on the financial system is that Chinese citizens have little choice but to put a large part of their savings into the banks. To a large extent, they are captive bank-depositors. But in a more open financial system, Chinese citizens would have many more options about how and where to invest their money. Banks would have to compete for deposits by offering higher returns, which would slash the profits they made from lending. And in order to retain the confidence of depositors, they would also have to be much more transparent about the risks they were taking with loans to pet government projects.

The Chinese authorities also use the tight control they have over the banking system to effectively set interest rates in the economy—another powerful tool that allows them to shape macroeconomic policy and keep credit cheap. But the power of the banks would be diminished by another necessary change. If foreign investors are going to hold a significant share of their assets in renminbi, they will need access to a large, liquid, and credible Chinese bond market. The global role of the dollar is underpinned by the huge U.S. government bond market, which gives investors an easy way to buy and sell large volumes of securities. It is that liquidity that makes it such a reliable store of value. Yet, in a large and transparent bond market, the price of credit is set by the market, not by government fiat. In essence, the decision to open up the economy to foreign capital would transform the position of the big state-owned banks. They would need to be run on much more stringent commercial principles and could no longer be used as piggy banks for other state-owned companies. And in the process, the Communist Party would lose a vital element of its current political control over the economy.

China would also need to transform the way it manages its exchange rate—another revolution in economic policy making. If China were to allow capital to flow more easily in and out of the country, it would have to adopt a much more flexible exchange rate in order to manage the volatility. China would probably end up floating its currency, at least partially. That means it would become much harder for Beijing to depress the value of its currency artificially to help its exporters—another central element of the economic model of the last few decades.

The implications do not end there. If foreign investors are going to park large sums of money in the Chinese financial system, then China would also need a much more independent legal system. Why invest in a Chinese security if a Communist Party official can tell a court what to decide in any legal disputes that might arise? The system of making economic policy would also need to be much more transparent. At present, it is not clear who actually makes decisions about interest rates in China, let alone why they are made. The central bank almost certainly does not make these decisions. But is it the premier? The Finance and Economics Leading Small Group? The Politburo? Or the Communist Party Standing Committee? If the world's central banks are going to put a large part of their reserves into Chinese government bonds, they will want to know more about the key economic decisions.

Over time, the Chinese renminbi will doubtless increase in importance and is likely to rank alongside the euro, the yen, and the British pound as one of the second-string reserve currencies, accounting for 10 to 20 percent of global reserves. But if it is to supplant the U.S. dollar and establish itself as the principal safe-haven currency, the harsh reality for China is that it has two options. It can keep its particular model of state capitalism. Or it can have a global reserve currency. But it cannot have both.

And that is, of course, the central irony of this whole discussion. The project to make the renminbi into an international force has been dressed up in the geopolitics of dethroning the U.S. dollar, a reflection of both the frustrations of the economic elite and the popular resentment of the U.S. Yet this project requires precisely the economic and political reforms that U.S. leaders have been calling for in China over the last couple of decades. Many of the frictions over economic issues that have built up between the U.S. and China in recent years would disappear if Beijing introduced these policies. The exchange-rate controversy would evaporate as China adopted a more market-based currency policy. And Beijing would be much less able to use its banks to subsidize its own companies with cheap loans—one of the core issues behind the current fears about a new wave of "state capitalism."

Indeed, some believe this has been the hidden agenda all along of Zhou Xiaochuan, the central-bank boss. Along with a group of other reform-minded officials, he has been trying for much of the last decade to get China to gradually open its financial system, which he thinks is essential for improving the efficiency of investment in China and maintaining high growth over the coming decades. But at almost every stage, he has been frustrated by the caution and conservatism of his Communist Party bosses, some of whom have legitimate complaints about financial capitalism, and some of whom fear an American conspiracy to weaken the Chinese economy. The push to take the Chinese currency global could end up as Zhou's Trojan Horse—a policy proposal which appears at first sight to have a nationalist, anti-American agenda but which, if followed through, will actually involve groundbreaking liberalization of the economy, the sort of things that American Treasury secretaries want to see happen. In its bid to end the dominance of the dollar, China could end up taking down its great financial wall much more quickly than Beijing would like. Challenging America's exorbitant economic privileges brings its own very high costs.

9

Post-American Globalization

For PETER BOSSHARD, the end of the Cold War was the moment when people finally started to pay attention. A Swiss national with a Ph.D. from Zurich University, Bosshard has spent most of his adult life trying to get foreign banks and engineering companies to rethink their support for large dams in developing countries. He would explain patiently why he thought these projects were white elephants that brought little benefit to the countries in question, other than to the officials who were able to cream off some of the contracts, while causing enormous damage to the surrounding environment. For years, his warnings were suffered in polite silence. Yet, after the fall of the Berlin Wall, development and environmental issues started to move center-stage. This was the era of the big UN conferences in Cairo, Rio, and Beijing on human rights and climate change, and Bosshard saw the mood shift. "People began to return my phone calls," he says.

One of the unexpected consequences of the end of the Cold War was the space it opened for activists. The 1990s became the era of the international NGO—the nongovernmental groups that lobby, campaign, and occasionally harass politicians and companies over issues in the developing world. During the Cold War, many of these NGOs struggled to find any oxygen, given that aid and finance to developing countries were wrapped up in the political expediency of bipolar competition. That started to change when the Wall fell. All of a sudden, clever young graduates wanted to work for Oxfam or ActionAid, instead of McKinsey. Bosshard, who wears wire-rimmed spectacles and Birkenstocks, is a soft-spoken engineer whose fluent English still carries a European accent. Since 2002, he has run International Rivers, an NGO based in a small office in Berkeley, California. "No one could accuse us anymore of doing Moscow's bidding," he says.

Before long, dams became one of the main political battlefields in this new wave of international activism. From the 1960s, large hydropower dams had been pushed as a silver bullet for developing economies. Under the leadership of Robert McNamara, the former U.S. defense secretary who had helped prosecute the Vietnam War, the World Bank put large amounts of resources behind these projects. The dams also became major earners for engineering multinationals such as Switzerland's ABB, one of the biggest companies in the world for much of the 1980s and 1990s. But with the end of the Cold War, activist NGOs started to point loudly to the failures and the high costs attached. As many as eighty million people had been displaced by large dams in the previous three decades, they claimed, many of whom did not manage to find a new livelihood. Bosshard, who fell in love with rivers while walking in the Alps as a child, started to go after the banks backing the projects, accusing them of "environmental money laundering." Under heavy pressure, the World Bank dramatically scaled back its lending to large dams. One senior executive complained in the mid-1990s that dams were "responsible for 95 percent of our headaches." Once the World Bank pulled out, most private banks also stood back. By the end of the 1990s, funding had dwindled so much that companies such as ABB exited the sector. The global approach to dam building had been completely transformed. It was one of the most successful lobbying campaigns by an NGO anywhere in the world. Then along came China.

Bosshard says he first started to take notice of China at the end of 2003, when Beijing agreed to build the Merowe Dam in northern Sudan, on one of the major tributaries of the Nile. The Sudanese government had been pushing the idea since the 1970s, and in the 1990s government delegations from Sudan toured Canada, Europe, and Southeast Asia, looking for financial backers for the project, only to return empty-handed each time. The World Bank also declined to get involved. Not only would the dam end up displacing tens of thousands of farmers who worked fertile Nile Valley land, but many governments were also put off by the Sudanese government's record of human-rights abuses. Yet for China's dam builders Merowe was a perfect chance to start taking their expertise global—expertise they had recently gleaned from the West.

In the 1990s, construction began on the massive and controversial Three Gorges Dam, on the Yangtze, the biggest hydroelectric power station in the world. Given that the market for dams had dried up elsewhere, the competition to get involved in the Three Gorges was intense. In order to get some of the multi-billion-dollar contracts that were on offer, Western groups had to enter joint ventures with Chinese companies, and under the terms of those agreements, they were obliged to hand over some of their technology. A decade later, the Chinese dam-building companies had absorbed these technologies and were ready to export them back overseas. Chinese banks also offered huge financing packages to convince other developing countries to begin construction, forging a powerful partnership with the new generation of dam-building companies. China has single-handedly revived the international market for large dams. By 2010, Chinese companies were involved in 220 dams in fifty different countries around the world and were constructing nineteen of the twenty-four largest hydropower stations ever built. Bosshard did not realize it at the time, but he was one of the first people to understand the potential for Chinese finance and investment to completely reshape globalization. "They are pretty much everywhere now," he says.

––––––

Mao Zedong was the central figure in the two events that produced the current era of globalization. The first was his 1972 meeting with Richard Nixon, which paved the way for China's re-entry into the international community. The second was his death. Deng Xiaoping was then able to launch the market reforms in the late 1970s that turned China from a centrally planned basket case into an economic juggernaut. During the three decades in which China has been on this reform path, Beijing and Washington have both placed a large strategic bet on economic integration. China felt that it needed access to American consumers and technology if it was to advance its economy; America decided that the global economy would be much stronger with China on the inside rather than outside. What we now call globalization was born.

China and the U.S. are approaching another critical crossroads in their economic relationship, which is as important as the 1972 meeting and will determine the future shape of the global economy. For the last three decades, globalization has been an American project, driven by American values, American capital, and American-led institutions. Peter Bosshard was one of the first witnesses of a new phase, in which Chinese finance and investment will play leading roles. The U.S. and China have to decide whether they now want to double down with a new stage of economic integration and cooperation. Down one road lies even greater interdependence between the two biggest economies on the planet, which will place restraints on their militaries and on other areas of competition. Yet down the other lies the formation of a two-track global economy, with a Western system revolving around the U.S. and a separate China-led economic sphere guided by Beijing's priorities. Will globalization break in half?

China's economic influence is usually thought of as a function of trade, all those T-shirts, widgets, and iPhones it makes for the world. China is now the world's largest exporter of manufactured goods, something that would have seemed preposterous to the officials who accompanied Mao and Nixon. In the process, it has displaced the U.S. as the largest trading partner of a host of countries, from Japan and South Korea to South Africa and Brazil, slowly turning the map of global commerce red. Trade is just the first stage, however. China is also now starting to become a global power in finance and investment. Until now, China has been a receiver rather than a giver of direct investment in factories and equipment. But that axis is shifting, as Chinese companies start to look overseas for investment opportunities and Chinese banks offer generous loans. The process began slowly in the late 1990s, after the government launched a "go out" strategy that led to a trickle of investments in mining and oil, and it is now gathering pace quickly in manufacturing and even services. As with so much else in modern China, the numbers will have an epic scale. Daniel Rosen, a China specialist at the Peterson Institute in Washington, D.C., calculates that if China follows the pattern of other developing economies, over the next decade it will invest overseas between $1 trillion and $2 trillion. This financial muscle will be one of the most important driving forces in the global economy over the coming decades. Corporate China's new export market will be its own money.

China is arriving at the same sort of inflection point that the U.S. economy reached in the 1890s. Before then, few American businessmen had even considered trying to operate abroad, as there was just too much money to be made at home. But eventually the lure of foreign markets started to become powerful. In the early 1890s, Senator Albert Beveridge of Indiana summed up the prevailing mood of a country ready to spread its commercial wings. "American factories are making more than the American people can use; American soil is producing more than they can consume," he said. "Fate has written our policy for us; the trade of the world must and shall be ours." Having reached a certain critical mass at home, many companies began to look for new markets and new investment opportunities overseas, particularly in the Americas. Before long, the United Fruit Company dominated banana production in Honduras, Guatemala, and elsewhere, to the extent that by 1925 it was the biggest employer in Central America. By the 1920s, American companies also owned 60 percent of Cuba's sugar plantations, and dominated the hotel-and-entertainment scene in Havana. And it was in the late 1890s that Washington started to push for an "Open Door" policy in China, which would allow American companies to trade and invest in China, along with the European colonial powers. Before long, Buicks had become the car of choice for the Chinese elite, with the list of proud owners including nationalist leader Sun Yat-sen and Pu Yi, the last Qing emperor.

As it contemplates this new stage in its development, the big strategic question for China is whether the U.S. should be at the forefront of its new investment plans. When Chinese companies survey the potential opportunities overseas, one instinct is to channel a large slice of this investment toward the U.S., which is still by far the largest economy in the world and the most powerful consumer market. America has a strong track record of consistent improvements in productivity, the real long-term guarantee of continued economic growth that companies are looking for when they make investment plans. It is basic business logic to go where the money is. As a result of shale oil and gas, the U.S. could be on the verge of a new energy boom, one of China's key priorities. Yet several Chinese companies that have tried to invest in the U.S. have suffered bruising political battles in Washington over their ties to the Chinese government. In 2006, the Chinese state oil company CNOOC tried to buy an American group called Unocal and put forward an offer bigger than the one already on the table from Chevron, another U.S. group. But after a storm of protest in Congress about Chinese interference in the U.S. energy sector, CNOOC decided to withdraw, feeling completely humiliated in the process by the political drubbing it had taken. Events such as this have left many Chinese companies in a wait-and-see mode, trying to work out whether or not they are really welcome in the U.S.

Even while they are testing the political mood in Washington, the Chinese also have a strong instinct to move in a very different direction, to use China's financial heft to fashion an alternative pattern of globalization that bypasses the U.S. The financial crisis was a profound shock for Beijing, revealing a level of dependence on the U.S. economy that left many in China deeply uncomfortable. Some of the Chinese officials who had supported close ties with the U.S. were dumbstruck to find that the U.S. financial system could have been so badly managed. The idea of trying to decouple China from the U.S. started to become more attractive. At the same time, it is part of the DNA of the aspirant great power to use its economic weight to begin shaping the rules and relationships that are at the heart of the global economy. China's efforts to challenge the role of the U.S. dollar are part of this mindset. There is now a lobby in Beijing that wishes to use the coming wave of investment to generate a new phase of globalization in which all the roads—business, financial, and political—converge on Beijing. Xu Shanda, a Chinese economist, argues for the launch of a Chinese "Marshall Plan" in the developing world, loans and aid that would create their own demand for Chinese goods. Some senior policy makers talk about how China's financial firepower could spark a new cycle of global growth among developing countries, with Beijing in the engine room, winning both new markets for China and new political partners, and all the time bypassing the developed markets of the U.S. and Europe. China is being tempted by the idea of post-American globalization.

To get a sense of what post-American globalization might look like, a good place to start is a small town called Açu, 175 miles north up the Atlantic coast from Rio de Janeiro in Brazil. Until recently, Açu used to be a small seaside village that attracted a modest crowd of weekenders to its long beaches. Now, it is a huge port with a two-mile-long pier and the ambition to be a strategic conduit between the Brazilian and Chinese economies. One of the world's largest dredging ships was used to carve a huge dock from the sand dunes, so that it will be able to house the new generation of Chinamax ships that can carry 400,000 tons of iron ore at a time across the oceans. A Chinese vice minister who came to visit the project described it as "a new highway to China."

The Açu port is the brainchild of Eike Batista, Brazil's most controversial businessman, whose spectacular rise and fall have become a potent symbol of the boom-and-bust cycles that have long scarred Brazilian capitalism. Batista made his first fortune as a gold trader in an area of the Amazon jungle that was undergoing a massive gold rush and which was a lawless place of legendary knife fights between the miners over who owned the precious metal. Over the last decade, he managed to ride the commodities boom that the China boom sparked, especially after he invested in a series of oilfields off the coast of Brazil in 2003. At one stage, his net worth was calculated at $34.5 billion, making him the seventh-richest person in the world. "Eike is a special kind of entrepreneur," Brazil's President Dilma Rousseff said during a visit to the Açu port project. "He comes up with extremely ambitious dreams and then seeks to fulfill them."

Once married to a *Playboy* cover girl and Carnival dancer, Batista once endorsed a new treatment for restoring the hair on his balding head, however, his wealth has demonstrated weaker roots. When Batista's oil wells produced much less oil than he had promised investors, his heavily indebted companies started to face a series of cash calls that have wiped billions off their market value in 2012 and early 2013. Batista could be forced into selling many of his businesses, which also include mining and shipbuilding.

Amid the scandals and schadenfreude that have accompanied the demise of Eike Batista's business fortunes, it is easy to lose sight of the fact that he has been a genuine trailblazer in ways that will have a lasting impact on Brazil. Batista was one of the first businessmen in Brazil to harness demand and finance from China, the country which has emerged over the last decade as Brazil's leading economic partner. "There is an endless market for us on the other side. China has endless pent-up demand," as Batista puts it.

One of the reasons America has maintained its dominant position in the world is that the size of its economy makes it a sort of customer of last resort, a constant source of demand that keeps the global economy ticking along. But China's growing ties with Brazil are one example of the way that it is starting to play the role of economic anchor in important relationships at the heart of the global economy. Brazil is good business and good politics for China. It is a fast-growing market of 200 million people, and China is building ties with a country in the backyard of its potential rival, a subtle intrusion into the Monroe Doctrine. The Brazil connection is part of a series of new economic links that have the potential to shape a different growth axis for the global economy, one that bypasses the West.

Brazil's improved economic performance over the last decade, including the China-style growth rate of 7.5 percent in 2010, was partly the result of demand from China for its natural resources, from iron ore and copper to beef and soybeans. In the process, China has become Brazil's biggest trading partner, overtaking the U.S. Batista was also one of the first in Brazil to understand the next phase, direct investment by Chinese companies. The Chinese group Wuhan Iron and Steel (Wisco) owns a large stake in MMX, the mining group he established. Before his troubles hit, Batista was talking to Wisco about an even bigger investment, a $5 billion steel plant in Açu next door to the port, which would have been the biggest ever Chinese investment in Brazil. Those talks may have floundered, but China has already become the biggest direct investor in Brazil in 2012, again outpacing the U.S. The investors have included car manufacturers and telecom companies, as well as natural resource businesses. "There is an enormous highway developing between Brazil and China," says Batista, who set up a high-end Chinese restaurant in Rio de Janeiro, called Mr. Lam, with two giant terra-cotta warriors flanking the entrance. "The world should start paying attention to it because it is fabulous." Batista might not manage to retain control of the Açu project, but there is a long list of potential investors lining up to finish the project that he started.

Brazil is involved in another interesting example of this new Chinese strategy to move beyond America-led globalization, the plan to create a BRICS bank. "BRICS" was a concept first invented by Jim O'Neill, an economist at Goldman Sachs, who wanted a catchy title to capture the exciting investment opportunities in a diverse group of emerging countries—Brazil, Russia, India, and China (South Africa was added later). Since then, the idea has taken on a geopolitical life of its own. The leaders of the five countries now hold annual summits, and some have high hopes that the BRICS can become an important political voice. Vladimir Putin, the Russian president, believes the group can develop into "a full-scale strategic cooperation mechanism that will allow us to look for solutions to key issues of global politics together." The leaders of the five countries are in detailed discussions to establish their own development bank, which would lend funds to other developing countries, providing a powerful alternative to the World Bank and International Monetary Fund. With China the driving force behind the project, the BRICS countries are discussing an initial capital injection of $50 billion.

It is one of the ironies of the international system the U.S. created after the end of the Second World War that so many of its institutions are deeply unpopular in the U.S. On the American right, the visceral dislike of the United Nations is so intense that the U.S. Senate cannot pass any UN agreement, even if it is something the U.S. initially proposed. In late 2012, the Senate refused to ratify a UN treaty to promote the rights of the disabled that was based on American legislation. The World Bank and the International Monetary Fund are sometimes the butt of the same disdain, criticized on the right for their cushy perks and on the left as bastions of neoliberalism. But the reality is that both the World Bank and the IMF, which are based a couple of blocks away from the White House, have been powerful instruments for pushing an American vision of politics and economics on the developing world. Especially since the end of the Cold War, the World Bank and the IMF have been important conduits for the promotion of privatization and free trade, the policies that have been the international priorities of the U.S. Treasury Department.

Their impact goes well beyond economics. These Washington-based institutions have also used their influence to encourage ideas about governance which have a strongly American flavor: a push for greater transparency, accountability, and respect for the rule of law. That makes the World Bank and the IMF hugely important and often underestimated tools in the global battle for influence. If China's banks really do start to undercut some of the authority of the World Bank, providing an alternative source of financing that comes with far fewer political and economic strings attached, that would have a significant impact on Washington's ability to shape attitudes in the developing world. Beijing does not want to tear up the World Bank or the IMF; indeed, it is lobbying hard for a bigger say in how they are managed. But without any announcement or grand design, it is also quietly setting up an alternative system of global development financing that has the potential to make the Washington institutions less relevant. "I sometimes ask the Chinese why they are making such an effort to be more involved at the World Bank," says a senior Brazilian official who used to work at the bank, "because they are at the same time effectively putting it out of business."

At the heart of most of China's new economic relationships is one institution: China Development Bank. In the space of just a few years, it has become one of the most influential banks in the world. The state owns almost all the main banks in China, but CDB is different. Like the China Export-Import Bank, it is defined as a "policy bank," which means that its objective is to support the overall economic goals of the government. China Development Bank is the sort of hybrid institution that can only really exist in Beijing, a branch of the Chinese state but for a long period it was also the political fiefdom of a very ambitious official from the Communist Party's aristocracy. In the late 1990s, the bank was effectively bankrupt when Chen Yuan, a former vice governor of the Chinese central bank, became its chairman. His father, Chen Yun, was one of the most influential of the first generation of Communist revolutionaries and one of the "Eight Immortals," the group of Deng's contemporaries who acted as a parallel power structure during the 1980s and 1990s, and who pushed for the military to take control of Tiananmen Square in 1989. Under Chen Yuan's leadership, CDB managed to follow a delicate path of supporting government goals while also being hugely profitable. Dragonomics, a Beijing consultancy, calls it "the best-run bank in China."

Chen used his close personal contacts within the Chinese system to create a central role for CDB in Chinese urban development. In the early part of the last decade, the bank used an innovative financing structure to help unleash a surge in infrastructure projects by Chinese local governments—all those new airports, highways, and high-speed trains that have attracted so much attention. Then, from the middle of the last decade, Chen decided to take his bank overseas. He bought a small stake in the U.K.'s Barclays Bank and flirted with a much bigger investment, before pulling out of the deal. Instead, when the financial crisis started, he realized there was a huge opportunity for China in the energy sector. Given the sharp drop in prices, energy-producing countries were "now in a difficult situation because they can't raise capital from the West," he said in 2008. "So they are shifting their focus to China. Therefore, we should grasp this opportunity to do deals." He decided to build up an informal branch network for the bank overseas. Each of the main offices in China was given responsibility for a different region of the world. The Henan branch, in northern China, was told to scout for business in southern Africa; the Chongqing office, from central China, was sent to develop contacts in the Balkans. By the end of 2009, the bank had teams in 141 countries, including almost all the fifty-four countries in Africa. In a book he wrote about his experiences working overseas for CDB, Shi Jiyang recalls sitting in his office in Shenzhen in 2006, looking at a map of the world, and wondering if he would ever get the chance to visit South America; a month later, he was sent there to find new business. "South America is going to be the hotspot for Chinese investment over the next ten years," he writes. "Entrepreneurs who want to 'challenge the blue ocean' should be ready to go to South America." In early 2013, Chen Yuan stepped down from CDB, after more than a decade in charge. His new job is to establish the BRICS development bank.

Ambitious companies, not the Foreign Ministry, are forging many of China's new international relationships. In a short period of time,

CDB started to sign a rapid succession of eye-catching deals. It provided the financing for the $2-billion Burma pipeline, as well as a series of big deals in Russia, Kazakhstan, and Turkmenistan. The bank was also behind a $9-billion development-financing deal that China signed with the government of Ghana. Africa gets most of the attention in China's overseas investments, but CDB has also made a big splash in Latin America. Kevin Gallagher, a development economist at Boston University, calculated the amount of loan commitments that China made to Latin America between 2005 and 2011. The figure he came up with, $75 billion, was more than the entire amount loaned to the region by the World Bank, the Inter-American Development Bank, and the U.S. government. Some of those funds went to countries such as Argentina and Bolivia, which had effectively been cut off from international financial markets. "The key thing is that the Chinese are financing the sorts of projects that Latin American governments actually want, rather than the projects that the Washington financial institutions think that they need for their development," says Gallagher.

The World Bank insists that it does not really compete with CDB and China Eximbank. In the strict sense, that is often correct. The Chinese are not involved in anything similar to many of the projects that the World Bank supports, such as microcredit schemes or health-care initiatives. According to World Bank officials, the Chinese are mostly interested in using their loans to get access to energy and natural resources, which is a different sort of business. But this explanation leaves out a number of things. It ignores the way in which Chinese money can alter the development priorities of governments. Dams are one of the best examples. After the World Bank succumbed to pressure from NGOs and withdrew from backing large dams in the 1990s, their construction ground to a halt. But when Chinese banks entered the fray, developing countries' governments could ignore Washington's advice about the risks of dam building. Whatever China's motives, the money it makes available gives governments new options and reduces the leverage of the Washington-based banks.

The World Bank's argument also ignores the broader political implications of China's overseas lending spurt. The China Development Bank's biggest client is Venezuela, whose firebrand leader, Hugo Chávez, liked nothing better than taking potshots at Washington until his death in 2013. From 2007 to 2012, the bank lent $42.5 billion to the government of Venezuela—roughly a quarter of its overseas loans during that period. Venezuela is one of the world's largest oil producers, and the loans are backed by oil revenues, which gives China some comfort about repayment. As part of the deal, Chinese companies are also getting access to some oil exploration projects which have become available because U.S. oil companies have been expelled. Most of the loans have gone into a development fund run by the Venezuelan government. It is not too much of an exaggeration to say that the Chinese money went a long way to securing Chávez's hold on power. "Venezuela's oil is at the service of China," Chávez once told Xi Jinping. Ecuador, another Latin American country with a left-populist government that enjoys snubbing its nose at Washington, has negotiated a similar oil-for-loans deal with China. The $7.3 billion in loans it has signed are equivalent to around one-third of its annual budget.

Venezuela's experience in recent years demonstrates the potential of Chinese financing to alter some of the dynamics of international politics. When its oil revenues plummeted during previous financial crises, Caracas was often obliged to look to the Washington institutions for support. The price of that help was to adopt some of their advice about how the economy should be run. During the 2009 crisis, Venezuela's finances were under heavy pressure as oil prices fell. But, courtesy of the Chinese money, Chávez was able to carry on as if nothing had happened. Indeed, as a result of Beijing's backing, Chávez went so far as to pull out of the World Bank and IMF formally in 2010. "We will no longer have to go to Washington," Chávez boasted.

Lurking behind the surge in Chinese lending there is also an economic philosophy that puts China at odds with the Washington institutions. When Deng Xiaoping decided to start opening up the Chinese economy, one of the first things the government did was to take out a large loan from Japan in 1978, on terms quite similar to the sorts of deals China has struck over the last five years in Africa and Latin America. China pledged to import $10 billion of Japanese technology and capital equipment, which it repaid with exports of coal and oil. (This was an era when Japan, not China, was the country scouring the world for natural resources to feed its rapid industrialization.) China used the funds to build new ports and roads, to construct power plants, and to build up its telecommunications network—the core industrial foundations it needed to help kick-start the economy. "China was getting a discount on finance the country needed for its modernization," according to Deborah Brautigam, an American academic who has done extensive research on China's links with Africa. China sees its hands-off financing in Africa and Latin America in a similar vein. Little of this is aid: the borrowing countries have to repay the loans, which are at international interest rates. But Chinese officials argue that economic development can only take place if governments are given the freedom to experiment with the sorts of projects that might work in their countries and which are important for their economy. "We had to learn from our own mistakes," as a senior Chinese official explained to me. "We are letting other countries do the same. We cannot tell them what they need or how to run their economy. All we can do is share some of our own recent experiences."

HACKED OFF

In 2004, a security officer at Nortel, a leading maker of telecommunications equipment, noticed something peculiar on the group's computer network. One of Nortel's senior executives appeared to be downloading a large series of sensitive documents about the company's technology and strategy. The executive claimed to know nothing about the downloads, so the company's IT-security staff started to investigate. They eventually followed the intrusion in Nortel's networks all the way back to Internet servers in China.

Over the next few years, Nortel continued to notice signals that hackers were still present in its system. Brian Shields, a longtime Nortel executive who led the company's internal investigation, concluded that the passwords of seven senior company officials, including the chief executive, had been stolen. Every so often, one of the company's computers would send a large packet of electronic data that would end up at one of the Internet addresses in China. The hacking had probably started as far back as 2000, Nortel concluded. "They had plenty of time to get pretty much anything they wanted," says Shields. "This is not the kind of thing that ordinary hackers can do. It has to be something organized by a state."

Nortel is already an also-ran of the fast-moving IT industry. One of the pioneers in making the electronic switches that power mobile-phone networks, the Canadian company filed for bankruptcy in 2009 and has since been sold off in different pieces. The company could never definitively prove that China was behind the hacking of its system, and Beijing has denied it. It is also not clear whether there was any link between the hacking and the company's deteriorating results. But the accusations that Shields has aired have become part of a familiar refrain in recent years, as American companies and politicians have started to accuse China of a staggering campaign of stealing trade secrets. The most detailed case has been compiled by Mandiant, a U.S. Internet-security company, which claims to have traced hacking attacks on 141 companies in the U.S. and fifteen other countries to one particular Chinese military unit based in Shanghai. According to the Mandiant report, a well-known group of hackers named APT1 is actually part of a PLA group called Unit 61398. By tracing a large volume of hacking activity back to telecom networks near the unit's base in a twelve-story building in central Shanghai, Mandiant concluded that the PLA had to be involved. Amid the increasing volume of evidence linking China to hacking, senior U.S. politicians and officials have taken to denouncing Beijing. In Congress, there is a strong move to try and find some sort of payback, to punish the companies that are benefiting from cybertheft. "What has been happening over the course of the last five years is that China—let's call it for what it is—has been hacking its way into every corporation it can find listed in Dun & Bradstreet," says Richard Clarke, former White House counterterrorism officer under Bill Clinton and George W. Bush. "Every corporation in the U.S., every corporation in Asia, every corporation in Germany. And using a vacuum cleaner to suck data out in terabytes and petabytes."

If China is having second thoughts about its close economic links with the U.S., then America is returning the compliment. The business community was once the most important supporter in the U.S. of strong ties with China, but over the last five years many companies have become much more wary. "I am not sure that in the end they want any of us to win, or any of us to be successful," Jeffrey Immelt, chief executive of General Electric, America's biggest manufacturing company, complained in 2010 at a dinner in Rome.

The hacking revelations have only added to the impression that China is stacking the cards against Western multinationals, especially when it comes to actually doing business in China. The country may be the second-largest economy in the world and the biggest market for many industries, but many foreign businesses have had a bruising experience over the last few years, which makes them think that the opportunities available to them in China are gradually being squeezed. They point to a complex web of Chinese industrial policies that affect their ability to compete, including generous financial subsidies for important Chinese state-owned companies, new industrial standards that favor Chinese competitors, and predatory regulations that seek to get foreign companies to hand over important technologies in return for market access. Chinese regulators believe that, because the Chinese market is so large, they can drive a very hard bargain with foreign companies who want to do business in the country. The fear that the Chinese military and security services are helping foreign companies' competitors steal their trade secrets has only added to the sense of disillusionment. "Many U.S. companies believe they are not competing with similar entities," says John Veroneau, a former deputy U.S. trade representative. "They are used to competing with market players, but not against governments. Not only are they up against subsidies, but they are also up against China's intelligence services."

The lightning rod for a lot of these suspicions has been a Chinese company called Huawei, one of the world's biggest makers of telecom equipment. Huawei has become a sort of Rorschach test for views on China: its supporters believe it is a shining example of Chinese innovation, whereas its critics argue it is a secretive, military-friendly corporation that could be a Trojan Horse for a future cyberwar. Along with Ericsson of Sweden and Cisco of the U.S., Huawei is one of the main companies making the essential infrastructure that goes into modern phone systems, including mobile networks. (Nortel used to be a leader in this market.) That is where the cyberwar fears come in. Security experts say that such expertise means that Huawei could leave devices in American phone systems that might be used to listen into telephone conversations, or it could hide corrupted computer code that would allow China to disable a phone network during a conflict.

Huawei has become such a sensitive political issue in part because of its background. The company was founded by Ren Zhengfei in 1987, when he started selling telephone-exchange equipment imported from Hong Kong. For much of the 1970s, however, Ren had served in the People's Liberation Army, latterly in its information-technology research unit. As a result of that PLA connection, Huawei has never been able to shake the impression that it cooperates with the military and China's security services. The suspicion is enhanced by the opaque management structure of the company, which revolves around the mercurial Ren. He has now become chairman of the company, but his idea of stepping back from the business has been to appoint three people to act as chief executive on a rotating basis, a recipe for backseat control.

Every time it has tried to expand in the U.S., Huawei has found itself frustrated. In 2008, its $2.2-billion attempt to buy an American company called 3Com, which makes Internet routers and networking equipment, was blocked on national security grounds. It had the same experience in 2011, when it tried to buy some assets from 3Leaf, another American technology company. The Intelligence Committee of the U.S. House of Representatives effectively fingered Huawei as a threat to national security in 2012 in a report which recommended not only that it be blocked from all U.S. government business, but that American telecom companies should not buy any equipment made by Huawei. "We simply cannot trust such vital systems to companies with known ties to the Chinese state, a country that is the largest perpetrator of cyberespionage against the U.S.," says Mike Rogers, chairman of the House Intelligence Committee. "You would have to be mad to let that company into our networks."

Not every Western country is quite as hostile to Huawei as is the U.S. In order to do business in the U.K., Huawei, which has invested $2 billion in the country, has established a separate testing center which works closely with British government agencies to ensure that the equipment and software sold by Huawei are reliable. Governments can never know for sure that the equipment they are buying is not compromised, but this British unit is as good a way as any of getting reassurance. There are also some members of the U.S. security establishment who are not opposed to Huawei. One former senior official at the U.S. National Security Agency says that if the Chinese wanted to set traps in U.S. communication networks or in its infrastructure, the last route they would use is equipment made by high-profile Chinese companies, because of the inevitable scrutiny: instead, they would look for ways to plant hidden code in the products of other suppliers. Yet the high-level political opposition to Huawei is so strong in Washington that it is hard to imagine a compromise emerging. One former senior Pentagon official says, "It is simply too dangerous to let a Chinese company near our phone networks, the potential problems are so great."

Perhaps telecom equipment in the twenty-first century is destined to be like the defense industry, a tightly controlled domain that is open only to companies from that nation. But the U.S. also runs a great risk in rejecting companies like Huawei so aggressively. There is bound to be retaliation: China is as afraid of Cisco as the U.S. is of Huawei. Banning major Chinese companies can also easily become a slippery slope. The initial focus has been on telecom equipment, but the U.S. Congress has started introducing restrictions in some areas for all Chinese information-technology products, from computers to smartphones. This sort of action raises the prospect that a core industry in the modern economy will end up being divided into two distinct camps, a group of companies that America politically approves of, and another group of companies that Washington does not trust, mostly from China. Such techno-nationalism can easily become the gateway to a broader outbreak of protectionism. The financial crisis and the great recession that followed did not lead to the flood of protectionist measures that many expected, but the panic over cybertheft of trade secrets might just do so.

———

Of all the China challenges facing Washington in the coming years, in many ways this is perhaps the most complex: how to prevent the political and protectionist pressures that are building up in both countries from splintering the rules and understandings at the heart of the global economy.

The postwar, liberal economic order that America promoted has survived so long because it has been attractive to enough countries that a decisive challenge never emerged. China has been one of the biggest beneficiaries of the existing system, but the clash between its model of state capitalism and America's free-market creed could easily tear it apart. While some in China want to tilt the system more to China's advantage, many in America think Beijing is defying the rules.

Over time, China's economic model will gradually change. Former premier Wen Jiabao described the Chinese economy as "unbalanced, uncoordinated, and unsustainable"—and he liked the phrase so much, he repeated it on several occasions. Among senior Chinese officials, there is a broad consensus on the direction of change toward an economy that depends less on heavy industry and investment and relies more on services and individual consumption. These reforms will inevitably reduce the power and importance in the economy of state-owned companies and banks, softening some of the edges of the system that have aggravated foreign businesses. But such changes will be fiercely resisted and will take a long time to implement, which means the tensions will remain. In the meantime, Washington needs to find new ways to build support for ideas for an open global economy and to steer China away from a major rupture with the system.

One way to do that is to try and establish more areas of common ground with China over the major issues of international economic governance. The last few years have served to demonstrate the big difference in their approaches to financing the developing world, as the China Development Bank has started to challenge the enormous political and economic influence of the World Bank. Yet, over time, this could be an area where the two sides end up with a more similar viewpoint.

For the Washington-based institutions, the obvious first step would be to abandon the charade of awarding the top jobs only to Westerners—the Americans currently get the leadership of the World Bank, while the Europeans have a hold on the post of managing director of the IMF. In order to remain relevant, the Bank and the Fund need to find ways to engage not just China but the other large developing countries, many of whom are deeply ambivalent about them. Opening up the leadership-selection process would be one obvious step. Competition from China will also likely lead to a gradual shift in philosophy. The World Bank and IMF have already been forced over the last decade into a thorough re-examination of some of the more rigid orthodoxies from the 1990s that were so heavily criticized after the Asia crisis. Whereas once they pushed for rapid budget cuts in the event of economic problems, the World Bank has become more sensitive to the importance of maintaining health care and other public goods. But there is still something to be learned from the Chinese emphasis on providing finance for the kinds of projects, including infrastructure, that the borrowing countries actually want to do.

China, too, is likely to find that its approach shifts. In a short space of time, China has issued a large volume of loans, mostly to countries with which it has quite shallow relations and only modest understanding. This lending boom has also taken place during one of the biggest bull markets in commodities the world has ever seen. Many of the Chinese loans are backed by oil, copper, or some other natural resource, which gives the Chinese banks the impression of complete security. But if commodity prices ever start to fall sharply and these economies suffer serious financial difficulties, there is a good chance that China will begin to suffer some defaults on its loans. Chinese bankers will learn the harsh lesson about all those difficult conditions that the World Bank and IMF attach to their loans: these conditions may force governments to adopt the sorts of free-market policies that Washington likes, but they are also partly designed to ensure the banks actually get repaid. If China is hit with a wave of defaults, its banks are likely to start paying a lot more attention to the way their clients are actually governed. The most likely candidate for a showdown could well be Venezuela, a country with incredibly opaque finances and looming economic problems, which is by far China Development Bank's biggest client. Even before the death of Hugo Chávez, CDB had realized it needed to be more hands-on in its approach to Caracas. The former CDB boss Chen Yuan at one stage presented Chávez with a six-hundred-page book of recommendations for how to run its economy. With Chávez no longer around, there is considerable uncertainty about the country's political future. It is possible that a revived opposition in Venezuela could seek to make the loans now owed to China into a political issue, just as the World Bank and IMF have often become political targets in the past in Latin America.

Even the recent explosion in dam building could become a source of compromise. After initially despairing at the way Chinese money had completely neutered the campaign against dams, Peter Bosshard at International Rivers is now trying to find a middle ground between the Chinese and Western approaches. Before the Chinese became so influential, his usual tactic would have been to put pressure on the financial backers of a dam-building project, but neither China Eximbank nor China Development Bank needs to go to international capital markets to get their funds, which meant there were no investors or partner banks he could lean on. With his leverage gone, he decided to engage. Bosshard started to visit China and talk with local NGOs, who he thought could become useful allies. He also tried to meet some of the companies involved in the industry. On his second trip to China, in 2006, he got a call out of the blue from China Eximbank, which was then bankrolling much of China's overseas dam building, asking him to come and meet its chairman, Li Ruogu. It was almost certainly the first-ever meeting between a Western, campaigning NGO and the head of a large state-owned bank.

Li Ruogu, a former deputy governor of the central bank and one of China's leading financial officials, has a reputation as something of a bully. But on the day when Bosshard was due to meet him, Li was suffering from a bad cold and had partly lost his voice, so he opened the meeting by asking Bosshard to outline his concerns. Then Li started to talk. Bosshard assumed he was about to hear the sort of evasions he used to get from Western banks in the 1980s and 1990s, to the effect that environmental and human-rights concerns were not really the responsibility of a bank. Instead, he received a lecture on how China had developed its economy using precisely these types of projects. "Li said that the bank had some responsibility for the social and environmental aspects of the projects it took on, but he also told me that China had needed to first grow out of poverty before it could start to worry about the environment," Bosshard says. "He said that China would not stand in the way of other developing countries that were trying to do the same thing. China was not just lending them money—it was exporting its development experience." At the end of the meeting, Li proposed a sort of informal collaboration. He said he would send a team to investigate problems at the Merowe Dam in Sudan and other cases brought up by Bosshard. But he asked that Bosshard talk to him before making any more public criticisms. Although he was aware that he risked being muzzled, Bosshard agreed. "If we believe that people are listening to us, that is not really a problem," he says, in justification of his acceptance of the deal.

The private dialogue with China Eximbank lasted for about a year. In May 2007, the African Development Bank held its annual meeting in Shanghai, another striking indicator of the new economic symbiosis between China and Africa. Bosshard decided to bring along two activists, one from the Merowe region of Sudan and the other from Mozambique, where Eximbank had signed another controversial dam-building agreement. He tried to organize a chance for them to talk to officials at the bank about their experiences, but after a lot of delaying, Eximbank declined to arrange a meeting. So Bosshard went to the media instead, offering a session with his two African visitors to the Shanghai Foreign Correspondents Club. Eximbank was furious and has not spoken to International Rivers since.

After falling out with China Eximbank, Bosshard began a similar dialogue with Sinohydro, the biggest dam-builder in the world. International Rivers has been discussing with the company a new policy of environmental guidelines. Sinohydro has ordered that all its overseas subsidiaries must use Chinese environmental law if they are working in countries that have weaker regulation, which Bosshard says could be an important step forward. He says they are taking it more slowly this time, after the bust-up with Eximbank, to see what sort of response the NGO gets from the company. But the revealing aspect of Bosshard's attempt to engage with China's hydropower sector is the way it has started to change some of his own views on dams and economic development. Bosshard is now married to a Chinese woman, and when I met him in Beijing, he had just come back from spending Chinese New Year with her family in Benxi, a rough mining town in the northeast. Even there, he said, it was clear how life has improved for the residents as a result of the booming economy. Western NGOs can be so focused on their particular human-rights or environmental issues, he says, that they can sometimes forget that economic growth is also a prerequisite for improving the welfare of ordinary people. He has not altered his views on the need to have much greater social and environmental protections attached to large dams, but he has come to see how major infrastructure projects do not always end up as huge boondoggles that hurt the poor. If well executed, they can have a major impact on the broader economy. "The years we have spent coming to China have definitely persuaded us that things are more complicated than we thought," he admits.

––––––––

Working more with China is one approach. At other times, the U.S. will need to work around Beijing. In a contest for influence, the country that prevails will be the one that manages to draw a larger number of other governments to its side. By building strong coalitions of support on specific issues, Washington can shape Chinese behavior, even in areas where they do not agree.

This approach is already being used in trade policy. As well as the Trans-Pacific Partnership (TPP), the trade agreement that brings together a group of countries from Asia and the Americas, the U.S. is also negotiating a trade agreement with the European Union which would unite into one economic zone 40 percent of the world's GDP. The two negotiations have a powerful theme in common: they are partly designed to take on Chinese state capitalism. The agendas of both agreements cover subjects like intellectual-property protection, generous financial subsidies, protection of foreign investment, and labor rights— precisely the areas that are becoming so contentious because of China's model of doing business. American negotiators see these agreements as a firewall against what they describe as Chinese abuse of trade rules. If Washington can get enough of the most important economies in the world to sign up for this sort of trade agreement, it can effectively set standards for the way international trade is conducted that China would find very hard to overturn.

These trade talks reflect a very different approach to dealing with China. American officials once talked about encouraging China to be a "responsible stakeholder" in the international system, and in the first year of the Obama administration there was a brief flirtation with a sort of G-2, an informal compact to try and solve some of the world's problems together. But by working around China in this way, Washington is almost trying to present China with a fait accompli. If the international consensus is strong enough, China could risk appearing like a pariah if it tried to resist the new rules. On many of these issues of economic governance, the U.S. is likely to find that the EU shares the exact same concerns—from cyberhacking, which is a huge issue for German manufacturing companies, to fears about Chinese subsidies. As China's economic influence grows, the U.S. and Europe are likely to find greater common ground, although Europe will likely remain divided on how to deal with China.

The talks are also the harbinger of a different way of trying to address global issues. The U.S. used to push its ideas through the ambitious global organizations it set up after the Second World War, including the UN, the World Bank, and the World Trade Organization. But whether it is the prolonged deadlock over the Doha round of trade talks or the endless series of climate-change talks that produce little, there is now a pervasive sense of gloom about the idea of big global agreements. TPP and the U.S.-EU trade talks are a reflection of a more modest approach, the idea that the best way to get things done now is through smaller agreements with like-minded governments, diplomatic coalitions of the willing.

The danger in such an approach, of course, is that it alienates China further and gives it more reason to break with the American-led system. Beijing is frank about what it thinks of the new trade talks. "The U.S. is trying to rewrite global trade rules behind our backs," says one senior Chinese official. A strategy based on sticks alone will likely only create a more frustrated China: Washington also needs to devise some carrots.

————

During the decade when he ran China, Hu Jintao rarely looked more relaxed than on the day he visited a Boeing factory in Seattle in 2006. He smiled broadly, donned a baseball cap with the Boeing logo, and gave a factory supervisor a hug. Hu's speech was somewhat leaden, but he still received a loud round of applause from the workers. As the event was coming to an end, the then head of Boeing's aircraft division, Alan Mulally, put one hand on Hu's shoulder, pumped his fist with the other, and shouted: "China rocks!" Such moments have been rare, however.

It has become so common to talk about the interconnectedness of the U.S. and Chinese economies that it is surprising just how shallow the personal links are in China. For all the powerful financial and trade ties that bind China to the U.S., the number of members of the Chinese elite with a direct stake in the U.S. economy is limited. China may own $2 trillion of U.S. assets, but those investments are handled by the small group of bureaucrats who manage the central bank's reserves. Trade offers a similar story. At least half of China's exports of consumer products are manufactured by foreign-owned companies in China. The number of Chinese firms that rely on the U.S. is much smaller than the headline figures would suggest. Investment has been even shallower. Of all the money that Chinese companies have started to invest in other countries in recent years, only 1 percent has come to the U.S. In terms of big-picture economics, China leans heavily on the U.S., but that does not translate into business careers and life experiences.

The coming wave of overseas Chinese investment is a new opportunity for the U.S. to think about what sort of relationship it really wants to have with China. Given the toxic politics over cybersecurity and the suspicions that Chinese companies enjoy unfair financial advantages, it would be easy to see a repeat of the Japan scare that accompanied Japanese investments in the early 1990s. Some politicians might be tempted to indulge in a round of China bashing. Yet that would be a big mistake. At a time when military rivalry between the two countries is accelerating, and when new economic tensions are swirling, one way to persuade China that the U.S. has no plans for containment would be to roll out the red carpet for Chinese investments that do not have clear national security implications. This is one of the tools America has at its disposal as it tries to influence China's long-term calculations.

The U.S. has an opportunity to build up its own lobby of supporters within the Chinese system. The bosses of the large Chinese state-owned companies are among the most important officials in the country, and if they have a personal stake in continued good relations with the U.S., this can only help Washington. Until China started to play hardball with foreign multinationals, the biggest supporter Beijing had in the U.S. was the business lobby. A surge in Chinese investment would also give the U.S. a bigger window to try and shape the behavior of large

Chinese companies as they become important global players. CNOOC, the oil group which was humiliated in its 2006 effort to buy Unocal, has since then acquired a group of smaller assets in the U.S. One upshot is that CNOOC and the rest of the Chinese oil industry have been relatively cooperative with the U.S. over the issue of Iran sanctions. Chinese companies have not progressed with the large investment deals they had signed in Iran and, under pressure from Washington, they have scaled back imports of oil from Iran. Encouraging Chinese state-owned groups to operate in the U.S. is one way of acquiring a little more leverage over them and the senior party officials who manage the companies.

America, it should be said, also needs the money. There is an odd disconnect between the way some in Washington see Chinese investment and the response in the rest of the country. In 2011, when Hu Jintao visited the U.S., the White House put on a grand state dinner in his honor, yet that evening the leaders of Congress—the speaker and the Senate minority and majority leaders—realized that they had somewhere else they would rather be. Not one wanted to be seen having dinner with the Chinese leader. The next day, Hu went to Chicago, which put on a lavish reception for him in the hope that China would send some investment its way. Richard M. Daley, the mayor and heir to his family's political dynasty in the town, called Hu a "man of vision."

During the 2012 election campaign, Barack Obama and Mitt Romney crisscrossed Ohio, slamming "Chinese cheaters" who were taking American jobs. On the same September day when both candidates were in Toledo, the city's mayor, Michael Bell, was hosting a conference for a group of 150 Chinese businessmen he had invited to try and attract investments. "I have to say, the campaign is really hindering us," Bell told me, referring to both candidates' China bashing. "The Chinese people we invited here are asking, 'Why are you picking on us?' or 'Why are we suddenly the big issue?'" Bell had made three trips to China in the previous two years to solicit investments. (His business card has his name in Chinese on the back.) In turn, he has received thirty different delegations of potential Chinese investors, many of whom have been treated to private performances of the Toledo Symphony.

Toledo is the vision of a rundown Midwestern city. The downtown area has plenty of old warehouses whose windows are boarded up or broken. Nearby, along the river, is a plot of unused land that the City Council has been trying to develop for a decade, only to see two deals with local developers fall through. In 2011, however, two Chinese investors bought the sixty-nine-acre stretch of land for $3.8 million in cash and have announced a $200-million retail-and-residential project on the riverfront plot, which is known as the Marina District. "We are planning on building it into an international city," said Yuan Xiaohong, one of the Chinese investors. Exactly how the project will develop is still not clear, but Mayor Bell thinks the reality is obvious. "There is a difference between the political rhetoric and what is actually happening in the country," says Bell, whose city faces a large budget deficit. "All we are trying to do is to get people to invest in our city."

The tidal wave of Chinese investment is coming. The only question is whether a significant slice of it is directed toward the U.S., or whether China ends up channeling more of its investment toward places like India or Brazil, in a bid to decouple from the U.S. and curry political favor elsewhere. This is a pivotal test for the U.S. It gives the U.S. an opportunity to deepen the links between the two countries, placing new restraints on China's more hawkish elements, and to build up its own vested interest within China. At the same time, if Washington routinely blocks Chinese companies from coming to the U.S., alleging national security and the excessive influence of the Chinese state, it would deeply antagonize Beijing, where large parts of the Chinese establishment would see this as concrete evidence that America is out to curtail its rise and weaken its economy. The rest of the world would interpret a Closed Door policy in America as a major failure of leadership, a sign that Washington was backing away from its basic commitments. America wants to cement its position as the leading power in a new age, and it aspires to continue setting the international agenda. To do so, the U.S. will need to remain open for business, including from China.

Conclusion

WHOSE PROBLEMS would you rather have?

On November 6, 2012, Barack Obama won what was in the end a comfortable re-election, but it followed a dispiriting campaign that rarely lifted above the resentful. Even before his second term began, Obama seemed mired in a never-ending series of budget crises and at the start of an era of grinding cuts. The following week, a new generation of leaders was unveiled in Beijing, the group of seven men who will run the country for the next decade. With the new party boss Xi Jinping at the head of the line, they filed onto a stage in the Great Hall of the People, a row of begonias and ferns separating them from the cameras. Standing in the center of the group, the new leader did not take any questions. Instead, he gave a brief speech laced with a few populist hints, which contrasted with his wooden predecessor but gave away little about his governing philosophy.

There have been three new Chinese leaders since the Tiananmen Square crackdown, and each one has assumed office amid the same sniping prediction in the West that only drastic action can fend off a looming crisis. Yet there does seem to be something different this time, a powerful sensation that China is approaching the end of a road. Chinese officials, scholars, and acquaintances almost universally acknowledge that the economic and political structures that have got them this far so fast are breaking down.

In domestic politics, the party's rigid control on power is being tested by a growing middle class that wants more rule of law and less corruption, by the irreverent irony and indignation of the Internet, and by Beijing's choking pollution. On the economic side, the growth model that relies on funneling cheap bank loans to investment projects is running out of steam and needs to be replaced by more emphasis on consumers. Most of the goals that China has set itself for the coming decades, whether it is encouraging more innovation or winning cultural recognition, are rooted in the initiative of private citizens. The next Chinese era will be less about the state and much more about the individual. Xi's challenge is to chart a series of reforms that start to address these demands without provoking a backlash from the party's many and powerful vested interests. Even in his very careful speech, Xi almost admitted as much. "We are not complacent . . ." he said. "Under the new conditions, our party faces many severe challenges, and there are also many pressing problems within the party that need to be resolved."

The bewildering series of domestic problems may grab all the attention, but this same reform agenda is also the key to unlocking Chinese influence abroad. To win a bigger role in the world, it is not enough to be wealthy; a country also needs to secure trust. Without a political system that embraces a greater degree of pluralism, allows more dissent, and is rooted in the rule of law, China will struggle to get the respect it needs to turn its economic weight into power and influence.

The link between domestic politics and soft power is the most obvious: China will not be truly admired abroad while it shows such disrespect to some of its more impressive citizens. But China's role in global economic affairs is also tied to its politics. The status of reserve currency is ultimately a question of trust and credibility. Having the biggest economy is an important but not sufficient condition. For the world's central banks to invest heavily in a currency, they must have a high level of confidence about why and how important decisions are made, a comfort that China does not yet provide.

The same goes for the PLA. China's military buildup was always bound to arouse intense suspicion in its Asian backyard, but the closed, opaque nature of the Chinese political system only adds to these tensions. The lack of transparency about its military spending, the absence of real discussion about China's long-term, strategic objectives, and the

PLA's ambiguous status within the country all make suspicion inevitable. Given such uncertainties, neighbors are forced to respond to China's rapidly expanding capabilities, not its intentions, which remain unclear. Over the last few years, China has contented itself by winning small tactical victories that advance its territorial claims, but in the process has sown even greater mistrust.

Ultimately, China's brittle domestic politics, with its squalls of nationalist anger, undermine its ability to forge the sorts of relationships with the peoples of other nations that are the route to enduring influence. The real way to alter the balance of power in Asia at the expense of the U.S. is not for China to bully its neighbors over small islands, but to win the lasting confidence of their populations. Instead, China has been doing the opposite.

The U.S. is also entering a critical period in which its economic problems are starting to undermine its role in the world. If the American economy remains sluggish and unemployment stays high, both allies and rivals will question its ability to meet future commitments. Indeed, the contest for influence that is emerging between the U.S. and China will be partly answered by the way both governments respond to the sense of malaise they both face. I am probably not the only person who has two mental lists about America's economic future, unsure on any given day which is correct. On the pessimistic list, there is a familiar litany of problems, including rising debt and health-care costs, stagnant wages, inequality, crumbling infrastructure, failing schools, and a pervasive sense that Washington politics will prevent any real solutions from emerging. On the other side of the ledger is the potential energy boom, the universities that attract the world's best and brightest, the unique ability to commercialize innovations, a cheaper currency, and the potential that the U.S., in the words of Australian Foreign Minister Bob Carr, is "only one budget deal away" from ending all the talk of decline. The single most important thing the U.S. can do to enhance its influence overseas is to get its domestic house in order.

The management of the domestic economy is so important because one of the central priorities for the U.S. in Asia is to demonstrate a sense of staying power. A large number of the tensions with China in recent years are rooted in the Chinese perception that the U.S. is in decline—

a view that was almost uniform in 2008 and which is still strong today. The best way to sway Chinese behavior and to deter adventurism is to demonstrate that the U.S. is not going anywhere. That means maintaining a robust military presence in the region, although without the sort of rapid buildup that would provoke China. It also means constructing a convincing long-term economic agenda that ties the U.S. to Asia.

A second priority is the patient, long-term task of fostering new partners in Asia and elsewhere who will support a U.S.-led order. The core ideas that the U.S. has promoted since the end of the Second World War—free trade, freedom of navigation, and open government—remain popular. But in a world where American dominance is being replaced by a more uncertain balance of power, the careful diplomacy of building different coalitions of support will become the deciding factor. The U.S. will sometimes have to take a backseat as other countries pick up the baton, an approach that some might even be inclined to call leading from behind. In Asia, China's belligerence over the past few years has done a lot of America's diplomatic work for it, allowing it to shore up alliances and strengthen other friendships. But even in Asia, managing these alliances will require skillful diplomacy that persuades other countries to do more to defend themselves.

Over time, the U.S. and China will eventually have to find a way to live together in the western Pacific, to establish a middle ground that respects each other's security interests. Before then, there is likely to be a lot of tension, and potentially some brinkmanship. But if Washington is successful in demonstrating staying power and in finding new sources of support, it will be in a much stronger position to influence China's choices and to steer Beijing away from a broader confrontation.

ACKNOWLEDGMENTS

First-time authors always underestimate the amount of effort and time that goes into writing a book, and I was no exception. But along the way, I had the immense good fortune to receive the help of some of the best professionals in the industry. Sarah Chalfant at the Wylie Agency was extremely generous with her time and indispensable with her advice: without her, my initial ideas would never have made it into print. Her colleague James Pullen was also endlessly helpful.

Through Sarah, I was lucky enough to meet Andrew Miller at Knopf, an incisive and perceptive editor, who provided just the right combination of support and pressure that any writer needs. I also owe huge thanks to his colleague Mark Chiusano for all his assistance and comments.

I would like to thank Lionel Barber, the editor of the *Financial Times,* for his indulgence during the writing of the book. I also received enormous help from a number of other colleagues at the *FT,* including Richard McGregor, Demetri Sevastopulo, David Pilling, Jamil Anderlini, and Kathrin Hille. During my years in China, I was fortunate to work closely with a number of Chinese journalists, without whom I really would have been lost and to whom I owe a special thanks—Helena Yu, Zhang Chenhao, Yang Jie, and Zhao Xue.

During the course of my research, I have benefited from the advice and wisdom of countless people, including good friends with whom I have talked regularly and occasional acquaintances whose insights I value highly. They include, in no particular order, Arthur Kroeber, Shi Yinhong, Joerg Wuttke, Jeff Wasserstrom, David Shambaugh, Shen Dingli, Stephanie Kleine-Ahlbrandt, Geoff Wade, Jim Holmes, Zhu

Feng, Bonnie Glaser, Chu Shulong, Chip Gregson, Michael Auslin, Jin Canrong, Mark Leonard, Andrew Small, Mike Green, Zha Daojiong, Paul Haenle, Chris Nelson, and Yan Xuetong.

Finally, I would like to thank my parents, Iain and Anne, for all their help in the early stages and my wife, Angelica, for her love and support. Without her, I really would never have made it through.

NOTES

INTRODUCTION

4 "remarkable symbols of China's defense muscle": http://news.xinhuanet.com/english/2009–10/01/content _ 12146098.htm.

5 the spontaneous greeting was restaged and edited: Geremie Barmé, "Chinese Military Parades," *East Asia Forum,* Oct. 31, 2009.

8 "No nation has ever experienced": Henry Kissinger, *Diplomacy* (New York: Simon & Schuster, 1995), p. 37.

10 "The veneration of an abstract idea": Fareed Zakaria, *The Post-American World* (New York: W. W. Norton, 2008), p. 125.

14 "Wall Street's crack-up": David Roche, "Another Empire Bites the Dust," *Far Eastern Economic Review,* Oct. 2008.

1 CHINA TAKES TO THE NEAR SEAS

21 "This is the most important communication": Walter Isaacson, *Kissinger* (New York: Simon & Schuster, 1992), p. 333.

24 "the great revitalization of the Chinese nation": quoted in Toshi Yoshihara and James R. Holmes, *Red Star over the Pacific* (Annapolis, Md.: Naval Institute Press, 2010), p. 64.

24 "When we look at history": Luo Yuan, "Call from Blue Sea to Protect the Development Interests of the Country," *Liaowang,* Feb. 9, 2009.

25 "Ignoring the oceans": quoted in Robert S. Ross, "China's Naval Nationalism," *International Security,* vol. 34, no. 2 (Fall 2009), pp. 46–81.

25 "Restricting China to the shallow seas": Zhang Wenmu, "Back to Yalta: A Roadmap for Sino-US Relations," *China Security,* issue no. 19, 2012.

28 "I am . . . devouring Captain Mahan's book": quoted in Robert K. Massie, *Dreadnought* (New York: Random House, 1991), p. 75.

28 "really responsible for the German Navy": *New York Times,* Dec. 2, 1914 (accessed at http://www.nytimes.com/learning/general/onthisday/bday/0927.html).

28 "Mahan was one of the causes": quoted in *Makers of Modern Strategy from Machiavelli to the Nuclear Age,* ed. Peter Paret with collaboration of Gordon A. Craig and Felix Gilbert (Princeton, N.J.: Princeton University Press, 1986), p. 474.

28 "A big country that builds": quoted in Yoshihara and Holmes, *Red Star over the Pacific*, p. 20.

29 "His sea power philosophy remains hypnotic": ibid., p. 18.

30 "China is knowingly, operationally and incrementally": transcript available at http://www.china-business-intelligence.com/content/transcript-remarks-capt-james-fanell-pacfleet.

32 "You, the US, take Hawaii East": quoted in Manu Pubby, "China Proposed Division of Pacific, Indian Ocean Regions, We Declined: US Admiral," *The Indian Express*, May 15, 2009.

33 "The commerce and command of the Pacific": quoted in Bruce Cumings, *Dominion from Sea to Sea* (New Haven, Conn.: Yale University Press, 2009), p. 138.

33 "U.S. does not hold its ground in the Pacific": *Lee Kuan Yew: Grand Master's Insights on China, the United States and the World*, interviews and selections by Graham Allison and Robert D. Blackwill (Cambridge, Mass.: MIT Press, 2012), p. 35.

37 "The navy of any great power": Mure Dickie and Kathrin Hille, "Chinese Army Turns on Charm," *Financial Times*, Nov. 16, 2008.

41 "If the U.S. can light a fire": Chris Buckley, "China PLA Officer Urges Challenging U.S. Dominance," *Reuters*, Feb. 28, 2010.

42 "the fundamental anti-Chinese force": Lyle Goldstein, "Chinese Naval Strategy in the South China Sea: An Abundance of Noise and Smoke, but Little Fire," *Contemporary Southeast Asia*, vol. 33, no. 3, p. 330.

45 "Deng had to explain": Ezra F. Vogel, *Deng Xiaoping and the Transformation of China* (Cambridge, Mass.: Harvard University Press, 2011), p. 578.

47 a Chinese "anti-navy": Andrew S. Erickson, U.S. Naval War College, "Are China's Near Seas 'Anti-Navy' Capabilities Aimed Directly at the United States?" June 14, 2012 article (http://www.informationdissemination.net/2012/06/are-chinas-near-seas-anti-navy.html).

48 "We want to spoof them": Spencer Ackerman, "How to Kill China's Carrier-Killer Missile": *Wired*, March 16, 2012.

2 THE LURE OF THE INDIAN OCEAN

52 The Battle of Ramree Island is better known: *Guinness Book of World Records*, 2012.

55 "No great power that has become a strong power": quoted in Robert S. Ross, "China's Naval Nationalism: Sources, Prospects, and the U.S. Response," *International Security*, vol. 34, no. 2 (Fall 2009), p. 69.

56 the same sort of "naval nationalism": ibid., pp. 46–81.

58 formed a "String of Pearls": "China Builds Up Strategic Sea Lanes," *Washington Times*, Jan. 17, 2005.

60 the government had asked China: "Pakistan Turns to China for Naval Base," *Financial Times*, May 22, 2011.

60 A peacetime naval strategy: Alfred Thayer Mahan, *The Influence of Sea Power upon History, 1660–1783* (Boston: Little, Brown, and Company, 1898), p. 22.

60 Secretary of State Hamilton Fish described Hawaii: quoted in Niall Ferguson, *Colossus: The Price of America's Empire* (New York: Penguin, 2004), p. 46.

65 "Rivalry has been a defining element": for more on India's looming naval rivalry with China, see C. Raja Mohan, *Samudra Manthan: Sino-Indian Rivalry in the*

Indo-Pacific (Washington, D.C.: Carnegie Endowment for International Peace, 2012).

3 THE ASIAN BACKLASH

71 **It settled the outstanding land-border disputes:** see M. Taylor Fravel, *Strong Borders, Secure Nation* (Princeton, N.J.: Princeton University Press, 2008).

72 **The mood toward China shifted:** see Joshua Kurlantzick, *Charm Offensive* (New Haven, Conn.: Yale University Press, 2007).

73 **"sometimes looked like a French bedroom farce":** Walter Russell Mead, *Via Meadia,* Sept. 26, 2010 (http://blogs.the-american-interest.com/wrm/2010/09/26/in-the-footsteps-of-the-kaiser-china-boosts-us-power-in-asia).

76 **Zheng He's fifteenth-century armadas:** Louise Levathes, *When China Ruled the Seas* (New York: Simon & Schuster, 1994), p. 20.

78 **"China's neighbors recognized the preponderance":** David C. Kang, *China Rising* (New York: Columbia University Press, 2007), p. 50.

78 **"Creating a community is easy":** Parag Khanna, *The Second World* (New York: Random House, 2008), p. 262.

79 **exercise in "shock and awe":** Geoffrey Wade, "The Zheng He Voyages: A Reassessment," Asian Research Institute working paper no. 31, National University of Singapore, Oct. 2004.

83 **"Japan and China now stand at ground zero":** Yoichi Funabashi, letter, *East Asia Forum,* Oct. 20, 2010.

90 **brings together oil, fish, and the potent nationalism:** see International Crisis Group, "Stirring Up the South China Sea (II)," Asia report no. 229, July 24, 2012.

91 **"China is not the maker of these problems":** Jane Perlez, "Political Worries in U.S. and China Color Obama Aide's Beijing Visit," *New York Times,* July 25, 2012.

91 **"There is no arable land here":** Patrick Boehler, "South China Sea City 'Could Become Chinese Business Hub,'" *Asian Correspondent,* March 10, 2013.

92 **government bureaucracies have overlapping:** see International Crisis Group, "Stirring Up the South China Sea (I)," Asia report no. 223, April 23, 2012.

93 **"Grab what you can on the sea":** ibid.

94 **"China's . . . 'blue-colored land' ":** Peng Guangqian, "China's Maritime Rights and Interests," in *Military Activities in the EEZ,* ed. Peter Dutton (Newport, R.I.: U.S. Naval War College, 2010), p. 15.

95 **"core interest":** "Chinese Military Seeks to Extend Its Naval Power," *New York Times,* April 23, 2010.

97 **publicly declare himself a "Monroista":** Tereza Maria Spyer Dulci, "O panamericanismo em Joaquim Nabuco e Olivera Lima," *Anais Eletrônicos do VII Encontro Internacional da ANPHLAC,* 2006.

100 **a role somewhat similar to France's:** David Uren, "Shifting Sands of Diplomacy," *Australian,* June 2, 2012.

100 **"while also preparing to deploy force":** "US Embassy Cables: Hillary Clinton Ponders US Relationship with Its Chinese 'Banker,'" *Guardian,* Dec. 4, 2010.

101 **"we are just an independent arts organisation":** "Chinese Hack Film Festival Site," *BBC News,* July 26, 2009 (news.bbc.co.uk/2/hi/8169123.stm).

101 **"America faces a choice of Euclidian clarity":** Hugh White, "Power Shift: Australia's Future Between Washington and Beijing," *Quarterly Essay,* issue no. 39, Sept. 2010.

102   **"the single, stupidest strategic document":** Greg Sheridan, "Distorted Vision of Future US-China Relations," *Australian,* Sept. 11, 2010.

103   **A caption at the Shaanxi History Museum:** Ross Terrill, *The New Chinese Empire* (New York: Basic Books, 2003), p. 45.

105   **Hanoi had been "too soft" on China:** "Patriotic Personalities Make Proposals on Defense and Development," *Vietnamnet,* July 16, 2011.

4 AMERICA'S CHOICE

115   **cover story for *The Atlantic*:** Robert Kaplan, "How We Would Fight China," *Atlantic,* June 1, 2005.

116   **"we own the sea":** CNO's Sailing Directions, Sept. 27, 2011.

117   **"blinding campaign":** AirSea Battle: A Point-of-Departure Operational Concept, Center for Strategic and Budgetary Assessments, May 2010.

117   **in the event of a conflict:** "Joint Operational Access Concept," Department of Defense, Jan. 17, 2012.

118   **"preposterously expensive":** Greg Jaffe, "U.S. Model for a Future War Fans Tensions with China and Inside Pentagon, *Washington Post,* August 1, 2012.

120   **"war limited by contingent":** Toshi Yoshihara and James R. Holmes, "Asymmetric Warfare, American Style," *U.S. Naval Institute Proceedings Magazine,* vol. 138, no. 4 (April 2012), p. 1310.

120   **In the event of a broader conflict:** see T. X. Hammes, "Offshore Control: A Proposed Strategy for an Unlikely Conflict," strategic forum no. 278, National Defense University, June 28, 2012.

122   **"big, expensive, vulnerable":** Henry Hendrix, "At What Cost a Carrier?" Center for a New American Security Disruptive Defense Papers, March 2013.

133   **"I informed the government":** "Eleven CEO: Amazing Changes in Myanmar," *Nation* (Thailand), May 14, 2012.

134   **"an explicit American project":** Henry Kissinger, *On China* (New York: Penguin, 2011), p. 526.

135   **U.S. military has reopened links:** Joshua Kurlantzick, "The Moral and Strategic Blindspot in Obama's Pivot to Asia," *New Republic,* Nov. 20, 2012.

136   **he visited Washington at the invitation of the Johnson administration:** Thant Myint-U, *Where China Meets India: Burma and the New Crossroads of Asia* (New York: Farrar, Straus and Giroux, 2011).

5 CHINA'S BRITTLE NATIONALISM

142   **China's pre-Olympics burst of learning English:** Evan Osnos, "Crazy English," *The New Yorker,* Apr. 28, 2008.

142   **posted pictures on the Internet:** "American Woman Gives Domestic Abuse a Face, and Voice, in China," NPR, Feb. 7, 2013.

144   **"The West is central to the construction":** Peter Hays Gries, *China's New Nationalism: Pride, Politics, and Diplomacy* (Berkeley: University of California Press, 2004), p. 35.

146   **Elgin had been dispatched to China:** Elgin's time in China is particularly well told in Stephen R. Platt, *Autumn in the Heavenly Kingdom* (New York: Alfred A. Knopf, 2012), pp. 25–32, 164–68.

147   **"We have often acted towards the Chinese":** ibid., p. 29.

149 "I am familiar with the history of foreign aggression": quoted in Suzanne Xiao Yang, *China in the UN Security Council Decision-Making on Iraq* (New York: Routledge, 2013), p. 218.

150 **To mark the 150th anniversary:** William A. Callahan, *China: The Pessoptimist Nation* (Oxford, U.K.: Oxford University Press, 2010), p. 38.

151 **"It is 1999, not 1899":** Han Zhongkun, "China, Not in 1899," *People's Daily,* May 12, 1999.

152 **blind nationalism and anti-foreigner sentiment:** Yuan Weishi, "Modernization and History Textbooks," *Freezing Point,* Jan. 11, 2006 (trans. available at http://www.zonaeuropa.com/20060126 _ 1.htm).

153 **"It would not be an exaggeration":** Callahan, *China,* p. 28.

154 **"youth, internationalism, and violence":** Rana Mitter, *A Bitter Revolution: China's Struggle with the Modern World* (New York: Oxford University Press, 2005), p. 11.

155 **the State Department classified its copy:** Jonathan Fenby, *Generalissimo: Chiang Kai-Shek and the China He Lost* (New York: Free Press, 2003), p. 401.

155 **"as familiar to Chinese schoolchildren":** Paul Cohen, *Speaking to History: The Story of King Goujian in Twentieth-Century China* (Berkeley: University of California Press, 2009), p. xix.

163 **"The humiliations of the past":** Ian Buruma, "Why They Hate Japan," *New York Review of Books,* Sept. 21, 2006.

164 **"How could Japanese imperialism dare":** Kirk A. Denton, "Heroic Resistance and Victims of Atrocity: Negotiating the Memory of Japanese Imperialism in Chinese Museums," *Japan Focus,* Oct. 17, 2007.

165 **"It was an extraordinary outpouring":** Interview with James Miles (http://www.cnn.com/2008/WORLD/asiapcf/03/20/tibet.miles.interview/index.html).

166 **"The question that now faces China's leaders":** Robert Barnett, "Thunder from Tibet," *New York Review of Books,* May 29, 2008.

172 **"simultaneous superficiality and depth":** quoted in Paul A. Cohen, *China Unbound: Evolving Perspectives on the Chinese Past* (London: Routledge Curzon, 2003), p. 164.

6 SOFT POWER

176 **"While our media empires are melting away":** David Barboza, "China Puts Best Face Forward in New English-Language Channel," *New York Times,* July 2, 2010.

177 **"lost the whole game due to a flaw in its soft power":** quoted in *Chinese Soft Power and Its Implications for the United States,* ed. Carola McGiffert (Washington, D.C.: CSIS, 2009), p. 13.

179 **what he calls "humane authority":** Yan Xuetong, *Ancient Chinese Thought, Modern Chinese Power,* ed. Daniel Bell and Sun Zhe (Princeton, N.J.: Princeton University Press, 2011), chaps. 1–3.

179 **"battle for the hearts and minds":** Yan Xuetong, "How China Can Defeat America," *New York Times,* Nov. 20, 2011.

180 **"The Chinese have always prided themselves":** Wang Gungwu, "China Rises Again," *YaleGlobal,* March 25, 2009.

181 **Zhao Tingyang is more oblique:** see Zhao Tingyang, "A Political World Philosophy in Terms of All-Under-Heaven (Tian-Xia)," *Diogenes,* vol. 221 (2009), pp. 5–18.

182   **"to love China, to long for China"**: Interview with Zhang Jigang, trans. *China Digital Times* from *PLA Times*, Aug. 1, 2008 (http://chinadigitaltimes.net/ 2008/08/interview-with-zhang-jigang-deputy-director-of-the-beijing-olympics -opening-ceremony/).

184   **"If Westerners feel dazed and confused"**: Nicolai Ouroussoff, "In Changing Face of Beijing, a Look at the New China," *New York Times,* July 13, 2008.

184   **"the most serious challenge"**: Ian Buruma, "China's Dark Triumph," *Los Angeles Times,* Jan. 13, 2008.

188   **"What we are left with"**: Robert Bridge, "America: Drugged Up, Dumbed Down and Crazy Dangerous," *Russia Today,* June 21, 2012.

193   **"Right now, foreigners are awarding Liu Xiaobo"**: Barbara Demick, "Chinese Dissident in U.S. Tells of Harassment, Torture," *Los Angeles Times,* Jan. 18, 2012.

196   **"a cause of a psychological disorder"**: Julia Lovell, *The Politics of Cultural Capital: China's Quest for a Nobel Prize in Literature* (Honolulu: University of Hawai'i Press, 2006), p. 4.

197   **" 'Mo Yan is a state writer' "**: quoted in Didi Kirsten Tatlow, "The Writer, the State and the Nobel," *International Herald Tribune,* Oct. 12, 2012.

7 "WE ARE NOT THE WORLD'S SAVIOR"

201   **If the twentieth century saw fierce ideological battles**: see James Traub, "The World According to China," *New York Times,* Sept. 3, 2006.

202   **"an intense desire among humiliated peoples"**: Pankaj Mishra, "America's Inevitable Retreat from the Middle East," *New York Times,* Sept. 23, 2012.

204   **"the most significant adjustment to national sovereignty"**: quoted in Lloyd Axworthy and Allan Rock, "The Unfulfilled Promise of UN Protection," *Globe and Mail,* Sept. 15, 2010.

208   **"Syria tells us that the era of humanitarian intervention"**: Michael Ignatieff, "How Syria Divided the World," *New York Review of Books,* July 11, 2012.

208   **she was known as Estela**: Simon Romero, "Leader's Torture in the '70s Stirs Ghosts in Brazil," *New York Times,* Aug. 4, 2012.

215   **he presented his Chinese hosts with two documents**: first told in International Crisis Group, "China's New Courtship in South Sudan," Africa report no. 186, April 4, 2012.

220   **Two Chinese engineers were on hand**: Jon Lee Anderson, "A History of Violence," *New Yorker,* July 23, 2012.

220   **the partition of Sudan was only the start**: see ICG, "China's New Courtship in South Sudan."

221   **"We are bystanders"**: ibid.

8 TAKING ON THE DOLLAR

228   **"We could be on the verge of a financial revolution"**: Robert Cookson and Geoff Dyer, "Currencies: Yuan Direction," *Financial Times,* Dec. 13, 2010.

228   **"the premier reserve currency"**: Arvind Subramanian, "Renminbi Rules: The Conditional Imminence of the Reserve Currency Transition," Peterson Institute for International Economics, working paper 11-14, Sept. 2011.

229   **"The real challenge to American and Western strategy"**: Edward Luttwak, "National Strategy: The Turning Point," Sept. 8, 2010 (http://www.abc.net.au/ unleashed/29746.html).

229 **"the fall of the dollar as the global reserve currency"**: National Intelligence Council, "Global Trends 2030: Alternative Worlds." Dec. 10, 2012.

232 **"How do you deal toughly with your banker?"**: Ewen MacAskill, "WikiLeaks: Hillary Clinton's Question: How Can We Stand Up to Beijing?" *Guardian*, Dec. 4, 2010.

232 **"Never before has the United States"**: Brad Setser, "China's $1.5 Trillion Bet," Council on Foreign Relations working paper, May 2009.

233 **"bargaining chip"**: Michael Pettis, "The 'Nuclear Threat' of Chinese Reserves," Aug. 8, 2007 (http://www.mpettis.com/2007/08/08/the-nuclear-threat-of-chinese -reserves/).

233 **"I won't say *kowtow*"**: James Fallows, "Be Nice to the Countries That Lend you Money," *The Atlantic Monthly*, Dec. 1, 2008.

235 **The harsh reality for China**: see Daniel W. Drezner, "Bad Debts: Assessing China's Financial Influence in Great Power Politics," vol. 34, no. 2 (Fall 2009) *International Security*, pp. 7–45.

236 **"disconnected to individual nations"**: Zhou Xiaochuan: "Reform the International Monetary System: Essay by Dr. Zhou Xiaochuan, Governor of the People's Bank of China," March 23, 2009 (http://www.bis.org/review/r090402c.pdf).

237 **"the financial crisis . . . let us clearly see"**: Geoff Dyer, David Pilling, and Henny Sender, "A Strategy to Straddle the Planet," *Financial Times*, Jan. 17, 2011.

237 **"The shortcomings of the current"**: quoted in Alan Wheatley, "China's Currency Foray Augurs Geopolitical Strains," Reuters, Oct. 3, 2012.

237 **"China becoming a nuclear power"**: quoted in "Redbacks for Greenbacks: Internationalising the Renminbi," European Council on Foreign Relations (http://ecfr.eu/content/entry/redbacks_for_greenbacks_the_internationalision _of_the_renminbi).

241 **just one decade after the bill was passed**: Barry Eichengreen, *Exorbitant Privilege* (New York: Oxford University Press, 2011), chap. 2.

243 **With the value of sterling plummeting**: ibid., p. 29.

9 POST-AMERICAN GLOBALIZATION

253 **"Fate has written our policy for us"**: quoted in Howard Zinn, *The Twentieth Century: A People's History* (New York: HarperCollins, 1980), p. 4.

256 **"There is an enormous highway developing"**: interview with Charlie Rose, Feb. 8, 2010 (http://www.charlierose.com/download/transcript/10851).

259 **he realized there was a huge opportunity for China**: see Erica Downs, *Inside China Inc* (Washington, D.C.: Brookings Institution, 2011).

262 **"China was getting a discount on finance the country needed"**: see also Deborah Brautigam, *The Dragon's Gift: The Real Story of China in Africa* (Oxford, U.K.: Oxford University Press, 2011).

262 **one of the company's computers would send a large packet**: the Nortel hacking case was first detailed in Siobhan Gorman, "Chinese Hackers Suspected in Long-Term Nortel Breach," *Wall Street Journal*, Feb. 14, 2012.

263 **"What has been happening"**: Michael Riley and John Walcott, "China-Based Hacking of 760 Companies Shows Cyber Cold War," Bloomberg, Dec. 14, 2011.

268 **presented Chávez with a six-hundred-page book**: Henry Sanderson and Michael Forsythe, "Hugo's Banker," *Foreign Policy*, March 7, 2013.

CONCLUSION

277   **"We are not complacent"**: "China Unveils New Leadership Team with Xi at the Helm," Agence Presse France, Nov. 15, 2012.

278   **"only one budget deal away"**: Maggie Haberman, "With Bob Carr's Permission," *Politico*, July 22, 2012.

BIBLIOGRAPHIC ESSAY

There is a rich literature that provides the background for the impact of China on Asia's politics and military balance. The expansion of China's influence during the period from the Asia crisis of the 1990s to the 2008 financial crisis is described in different and interesting ways in David Shambaugh, ed., *China Engages Asia* (Cambridge, Mass.: MIT Press 2005); David C. Kang, *China Rising* (New York: Columbia University Press, 2007); and Joshua Kurlantzick, *Charm Offensive* (New Haven, Conn.: Yale University Press, 2007). Ross Terrill's *The New Chinese Empire* (New York: Basic Books, 2003) provides rich insights into China's historical legacy in the region. Hugh White's essay "Power Shift" (*Quarterly Essay*, issue no. 39, Sept. 2010), which lays out many of the strategic issues now facing the region in a lucid manner, has been published in book form as *The China Choice* (Collingwood, Australia: Black Inc., 2012).

The growing strategic importance of the Indian Ocean is beautifully told in Robert D. Kaplan, *Monsoon: The Indian Ocean and the Future of American Power* (New York: Random House, 2010). China's complex links with Burma are outlined by Thant Myint-U in *Where China Meets India: Burma and the New Crossroads of Asia* (New York: Farrar, Straus and Giroux, 2011). The single best source for information on maritime disputes involving China is the reports of the International Crisis Group, notably "Stirring Up the South China Sea" (pt. I, Asia report no. 223, April 2012; pt. II, Asia report no. 229, July 2012).

The US Naval War College's James R. Holmes and Toshi Yoshihara have produced a series of writings over the last decade that lift the lid on China's growing naval fascination, including *Red Star over the Pacific* (Annapolis, Md.: Naval Institute Press, 2010). Their colleague at the Naval War College Andrew S. Erickson is another source of great insight into the capabilities of the Chinese military (his writings are collected at www.andrewerickson.com).

China's revival of "national humiliation" education is well told by both William A. Callahan in *The Pessoptimist Nation* (Oxford: Oxford University Press, 2010) and Zheng Wang in *Never Forget National Humiliation* (New York: Columbia University Press, 2012). For the growth in nationalism over the last two decades, see also Peter Hays Gries, *China's New Nationalism* (Berkeley: University of California Press, 2004), and Christopher R. Hughes, *Chinese Nationalism in the Global Era* (New York: Routledge, 2004). For the debates at the UN over Sudan and the "Responsibility to Protect," see James Traub, *The Best Intentions: Kofi Annan and the UN in the Era of American World Power* (New York: Farrar, Straus and Giroux, 2006).

The risk of imperial overstretch has been widely chronicled over the last few decades, from Paul Kennedy's *The Rise and Fall of the Great Powers* (New York: Random House, 1987) to David P. Calleo's *The Imperious Economy* (Cambridge, Mass.: Harvard University Press, 1982). But the best introduction to the contemporary dilemmas facing the U.S. dollar and the Chinese renminbi is Barry Eichengreen's *Exorbitant Privilege* (New York: Oxford University Press, 2011).

INDEX

Page numbers beginning with 283 refer to endnotes.

ABB Group, 250
ABC, 185
Abe, Shinzo, 83, 162
abortions, forced, 192
Action Aid, 250
Açu, 255–7
Addis Ababa, 221
A'Er (poet), 193
Afghanistan, 64
Afghanistan War, 33, 44, 72
Africa, 187, 200, 212, 219, 261–2
    genocide in, 201, 207, 209, 215, 217, 218
African Development Bank, 270
African National Congress, 210
African Union, 207, 212–13
Agriculture Ministry, Chinese, 93
air pollution, 227–8
Ai Weiwei, 195
Aldrich, Nelson, 240
Alexandria Library, 147
Al Jazeera, 178, 185–6
    English language, 186, 190–1
Amorim, Celso, 209
Andrew, Abraham Piatt, 240–1
Annan, Kofi, 203, 207
anti-Americanism, 41, 84, 97, 156–7, 171–2,
    174, 188–9
anti-colonialism, 65, 97, 145–9, 202, 206,
    209
anti-communism, 155, 212
anti-Semitism, 238–9
anti-Vietnam War campaigns, 82
APT1 hacker group, 263
Aquino, Benito, 95
Arabian Sea, 59–60
Arabic language, 186
Arab League, 213
Arab Spring, 190–1
Argentina, 27, 260
Arrow, 146
Arroyo, Gloria, 72, 95

Asia
    backlash against China in, 13, 69–109, 123,
        131
    balance of power in, 33, 73–4, 111, 123
    as center of global power, 32–3
    China as biggest economy and trading
        partner in, 70, 128
    China as "Sick Man" of, 165
    Chinese ambitions in, 13, 15, 22–3, 45, 49,
        51–5, 58, 78–81
    Chinese rivalries in, 6, 10, 13, 25, 29, 69–109
    colonialism in, 25, 51, 62, 77–8
    destabilizing of maritime environment in,
        29–31
    East, 78, 82
    economic miracle of, 21, 22
    financial crisis of 1997 in, 71–2
    four pillars of U.S. approach to, 113
    international trade policy in, 126–8
    manufacturing in, 21, 22, 31, 71, 86
    Northeast, 81, 88, 96
    regional organization in, 124–5, 127–8,
        136
    Southeast, 61, 72, 75, 79, 88–96
    twenty-first-century contest for power in,
        33, 90
    2004 tsunami in, 67
    U.S. alliances in, 23, 25, 32, 64, 65–6, 71,
        81–8, 95, 122, 123, 279
    U.S. military dominance in, 22, 24, 33, 46
    U.S. objectives in, 131
Asia-Pacific Summit of 2010, 69–70, 73
Asia Society Center on U.S.-China Relations,
    176
Asia World, 132
Assad, Bashar al-, 207
Assange, Julian, 188
Associated Press, 187
Association of Southeast Asian Nations
    (ASEAN), 70, 124, 128
Atlantic, 115

Australia, 48, 97, 125, 127
  Chinese relations with, 70, 77, 98–102, 103, 109
  democratic government of, 101
  foreign trade of, 98, 100
  mining industry in, 98, 101
  Muslim population of, 101
  Parliament of, 99–100
  Pilbara region of, 98
  population of, 98
  tourism in, 99
  U.S. alliance with, 99–102
Australian, 102
Australian Financial Review, 100
Austria, 73
Austro-Hungarian Empire, 110
Aviation Week, 34

Bader, Jeff, 94–5
Bahrain, 67–8
Baker, James, 69–70
Balkans, 259
Bangkok, 50, 71
Barclays Bank, 259
Barmé, Geremie, 4–5, 168
Barnett, Robert, 166
Bashir, Omar al-, 199, 200, 221
Batista, Eike, 255–7
Bay of Bengal, 51, 52, 59, 63, 137
BBC, 176, 187, 188
Beijing, 3–6, 11–15, 20–4, 34, 36, 40, 43, 47, 56, 75, 82, 98, 154
  Apple Store in, 173
  "Bird's Nest" stadium in, 183, 195
  Dongzhimen Avenue in, 240
  Forbidden City in, 5, 146
  "Giant Egg" concert hall in, 183
  Great Hall of the People in, 200, 276
  international airport at, 183, 184
  Jianguomen Avenue in, 3
  Legation Quarter in, 148
  modern architecture of, 183–4, 195
  security in, 3–4, 6, 11, 39–40
  U.S. Embassy in, 113, 156, 172, 233
  see also Tiananmen Square
Beijing University of Politics and Law, 192
Beijing Women's Militia, 5
Belgrade, NATO bombing of Chinese Embassy in, 151, 160, 172
Bell, Michael, 274–5
Benghazi, 190
Berlin Wall, fall of, 8, 177, 249, 250,
Beveridge, Albert, 253
Biden, Joe, 233
bin Laden, Osama, 200
Bismarck, Otto von, 56, 72–3, 81, 96, 110
Blair, Dennis, 46–7
Bloomberg News, 190
Boeing Aircraft, 272

Bolivia, 260
Booz Allen Hamilton, 58
Bosnian War, 188, 203
Bosshard, Peter, 249–50, 252, 269–71
Boston University, 260
Bowlby, Thomas, 147
Boxer Rebellion, 148, 149, 152
Bo Xilai, 189–90
Brazil, 14, 187, 206, 213
  abolition of slavery in, 97
  Chinese investment in, 255–8, 275
  Chinese iron ore imports from, 10, 255
  dictatorships in, 209
  guerrilla activity in, 208–9
  human rights abuses in, 208–9
  offshore oilfields of, 255
  Palacio Monroe in, 97
  U.S. relations with, 97, 214
BRICS nations, 257, 259
Bridge, Robert, 188
British Army, 24, 146–7
British Council, 142
British Empire, 44, 51–3, 62, 169, 229
  cultural "vandalism" of, 145–9
  decline of, 24, 25, 27, 33
  Opium Wars of, 25, 146, 150–1, 160, 168
  see also United Kingdom
British Museum, Elgin marbles in, 145–6
British Navy, 23, 24, 25, 28, 60
Brokaw, Tom, 187
Brookings Institution, 36
Brunei, 89
Brussels, 65
Buffett, Warren, 40
Bureau of Fisheries Administration, Chinese, 93
Burma, 50–3, 129–38
  British era in, 51, 62
  Chinese oil-and-gas pipeline development in, 51–3, 61–3, 137, 260
  Chinese relations with, 64, 66, 71, 130–3
  1824 British invasion of, 62
  ethnic conflict in, 137–8
  former military regime of, 129–30, 135, 136
  human rights abuses in, 131, 137–8
  Kachin State in, 132
  lagging economy and banking system of, 50–1
  Myitsone Dam in, 130, 132, 135, 137
  new democratic civilian government in, 63–4, 130
  Parliament of, 129
  political revolution in, 130
  U.S. relations with, 129–30, 131, 133–8
  Western sanctions against, 129, 131, 132
Buruma, Ian, 163, 184
Bush, George H. W., 69–70, 72
Bush, George W., 72, 77, 99–100, 124, 215, 231
  antiterror campaign of, 99, 263

"axis of evil" rhetoric of, 84
Iraq War and, 190

Cairo, 190, 249
Tahrir Square in, 188
Calcutta, 51, 146
California software and design industries, 21
Callahan, William, 153–4
Calleo, David, 231
Cambodia, 124, 135, 203
Cam Ranh naval base, 109
Canada, 110, 250, 263
Canberra, 98–100, 102
Cao Rulin, 154
capitalism, 201, 248, 255
Cardoso, Fernando Henrique, 209
Caribbean Sea, 28, 45, 60
Carr, Bob, 278
Carrefour, 168–9
CCTV America, 185, 187–91
Center for Strategic and Budgetary
    Assessments, 117, 119
Central Military Commission (China), 41, 45
Chan, Melissa, 191
Chang, Iris, 163
Charter 08 pro-democracy petition, 192
Chávez, Hugo, 200, 260–1, 268
Cheney, Dick, 231
Chengdu, 34–5, 189
Cheng Li, 36
Chen Guangcheng, 233
Chen Shaokuan, 55
Chen Yonglin, 100
Chen Yuan, 258–9, 268
Chen Yun, 258
Cheonan, 85–8
Chevron, 254
Chiang Kai-shek, 89, 154–5
Chiang Kai-shek, Madame (Soong Meiling), 155
Chicago, Ill., 145, 274
Chile, 27, 97, 104, 127, 209, 230
China, Imperial, 74–81, 162
    Ming dynasty of, 75, 77, 79–80, 103, 146,
        150, 153
    Qing dynasty of, 4, 146–8, 150, 152–3
    Warring States period of, 155–6
    Western exploitation and humiliation of,
        25, 36, 145–56, 161, 167–8, 205, 253
China, People's Republic of, 3–15
    ancient ethical and moral traditions of,
        179–82
    Anhui Province in, 158
    authoritarianism of, 9, 211
    censorship in, 35, 152, 195
    Communist revolution and 1949 victory of,
        150, 155, 161, 178, 195
    conspiratorial view of, 61, 90–1, 194, 248
    continental size of, 20, 94
    creativity suppressed in, 14–15

cultural and intellectual influence of, 77–8,
    79, 107–98
Cultural Revolution in, 148, 149, 152, 171,
    178–81, 192
cyberwar capabilities of, 38, 48–9, 117,
    262–6, 273, 289
decades of inward focus and restraint of, 6,
    9, 10, 11–12, 73, 179
defense spending of, 4, 9, 11, 23, 44–8, 53–8,
    277
demonizing and exoticizing of, 11
domestic violence in, 142–3
economic blackmail in foreign disputes
    by, 31
economic reforms in, 7, 11, 144, 161, 236,
    245, 247–8, 251, 267
education in, 141–5, 150–3, 155–6, 170–3, 179
energy needs of, 10, 26, 51–3, 61–3, 121
English speaking in, 141–5, 170
entrepreneurism in, 40, 259
era of economic isolation in, 90
exchange rate controversy in, 247–8
expanding overseas interests of, 215–23
film industry of, 101
"first island chain" barrier around, 25, 28,
    60, 120
fishing industry of, 90
focus on economic development of, 6,
    9–10, 11, 12
foreign criticism of, 6, 11, 43, 127, 204,
    207–8
foreign-currency reserves of, 234, 277,
    289
foreign development and investments of,
    13, 51–3, 61–4, 252–62, 273–5
foreign exports of, 22, 31, 90, 234, 245,
    252–3, 273
foreign imports of, 10, 21, 22, 26, 31, 52,
    201, 234
foreign policy of, 6–7, 9–10, 11, 36, 39, 63–6,
    69–109, 179, 182, 199–223
founding of, 3
fragmentation of power in, 9, 36, 92
global ambitions of, 9, 10, 11, 14–15, 30–1,
    55, 67, 176–7, 179
gross domestic product (GDP) of, 61–2, 176
Guangxi Province in, 104
Heilongjiang Province in, 178
human rights offenses in, 11, 13
insecurity and paranoia in, 3–4, 10–11,
    25–6, 28, 170
intelligence services of, 264
isolationist rhetoric in, 64–5
Jiangxi Province in, 20, 113
local government in, 36, 61, 63, 92
manufacturing in, 21, 22, 31, 39
Maoist era in, 19, 36, 71, 85–7, 90, 149, 161
map of, viii–ix
middle class in, 9, 36, 142, 154

China, People's Republic of (*continued*)
    military buildup and strength of, 4–5, 6, 9,
      13, 21–49, 111–15, 277–8
    military parades in, 3–6, 11, 12, 24
    modernization of, 6, 8, 183–4, 195, 262
    modern turning points of, 6–7, 214–15
    Mukden incident in, 163–4
    National Day celebration in, 3–6, 11, 12
    and "national humiliation," 25, 36, 145–57,
      159–64
    nationalism in, 7, 9–11, 13, 36, 39, 42–3, 56,
      59, 141–74, 198, 233, 278, 287
    need for outside commercial ports by,
      52–4, 58–64
    new energies, ambitions, and tensions of, 7,
      8, 9, 13, 29–31, 171
    New Year holiday in, 42, 141–3, 171, 270
    oilfields and offshore oil of, 90, 93, 94,
      200–1, 254
    oil imports of, 10, 26, 52
    Olympic Games of 2008 in, 142, 165, 168,
      170, 173, 182–4, 193, 195, 198, 286
    opacity of political process in, 11, 14–15, 61
    periodic arrests of dissidents in, 11
    political leaders and officer class of, 9
    political propaganda of, 4, 10, 59, 85, 90,
      163, 175–8, 182, 183
    political reform in, 181
    ports of, 24, 25, 55
    predicted overtake of U.S. economy by, 14
    projected "String of Pearls" military bases
      of, 58–61, 63–4, 66
    promotion of national interests by, 7, 9,
      10, 36
    public works programs in, 244, 250–1, 262
    renminbi currency of, 228–9, 236, 242,
      245–6
    rigid sovereignty principles of, 13, 93–4, 151,
      169, 202, 204–6, 209, 217
    rising economic and political strength of,
      3–11, 13–15, 22–4, 31–3, 36, 44, 45, 62, 66,
      70–1, 73, 80, 82, 98, 104, 108, 110–11
    sanctions imposed on, 149
    seaborne trade of, 10, 22, 26, 31
    security concerns of, 3–4, 6, 10–11, 22,
      25–6, 27, 28, 63
    sense of exceptionalism in, 180
    shoddy consumer products from, 185
    sixtieth anniversary of, 3–6
    "state capitalism" in, 244–5, 271
    state media in, 4–5, 57, 175–8, 183, 185–91
    state-owned companies in, 19, 36, 62, 63,
      136, 183, 240, 254, 273
    surveillance technologies of, 122
    three "core interests" of, 95
    tourism in, 19–20, 183, 193
    "tributary" system of, 78
    Uighur population of, 218
    urbanization of, 10

    urban professionals in, 36
    U.S. debt held by, 232–5, 238
    as world's biggest energy consumer, 26, 53
    as World's biggest exporter of
      manufactured goods, 22, 245
    as World's biggest seafood consumer, 90
    as World's second-largest economy, 73
    worldview of, 38, 39, 177–8, 182
    Xinjiang Province in, 101, 142, 218
    Yunnan Province in, 61–2, 75
China, Republic of, 169
    Japanese war crimes in, 160–1, 162
    May Fourth Movement in, 154
    "national humiliation" mentality in, 153–5,
      156
    see also Nationalist China; Taiwan
China Can Say No, 156
China Central Television (CCTV), 55, 183–91
    see also CCTV America
China Daily (Beijing), 176, 186–7
China Development Bank (CDB), 258–61,
    267, 268
China Dream (Liu Mingfu), 39–40, 41
China Export-Import Bank, 237, 260, 269–70
China Harbour Engineering Company, 59
China Marine Surveillance, 93
Chinamax ships, 255
China National Offshore Oil Corporation,
    (CNOOC), 93, 94, 254, 274
China National Petroleum Corporation
    (CNPC), 62, 201
China Ocean Shipping Company (COSCO),
    216
China Power Investment (CPI)m, 132
China Radio International, 176, 187
China Rising (Kang), 78
China's Destiny (Chiang Kai-shek), 155
China Southern Airlines, 43
Chinese Academy of Social Sciences, 29, 177,
    179
Chinese Air Force, 41, 114
    aircraft of, 4, 34–5, 38, 47, 57
Chinese Army, 25, 35–9, 41–3, 149, 233
    boosting of morale in, 38
    British consulate destroyed by, 149
    buildup of, 45–6, 277–8
    civilian control of, 42
    domestic politics and, 38, 42, 45
    foreign-affairs office of, 37
    hawkish views in, 39–43, 94
    leadership of, 38, 41, 42
    Long March of, 37
    political commissars of, 38
    professional soldiers and officer class of,
      38
    Red Guards of, 180, 192
    relationship of Communist Party and, 37–9
    Second Artillery Force of, 47
    signs of restlessness in, 36, 38, 42, 44–5

skepticism and hostility toward U.S.
  military in, 39–42
song-and-dance troupe of, 42
in Tiananmen Square protest of 1989, 46
Unit 61398 in, 263
U.S. Army and, 39–42, 126
Chinese Central Television (CCTV), 176
Chinese Communist Party (CCP), 4–6, 61, 65,
  89, 90, 107, 149–50, 153, 157, 172, 189, 204
  bureaucratic domination of, 38
  Central Committee of, 186
  changing message of, 180–1
  fixed retirement age and leadership
    transition set by, 36
  leadership of, 10, 36, 37–8, 42, 166, 167, 221,
    248
  legitimacy threat to, 11, 150, 152, 198
  Politburo of, 36, 177, 189, 247
  propaganda of, 163, 175, 180–1, 185–6
  relationship of Chinese Army and, 37–9
  sixtieth anniversary of, 24
  Standing Committee of, 5–6, 54, 185, 189,
    199, 247
  strength of, 6, 7, 174
Chinese Defense Ministry, 37, 39
"Chinese dream," 43
Chinese Foreign Ministry, 36, 38
Chinese language, 32, 72, 99, 168, 186
  Mandarin, 20, 99
Chinese Military Science Society, 24
Chinese Navy, 10, 20–1, 25, 29, 32, 93, 120
  aircraft carriers of, 37, 54–8
  "anti-navy" weaponry of, 47–8, 58
  "asymmetric" fighting capabilities of, 48–9
  buildup and modernization of, 13, 23–4, 25,
    26–7, 29, 33, 44–9, 54–9, 63–6, 76–7
  celebration and review of, 24
  civilian control of, 55
  control over "Near Seas" sought by, 29–31,
    49, 53, 55, 58, 67, 96
  as an expression of power, 23, 24, 37
  fifteenth-century, 74–80, 285
  Houbei-class vessels of, 48
  investment in, 22–3, 45–9, 53–8, 63
  lure of a "blue water" navy to, 53, 58
  as means to a diplomatic end, 23
  "million-man swim" era of, 44, 49
  mobile patrol craft of, 48
  "naval nationalism" of, 56
  need for Indian Ocean access by, 13, 58–67,
    52, 54
  patrol of South China Sea by, 43, 46, 52
  political commissars of, 42
  seamanship training in, 57
  supply and protection of vessels in, 58
  Taiwan as primary focus of, 44, 46
  Type 054 frigate of, 20
  U.S. naval dominance challenged by, 13,
    22–3, 29–31, 42–9, 53–4, 63–4, 67–8

vulnerability of, 25, 49
warships, submarines, and small boats of,
  20, 23, 24, 29, 43–7, 54, 55, 59, 68, 91, 217
"wolf pack" operations of, 48
Chinese-U.S. competition, 6–8, 9–10, 12–15,
  110–38
  attempted U.S. deflection of, 8, 15
  Chinese plan of gradual success in, 12
  diplomatic front of, 113, 123–6, 133–6
  economic front of, 13, 14, 20, 26, 113, 120,
    126–8, 225–75, 277
  military front of, 13, 20–49, 53–4, 108,
    113–22, 125–6
  political front of, 13, 24–5, 45, 113, 120, 123–4
  predicted overtake of U.S. economy
    (*sorpasso* moment) in, 14, 242
  question of Chinese regime change in, 24–5
  role of U.S. dollar in, 13, 14, 228–32, 235–8,
    240–3, 246–7, 254, 289
  shifting power in, 39
  soft power and, 175–98, 277, 287
  three fronts of, 13
  U.S. decline and, 8, 12–14, 33, 208, 210,
    278–9
  see also United States
Chinese Writers Association, 196
Chongqing, 259
  murder scandal in, 189–90
Christians, 218, 219
Churchill, Winston, 204
Chu Shulong, 26, 41
Cisco, 264, 266
Civil War, U.S., 9
Clarke, Richard, 263
climate change, 66, 249
Clinton, Bill, 6, 263
Clinton, Hillary, 100–1, 289
  as Secretary of State, 69–71, 95, 133, 135,
    177–8, 194, 222, 232
  Senate career of, 233
CNC World, 175
CNN, 168, 176, 187, 188
Cohen, Paul, 156
Cold War, 7, 11, 24, 29, 84, 101, 107, 112, 123, 136
  arms race in, 118, 231
  end of, 8, 14, 21, 47, 118, 162, 194, 203, 205,
    209–10, 249–50
  U.S. era of growth after, 14, 21
  U.S. goal and victory in, 33, 177
Colombia, 194
colonialism
  Chinese, 79–80
  decay of, 110
  European, 25, 53, 97, 110, 133
  maritime, 79
Columbia University, 166
Columbus, Christopher, 79
Communist Party, Chinese, *see* Chinese
  Communist Party

Confucianism, 11, 76, 103, 143, 152, 161, 180–1, 183, 198
Confucius from the Heart (Yu Dan), 190
Confucius Institutes, 186
Congo
  Chinese copper imports from, 10, 215–16
  Katanga Province in, 215–16
Congress, U.S., 9, 177–8, 243, 254, 266, 274
  see also House of Representatives, U.S.; Senate, U.S.
Connally, John, 231
Copenhagen climate-change conference, 66
Coulter, Ann, 156
Cuba, 187–8, 194, 218
  Guantánamo Bay in, 60
  Soviet relations with, 108
  sugar plantations of, 253
  U.S. relations with, 44, 108
Cui Tiankai, 91
Cultural Revolution, 148, 149, 152, 171
  negative effects of, 178–81, 192
Currency Wars (Song Hongbing), 238–40
Czechoslovakia, Charter 77 of, 192

Dai Bingguo, 87–8, 95, 194
Dai Xu, 41
Dalai Lama, 166, 170, 233
Daley, Richard M., 274
Dalian, 55
Danang, 106
Danwei, 160
Daqing oilfield, 90
Darfur, 206–7, 213, 219
  conflict and genocide in, 201, 209, 215, 217, 218
Davison, Henry, 240
Davison, Rosanna, 19
Davos, 9–10
"Dear American," 84
de Burgh, Chris, 19
Defense Department, U.S., 34–5, 57, 58, 114, 115, 126, 135–6, 190
  AirLand Battle concept of, 115
  AirSea Battle concept of, 115, 116–20
de Gaulle, Charles, 211, 237
democracy, 21, 101, 130, 176, 188–9, 201, 204, 212–14
Democratic Party, 233
Deng Xiaoping, 35–6, 85, 149–51, 258
  balance-of-power strategy of, 81
  eightieth birthday of, 5
  foreign policy of, 6, 9–12, 35, 39, 71
  hard-liner opposition to, 11
  market reforms of, 251, 261
  military history of, 37
  national restraint urged by, 6, 9, 10, 11, 12, 35, 39, 45–6, 55, 71, 215
"Desperate States of America, The," 14
Development Research Center, 233

DF-31A intercontinental ballistic missiles, 4
Dien Bien Phu, Battle of, 105
Doha trade talks, 272
Downer, Alexander, 100
Drepung Monastery, 164
drones, unmanned, 47
Duara, Prasenjit, 172
Dublin, 19
Duke University, 169
Dun & Bradstreet, 263
Dutton, Peter, 31
Dyer, Angelica, 72, 157

East
  Chinese rivals in, 6, 10
  transfer of wealth and influence from West to, 8
East Africa, 67–8, 146
East China Sea, 22, 173
East Timor, 135
Economist, 165
Ecuador, 261
Egypt, 188
Eichengreen, Barry, 241
"Eight Immortals," 258–9
Eisenhower, Dwight D., 232
Eleven Media Group, 132, 133
Elgin, James Bruce, 8th Earl of, 146–9, 150, 286
Elgin, Thomas Bruce, 7th Earl of, 145–6, 150
English language, 20, 32, 69, 141–5, 148, 155, 170, 250
  media in, 175–6, 178, 185–91
Ericsson, 264
Estela, 208, 288
Ethiopia, 217
  Sinopec facility in, 216
eunuchs, 75, 76
Eurasia, 33
Europe, 33, 45, 73
  Asian trade with, 21
  colonialism in, 25, 27, 62, 77–8, 222
  fifteenth-century, 76
  German aggression in, 33
  integration of, 124
  nineteenth-century territorial expansion in, 12, 27, 62
  territorial conflict in, 78
  U.S. relations in, 15, 27, 33
European Council on Foreign Relations, 208
European Union (EU), 271–2
Evans, Gareth, 203
exclusive economic zones (EEZ), 30, 92, 93
Exxon Mobil, 92

F-18 naval aircraft, 67
Fallows, James, 233
Fanell, James, 30–1
Fang Lizhi, 156
Fannie Mae, 234, 239

"Far Seas," 54
fascism, 184, 201
Federal Reserve, U.S., 234, 238–9, 241
Finance and Economics Small Group, 247
financial crisis of 2008, 239
  Chinese response to, 12, 39, 184, 234, 238,
    244–5, 254
  currency concerns in, 229–32
  fiscal retrenchment in, 23
  U.S. decline and, 14
  Wall Street crack-up in, 12, 14, 236, 244
Financial Times (London), 168, 190
Fish, Hamilton, 60, 284
Flying Dutchman, The (Wagner), 56
Foreign Ministry, Chinese, 93–4, 160, 165, 177,
  189, 194, 205–6, 217
Foster, Norman, 183
Fox News, 157
France, 100, 120, 209, 213
  colonial era of, 25, 53
  U.S. relations with, 237
Frankfurt Book Fair, 197
Franz Ferdinand, Archduke, 8
Fraser, Malcolm, 101
Freddie Mac, 234, 239
freedom of navigation, 15, 30, 31
  modern consumer economy and, 21
Freezing Point, 152–3
French Army, 146–7
French Navy, 25, 56
Fudan University, 59, 159, 176–7
Furious, 146

G-7 nations, 149
Gallagher, Kevin, 260
Galveston, Tex., 187
Gama, Vasco da, 75, 77, 79
"Gangnam Style" video, 84
Gao Xiqing, 233
Gates, Bill, 9, 40, 238
Gates, Robert, 34–5, 38, 47, 114, 116
Geithner, Tim, 238
General Electric, 264
Geng Biao, 42
geopolitics, 9–10, 27, 61
  balance of power in, 15, 23, 33
  competition and struggle in, 10, 13, 20–3
  developing world in, 14
  diffusion of economic power in, 14
  economic interdependence and, 9–10, 12, 21
  international trading system of, 22
  modern consumer economy of, 21
  rules, institutions, and power dynamics of,
    13, 14, 15, 23
  see also Chinese-U.S. competition
German Navy, 23, 28, 283
  battleship fleet of, 56
Germany, Imperial, 7, 22, 23, 110, 150, 154
  foreign relations of, 72–3

Germany, Nazi, 202
  European aggression of, 33
Germany, Unified, 73
Ghana, 260
Giap, Vo Nguyen, 105
Gilbert, Martin, 204
Giscard d'Estaing, Valéry, 237
Global Business and Finance Institute,
  239–40
globalization, 7, 12
  centrality of sea trade in, 30
  Chinese growth and reshaping of, 13, 20, 23
  container ship as symbol of, 21
  expansion of trade and manufacturing in,
    8, 21
  impact on U.S. of, 127, 128
  interdependence of nations in, 9–10
  international politics transformed by, 10
  post-American, 249–75
Global Times (China), 157, 194
Godement, François, 208
gold, 231, 237, 255
Gordon, Charles George, 147
Goujian, King of Yue, 155–6
Greater East Asian Co-Prosperity Sphere, 78
"great power" status, 8
  aircraft carriers as concentrated expression
    of, 54, 56
  China's aspirations to, 11, 12, 20–3, 30–1, 43,
    54–6, 59, 80
  economic dynamism, construction, and
    engineering in, 8
  expectations of middle class and, 8, 9
  global expansion and, 8
  importance of powerful navies to, 23–9, 37,
    46, 55–6
  mixture of confidence and insecurity in, 22
  molding of international trends by, 8
  respect, recognition, and influence
    demanded in, 8
  security concerns of, 8, 26–9
Great Wall, Badaling Station on, 192
Greece, 145–6
  ancient, 23, 56
Greenert, Jonathan, 48, 116
Greenspan, Alan, 236
Gries, Peter Hays, 144
Guangzhou, 142–3, 173
Guatemala, 253
  U.S. interference in, 97
Guinness Book of World Records, 52
Gu Kailai, 189
Gulf of Aden, pirates in, 67–8, 126, 230
Gulf War (1990–91), 40, 46
"gunboat diplomacy," 25, 79
Gwadar, 59–60, 64

Hague, 199
Haikou, 43

Hainan Island, 19–21, 31, 91, 92–3
  Chinese naval base on, 20–1, 22, 26, 46, 92
Haiti, 213
Hambantota, 59, 64
Hammes, T. X., 116
Han Chinese, 164–6, 167, 169
Han dynasty, 103, 148
Hanfeizi, 181
Hanoi, 69–71, 73, 102–9
  Ba Trung neighborhood in, 103
  convention center in, 69
  Ho Loa Prison in, 102
Han Thar Myint, U, 130
Harare, Chinese Embassy in, 200
Hatoyama, Yukio, 82
Havana, 187, 253
Havel, Václav, 192
Hawaii, 32, 81, 113
  statehood of, 60
Hawke, Bob, 98
Hefei, 169
Heglig, 221
Hendrix, Henry, 122
Herzog & de Meuron, 183
He Yafei, 86
Heywood, Neil, 189–90
Himalayan Mountains, 176, 192
  disputed borders in, 65
Hoan Kiem Lake, 102–3
Holmes, James, 29, 120
Holocaust, 163, 204
Honduras, 253
Hong Kong, 39, 185, 236, 245
  Admiralty District of, 227
  competition of Shanghai and, 227–8
  end of British rule in, 151
  Harbor of, 228
Honiara, 216
Hornet, 115
House of Representatives, U.S., Intelligence
  Committee of, 265
How to Be a Great Power (Xue Yong), 9
"How We Would Fight China" (Kaplan),
  115–16
HSBC, 228
Hu, Stern, 101
Huawei, 264–6
Hua Ze, 192
Hugo, Victor, 147
Hui Muslims, 164–5
Hu Jintao, 6
  development of Chinese naval power
    defined by, 24
  domestic criticism of, 39
  presidency of, 5, 12, 26, 34–5, 42, 54, 74,
    77–8, 82, 99–100, 170, 201, 215, 220,
    235
  soft power approved by, 177, 198
  U.S. visit of, 186, 272, 274

human rights abuses, 13, 135, 176, 191, 208–9
  in Brazil, 208–9
  in Burma, 131, 137–8
  in China, 11, 13
  in North Korea, 84
  UN focus on, 202–8, 213–14, 249
Human Rights Watch, 206
Hun Sen, 135
Huntsman, Jon, 34
Hu Shi, 197–8
Hu Yanlin, 42
Hu Yaobang, 98
Hyundai Corporation, 84

Ignatieff, Michael, 208, 222
Immelt, Jeffrey, 264
Impeccable, USNS, 29, 30
India, 14, 65–6, 110, 131, 185, 206, 210, 213
  British era in, 51, 62, 133, 146, 147
  Chinese encirclement feared by, 59, 66
  Chinese relations with, 65–7, 275
  democratic government of, 66
  English speaking in, 142
  foreign trade of, 65
  growth and development of, 32, 65
  independence gained by, 65
  Japanese relations with, 125
  neutral history of, 66
  nuclear weapons of, 66
  security concerns of, 59, 66
  U.S. relations with, 66, 123
Indian Army, 52
Indian Navy, 65–6, 125
  aircraft carriers in, 65
  joint exercises of U.S. Navy and, 66
Indian Ocean, 32, 49, 74–6, 125
  China's need for access to, 13, 52–4, 58–67
  U.S. dominance in, 24, 58, 63–4
Indignation of National Humiliation, 151
Indonesia, 14, 26, 80–1, 110, 124, 125, 210
  anti-Chinese sentiment in, 72
  Chinese coal imports from, 10
Influence of Sea Power upon History,
  1680–1783, The (Mahan), 27–9
Inter-American Development Bank, 260
international anti-piracy coalition, 67–8
International Criminal Court, 199, 203
International Crisis Group, 221
international law, 15, 88, 92
  Chinese version of, 30–1
International Monetary Fund (IMF), 71, 209,
  232, 257–8, 261, 267–8
International Rivers, 269–70
Internet, 173
  Chinese censorship of, 35
  Chinese hacking of commercial sites on,
    48, 262–4, 289
  Chinese Web sites on, 34, 36, 86, 142–3, 158,
    160, 169, 196, 217

cyberwar and, 38, 48–9, 117, 262–6, 273, 289
  U.S. Web sites on, 34
Iran, 64
  Indian trade with, 66
Iraq, 84
  in Kuwait defeat, 46
Iraq War, 72, 78, 190, 206, 213
  ending of, 33
  military costs of, 44
Irrawaddy River, 132
Ishihara, Shintaro, 83
Islamist terrorism, 72
Israel
  human rights abuses charged to, 205
  Likud party of, 163
  U.S. relations with, 205
Istanbul, 55
Italian language, 99

J-10 fighter jet, 4
J-20 stealth bomber, 34–5, 38, 47
Jackson, Andrew, 32
Jagland, Thorbjorn, 194
Jane's Fighting Ships, 1990 edition, 44
Janjaweed militia, 207
Japan, 22, 32, 33, 73, 112, 115, 127, 148, 150, 154, 186, 232
  Chinese relations with, 10, 21, 31, 39, 70, 71, 82–4, 157–64, 172, 173, 174, 261–2
  economy of, 78, 110, 128
  imports of, 31
  Indian relations with, 125
  manufacturing in, 31, 71
  Meiji Restoration in, 161–2
  new dynamic defense rhetoric of, 84
  1945 Allied defeat of, 21, 52
  nineteenth-century rise of, 161
  pacifism espoused by, 84
  politics in, 82, 83–4
  rise of, 32, 39, 60, 211
  U.S. alliance with, 23, 25, 81–4, 123, 128, 173
  U.S. blockade of, 120
  U.S. soldiers in, 81, 82, 162
  war crimes of, 158, 160–4
Japanese Air Force, kamikaze pilots in, 162
Japanese Army, 84
  in World War II, 52, 162
Japanese coast guard, 31, 82
Japanese Democratic Party, 82
Japanese Liberal Democratic Party (LDP), 82, 83
Japanese Navy, 110, 173
Jekyll Island, 240–1, 243
Jesuit missionaries, 148
Jiang Yu, 194
Jiang Zemin, 55, 149, 151
Jiao Tong University, 72
Jia Qinglin, 221
Jin Jing, 168

John C. Stennis, USS, 106
John S. McCain, USS, 106
Johnson, Lyndon B., 136, 231, 286
Joint Chiefs of Staff, U.S., 67
Ju (writer), 132
Juba, 220
Jungle Book, The (Kipling), 51

Kachin Independence Army, 137
Kadeer, Rebiya, 101
Kang, David, 78
Kang Youwei, 162
Kaplan, Robert, 115–16
Karchi, 64
Kazakhstan, 260
Keating, Timothy, 32
Ke Chunqiao, 233
Kennedy, Paul, 231
Kenya, 75
Khanfar, Wadah, 190–1
Khanna, Parag, 78
Khartoum, 199–201, 206–7, 215, 218
Kiev, 56
Kiir, Salva, 214–15, 218, 219, 221
Kim Dae-jung, 84
Kim Il-sung, 85
Kim Jong-il, 84, 86–7, 153, 199
Kim Jong-un, 87, 199, 200
Kipling, Rudyard, 51, 222
Kissinger, Henry, 8, 21, 134, 237
Koizumi, Junichiro, 162–3
Koolhaas, Rem, 183–4
Korean War, 84, 153
  Chinese forces in, 85, 86–7
Kosovo, 203, 218
Ko Tar, 132
Kunming, 51
Kushites, 219
Kuwait, Iraq ousted from, 45

"Lady in Red" (de Burgh), 19
Lahore, 64
  siege of the Red Mosque in, 216
land seizures, illegal, 192
Lang Lang, 186
Laos, 61
Laozi, 181
Latin America, 212
  U.S. relations in, 96–7
Laurie, Jim, 185–7
Law of the Sea Treaty, 88
  exclusive economic zones (EEZ) defined in, 30, 92, 93
League of Nations, 202
Lee, Kim, 142–3
Lee Kuan Yew, 33, 71
Lee Myung-bak, 88
Lehman Brothers, 12, 236, 244
Le Loi, Emperor of Vietnam, 103

Leping, 113
Levathes, Louise, 75–6
Lhasa
    Jokhang Temple in, 166–7
    protests of monks in, 164–7
    racial violence in, 164–8, 170
Liang Guanglie, 34–5
Liaoning, 55, 57
Liberia, 205
Libya
    civil conflict in, 217
    2011 U.S. operation in, 125, 213–14
Li Chenyang, 61
Li Congjun, 175
Li Datong, 153
Lijiang, 193
Li Jie, 55–6
Lima, English Club in, 27
Li Ruogu, 237, 269–70
Liu Guijin, 219
Liu Huaqing, 54, 55, 58
Liu Mingfu, 39–41
Liu Xia, 191–2
Liu Xiaobo, 288
    jailing of, 4, 191, 192, 199
    Nobel Peace Prize of, 4, 191–5, 196
Liu Yazhou, 41
Liu Yingcai, 221
Li Yang, 141–5, 170–1, 172
Li Zhiguo, 220
Loch, Henry, 147
Locke Gary, 238
London, 168
Longqing Gorge, 192
Loos, Adolf, 184
Los Angeles, Calif., 4, 60
Lovell, Julia, 196
Lowy Institute, 99
Lula da Silva, Luiz Inácio, 209
Luo Jialun, 154
Luo Ping, 235
Luo Yan, 233
Luo Yuan, 24
Luttwak, Edward, 229
Lu Xun, 143

Macartney, George, Lord, 167–8
Macartney, Jane, 167–8
Macclesfield Bank, 89
Magellan, Ferdinand, 79
Mahan, Alfred Thayer, 27–9, 32, 44, 60, 65, 283
    Chinese navalists influenced by, 28–9
Malacca, 74–6, 79
Malaysia, 26, 74–6, 78, 88–90, 236
Manchus, 148
Mandiant, 263
manga comics, 162
Mao Yushi, 192

Mao Zedong, 19, 36, 42, 71, 85–7, 90, 143, 149, 180
    Communist revolution led by, 161, 178, 195
    death of, 7, 251
    iconic tunic of, 5
    meeting of Nixon and, 21–2, 212, 251, 252
    personality cult of, 152
    public portrait of, 5
maritime law, 30–1
Marx, Karl, 11, 104, 152
Marxism-Leninism, 40, 104, 107–8
    declining influence of, 38, 161
Maui, 136
Maw Tun Aung, Ko, 132, 135
Ma Xiaotian, 35
May Fourth Movement, 154
McCain, John, 102, 106
McDonald's Corporation, 228
McNamara, Robert, 250
McVadon, Eric, 67
Mead, Walter Russell, 73
Mediterranean Sea, 217
Melbourne Film Festival, 101
Mencius, 181
Mercosur, 213
Mexico, 110, 127, 230
Mexico City, 43
Middle East, 70
    Chinese oil imports from, 10, 26, 52, 121
Midway archipelago, 60
Miles, James, 165
Ming dynasty, 75, 77, 79–80, 103, 146, 150, 153
Ministry of Culture, Chinese, 197
Mischief Reef, 89
Mishra, Pankaj, 202
missiles, 53, 55
    ballistic, 4, 47
    carrier-killer, 47–8
    Chinese buildup of, 47–8, 114, 117
    cruise, 48
    defense against, 47, 48
    deployment of, 47
    DF-31A intercontinental ballistic, 4
    land-based, 38
    range of, 4, 47
    "seeker" technology of, 48
Miss World beauty pageant, 19
Mitter, Rana, 154
MMX mining group, 256
Mohan, Raja, 65, 125
Mongolia, 70, 76, 142
Monroe, James, 27
Monroe Doctrine, 27, 96–7, 256
Moore, Richard, 101
Morgan, J. P., 27, 240–1
Morgan Stanley, 14
Moscow, 211–12
Mo Yan, 196–7
Mozambique, 270

Mubarak, Hosni, 205
Mugabe, Robert, 200, 205
Mulally, Alan, 272
Mullen, Michael, 67
Mumbai, 65
Muslims, 75, 219
  Uighur, 218

Nabuco, Joaquim, 97
Nairobi, 187
Nanjing, 79
  Japanese massacre at, 160–4
Nanning, 104
Napoleon I, Emperor of France, 120, 238
National Defense University (China), 40
National Intelligence Council, 229
Nationalist China, 154–5, 253
  Communist war against, 37, 42, 89, 155
  see also China, Republic of; Taiwan
National League for Democracy (NLD), 130,
  132–3
National People's Congress, 164
National Reform and Development
  Commission, 244
National Security Agency, U.S., 266
National Security Council, U.S., 35, 94
Naval Research Institute, Chinese, 55
NBC, 185
Near Seas, 22, 28, 54
  rivalry of China with U.S. in, 29–31, 44, 49,
    53, 55, 58, 67, 96
Nehru, Jawaharlal, 65
Nemesis, 25
neo-Confucianism, 180–1, 182, 186, 195
Netherlands, 68, 77
Never Forget National Humiliation, 151
New Delhi, 65–6
Ne Win, 136
New York, N.Y., 130, 184
  Times Square in, 175, 186, 187
New York Times, 28, 95, 175, 176, 184
Ngoc Son Temple, 103
Nigeria, 216
Nile River, 250–1
Nixon, Richard M.
  gold standard abandoned by, 231
  historic China visit of, 21–2, 161, 212, 237,
    251, 252
Nobel Prize, 191–8
  for Literature, 196–7
  for Peace, 4, 191–5, 196
Non-Aligned Movement, 65, 210
nongovernmental organizations (NGOs),
  249–50, 260, 269, 270
Nortel, 262–3
North American Treaty Organization
  (NATO), 40, 123, 151, 160, 172, 211, 237
North Korea, 153, 183
  Chinese relations with, 84–8, 157, 200

mass military displays of, 4
  nuclear capability of, 85, 87
  poverty and starvation in, 85
  South Korean relations with, 84–8
North Korean Army, 85
North Vietnam, 102
Norway, 194, 196
nuclear weapons, 112, 233, 237
  China and, 237, 289
  deterrence and, 12
  escalation of, 119
  of India, 66
  of North Korea, 85, 87
Nye, Joseph, 176

Obama, Barack, 32, 46–7, 100, 112, 129, 133–5,
  210, 271
  budget crises of, 276
  China trip of, 199–200
  criticism of, 125
  election campaigns of, 122, 127, 144–5, 274,
    276
  "pivot" to Asia thrust of, 33, 70, 71, 113
  on U.S. dominance, 40
Office of Metropolitan Architecture,
  Rotterdam, 183
oil, 10, 26, 60
  in China, 63, 90, 93, 94, 200–1
  Chinese import of, 10, 26, 52
  Chinese pipeline development for, 51–3,
    61–3, 137, 260
  in Southeast Asia, 90, 92–4
Okinawa, Futenma base in, 82
Olympic Games of 2008, 142, 165, 168, 170,
  173, 182–4, 193, 198, 286
  architectural triumphs of, 183–4, 195
  opening ceremony of, 182–3
On China (Kissinger), 134
Opium War of 1840, 25, 150–1, 161, 168
Opium War of 1856–60, 146, 161, 168
Oslow, 194, 196
Ottoman Empire, 110
Ouroussoff, Nicolai, 184
Oxfam, 250
Ozawa, Ichiro, 82

Pacific Command, U.S., 32, 126
Pacific Ocean, 28, 32–4, 60, 96
  Arctic region in, 212
  eastern, 32
  military rivalry of China and U.S. in, 21,
    22–3, 32–3, 45, 49
  U.S. dominance in, 13, 21, 22, 24, 26, 29,
    32–3, 49, 99, 111–13, 115, 116
  western, 13, 22–3, 25, 29, 32, 45, 49, 81, 111,
    279
Pakistan, 59–60, 67, 216
  Baluchistan Province of, 64
  Chinese relations with, 64, 66

Palmares Armed Revolutionary Vanguard, 209
Palmerston, Henry John Temple, Lord, 146
Panama, Isthmus of, 28
Panama Canal, 28, 60, 232
Panetta, Leon, 109
Papua New Guinea, 216
Paracel Islands, 89, 91, 92–3, 104
Paraguay, 213
Paralympics, 168
Paris, 116, 168, 202
Parkes, Harry, 146–7
Parthenon, 145
Paul, Ron, 239, 241
Pax Americana, 21
Peacock, USS, 32
Peking University, 5, 26, 41, 86, 238
Peng Guangqian, 94
Peng Liyuan, 42
People's Daily (China), 34, 151, 157, 160, 194, 196
People's Liberation Army (PLA), *see* Chinese Army
People's Liberation Army Navy (PLAN), *see* Chinese Navy
Perry, Matthew, 32
Persian Gulf, 53, 58, 64
Peru, 27, 215
Peterson Institute, 252
Petrodar, 221
PetroVietnam, 92
Philippines, 89, 125, 194
 banana exports of, 31
 Chinese relations with, 29, 31, 91–2, 95, 108
 U.S. alliance with, 23, 25, 44, 72, 95
 U.S. conquest of, 148
Piano, Renzo, 175
Pinggu, 193
plague, 160
Playboy, 255
Plot to Demonize China, The, 156
Port Sudan, 218
Portugal, 24, 110, 120
Portuguese language, 32
Portuguese Navy, 75, 77
Post-American World, The (Zakaria), 10
"Power Shift" (White), 101–2
Presley, Elvis, 162
Primark, 21
PSA International, 60
Psy (rapper), 84
Putin, Vladimir, 211, 257
Pu Yi, Emperor of China, 253
Pyongyang, 84–8, 199

Qaddafi, Muammar, 214
Qatar, 185
Qian Lihua, 37
Qianlong Emperor, 167–8

Qiao Damo, 196
Qi Guan, 19
Qi Kang, 163
Qingdao, 24, 86, 169
Qing dynasty, 4, 146–8, 150, 152–3, 253
Qu Hongbin, 228

Raby, Geoff, 98
radar, 34, 47–8, 117
Rajapaksa, Mahinda, 59
Rama III, King of Siam, 32
Ramoche Monastery, 164
Ramree Island, 51–3, 61–3
 Battle of, 52, 284
Rand Corporation, 35
Rape of Nanking, The (Chang), 163
rare earth commodities, 31
Reagan, Ronald, 231
Red Flag limousines, 5
Regional Comprehensive Economic Partnership (RCEP), 128
Renmin University, 81
Ren Zhengfei, 265
"Responsibility While Protecting," 214
Reuters, 187
Rice, Susan, 210
Richard E. Byrd, USS, 109
Rio de Janeiro, 249, 255, 256–7
Rio Tinto, 101
Rise and Fall of the Great Powers, The (Kennedy), 231
Robbins, Tony, 145
Roberts, Edmund, 32
Roche, David, 14
Rockefeller, John D., Jr., 240
Rogers, Mike, 265
Rome, 56, 264
Romney, Mitt, 122, 127, 211, 274
Roosevelt, Franklin D., 135, 222
Roosevelt, Theodore, 44, 97
 importance of Asia seen by, 32–3
Root, Elihu, 97
Rosen, Daniel, 252–3
Ross, Robert, 56
Rothschild family, 238
Rousseff, Dilma, 209, 214, 255
Rudd, Kevin, 98–9, 100–1
Rumsfeld, Donald, 46, 126
Russia, 110, 125, 186, 202
 Chinese relations with, 47, 71, 194, 207–9, 210–12, 260
 submarines supplied to China and Vietnam by, 47, 106
 U.S. relations with, 211–12
 see also Soviet Union
Russian language, 20
Russia Today, 188
Rwanda, 203, 207
Ryan, Paul, 233

Sahnoun, Mohamed, 203
Saigon, 106
　fall of, 185
San Diego, Calif., 44, 56, 81
Sansha, 91
Sanya, 19–20
　submarine base at, 43
Sarajevo, 188
SARS, 228
satellites, 38, 47, 49, 91
Saudi Arabia, 90, 205
　Chinese oil imports from, 10
Scarborough Shoal, 89, 108, 123
Scheeren, Ole, 184
Schell, Orville, 176
Schreer, Ben, 119
Science of Military Strategy, 25
Scobell, Andrew, 35
Seattle, Wash., 272
Second World, The (Khanna), 78
Senate, U.S., 233
　Finance Committee of, 240
Senkaku/Diaoyu Islands dispute, 82, 83, 160,
　　161, 173
Seoul, 71, 84, 85
Sepoy Mutiny, 146
Serbia, 218
Serra, José, 209
Setser, Brad, 232
Shaanxi History Museum, 103, 286
Shanghai, 59, 60, 72, 115, 133, 154, 157–9, 168–9
　Bund in, 158
　colonial era of, 25, 157
　competition of Hong Kong and, 227–8
　French Concession in, 157
　Hongqiao district in, 159
　Huai Hai Road in, 157–8
　Japanese in, 158–9
Shanghai Co-operation Organisation, 211
Shanghai Institutes for International Studies,
　237
"Shanghai smile," 10
Shared Awareness and Deconfliction Group
　(SHADE), 68
Shen Dingli, 59
Shengping Yuan Hotel, 191
Shen Jiru, 177
Shenyang, 85
　September 18 History Museum in, 163–4
Shenzhen, 172
Sheridan, Greg, 102
Shields, Brian, 262–3
Shi Yinhong, 81, 96
Shona language, 200
Siamese-American Treaty of Amity and
　Commerce, 32
Siamese language, 32
Siberia, 20, 178, 212
Sikh cavalry, 147

Singapore, 26, 46, 50, 58, 60, 74, 124, 127, 172,
　192
Sino-Japanese War of 1894–95, 161, 162
Sittwe, 62
socialism, 6, 70, 107–8, 198
soft power, Chinese, 175–98, 287
　cultural, philosophical, and intellectual
　　elements of, 176–91
　definition of, 176
　media elements of, 175–8, 183, 185–91, 194,
　　196
Solomon Islands, 216
Somalia, 67, 126, 207, 230
Song Hongbing, 238–40
Soros, George, 239, 240
South Africa, 210
South China Sea, 20, 22, 32, 71, 74, 75, 109, 125
　China as dominant power in, 29–31, 46,
　　69–70, 88–96, 104, 154
　Chinese fishing moratorium in, 92, 94
　Chinese patrol of, 43, 46, 52
　disputed territories in, 82, 83, 89–93, 104,
　　108, 123, 124, 160, 161, 173
　"nine-dash-line" map of, 29–30, 88–9, 92,
　　93–4, 96, 105, 154
　risk of confrontation and escalation in,
　　29, 31, 42
Southern Sudan Referendum Commission,
　219
South Kordofan, 221
South Korea, 80–1, 110, 112, 127, 173, 210
　Chinese relations with, 84–8, 98
　Foreign Ministry of, 88
　Japanese occupation of, 162–3
　manufacturing in, 71
　North Korean relations with, 84–8
　sophisticated screen technology of, 21
　"sunshine" policy of, 84
　U.S. alliance with, 23, 81–2, 84–5, 87–8, 230
　U.S. soldiers in, 81, 84, 88
South Sudan, 214–16, 219–21, 223
South Vietnam, 89
Soviet Union, 116, 177
　Chinese relations with, 4, 54–7, 212
　economic failure in, 231
　May Day celebrations of, 4
　military buildup of, 115, 118, 231
　rise of, 39
　U.S. competition with, 33, 107, 203, 231
　see also Russia
Spain, 110, 120
　U.S. conflicts with, 44
Spanish Navy, 23, 56
Spiegel, Der, 14
Spielberg, Steven, 183
Spratly Islands, 91, 92, 104
Sri Lanka, 64, 66, 79, 194
　civil war in, 59
Stalin, Joseph, 85

Standard & Poor's, 243
State Department, U.S., 155, 287
Steinberg, James, 94–5
sterling silver, 229, 243
Stokes, Mark, 113–14
Strait of Hormuz, 59–60, 63
Strait of Lombok, 121
Strait of Malacca, 26, 28, 52–3, 61, 74, 79, 121
Strait of Sunda, 121
Strong, Benjamin, 240
Subic Bay, 95
submarines, 23, 106
    diesel, 47
    nuclear, 24, 47
Subramanian, Arvind, 228
Sudan, 183, 194, 206–7, 209, 215–23, 250–1
    Chinese relations with, 199, 200–2, 205,
        215, 217–20
    civil war in, 215, 218–20, 222
    human-rights abuses in, 207, 251
    Merowe Dam in, 250–1, 270
    oil reserves in, 200–1, 215–16, 218–21
    see also South Sudan
Sudan People's Liberation Movement
    (SPLM), 215, 218, 221
Suez Canal, 74, 232
Suharto, 72
Sumatra, 74, 79
Summers, Larry, 234
Sun Yat-sen, 162, 253
Suu Kyi, Aung San, 132–3, 137
    Congressional Gold Medal of, 129
    house arrest of, 129–30
Sweden, 264
Sweetman, Bill, 34
Switzerland, 20, 250
Sydney, 99, 100
Syngenta, 20
Syria, 207–10, 213, 222
    civil war in, 200, 207

Taiping Rebellion, 150
Taiwan, 67, 95, 114, 216
    manufacturing in, 71
    planned Chinese takeover of, 44, 46
    U.S. alliance with, 25, 34
    U.S. arms sales to, 34, 233
    see also China, Republic of; Nationalist
        China
Taiwan Strait, 114
Tanaka, Kakuei, 161
Tea Party, 234
television, 42, 57
    Chinese, 41, 55, 165, 175–6, 178, 185–91, 192
    Gulf War as seen on, 46
    U.S. military comment on, 40–1
Teng Biao, 191–3
terrorist attacks of 9/11, 72, 173
    U.S. conservatives empowered by, 12

Thailand, 20, 32, 130, 131
Than Htut Aung, 133
Thein Sein, 129–31
think tanks, 55, 117, 119, 233
Third Pan-American Conference of 1906, 97
3Com, 265
Three Gorges Dam, 132, 251
Tiananmen Square, 154
    National Museum in, 180
    1989 protests and massacre in, 6, 11, 42, 46,
        55, 70, 149–50, 152–3, 156, 158, 189, 259, 276
    2009 National Day parade in, 3–6, 11, 12,
        15, 195
Tianjin theme park, 56
tianxia "all under heaven" concept, 179, 181
Tianxia System, The (Zhao Tingyang), 181
Tibet, 69–70, 95, 164–70
    Chinese claims to, 167–70
    ethnic minorities in, 164–7, 169–70, 218
    foreign journalists banned in, 165, 167–8,
        170
    1903 British invasion of, 169
    see also Lhasa
Tibetan Buddhism, 166
Time, 237
Times (London), 147, 167
Tin Oo, U, 133
Tojo, Hideki, 162
Tokyo, 31, 83
    Yasukuni Shrine in, 162
Toledo, Ohio, 274–5
Toledo Symphony, 274
Trans-Pacific Partnership (TPP), 127–8, 271
Treasury Department, U.S., 71, 132, 241
    bond market of, 230, 234–5, 243
Trong Vinh, Nguyen, 105
Tsinghua University, 80, 179
Tunisia, 190
Turkey, 55, 210
Turkmenistan, 260
Twain, Mark, 7
Twitter, 193

Uganda, 203
Ukraine, military sales to China by, 54, 56–7
Unhappy China, 156–7
United Fruit Company, 253
United Kingdom, 23, 24, 25, 27, 213
    economy of, 73
    pound currency of, 241, 243
    U.S. relations with, 66, 232
    see also British Empire
United Nations, 90, 129, 201–7, 211–14
    Charter of, 202, 213, 221–2
    Chinese veto in, 59, 207–9, 222
    Commission on the Limits of the
        Continental Shelf in, 88
    defense of sovereignty in, 202–3, 206, 210,
        213

founding of, 202–3
human rights and protection of minorities focus in, 202–8, 213–14, 249
Human Rights Council of, 204
Law of the Sea Treaty of, 30, 88
peacekeeping operations of, 207–8, 221
"Responsibility to Protect" formula of, 203–4, 206, 207, 209
Russian veto in, 207–9, 222
Security Council of, 201, 206, 209, 221
U.S. veto in, 205
United States
budget deficits and foreign debt in, 14, 231, 232–5, 238, 242
Chinese relations and trade with, 10, 12–13, 15, 21, 22–7, 29–32, 34–5, 40–1, 110–38, 160, 223, 271–5
Chinese resentment of, 12, 25–6, 40–2, 156–7, 171, 174, 247–8
decisive influence of presidency in, 9
decline of, 8, 12, 13–14, 33, 208, 210, 278–9
deep roots of power and strength in, 8, 14–15
defense budget of, 44
democratic values of, 21, 24, 66, 176
economic interdependence of China and, 9–10, 12, 121, 252–4, 263
election of 2012 in, 122, 127
fiscal retrenchment in, 23
foreign criticism of, 101–2, 145
foreign policy of, 9, 14, 21–2, 60, 66
fragmented politics of 1870s–1880s in, 9
free trade and navigation system of, 15, 21, 24, 30, 267, 268, 279
hawkish voices in, 58–9, 111–12
innovative history of, 14
intelligence services in, 46–7, 49, 229
international role and influence of, 9, 12, 14–15
issue of confrontation vs. isolation in, 8
late nineteenth-century growth in, 8, 9
military strength and dominance of, 14, 15, 35
multiculture of, 66
need for financial reform in, 8, 14
nineteenth-century security and sovereignty concerns of, 27
political polarization in, 23
security needs of, 33
sense of exceptionalism in, 180
shale oil and gas production in, 253–4
unresolved problems of, 14, 23
vulnerability of dollar in, 13, 14, 228–32, 235–8, 240–3, 246–7, 254, 289
as world's largest economy, 253
see also Chinese-U.S. competition
United States Air Force, 106
Chinese downing of spy plane of, 151
fighter jets of, 49
information system of, 49
superiority of, 24, 58

United States Army, 126
Chinese hostility toward, 39–42, 126
operational skills and technology of, 41
United States Marines, 100–1, 102, 118, 148
United States Navy, 10, 32, 35, 95, 106–7, 109, 126
Aegis missile-defense cruisers of, 48
aircraft carriers of, 24, 40, 47–8, 67, 77, 106, 114–15, 120, 122
destroyers in, 68
development of, 27, 44, 60
Fifth Fleet of, 53
information system of, 49
joint exercises of Indian Navy and, 66
nineteenth-century strength of, 27, 44, 60, 96
overseas bases of, 60, 95
Pacific dominance by, 13, 21, 22, 24, 26, 29
Pacific Fleet of, 30
predicted Chinese Navy superiority to, 45
relations of Chinese Navy and, 13, 22–3, 29–31, 42–9, 67–8
seamanship training in, 57
Seventh Fleet of, 67–8
submarines of, 120
see also Chinese-U.S. competition
Universal Declaration of Human Rights, 202
Unocal, 254, 274
USS *Midway* Museum, 56

Vanderlip, Frank, 240
Varyag, 54–5, 56
Vatican, Chinese relations with, 188
Venezuela, 200, 213, 260–1, 268
Venice, 23, 26
Veroneau, John, 264
Versailles Treaty of 1919, 150, 154, 162
Vietnam, 61, 79–81, 88–91, 97, 112
anti-Chinese nationalism in, 105, 108
Chinese invasions of, 71, 79–80, 103
Chinese relations with, 29, 69–70, 91–2, 102–9
economy of, 104
exclusive economic zone of, 92, 93
French rule era of, 102, 105
off-shore oil and gas of, 92
overseas diaspora of, 105
political system of, 104
U.S. relations with, 102, 106–9, 125, 133
Vietnamese Communist Party, 70, 104, 107, 185
Politburo of, 105
Vietnam War, 105, 108–9, 250
deaths in, 102
Vogel, Ezra, 45
Voss, Mike, 187

Wade, Geoffrey, 79
Wagner, Richard, 56
Wall Street Journal, 190

Walmart, 21, 127
Wang, Grace, 169
Wang Gungwu, 180
Wang Hongli, 159
Wang Huning, 176–7
Wang Lijun, 189
Warburg, Paul, 240
war games, 117
Washington, D.C., 12, 15, 22, 27, 36, 44, 48, 58,
    252, 257–8
  fin-de-siècle anxiety in, 13–14, 65
  U.S. Capitol in, 91
Washington Post, 187
Washington Times, 58
Webster, Charles, 28
Weekly Standard, 187
Wei Zhixin, 219–20
Welch, Jack, 9
Wellington, Arthur Wellesley, Duke of, 120
Wen Jiabao, 77, 234, 239, 245, 267
Wesley, Michael, 99
West Point Military Academy, 135
When China Ruled the Seas (Levathes), 75–6
White, Hugh, 101–2
White House, 125, 136, 214–15, 232, 257
  Hu Jintao's visit to, 274
  military communication with, 35
"White Man's Burden" (Kipling), 222
WikiLeaks, 86, 188
Wilde, Oscar, 44
Wilhelm II, Emperor of Germany, 23, 28, 56
Wilson, Woodrow, 134
Woody Island, 89, 91
Workers' Party of Brazil, 209
World Bank, 251, 257–8, 260–1, 267–8, 272
World Cup of 2011, 59
World Economic Forum (Davos), 9–10
World Trade Organization, 272
World War I, 22, 28, 33, 76
World War II, 10, 15, 21, 24, 97, 229, 279
  Allies in, 21, 52
  economic roots of, 22
  end of, 21, 24, 33, 82, 99, 116, 124, 202
  Japanese defeat in, 21, 52, 162
  new international order after, 210–11
  Pacific theater of, 21, 52, 115, 120, 162–3
  U.S. goal in, 33
Wortzel, Larry, 47
Wuhan Iron and Steel (Wisco), 256
Wu Hung, 148–9
Wu Shengli, 24

Xia Bin, 232–3
Xian, 103, 160
Xianfeng, Emperor of China, 146–7
Xiao Jie, 91
Xi Jinping, 41–3, 54, 87, 130, 180, 197, 261,
    276–7
Xin Buyang, 26

Xinhua News Agency, 4, 82, 175–6, 187, 233
Xi Zhongxun, 42
Xue Yong, 9
Xu Shanda, 254
Xuzhou, 217
Xu Zuyuan, 77

Yalong Bay, 19–21, 22, 43
Yan'an guerrilla base, 42
Yanghe liquor company, 39
Yang Jiechi, 69–70, 73–4, 221
Yangon, 50, 63, 129–33
  Ice Wonderland in, 131
  Shwedagon Pagoda in, 131
Yangtze River, 251
Yang Yong, 25
Yan Xuetong, 80, 178–82
Yao Ming, 186
Ye Hailin, 29
Yellow Sea, 22
Yongle, Emperor of China, 75–6
Yoshihara, Toshi, 29, 120
You Ji, 58
YouTube, 84
Yuan dynasty, 103
Yuanming Yuan (Garden of Perfect
    Brightness)
  Summer Palace at, 146–52
  Zhengjue Temple in, 148
Yuan Weishi, 152–3
Yuan Youfei, 40
Yu Dan, 180
Yu Jie, 192–3
Yunnan University, 61

Zakaria, Fareed, 10
Zarganar, 130
Zha Daojiong, 62
Zhang Jigang, 182
Zhang Qingli, 166
Zhang Wenmu, 25, 56
Zhang Yimou, 182–3, 195
Zhang Zheng, 55, 57
Zhang Zilin, 19
Zhang Zongxiang, 154
Zhao Tingyang, 179, 181–2, 287
Zhao Ziyang, 149
Zha Xiaogang, 237
Zheng He, 74–81, 285
  voyages of, 74–80
Zheng Wang, 151
Zhongshan University, 152
Zhou Xiaochuan, 236, 248
Zhou Yongkang, 199–201
Zhu Chenghu, 233
Zhu Di, 75
Zhu Feng, 65, 86
Zimbabwe, 200, 205
Zurich University, 249

A NOTE ABOUT THE AUTHOR

GEOFF DYER is a journalist for the *Financial Times* and has been
a correspondent in China, the United States, and Brazil. He is the
recipient of a Fulbright award and of several journalism awards,
including a Society of Publishers in Asia award for a series of 2010
opinion pieces about China's role in the world. He studied at Cambridge University and the Johns Hopkins School of Advanced
International Studies. He lives with his family in Washington, D.C.

A NOTE ON THE TYPE

This book was set in Minion, a typeface produced by the Adobe Corporation specifically for the Macintosh personal computer, and released in 1990. Designed by Robert Slimbach, Minion combines the classic characteristics of old style faces with the full complement of weights required for modern typesetting.

Typeset by Scribe,
Philadelphia, Pennsylvania

Printed and bound by Berryville Graphics,
Berryville, Virginia

Designed by Cassandra J. Pappas